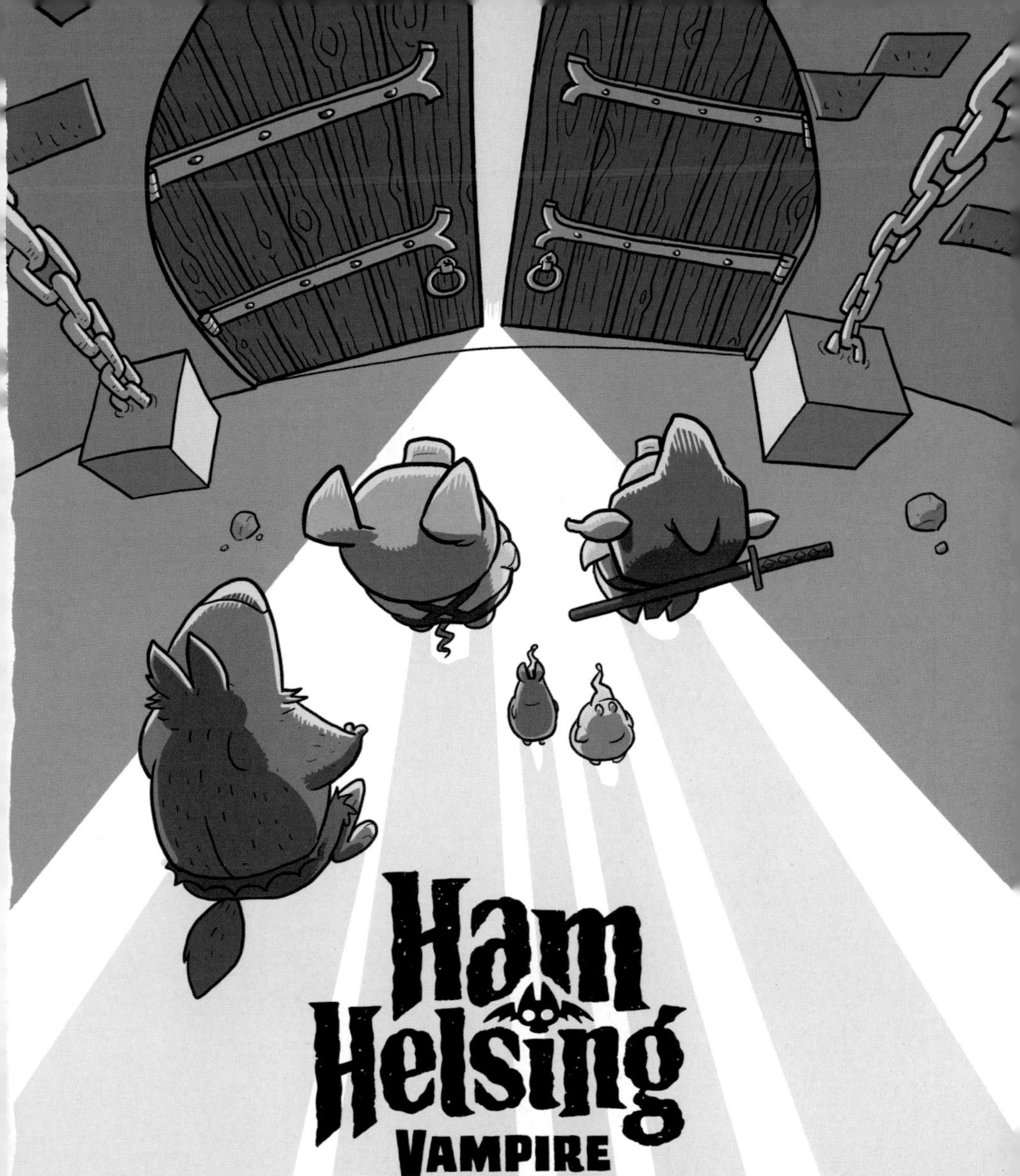

Ham Helsing
Vampire Hunter

Rich Moyer

With color by Josh Lewis

Crown Books for Young Readers
New York

Visit us on the Web! rhcbooks.com

Educators and librarians, for a variety of teaching tools, visit us at
RHTeachersLibrarians.com

Library of Congress Cataloging-in-Publication Data
Names: Moyer, Rich, author, illustrator.
Title: Ham Helsing: vampire hunter. #1 / Rich Moyer.
Description: New York: Crown Books for Young Readers, 2021. | Audience:
Ages 8–12. | Audience: Grades 4–6. | Summary: Descended from a long line of adventurers
and monster hunters, a gentle pig who prefers poetry writing to catching dangerous
creatures reluctantly sets out on his first assignment, to hunt a dangerous vampire.
Identifiers: LCCN 2020038349 (print) | LCCN 2020038350 (ebook) |
ISBN 978-0-593-30891-2 (hardcover) | ISBN 978-0-593-30892-9 (library binding) |
ISBN 978-0-593-30893-6 (ebook)
Subjects: LCSH: Graphic novels. | CYAC: Graphic novels. | Pigs—Fiction. |
Vampires—Fiction. | Humorous stories.
Classification: LCC PZ7.7.M74 Ham 2021 (print) | LCC PZ7.7.M74 (ebook) |
DDC 741.5/973—dc23

Cover design, logo, and inside color by Josh Lewis

MANUFACTURED IN CHINA
10 9 8 7 6 5 4 3 2
First Edition

Random House Children's Books supports the
First Amendment and celebrates the right to read.

This book is dedicated to
Juno and Cleo.

I was frustrated at first that
you two didn't come with an
owner's manual . . . until
I realized that was the
point.

Love you forever and
without conditions, Dad.

PROLOGUE

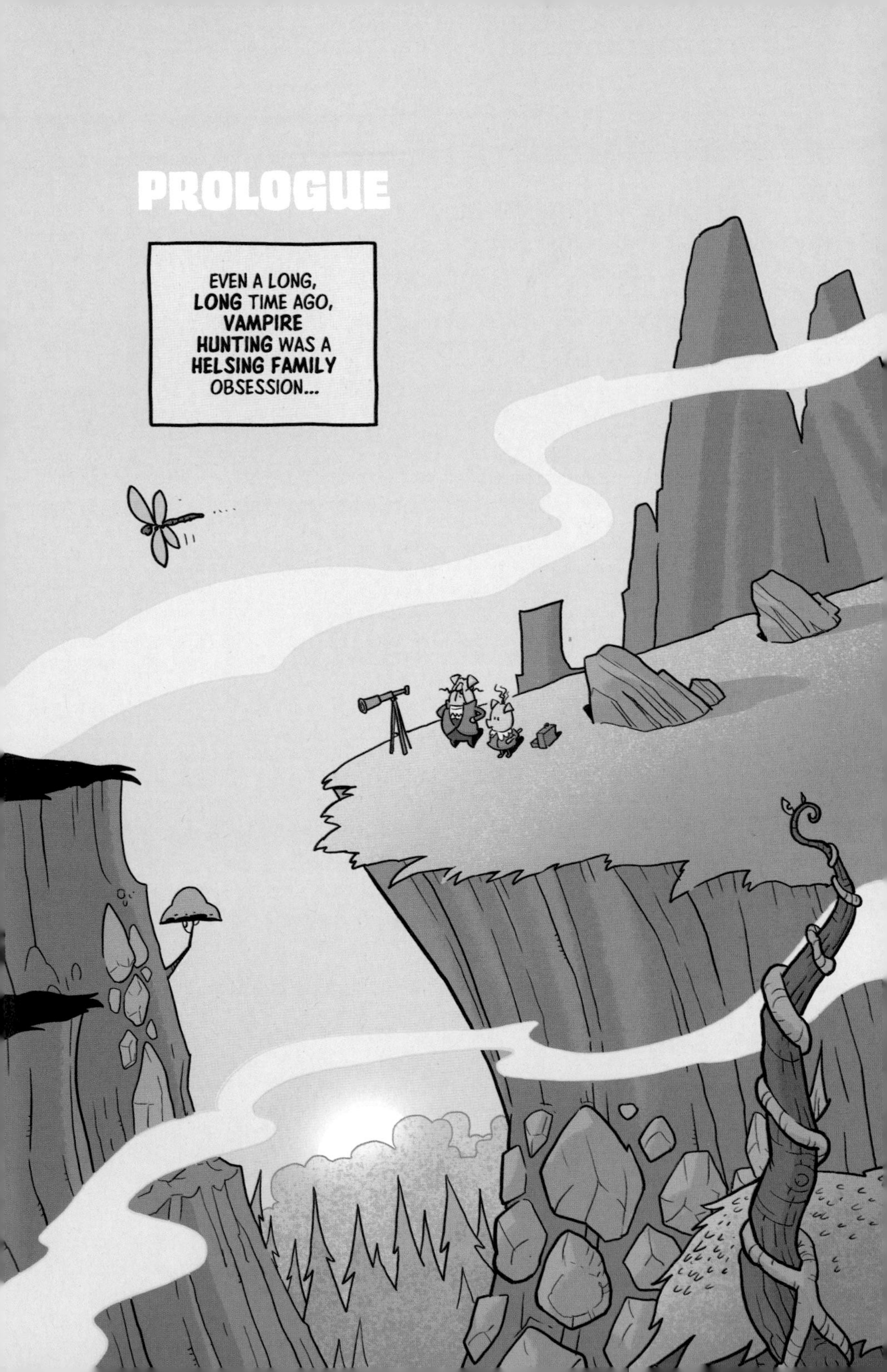
EVEN A LONG, LONG TIME AGO, VAMPIRE HUNTING WAS A HELSING FAMILY OBSESSION...

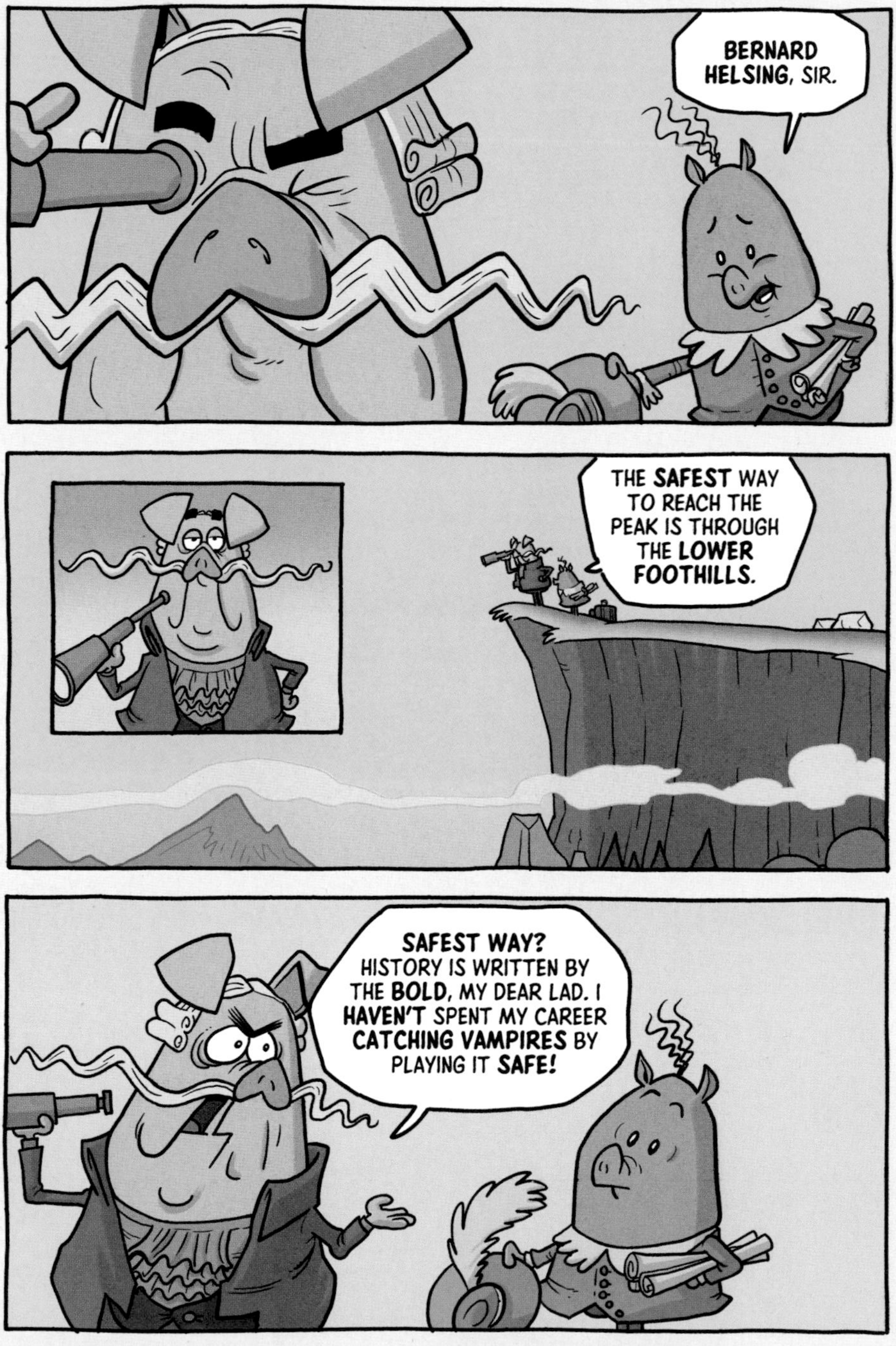
BERNARD HELSING, SIR.
THE SAFEST WAY TO REACH THE PEAK IS THROUGH THE LOWER FOOTHILLS.
SAFEST WAY? HISTORY IS WRITTEN BY THE BOLD, MY DEAR LAD. I HAVEN'T SPENT MY CAREER CATCHING VAMPIRES BY PLAYING IT SAFE!

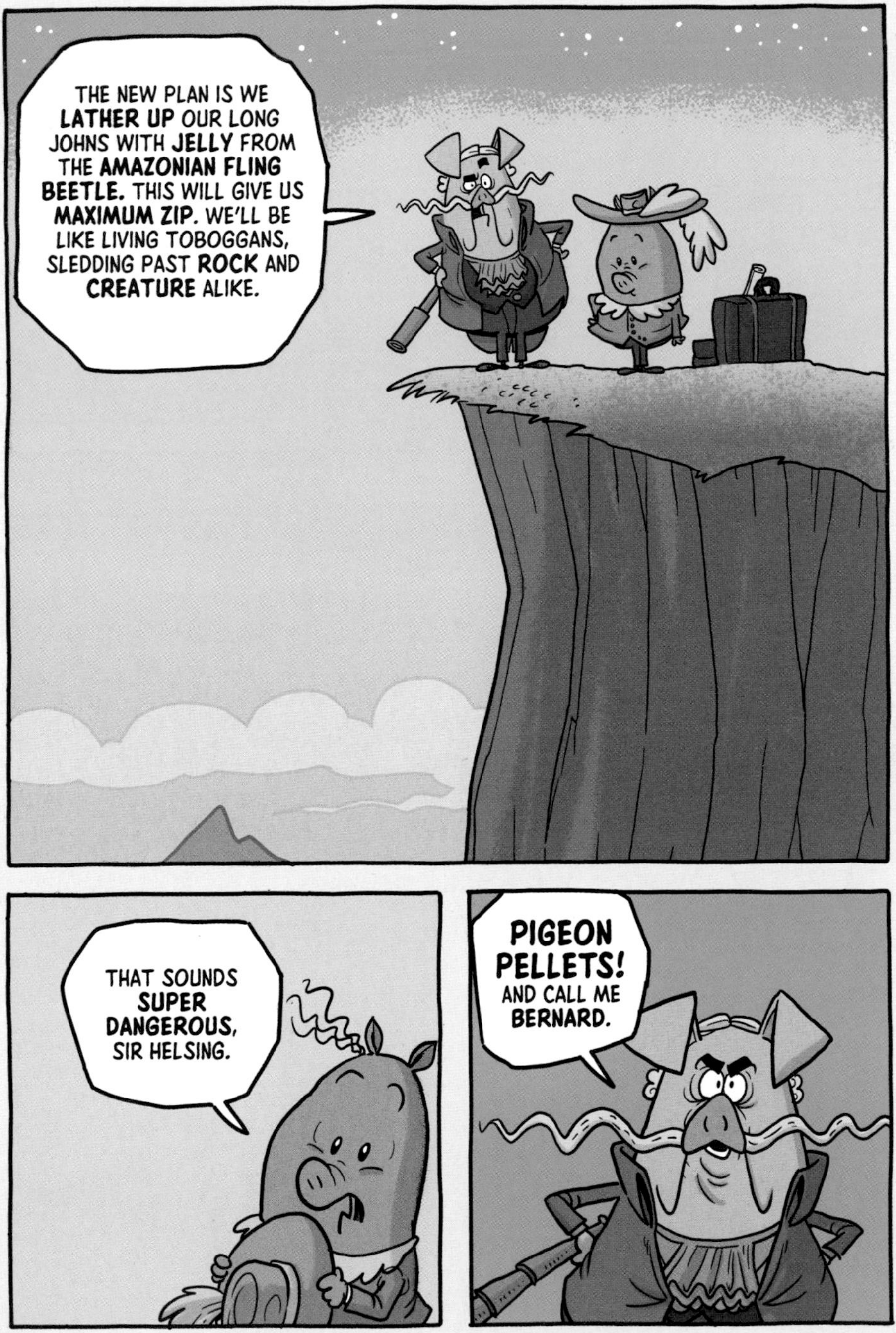
THE NEW PLAN IS WE **LATHER UP** OUR LONG JOHNS WITH **JELLY** FROM THE **AMAZONIAN FLING BEETLE.** THIS WILL GIVE US **MAXIMUM ZIP**. WE'LL BE LIKE LIVING TOBOGGANS, SLEDDING PAST **ROCK** AND **CREATURE** ALIKE.
THAT SOUNDS **SUPER DANGEROUS,** SIR HELSING.
PIGEON PELLETS! AND CALL ME **BERNARD.**

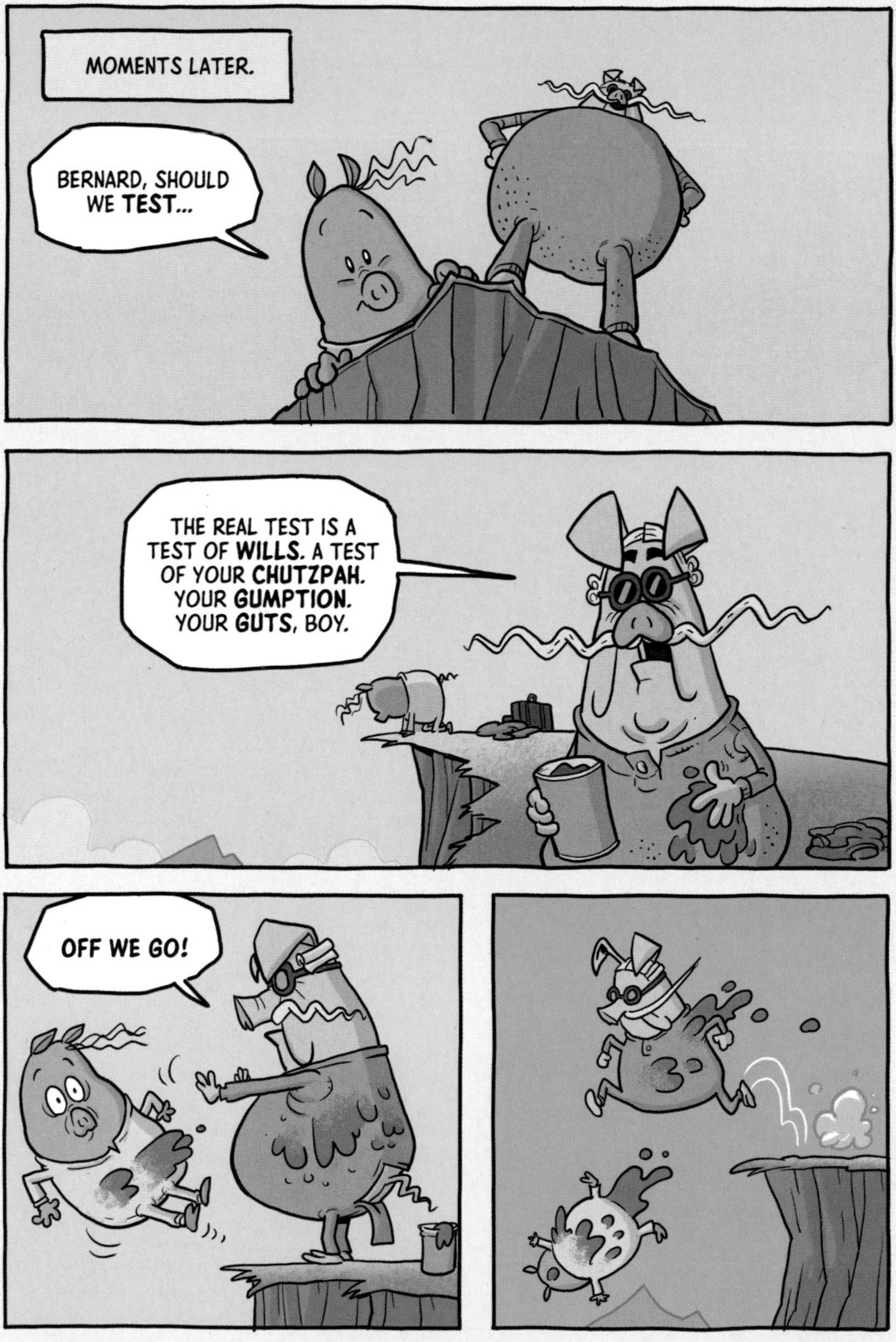
MOMENTS LATER.
BERNARD, SHOULD WE TEST...
THE REAL TEST IS A TEST OF WILLS. A TEST OF YOUR CHUTZPAH. YOUR GUMPTION. YOUR GUTS, BOY.
OFF WE GO!

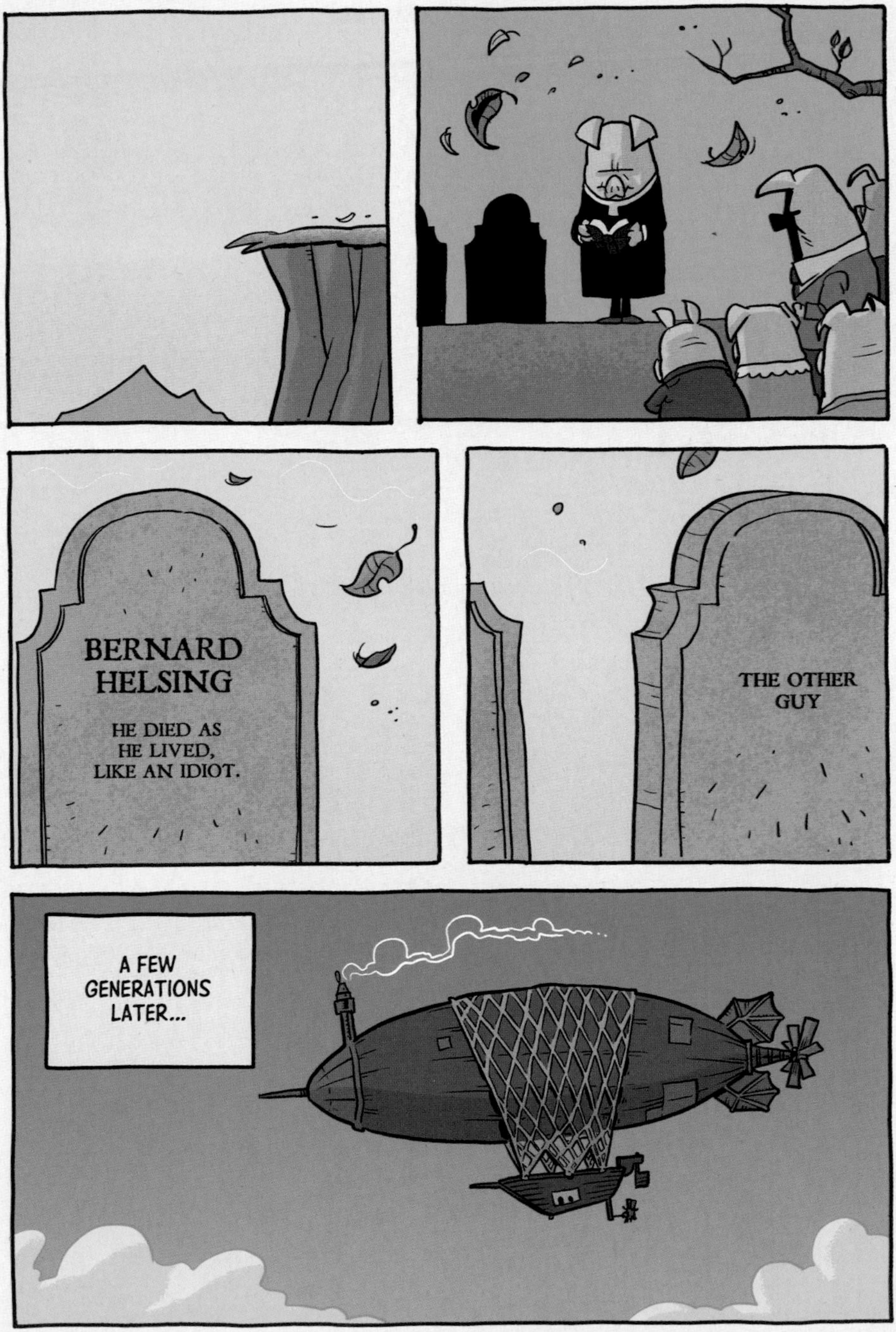
BERNARD HELSING
HE DIED AS HE LIVED, LIKE AN IDIOT.
THE OTHER GUY
A FEW GENERATIONS LATER...

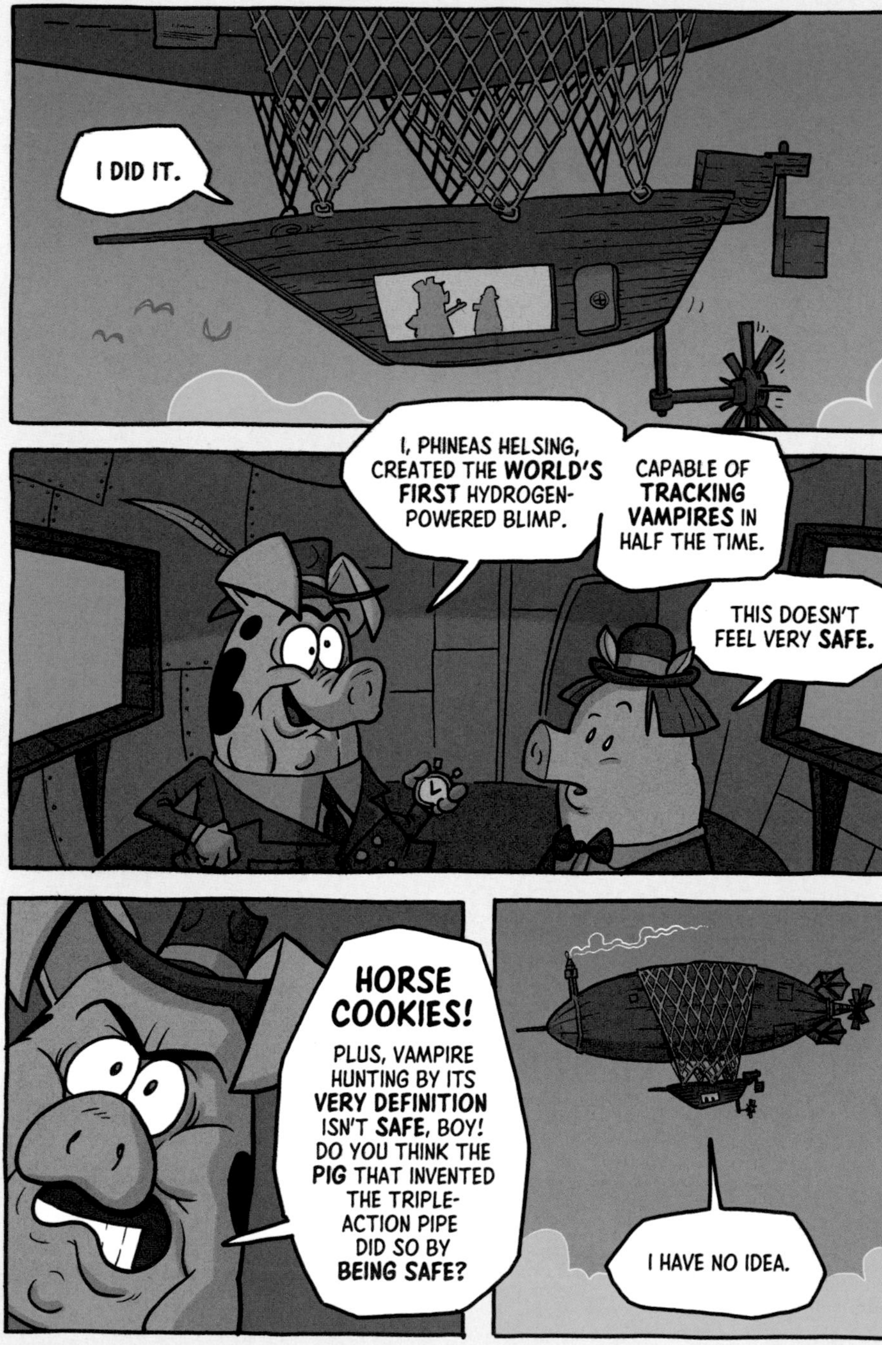
I DID IT.
I, PHINEAS HELSING, CREATED THE WORLD'S FIRST HYDROGEN-POWERED BLIMP.
CAPABLE OF TRACKING VAMPIRES IN HALF THE TIME.
THIS DOESN'T FEEL VERY SAFE.
HORSE COOKIES!
PLUS, VAMPIRE HUNTING BY ITS VERY DEFINITION ISN'T SAFE, BOY! DO YOU THINK THE PIG THAT INVENTED THE TRIPLE-ACTION PIPE DID SO BY BEING SAFE?
I HAVE NO IDEA.

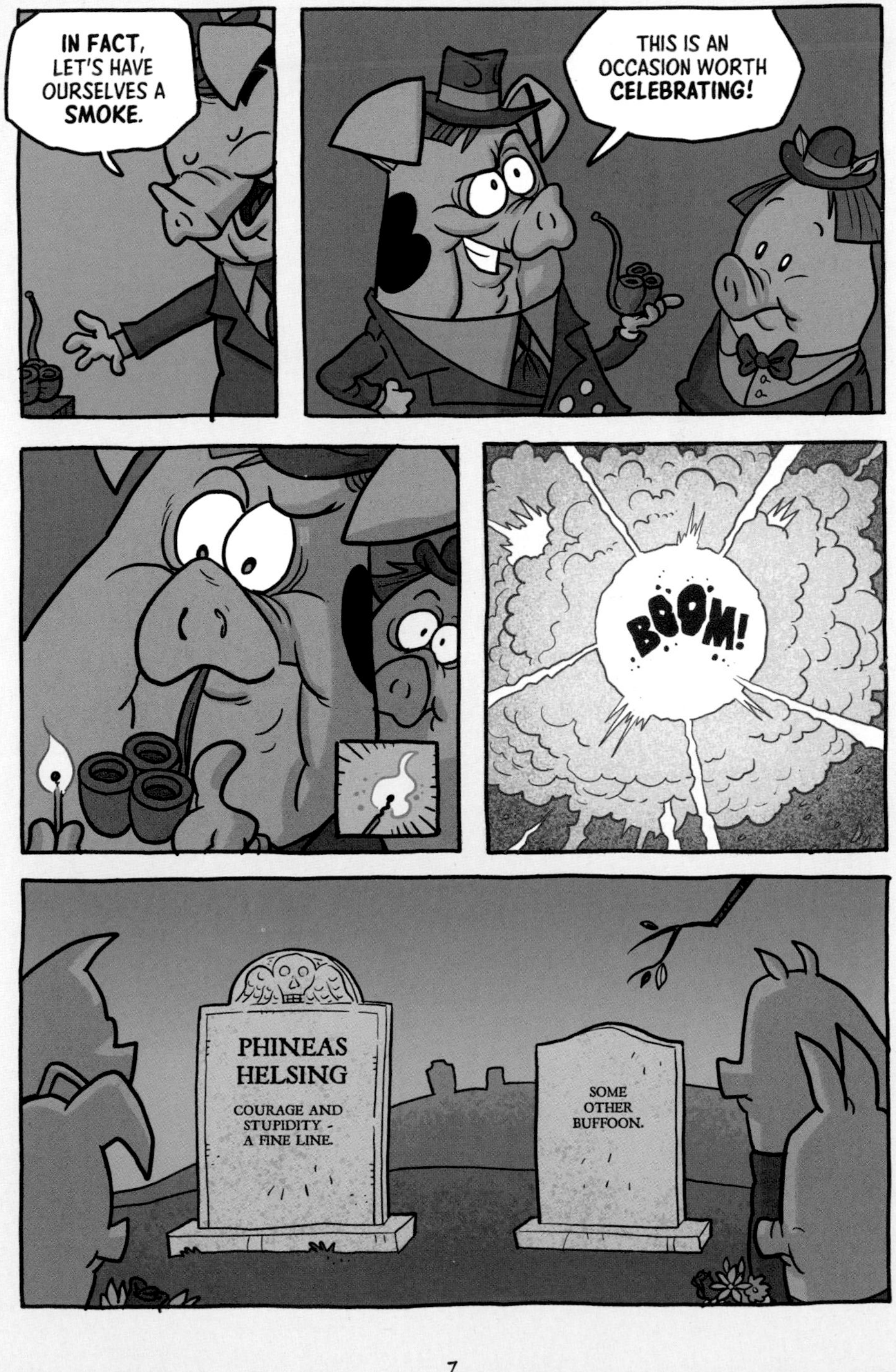
IN FACT, LET'S HAVE OURSELVES A SMOKE.
THIS IS AN OCCASION WORTH CELEBRATING!
BOOM!
PHINEAS HELSING
COURAGE AND STUPIDITY - A FINE LINE.
SOME OTHER BUFFOON.

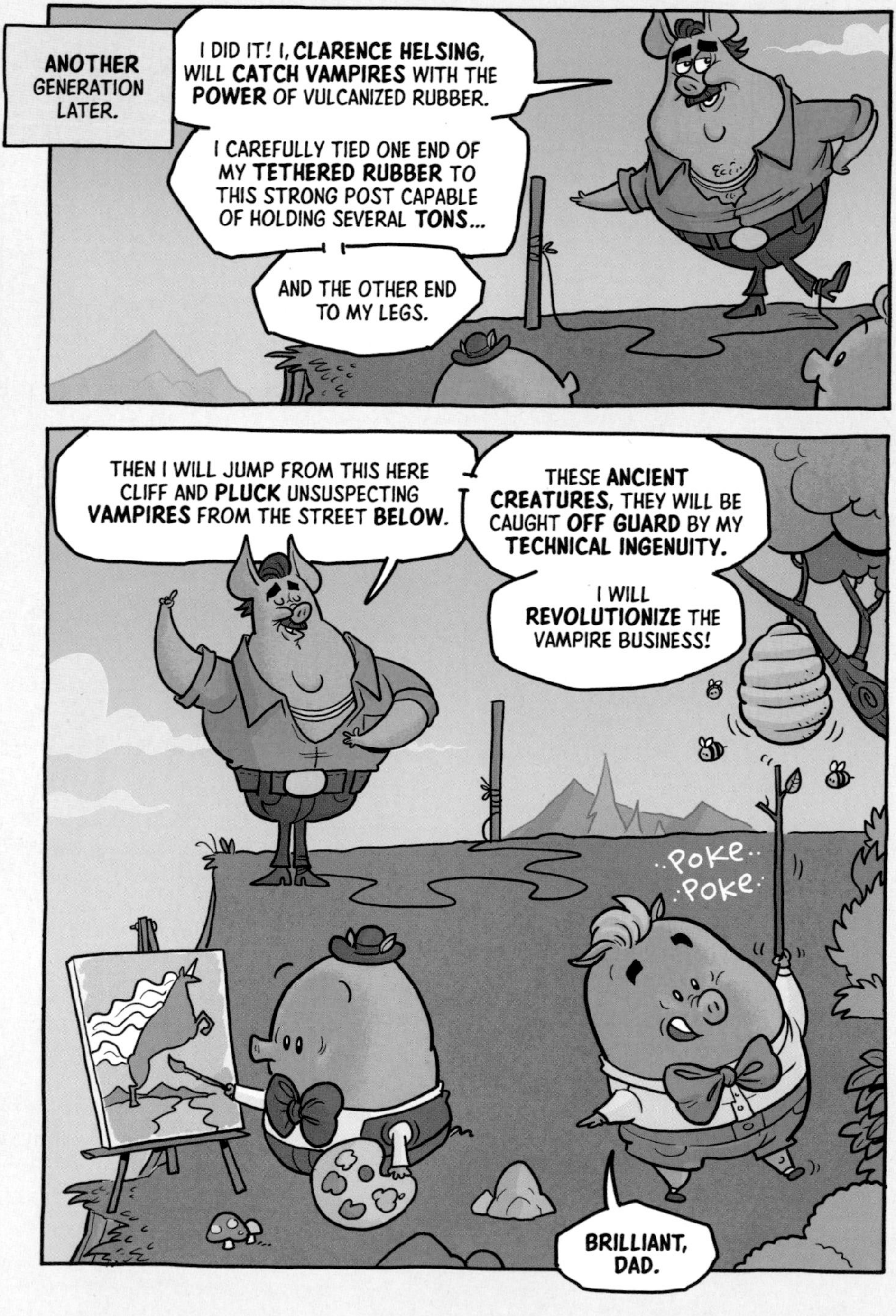
ANOTHER GENERATION LATER.
I DID IT! I, CLARENCE HELSING, WILL CATCH VAMPIRES WITH THE POWER OF VULCANIZED RUBBER.
I CAREFULLY TIED ONE END OF MY TETHERED RUBBER TO THIS STRONG POST CAPABLE OF HOLDING SEVERAL TONS...
AND THE OTHER END TO MY LEGS.
THEN I WILL JUMP FROM THIS HERE CLIFF AND PLUCK UNSUSPECTING VAMPIRES FROM THE STREET BELOW.
THESE ANCIENT CREATURES, THEY WILL BE CAUGHT OFF GUARD BY MY TECHNICAL INGENUITY.
I WILL REVOLUTIONIZE THE VAMPIRE BUSINESS!
POKE
POKE
BRILLIANT, DAD.

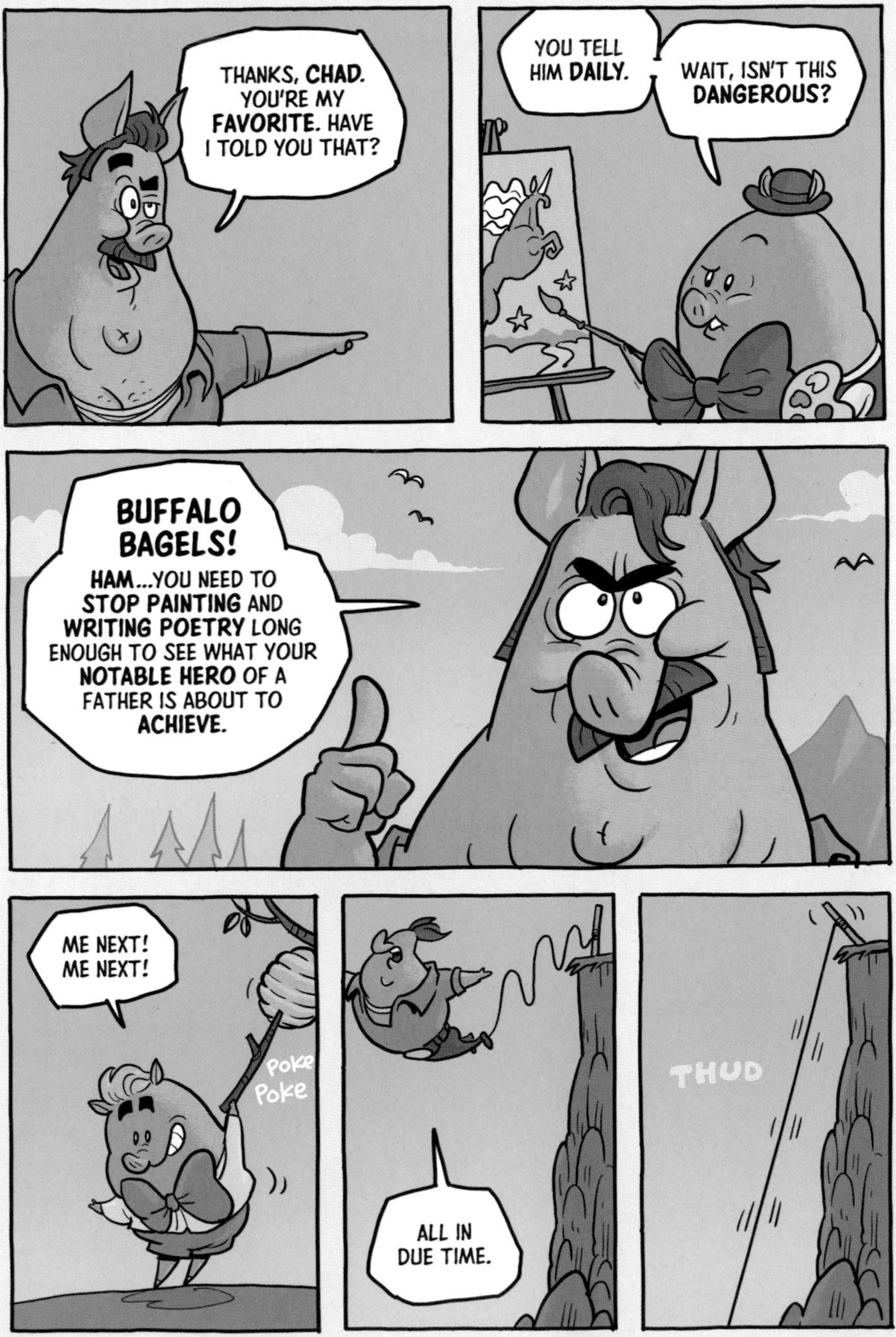
THANKS, CHAD. YOU'RE MY FAVORITE. HAVE I TOLD YOU THAT?
YOU TELL HIM DAILY.
WAIT, ISN'T THIS DANGEROUS?
BUFFALO BAGELS!
HAM...YOU NEED TO STOP PAINTING AND WRITING POETRY LONG ENOUGH TO SEE WHAT YOUR NOTABLE HERO OF A FATHER IS ABOUT TO ACHIEVE.
ME NEXT! ME NEXT!
POKE POKE
ALL IN DUE TIME.
THUD

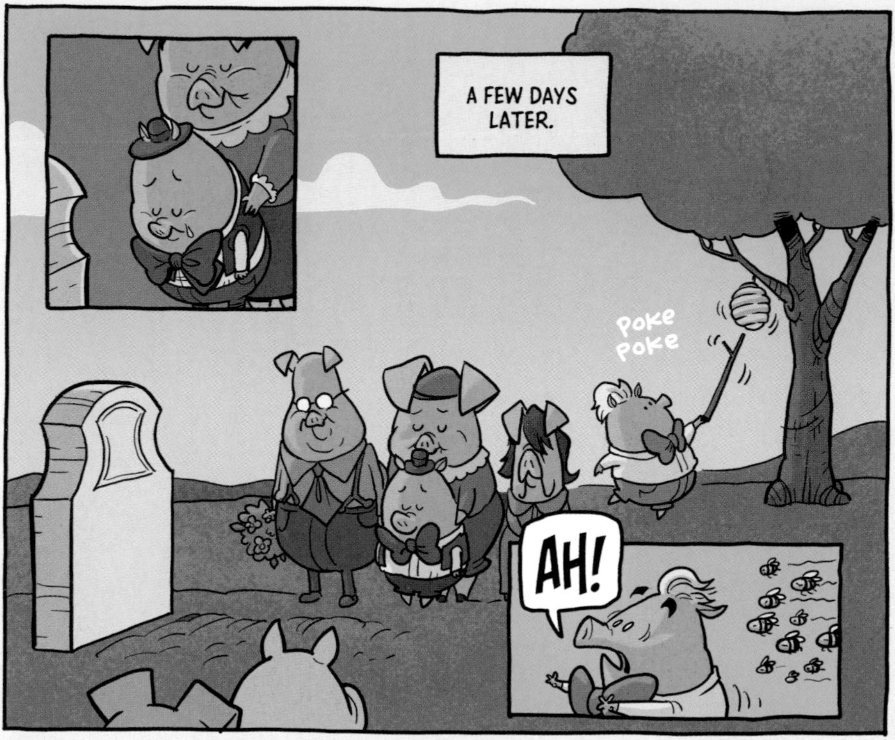
A FEW DAYS LATER.
POKE POKE
AH!

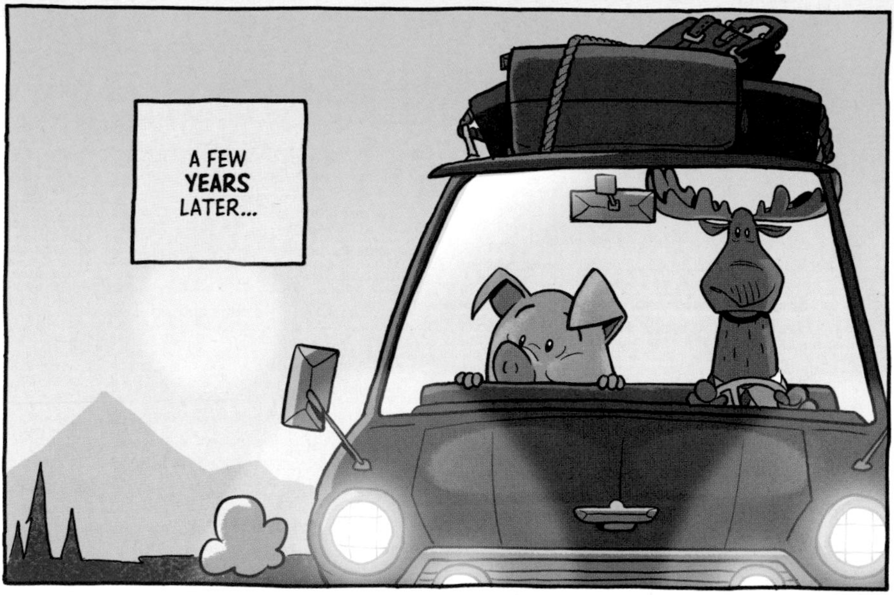
A FEW YEARS LATER...

CHAPTER ONE

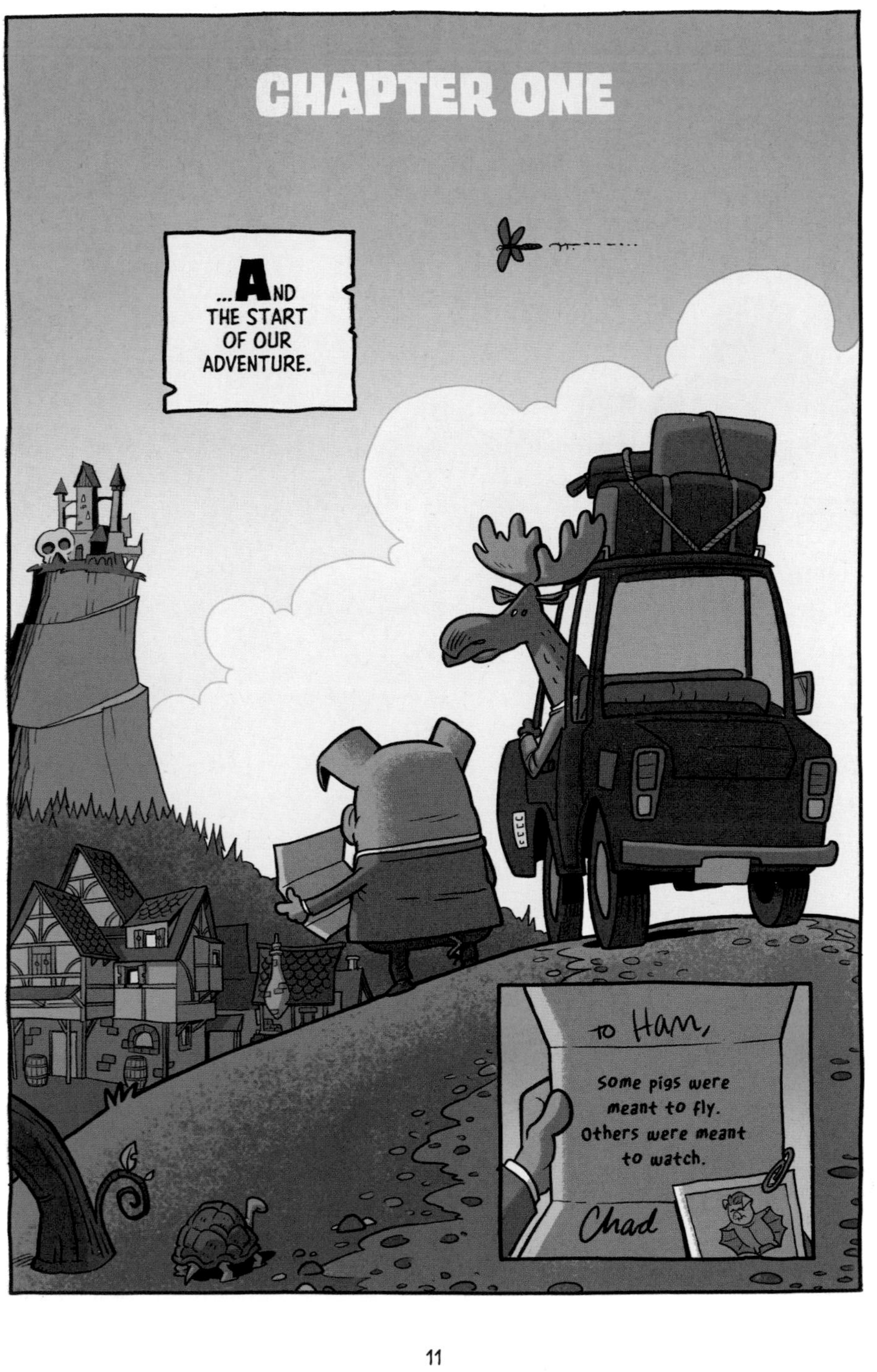

...AND THE START OF OUR ADVENTURE.
to Ham,
Some pigs were meant to fly. Others were meant to watch.
Chad

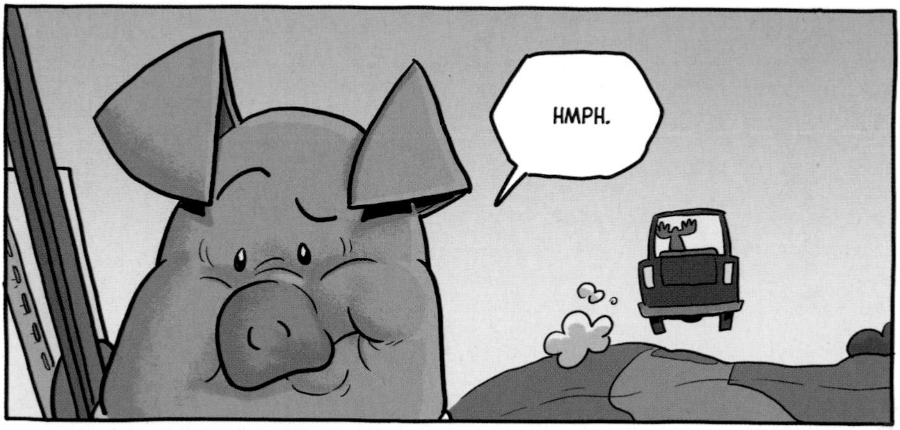
HMPH.

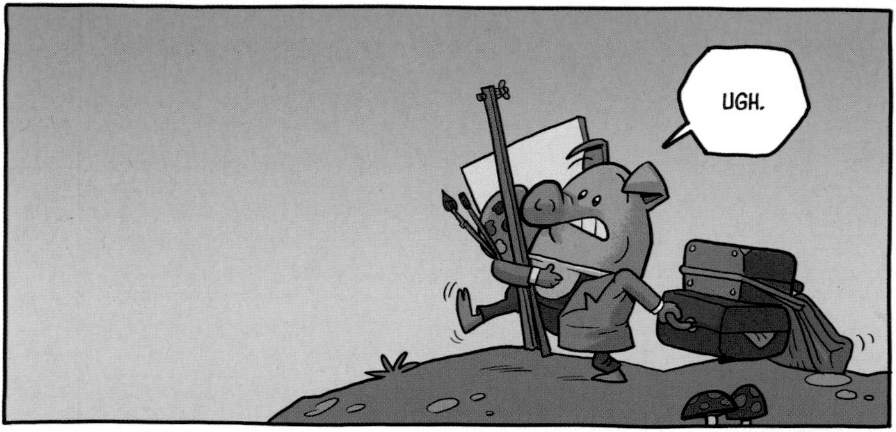
UGH.

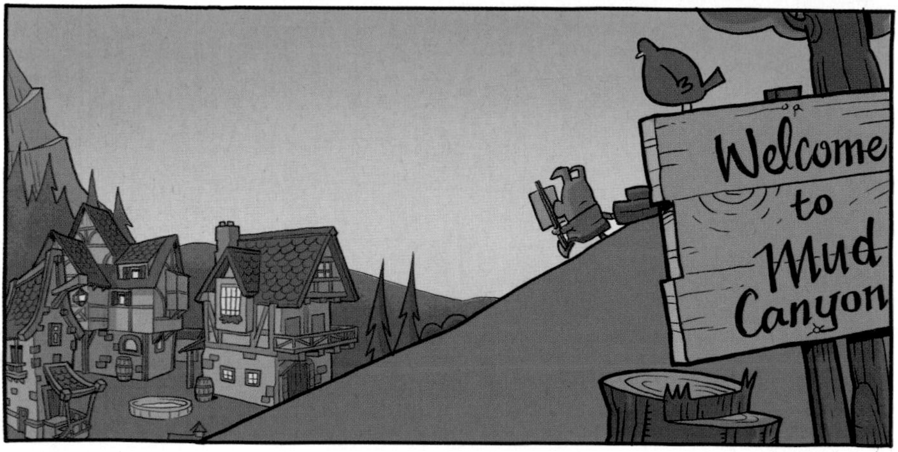
Welcome to Mud Canyon

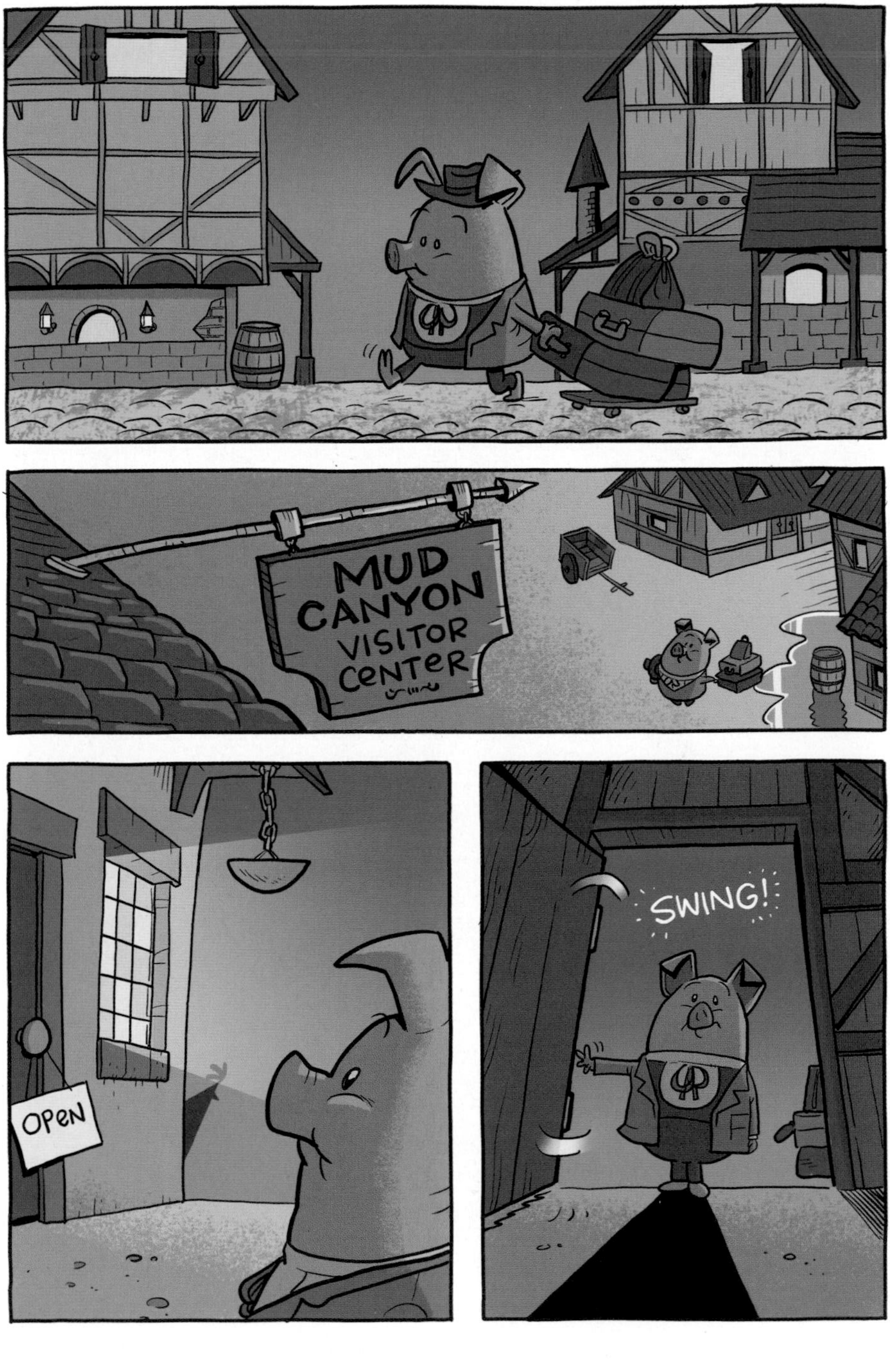
MUD CANYON VISITOR CENTER
OPEN
SWING!

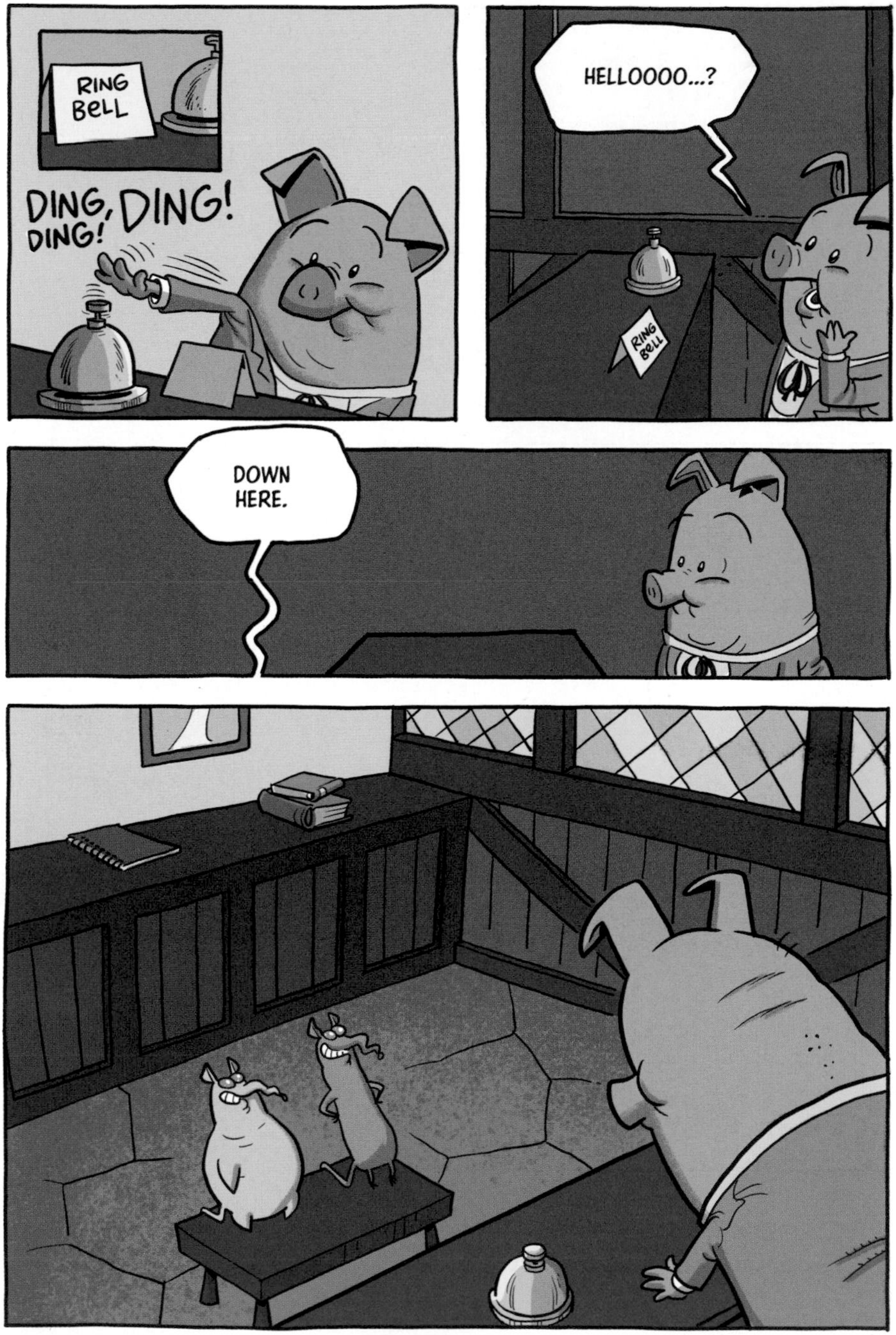
RING
BeLL
DING, DING! DING!
HELLOOOO...?
RING
BeLL
DOWN
HERE.

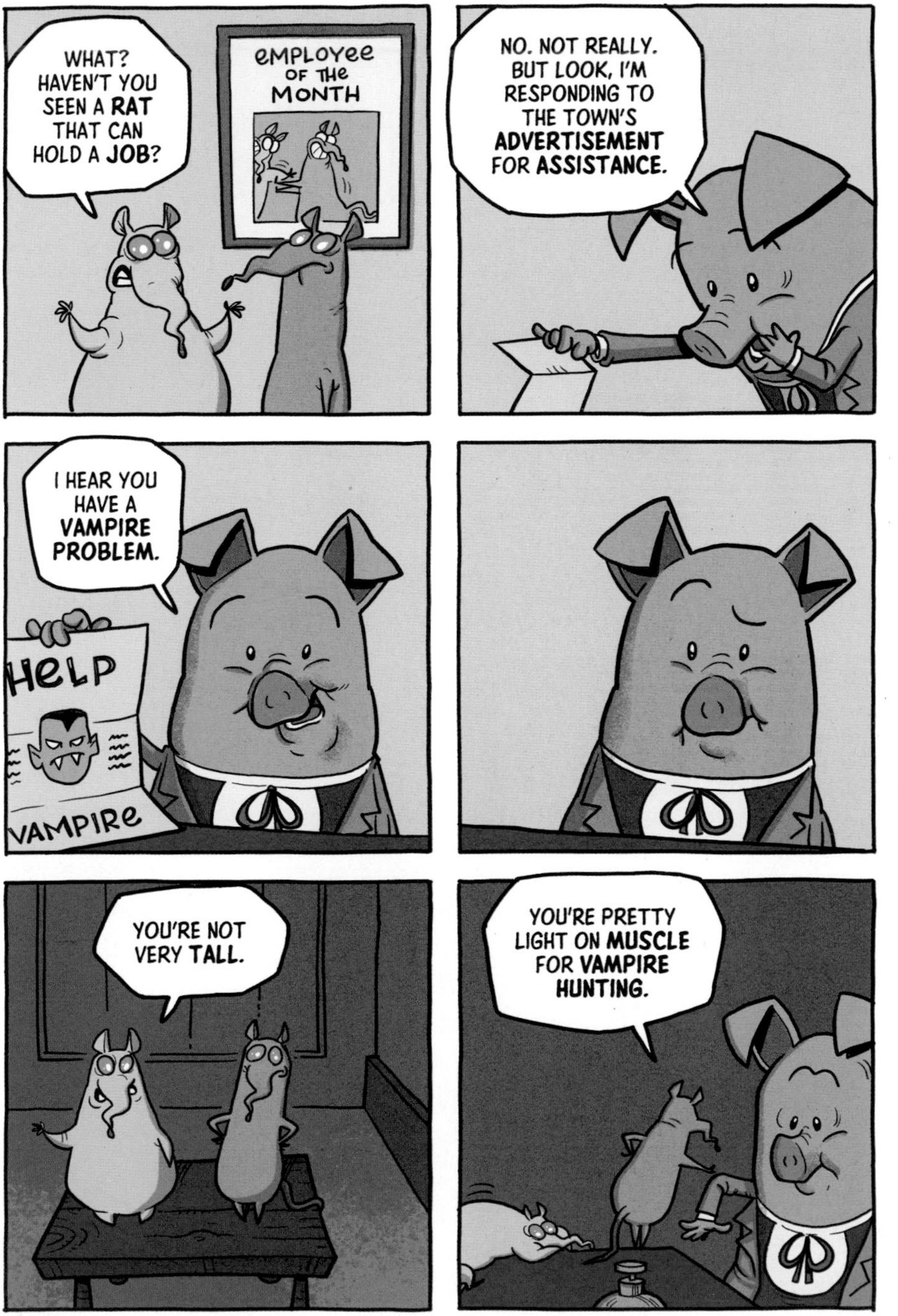
WHAT? HAVEN'T YOU SEEN A RAT THAT CAN HOLD A JOB?
EMPLOYEE OF THE MONTH
NO. NOT REALLY. BUT LOOK, I'M RESPONDING TO THE TOWN'S ADVERTISEMENT FOR ASSISTANCE.
I HEAR YOU HAVE A VAMPIRE PROBLEM.
HELP
VAMPIRE
YOU'RE NOT VERY TALL.
YOU'RE PRETTY LIGHT ON MUSCLE FOR VAMPIRE HUNTING.

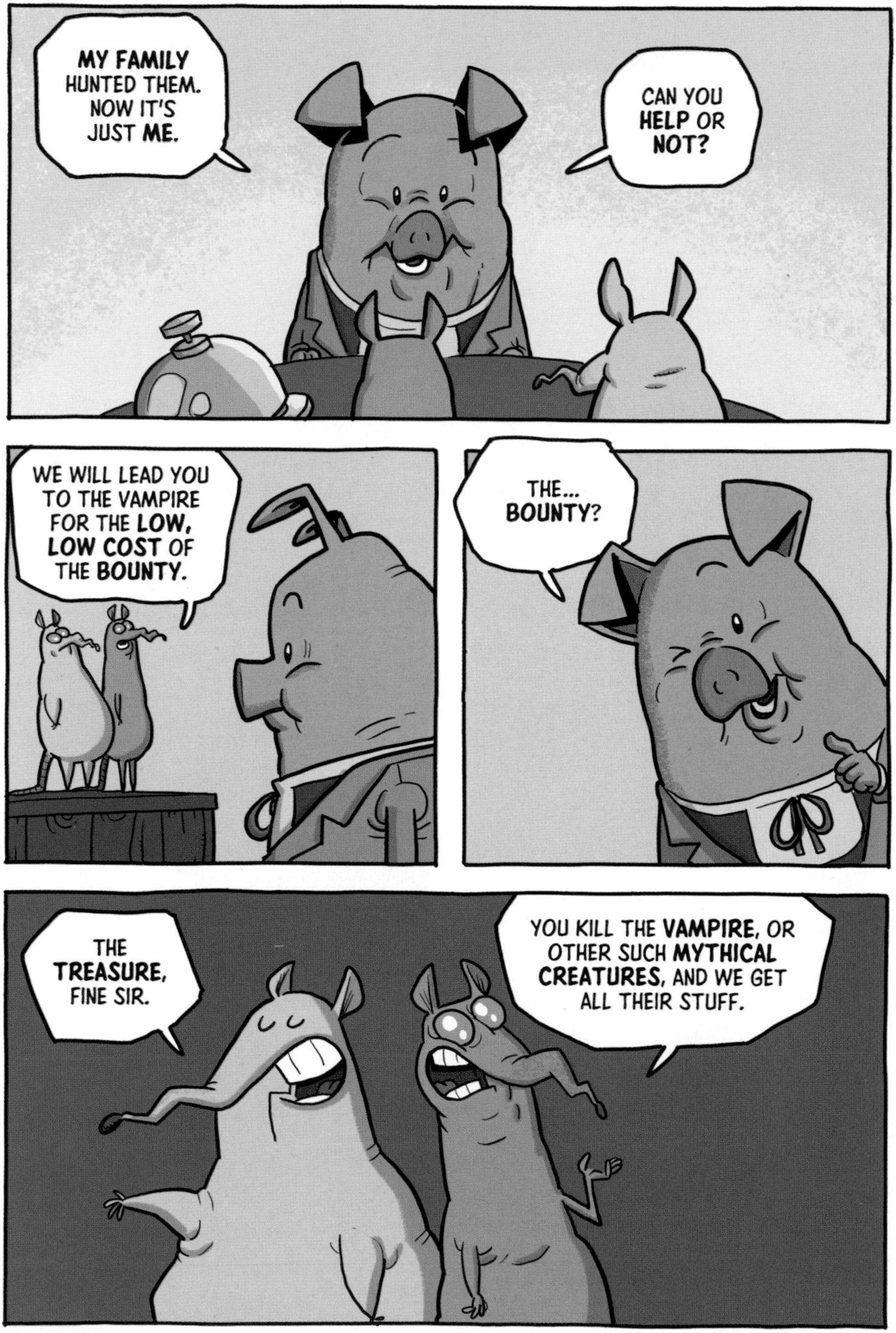
MY FAMILY HUNTED THEM. NOW IT'S JUST ME.
CAN YOU HELP OR NOT?
WE WILL LEAD YOU TO THE VAMPIRE FOR THE LOW, LOW COST OF THE BOUNTY.
THE... BOUNTY?
THE TREASURE, FINE SIR.
YOU KILL THE VAMPIRE, OR OTHER SUCH MYTHICAL CREATURES, AND WE GET ALL THEIR STUFF.

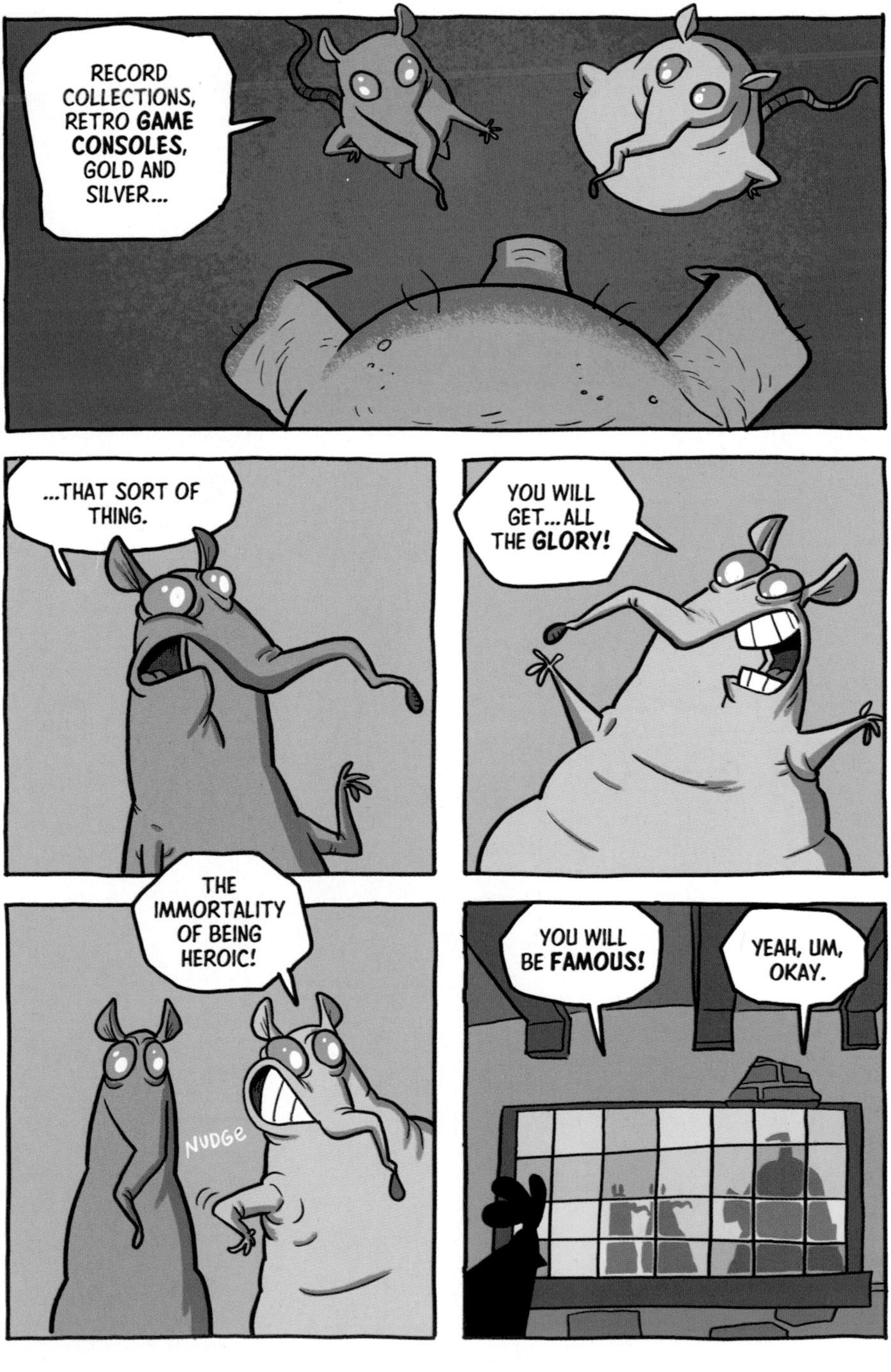
RECORD COLLECTIONS, RETRO GAME CONSOLES, GOLD AND SILVER...
...THAT SORT OF THING.
YOU WILL GET... ALL THE GLORY!
THE IMMORTALITY OF BEING HEROIC!
NUDGE
YOU WILL BE FAMOUS!
YEAH, UM, OKAY.

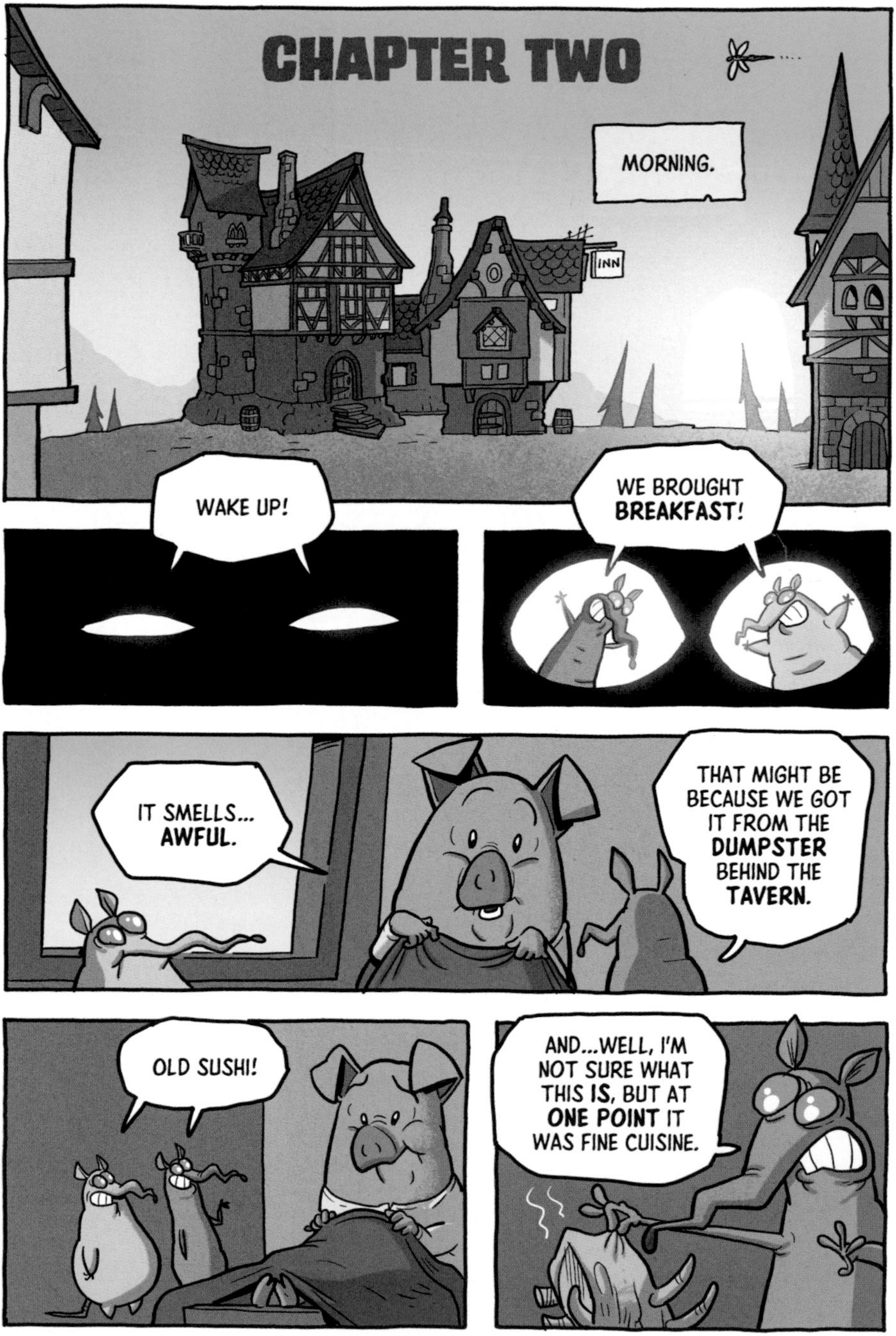
CHAPTER TWO
MORNING.
INN
WAKE UP!
WE BROUGHT BREAKFAST!
IT SMELLS... AWFUL.
THAT MIGHT BE BECAUSE WE GOT IT FROM THE DUMPSTER BEHIND THE TAVERN.
OLD SUSHI!
AND...WELL, I'M NOT SURE WHAT THIS IS, BUT AT ONE POINT IT WAS FINE CUISINE.

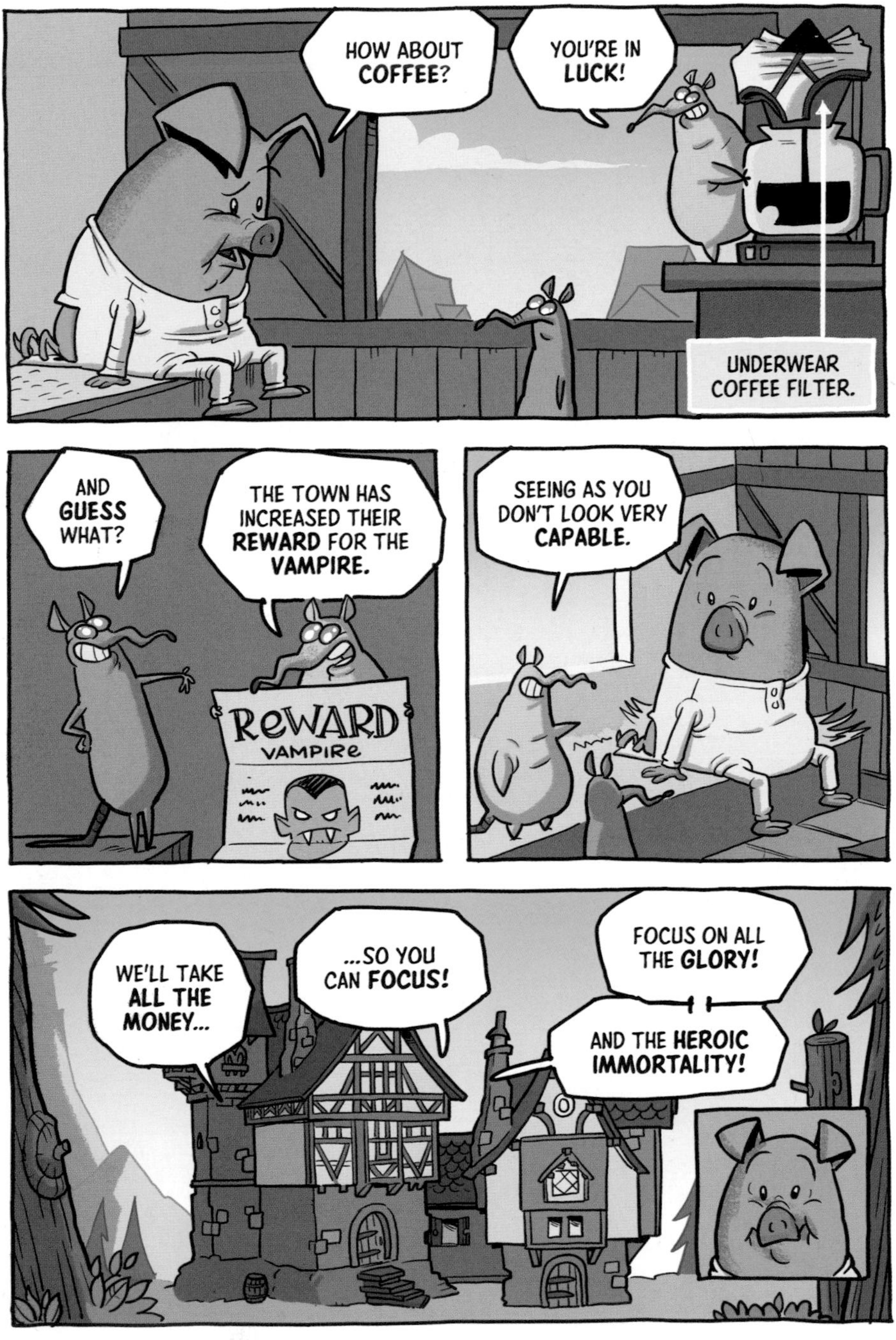
HOW ABOUT **COFFEE?**
YOU'RE IN **LUCK!**
UNDERWEAR COFFEE FILTER.
AND **GUESS** WHAT?
THE TOWN HAS INCREASED THEIR **REWARD** FOR THE **VAMPIRE.**
REWARD
VAMPIRE
SEEING AS YOU DON'T LOOK VERY **CAPABLE.**
WE'LL TAKE **ALL THE MONEY...**
...SO YOU CAN **FOCUS!**
FOCUS ON ALL THE **GLORY!**
AND THE **HEROIC IMMORTALITY!**

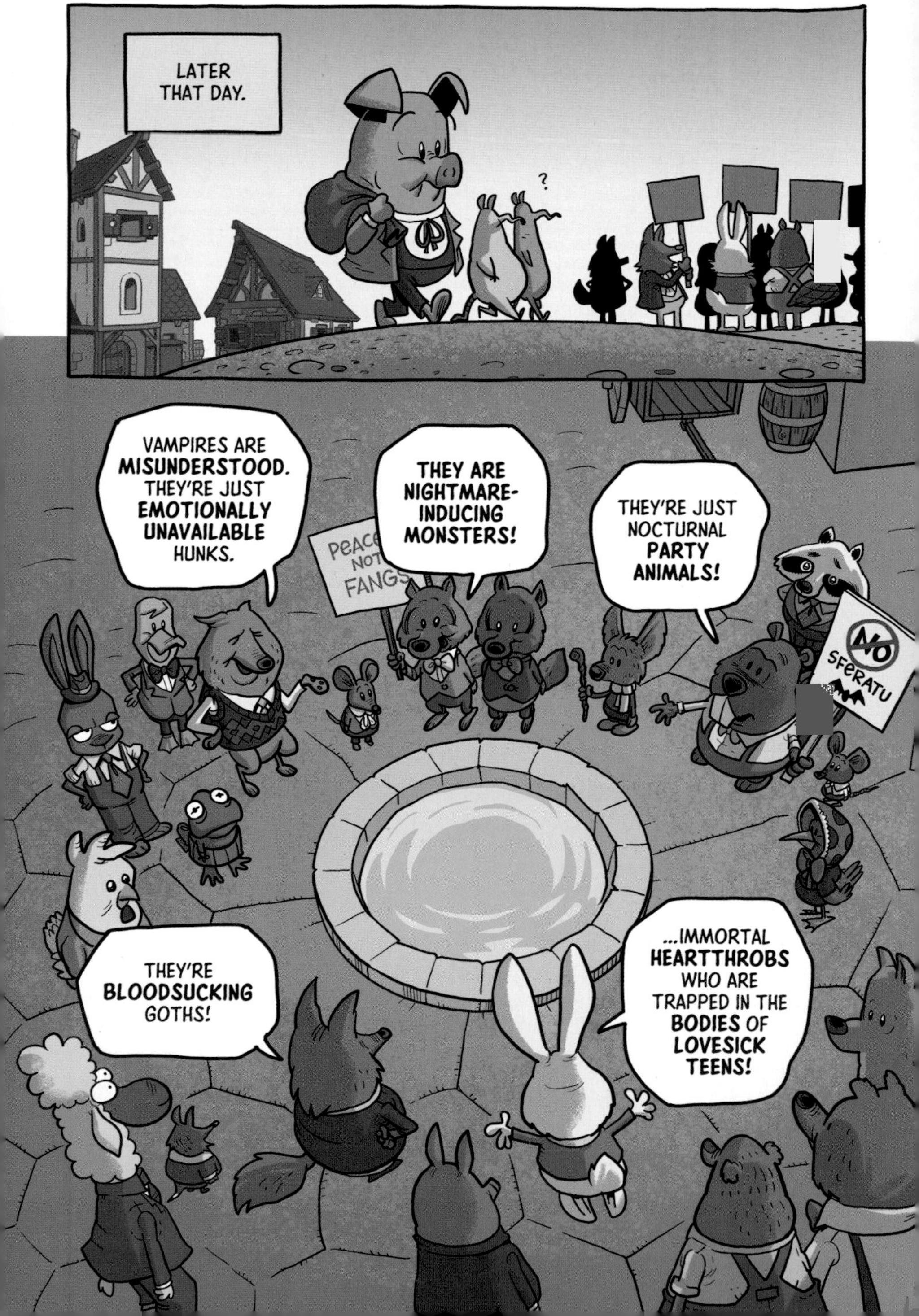
LATER THAT DAY.
?
VAMPIRES ARE **MISUNDERSTOOD.** THEY'RE JUST **EMOTIONALLY UNAVAILABLE** HUNKS.
PEACE NOT FANGS
THEY ARE NIGHTMARE-INDUCING MONSTERS!
THEY'RE JUST NOCTURNAL **PARTY ANIMALS!**
NO SFERATU
THEY'RE **BLOODSUCKING** GOTHS!
...IMMORTAL **HEARTTHROBS** WHO ARE TRAPPED IN THE **BODIES** OF **LOVESICK TEENS!**

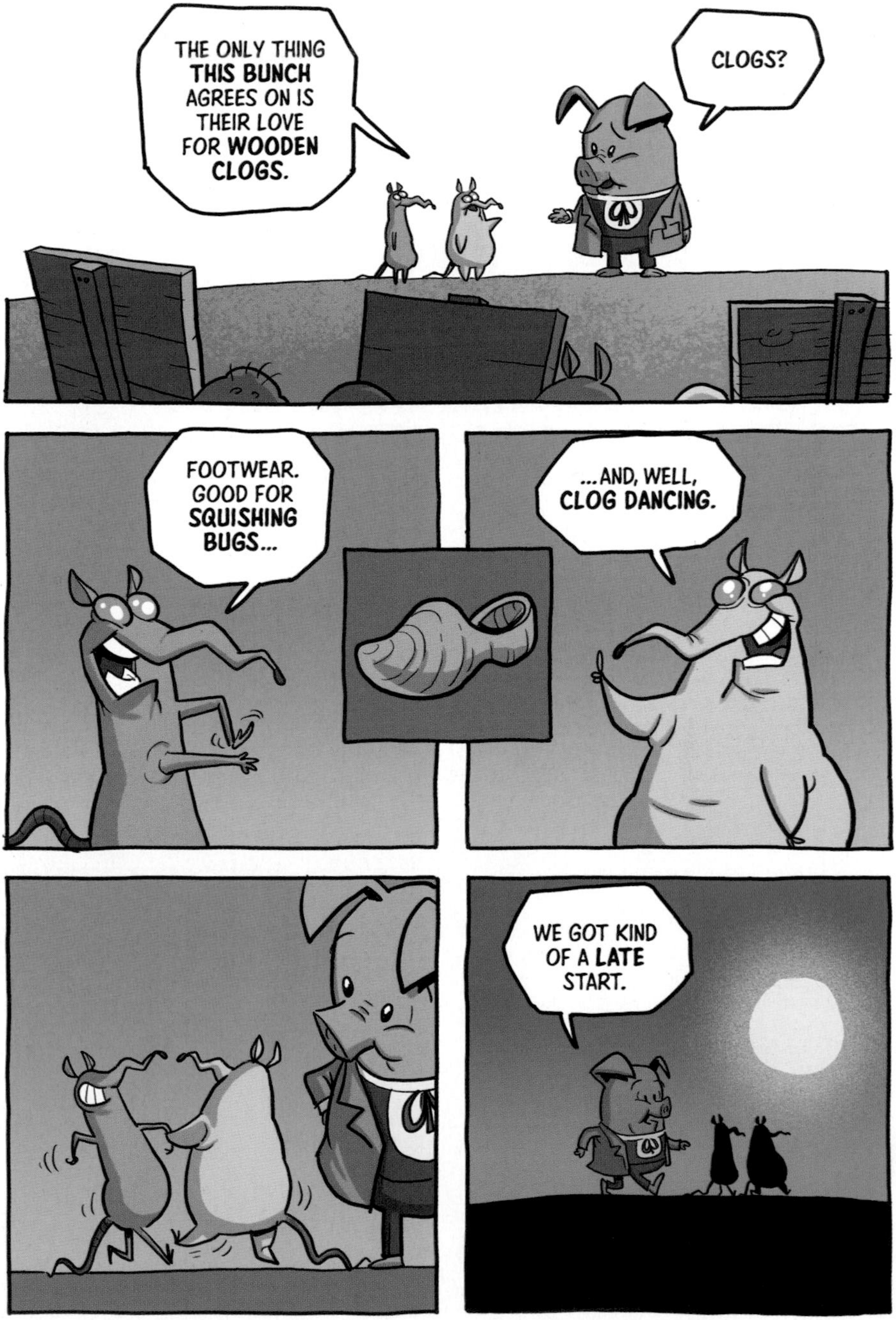
THE ONLY THING THIS BUNCH AGREES ON IS THEIR LOVE FOR WOODEN CLOGS.
CLOGS?
FOOTWEAR. GOOD FOR SQUISHING BUGS...
...AND, WELL, CLOG DANCING.
WE GOT KIND OF A LATE START.

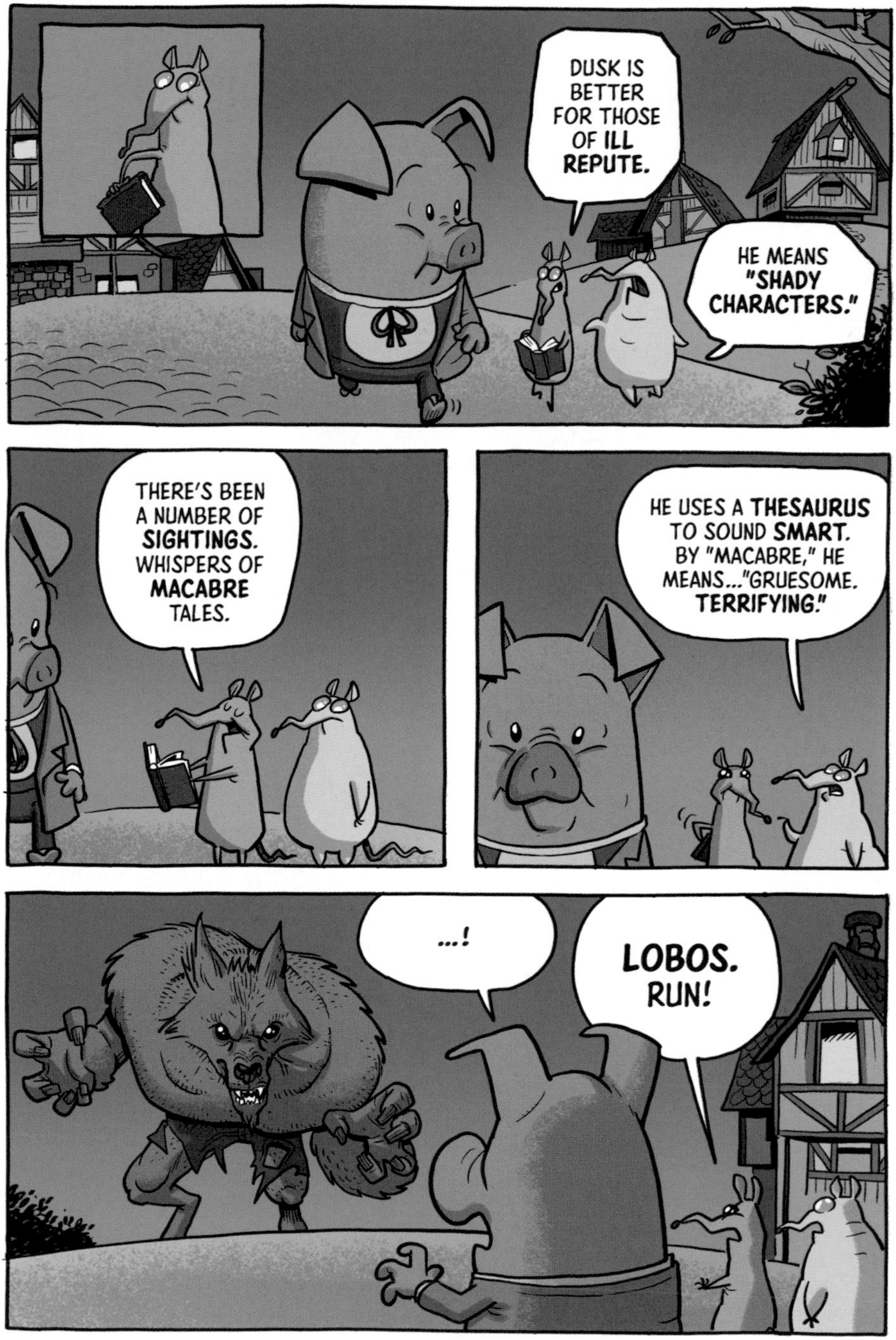
DUSK IS BETTER FOR THOSE OF ILL REPUTE.
HE MEANS "SHADY CHARACTERS."
THERE'S BEEN A NUMBER OF SIGHTINGS. WHISPERS OF MACABRE TALES.
HE USES A THESAURUS TO SOUND SMART. BY "MACABRE," HE MEANS..."GRUESOME. TERRIFYING."
...!
LOBOS. RUN!

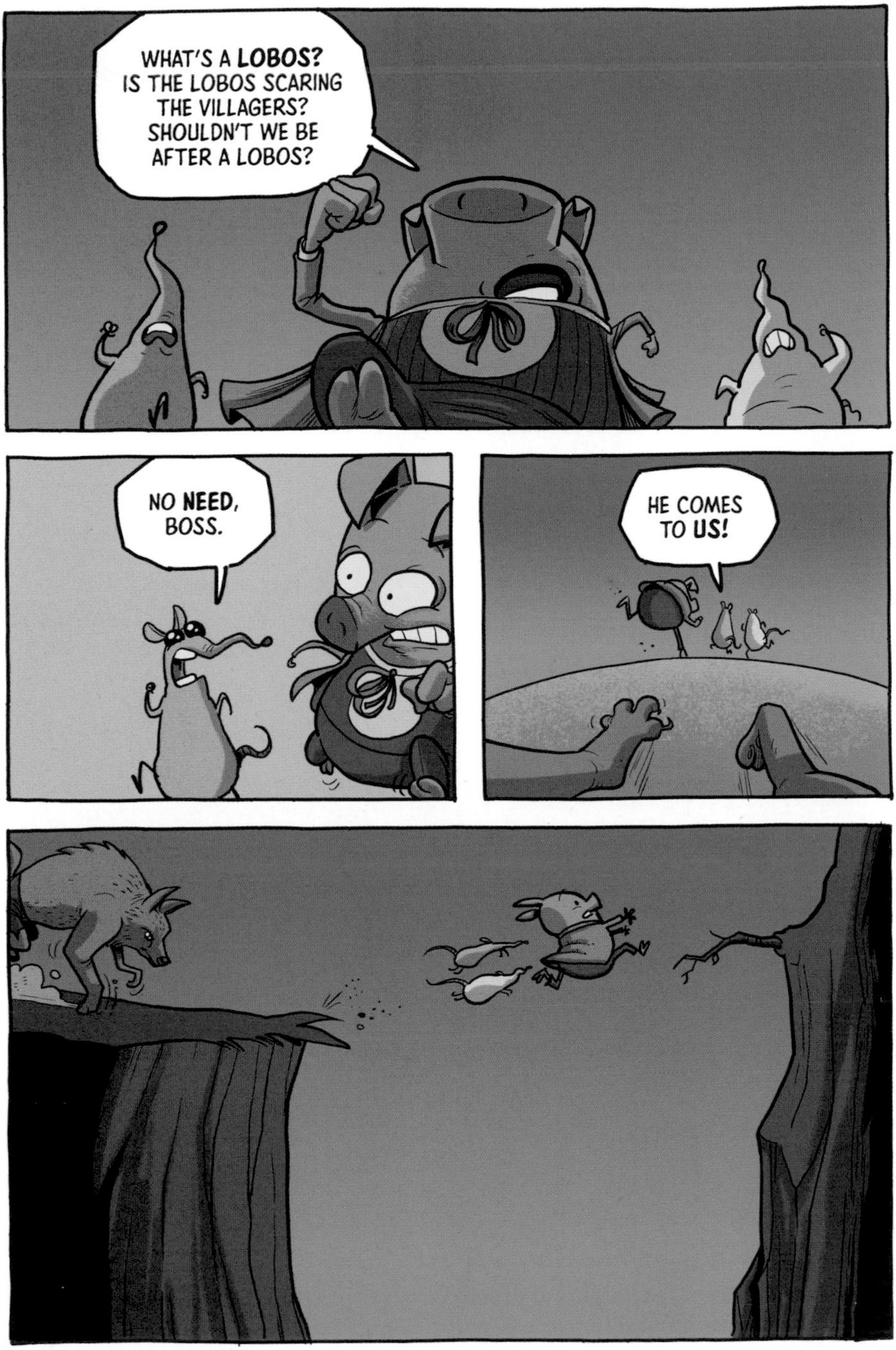
WHAT'S A **LOBOS?** IS THE LOBOS SCARING THE VILLAGERS? SHOULDN'T WE BE AFTER A LOBOS?
NO **NEED,** BOSS.
HE COMES TO **US!**

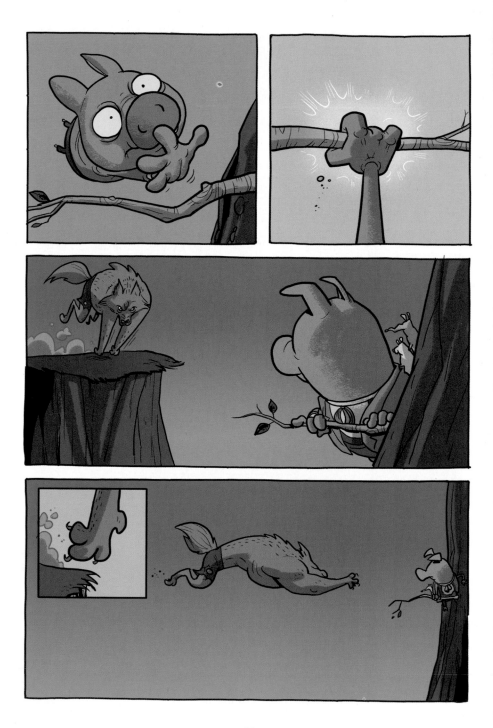

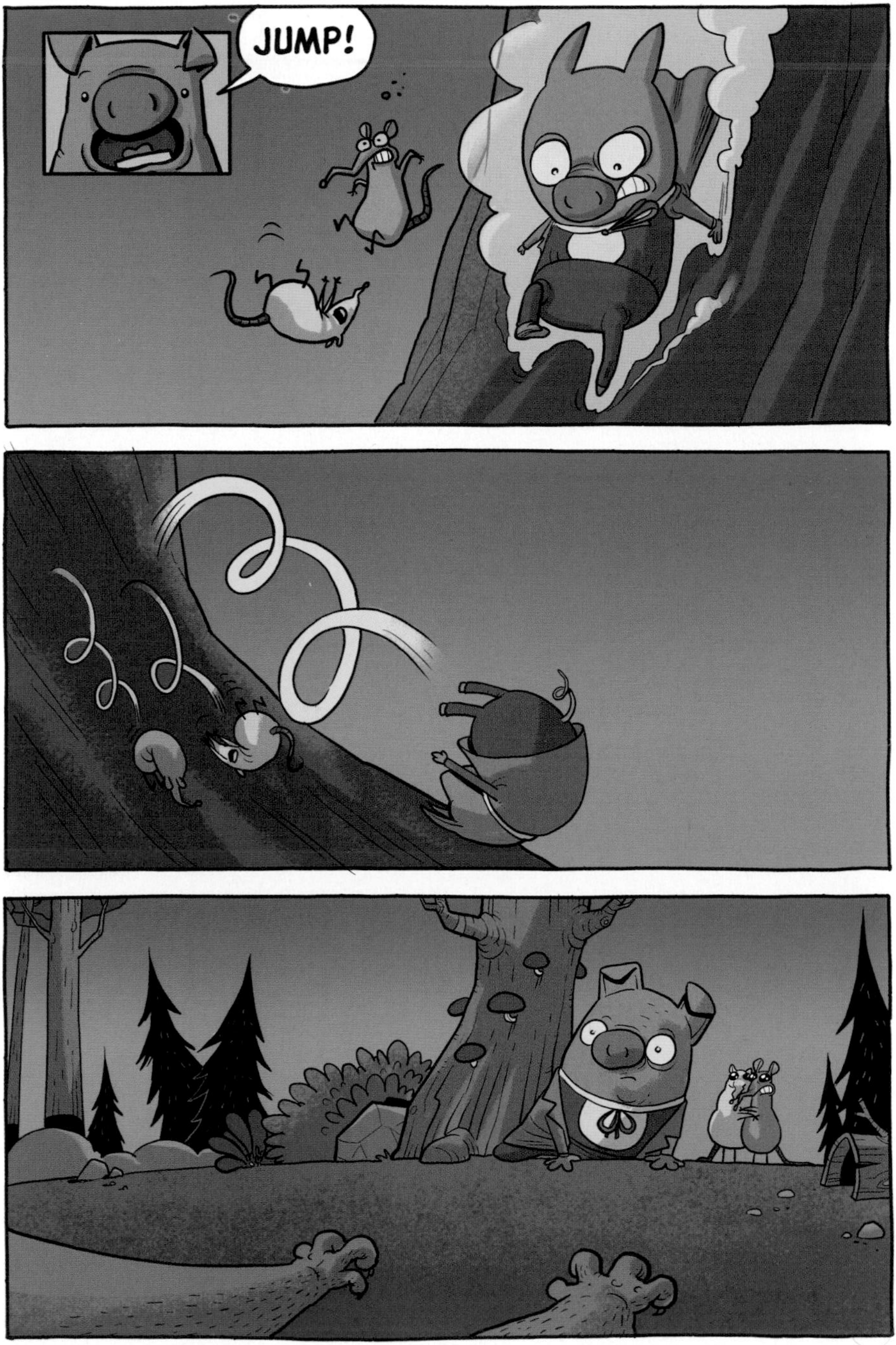
JUMP!

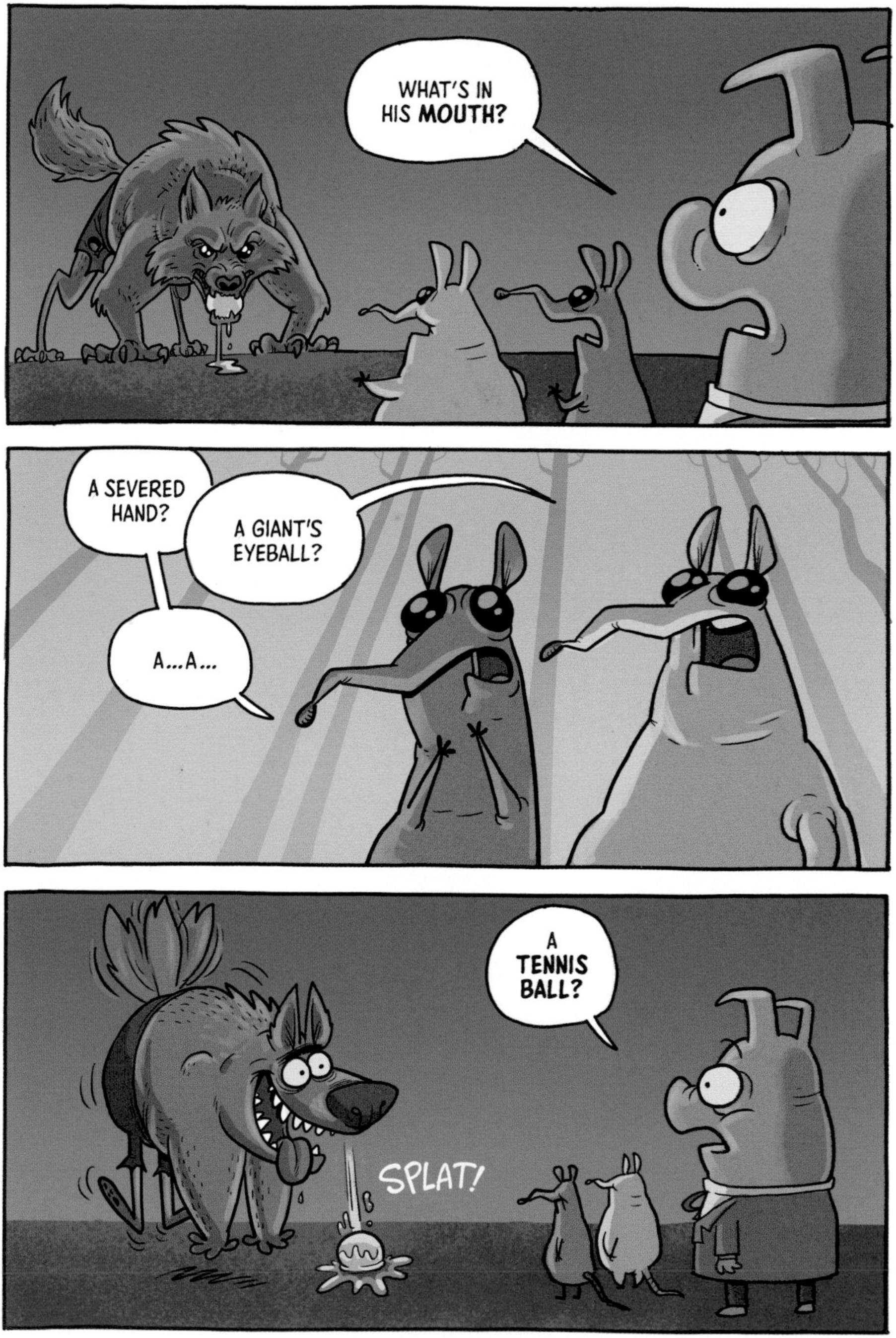
WHAT'S IN HIS MOUTH?
A SEVERED HAND?
A GIANT'S EYEBALL?
A...A...
A TENNIS BALL?
SPLAT!

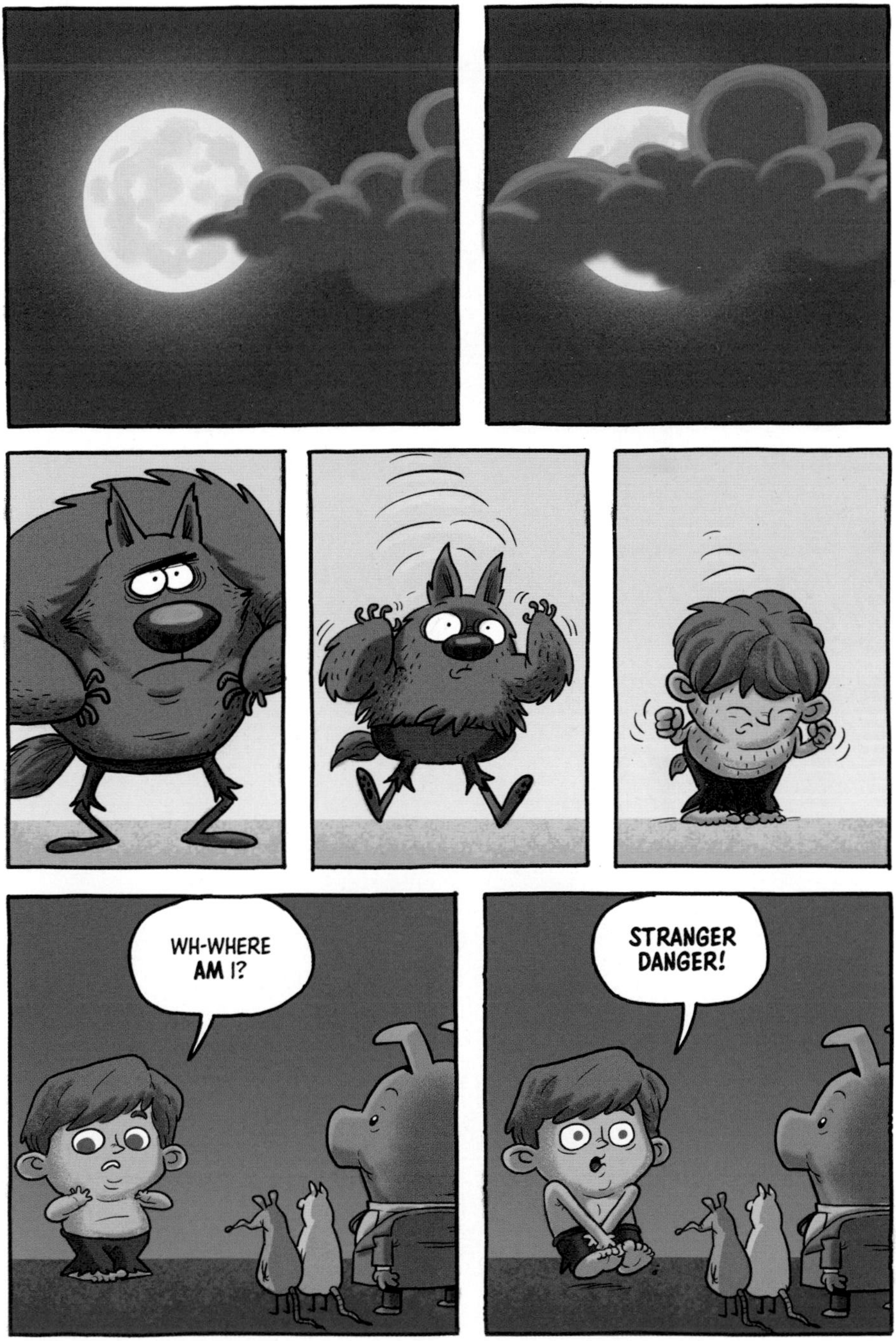
WH-WHERE AM I?
STRANGER DANGER!

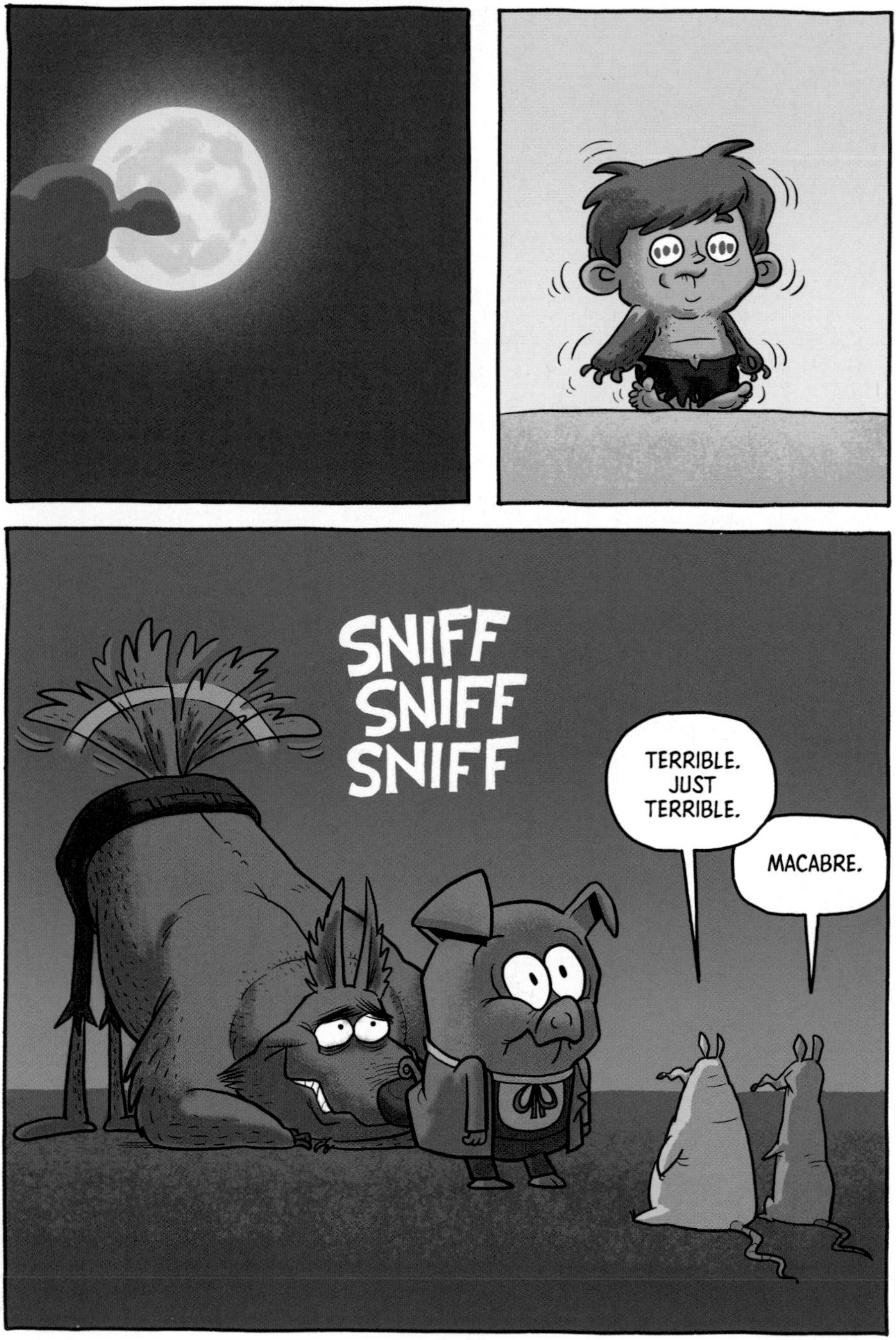
SNIFF
SNIFF
SNIFF
TERRIBLE. JUST TERRIBLE.
MACABRE.

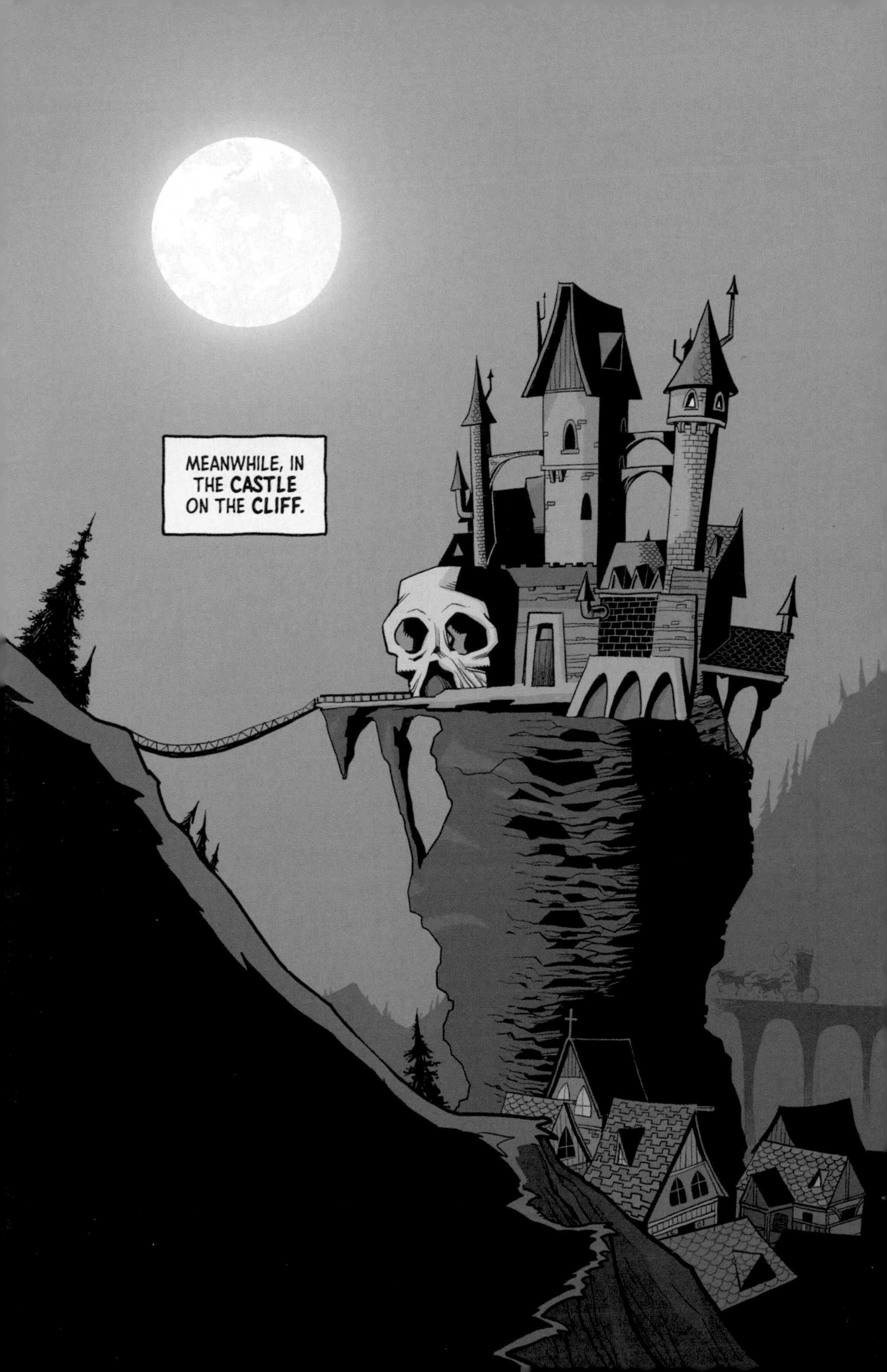
MEANWHILE, IN THE CASTLE ON THE CLIFF.

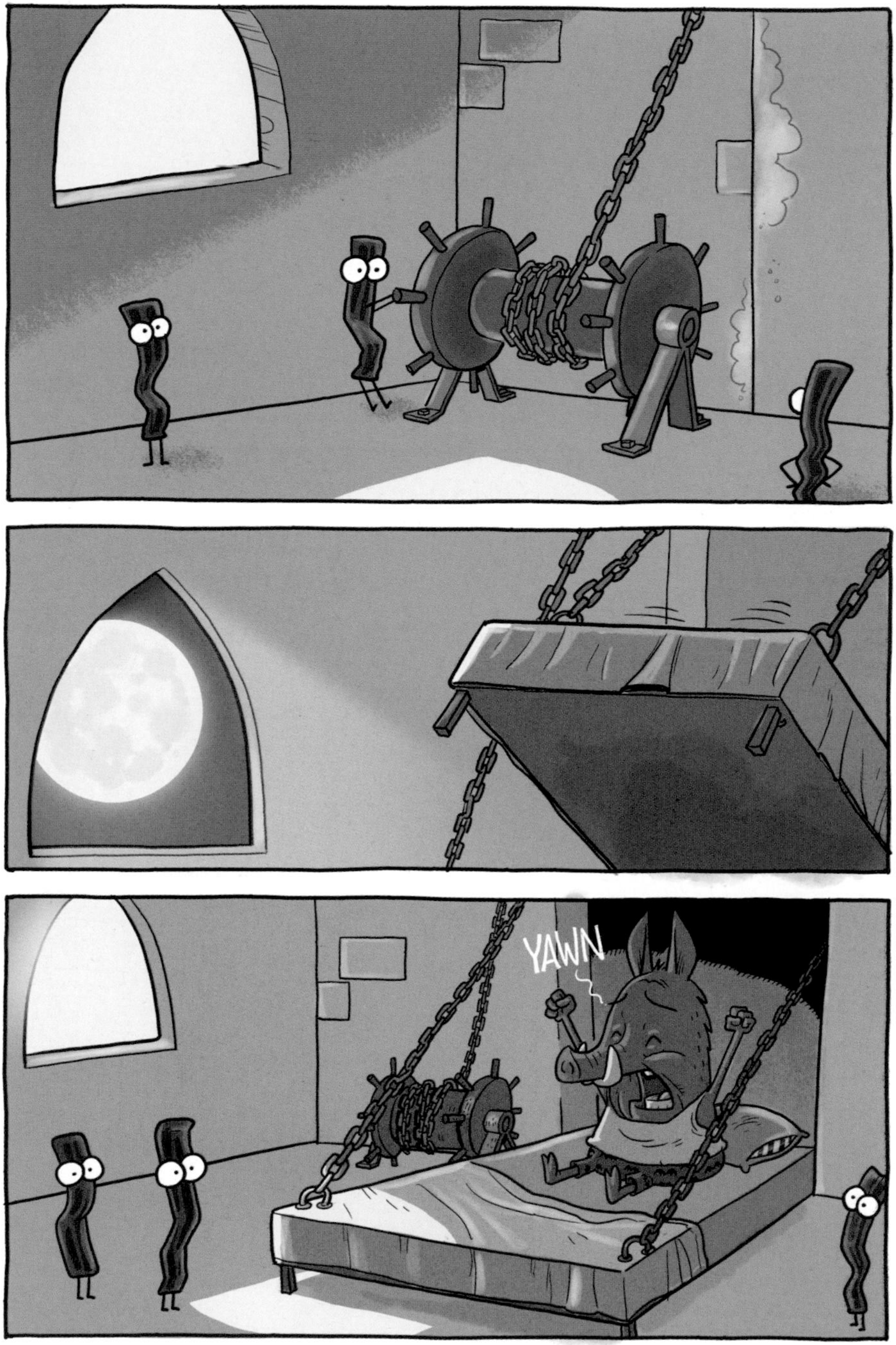
YAWN

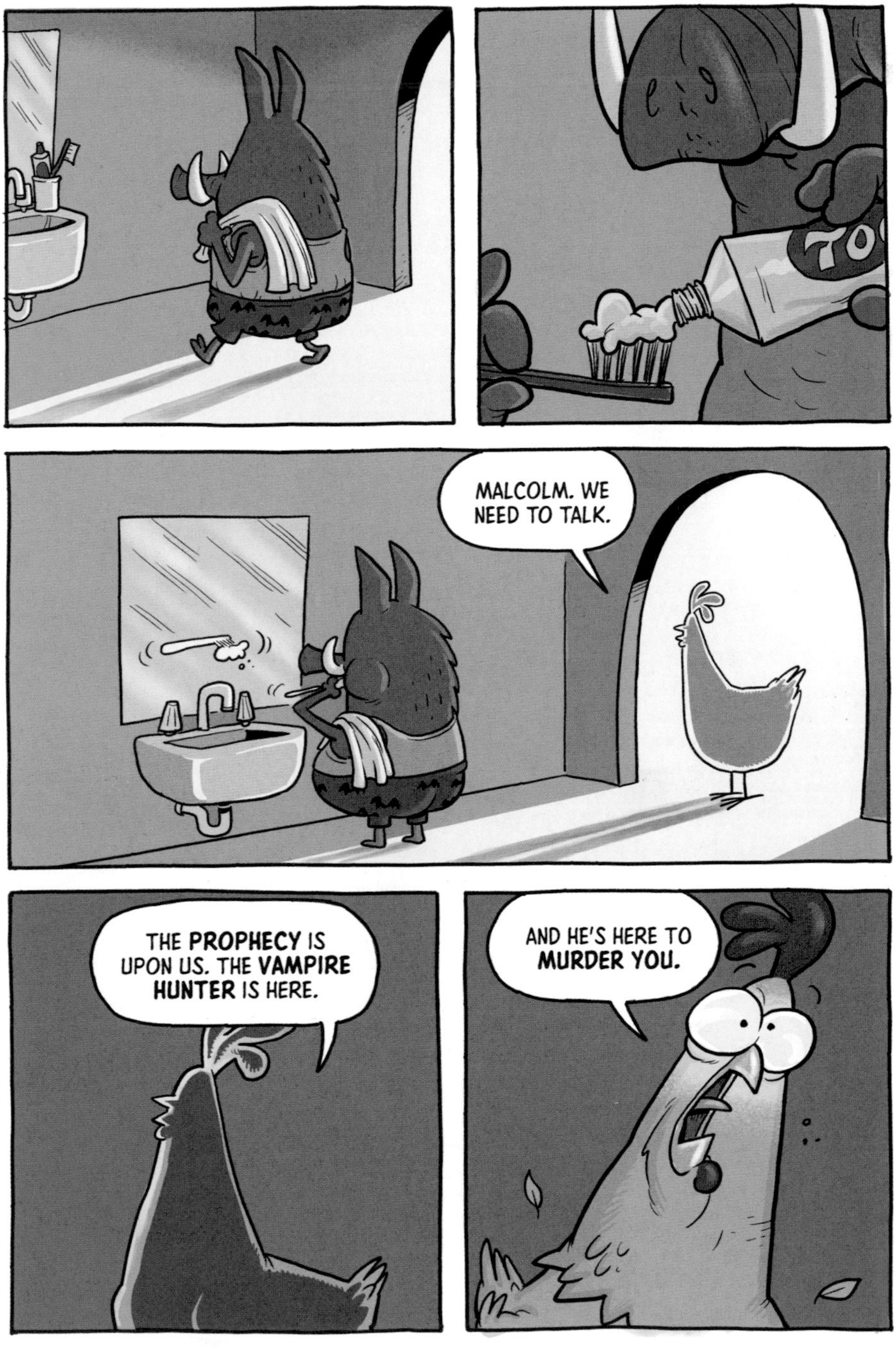
MALCOLM. WE NEED TO TALK.
THE **PROPHECY** IS UPON US. THE **VAMPIRE HUNTER** IS HERE.
AND HE'S HERE TO **MURDER YOU.**

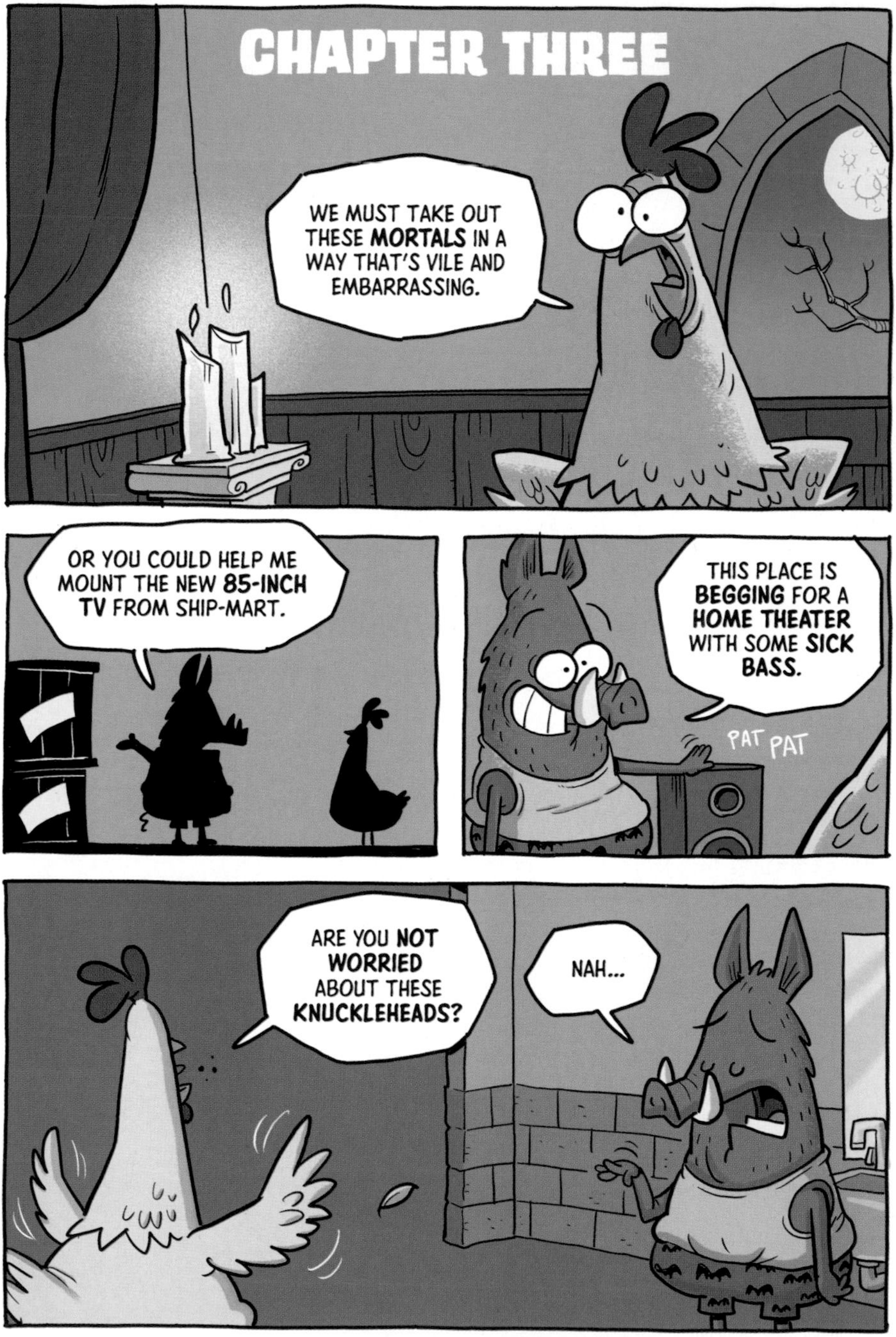
CHAPTER THREE
WE MUST TAKE OUT THESE MORTALS IN A WAY THAT'S VILE AND EMBARRASSING.
OR YOU COULD HELP ME MOUNT THE NEW 85-INCH TV FROM SHIP-MART.
THIS PLACE IS BEGGING FOR A HOME THEATER WITH SOME SICK BASS.
PAT PAT
ARE YOU NOT WORRIED ABOUT THESE KNUCKLEHEADS?
NAH...

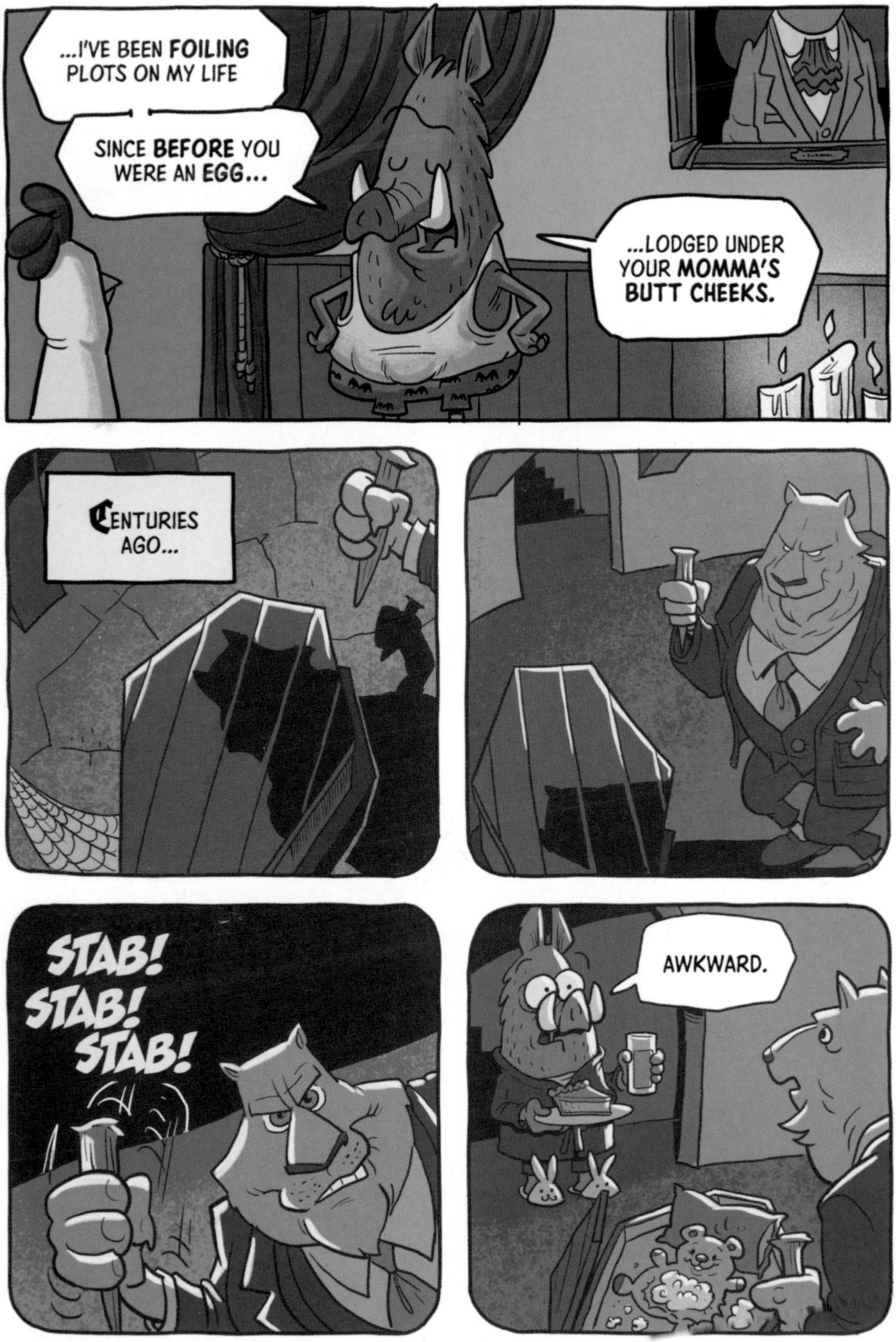
...I'VE BEEN FOILING PLOTS ON MY LIFE
SINCE BEFORE YOU WERE AN EGG...
...LODGED UNDER YOUR MOMMA'S BUTT CHEEKS.
CENTURIES AGO...
STAB! STAB! STAB!
AWKWARD.

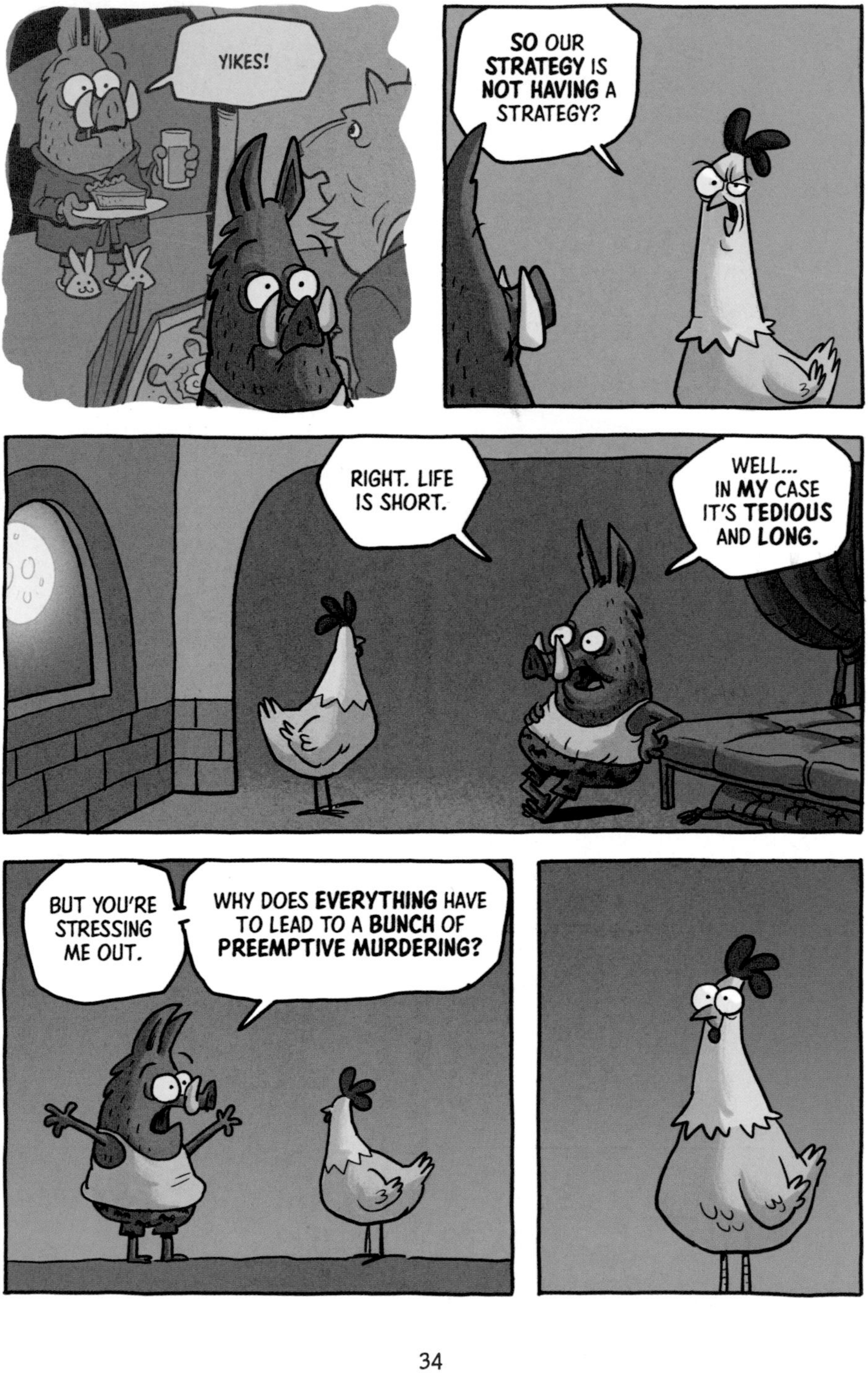
YIKES!
SO OUR STRATEGY IS NOT HAVING A STRATEGY?
RIGHT. LIFE IS SHORT.
WELL... IN MY CASE IT'S TEDIOUS AND LONG.
BUT YOU'RE STRESSING ME OUT.
WHY DOES EVERYTHING HAVE TO LEAD TO A BUNCH OF PREEMPTIVE MURDERING?

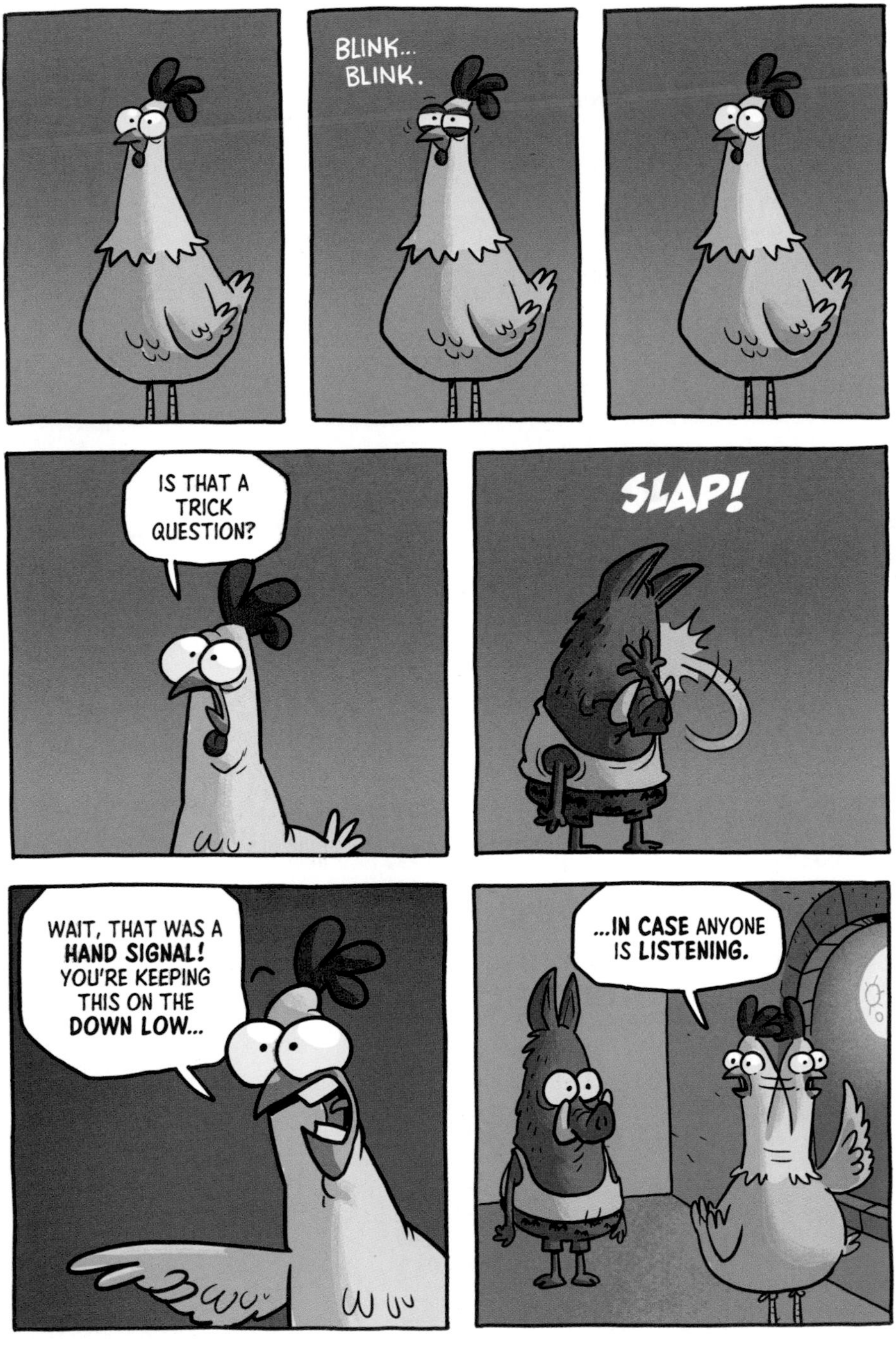
BLINK...
BLINK.
IS THAT A TRICK QUESTION?
SLAP!
WAIT, THAT WAS A HAND SIGNAL! YOU'RE KEEPING THIS ON THE DOWN LOW...
...IN CASE ANYONE IS LISTENING.

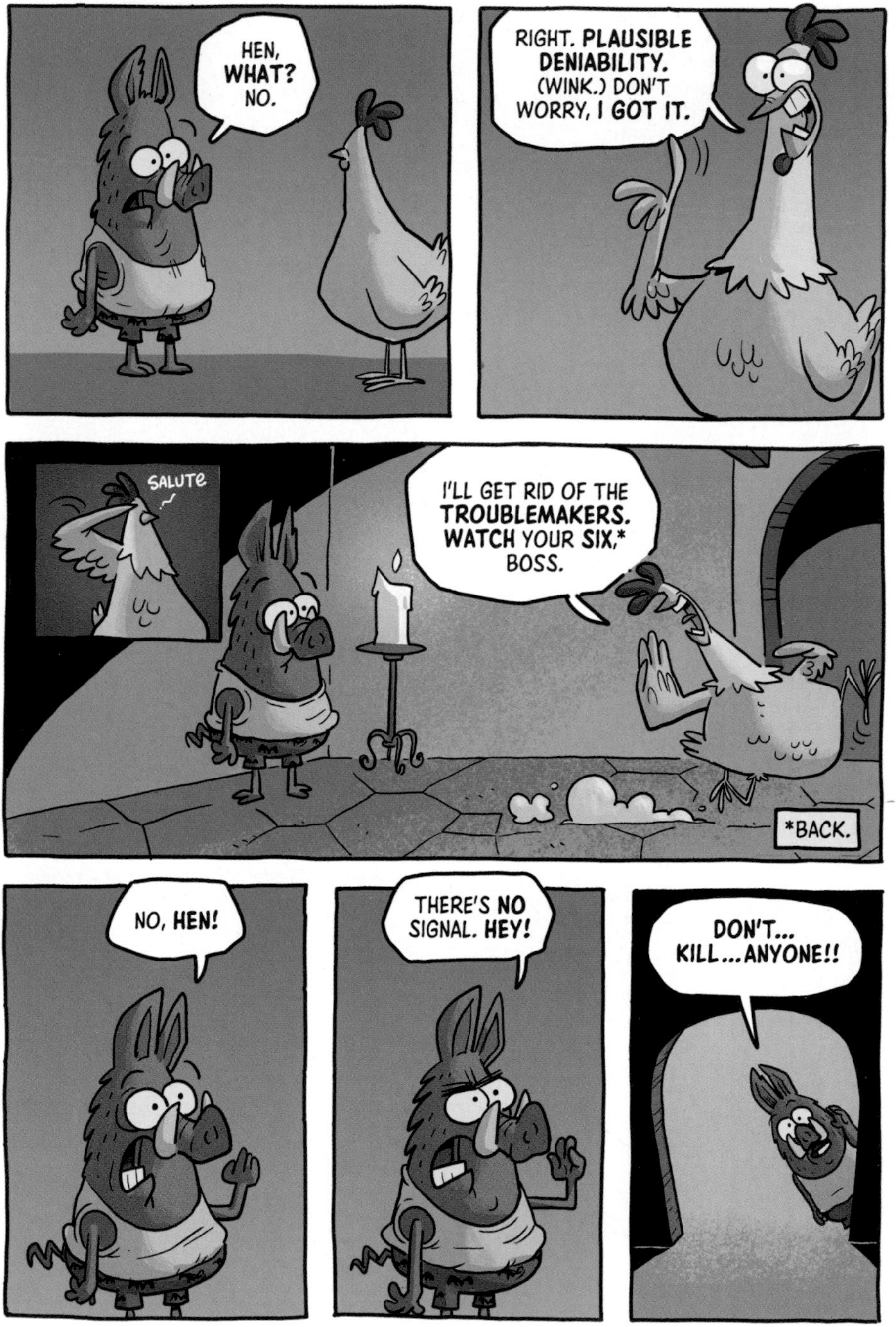
HEN, WHAT? NO.
RIGHT. PLAUSIBLE DENIABILITY. (WINK.) DON'T WORRY, I GOT IT.
SALUTE
I'LL GET RID OF THE TROUBLEMAKERS. WATCH YOUR SIX,* BOSS.
*BACK.
NO, HEN!
THERE'S NO SIGNAL. HEY!
DON'T... KILL... ANYONE!!

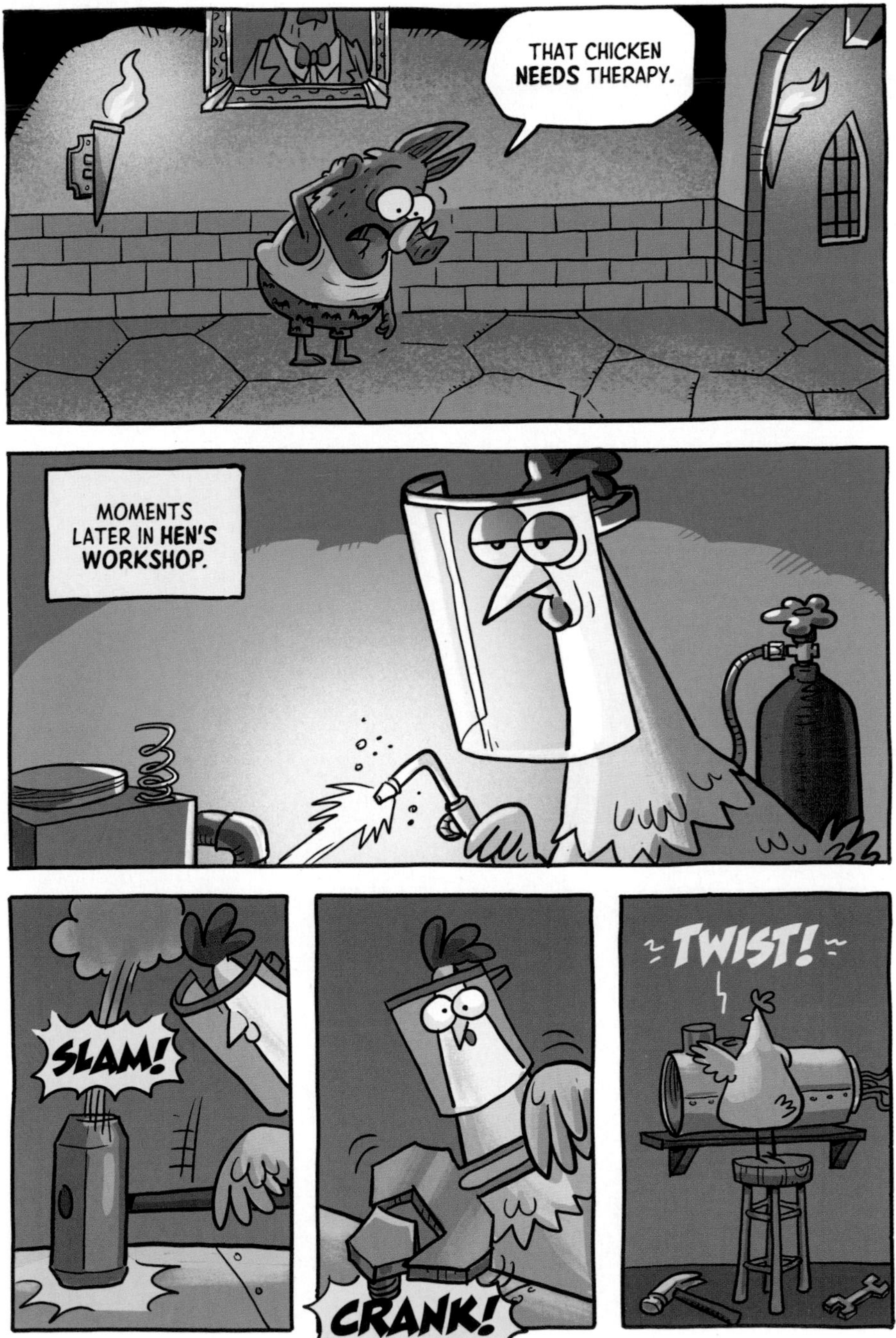
THAT CHICKEN NEEDS THERAPY.
MOMENTS LATER IN HEN'S WORKSHOP.
SLAM!
CRANK!
TWIST!

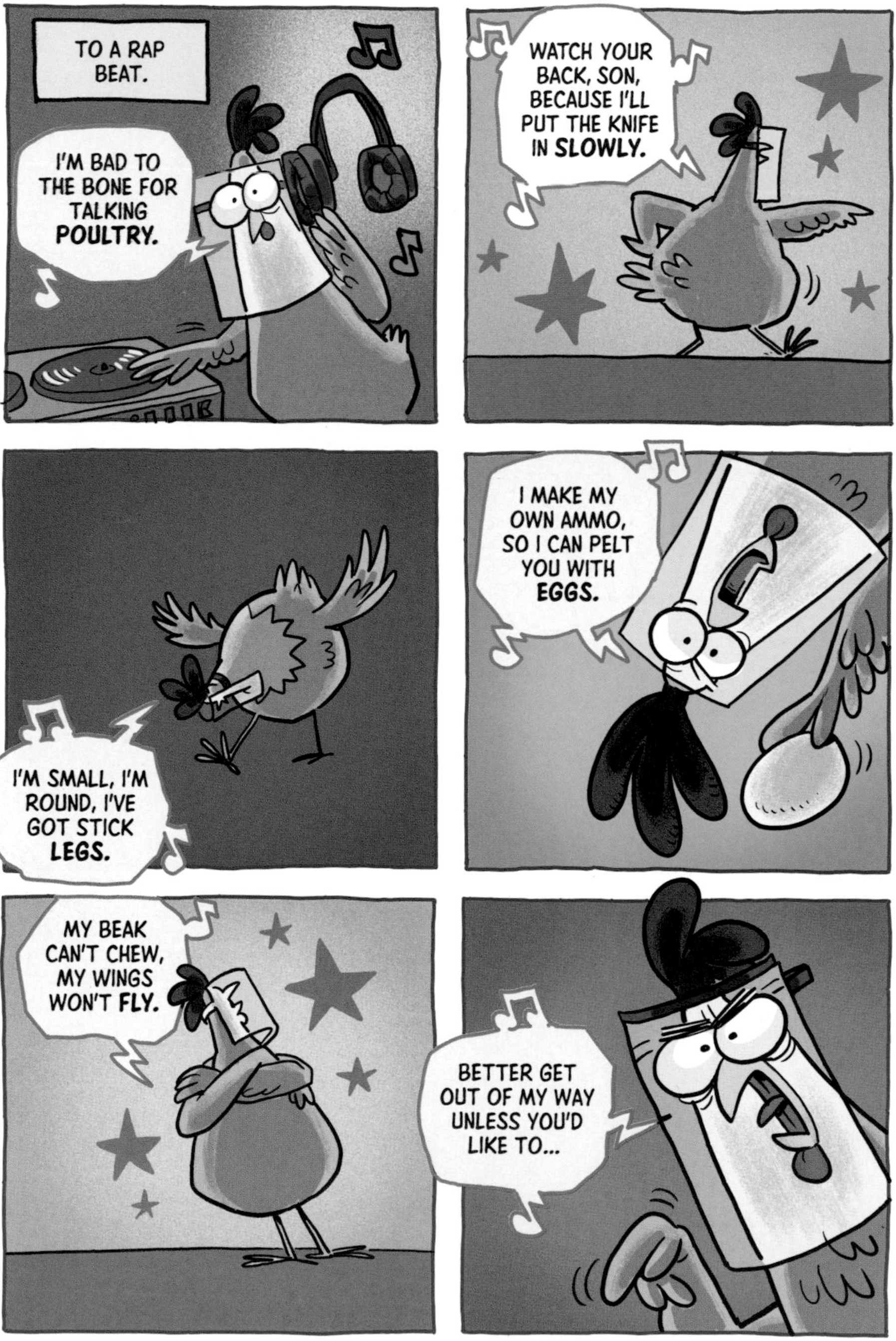
TO A RAP BEAT.
I'M BAD TO THE BONE FOR TALKING POULTRY.
WATCH YOUR BACK, SON, BECAUSE I'LL PUT THE KNIFE IN SLOWLY.
I'M SMALL, I'M ROUND, I'VE GOT STICK LEGS.
I MAKE MY OWN AMMO, SO I CAN PELT YOU WITH EGGS.
MY BEAK CAN'T CHEW, MY WINGS WON'T FLY.
BETTER GET OUT OF MY WAY UNLESS YOU'D LIKE TO...

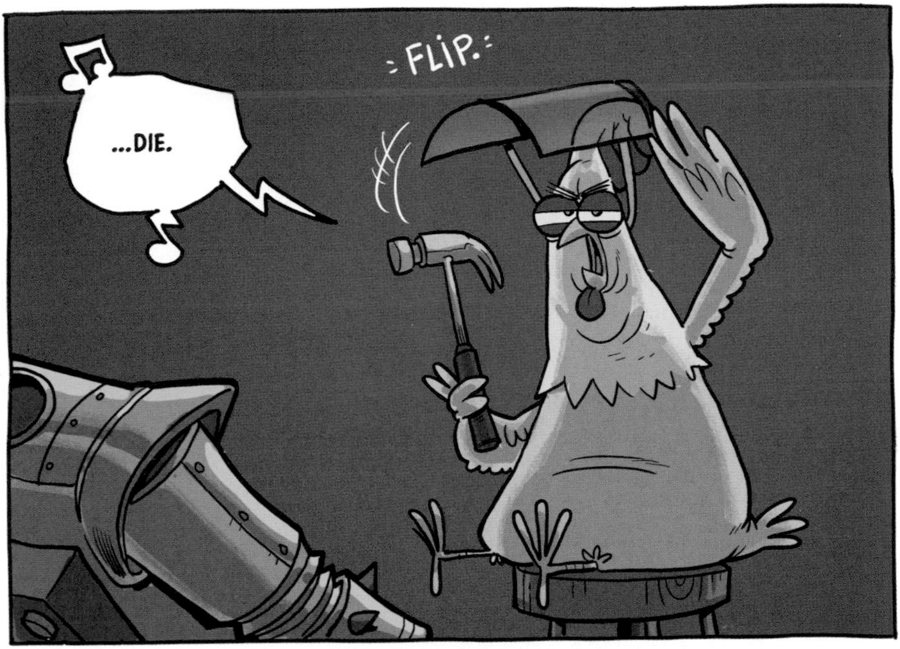
...DIE.
FLIP.

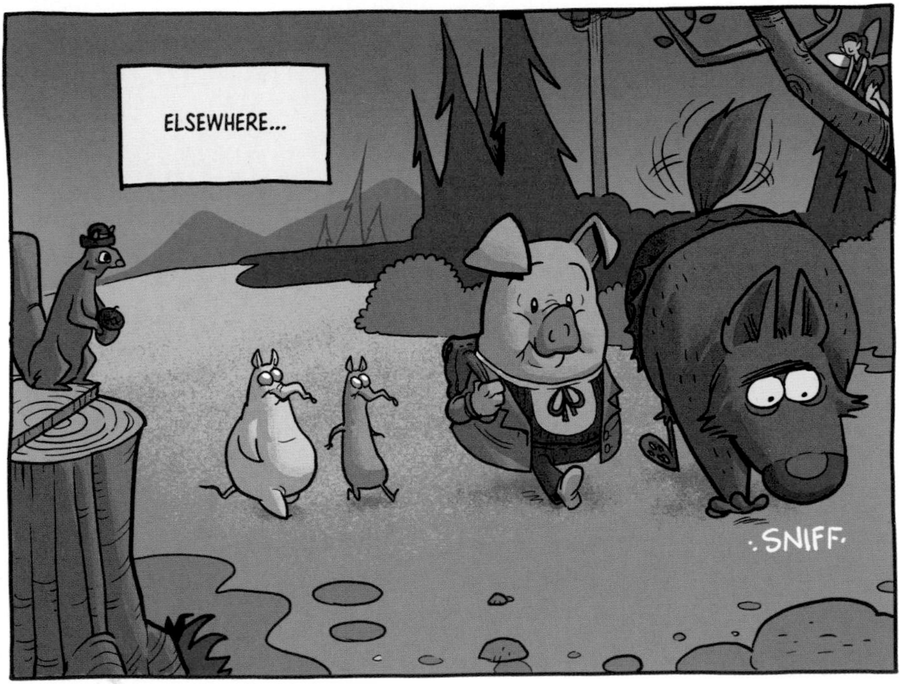
ELSEWHERE...
SNIFF.

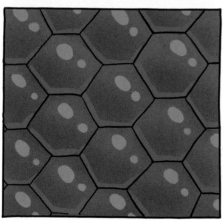

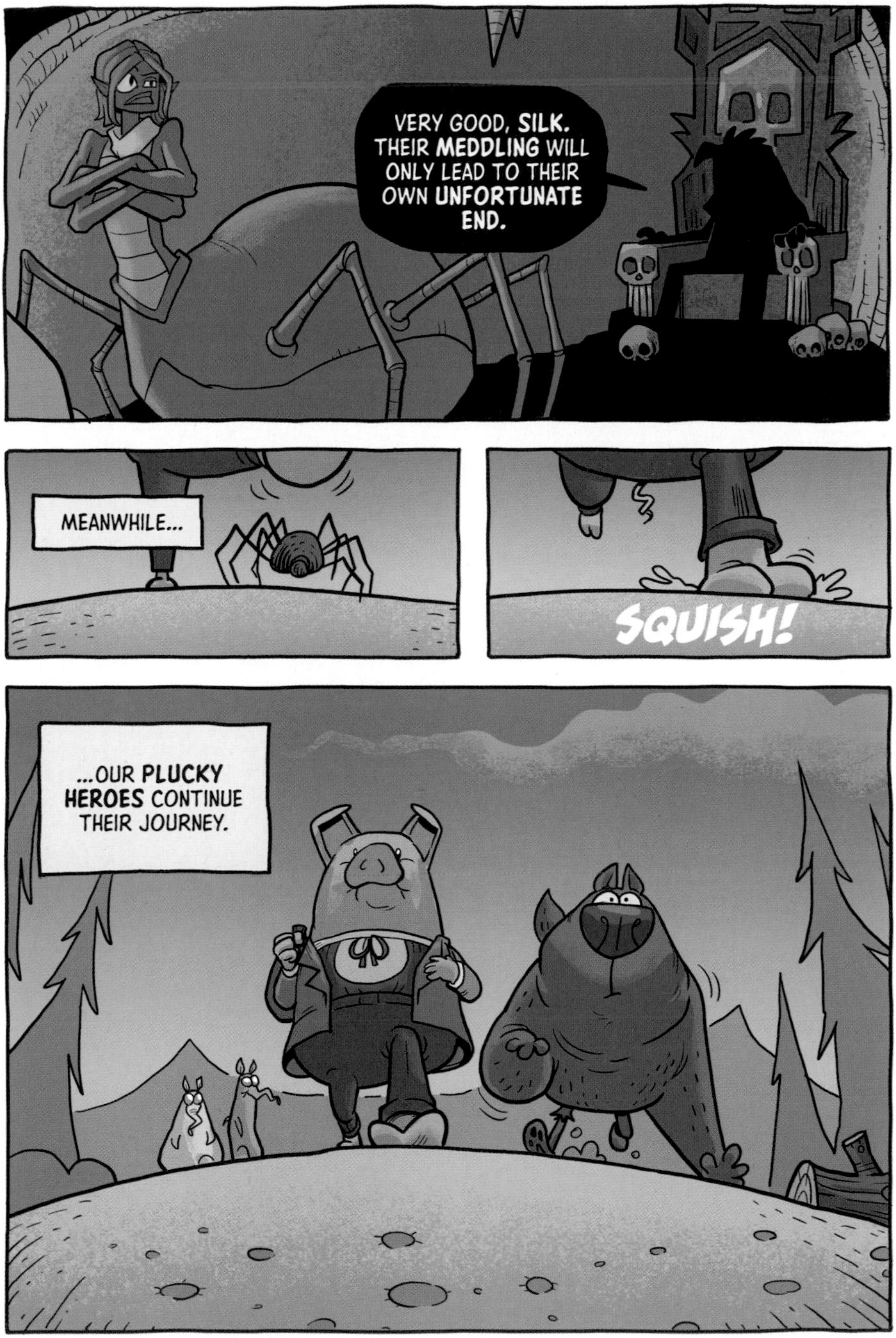
VERY GOOD, **SILK.** THEIR **MEDDLING** WILL ONLY LEAD TO THEIR OWN **UNFORTUNATE END.**
MEANWHILE...
SQUISH!
...OUR **PLUCKY HEROES** CONTINUE THEIR JOURNEY.

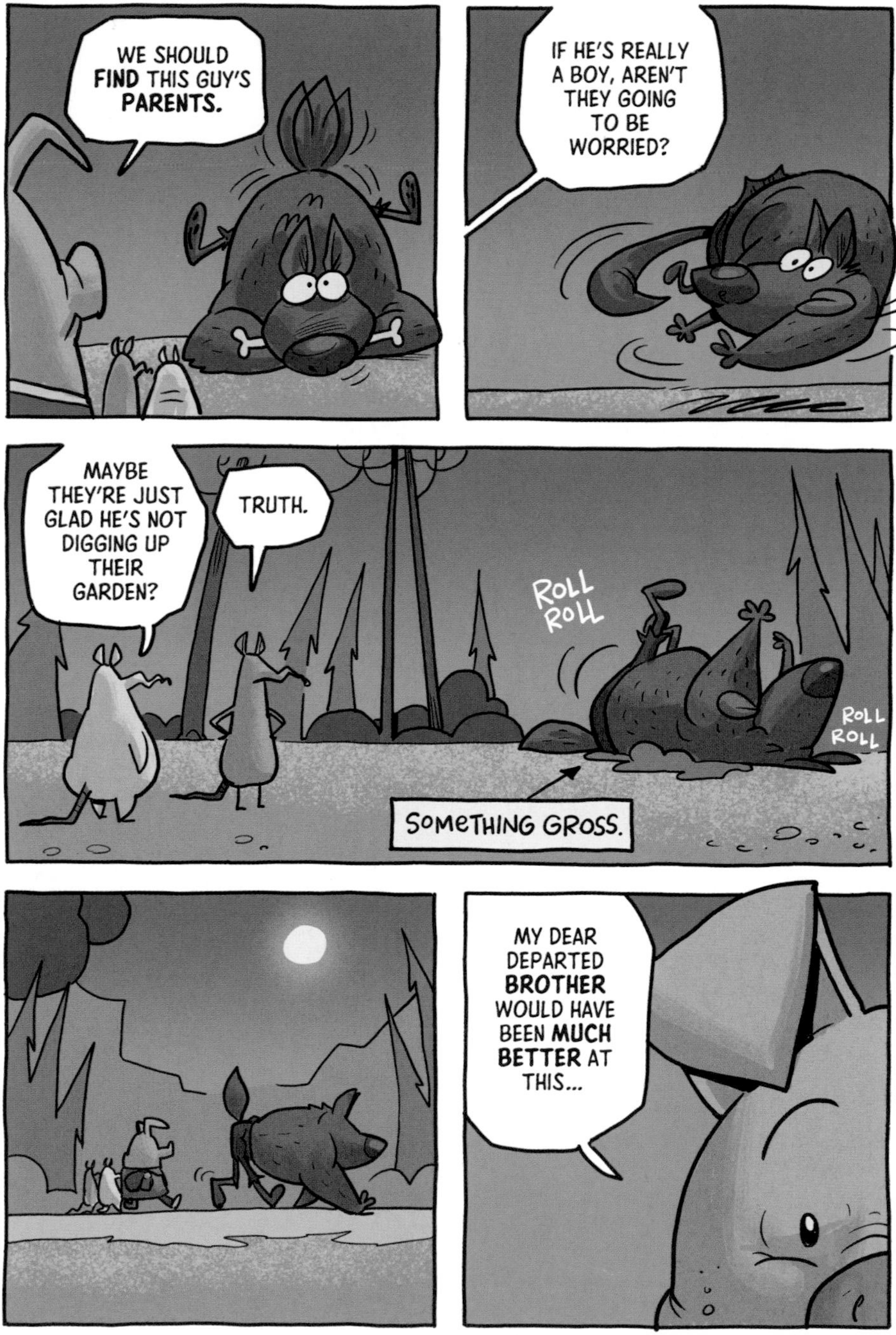

WE SHOULD FIND THIS GUY'S PARENTS.
IF HE'S REALLY A BOY, AREN'T THEY GOING TO BE WORRIED?
MAYBE THEY'RE JUST GLAD HE'S NOT DIGGING UP THEIR GARDEN?
TRUTH.
ROLL ROLL
ROLL ROLL
SOMETHING GROSS.
MY DEAR DEPARTED BROTHER WOULD HAVE BEEN MUCH BETTER AT THIS...

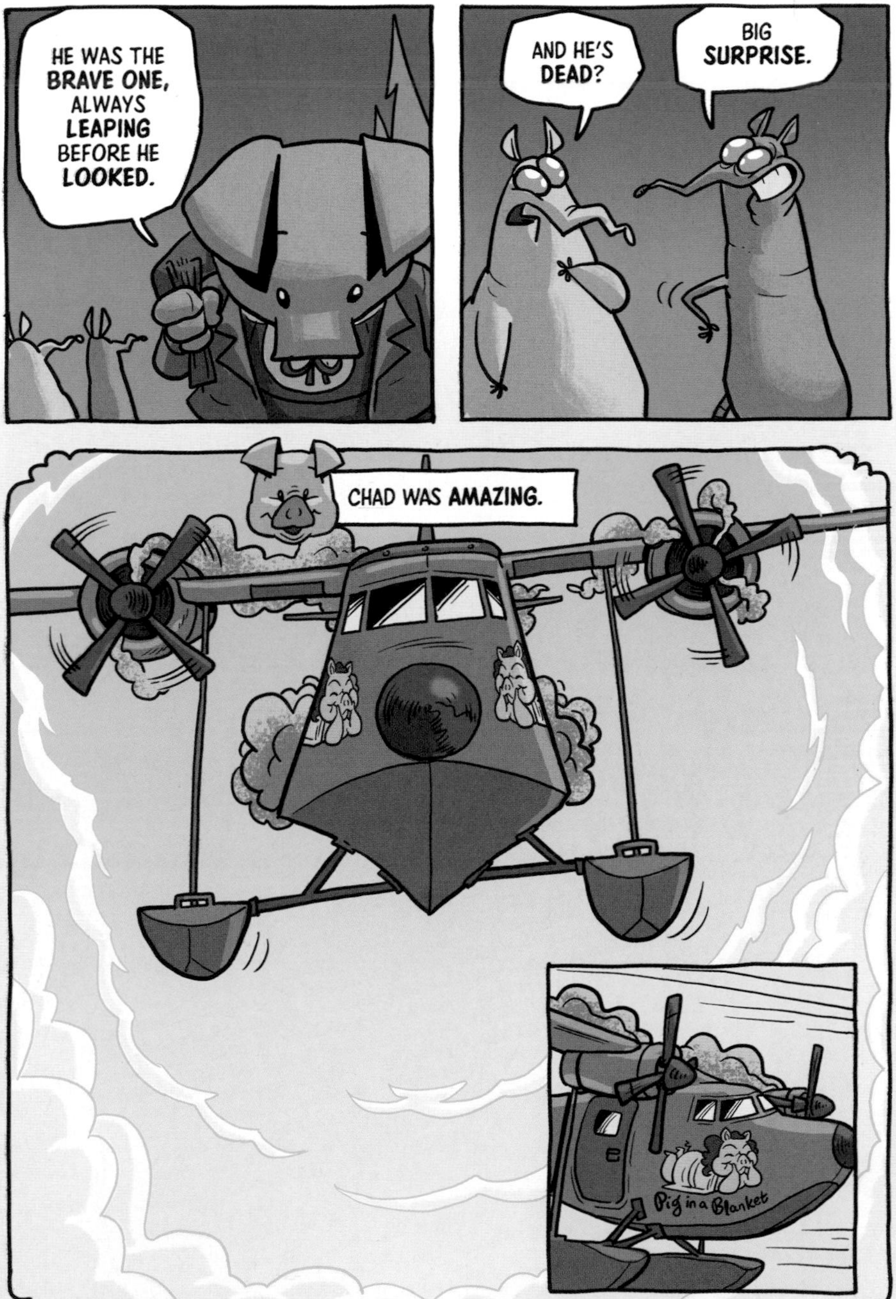

HE WAS THE **BRAVE ONE**, ALWAYS **LEAPING** BEFORE HE **LOOKED**.
AND HE'S **DEAD**?
BIG **SURPRISE**.
CHAD WAS **AMAZING**.
Pig in a Blanket

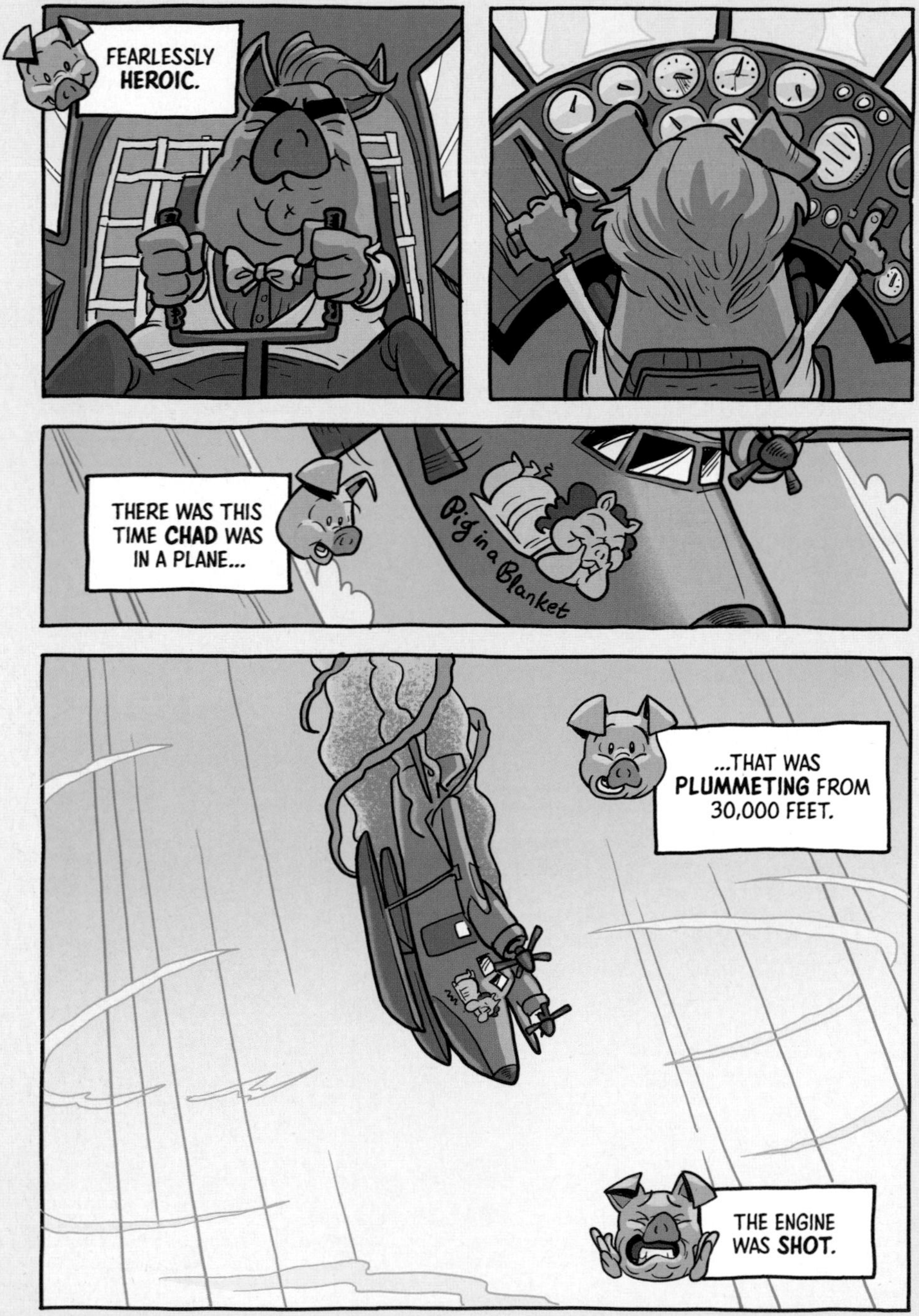
FEARLESSLY HEROIC.
THERE WAS THIS TIME CHAD WAS IN A PLANE...
Pig in a Blanket
...THAT WAS PLUMMETING FROM 30,000 FEET.
THE ENGINE WAS SHOT.

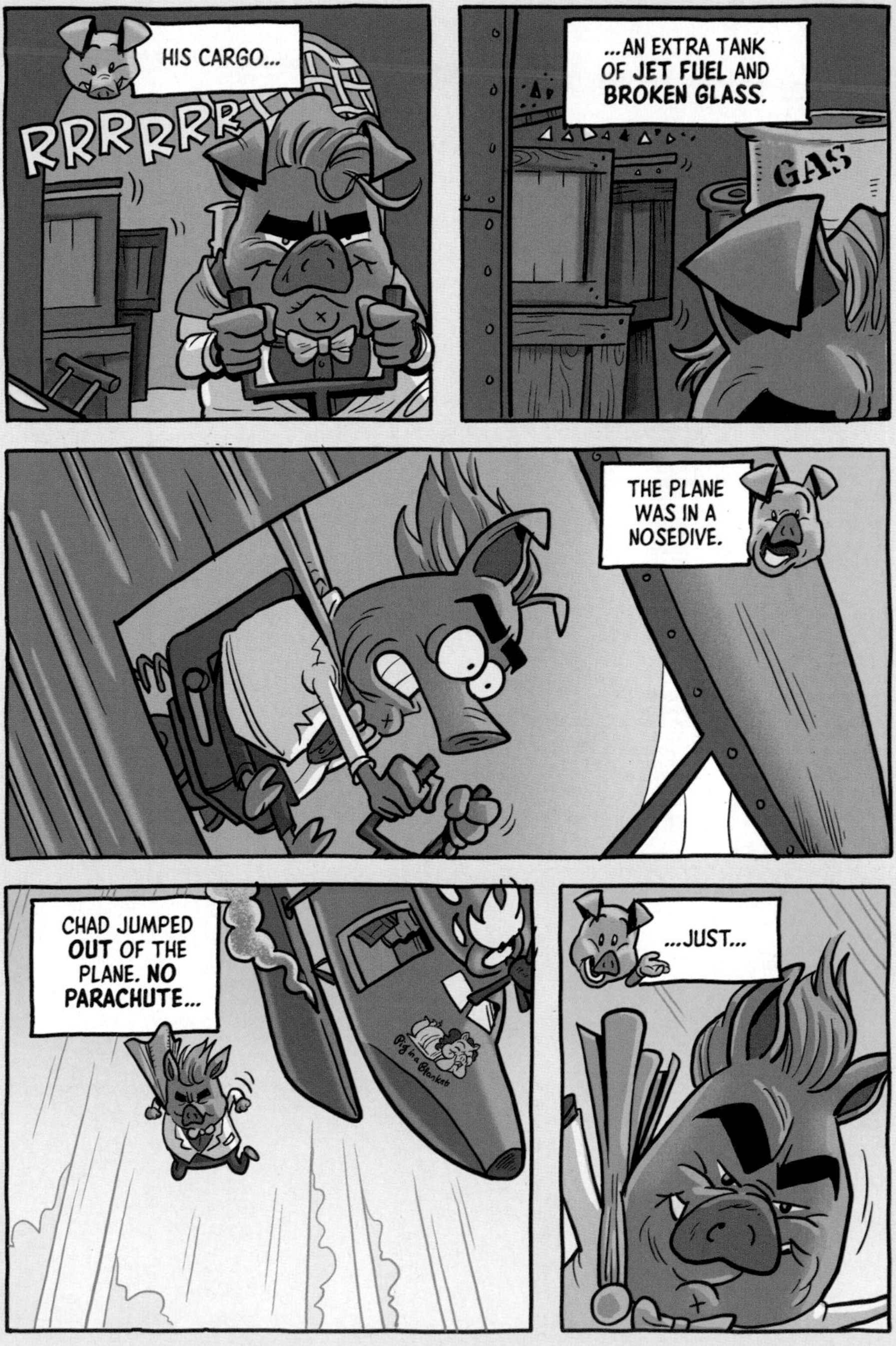
HIS CARGO...
RRRRRR
...AN EXTRA TANK OF JET FUEL AND BROKEN GLASS.
GAS
THE PLANE WAS IN A NOSEDIVE.
CHAD JUMPED OUT OF THE PLANE. NO PARACHUTE...
Pig in a Blanket
...JUST...

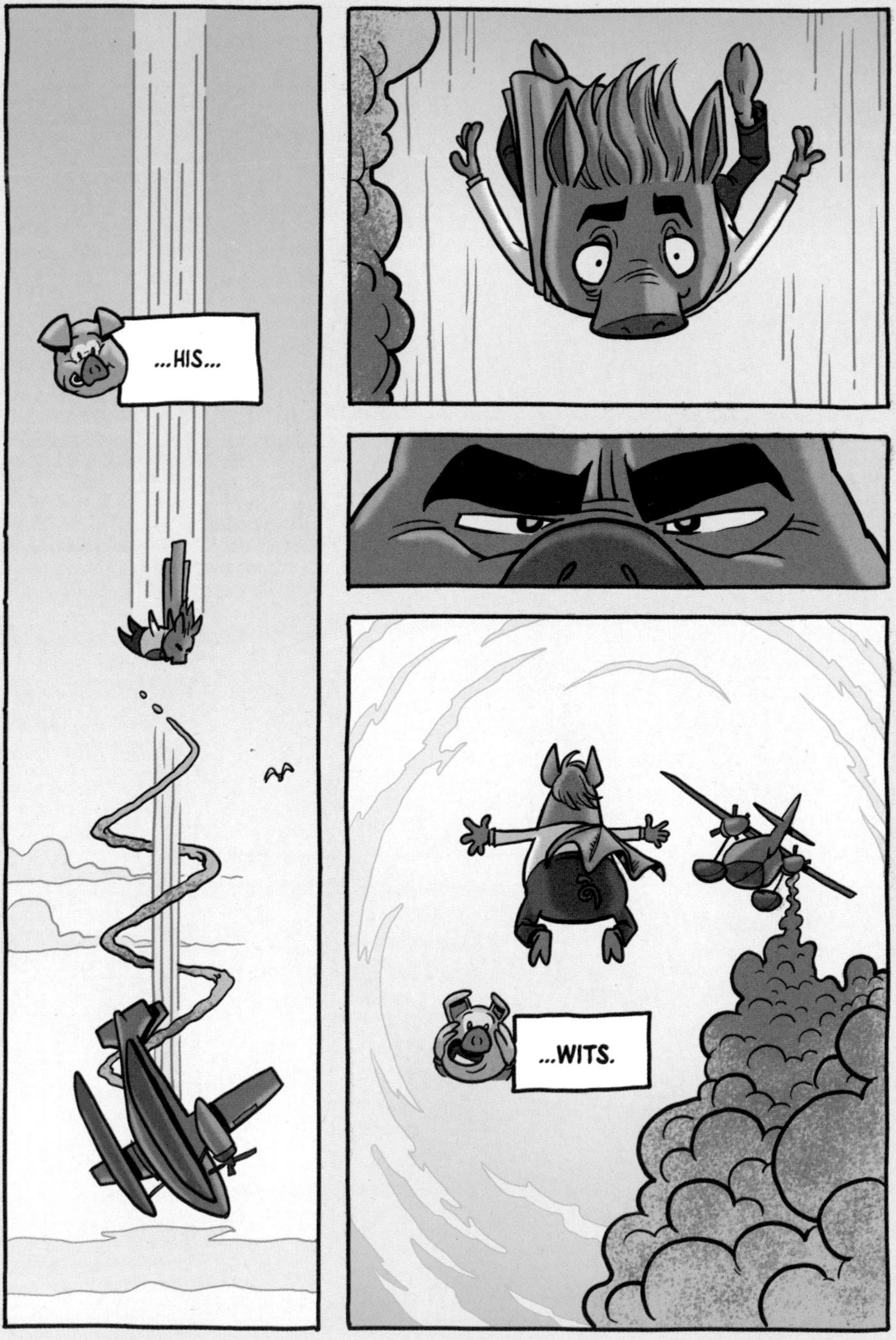
...HIS...
...WITS.

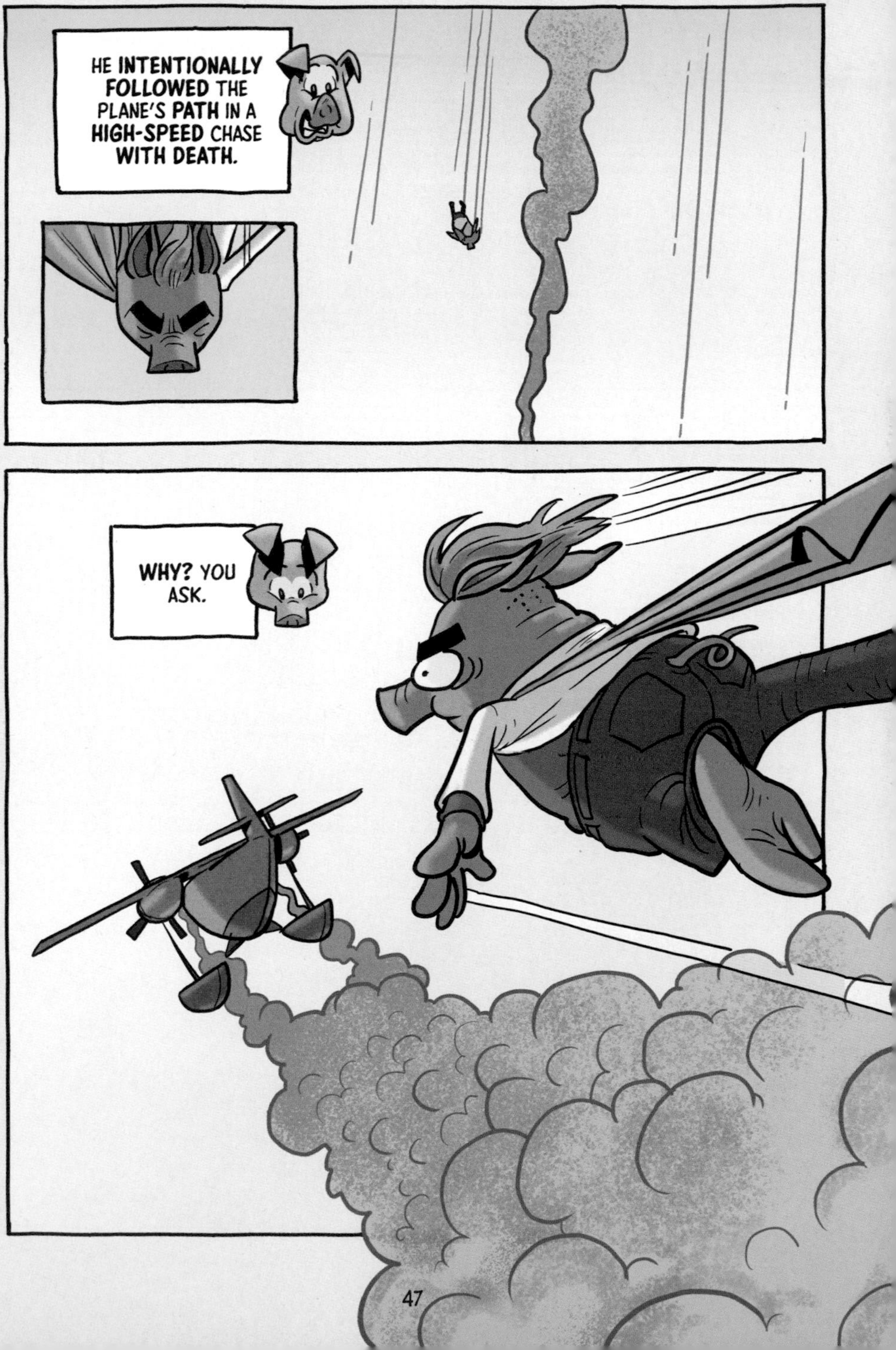
HE INTENTIONALLY FOLLOWED THE PLANE'S PATH IN A HIGH-SPEED CHASE WITH DEATH.
WHY? YOU ASK.

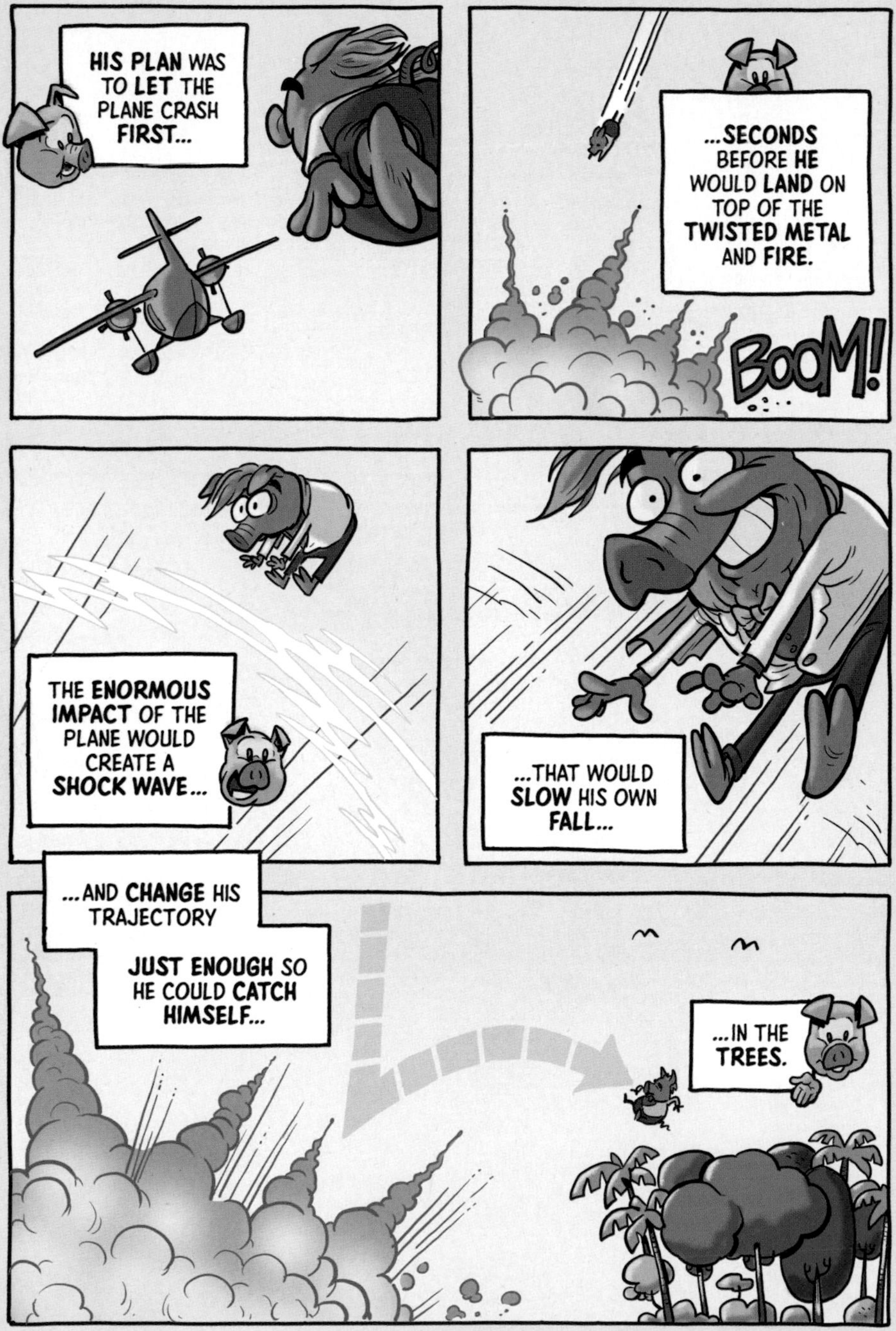
HIS PLAN WAS TO LET THE PLANE CRASH FIRST...
...SECONDS BEFORE HE WOULD LAND ON TOP OF THE TWISTED METAL AND FIRE.
BOOM!
THE ENORMOUS IMPACT OF THE PLANE WOULD CREATE A SHOCK WAVE...
...THAT WOULD SLOW HIS OWN FALL...
...AND CHANGE HIS TRAJECTORY
JUST ENOUGH SO HE COULD CATCH HIMSELF...
...IN THE TREES.

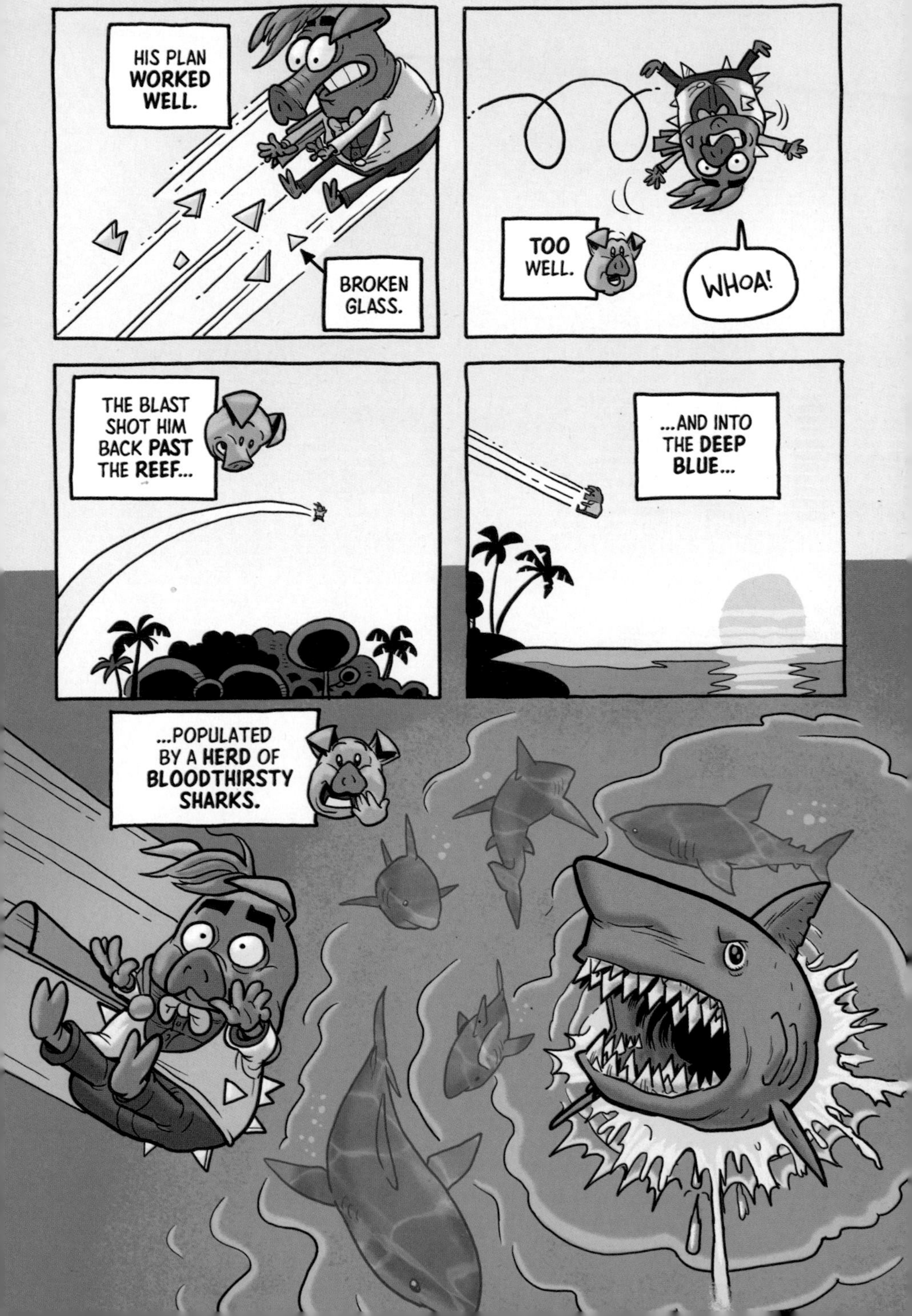
HIS PLAN WORKED WELL.
BROKEN GLASS.
TOO WELL.
WHOA!
THE BLAST SHOT HIM BACK PAST THE REEF...
...AND INTO THE DEEP BLUE...
...POPULATED BY A HERD OF BLOODTHIRSTY SHARKS.

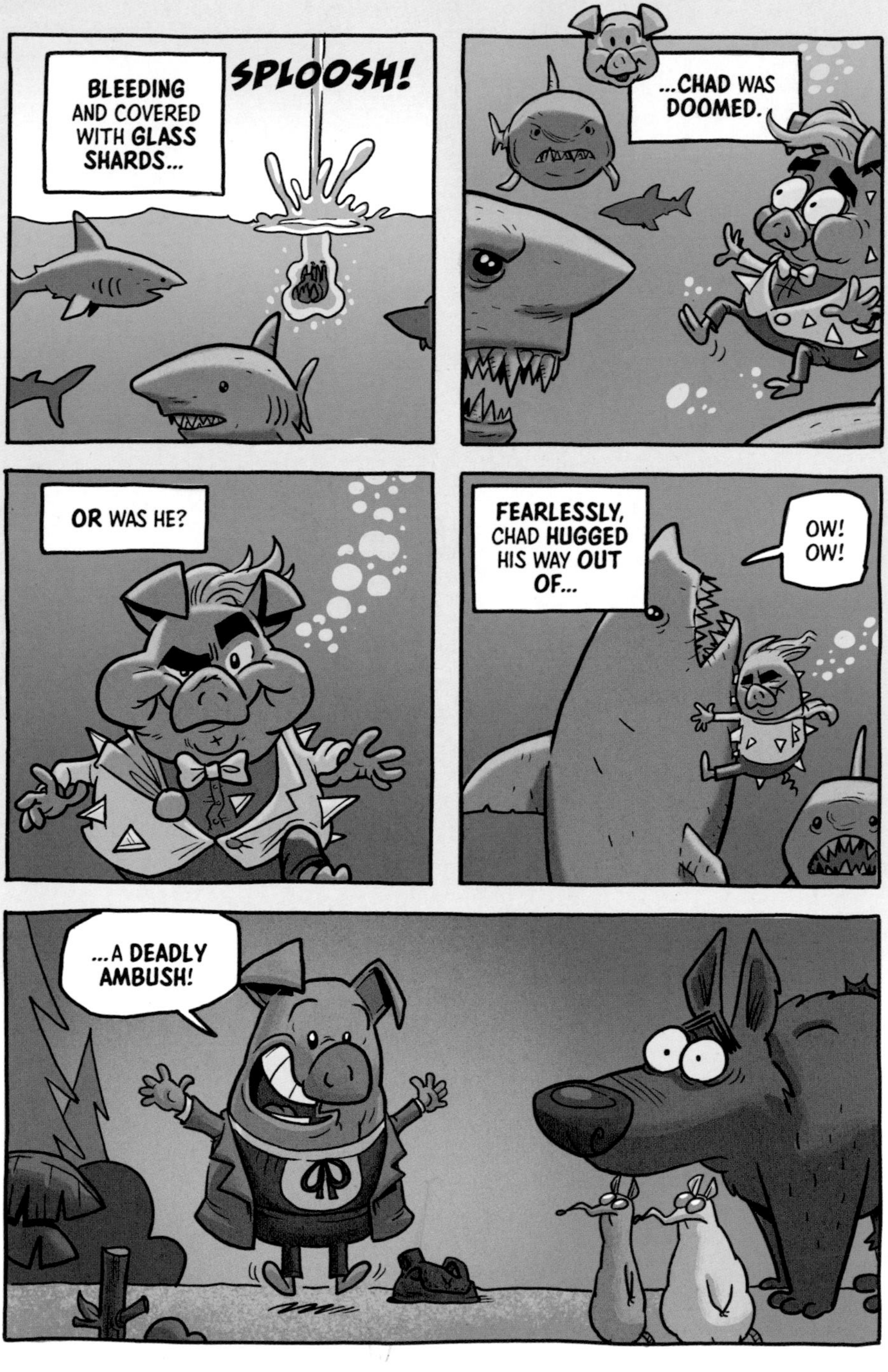
BLEEDING AND COVERED WITH GLASS SHARDS...
SPLOOSH!
...CHAD WAS DOOMED.
OR WAS HE?
FEARLESSLY, CHAD HUGGED HIS WAY OUT OF...
OW! OW!
...A DEADLY AMBUSH!

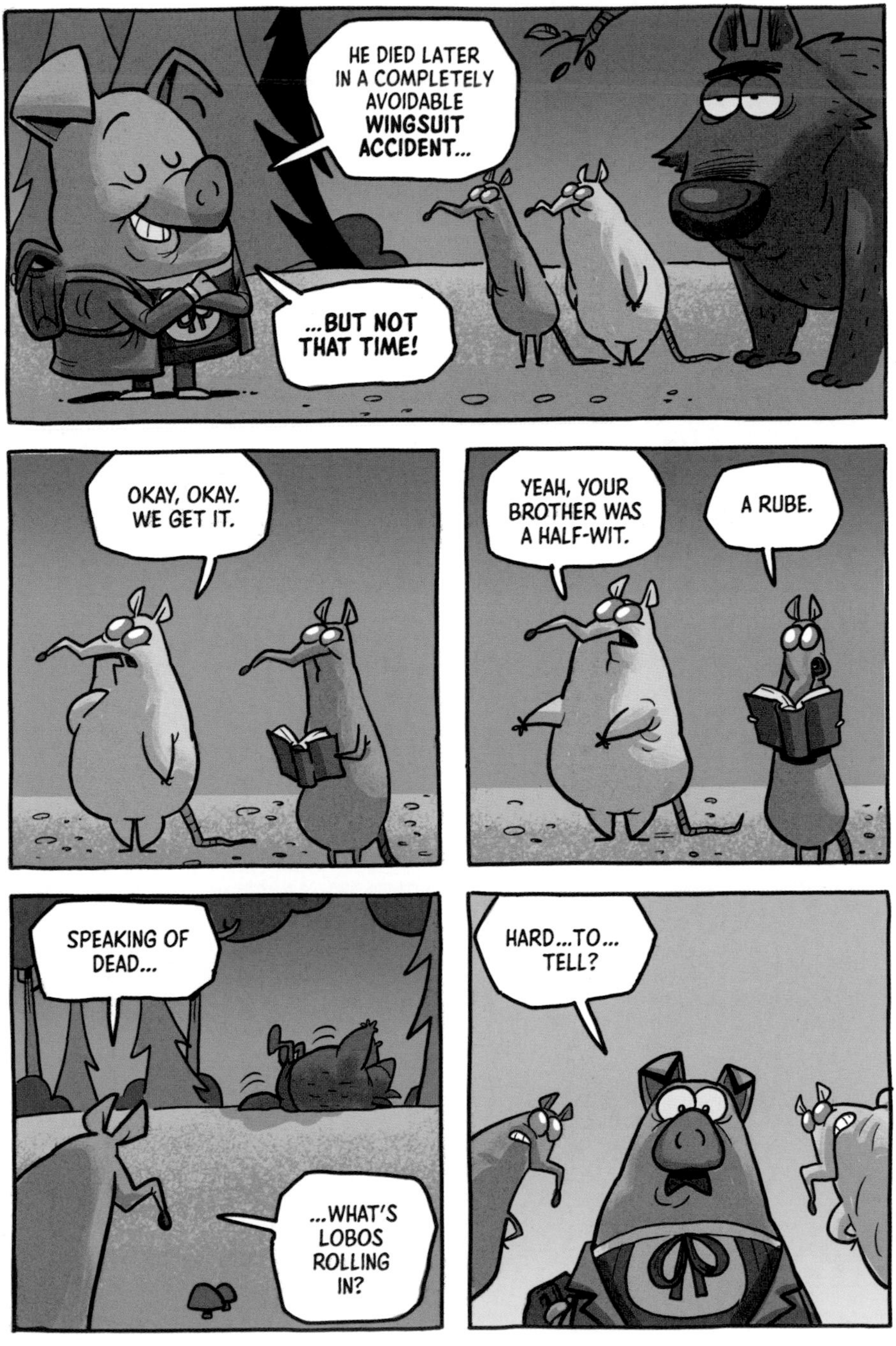
HE DIED LATER IN A COMPLETELY AVOIDABLE **WINGSUIT ACCIDENT**...
...BUT NOT THAT TIME!
OKAY, OKAY. WE GET IT.
YEAH, YOUR BROTHER WAS A HALF-WIT.
A RUBE.
SPEAKING OF DEAD...
...WHAT'S LOBOS ROLLING IN?
HARD...TO... TELL?

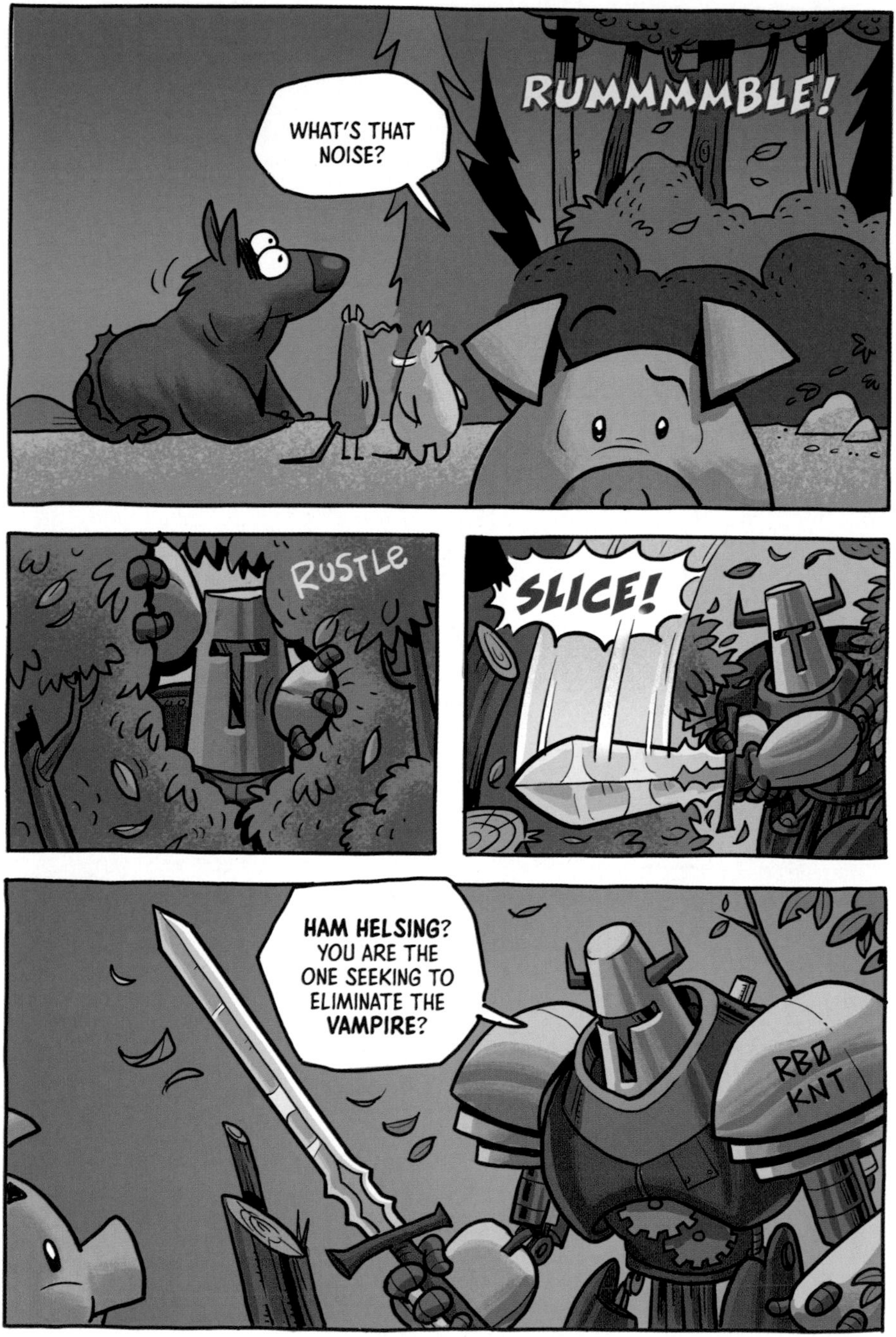
WHAT'S THAT NOISE?
RUMMMMBLE!
RUSTLE
SLICE!
HAM HELSING? YOU ARE THE ONE SEEKING TO ELIMINATE THE VAMPIRE?
RBO KNT

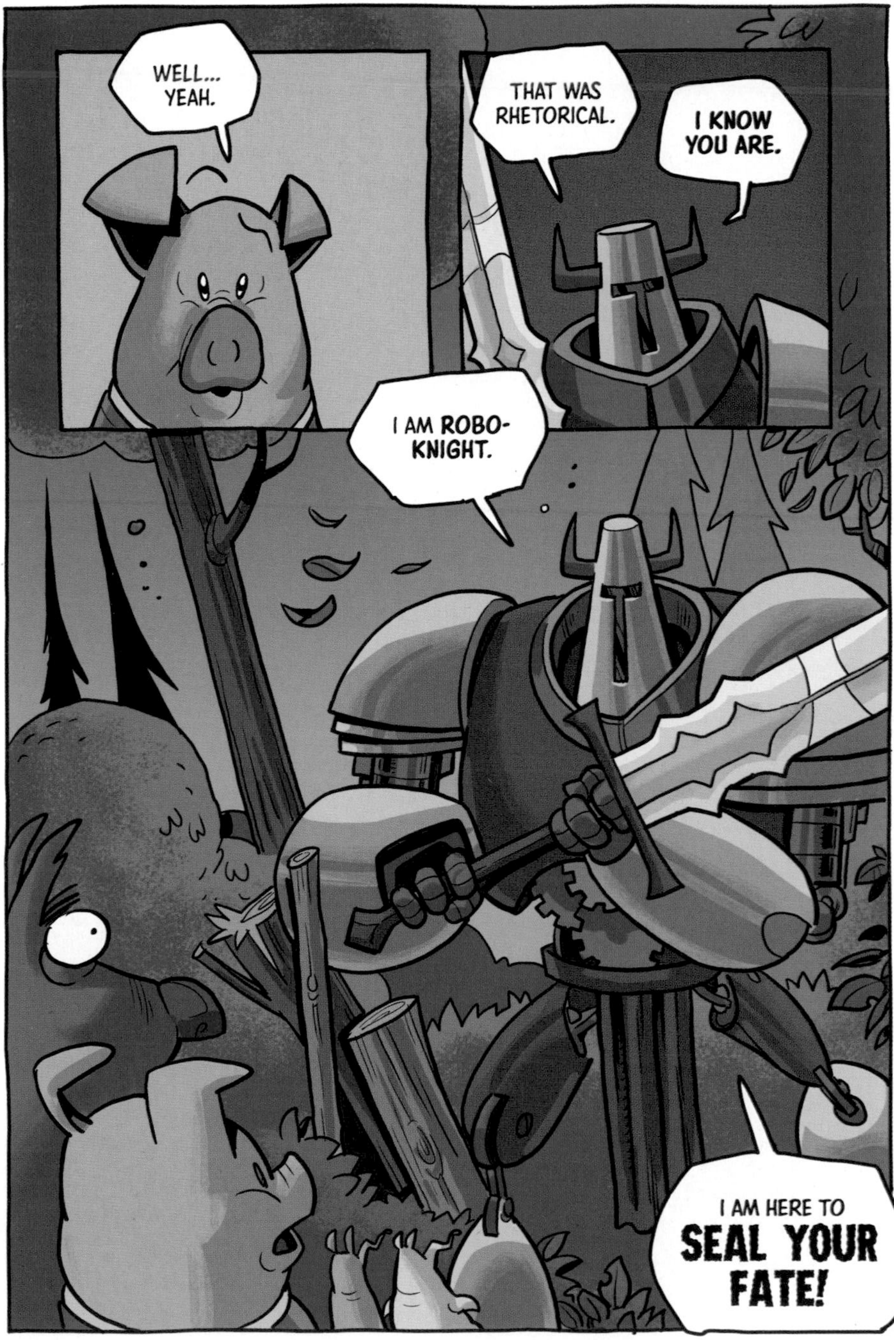
WELL... YEAH.
THAT WAS RHETORICAL.
I KNOW YOU ARE.
I AM ROBO-KNIGHT.
I AM HERE TO SEAL YOUR FATE!

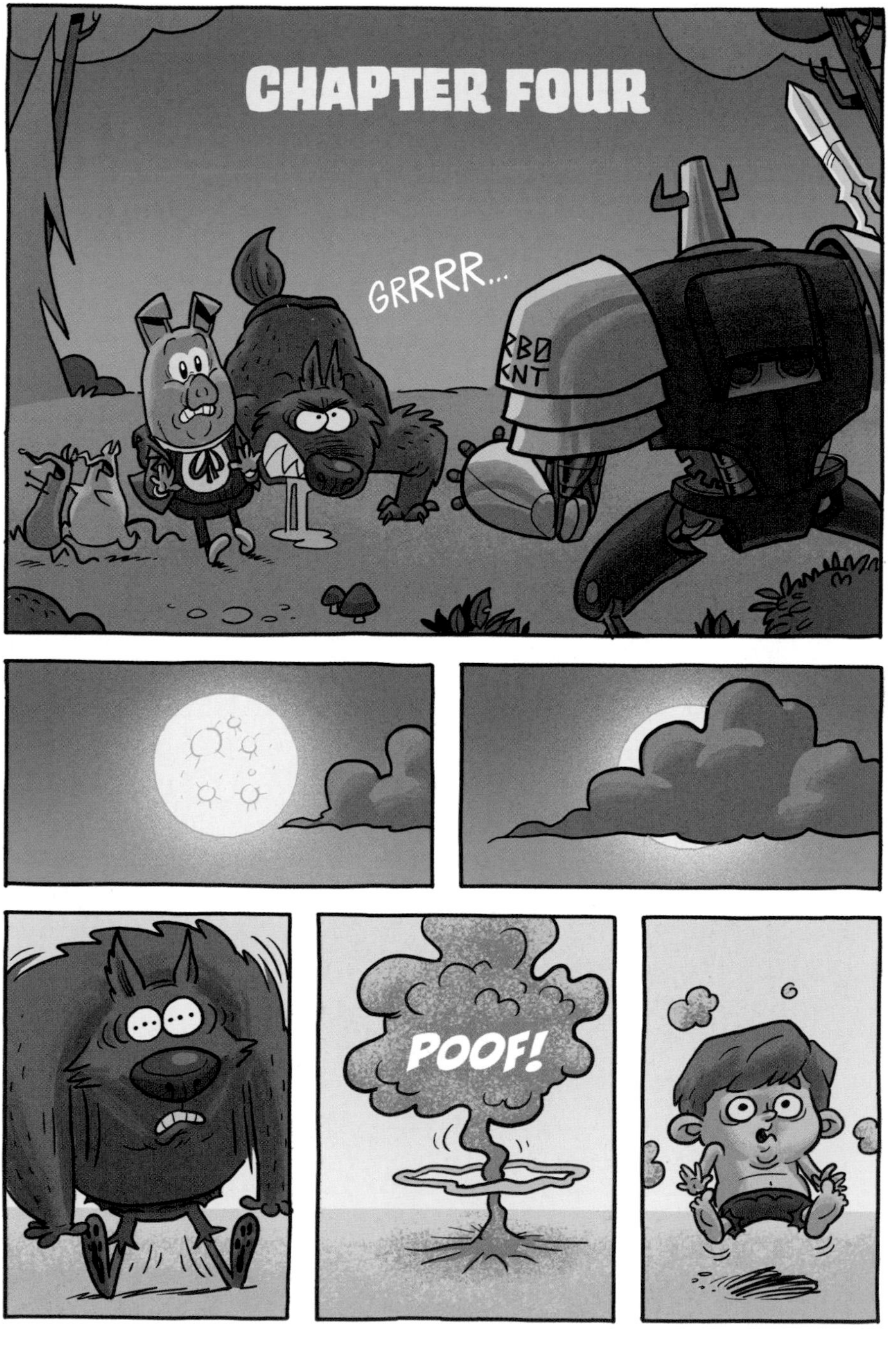
CHAPTER FOUR
GRRRR...
RBO
KNT
POOF!

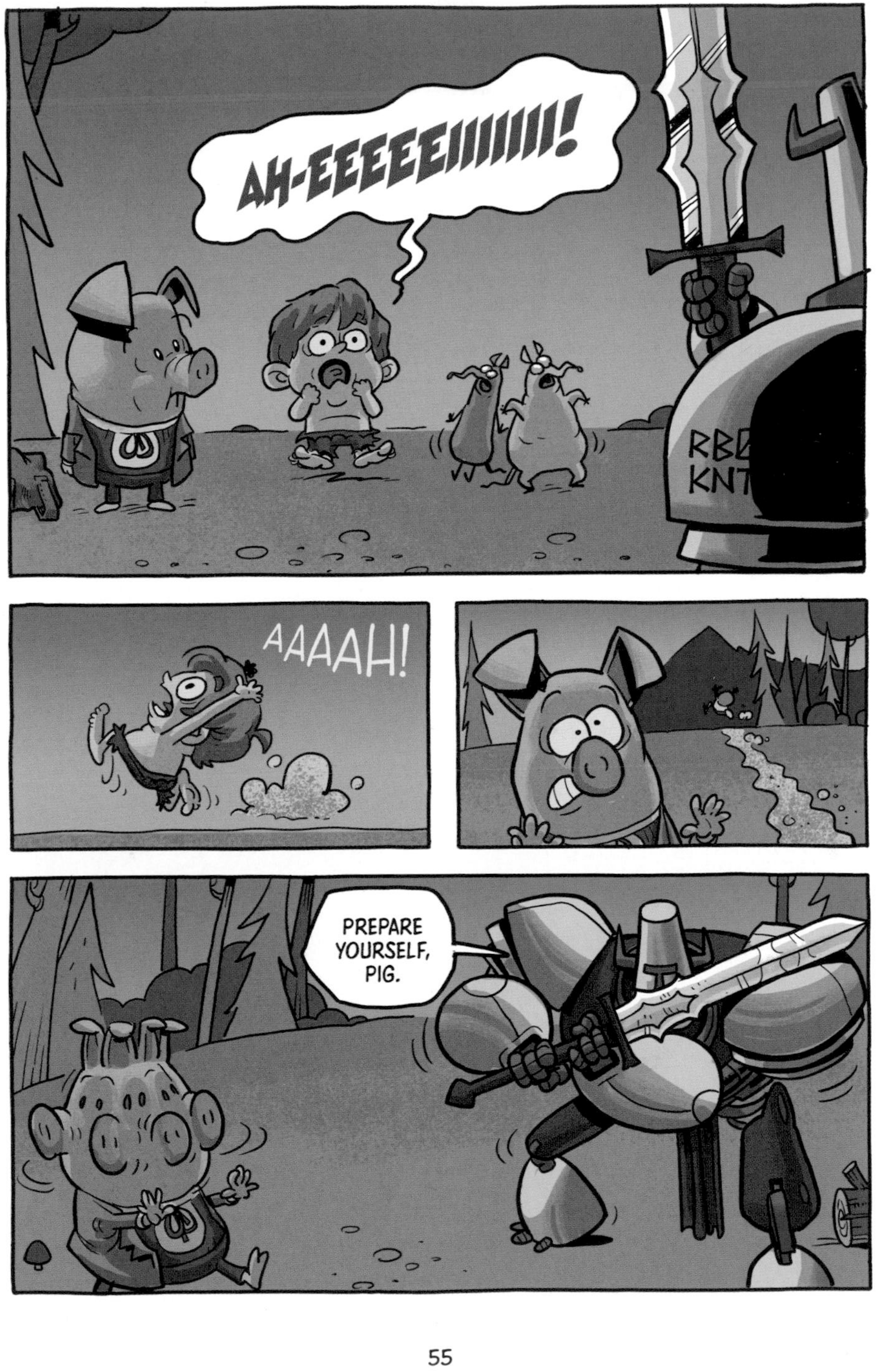
AH-EEEEEIIIIIII!
RBO
KNT
AAAAH!
PREPARE YOURSELF, PIG.

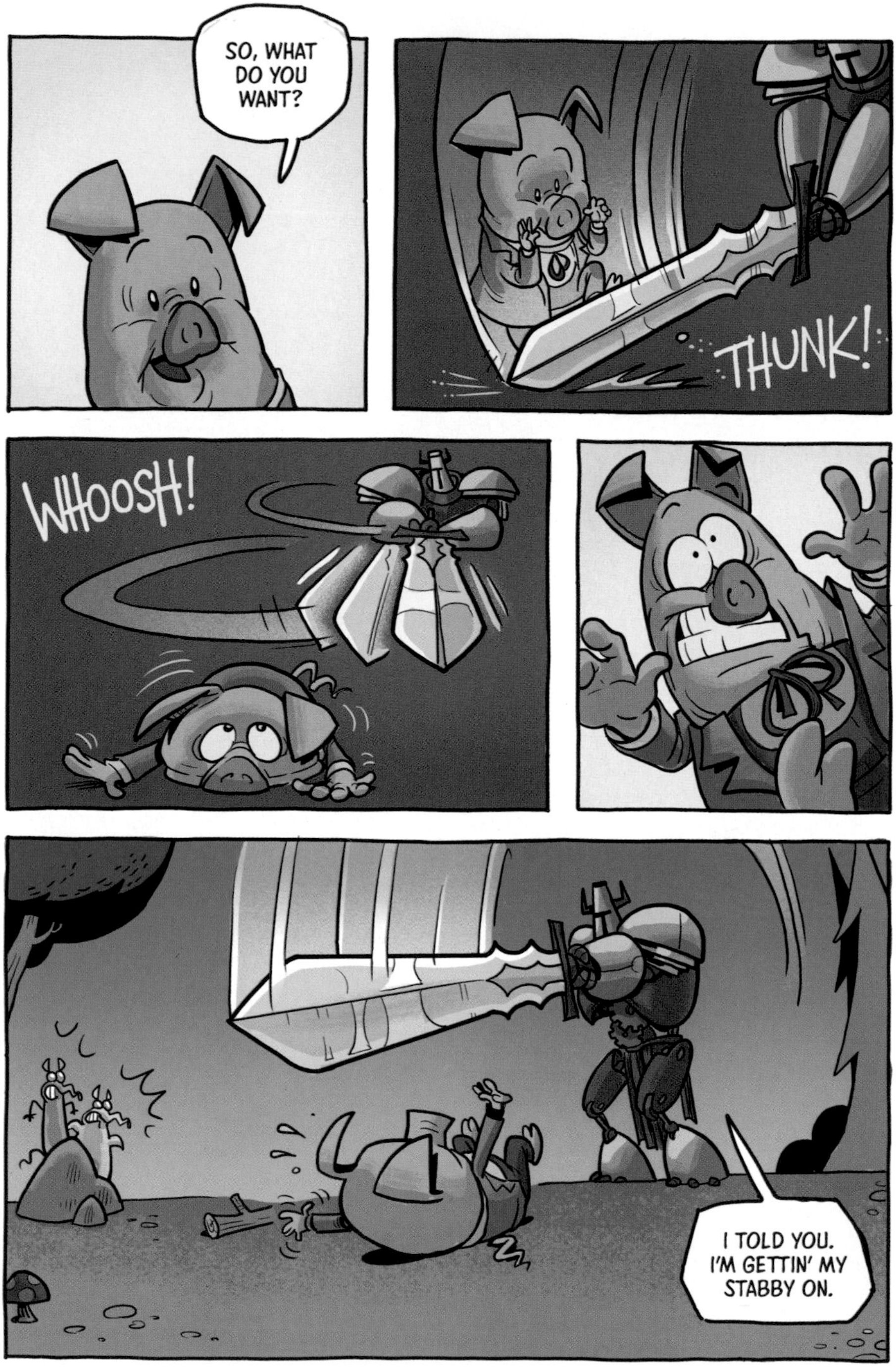
SO, WHAT DO YOU WANT?
THUNK!
WHOOSH!
I TOLD YOU. I'M GETTIN' MY STABBY ON.

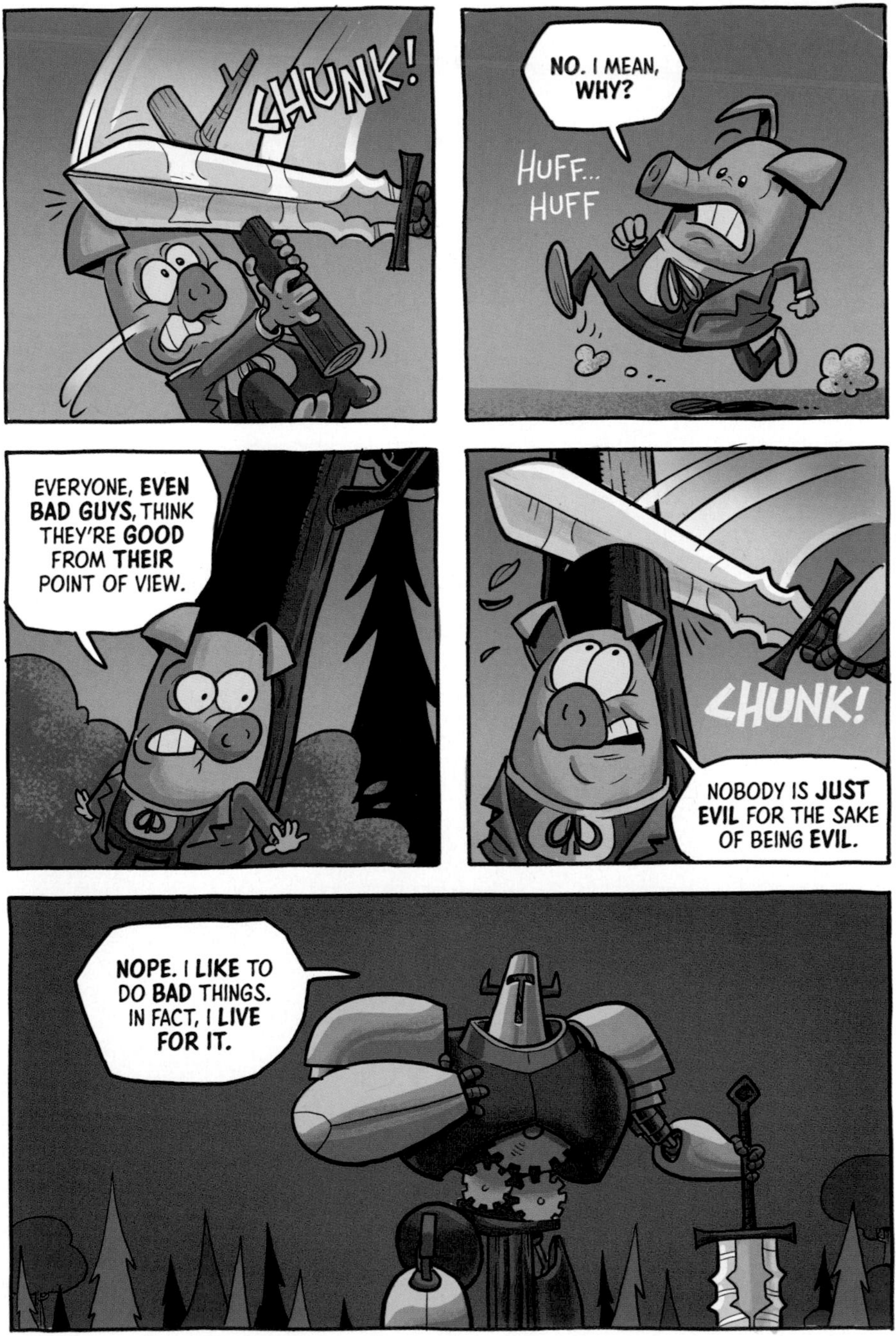
CHUNK!
NO. I MEAN, WHY?
HUFF... HUFF
EVERYONE, EVEN BAD GUYS, THINK THEY'RE GOOD FROM THEIR POINT OF VIEW.
CHUNK!
NOBODY IS JUST EVIL FOR THE SAKE OF BEING EVIL.
NOPE. I LIKE TO DO BAD THINGS. IN FACT, I LIVE FOR IT.

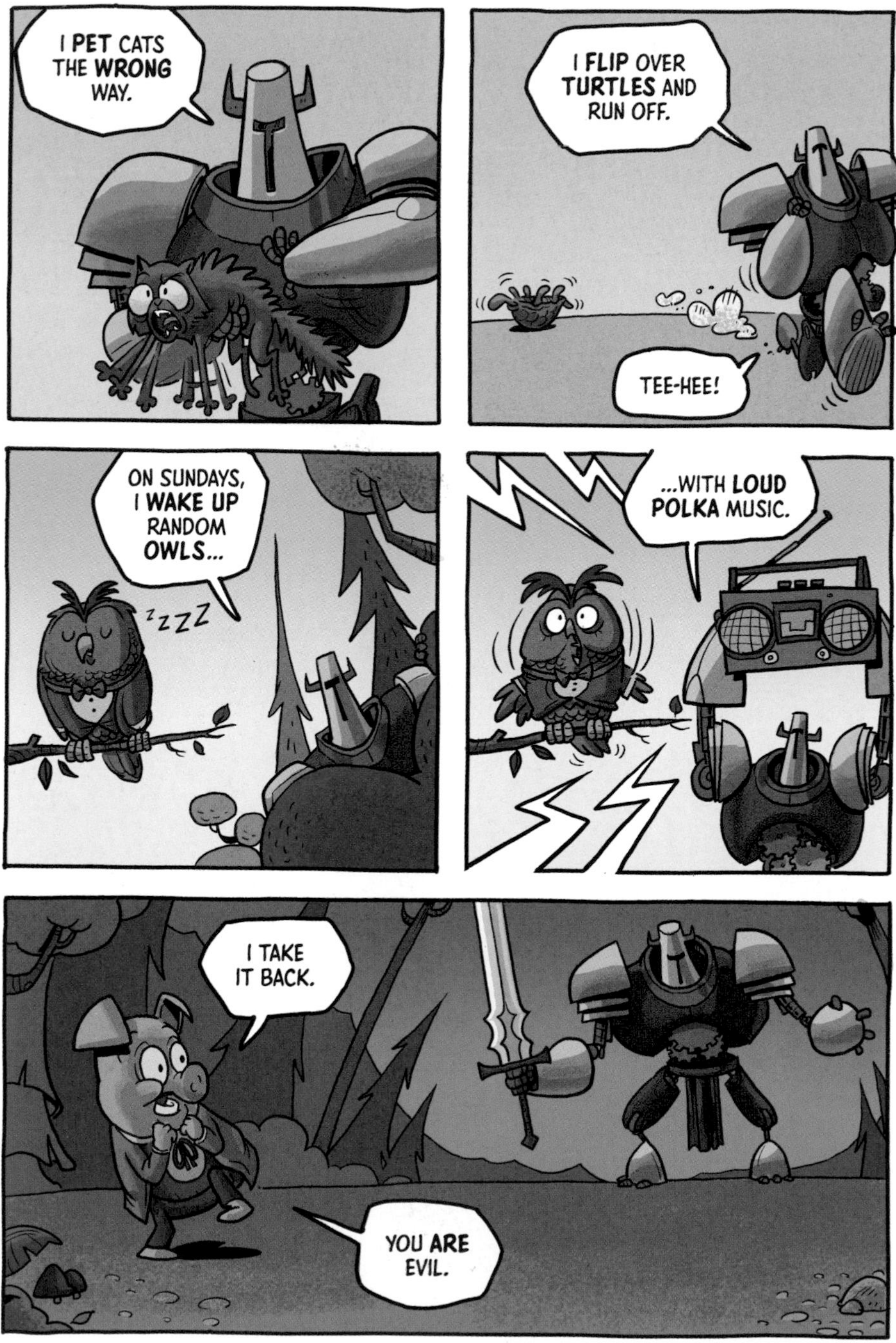
I **PET** CATS THE **WRONG** WAY.
I **FLIP** OVER **TURTLES** AND RUN OFF.
TEE-HEE!
ON SUNDAYS, I **WAKE UP** RANDOM **OWLS**...
ZZZZ
...WITH **LOUD POLKA** MUSIC.
I TAKE IT BACK.
YOU **ARE** EVIL.

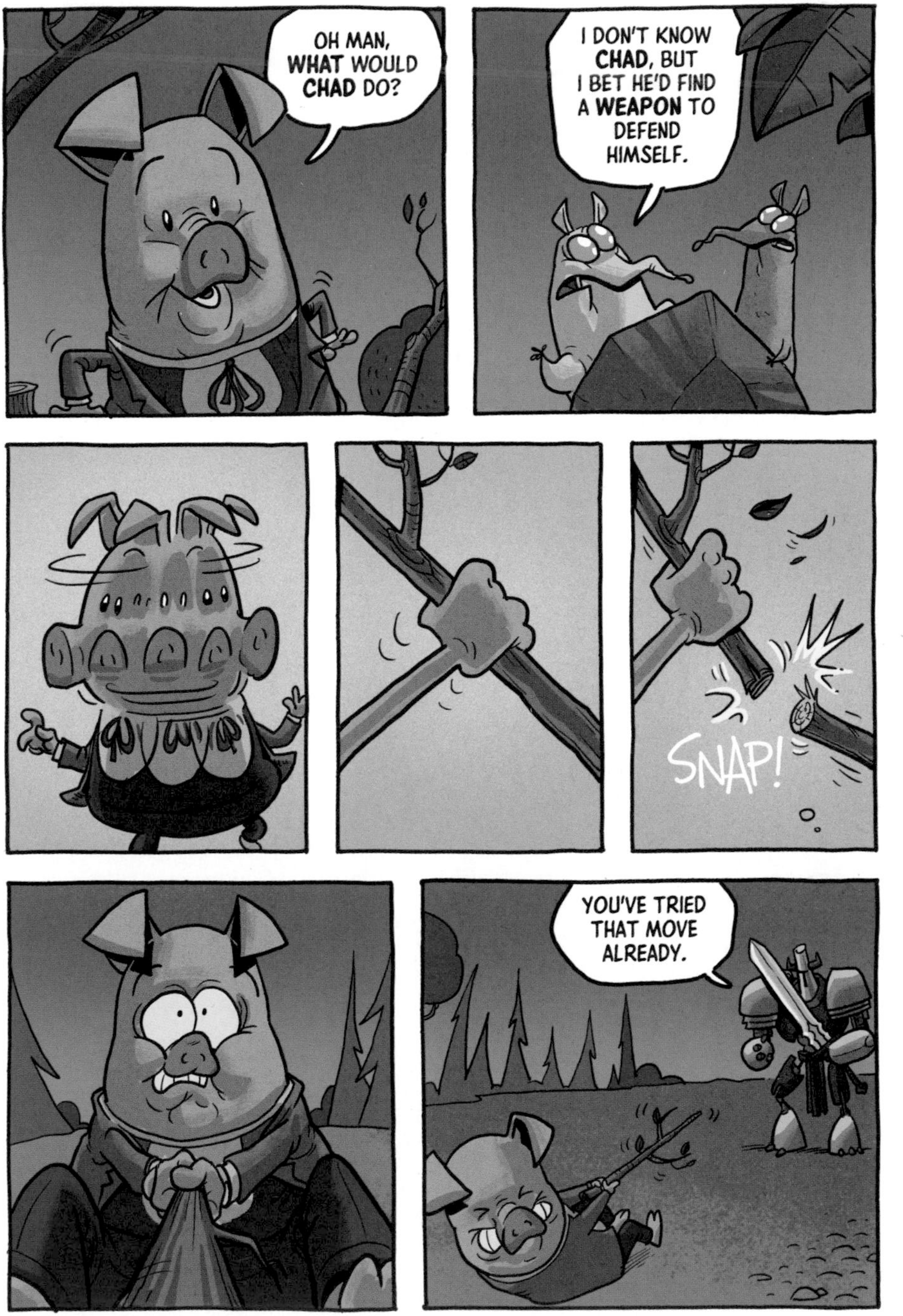

OH MAN, WHAT WOULD CHAD DO?
I DON'T KNOW CHAD, BUT I BET HE'D FIND A WEAPON TO DEFEND HIMSELF.
SNAP!
YOU'VE TRIED THAT MOVE ALREADY.

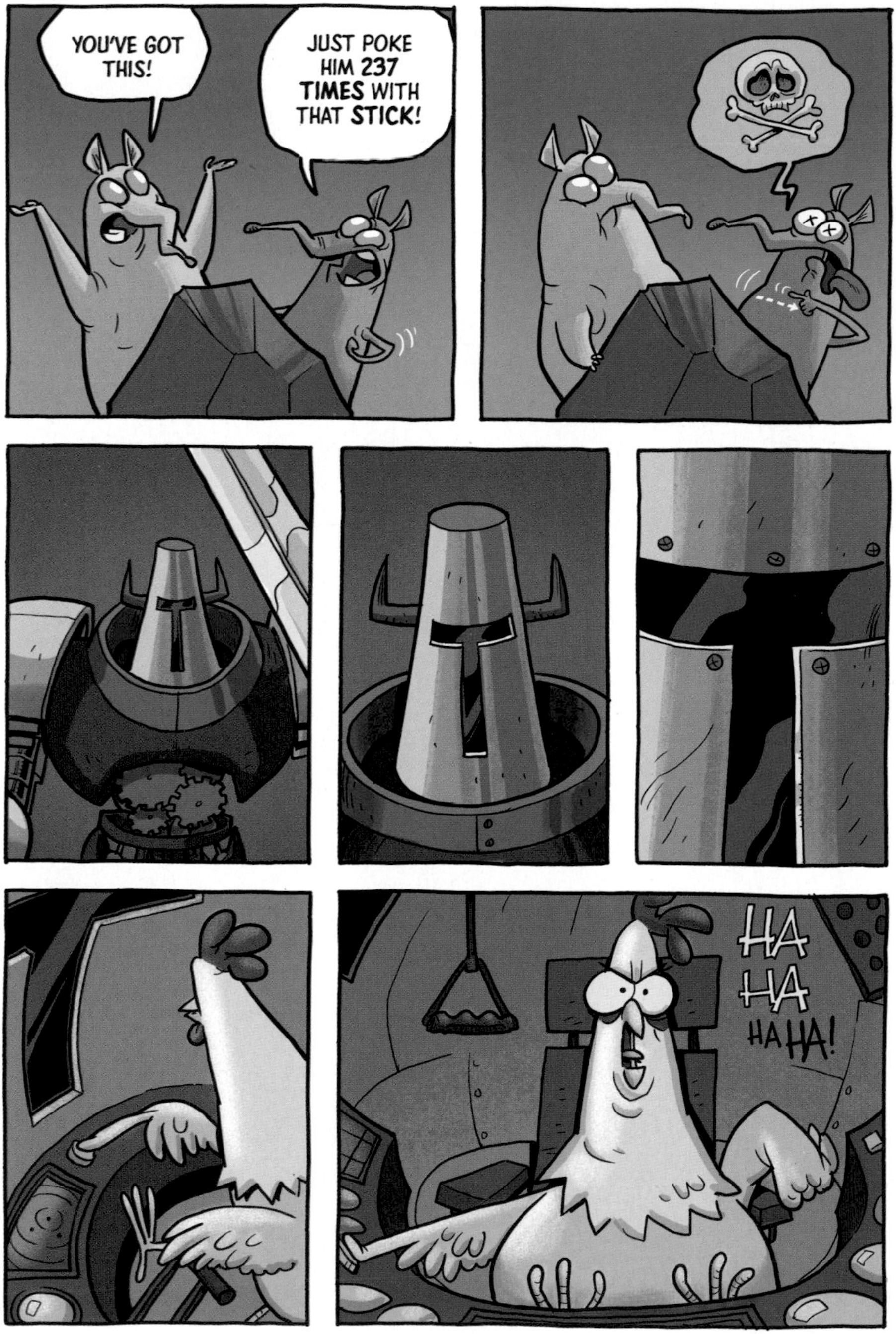
YOU'VE GOT THIS!
JUST POKE HIM 237 TIMES WITH THAT STICK!
HA
HA
HAHA!

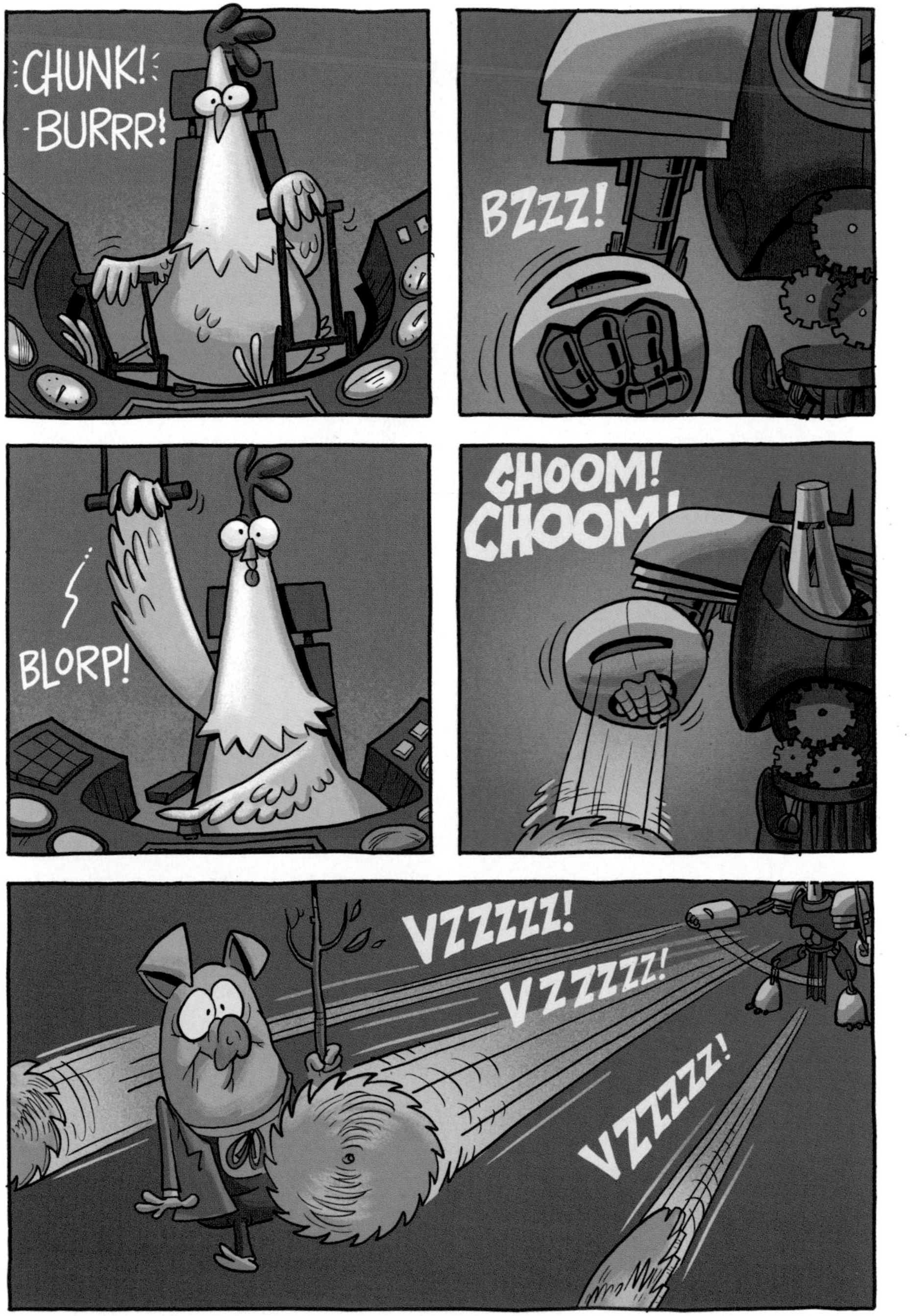
CHUNK!
BURRR!
BZZZ!
BLORP!
CHOOM!
CHOOM!
VZZZZZ!
VZZZZZ!
VZZZZZ!

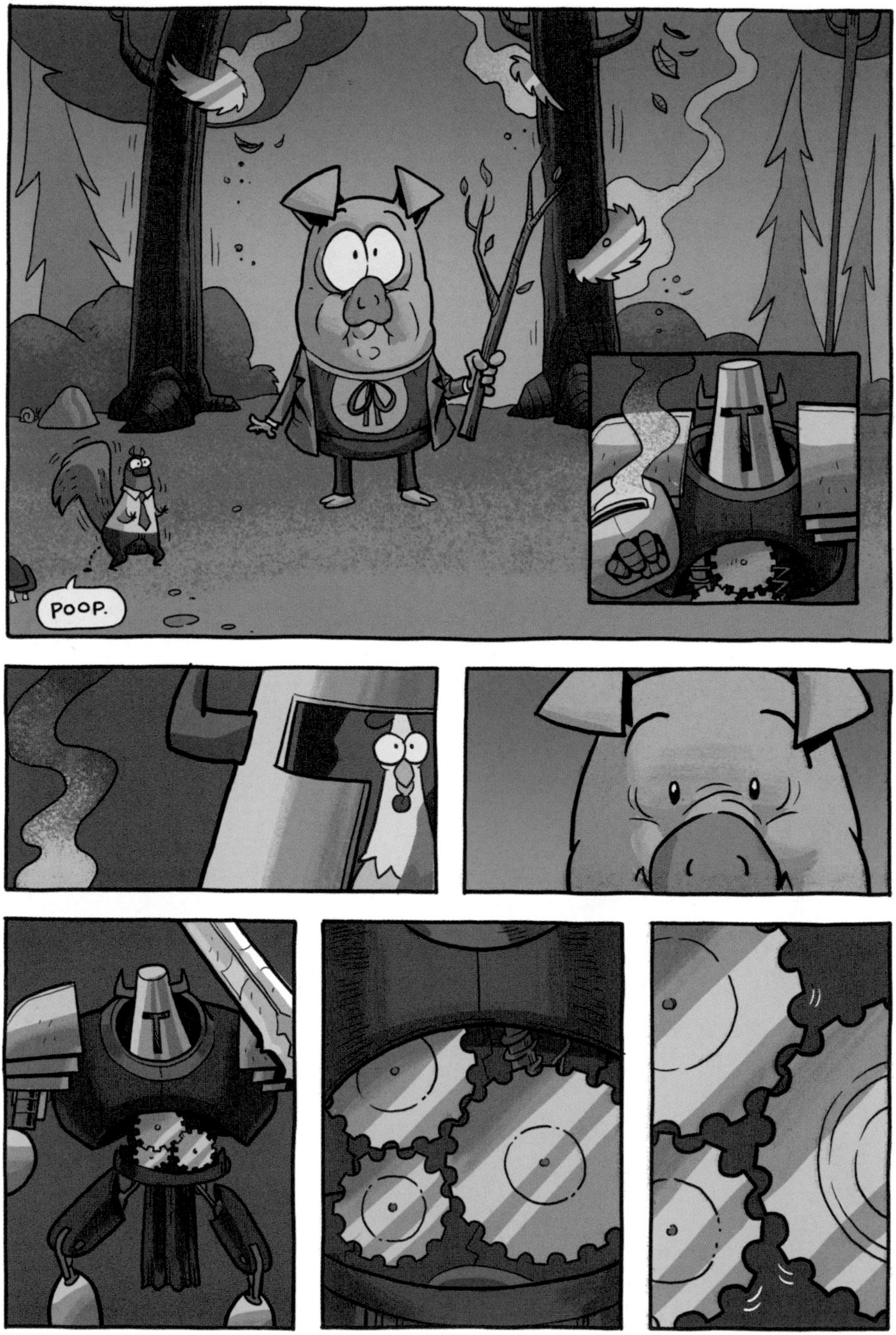
POOP.

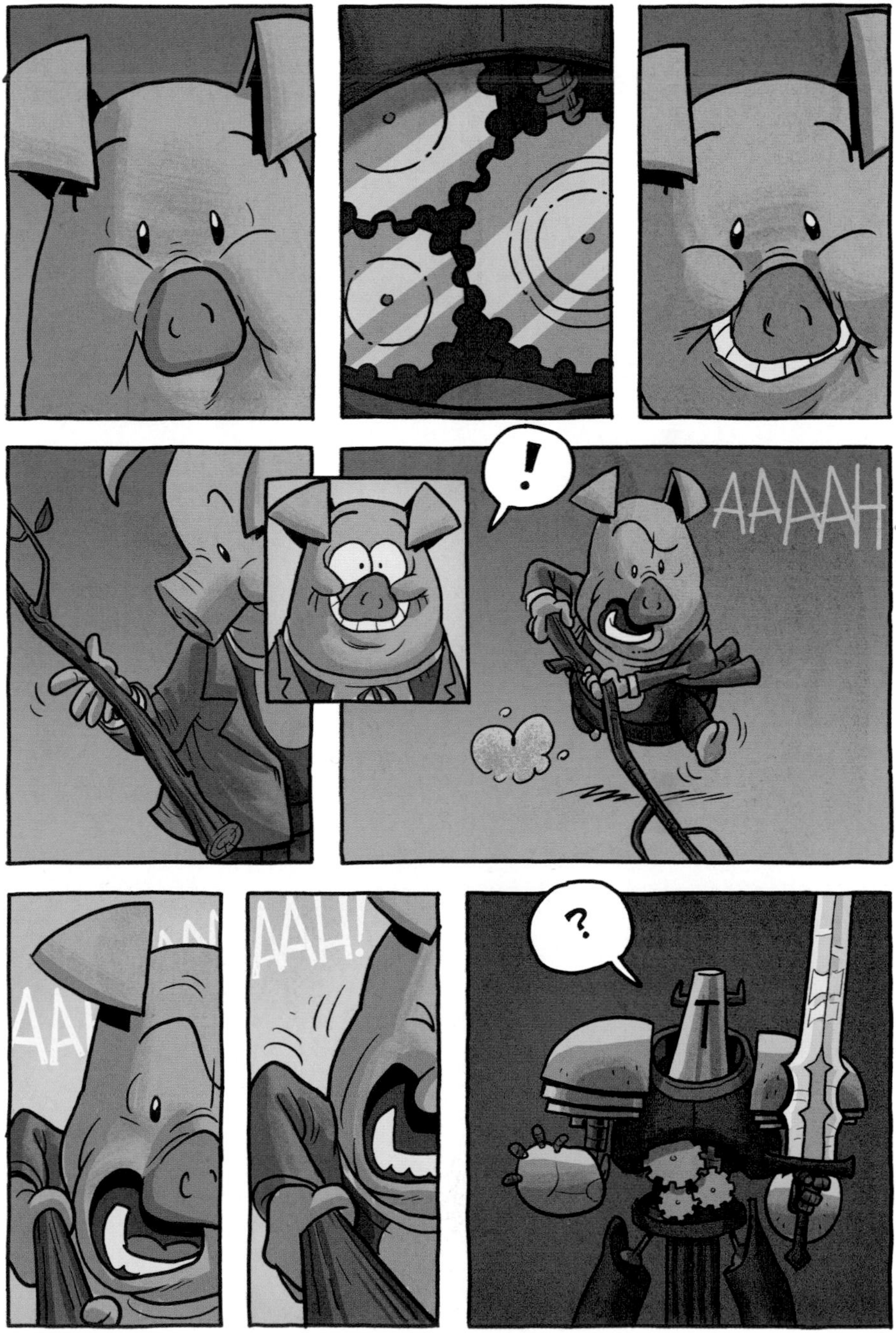
!
AAAAH!
AAAAAAAH!
?

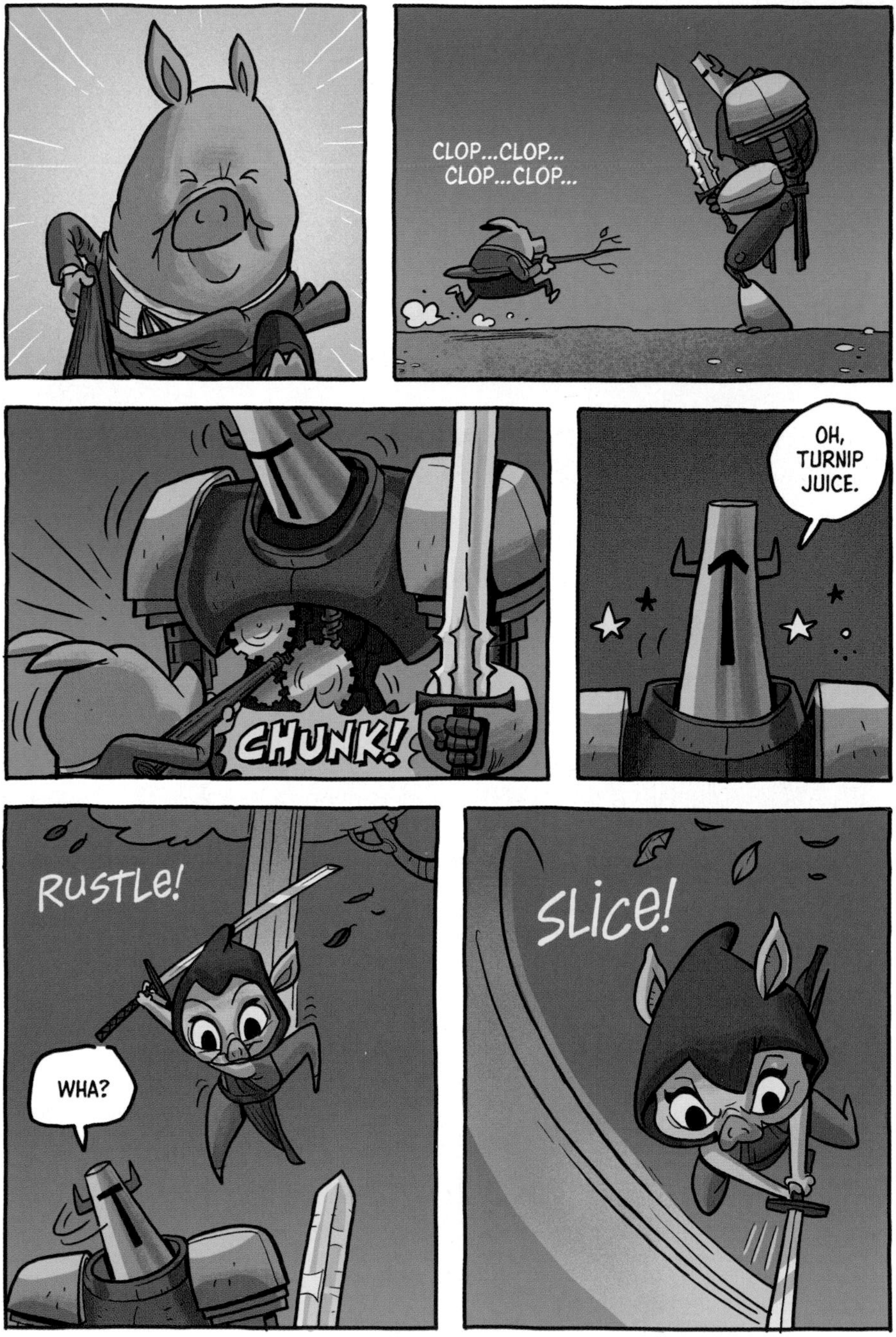

CLOP...CLOP...
CLOP...CLOP...
CHUNK!
OH, TURNIP JUICE.
RUSTLE!
WHA?
SLICE!

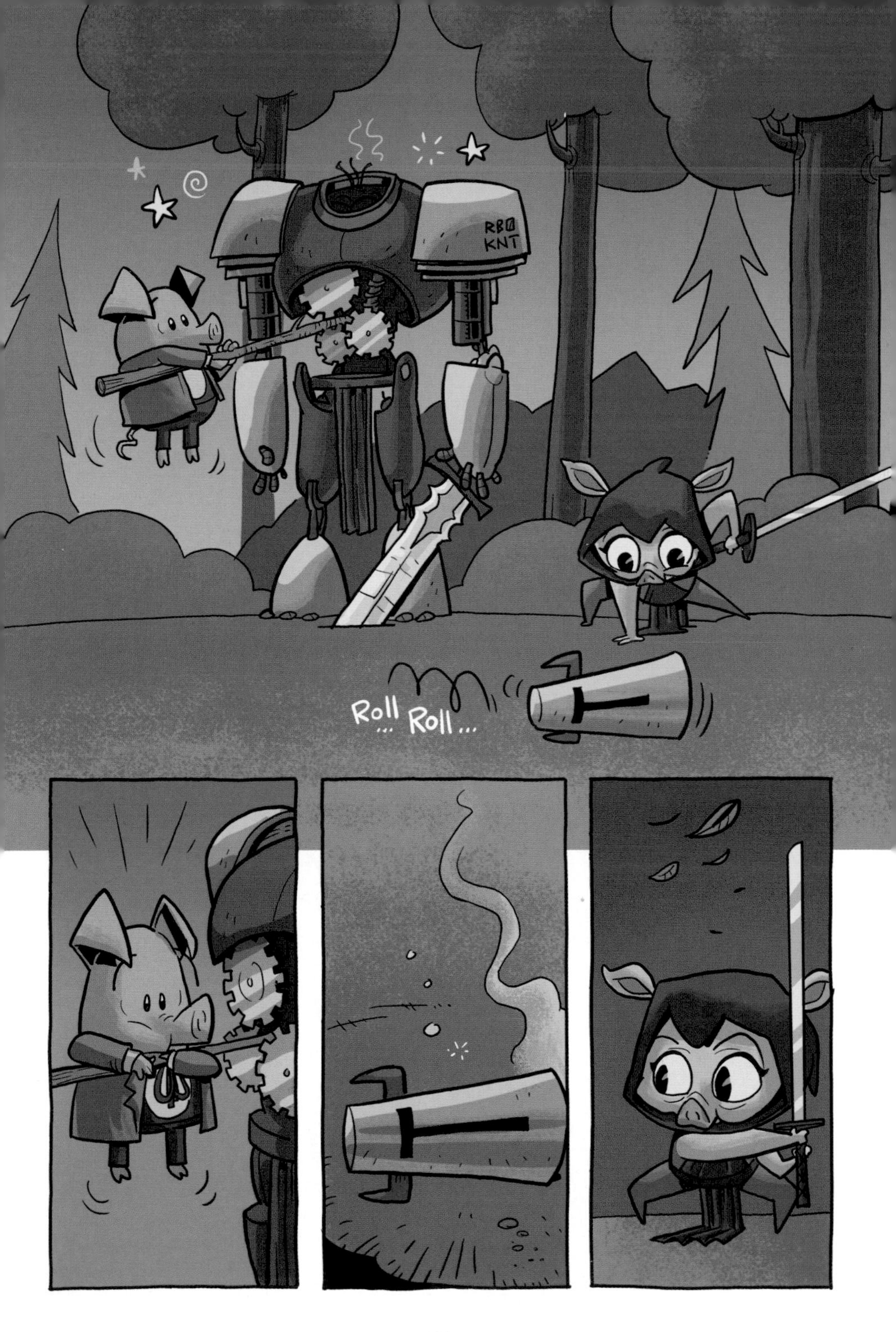
RB0 KNT
Roll... Roll...

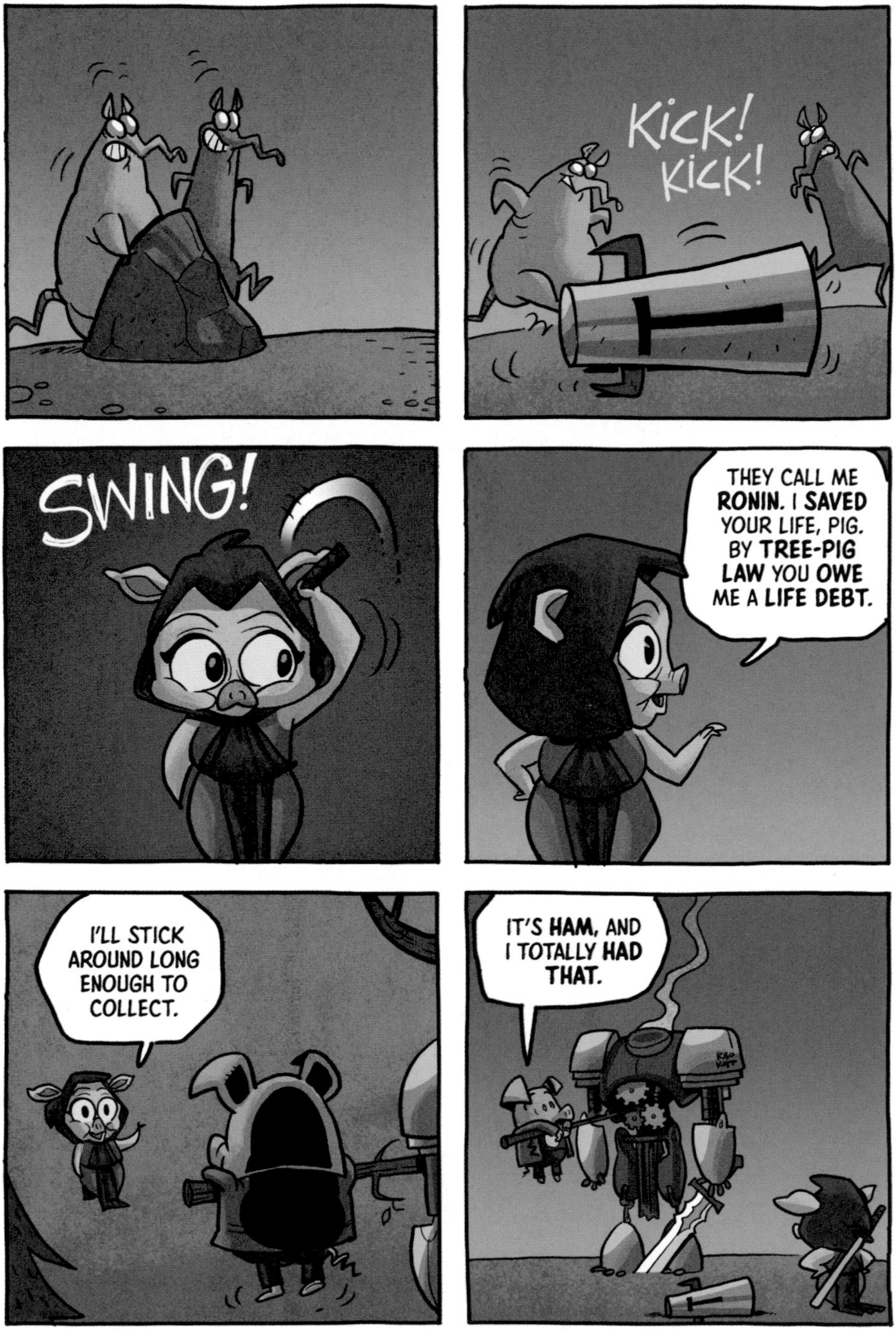
KICK!
KICK!
SWING!
THEY CALL ME RONIN. I SAVED YOUR LIFE, PIG. BY TREE-PIG LAW YOU OWE ME A LIFE DEBT.
I'LL STICK AROUND LONG ENOUGH TO COLLECT.
IT'S HAM, AND I TOTALLY HAD THAT.

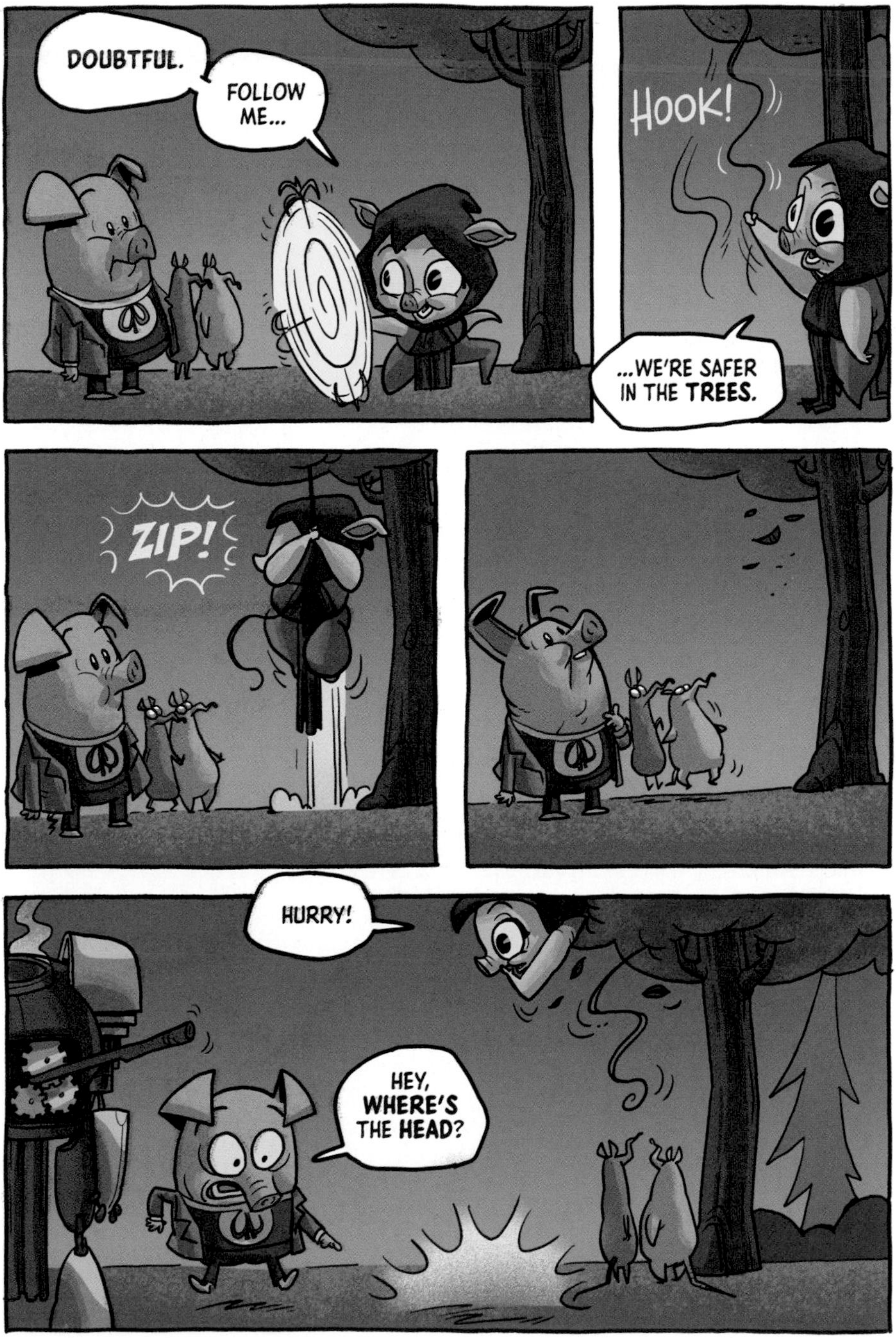
DOUBTFUL.
FOLLOW ME...
HOOK!
...WE'RE SAFER IN THE TREES.
ZIP!
HURRY!
HEY, WHERE'S THE HEAD?

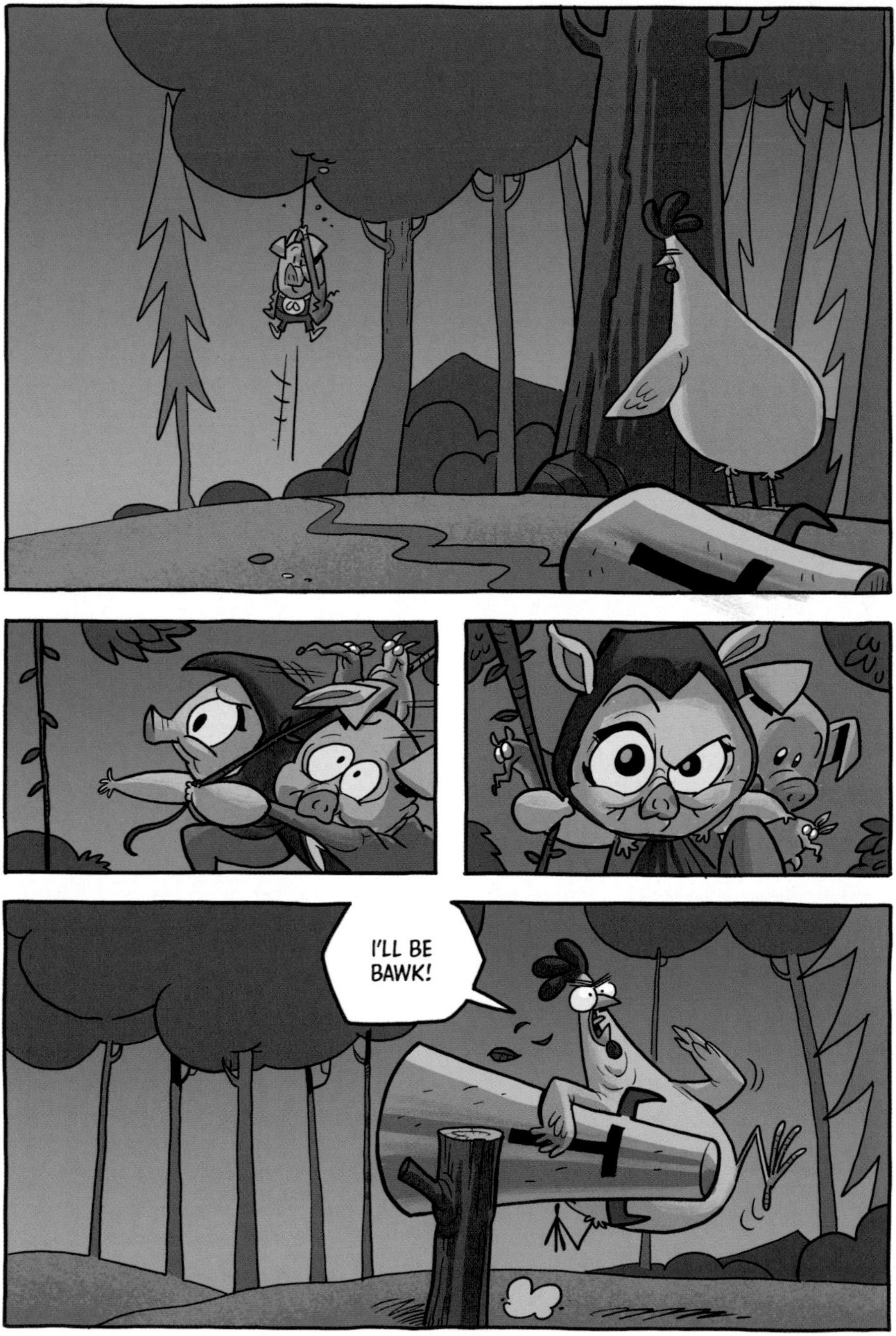
I'LL BE BAWK!

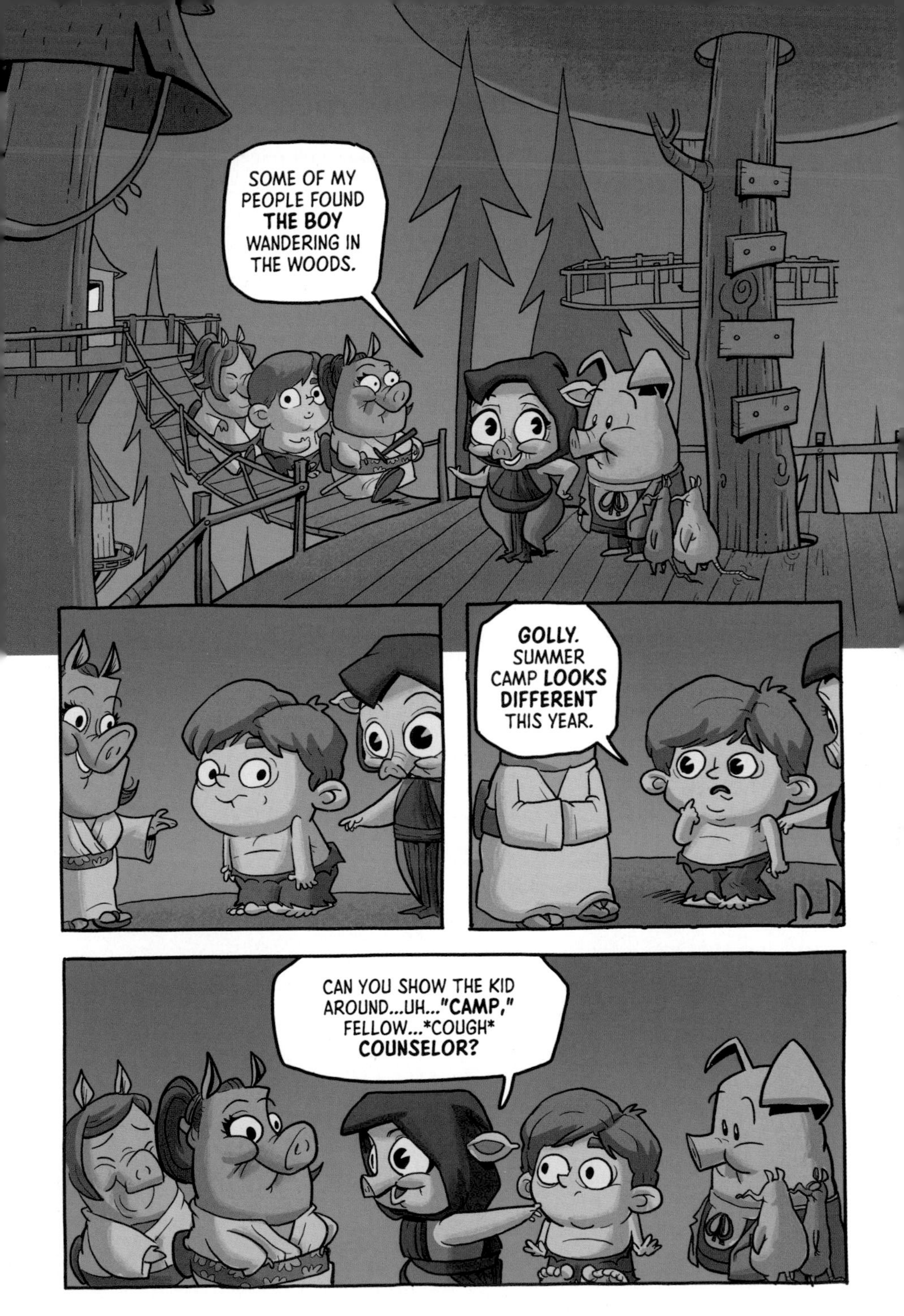
SOME OF MY PEOPLE FOUND **THE BOY** WANDERING IN THE WOODS.
GOLLY. SUMMER CAMP **LOOKS DIFFERENT** THIS YEAR.
CAN YOU SHOW THE KID AROUND...UH...**"CAMP,"** FELLOW...*COUGH* **COUNSELOR?**

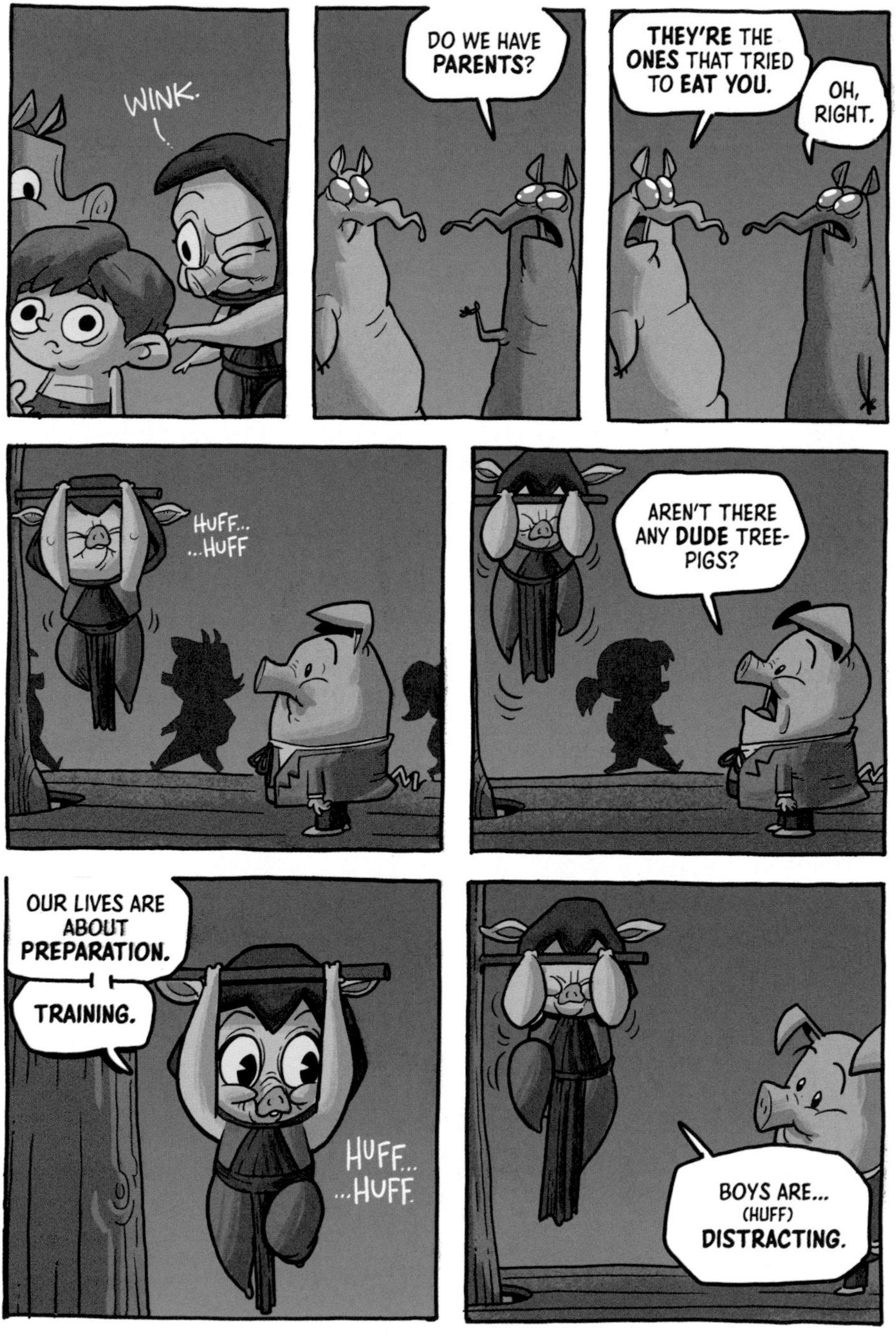
WINK.
DO WE HAVE PARENTS?
THEY'RE THE ONES THAT TRIED TO EAT YOU.
OH, RIGHT.
HUFF... ...HUFF
AREN'T THERE ANY DUDE TREE-PIGS?
OUR LIVES ARE ABOUT PREPARATION.
TRAINING.
HUFF... ...HUFF.
BOYS ARE... (HUFF) DISTRACTING.

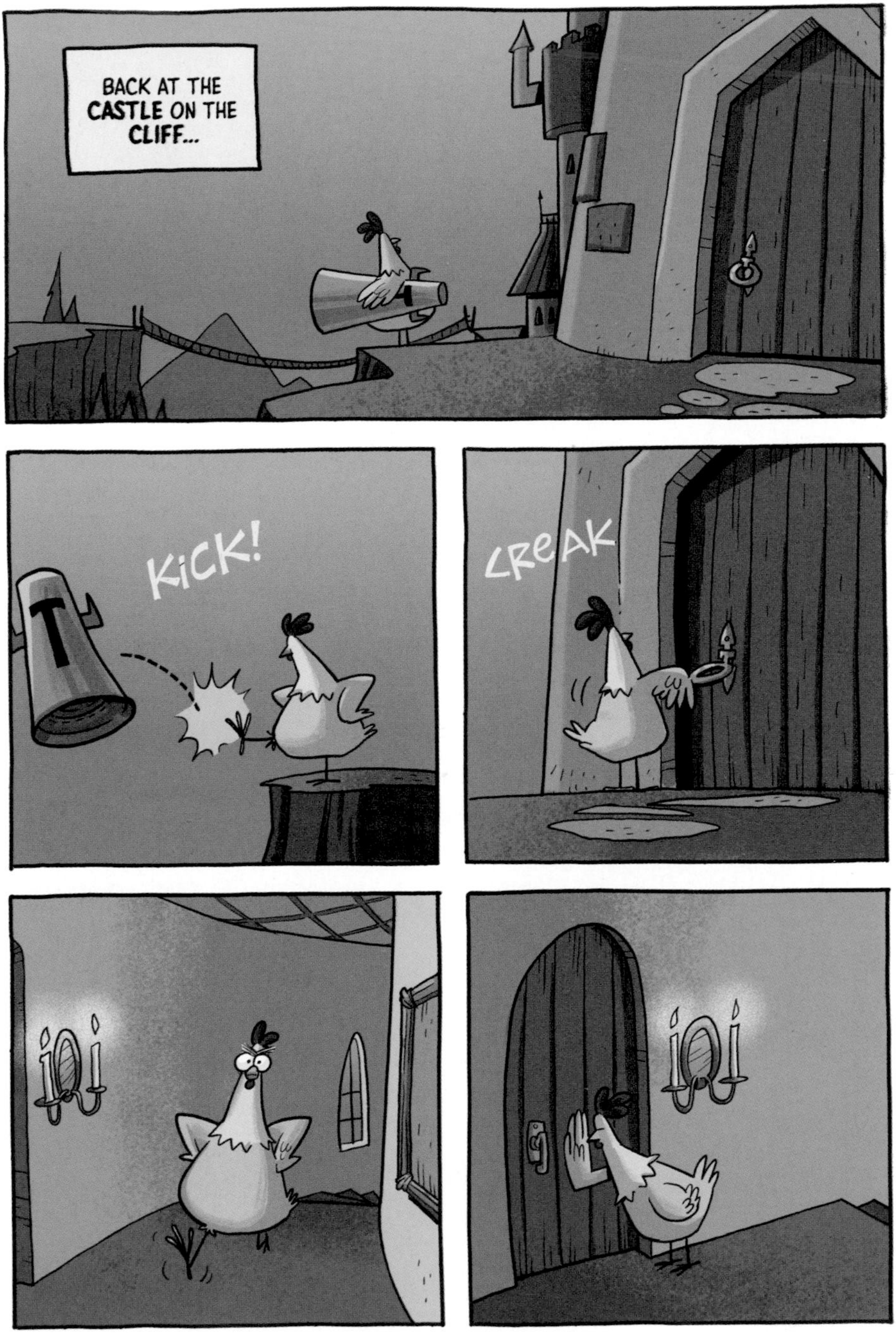
BACK AT THE CASTLE ON THE CLIFF...
KICK!
CREAK

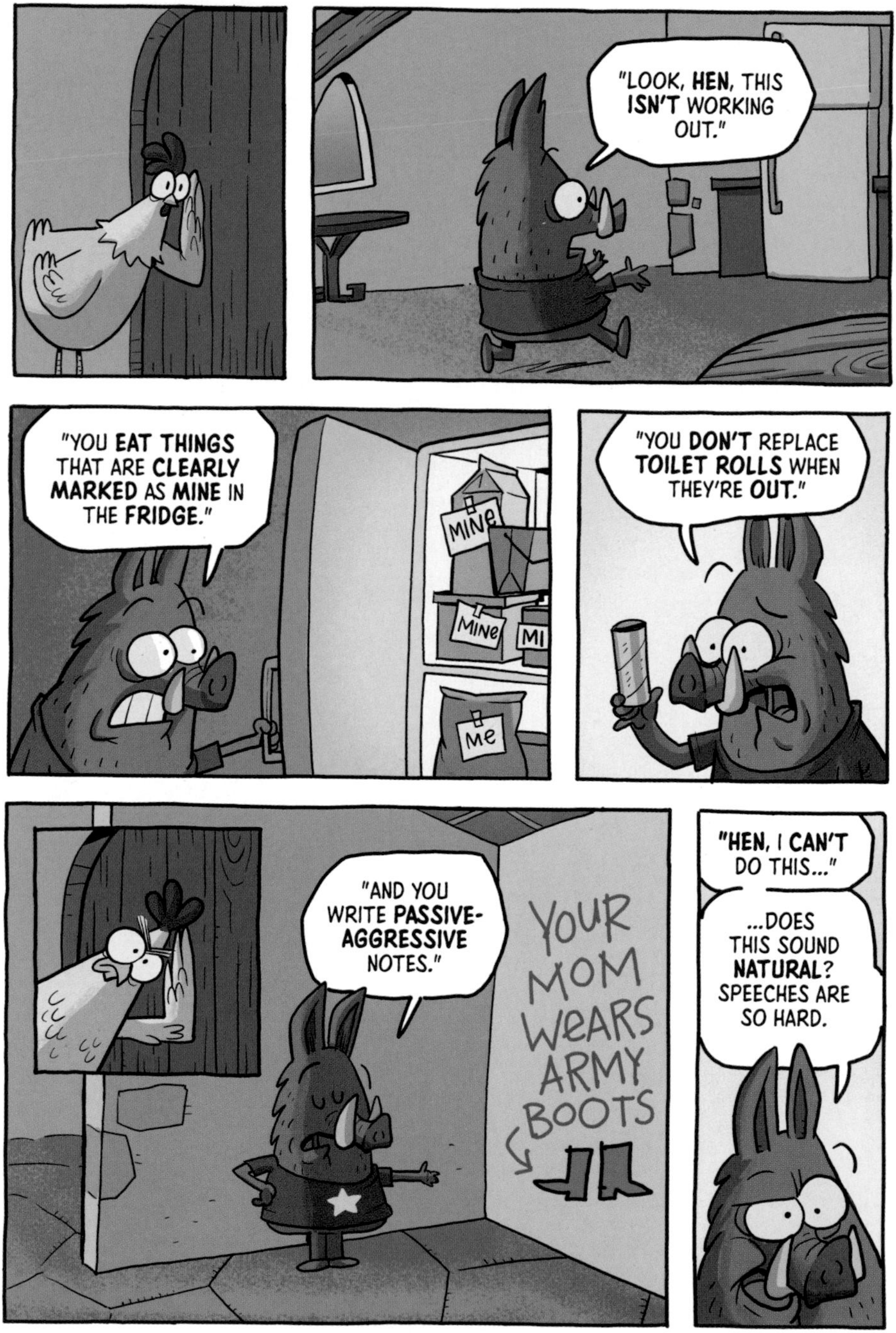
"LOOK, **HEN**, THIS **ISN'T** WORKING OUT."
"YOU **EAT THINGS** THAT ARE **CLEARLY MARKED** AS **MINE** IN THE **FRIDGE**."
MINE
MINE
MI
ME
"YOU **DON'T** REPLACE **TOILET ROLLS** WHEN THEY'RE **OUT**."
"AND YOU WRITE **PASSIVE-AGGRESSIVE** NOTES."
YOUR MOM WEARS ARMY BOOTS
"HEN, I CAN'T DO THIS..."
...DOES THIS SOUND **NATURAL**? SPEECHES ARE SO HARD.

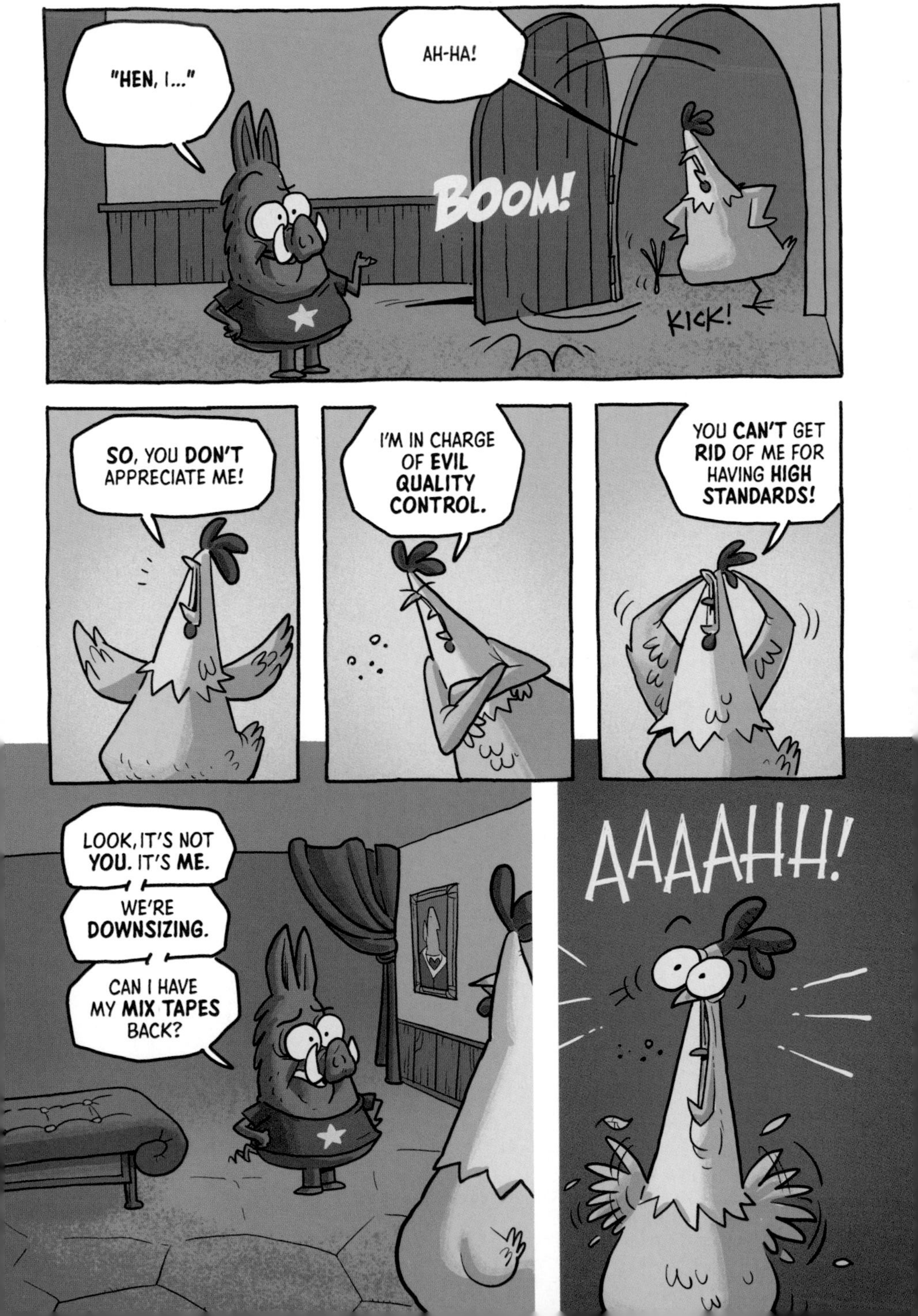

"HEN, I..."
AH-HA!
BOOM!
KICK!
SO, YOU DON'T APPRECIATE ME!
I'M IN CHARGE OF EVIL QUALITY CONTROL.
YOU CAN'T GET RID OF ME FOR HAVING HIGH STANDARDS!
LOOK, IT'S NOT YOU. IT'S ME.
WE'RE DOWNSIZING.
CAN I HAVE MY MIX TAPES BACK?
AAAAHH!

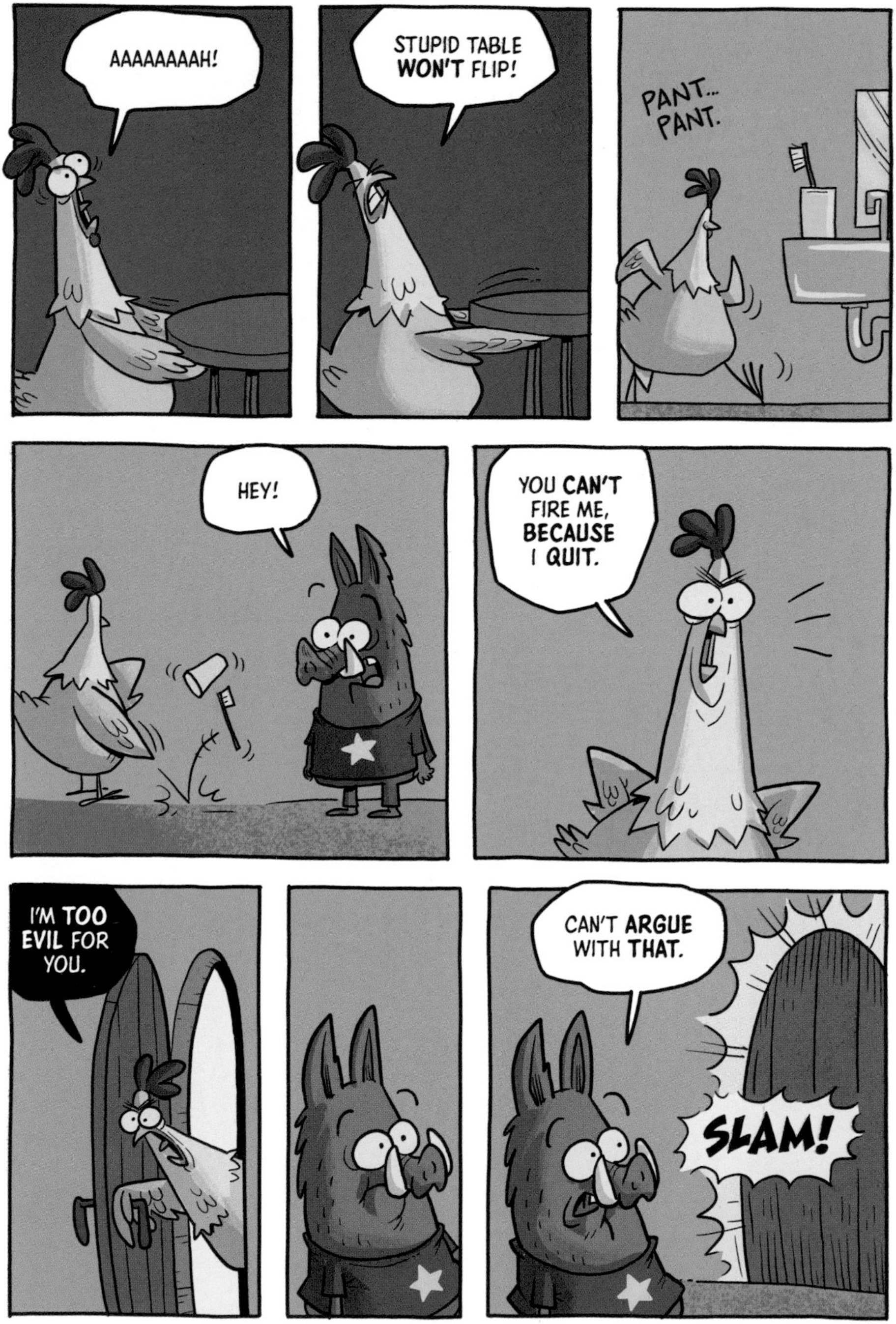
AAAAAAAAH!
STUPID TABLE WON'T FLIP!
PANT... PANT.
HEY!
YOU CAN'T FIRE ME, BECAUSE I QUIT.
I'M TOO EVIL FOR YOU.
CAN'T ARGUE WITH THAT.
SLAM!

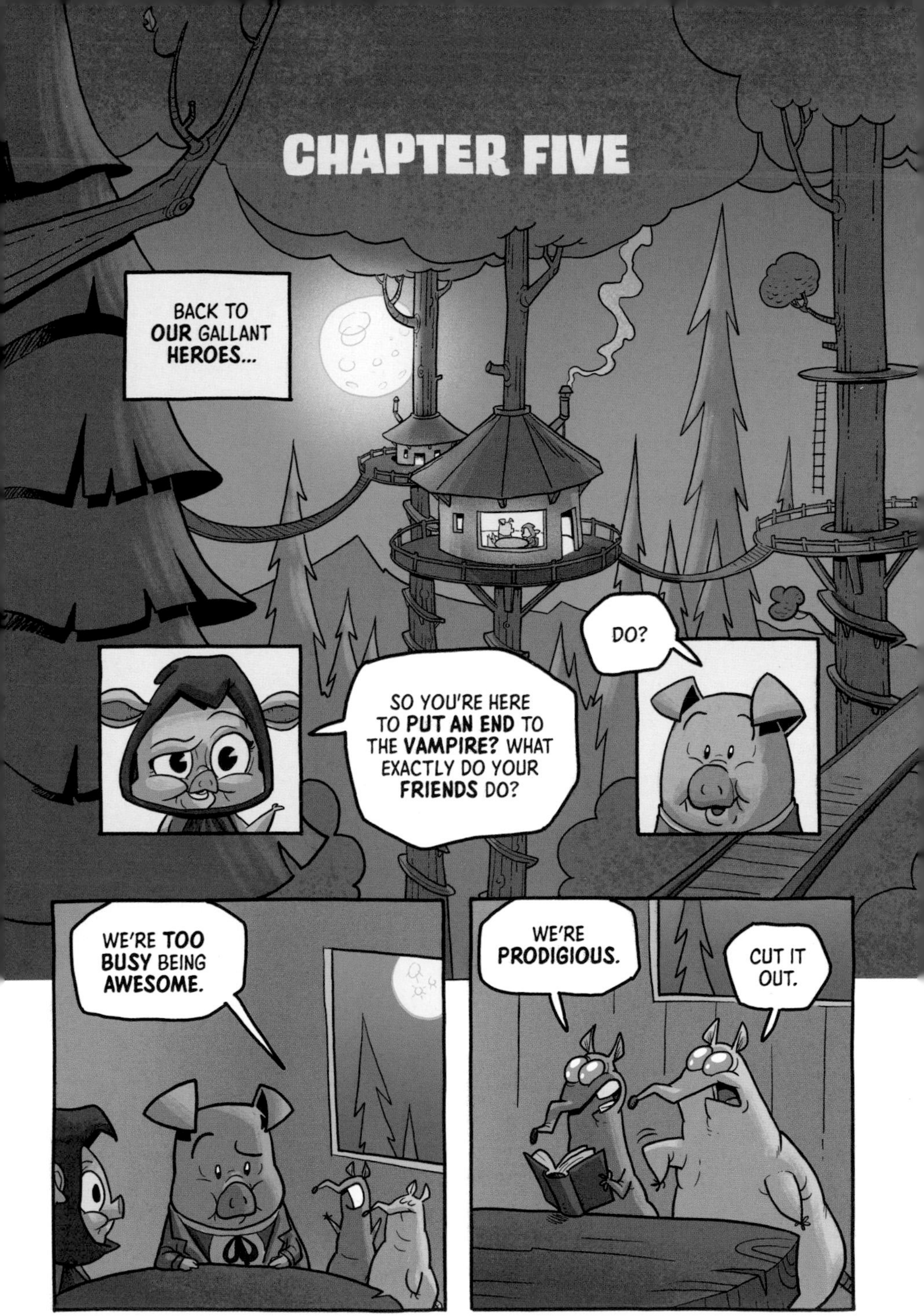
CHAPTER FIVE
BACK TO OUR GALLANT HEROES...
SO YOU'RE HERE TO PUT AN END TO THE VAMPIRE? WHAT EXACTLY DO YOUR FRIENDS DO?
DO?
WE'RE TOO BUSY BEING AWESOME.
WE'RE PRODIGIOUS.
CUT IT OUT.

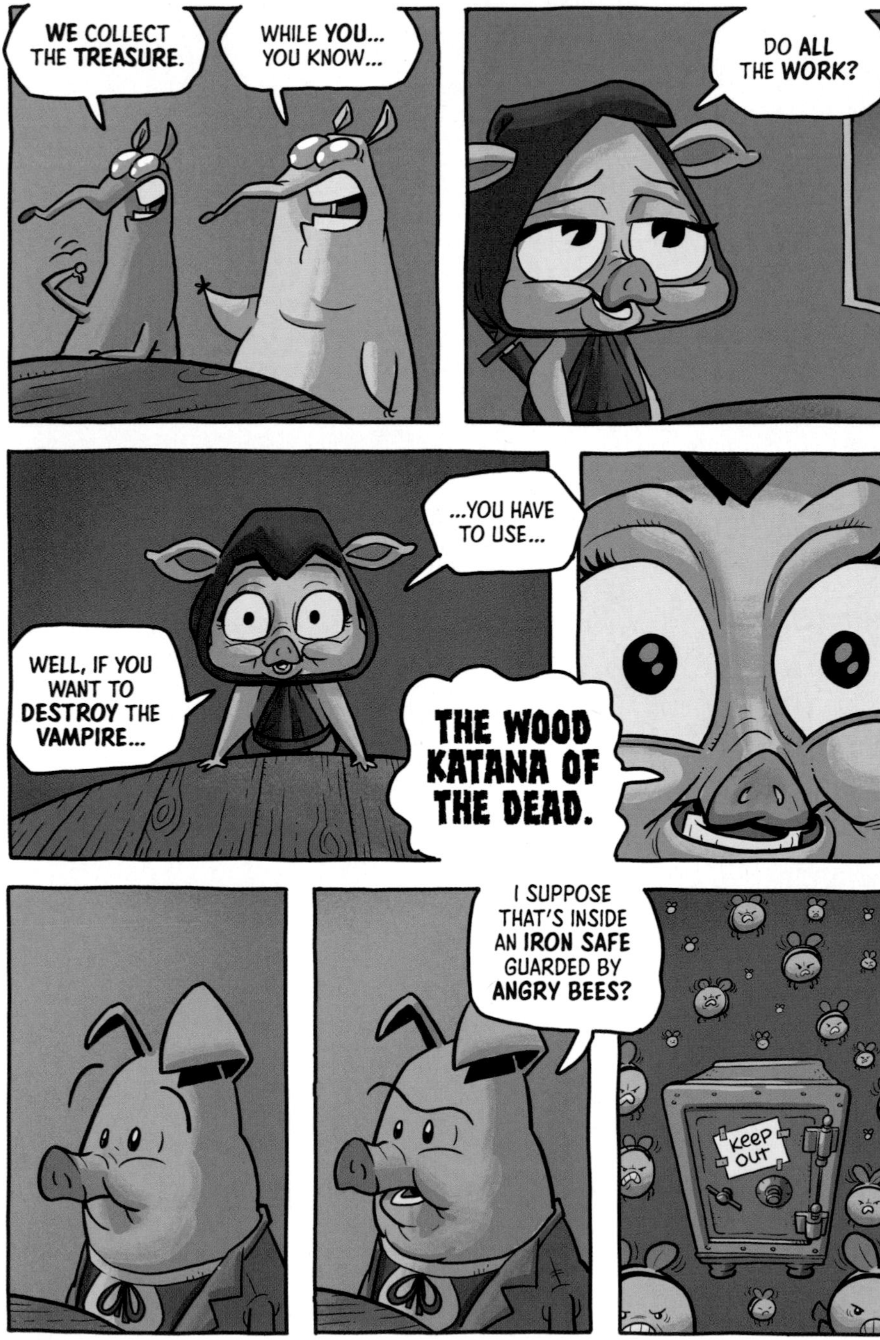
WE COLLECT THE TREASURE.
WHILE YOU... YOU KNOW...
DO ALL THE WORK?
WELL, IF YOU WANT TO DESTROY THE VAMPIRE...
...YOU HAVE TO USE...
THE WOOD KATANA OF THE DEAD.
I SUPPOSE THAT'S INSIDE AN IRON SAFE GUARDED BY ANGRY BEES?
KEEP OUT

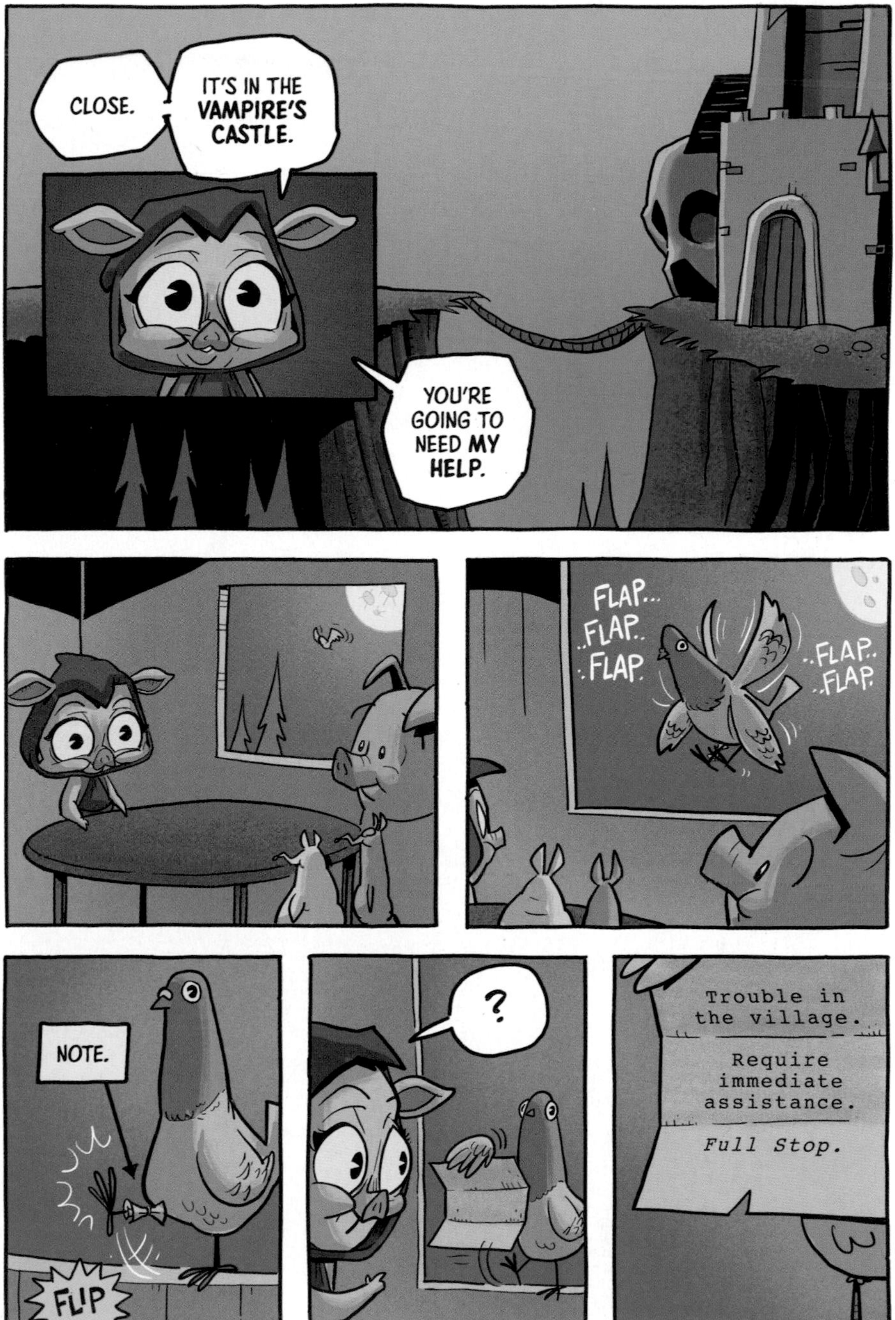
CLOSE.
IT'S IN THE VAMPIRE'S CASTLE.
YOU'RE GOING TO NEED MY HELP.
FLAP... FLAP.. FLAP.
..FLAP.. ..FLAP.
NOTE.
FLIP
?
Trouble in the village.
Require immediate assistance.
Full Stop.

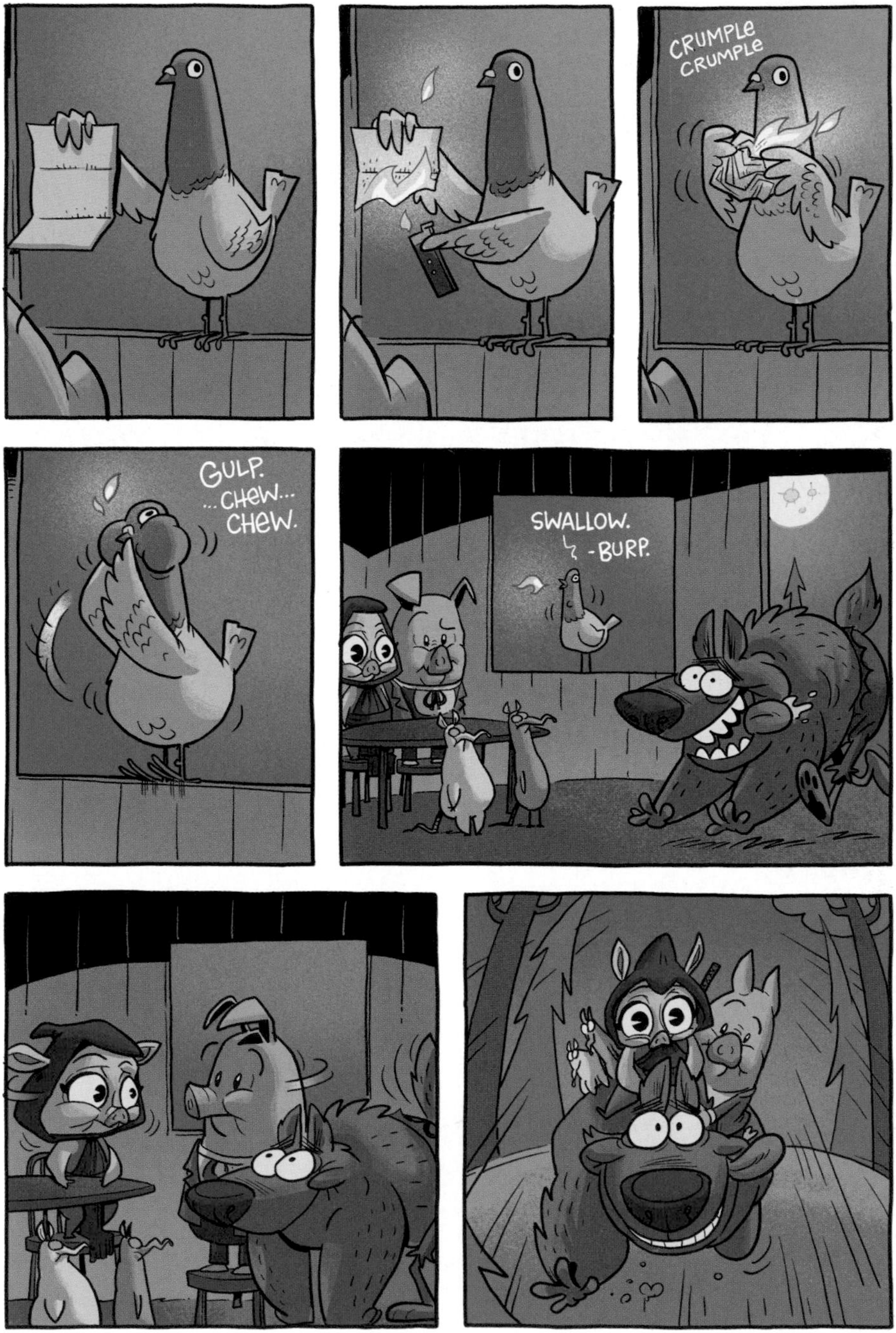
CRUMPLE
CRUMPLE
GULP.
...CHEW...
CHEW.
SWALLOW.
-BURP.

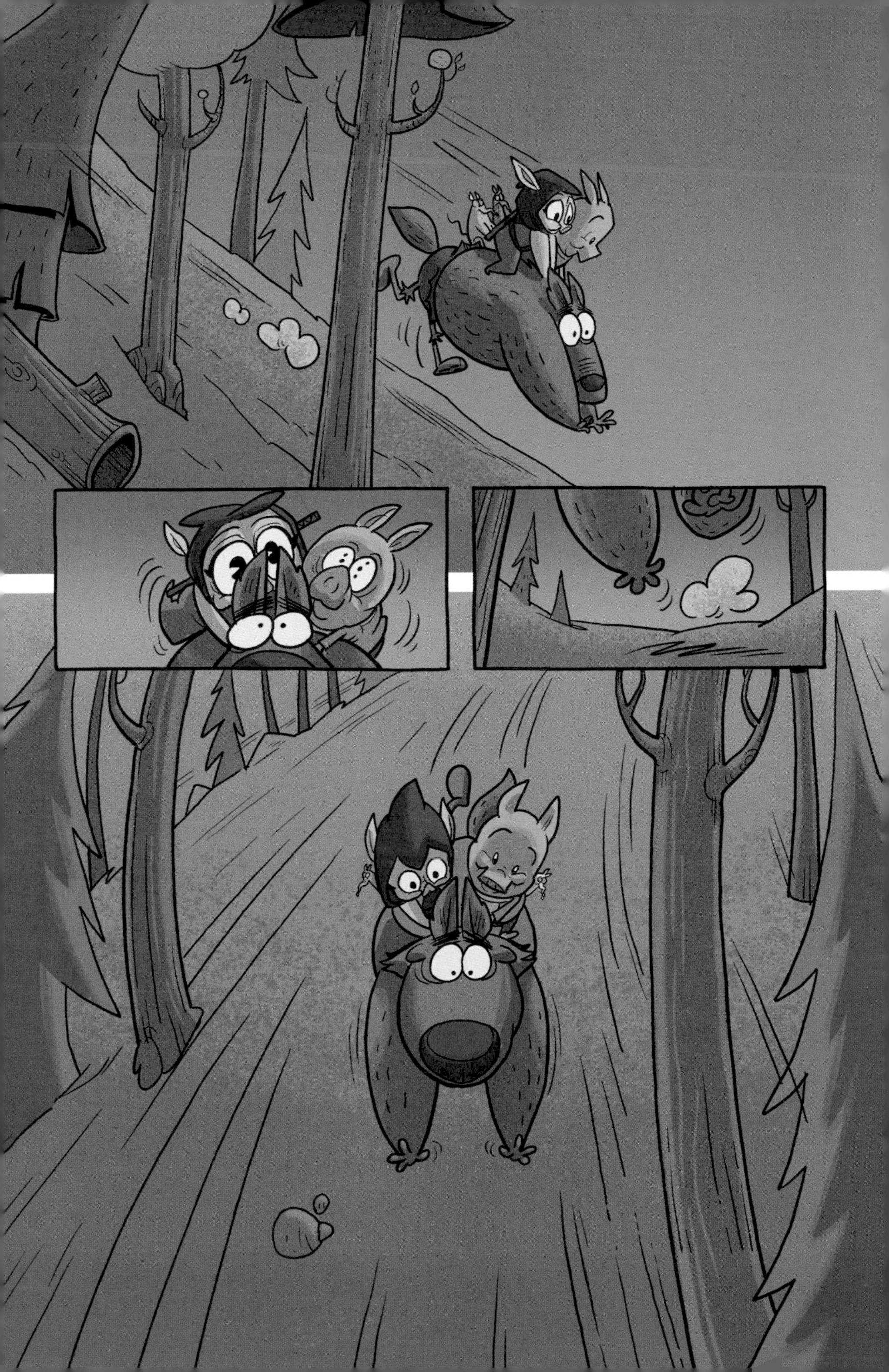

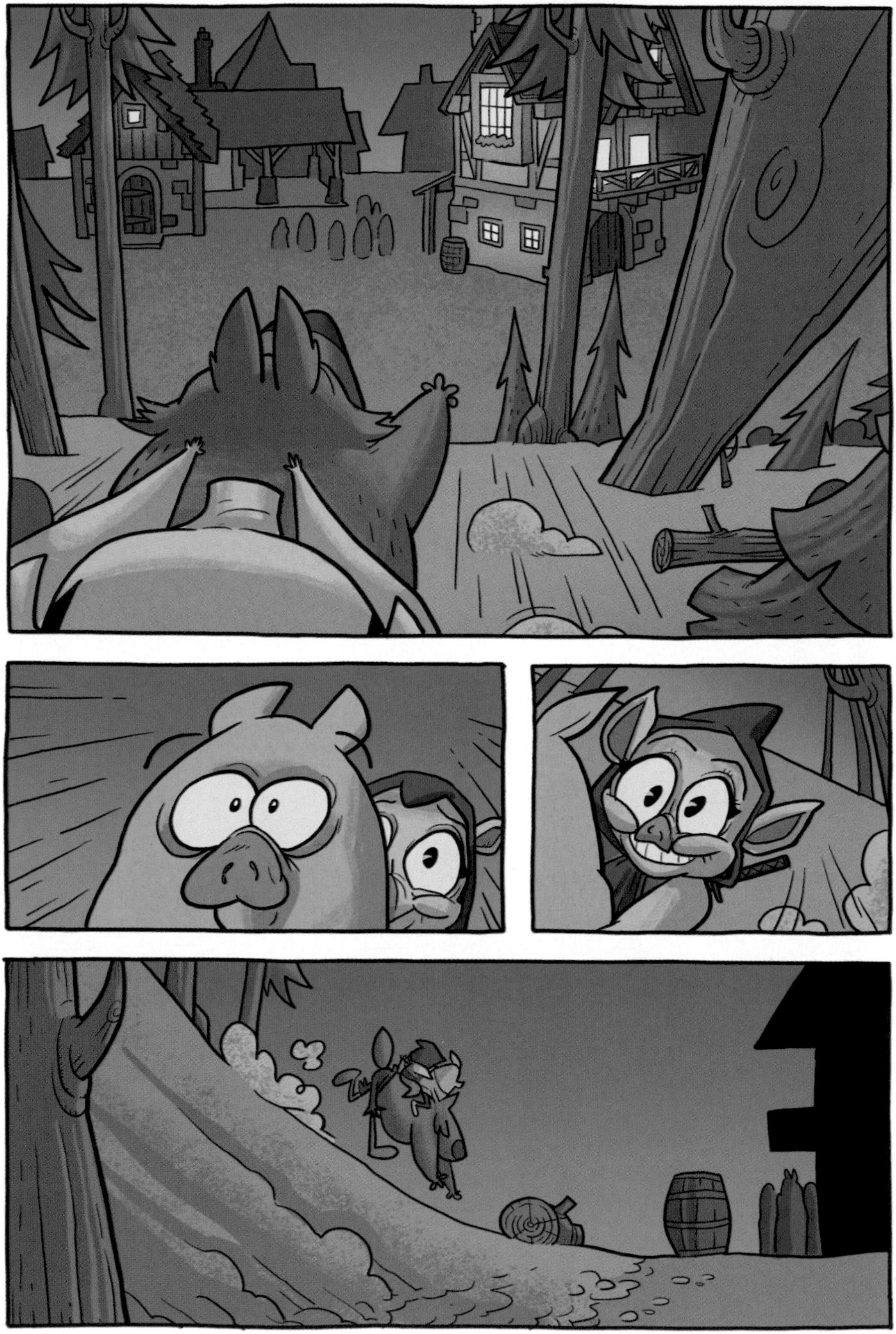

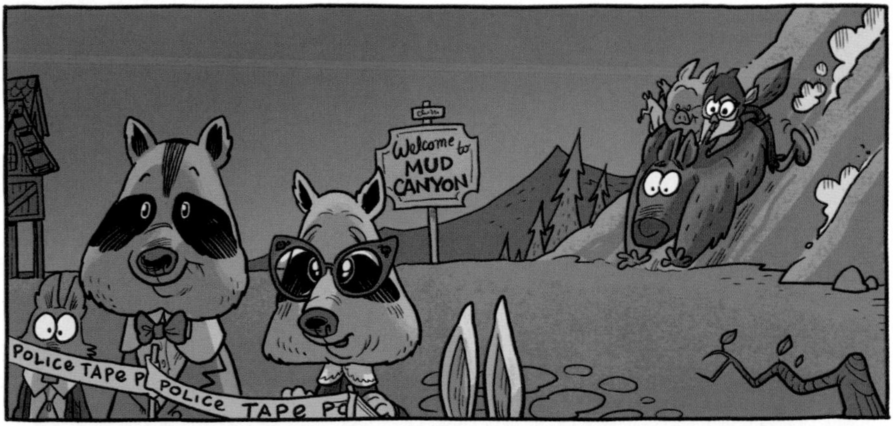
Welcome to
MUD
CANYON
POLICE TAPE P
POLICE TAPE P

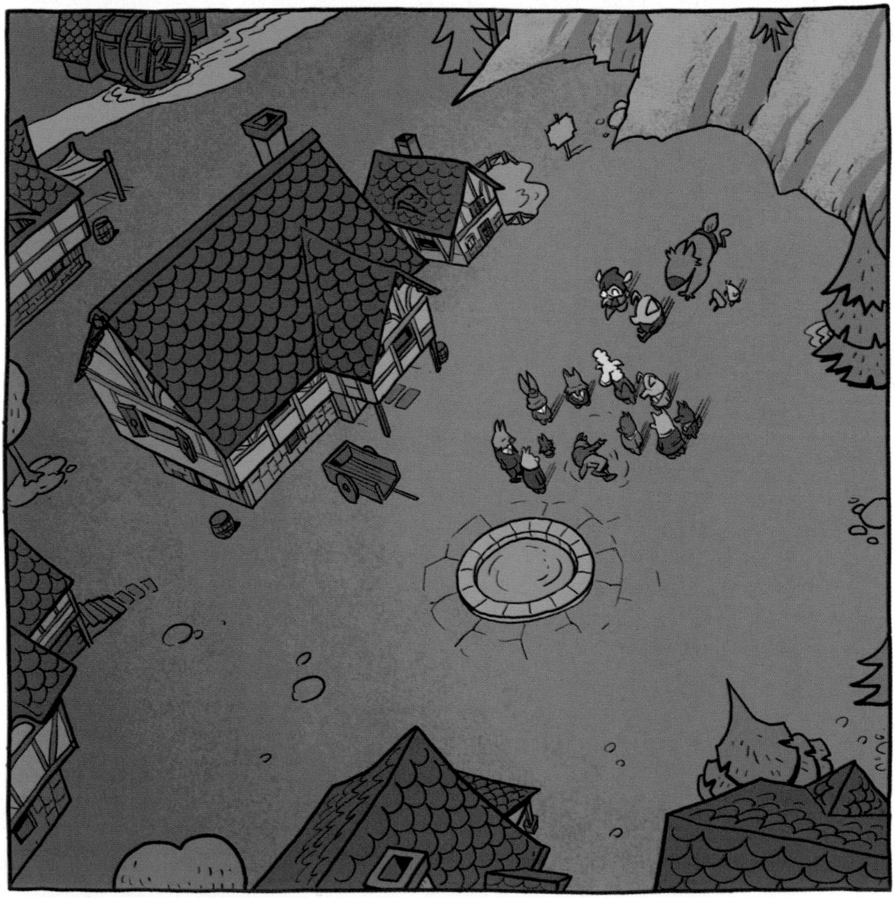

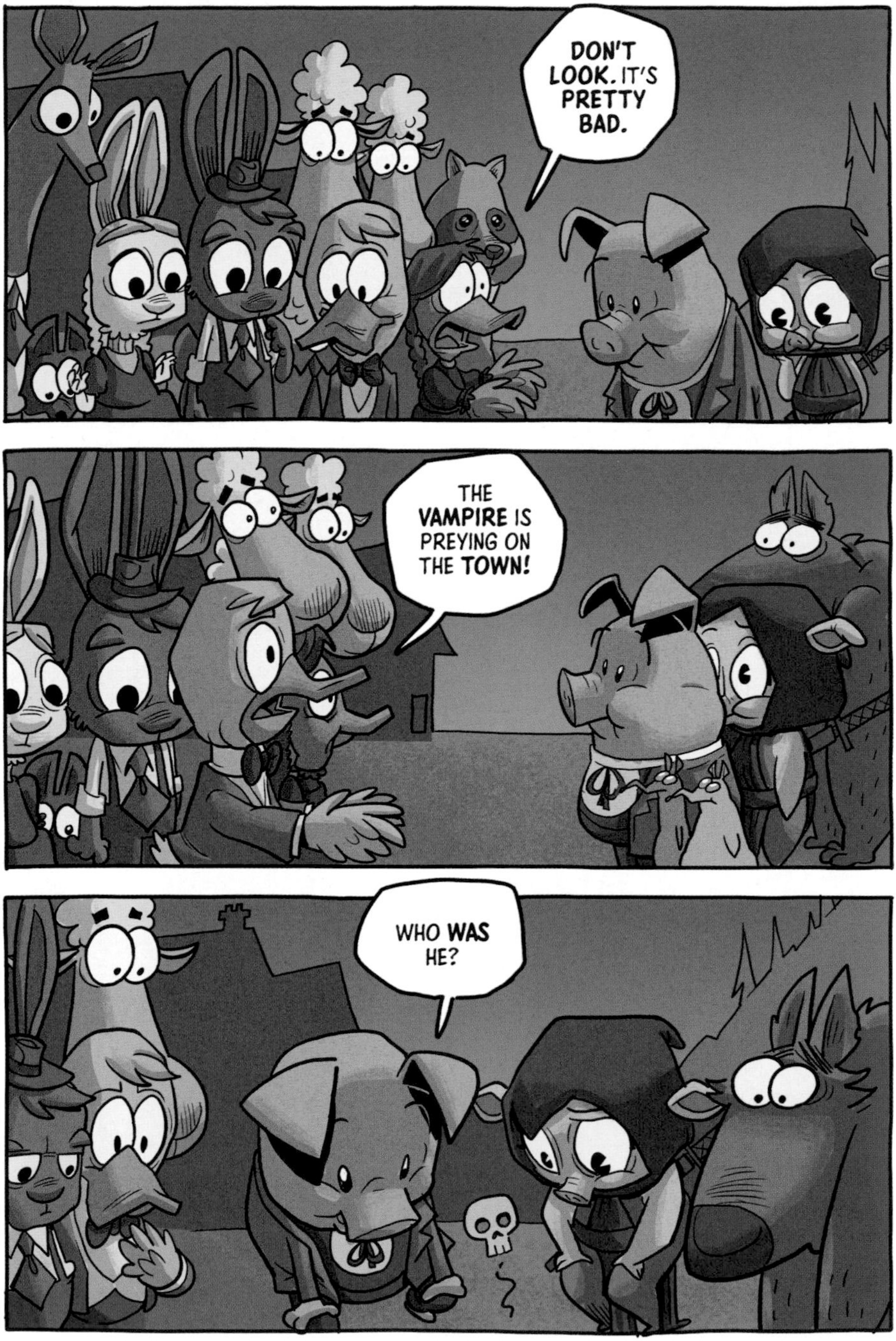
DON'T LOOK. IT'S PRETTY BAD.
THE VAMPIRE IS PREYING ON THE TOWN!
WHO WAS HE?

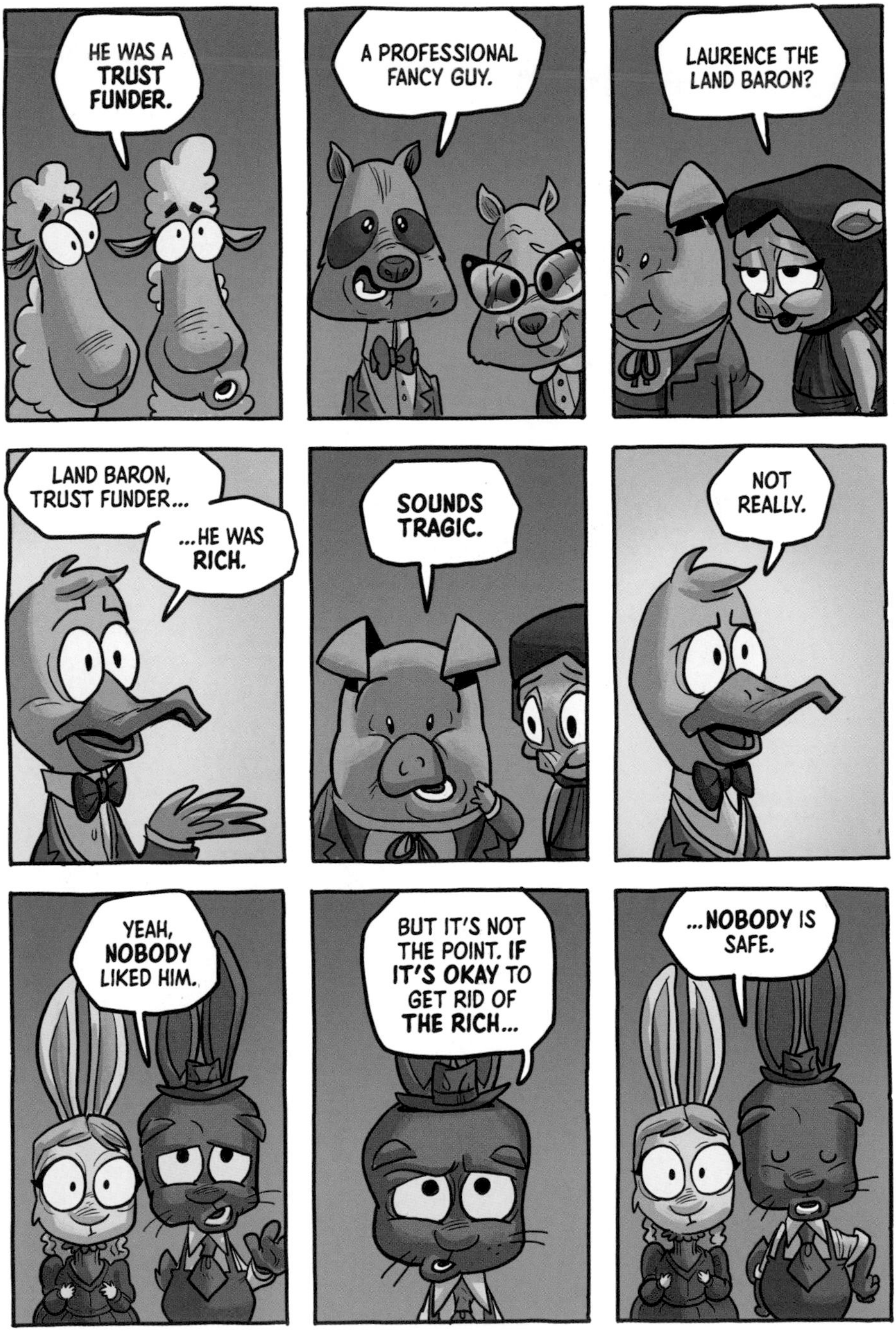
HE WAS A **TRUST FUNDER.**
A PROFESSIONAL FANCY GUY.
LAURENCE THE LAND BARON?
LAND BARON, TRUST FUNDER...
...HE WAS **RICH.**
SOUNDS TRAGIC.
NOT REALLY.
YEAH, **NOBODY** LIKED HIM.
BUT IT'S NOT THE POINT. **IF IT'S OKAY** TO GET RID OF **THE RICH...**
...NOBODY IS SAFE.

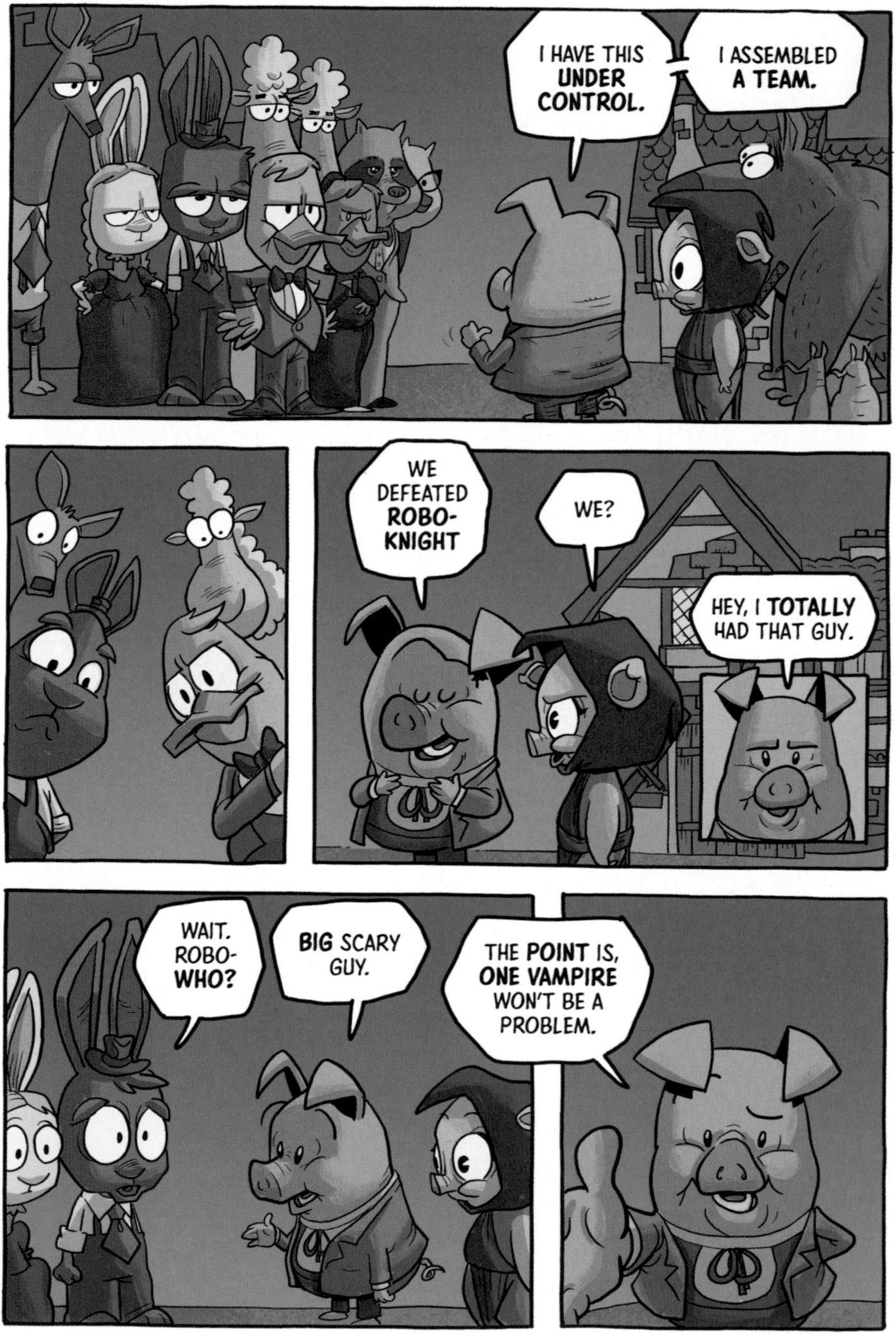
I HAVE THIS UNDER CONTROL.
I ASSEMBLED A TEAM.
WE DEFEATED ROBO-KNIGHT
WE?
HEY, I TOTALLY HAD THAT GUY.
WAIT. ROBO-WHO?
BIG SCARY GUY.
THE POINT IS, ONE VAMPIRE WON'T BE A PROBLEM.

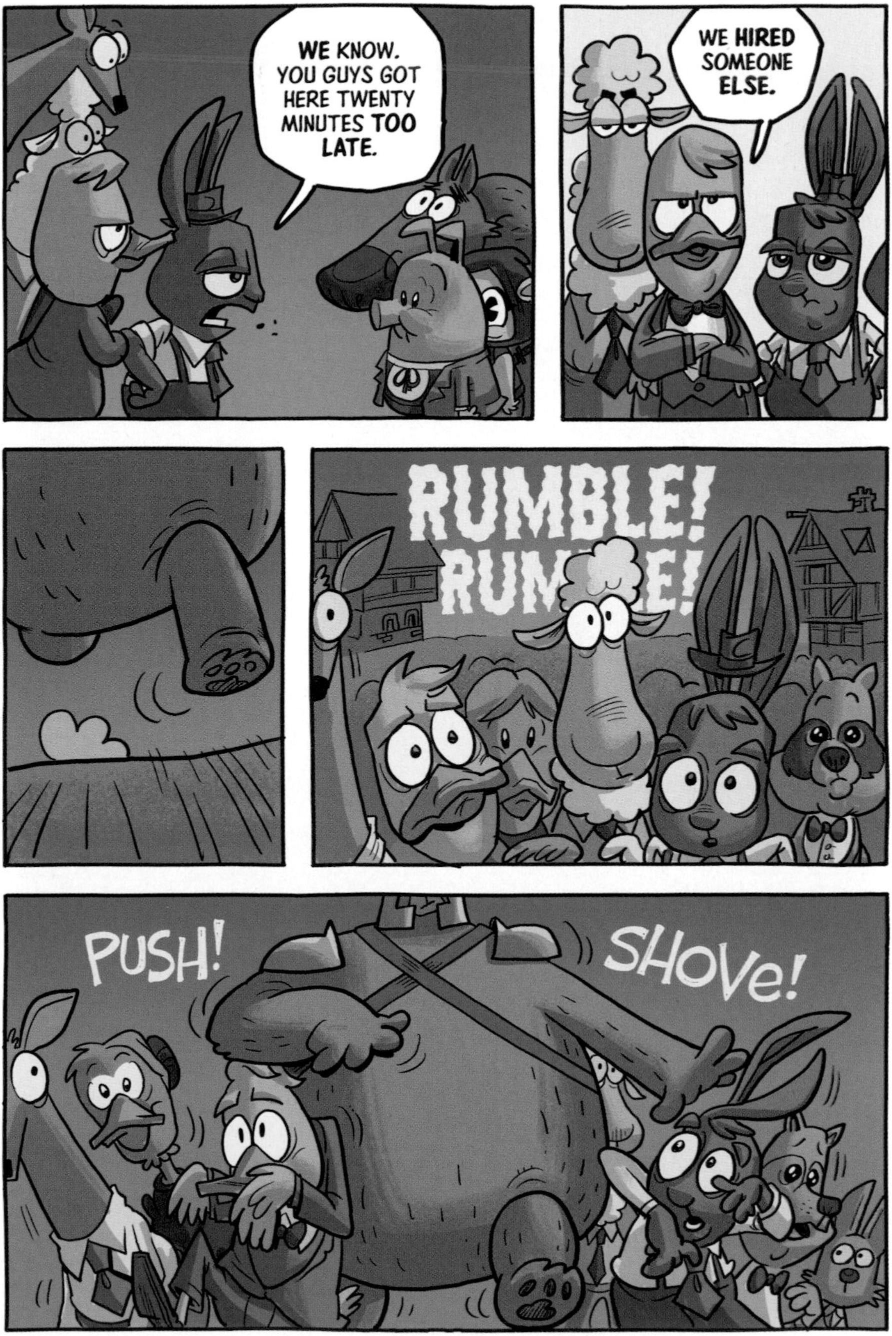
WE KNOW. YOU GUYS GOT HERE TWENTY MINUTES TOO LATE.
WE HIRED SOMEONE ELSE.
RUMBLE!
PUSH!
SHOVE!

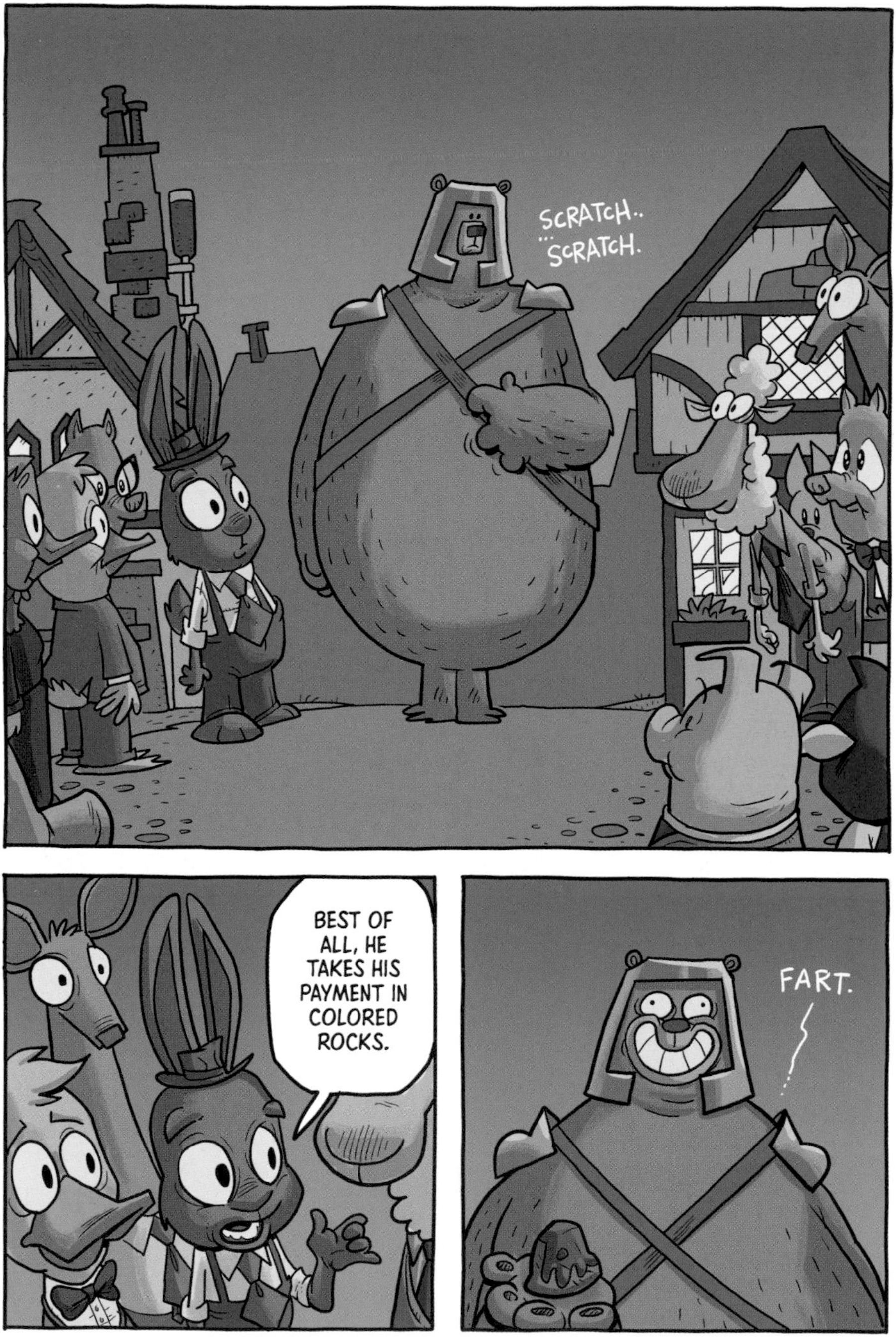
SCRATCH..
...SCRATCH.
BEST OF ALL, HE TAKES HIS PAYMENT IN COLORED ROCKS.
FART.

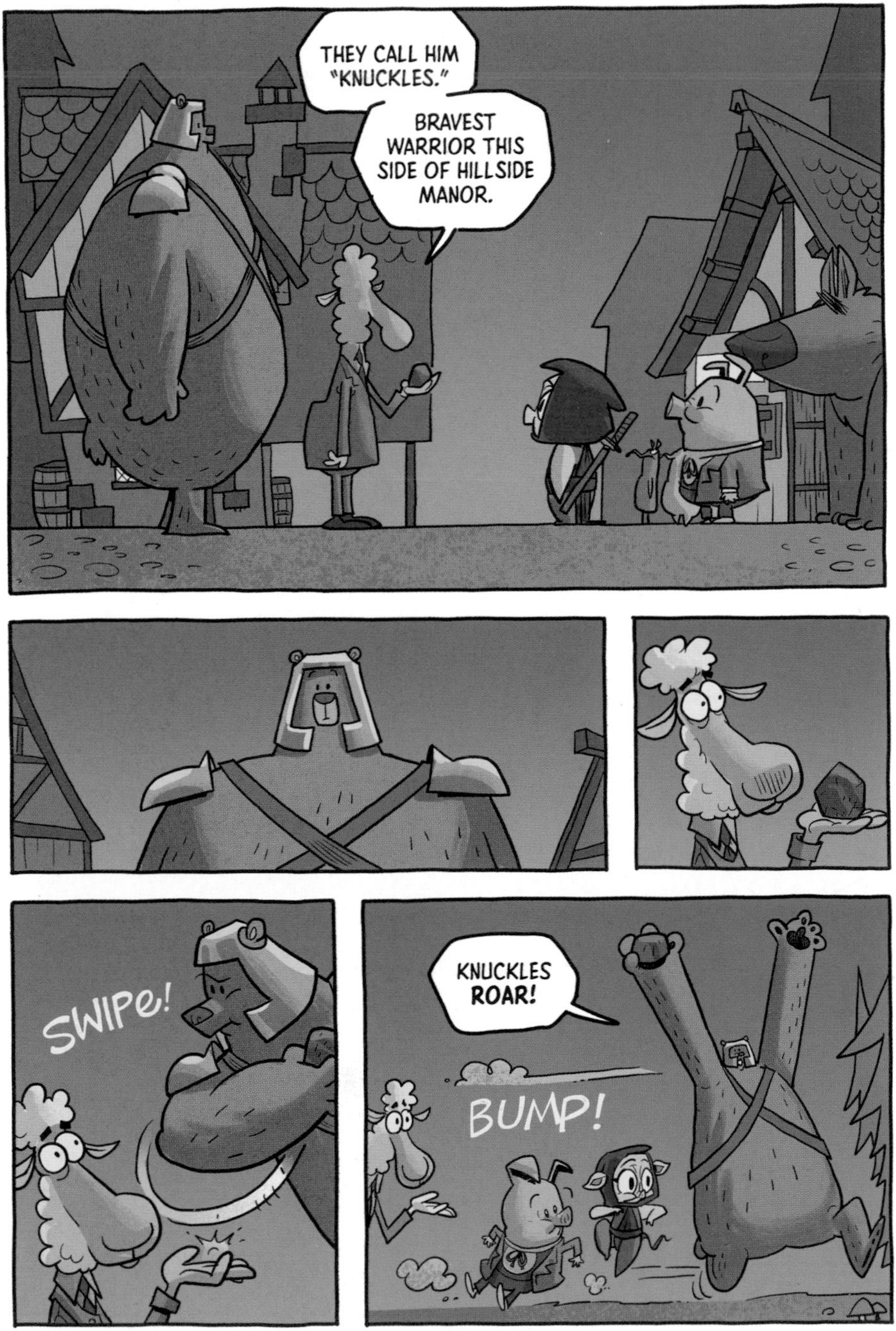
THEY CALL HIM "KNUCKLES."
BRAVEST WARRIOR THIS SIDE OF HILLSIDE MANOR.
SWIPE!
KNUCKLES ROAR!
BUMP!

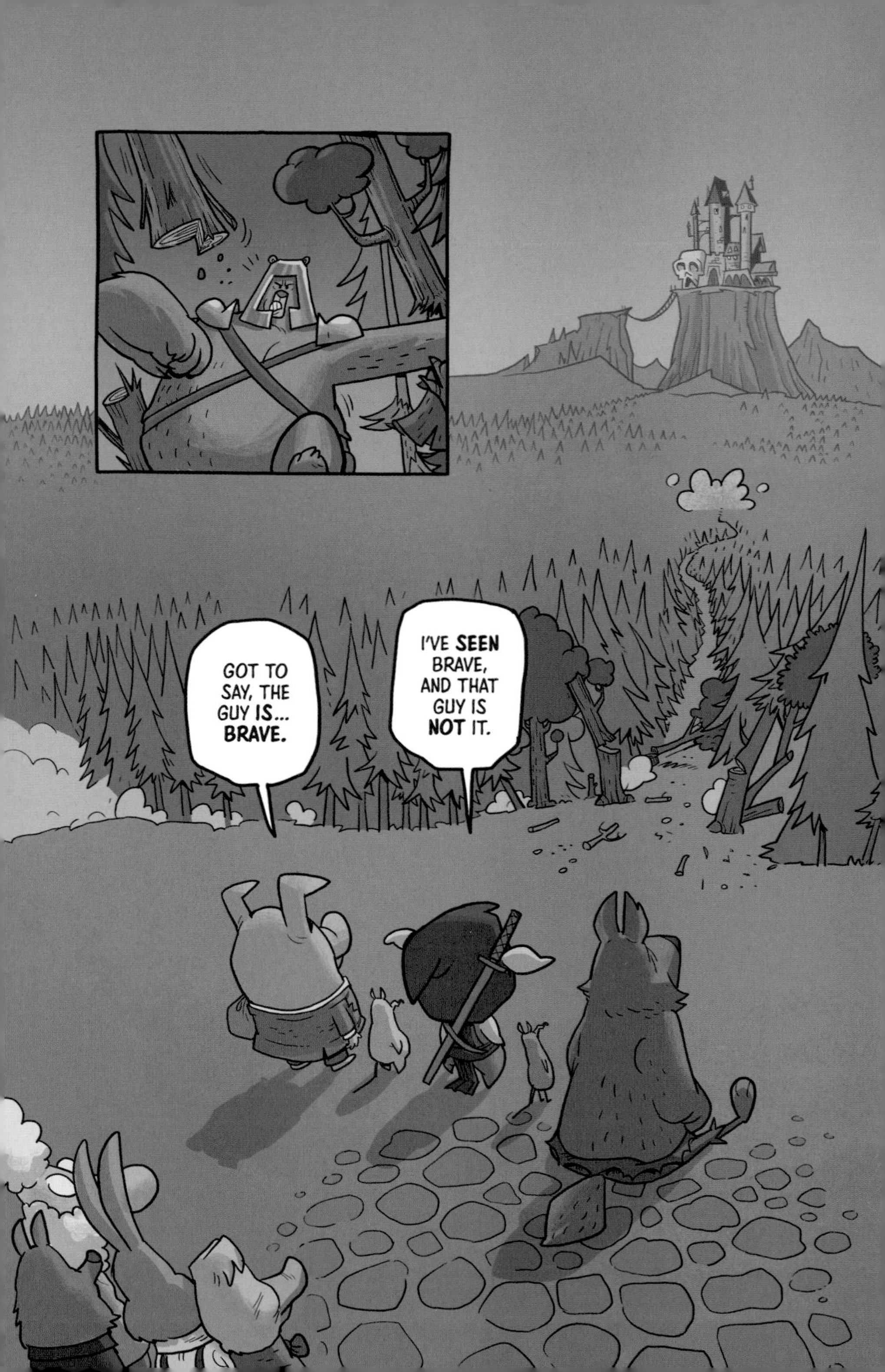

GOT TO SAY, THE GUY IS... BRAVE.
I'VE SEEN BRAVE, AND THAT GUY IS NOT IT.

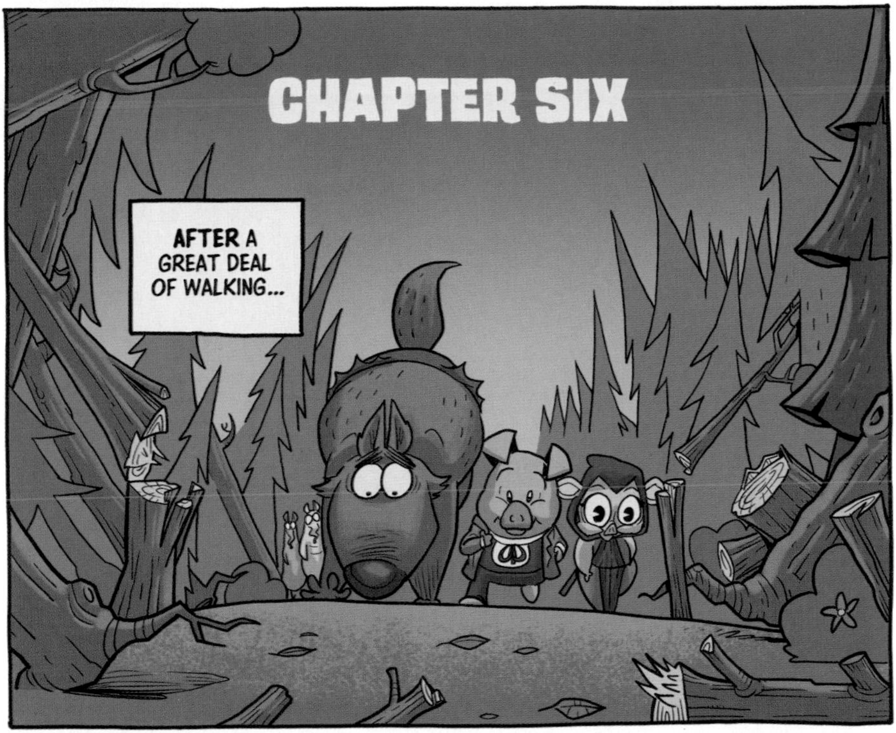
CHAPTER SIX
AFTER A GREAT DEAL OF WALKING...

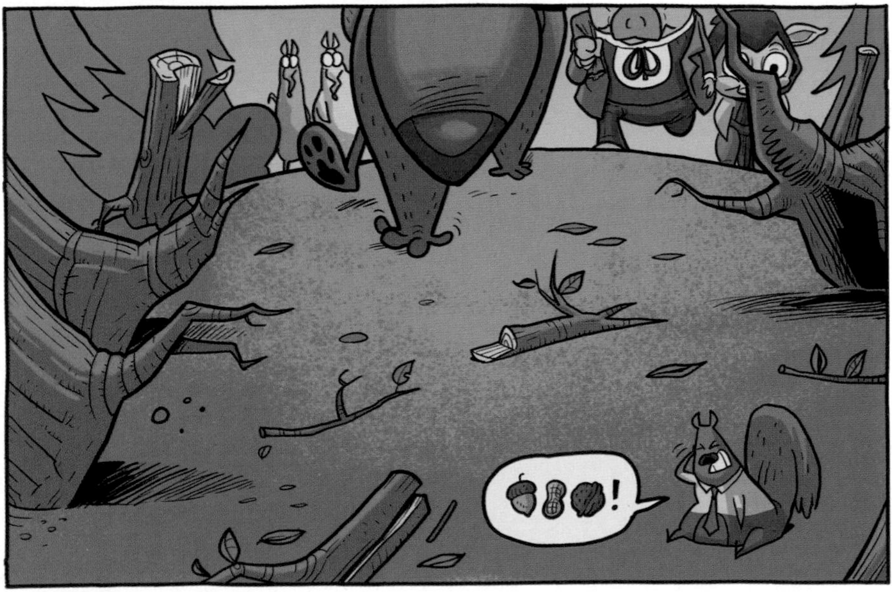

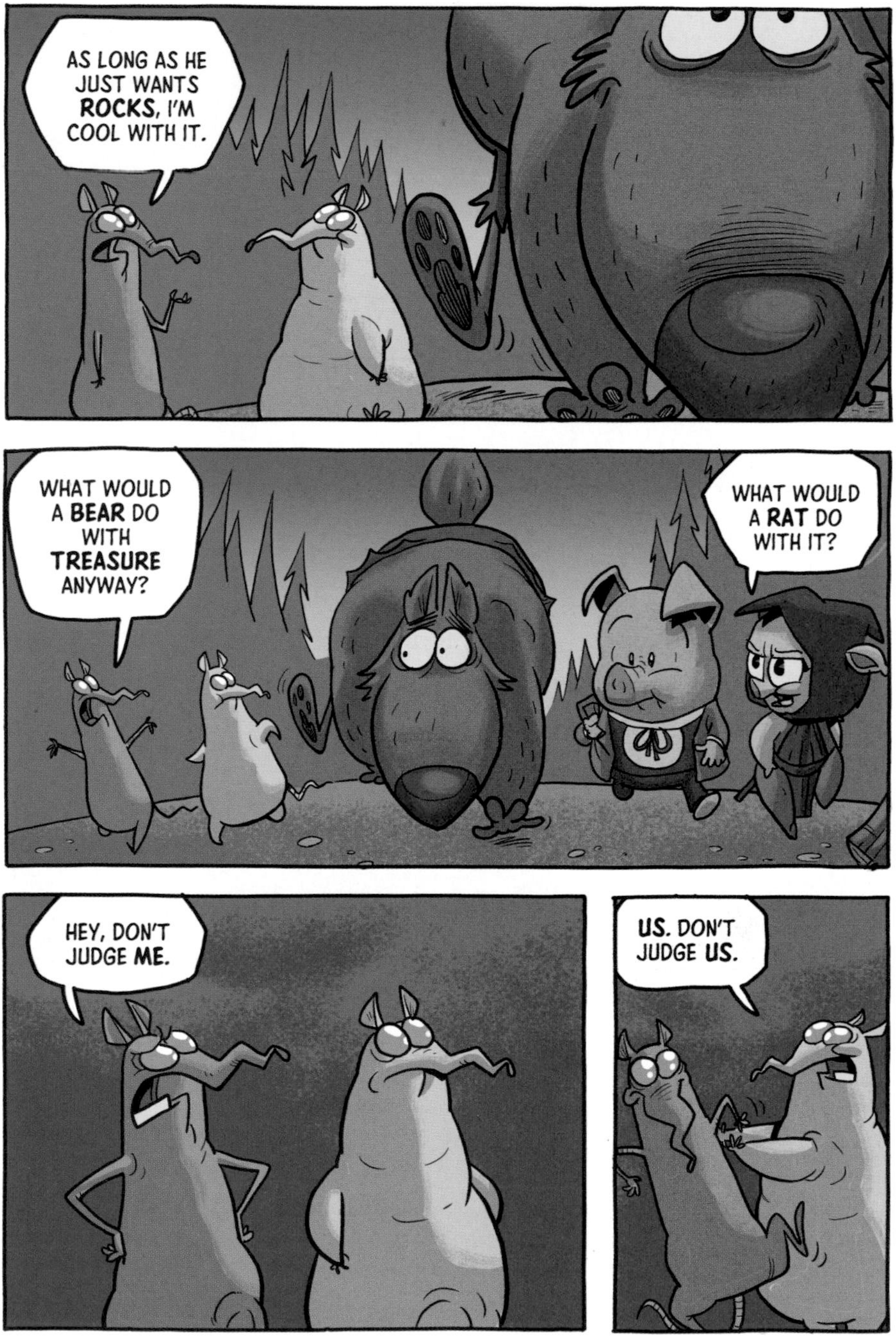
AS LONG AS HE JUST WANTS **ROCKS**, I'M COOL WITH IT.
WHAT WOULD A **BEAR** DO WITH **TREASURE** ANYWAY?
WHAT WOULD A **RAT** DO WITH IT?
HEY, DON'T JUDGE **ME**.
US. DON'T JUDGE **US.**

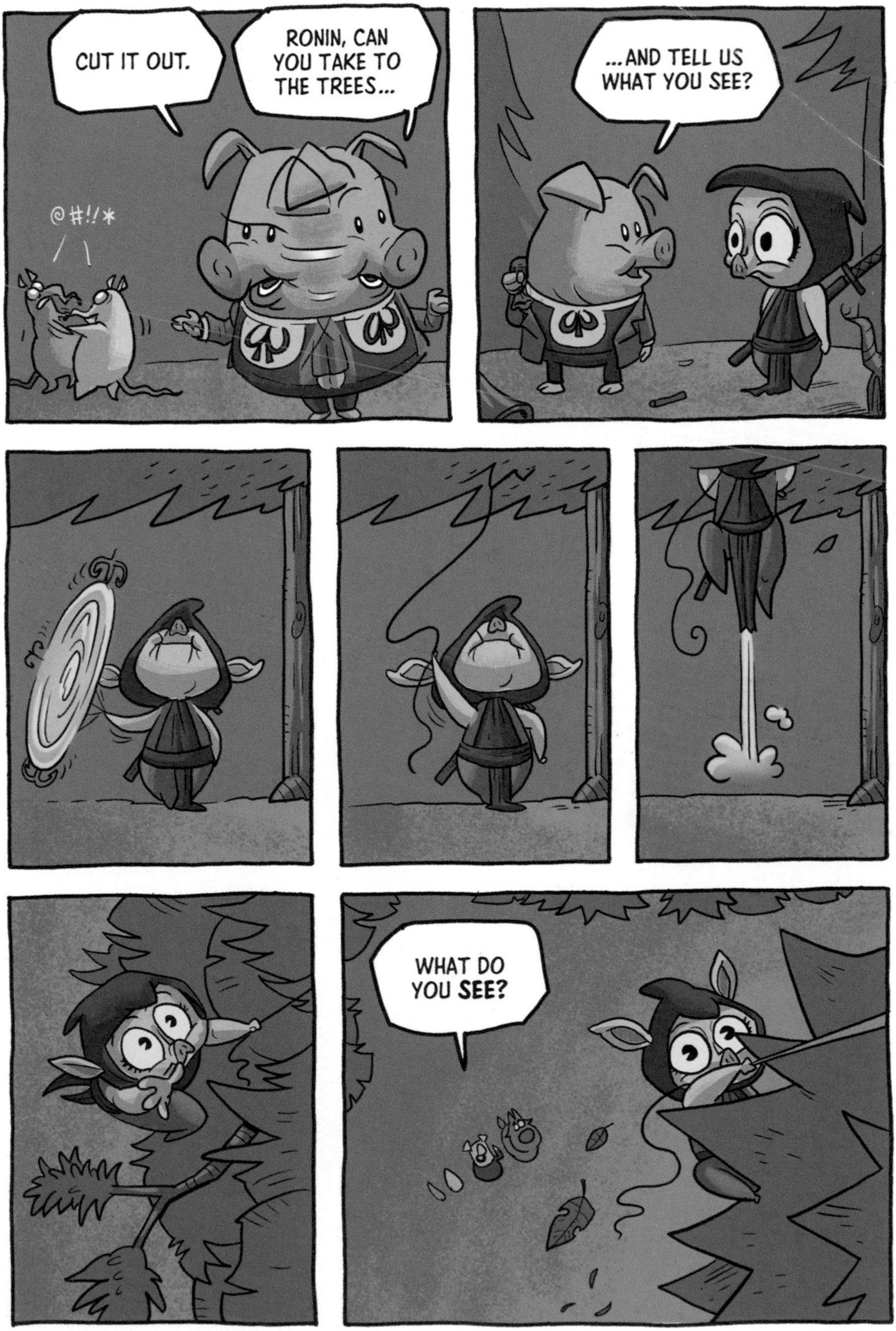
CUT IT OUT.
RONIN, CAN YOU TAKE TO THE TREES...
@#!/*
...AND TELL US WHAT YOU SEE?
WHAT DO YOU **SEE?**

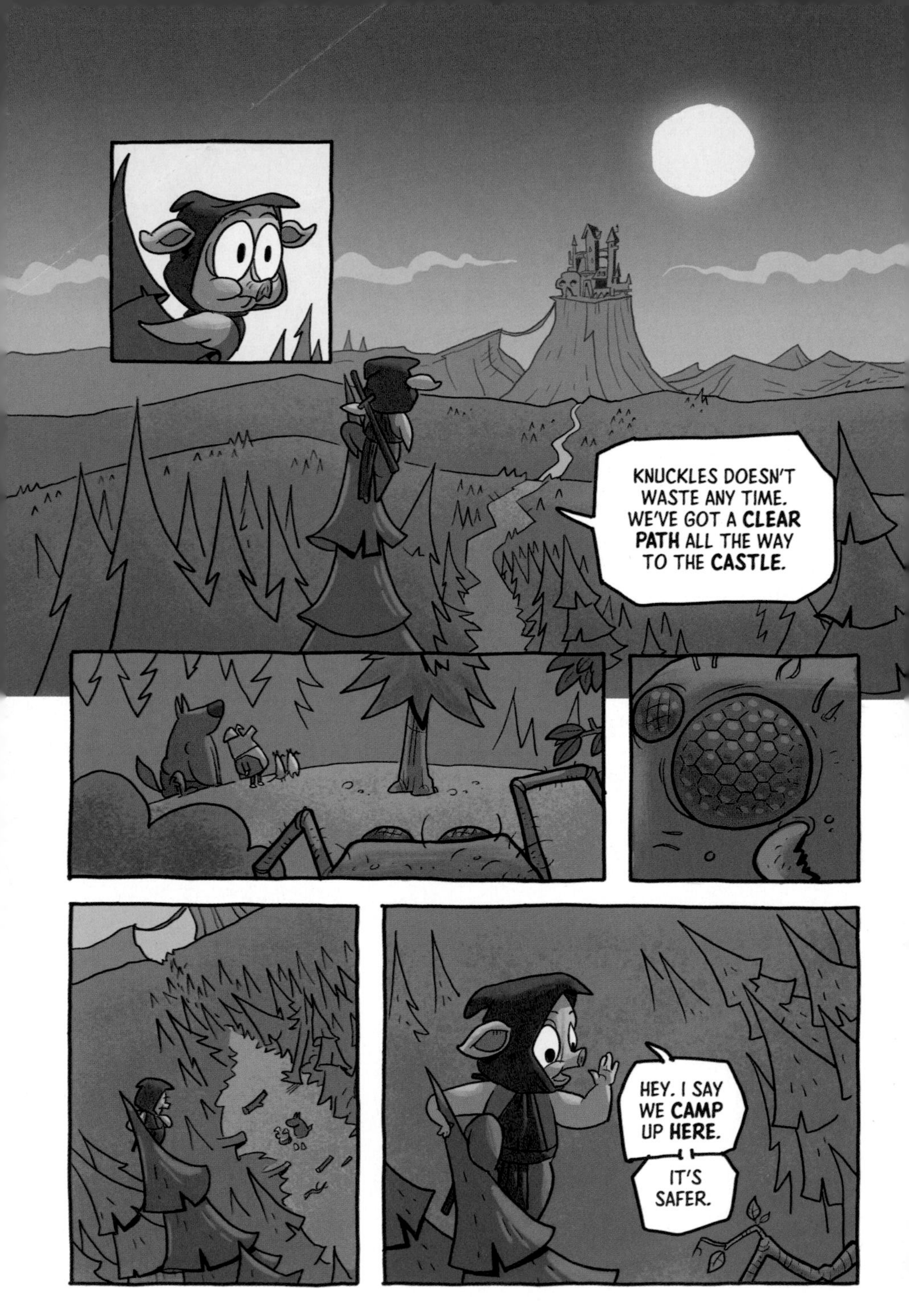

KNUCKLES DOESN'T WASTE ANY TIME. WE'VE GOT A **CLEAR PATH** ALL THE WAY TO THE **CASTLE.**
HEY. I SAY WE **CAMP** UP **HERE.**
IT'S SAFER.

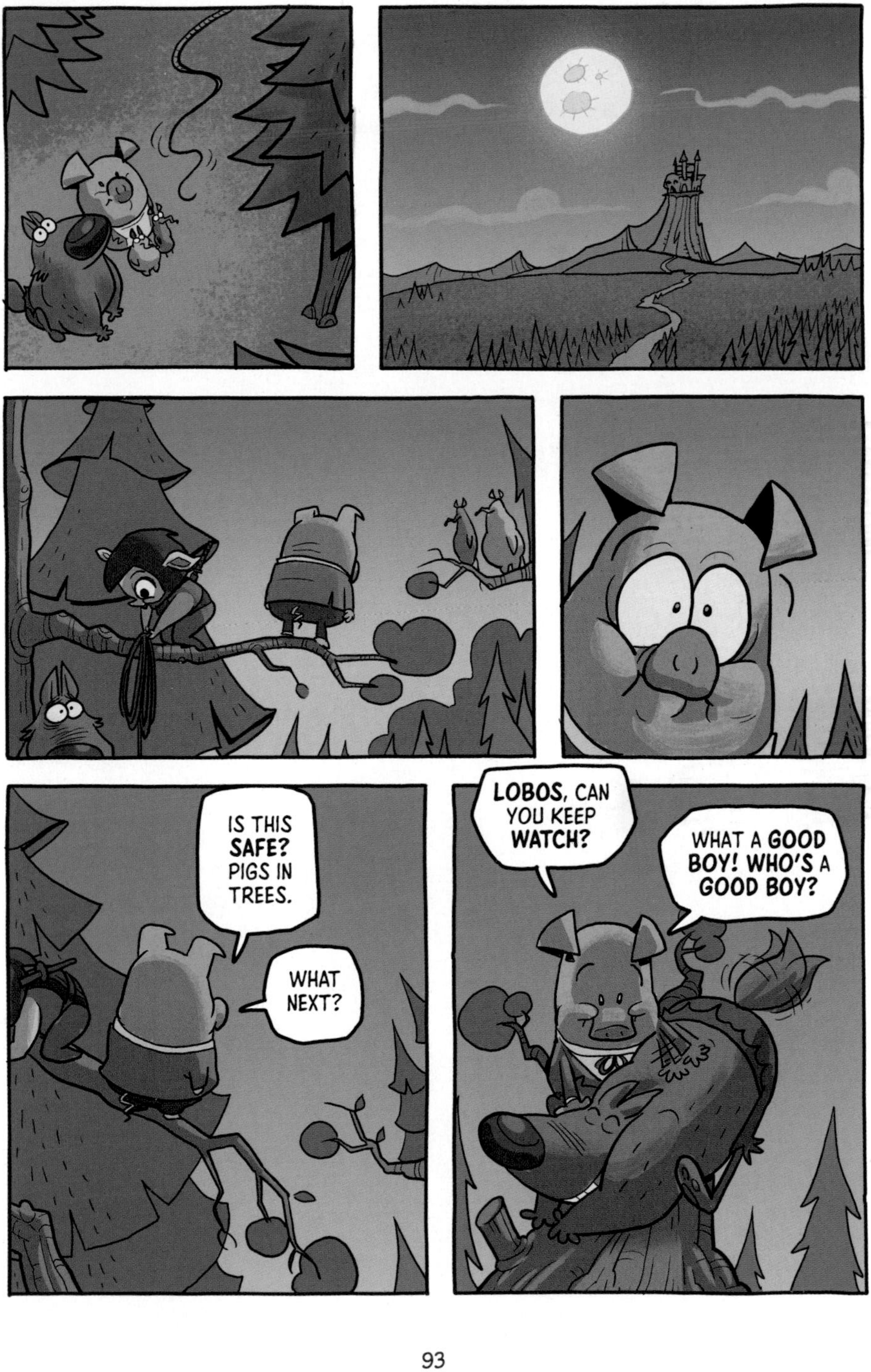
IS THIS SAFE? PIGS IN TREES.
WHAT NEXT?
LOBOS, CAN YOU KEEP WATCH?
WHAT A GOOD BOY! WHO'S A GOOD BOY?

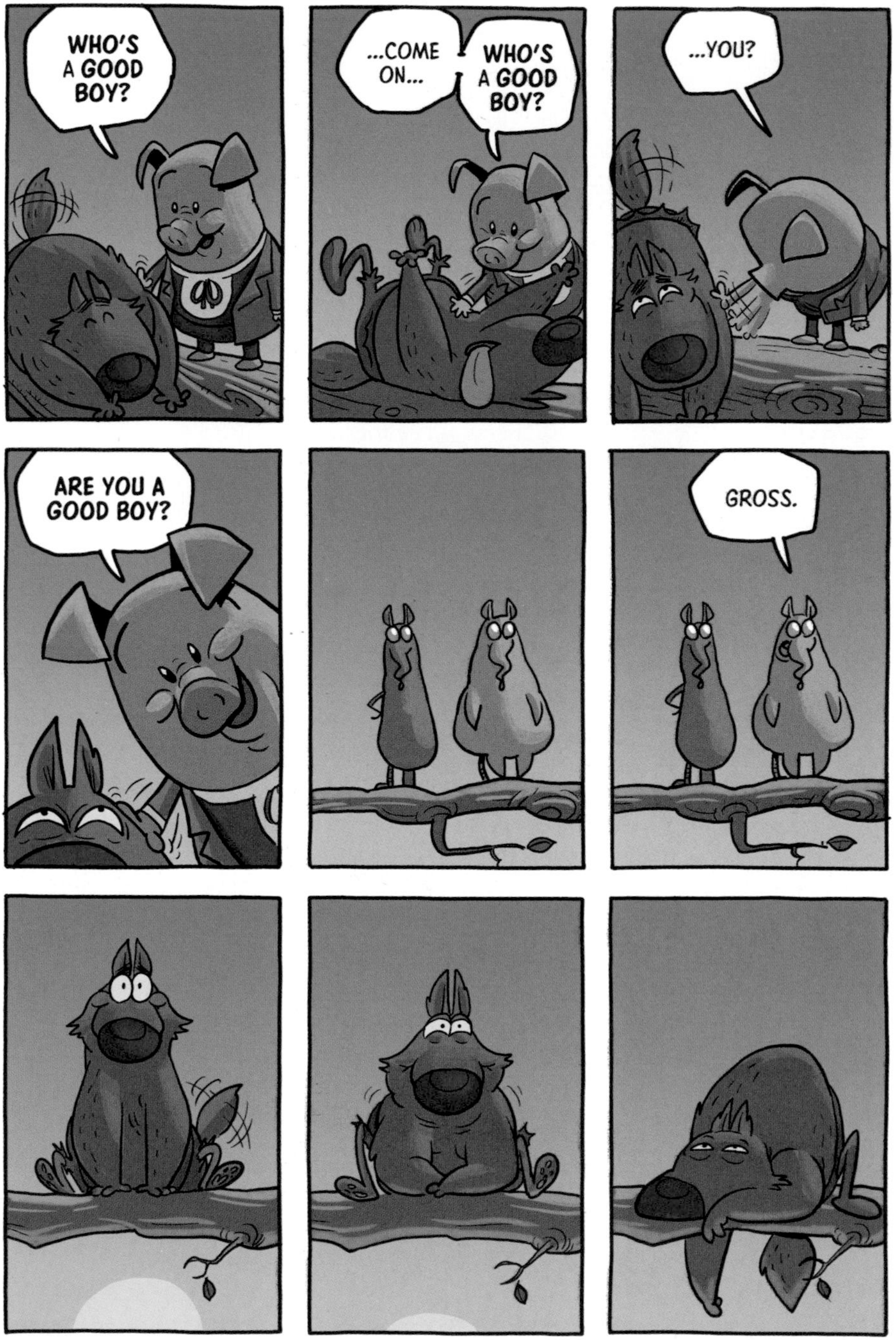
WHO'S A GOOD BOY?
...COME ON...
WHO'S A GOOD BOY?
...YOU?
ARE YOU A GOOD BOY?
GROSS.

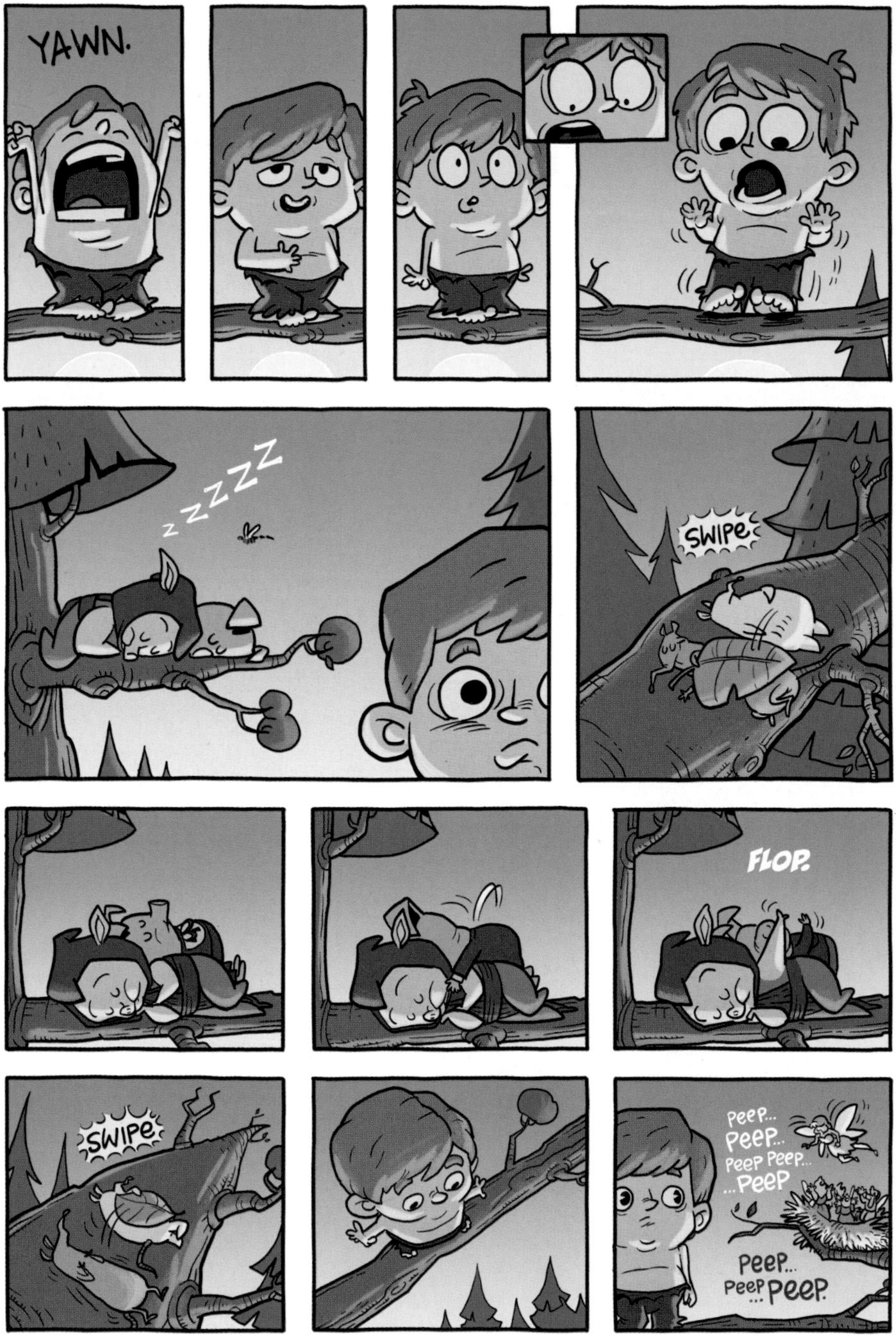
YAWN.
zZZZZ
SWIPE
FLOP.
SWIPE
PEEP... PEEP... PEEP PEEP... ...PEEP
PEEP... PEEP ...PEEP.

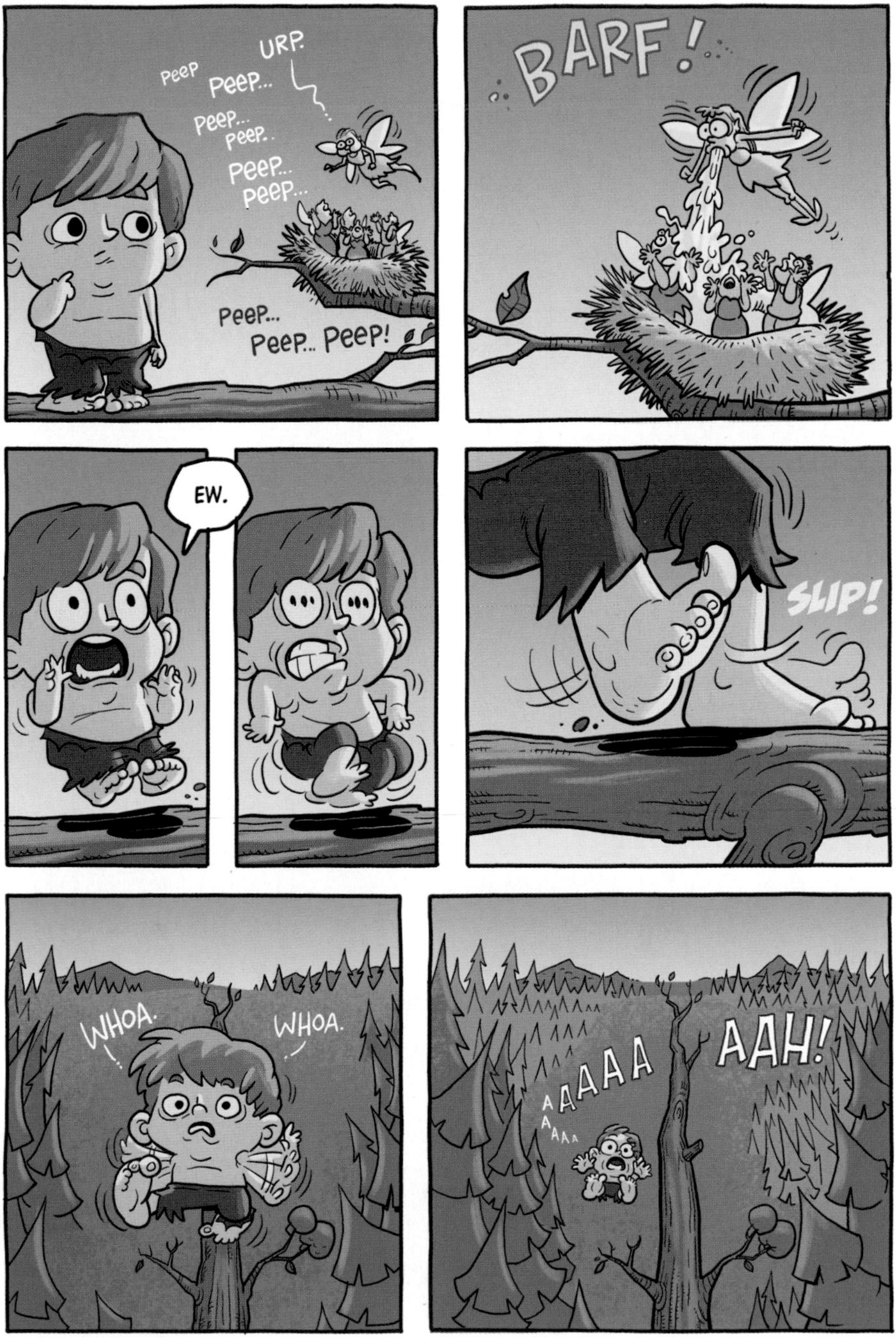
PEEP
PEEP...
URP.
PEEP...
PEEP..
PEEP...
PEEP...
PEEP...
PEEP... PEEP!
BARF!
EW.
SLIP!
WHOA.
WHOA.
AAAAAAAAA
AAH!

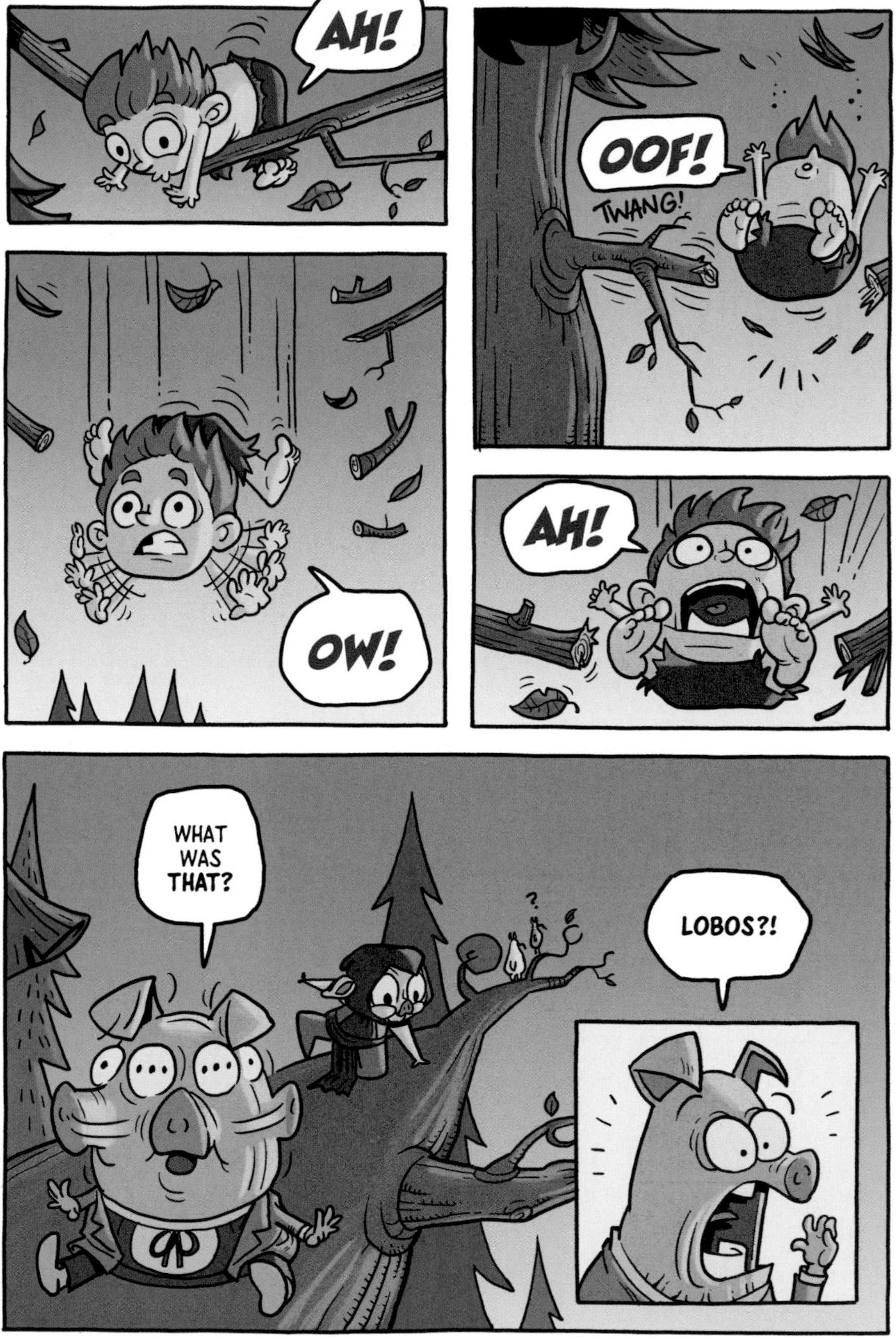
AH!
OOF!
TWANG!
OW!
AH!
WHAT WAS THAT?
LOBOS?!

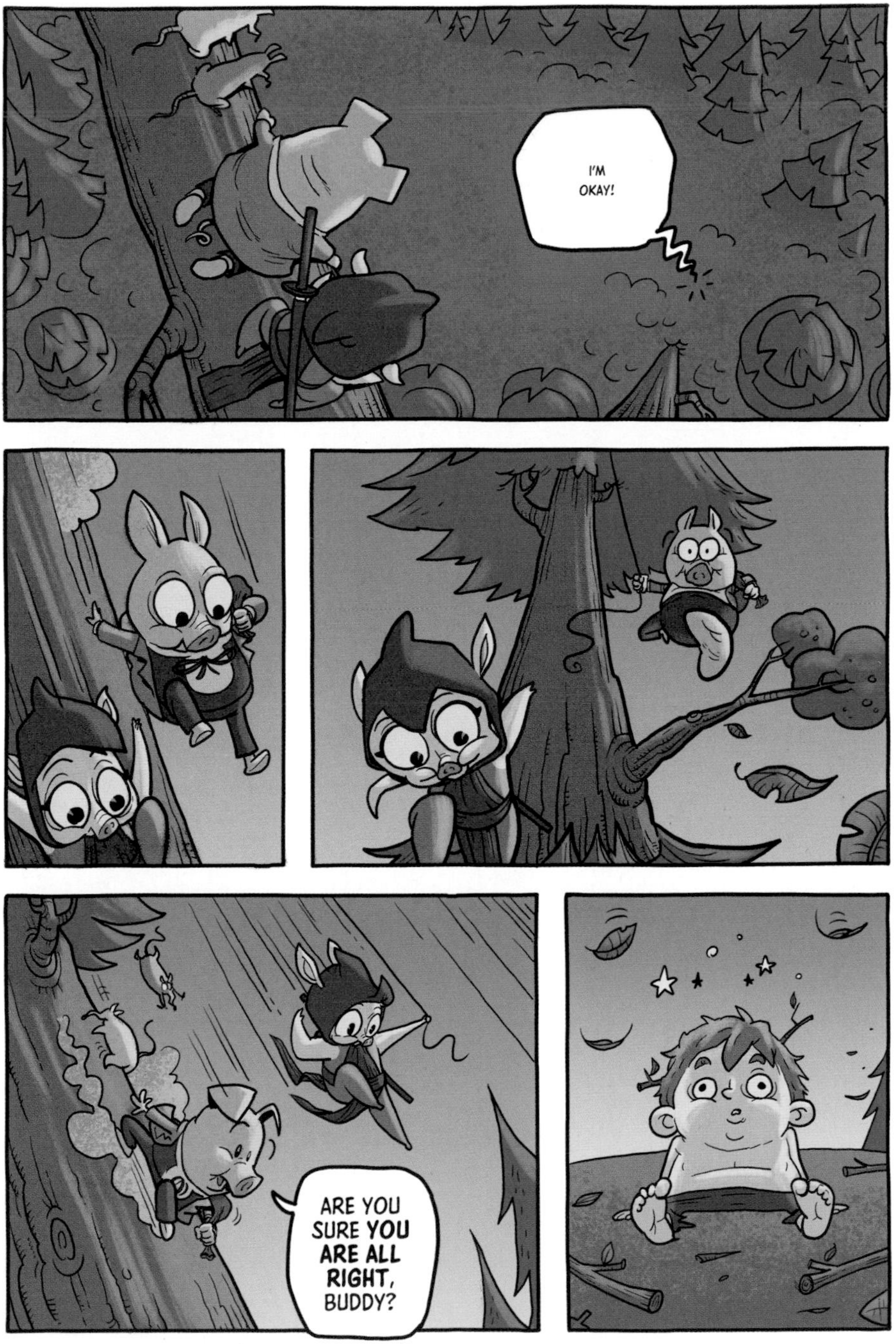
I'M OKAY!
ARE YOU SURE YOU ARE ALL RIGHT, BUDDY?

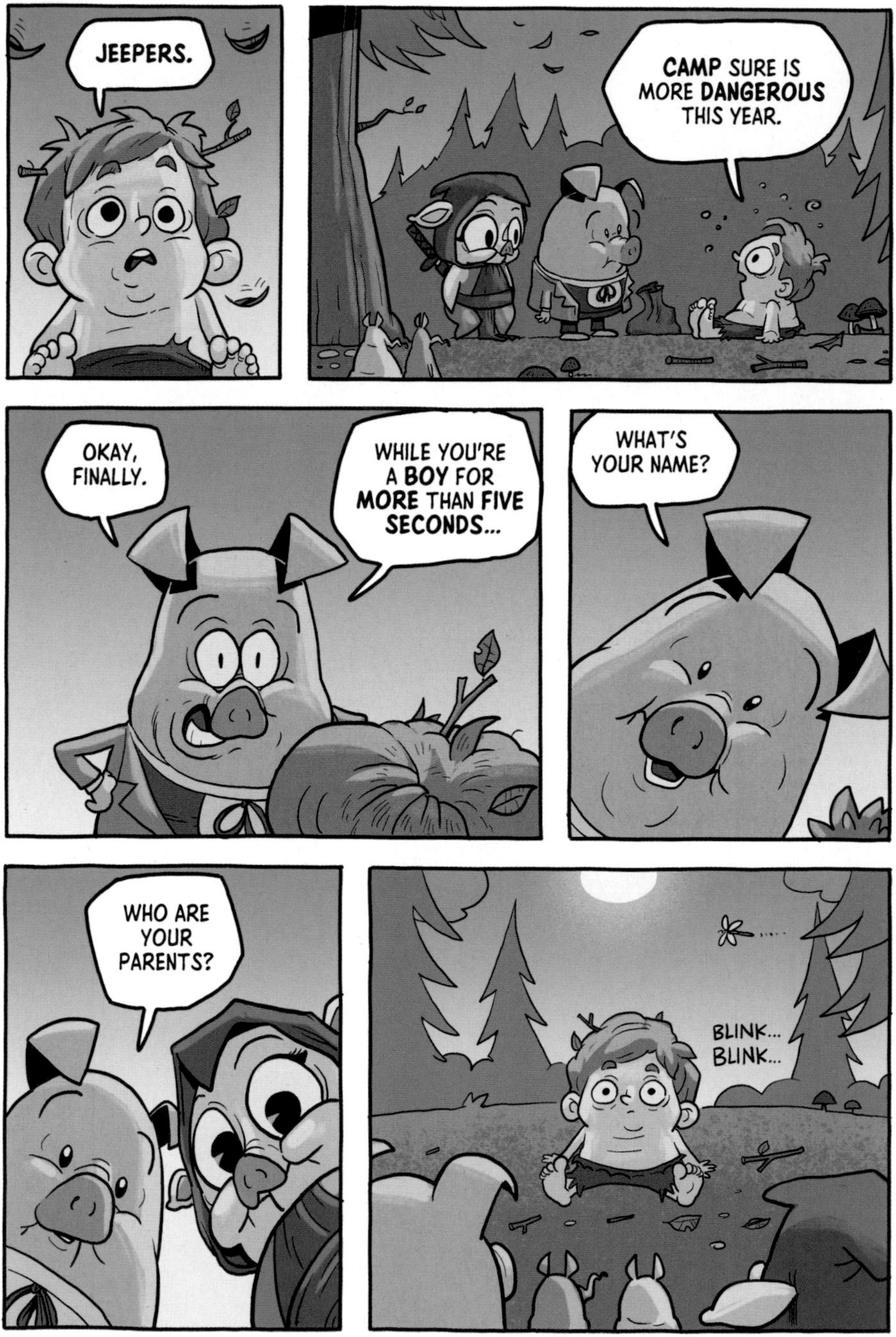
JEEPERS.
CAMP SURE IS MORE DANGEROUS THIS YEAR.
OKAY, FINALLY.
WHILE YOU'RE A BOY FOR MORE THAN FIVE SECONDS...
WHAT'S YOUR NAME?
WHO ARE YOUR PARENTS?
BLINK... BLINK...

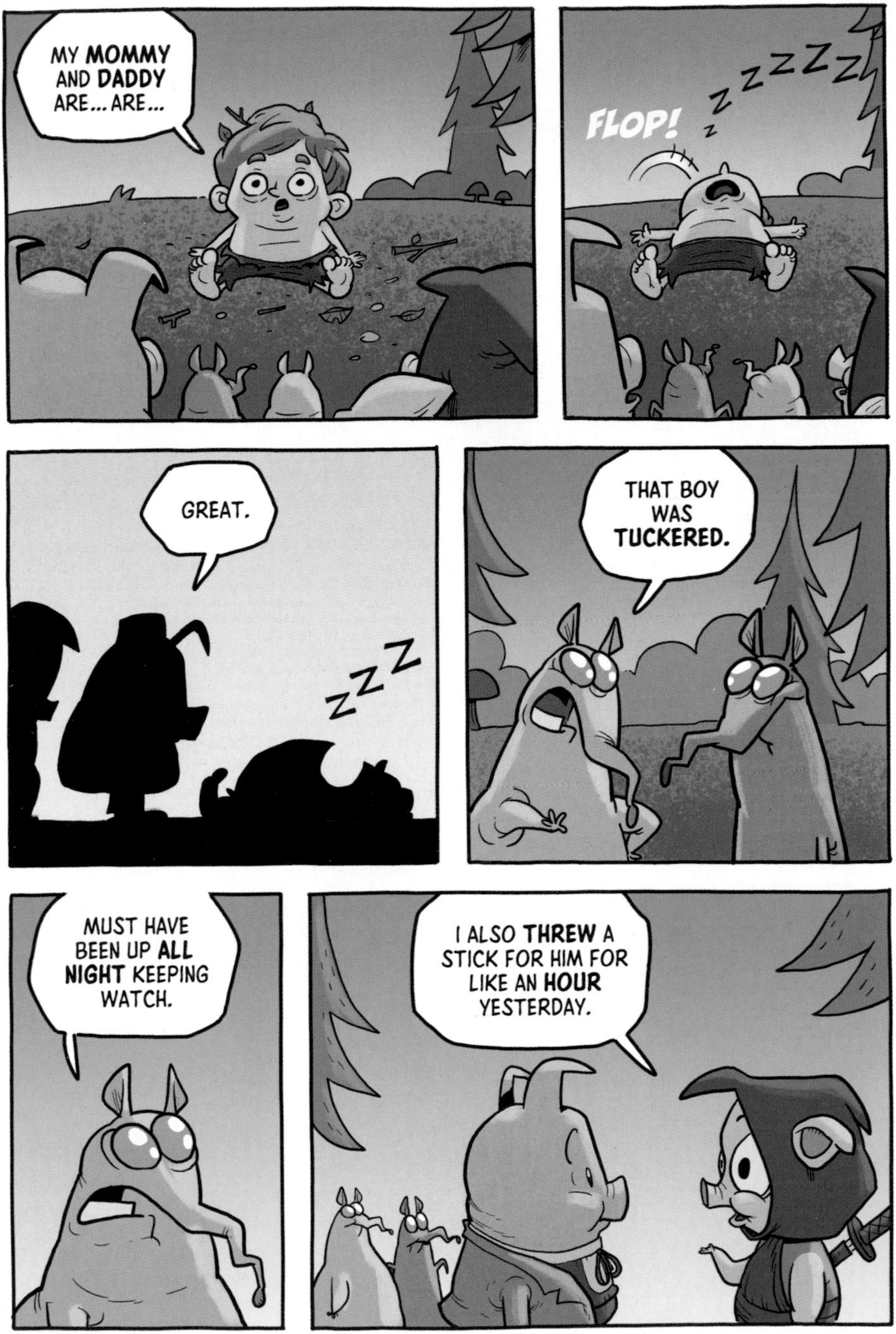
MY **MOMMY** AND **DADDY** ARE... ARE...
FLOP!
ZZZZZZZ
GREAT.
ZZZ
THAT BOY WAS **TUCKERED.**
MUST HAVE BEEN UP **ALL NIGHT** KEEPING WATCH.
I ALSO **THREW** A STICK FOR HIM FOR LIKE AN **HOUR** YESTERDAY.

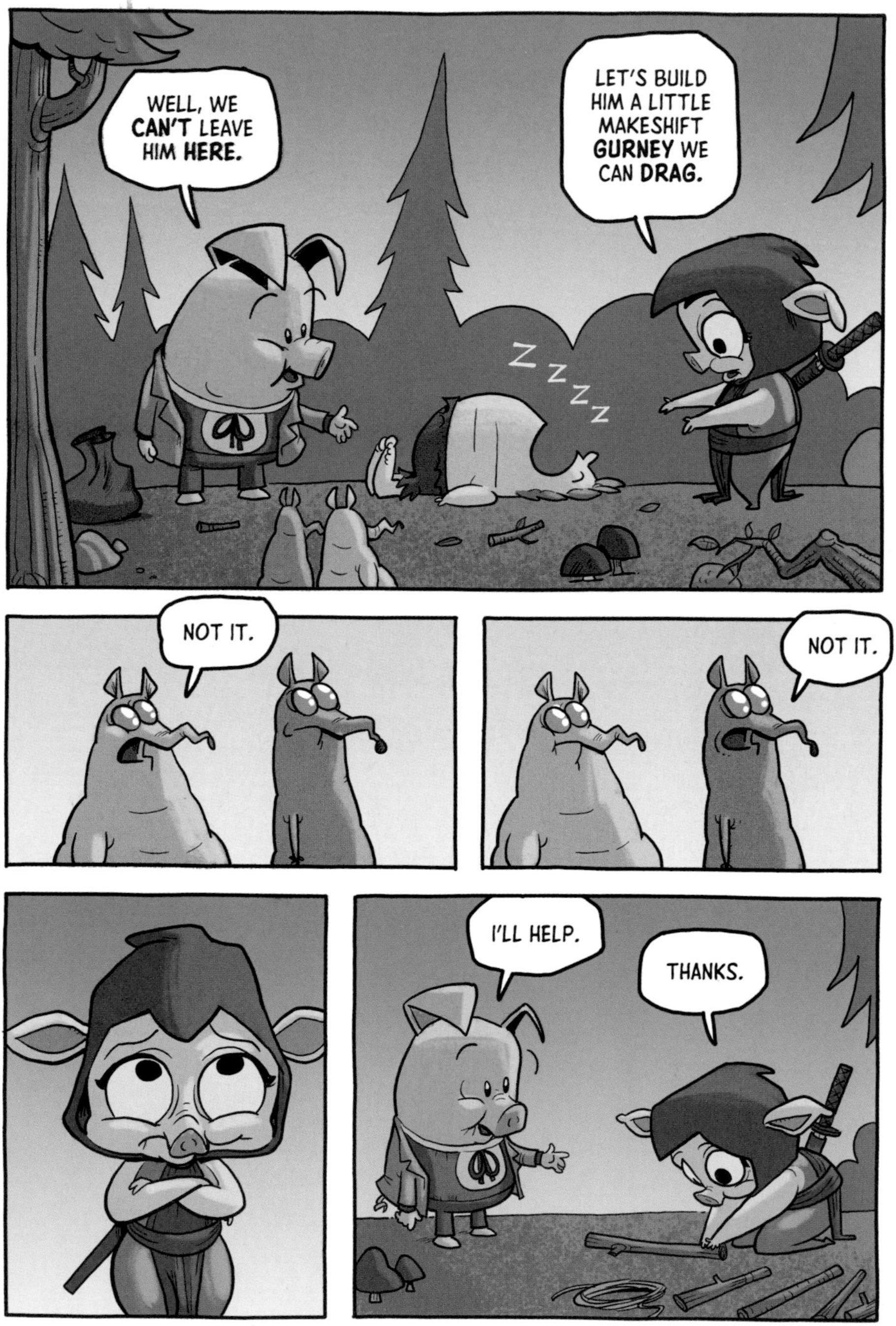
WELL, WE CAN'T LEAVE HIM HERE.
LET'S BUILD HIM A LITTLE MAKESHIFT GURNEY WE CAN DRAG.
Z Z Z Z
NOT IT.
NOT IT.
I'LL HELP.
THANKS.

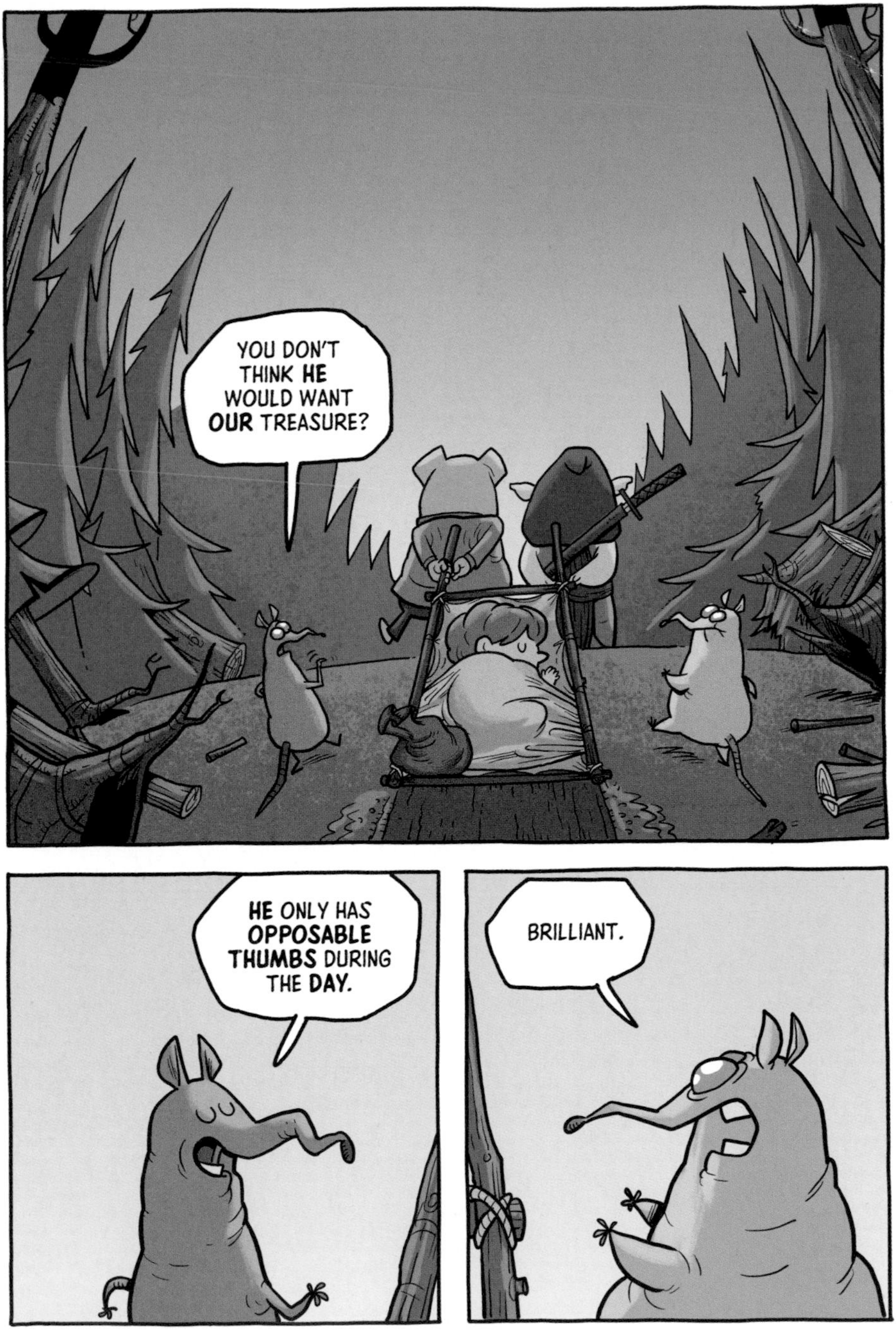
YOU DON'T THINK **HE** WOULD WANT **OUR** TREASURE?
HE ONLY HAS **OPPOSABLE THUMBS** DURING THE **DAY.**
BRILLIANT.

CHAPTER SEVEN

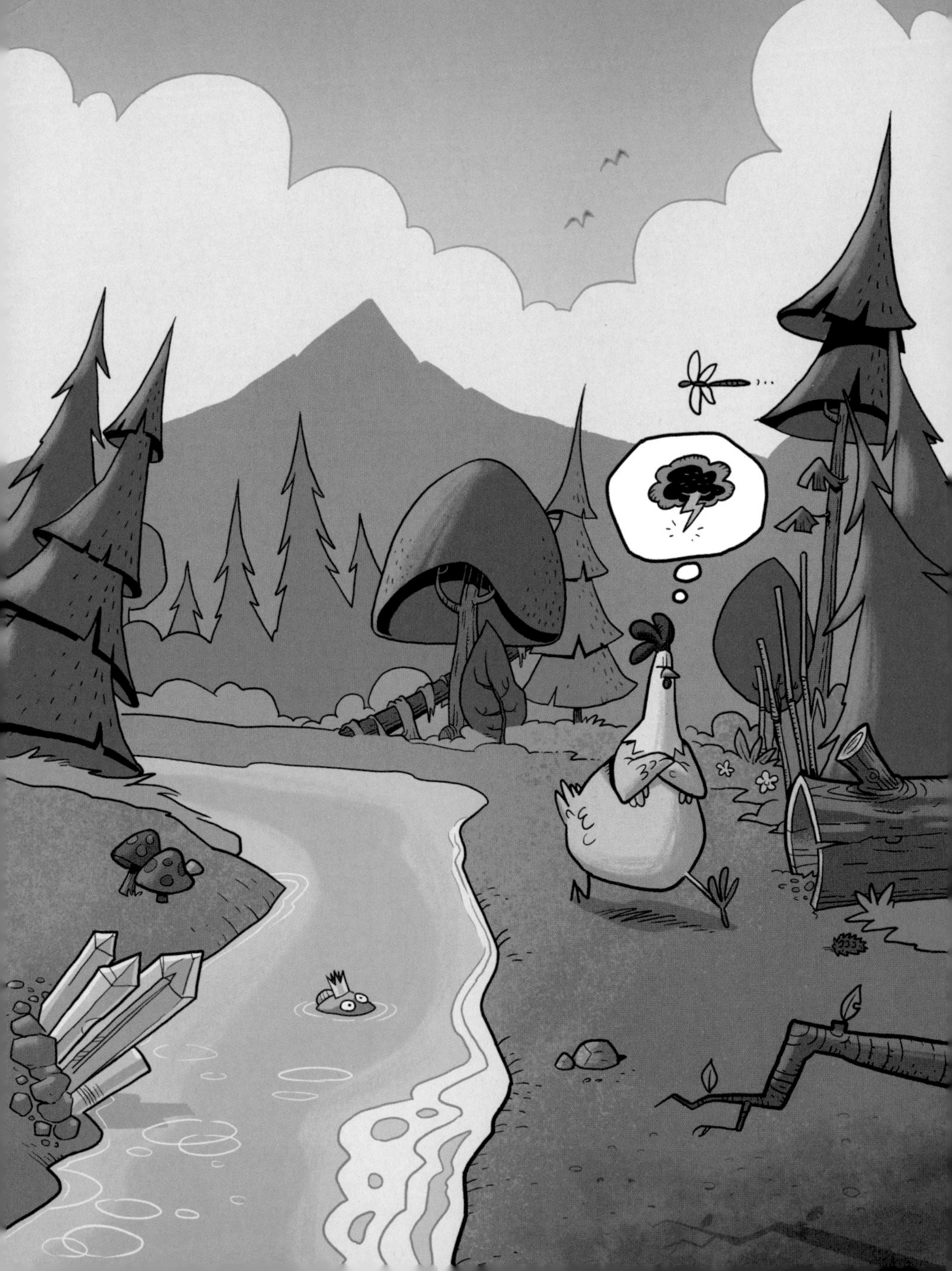

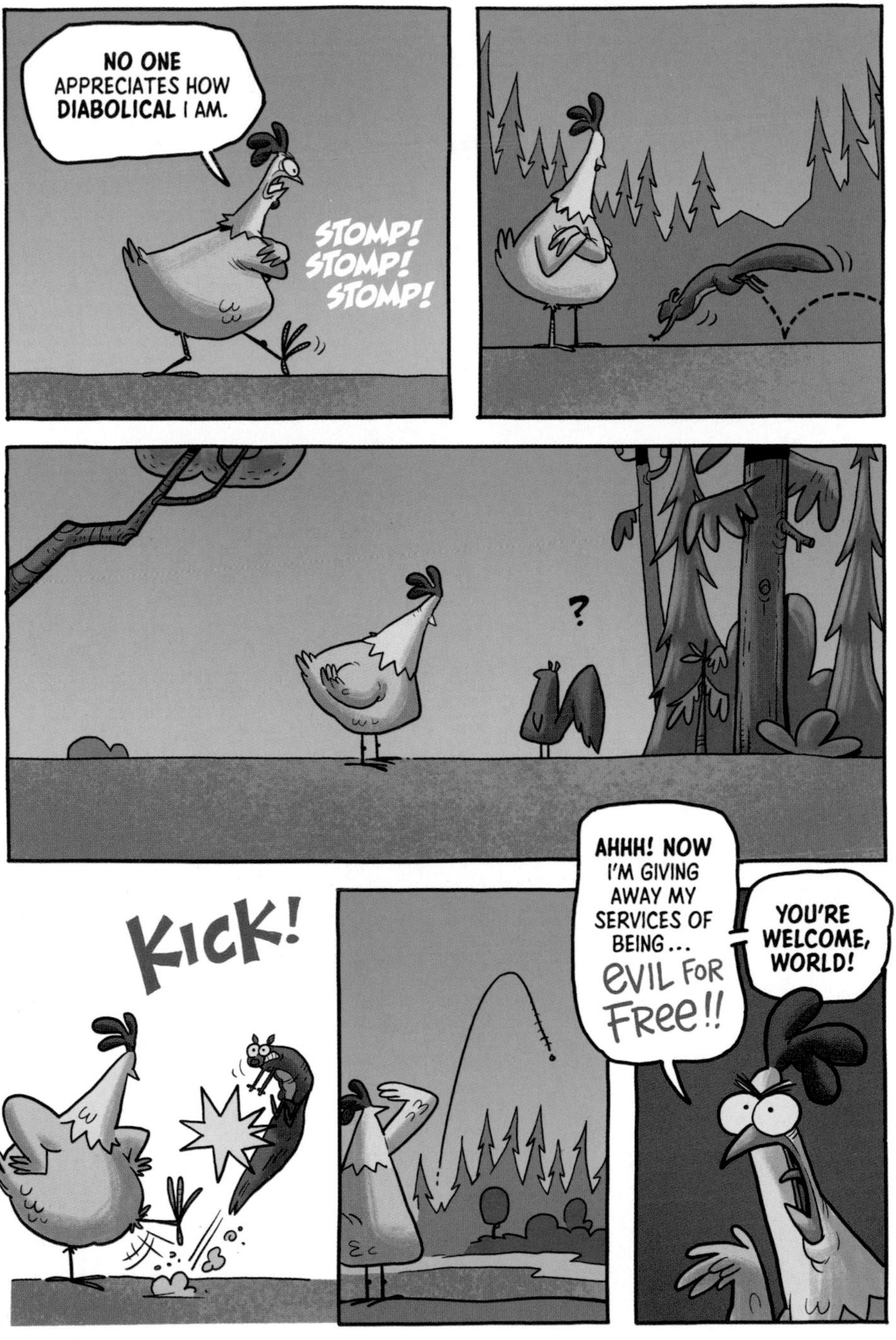
NO ONE APPRECIATES HOW DIABOLICAL I AM.
STOMP! STOMP! STOMP!
?
KICK!
AHHH! NOW I'M GIVING AWAY MY SERVICES OF BEING... EVIL FOR FREE!!
YOU'RE WELCOME, WORLD!

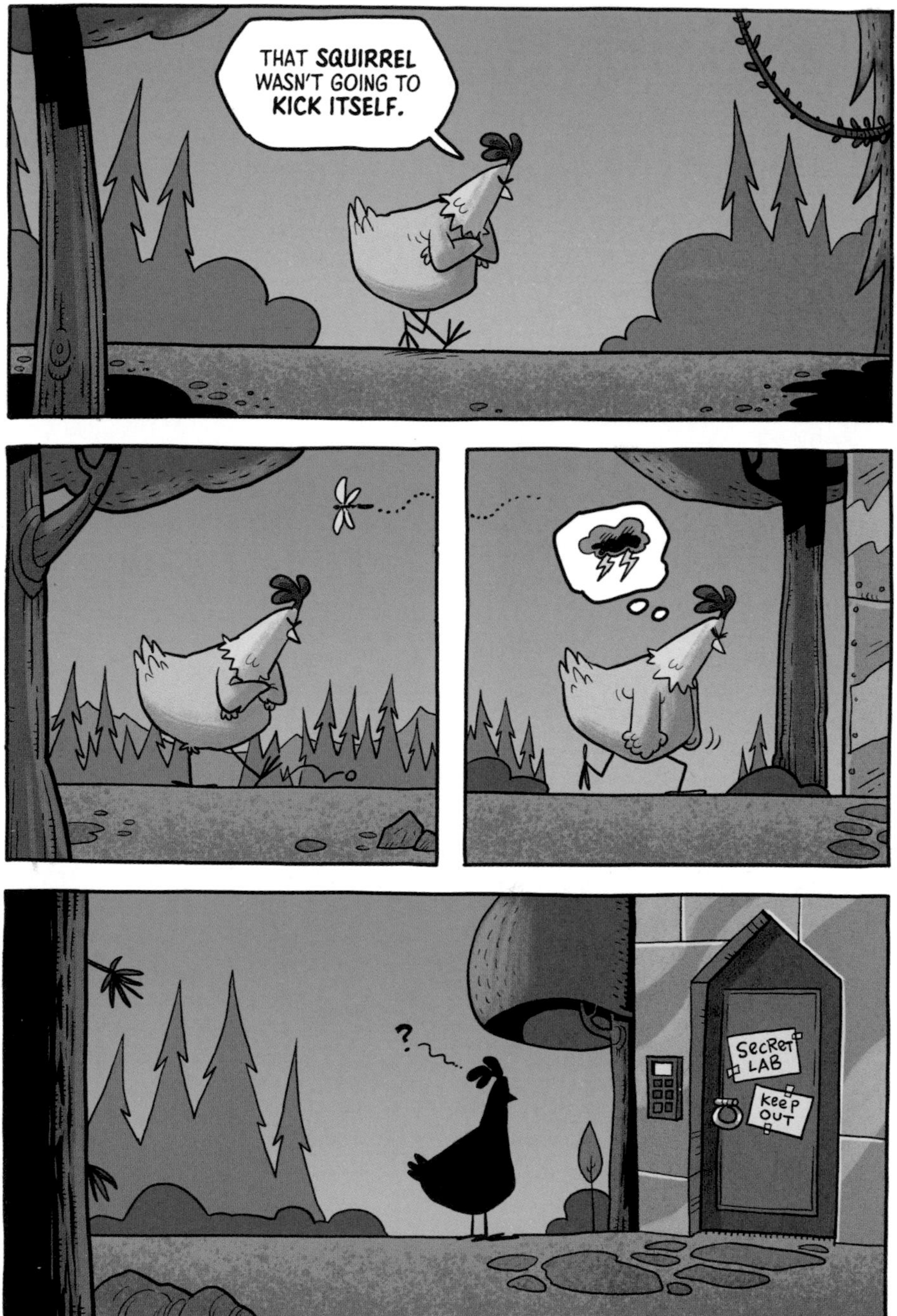
THAT SQUIRREL WASN'T GOING TO KICK ITSELF.
?
SECRET LAB
KEEP OUT

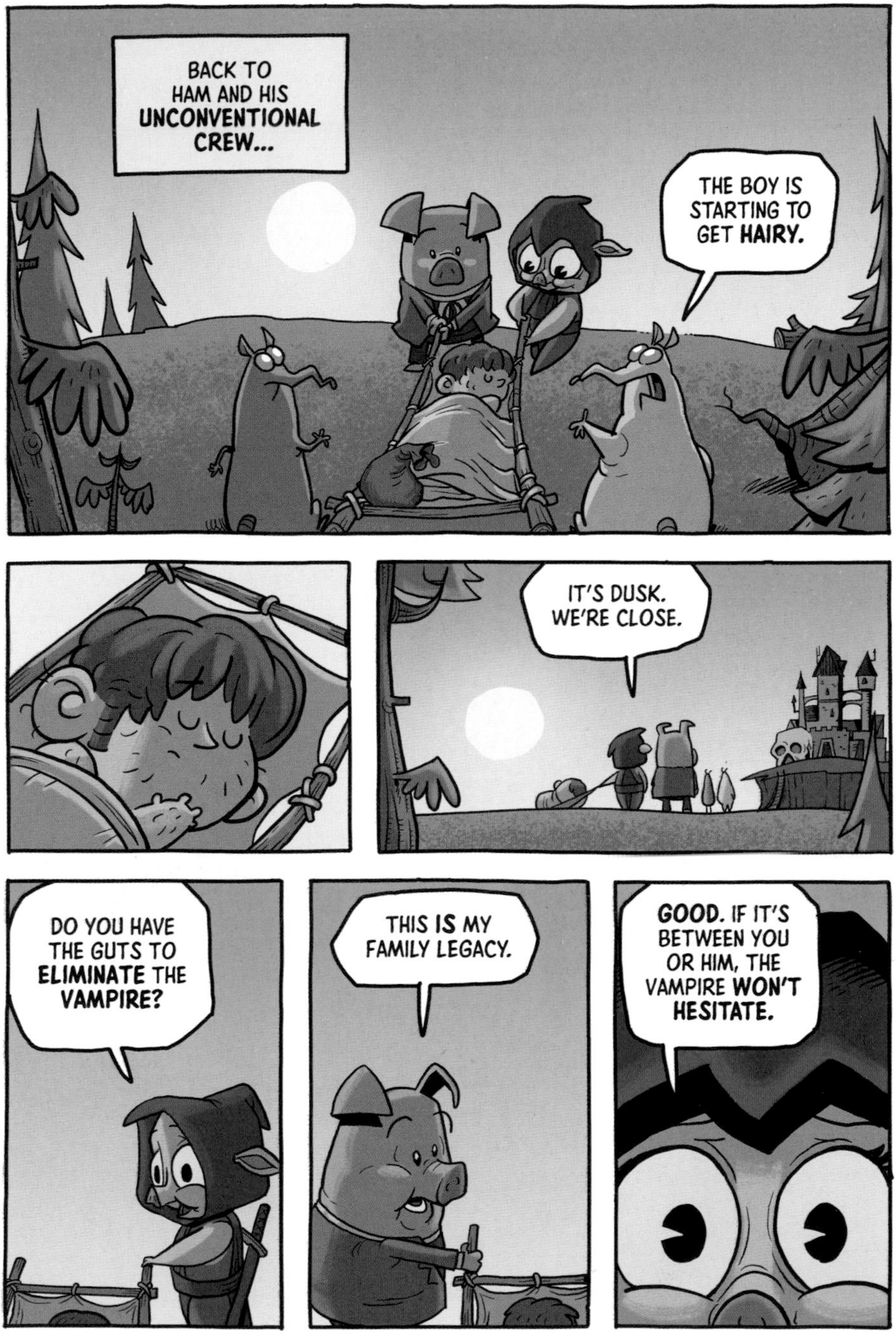
BACK TO HAM AND HIS UNCONVENTIONAL CREW...
THE BOY IS STARTING TO GET HAIRY.
IT'S DUSK. WE'RE CLOSE.
DO YOU HAVE THE GUTS TO ELIMINATE THE VAMPIRE?
THIS IS MY FAMILY LEGACY.
GOOD. IF IT'S BETWEEN YOU OR HIM, THE VAMPIRE WON'T HESITATE.

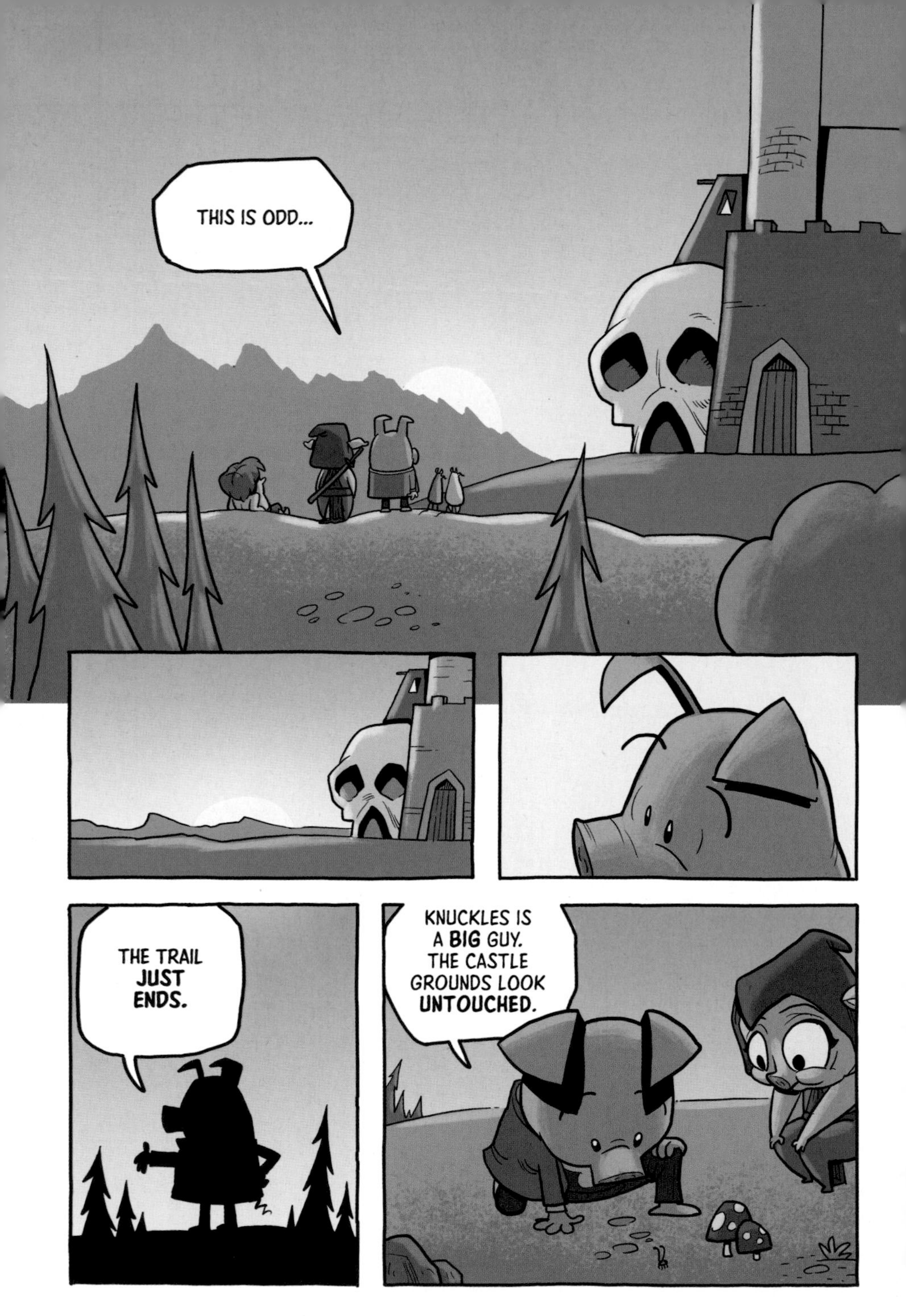

THIS IS ODD...
THE TRAIL JUST ENDS.
KNUCKLES IS A BIG GUY. THE CASTLE GROUNDS LOOK UNTOUCHED.

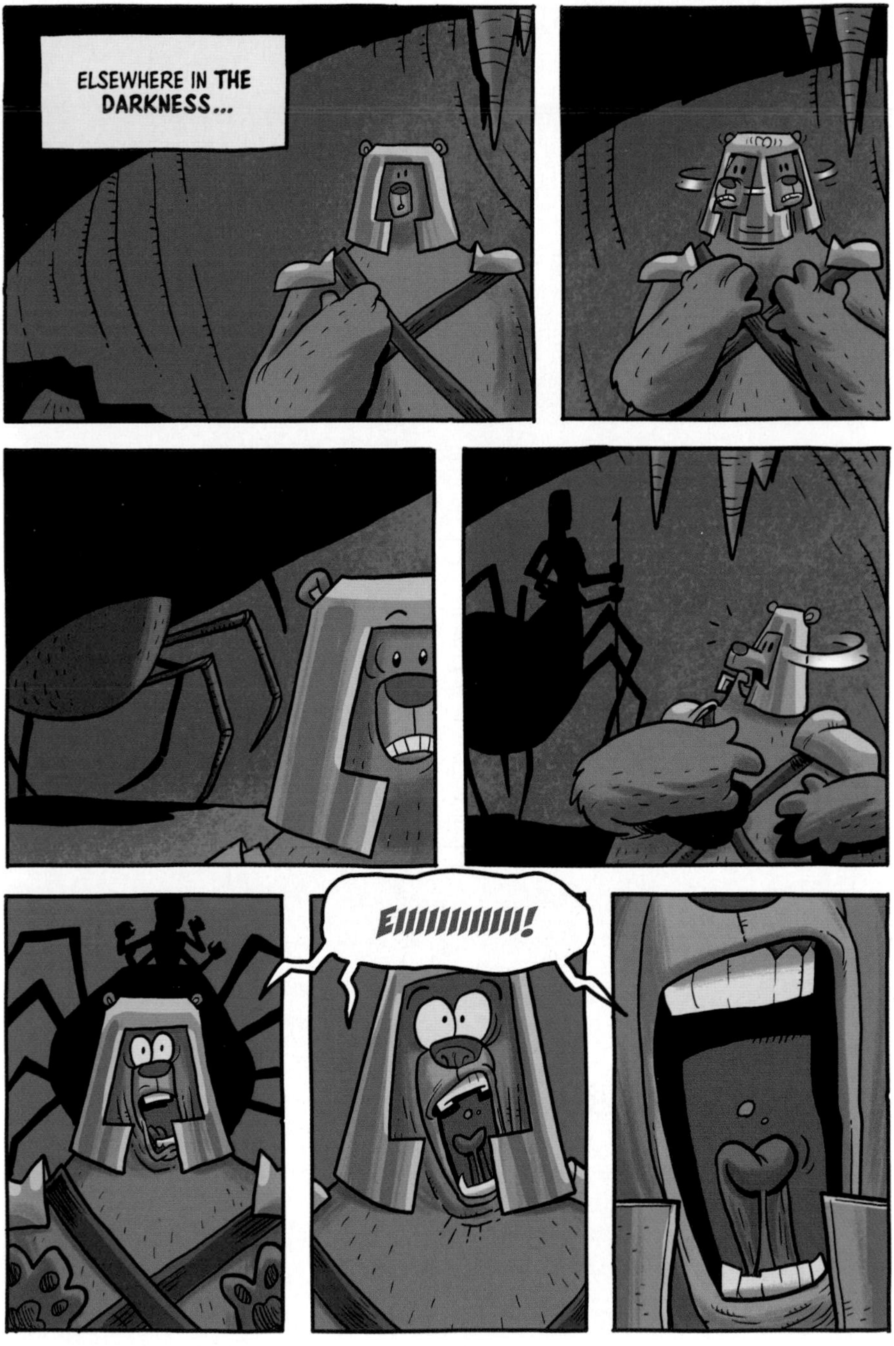
ELSEWHERE IN THE DARKNESS...
EIIIIIIIIIII!

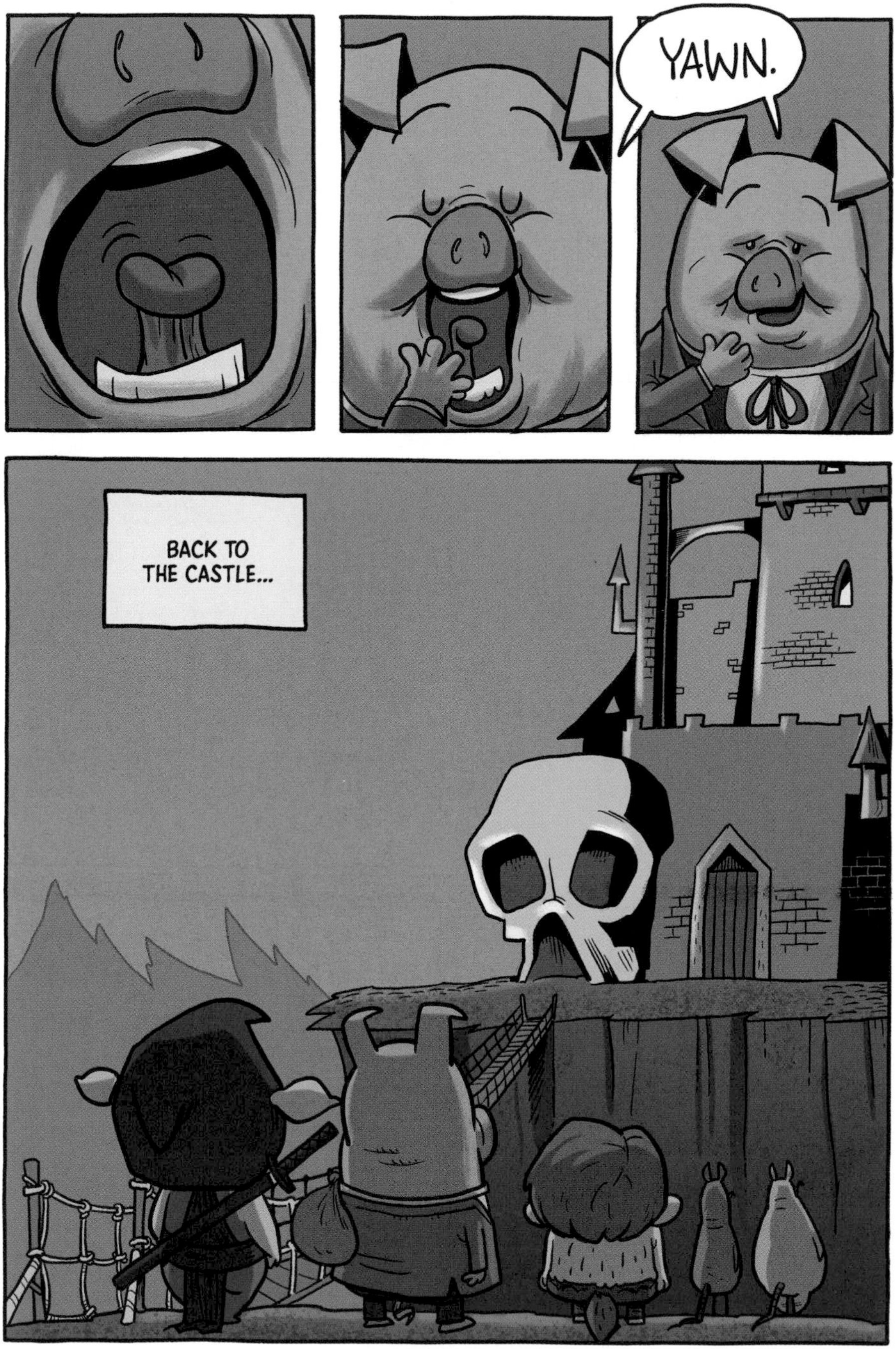
YAWN.
BACK TO THE CASTLE...

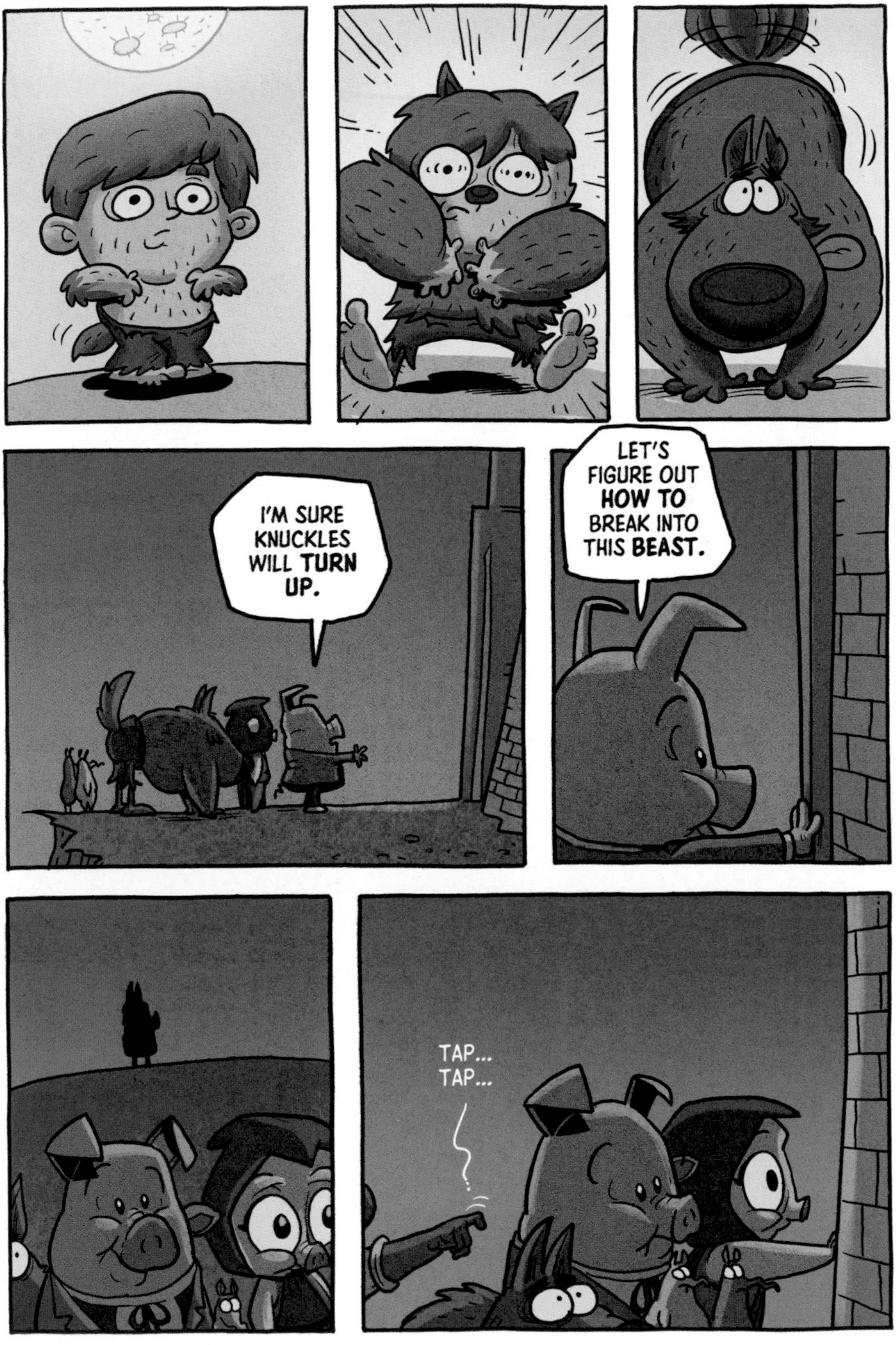

I'M SURE KNUCKLES WILL TURN UP.
LET'S FIGURE OUT HOW TO BREAK INTO THIS BEAST.
TAP... TAP...

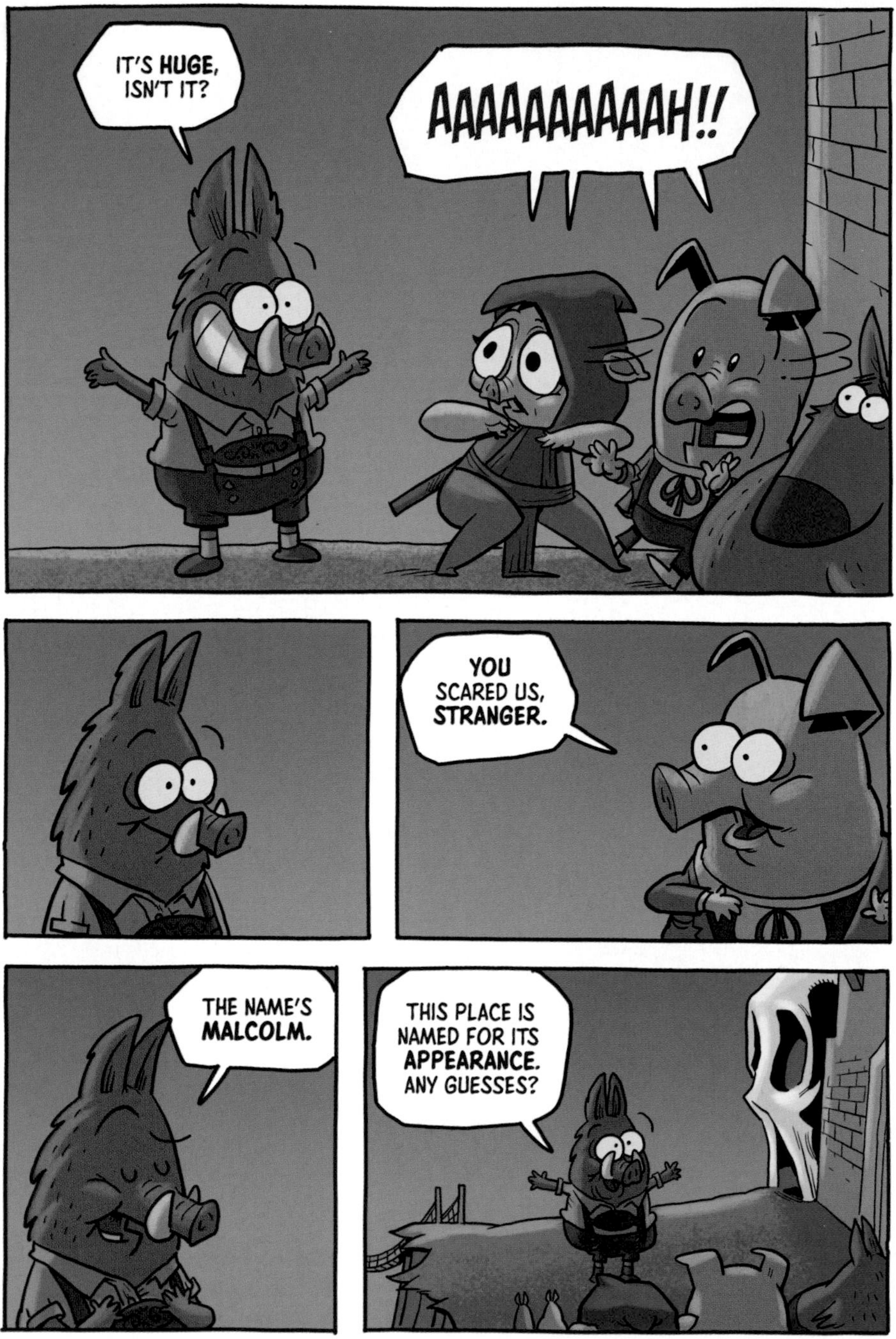
IT'S HUGE, ISN'T IT?
AAAAAAAAAAH!!
YOU SCARED US, STRANGER.
THE NAME'S MALCOLM.
THIS PLACE IS NAMED FOR ITS APPEARANCE. ANY GUESSES?

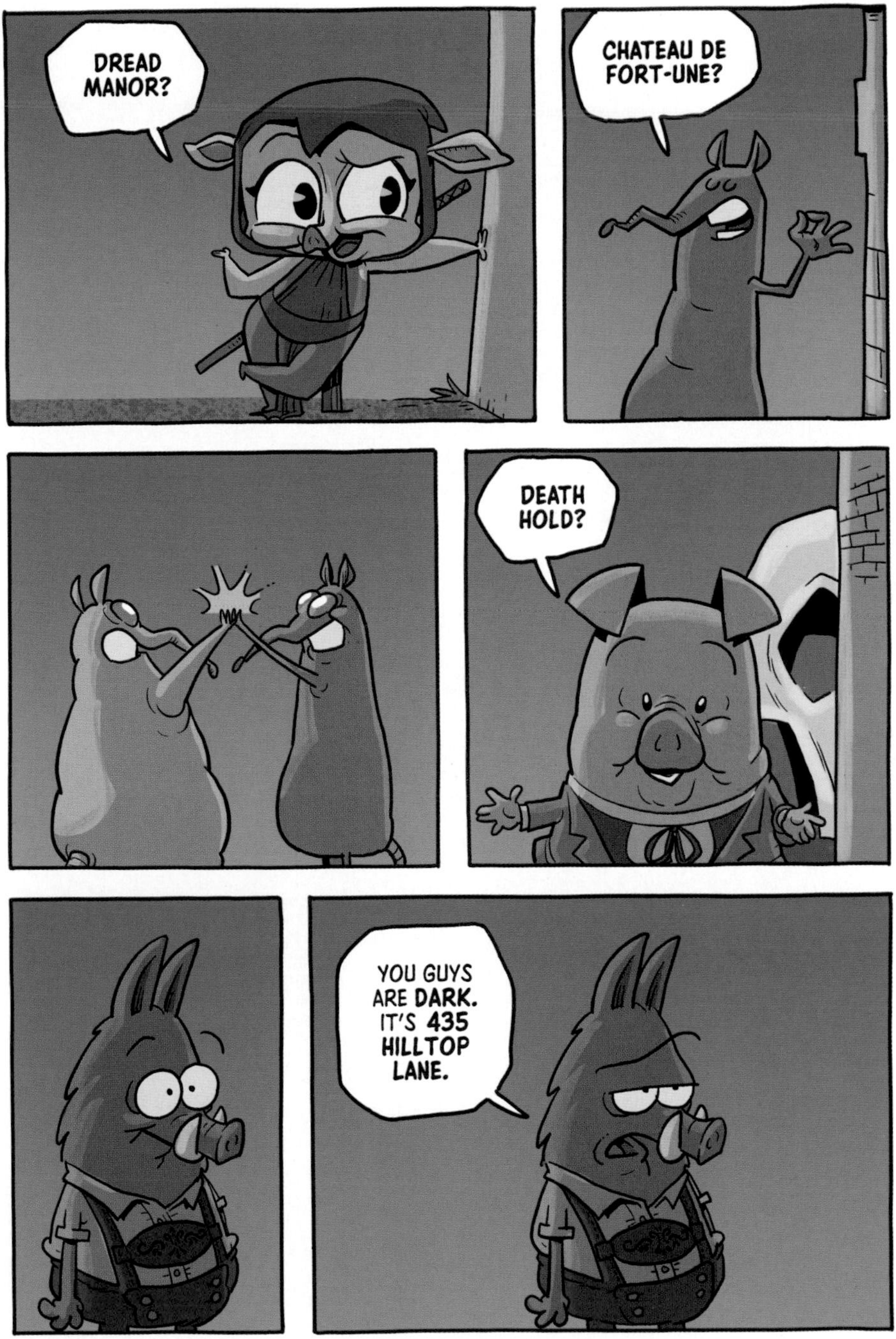
DREAD MANOR?
CHATEAU DE FORT-UNE?
DEATH HOLD?
YOU GUYS ARE **DARK.** IT'S **435 HILLTOP LANE.**

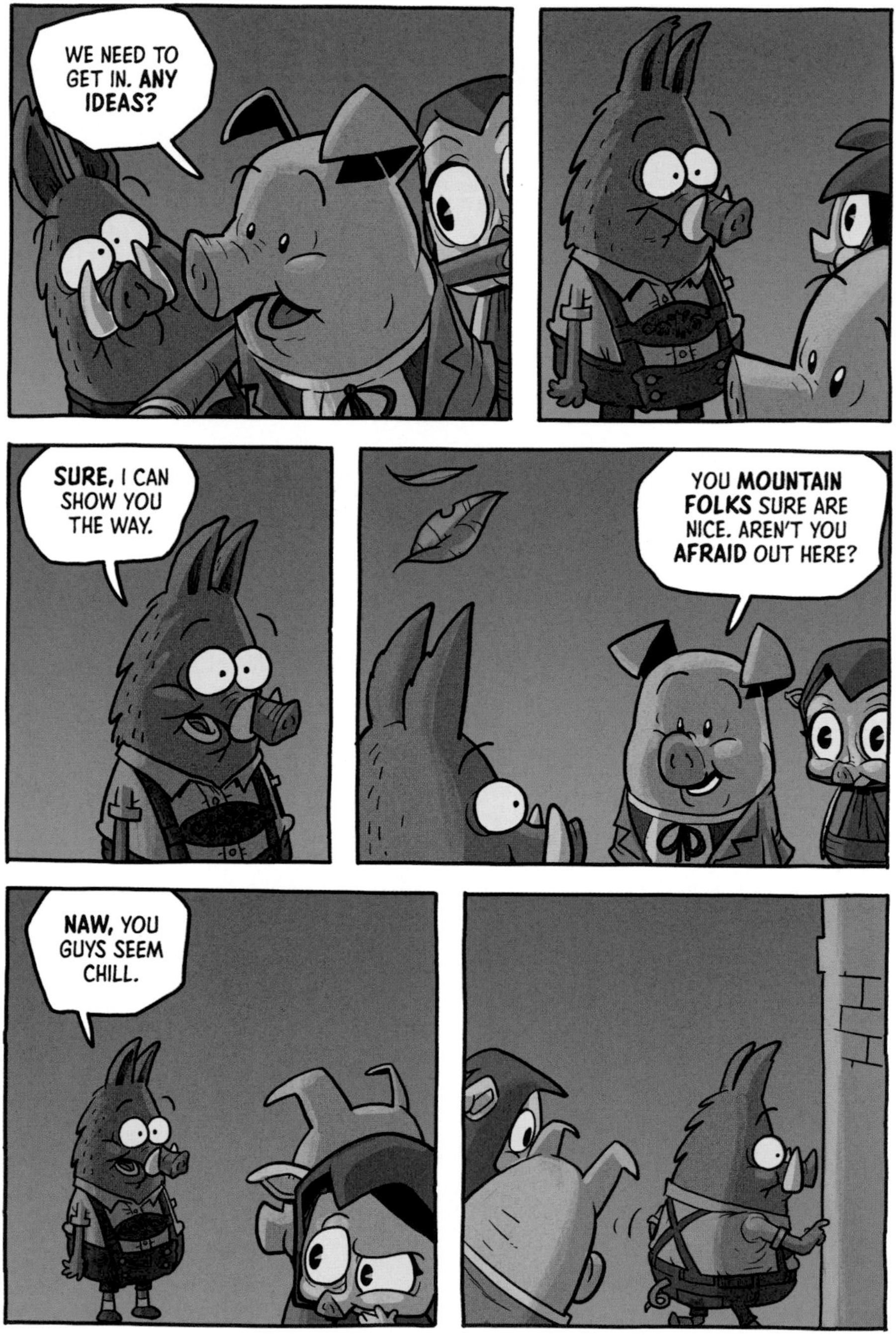
WE NEED TO GET IN. ANY IDEAS?
SURE, I CAN SHOW YOU THE WAY.
YOU MOUNTAIN FOLKS SURE ARE NICE. AREN'T YOU AFRAID OUT HERE?
NAW, YOU GUYS SEEM CHILL.

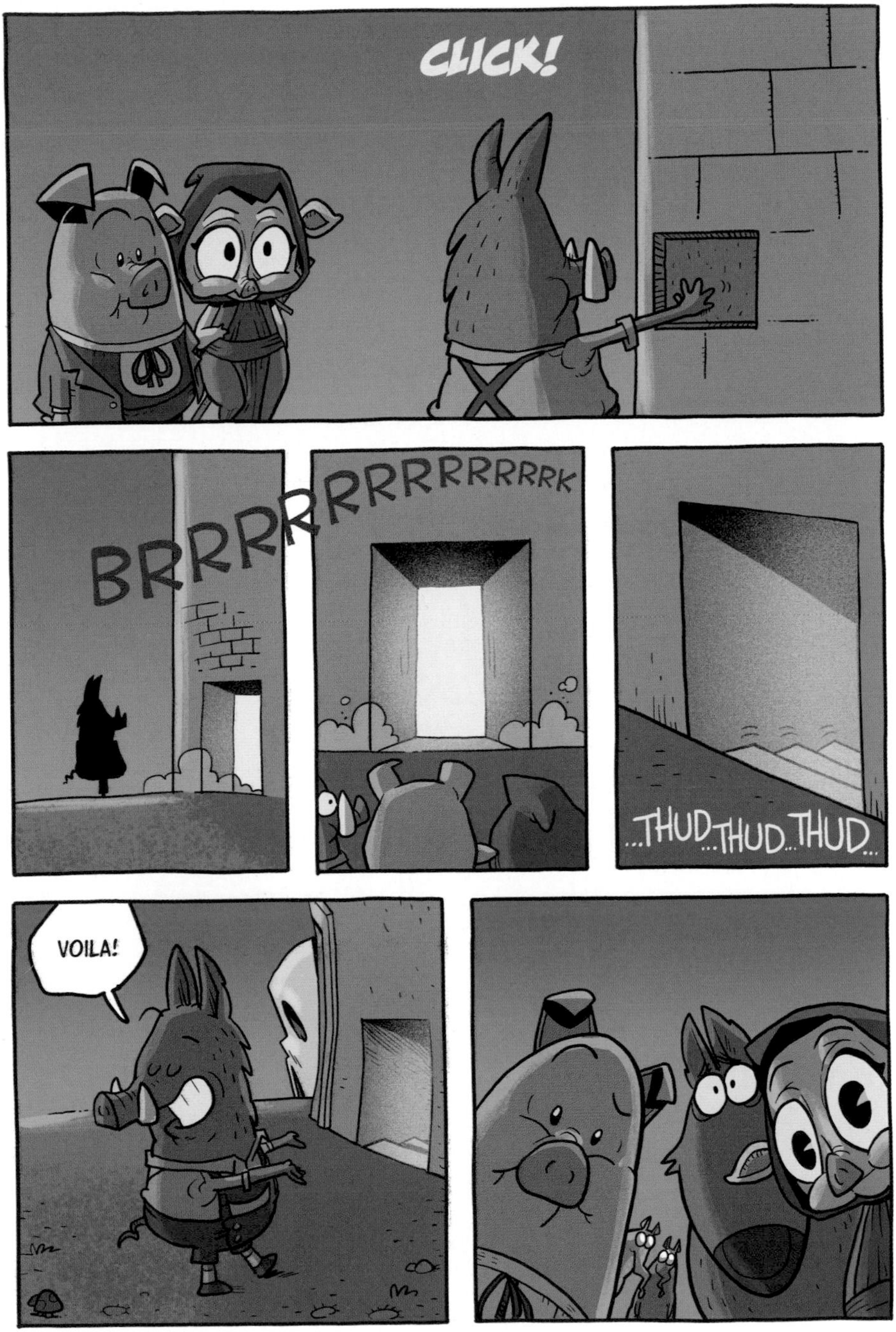
CLICK!
BRRRRRRRRRRRRK
...THUD...THUD...THUD...
VOILA!

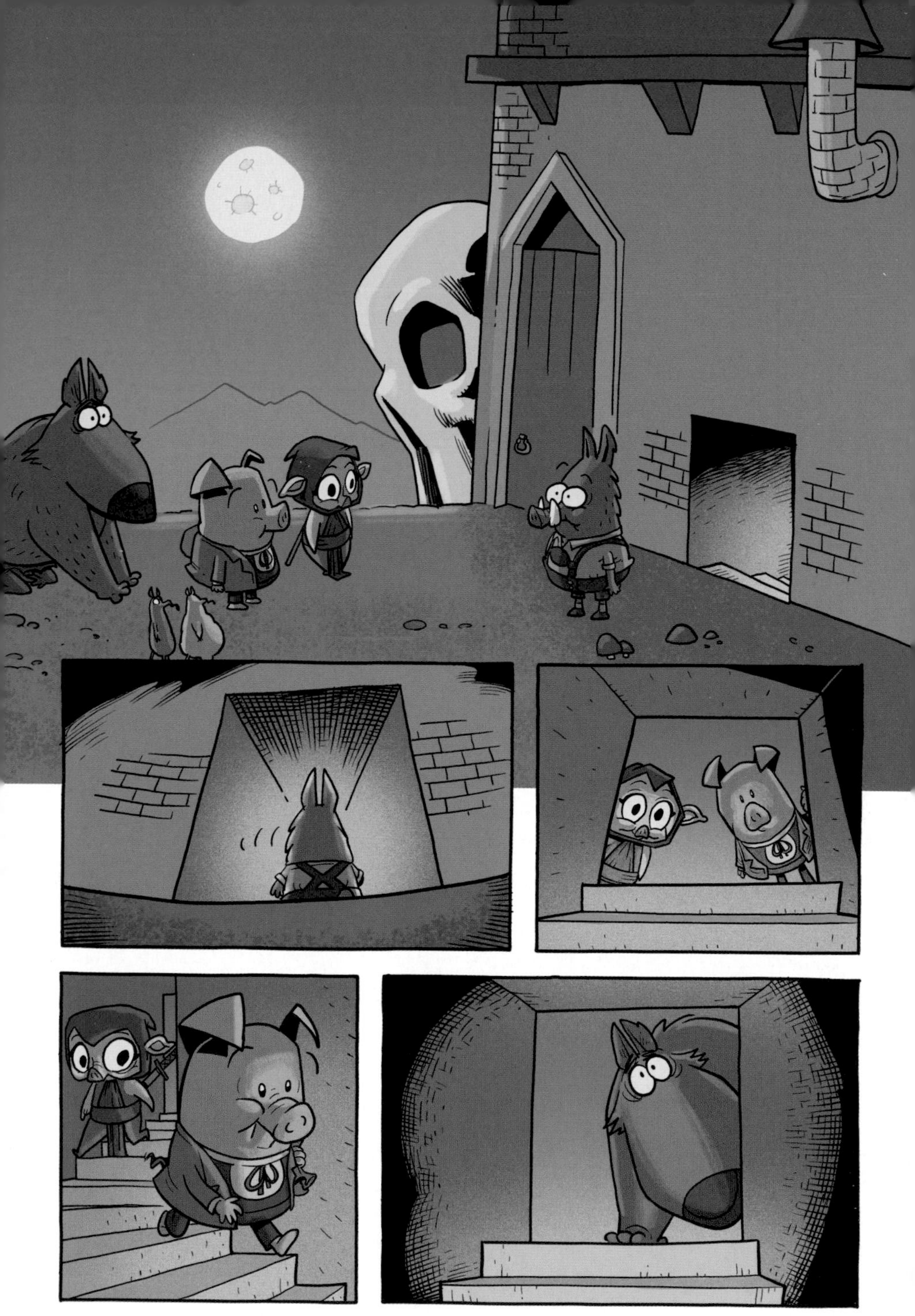

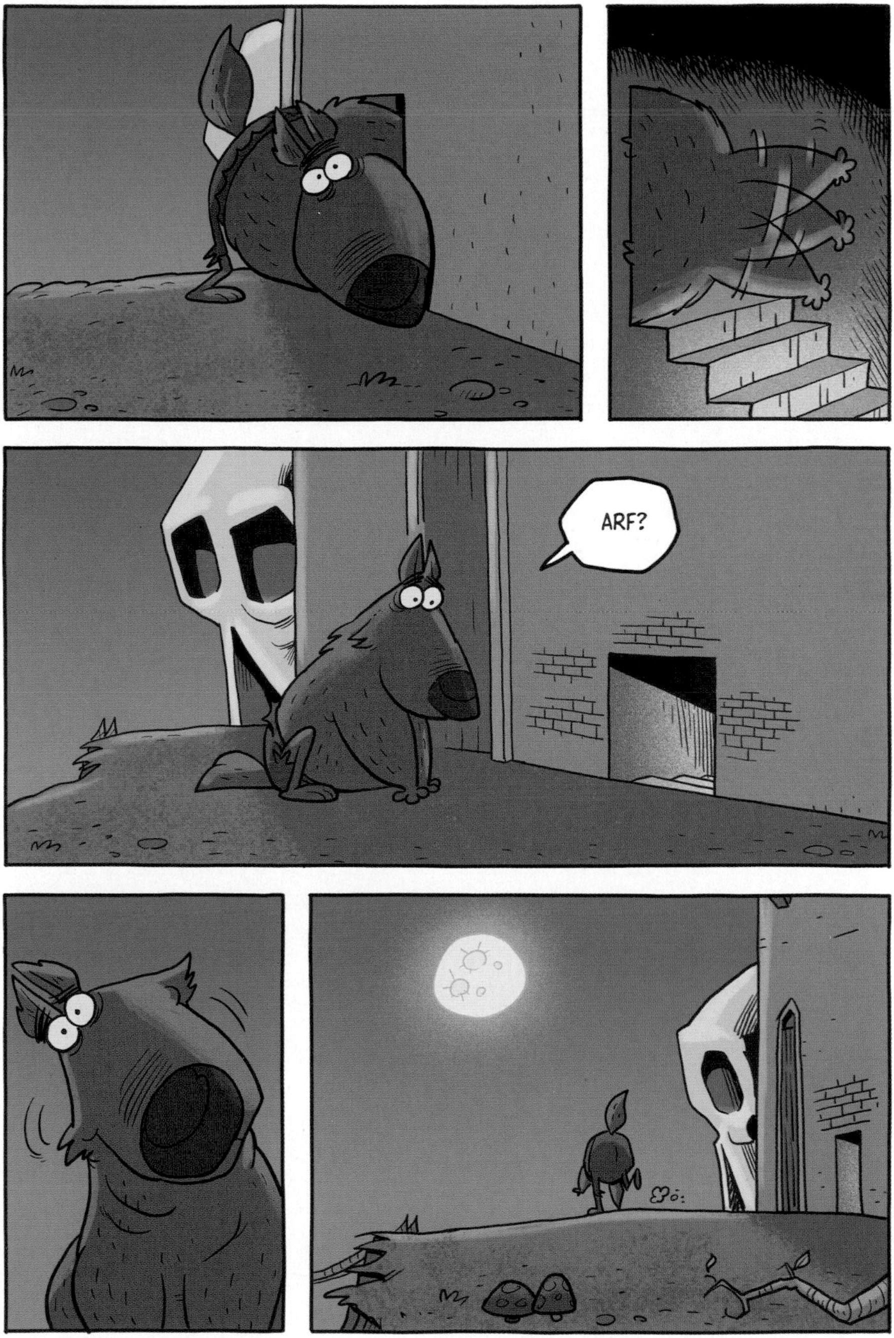
ARF?

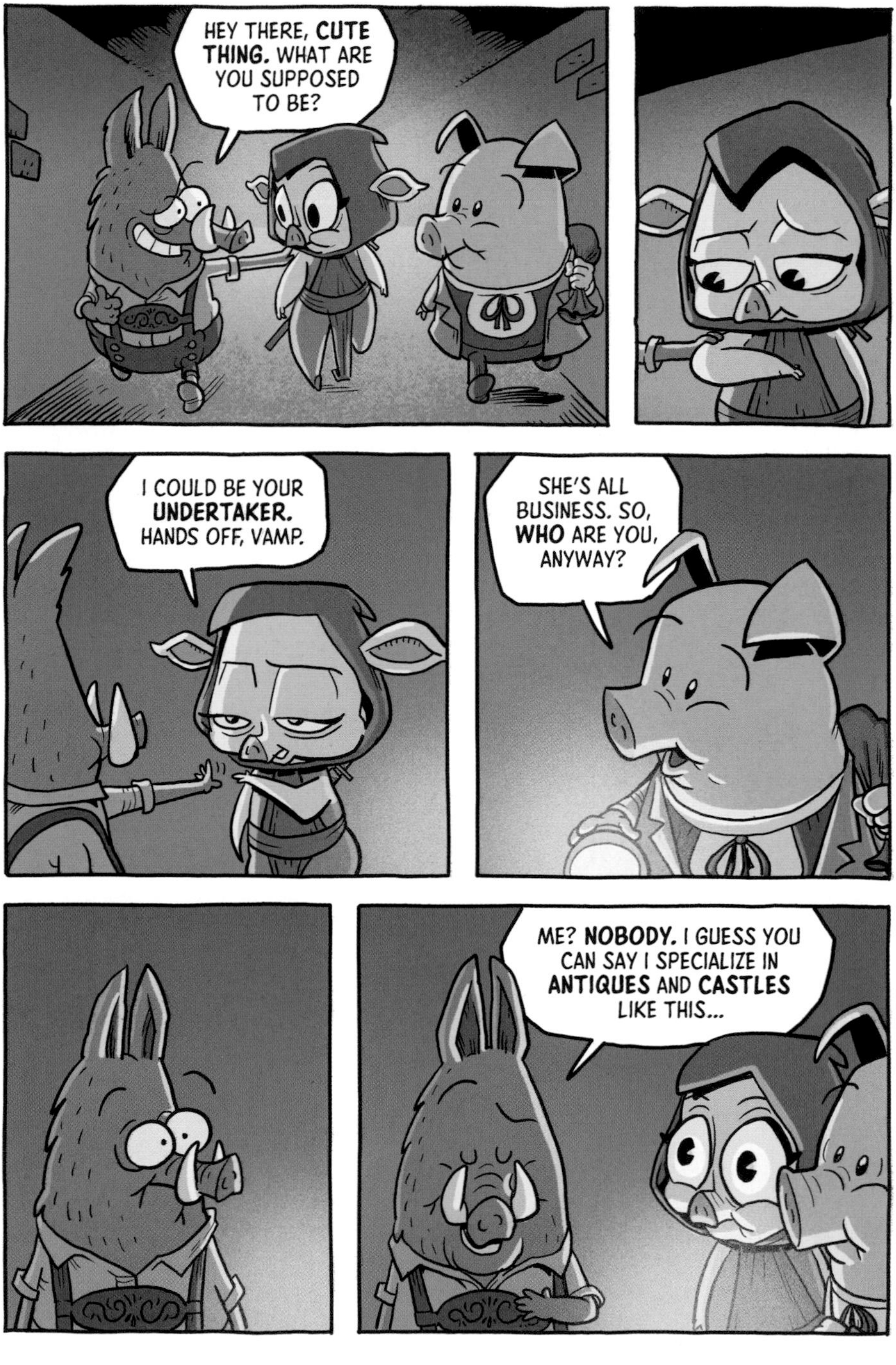
HEY THERE, **CUTE THING.** WHAT ARE YOU SUPPOSED TO BE?
I COULD BE YOUR **UNDERTAKER.** HANDS OFF, VAMP.
SHE'S ALL BUSINESS. SO, **WHO** ARE YOU, ANYWAY?
ME? **NOBODY.** I GUESS YOU CAN SAY I SPECIALIZE IN **ANTIQUES** AND **CASTLES** LIKE THIS...

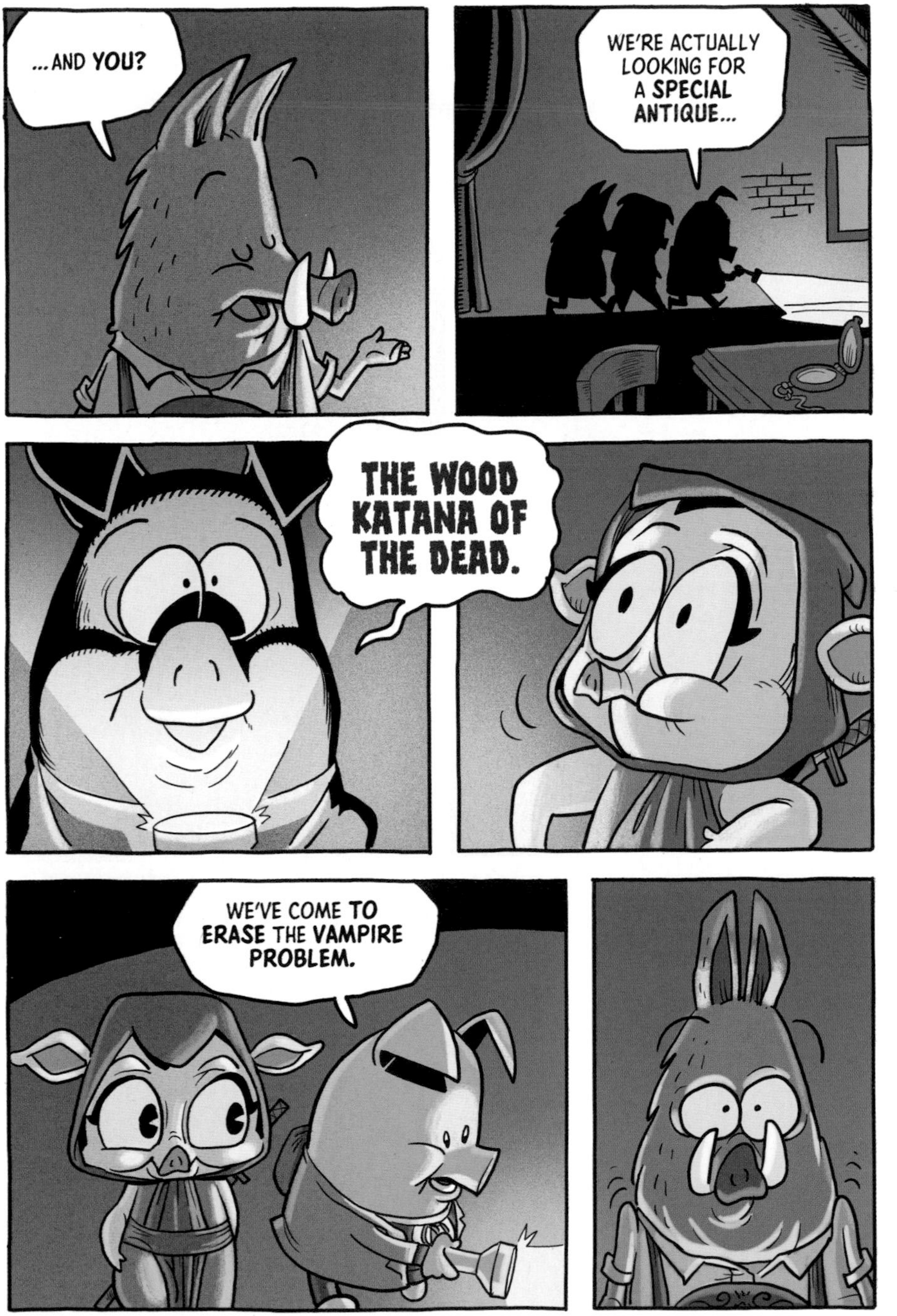
...AND YOU?
WE'RE ACTUALLY LOOKING FOR A SPECIAL ANTIQUE...
THE WOOD KATANA OF THE DEAD.
WE'VE COME TO ERASE THE VAMPIRE PROBLEM.

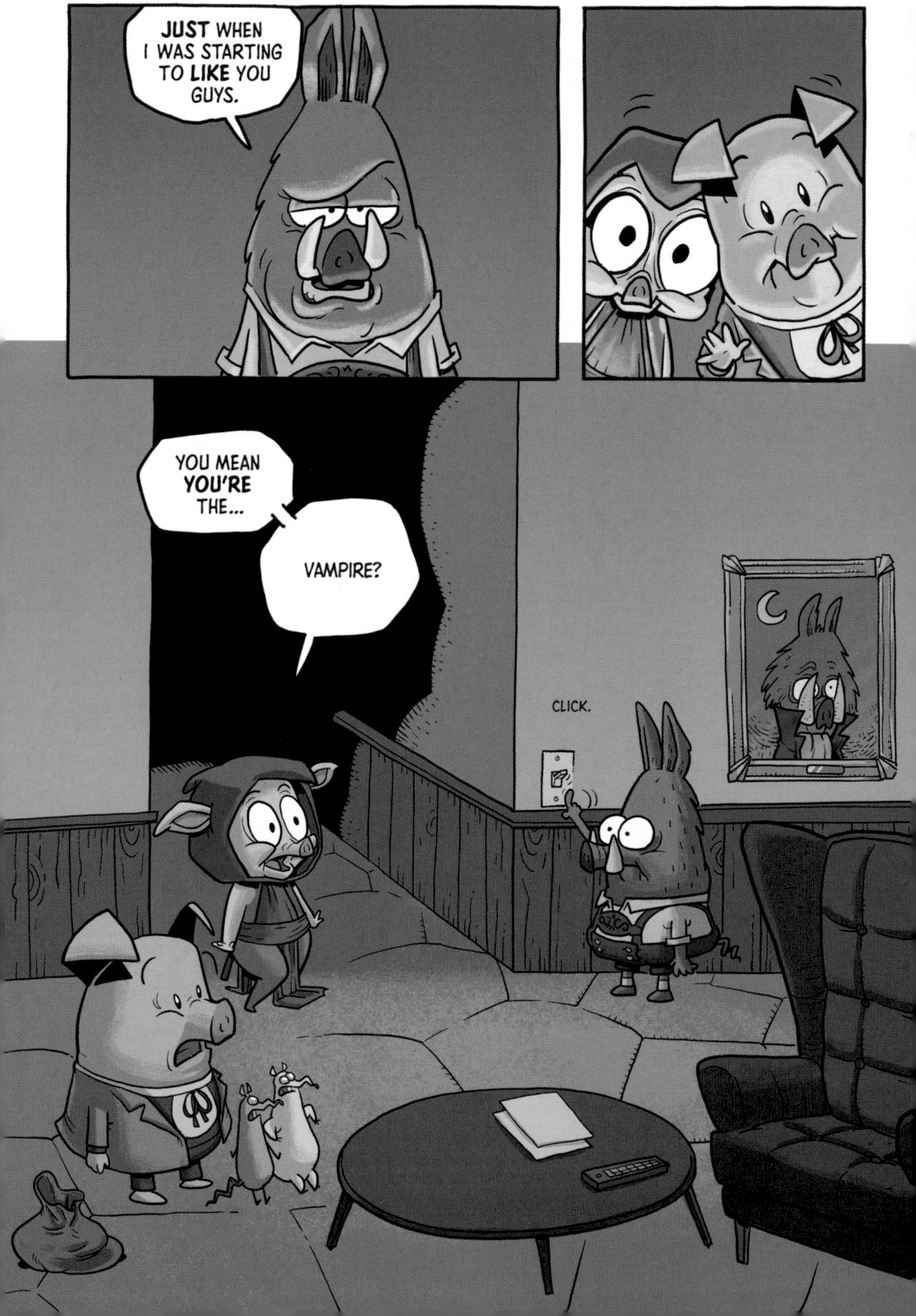
JUST WHEN I WAS STARTING TO LIKE YOU GUYS.
YOU MEAN YOU'RE THE...
VAMPIRE?
CLICK.

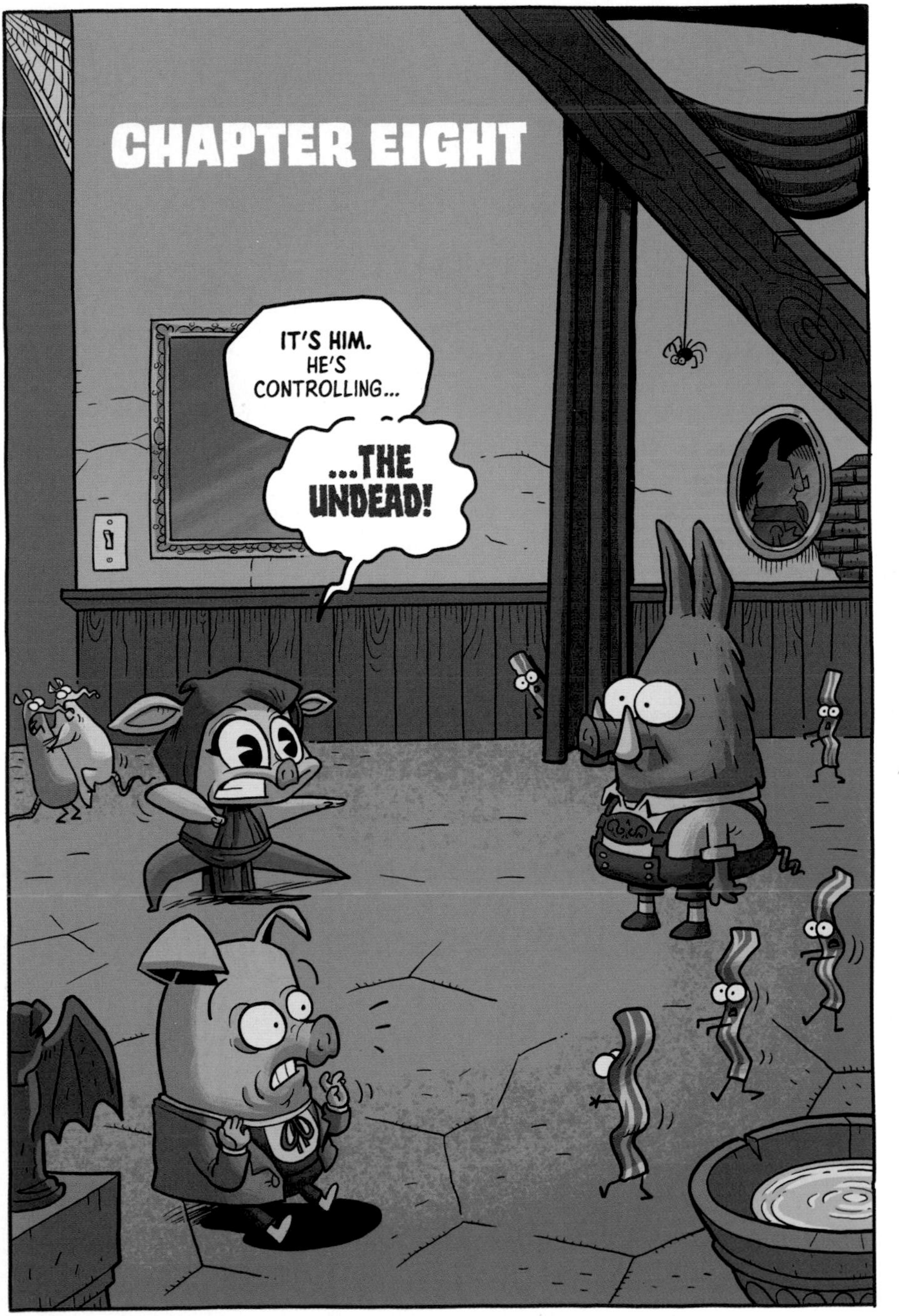
CHAPTER EIGHT
IT'S HIM. HE'S CONTROLLING...
...THE UNDEAD!

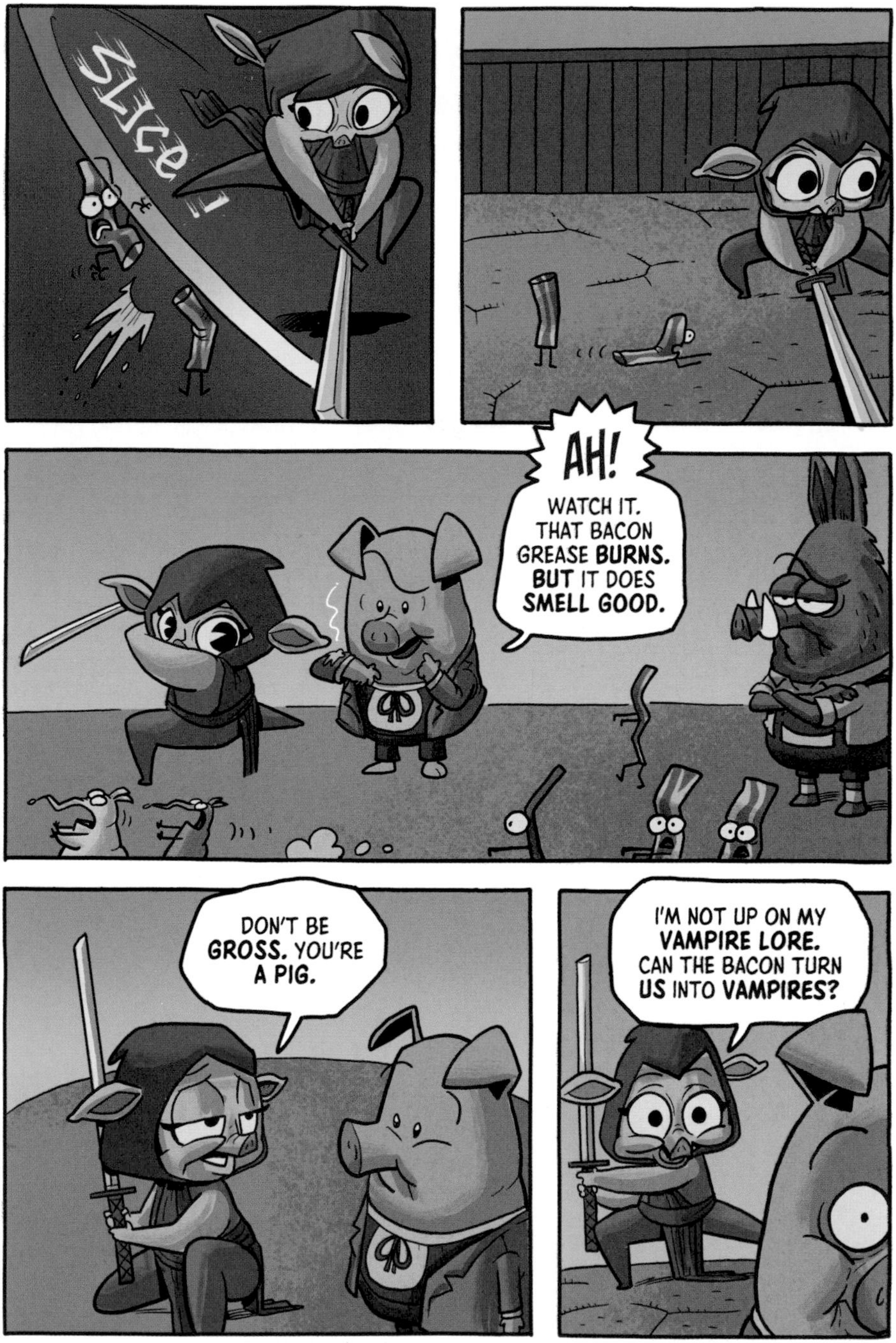
SLICE!
AH!
WATCH IT. THAT BACON GREASE BURNS. BUT IT DOES SMELL GOOD.
DON'T BE GROSS. YOU'RE A PIG.
I'M NOT UP ON MY VAMPIRE LORE. CAN THE BACON TURN US INTO VAMPIRES?

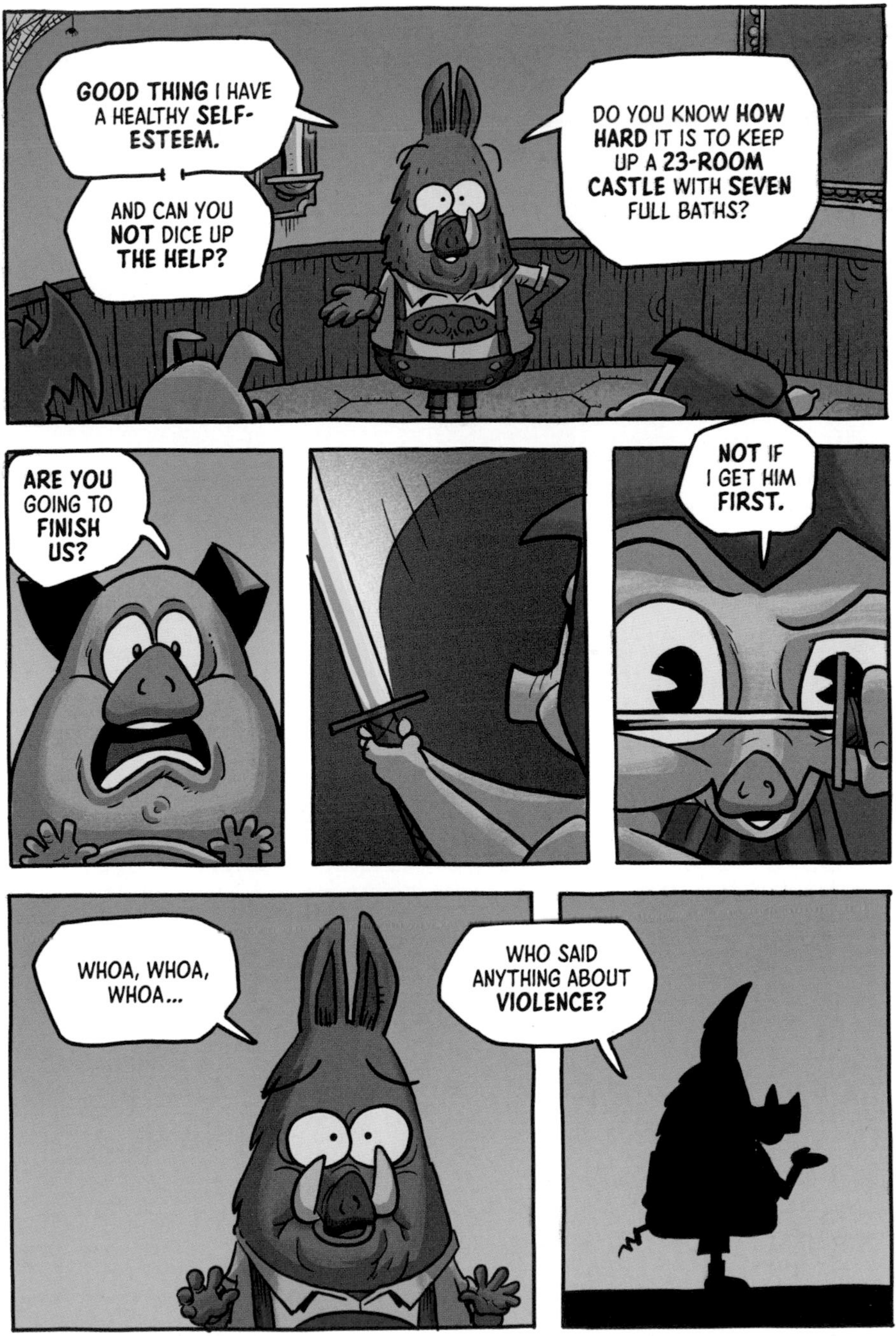
GOOD THING I HAVE A HEALTHY SELF-ESTEEM.
AND CAN YOU NOT DICE UP THE HELP?
DO YOU KNOW HOW HARD IT IS TO KEEP UP A 23-ROOM CASTLE WITH SEVEN FULL BATHS?
ARE YOU GOING TO FINISH US?
NOT IF I GET HIM FIRST.
WHOA, WHOA, WHOA...
WHO SAID ANYTHING ABOUT VIOLENCE?

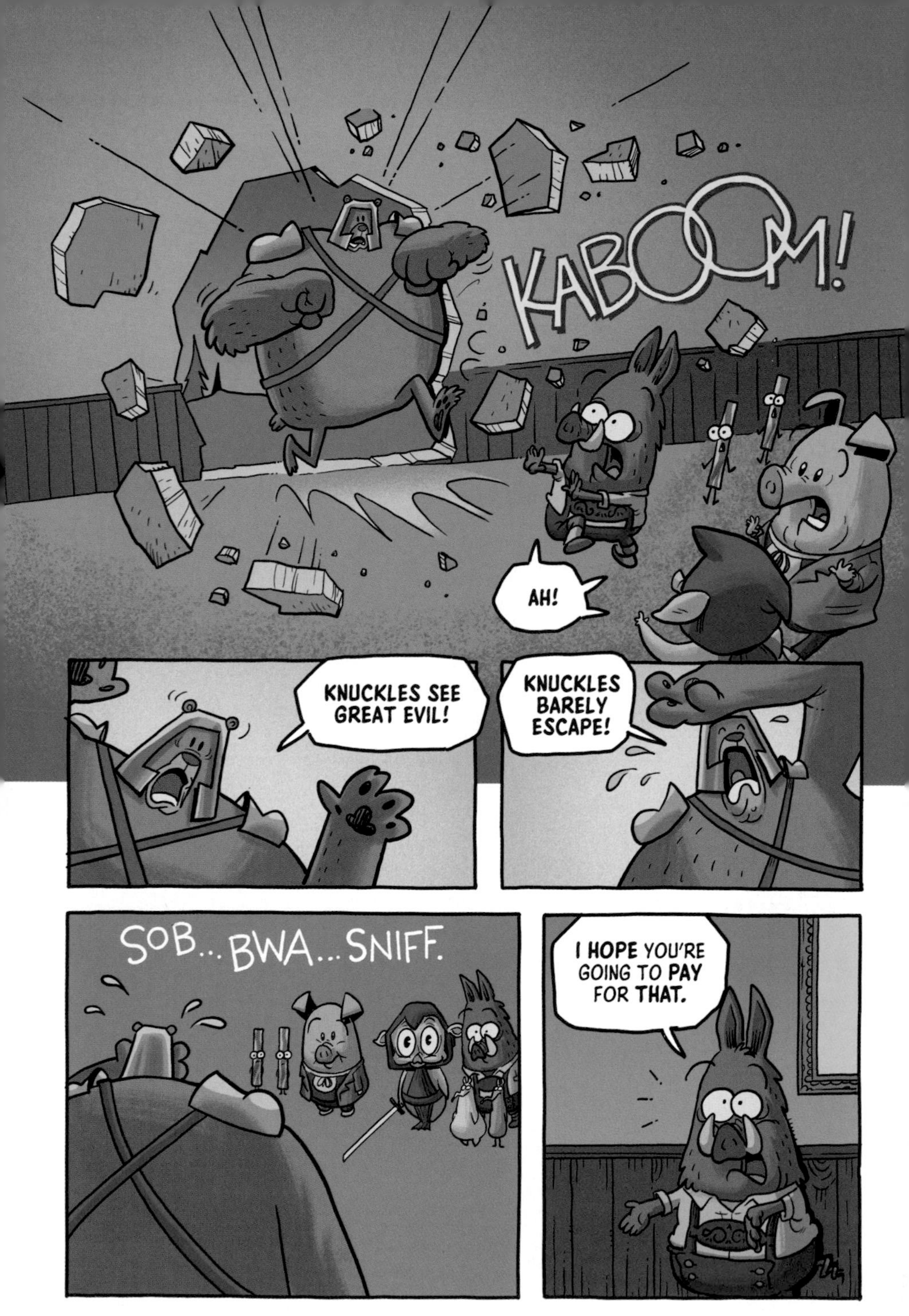
KABOOOM!
AH!
KNUCKLES SEE GREAT EVIL!
KNUCKLES BARELY ESCAPE!
SOB... BWA... SNIFF.
I HOPE YOU'RE GOING TO PAY FOR THAT.

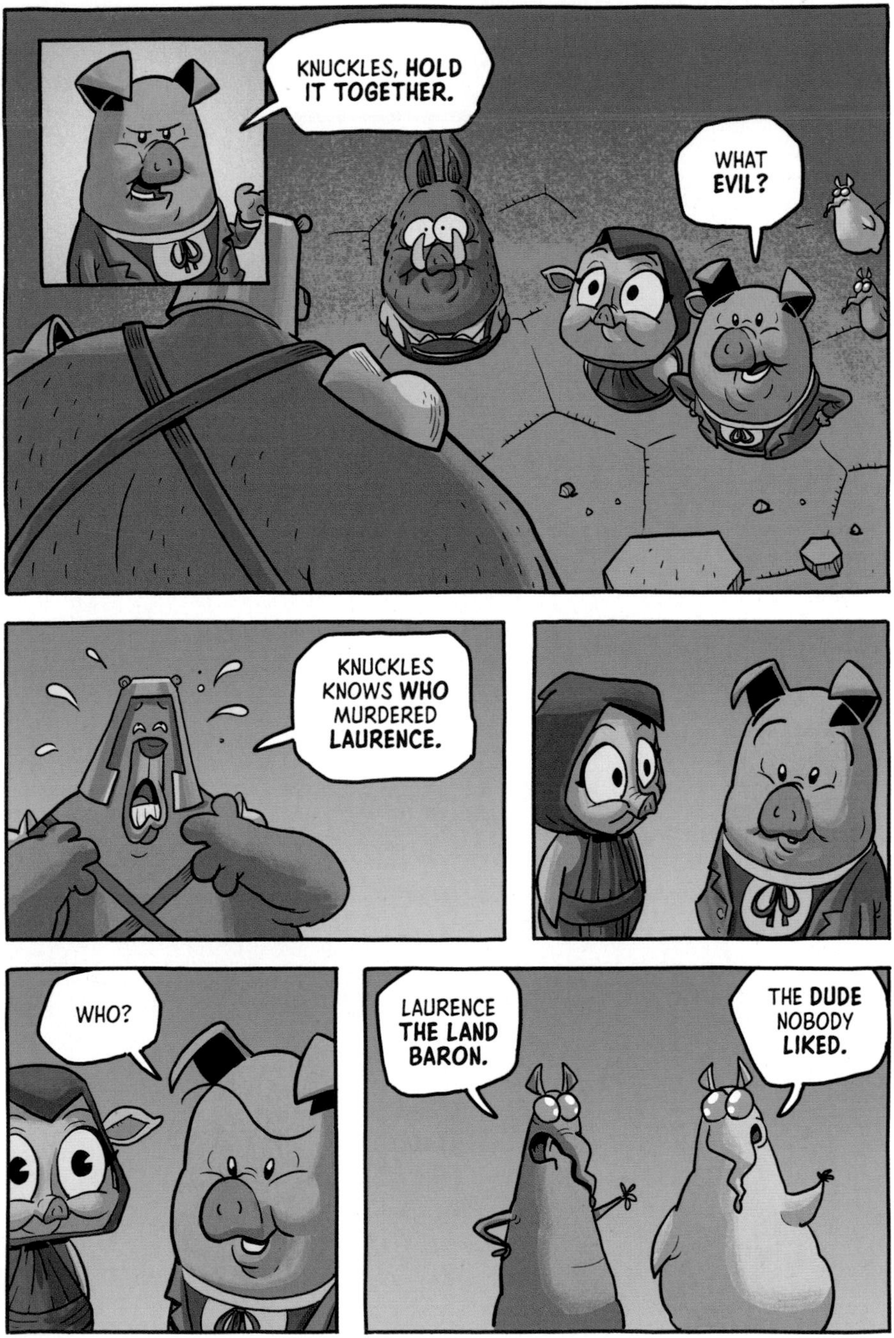
KNUCKLES, HOLD IT TOGETHER.
WHAT EVIL?
KNUCKLES KNOWS WHO MURDERED LAURENCE.
WHO?
LAURENCE THE LAND BARON.
THE DUDE NOBODY LIKED.

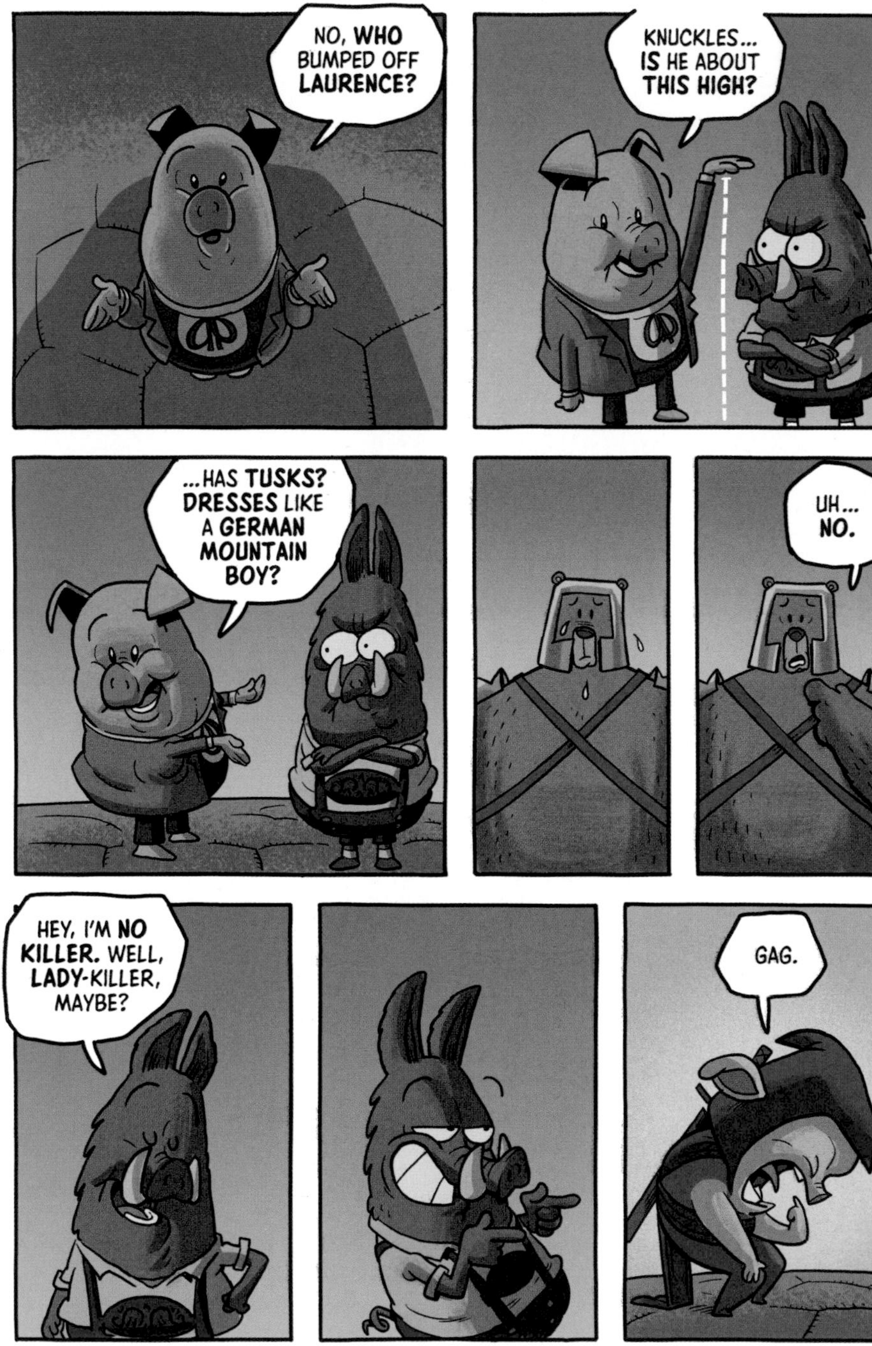
NO, WHO BUMPED OFF LAURENCE?
KNUCKLES... IS HE ABOUT THIS HIGH?
...HAS TUSKS? DRESSES LIKE A GERMAN MOUNTAIN BOY?
UH... NO.
HEY, I'M NO KILLER. WELL, LADY-KILLER, MAYBE?
GAG.

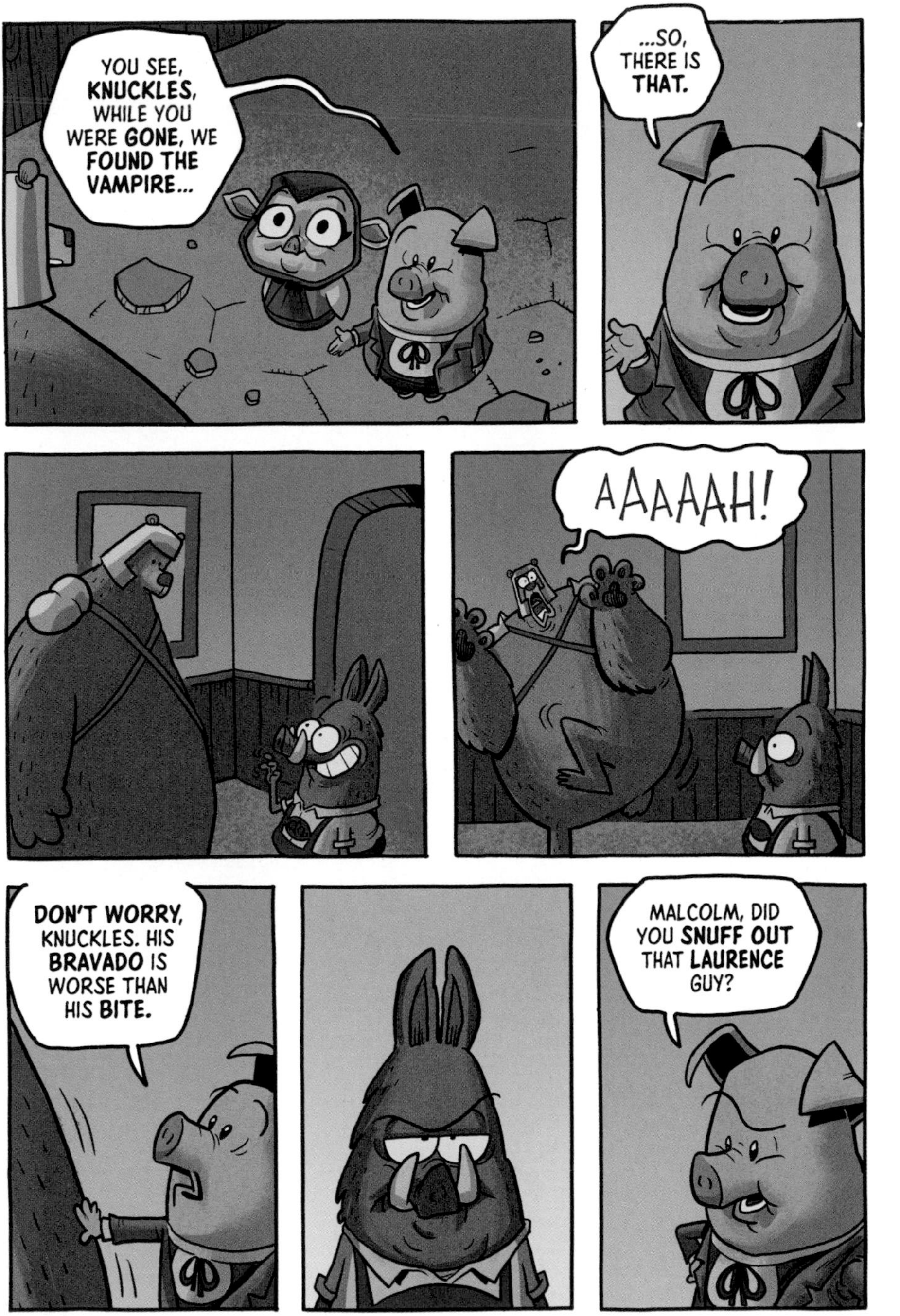
YOU SEE, KNUCKLES, WHILE YOU WERE GONE, WE FOUND THE VAMPIRE...
...SO, THERE IS THAT.
AAAAAH!
DON'T WORRY, KNUCKLES. HIS BRAVADO IS WORSE THAN HIS BITE.
MALCOLM, DID YOU SNUFF OUT THAT LAURENCE GUY?

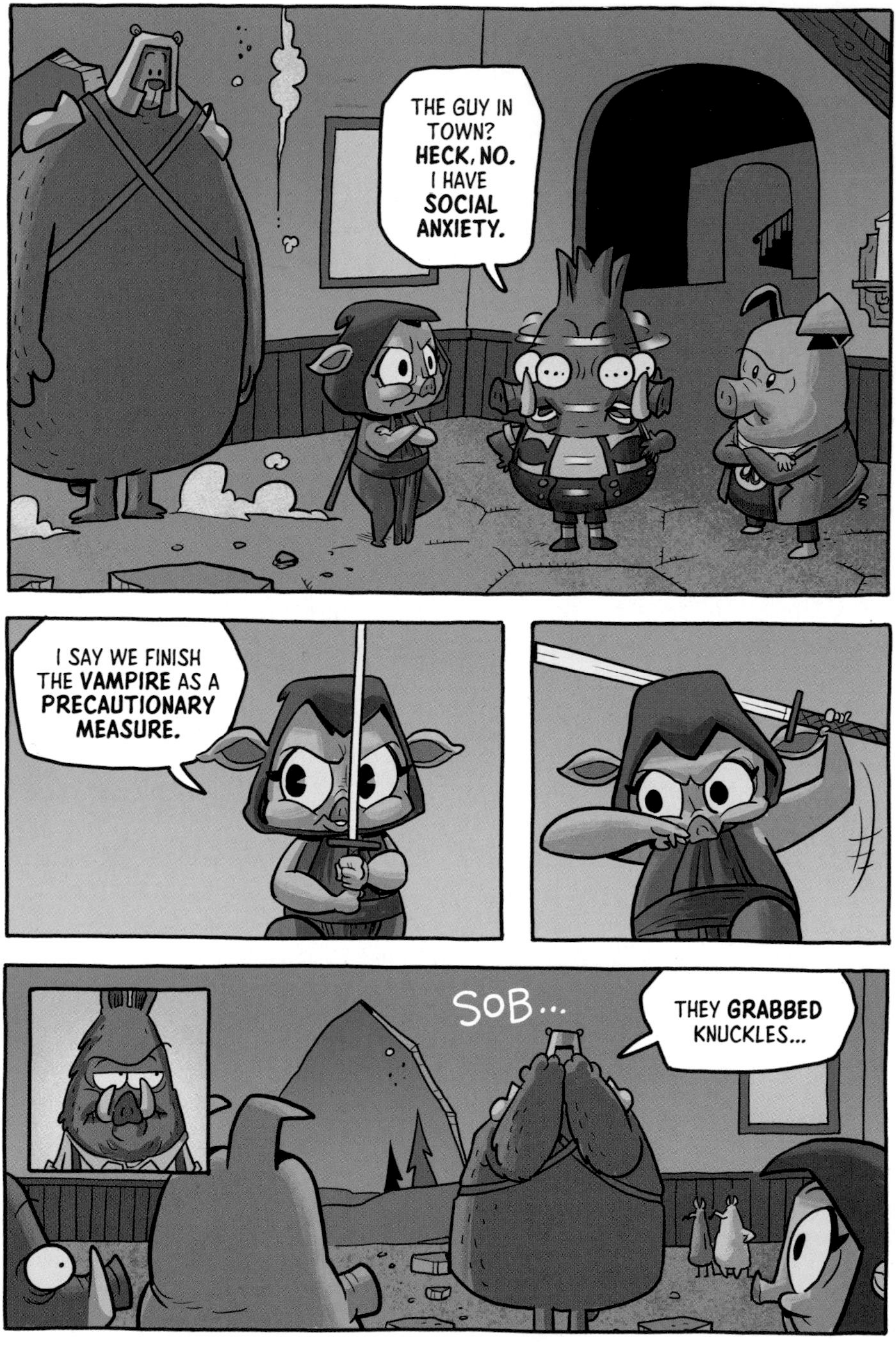
THE GUY IN TOWN? HECK, NO. I HAVE SOCIAL ANXIETY.
I SAY WE FINISH THE VAMPIRE AS A PRECAUTIONARY MEASURE.
SOB...
THEY GRABBED KNUCKLES...

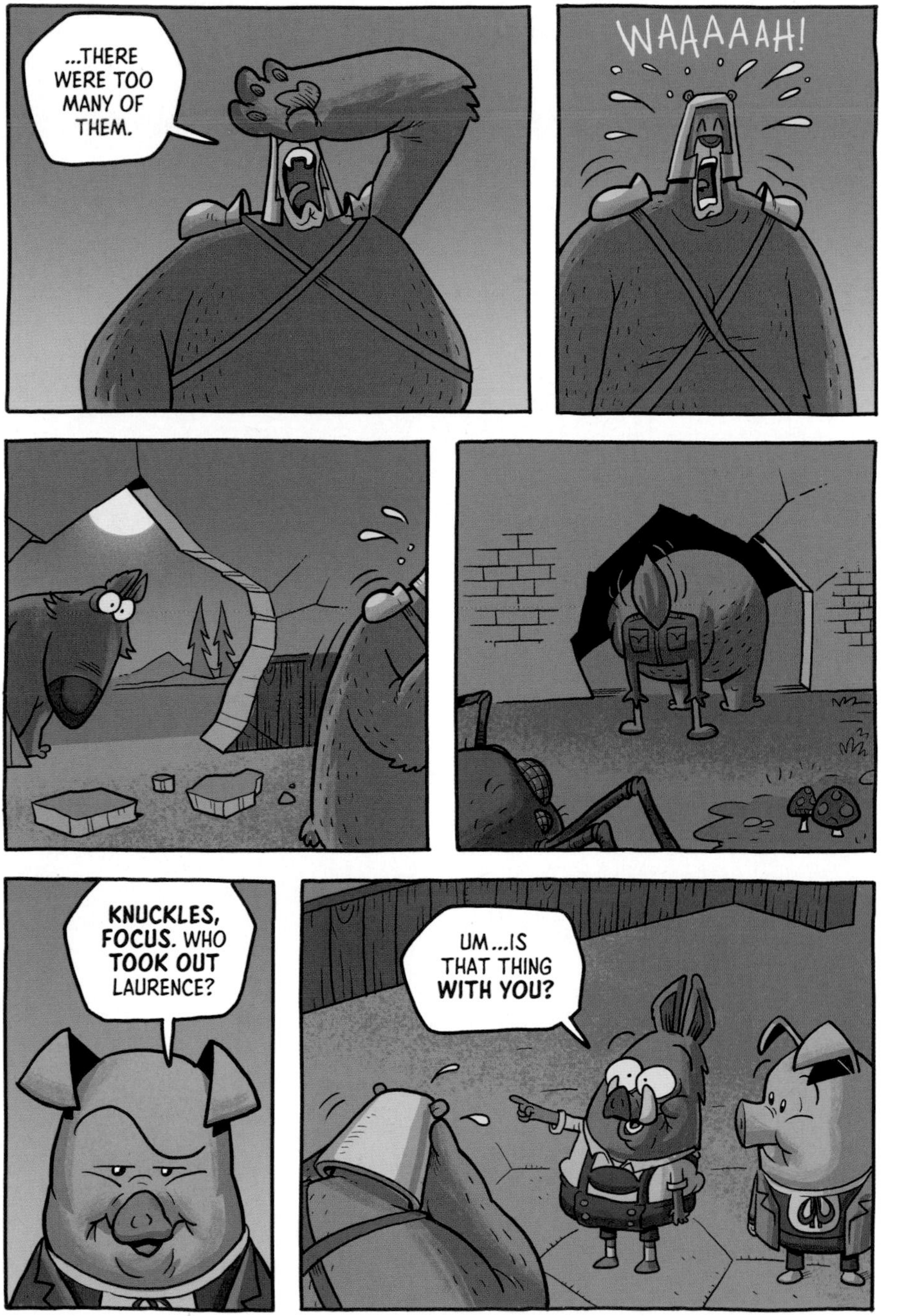
...THERE WERE TOO MANY OF THEM.
WAAAAAH!
KNUCKLES, FOCUS. WHO TOOK OUT LAURENCE?
UM...IS THAT THING WITH YOU?

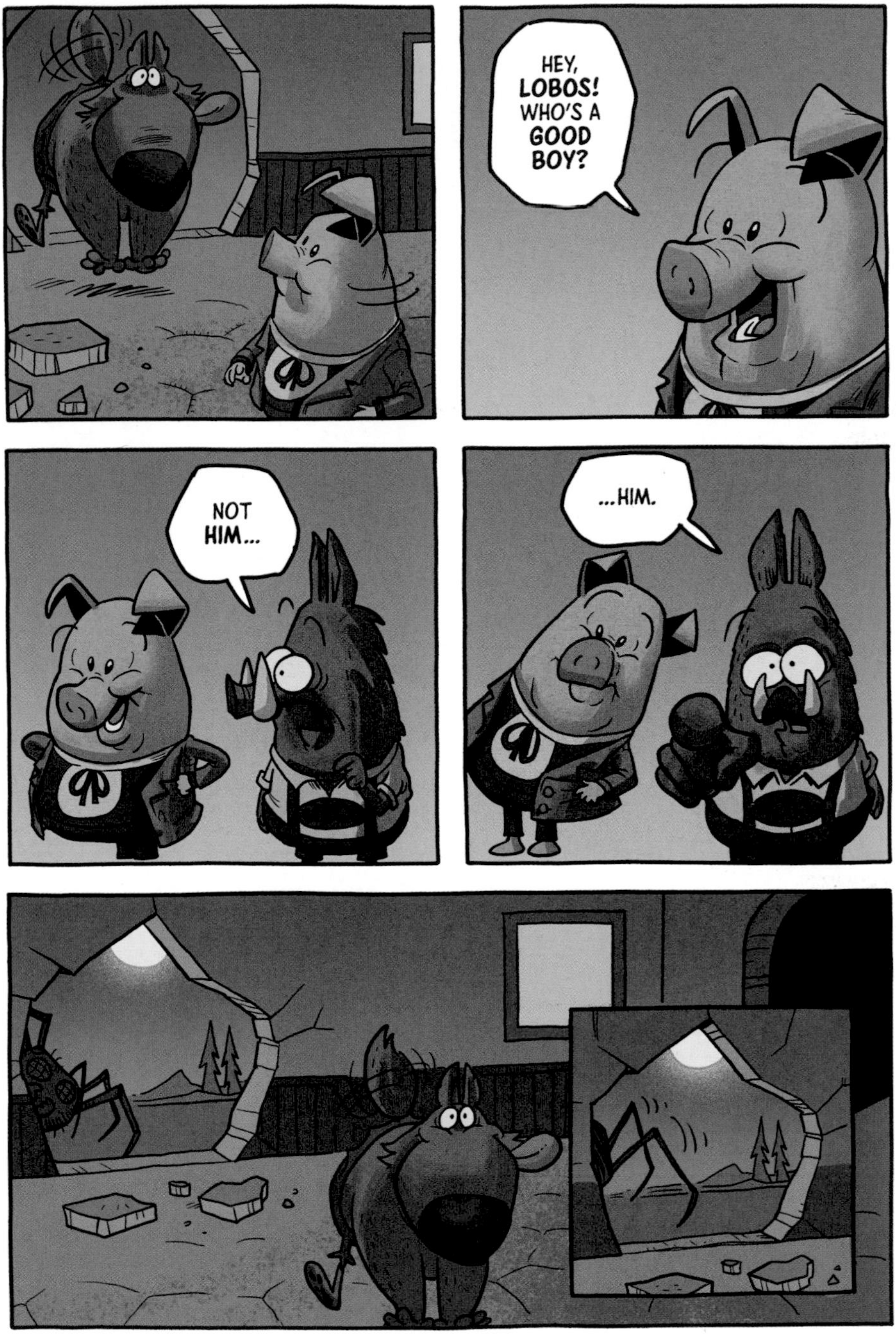
HEY, LOBOS! WHO'S A GOOD BOY?
NOT HIM...
...HIM.

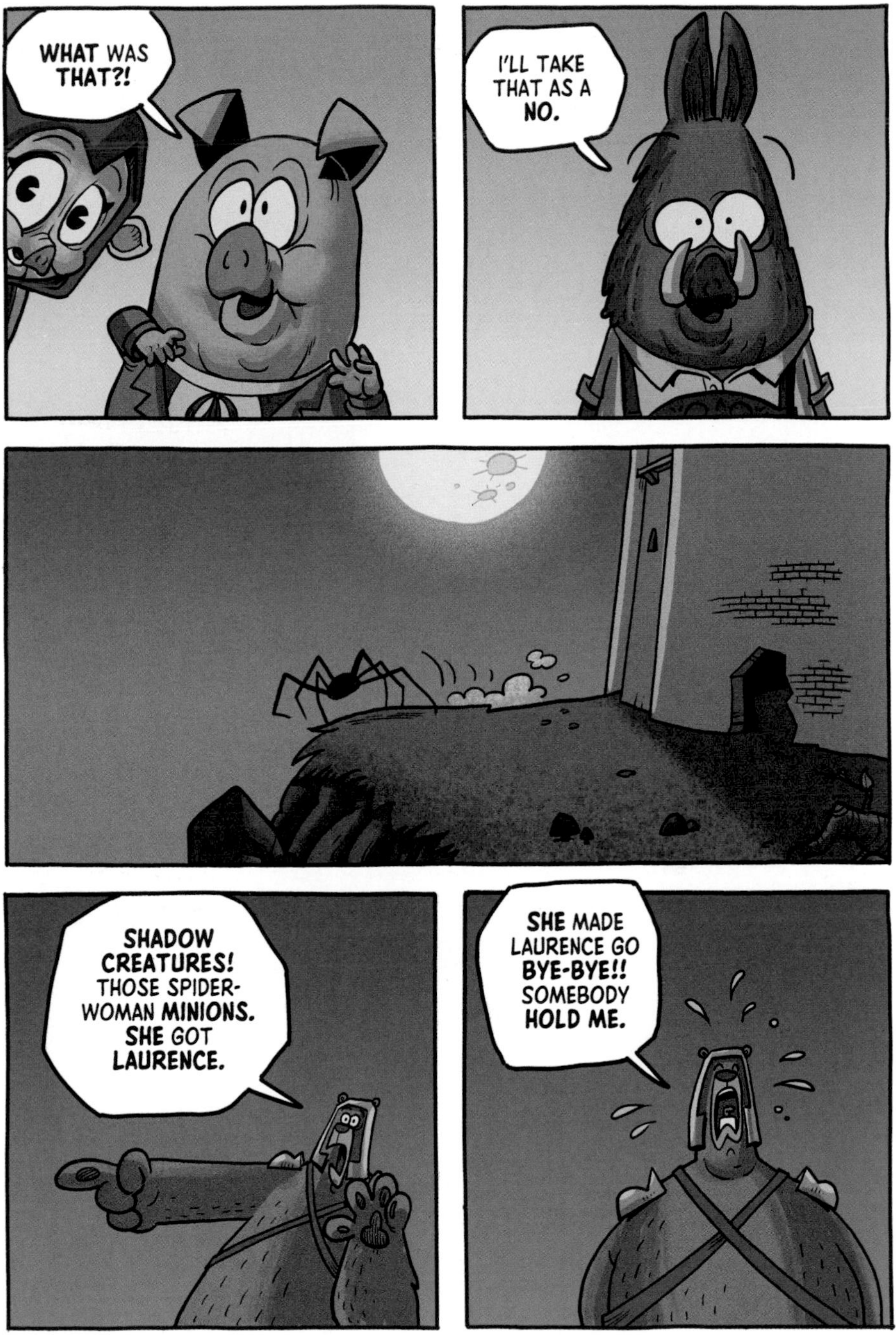
WHAT WAS THAT?!
I'LL TAKE THAT AS A NO.
SHADOW CREATURES! THOSE SPIDER-WOMAN MINIONS. SHE GOT LAURENCE.
SHE MADE LAURENCE GO BYE-BYE!! SOMEBODY HOLD ME.

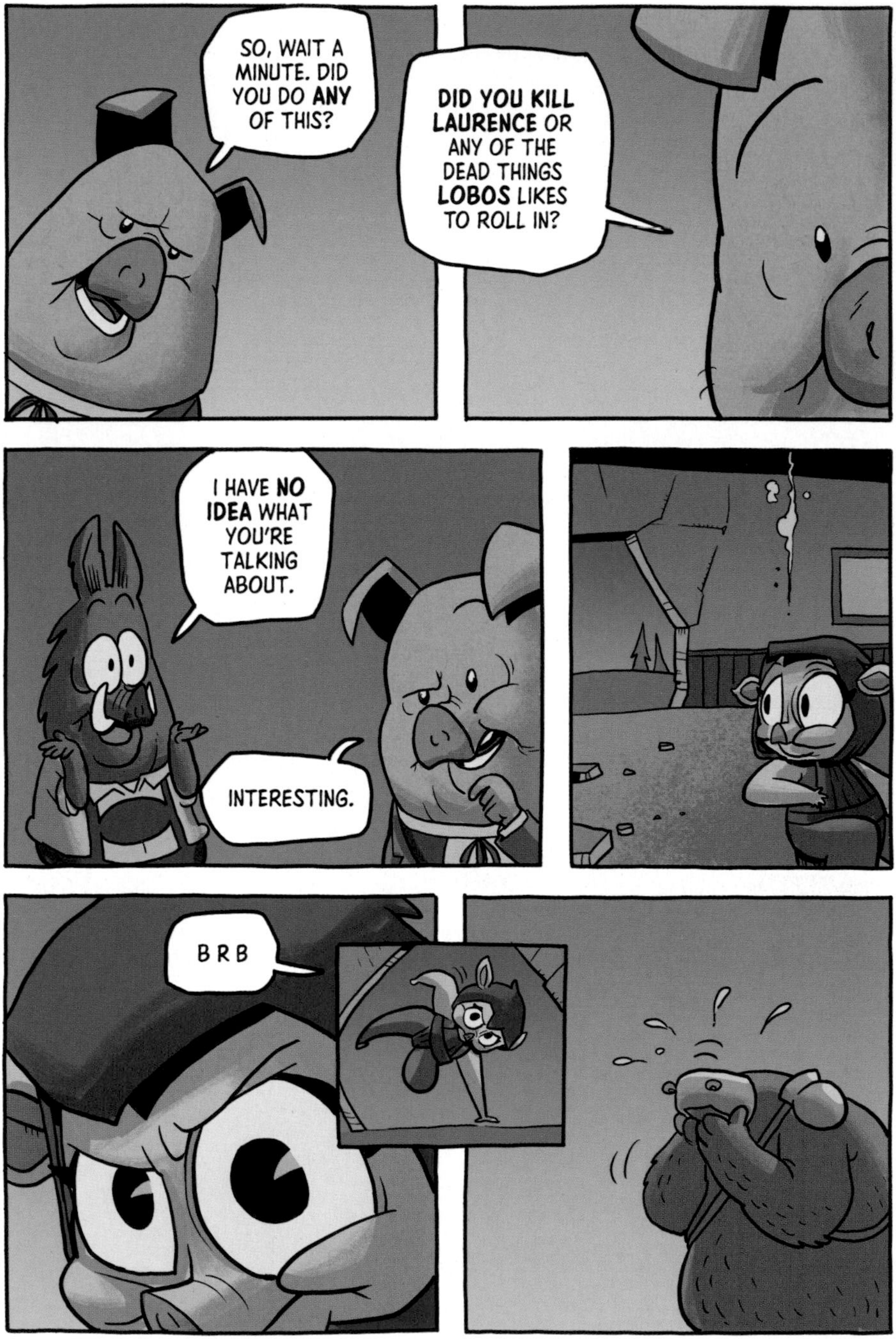
SO, WAIT A MINUTE. DID YOU DO ANY OF THIS?
DID YOU KILL LAURENCE OR ANY OF THE DEAD THINGS LOBOS LIKES TO ROLL IN?
I HAVE NO IDEA WHAT YOU'RE TALKING ABOUT.
INTERESTING.
B R B

CHAPTER NINE

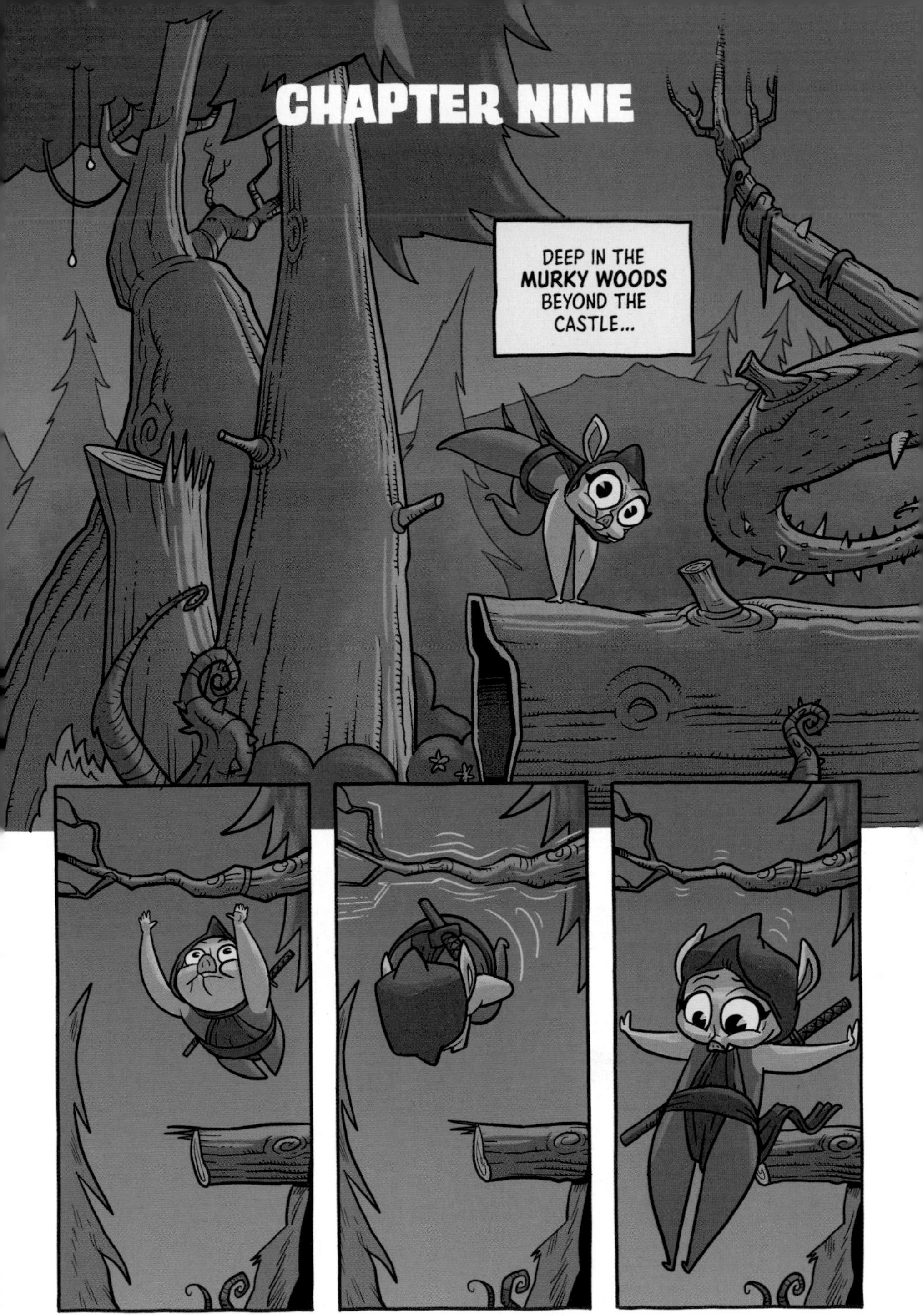
DEEP IN THE
MURKY WOODS
BEYOND THE
CASTLE...

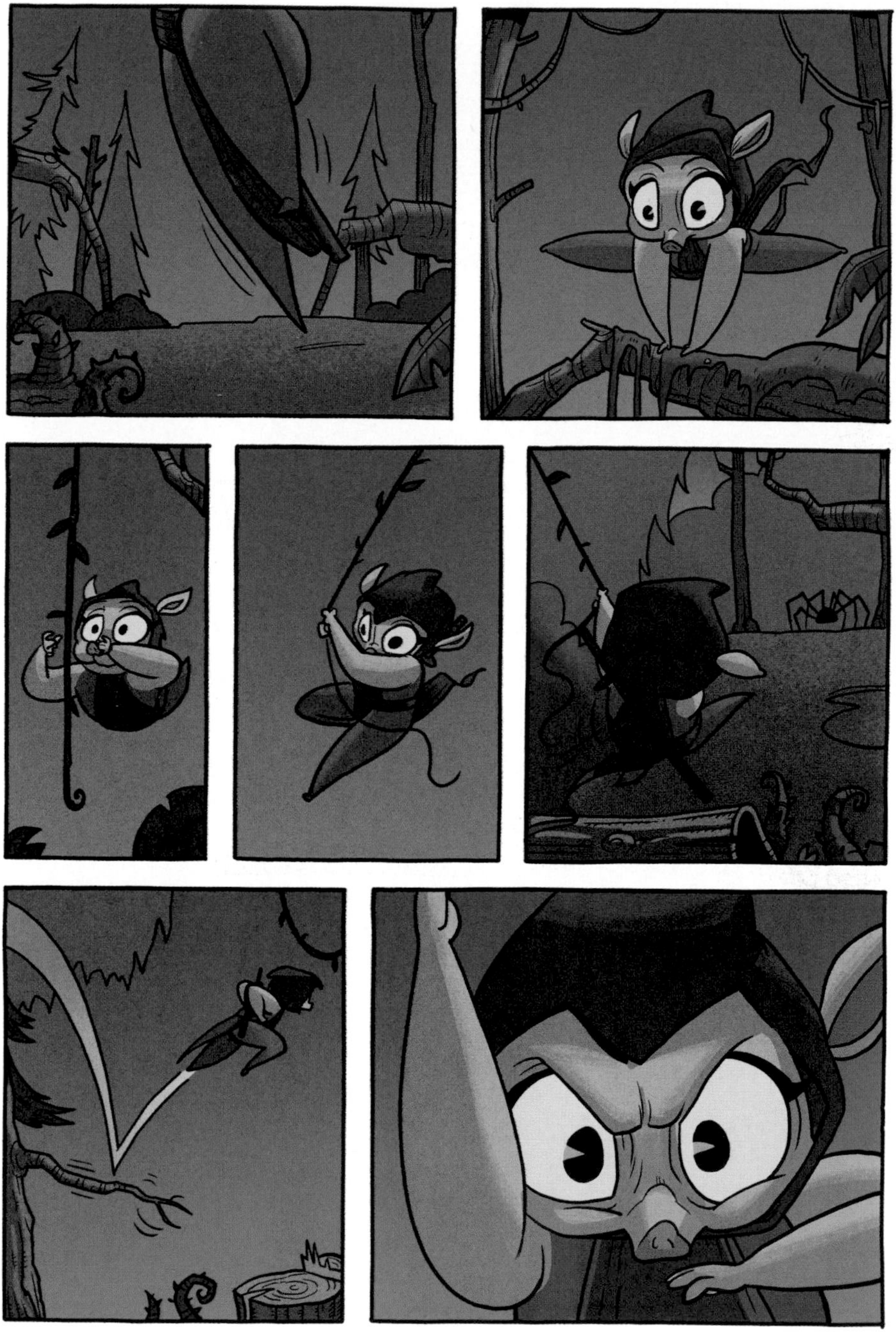

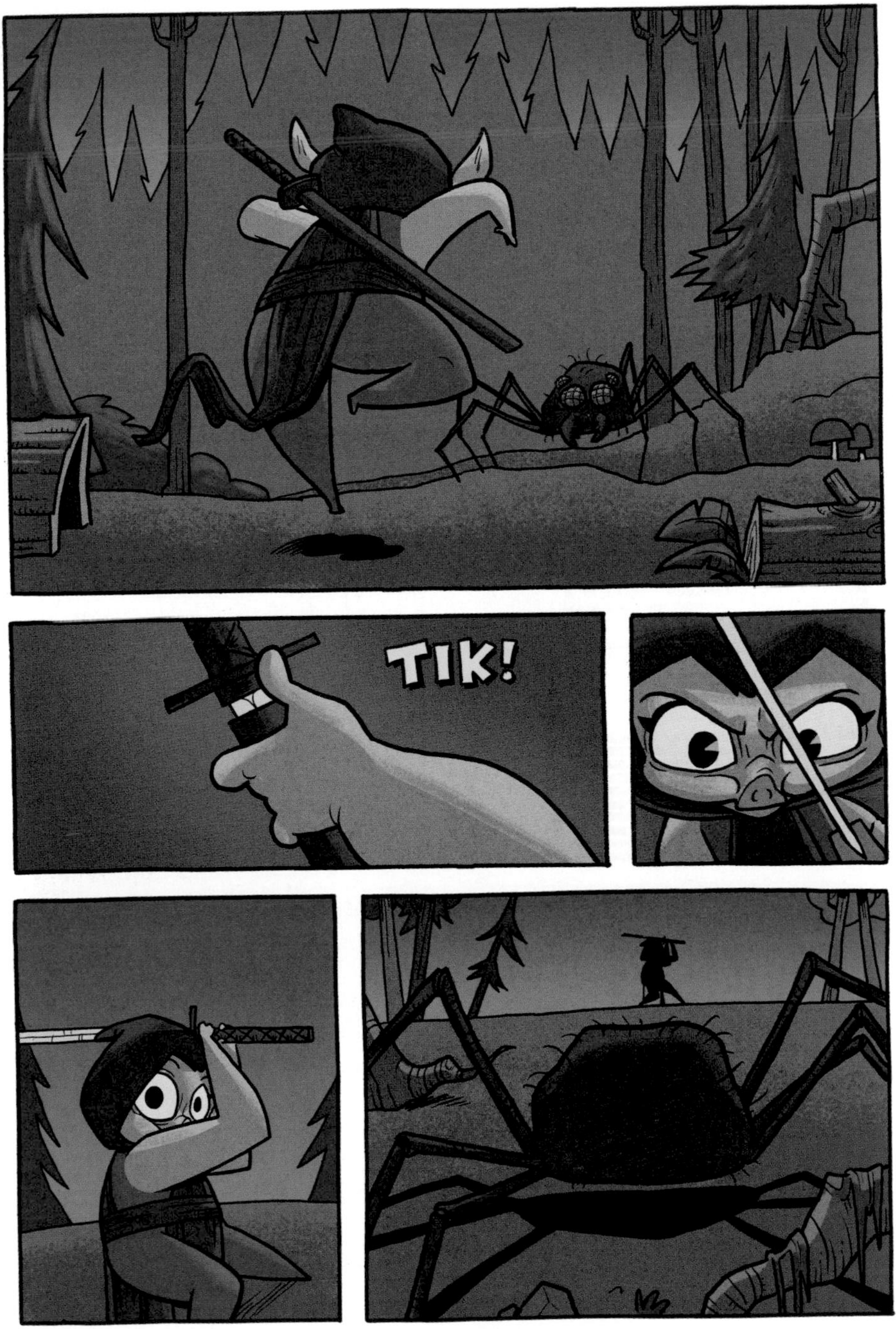
TIK!

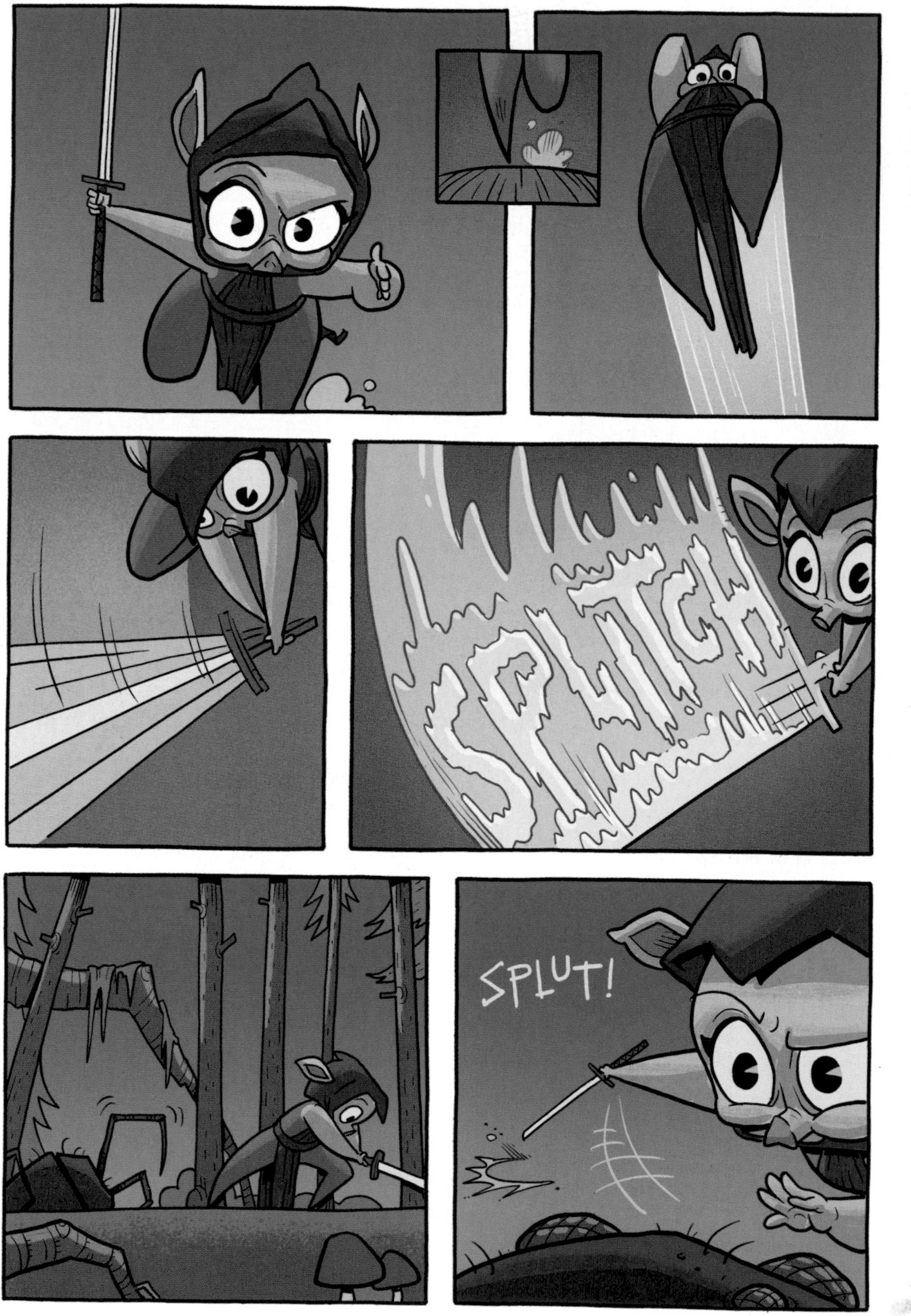
SPLITCH
SPLUT!

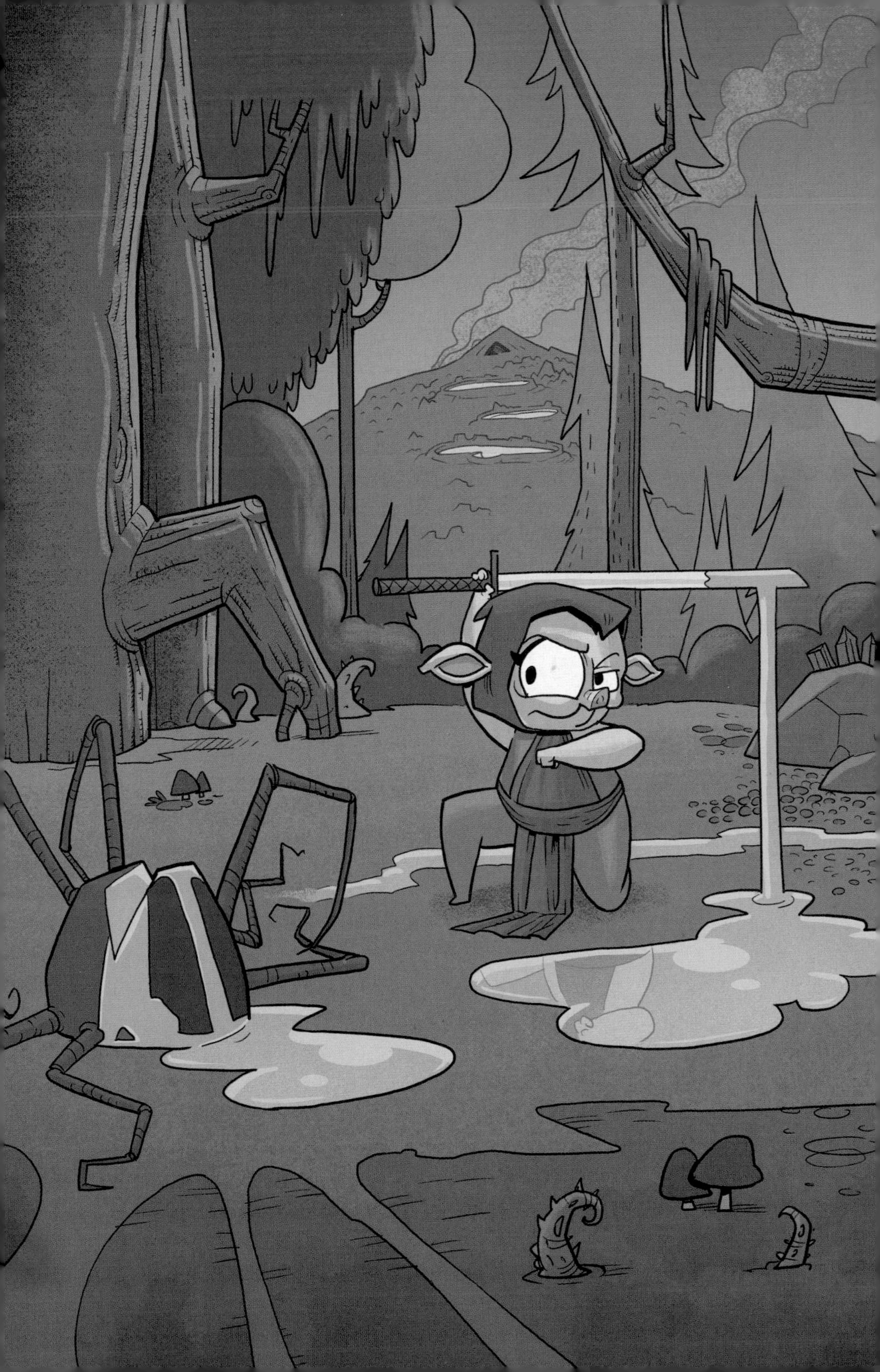

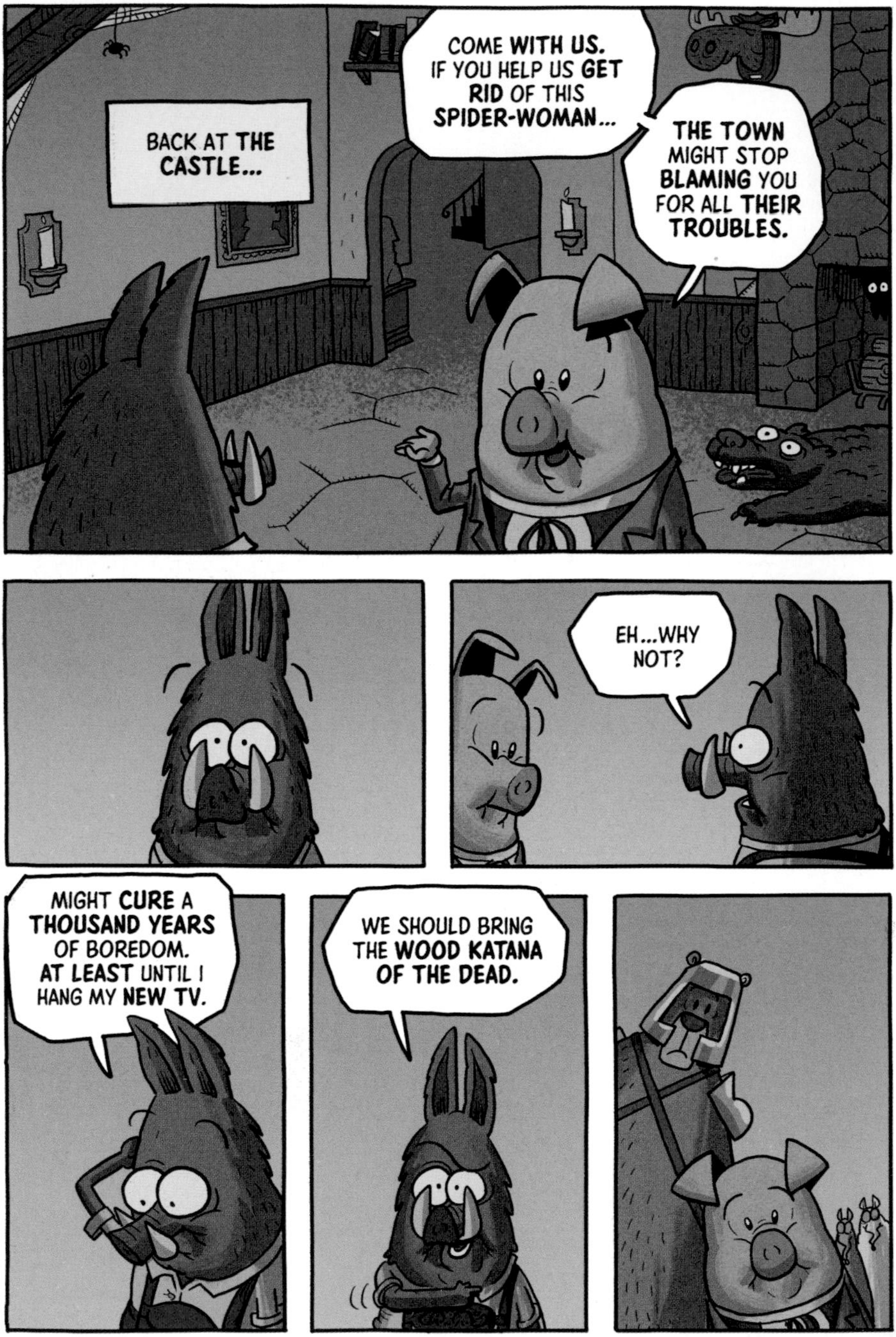
BACK AT THE CASTLE...
COME WITH US. IF YOU HELP US GET RID OF THIS SPIDER-WOMAN...
THE TOWN MIGHT STOP BLAMING YOU FOR ALL THEIR TROUBLES.
EH...WHY NOT?
MIGHT CURE A THOUSAND YEARS OF BOREDOM. AT LEAST UNTIL I HANG MY NEW TV.
WE SHOULD BRING THE WOOD KATANA OF THE DEAD.

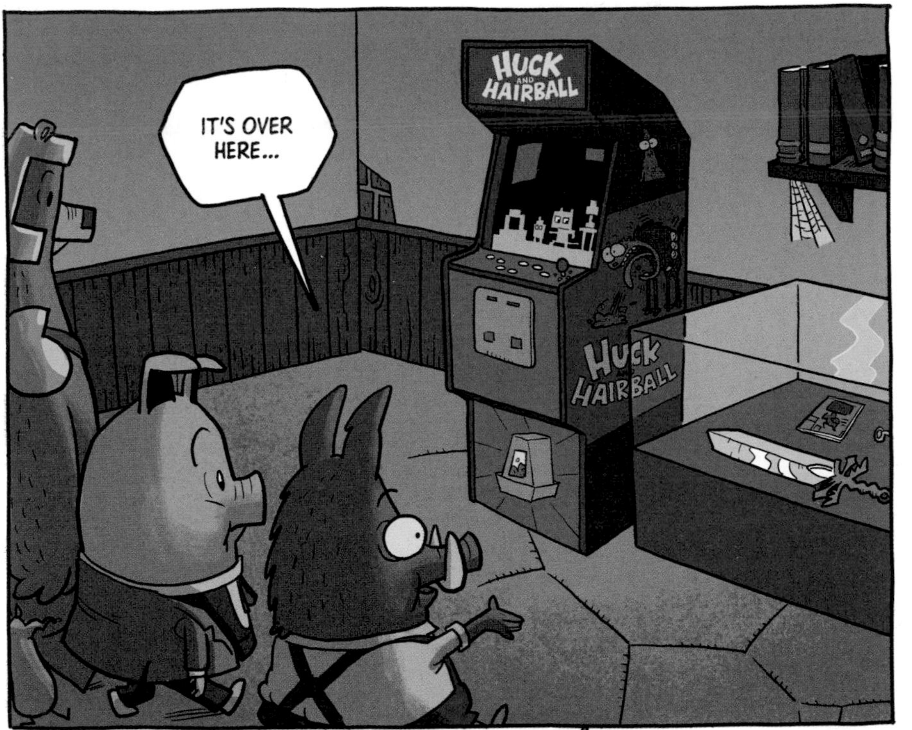
HUCK AND HAIRBALL
IT'S OVER HERE...
HUCK AND HAIRBALL

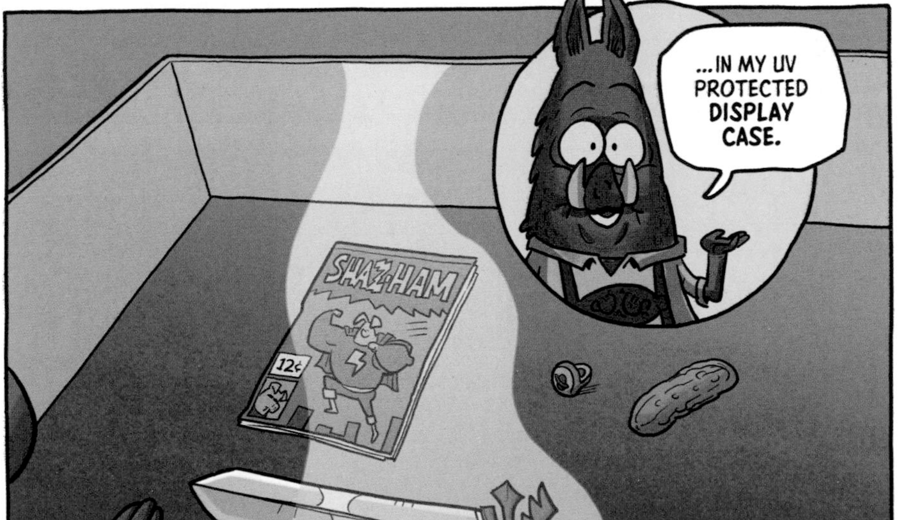
...IN MY UV PROTECTED DISPLAY CASE.
SHAZ-HAM
12¢

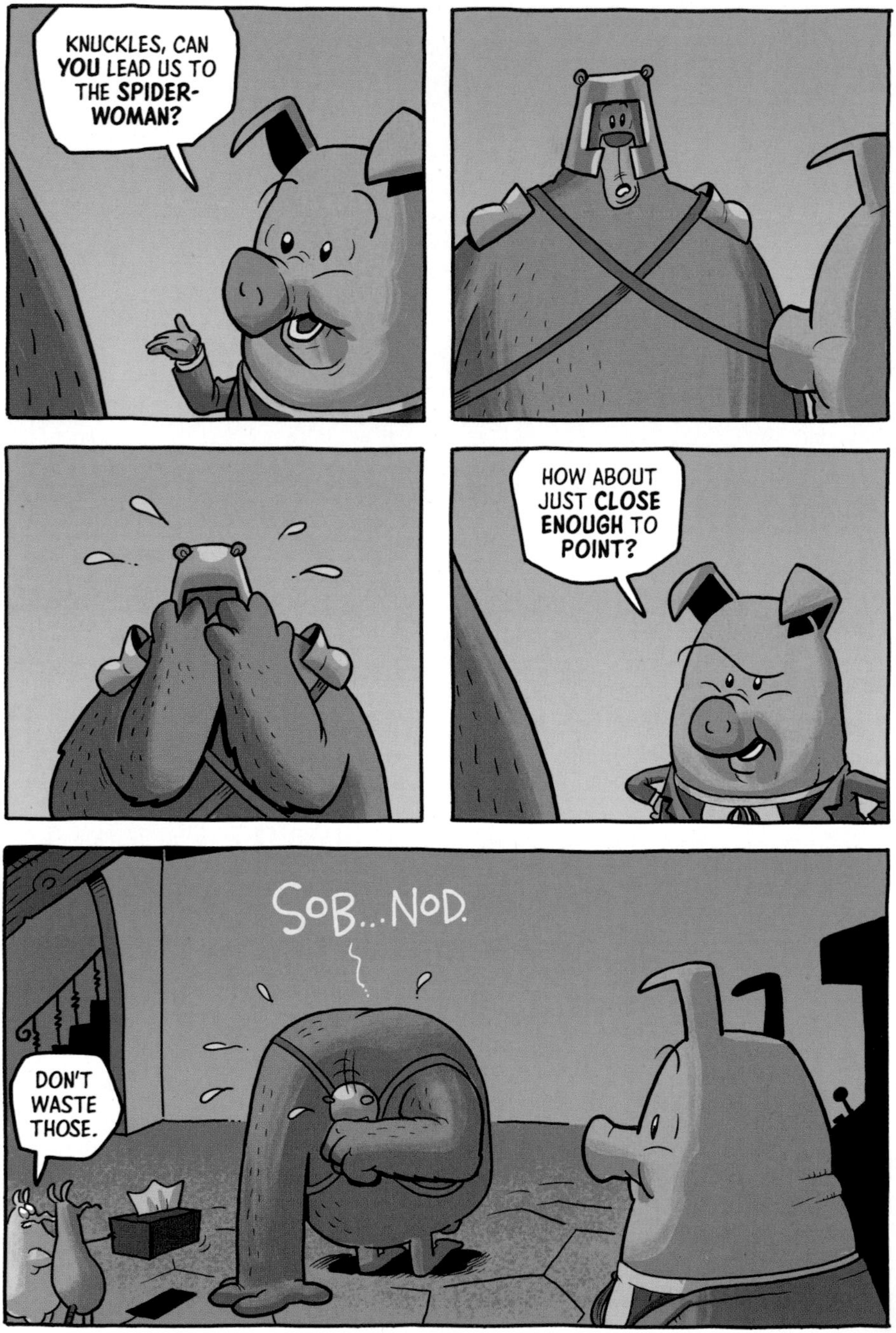
KNUCKLES, CAN YOU LEAD US TO THE SPIDER-WOMAN?
HOW ABOUT JUST CLOSE ENOUGH TO POINT?
SOB...NOD.
DON'T WASTE THOSE.

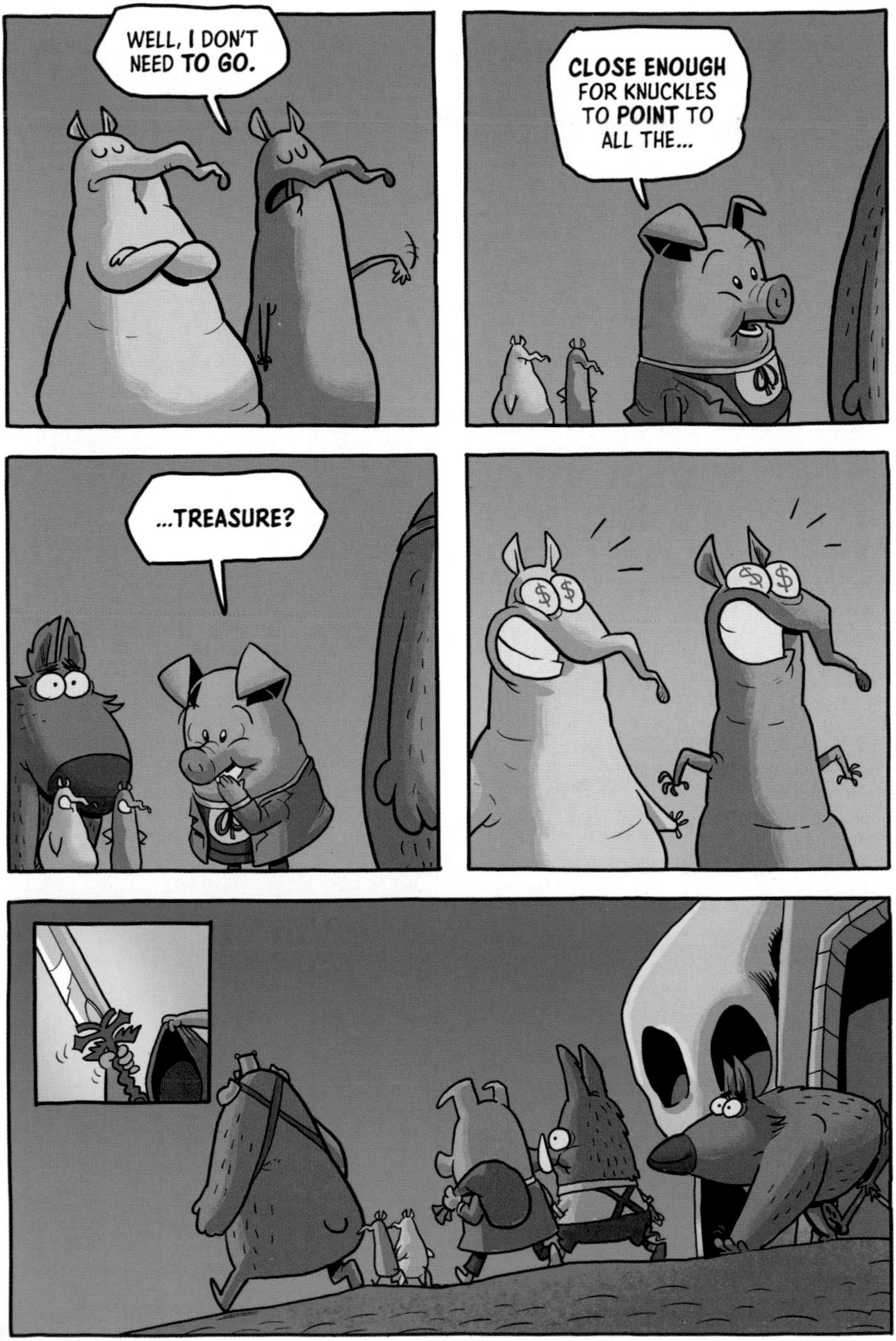
WELL, I DON'T NEED TO GO.
CLOSE ENOUGH FOR KNUCKLES TO POINT TO ALL THE...
...TREASURE?

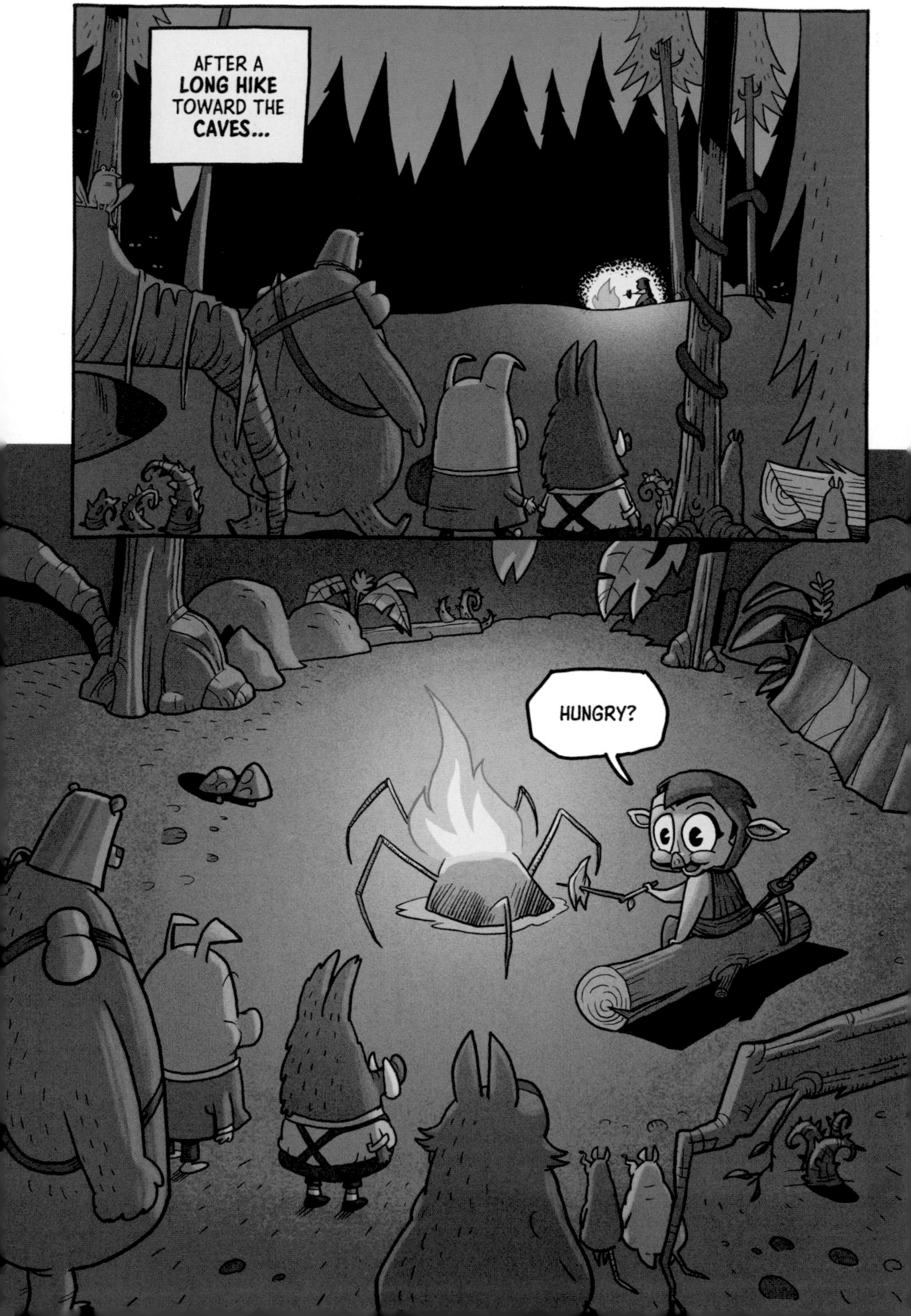

AFTER A LONG HIKE TOWARD THE CAVES...
HUNGRY?

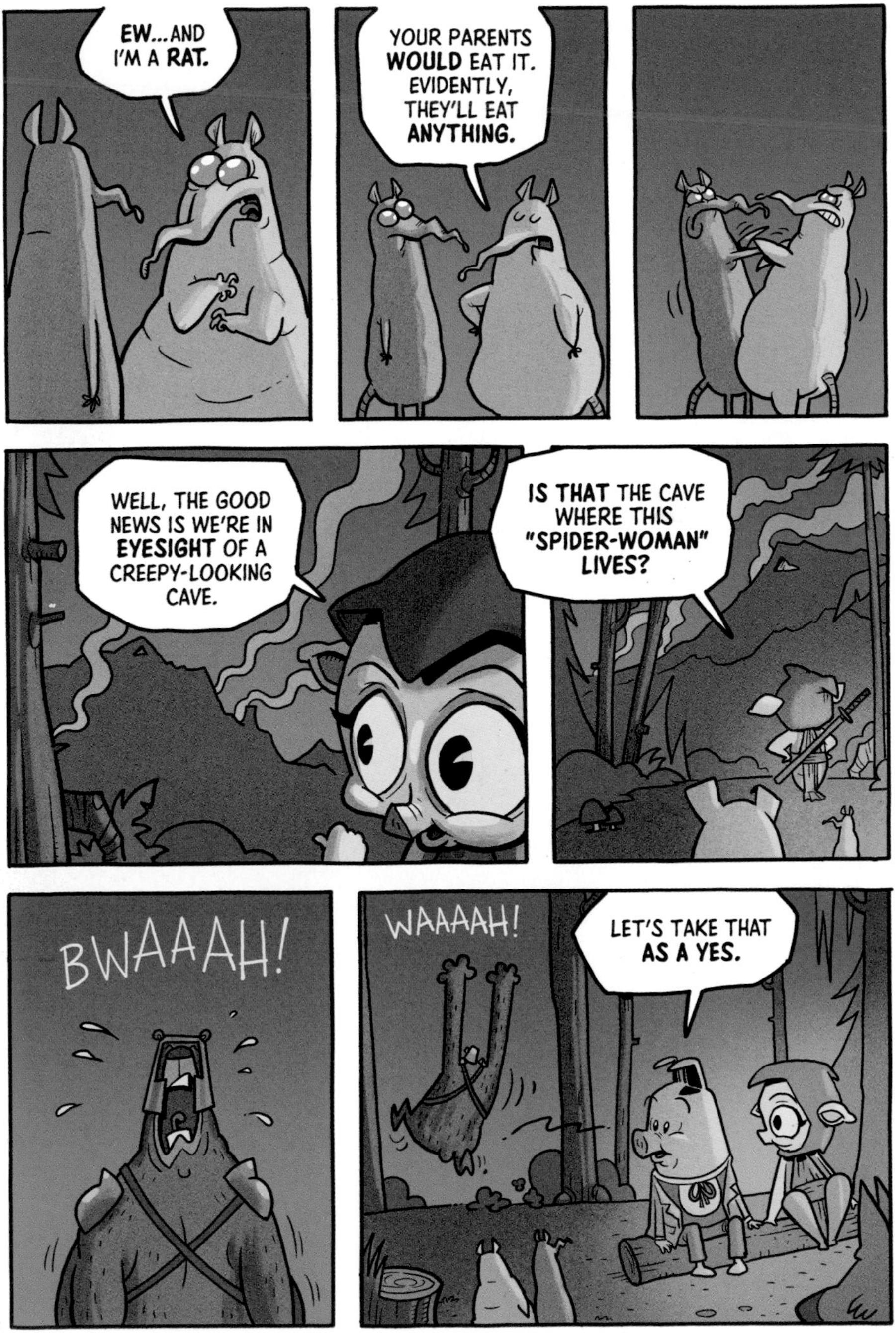
EW...AND I'M A RAT.
YOUR PARENTS WOULD EAT IT. EVIDENTLY, THEY'LL EAT ANYTHING.
WELL, THE GOOD NEWS IS WE'RE IN EYESIGHT OF A CREEPY-LOOKING CAVE.
IS THAT THE CAVE WHERE THIS "SPIDER-WOMAN" LIVES?
BWAAAH!
WAAAAH!
LET'S TAKE THAT AS A YES.

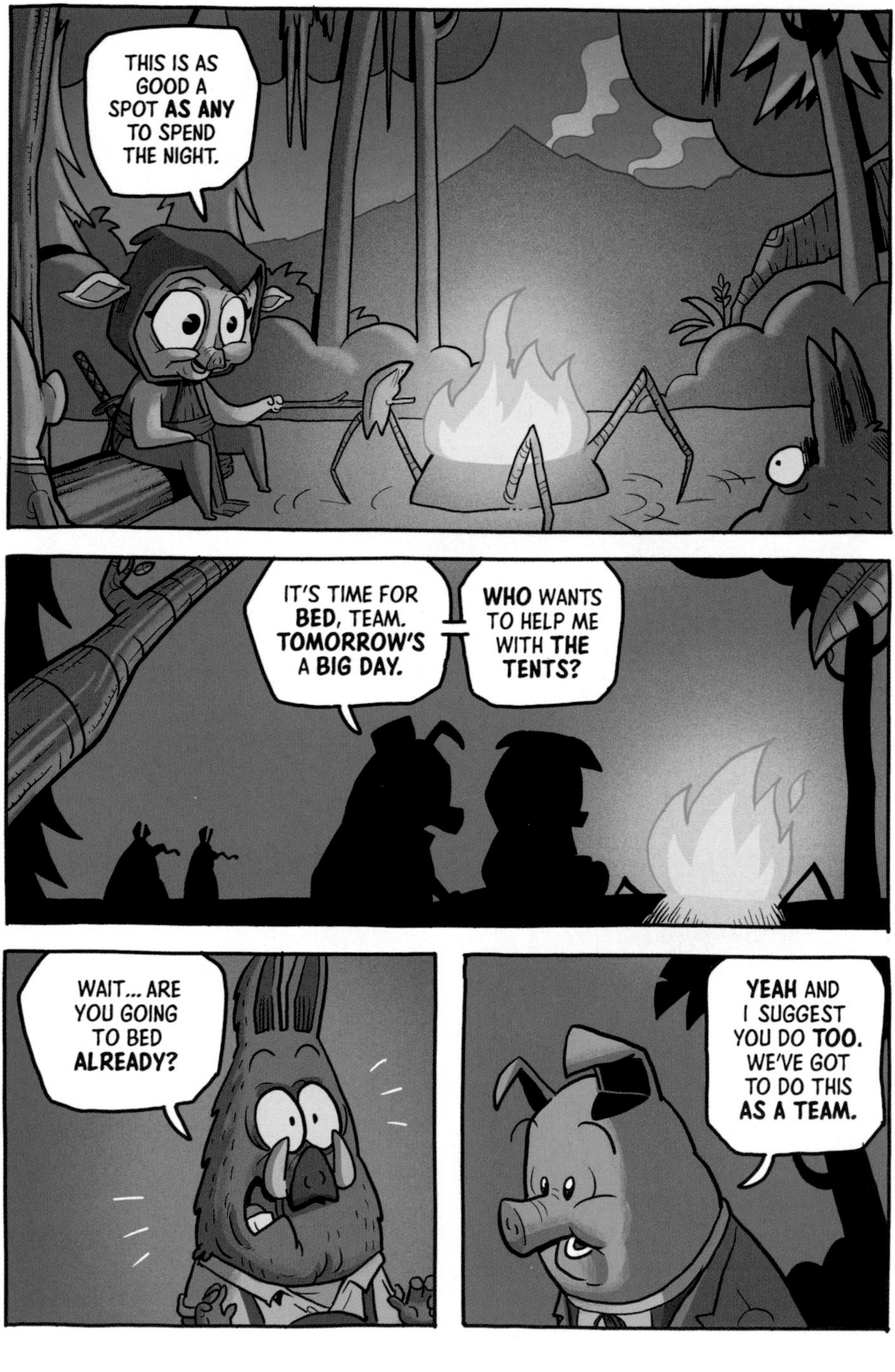
THIS IS AS GOOD A SPOT AS ANY TO SPEND THE NIGHT.
IT'S TIME FOR BED, TEAM. TOMORROW'S A BIG DAY.
WHO WANTS TO HELP ME WITH THE TENTS?
WAIT... ARE YOU GOING TO BED ALREADY?
YEAH AND I SUGGEST YOU DO TOO. WE'VE GOT TO DO THIS AS A TEAM.

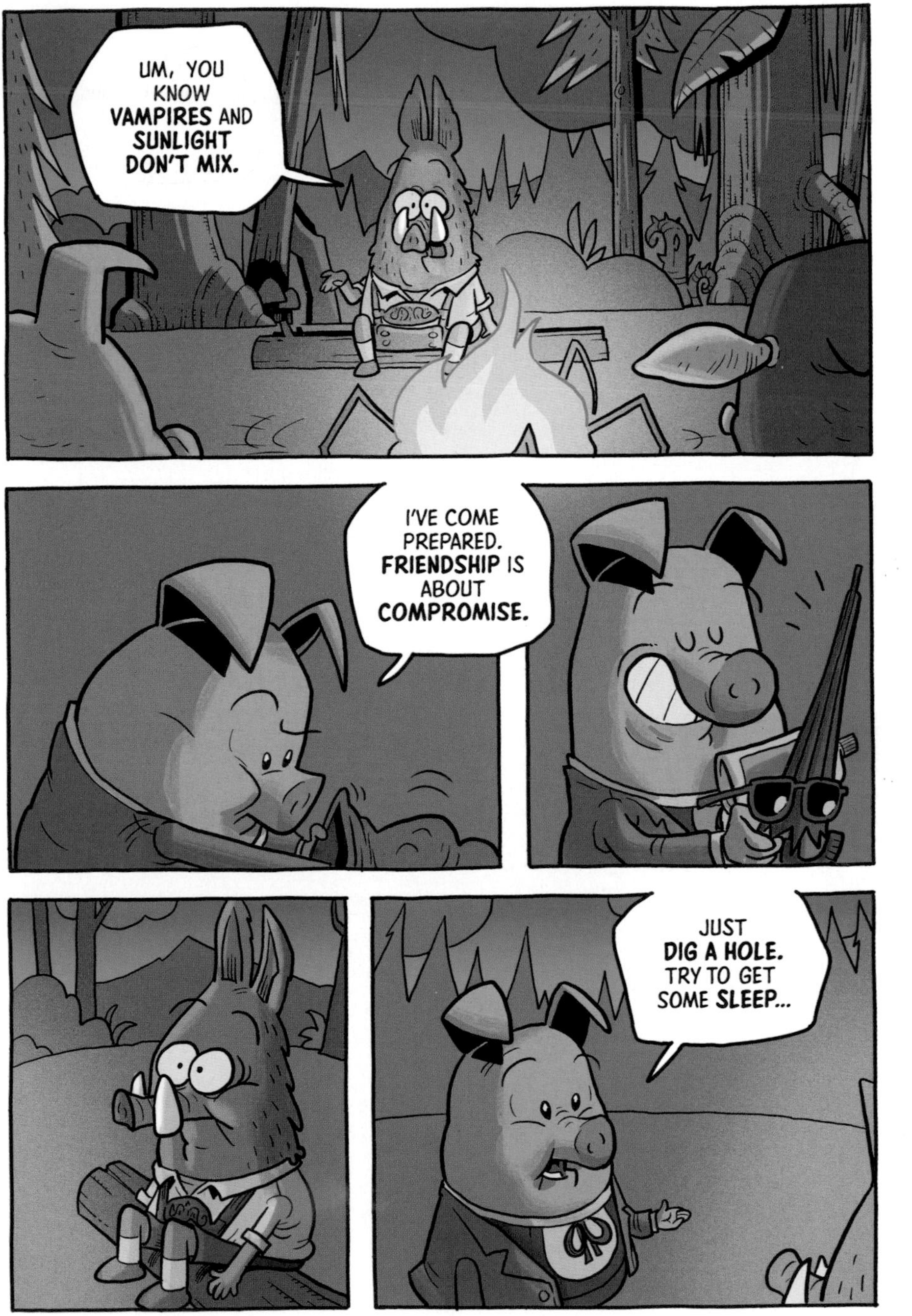
UM, YOU KNOW VAMPIRES AND SUNLIGHT DON'T MIX.
I'VE COME PREPARED. FRIENDSHIP IS ABOUT COMPROMISE.
JUST DIG A HOLE. TRY TO GET SOME SLEEP...

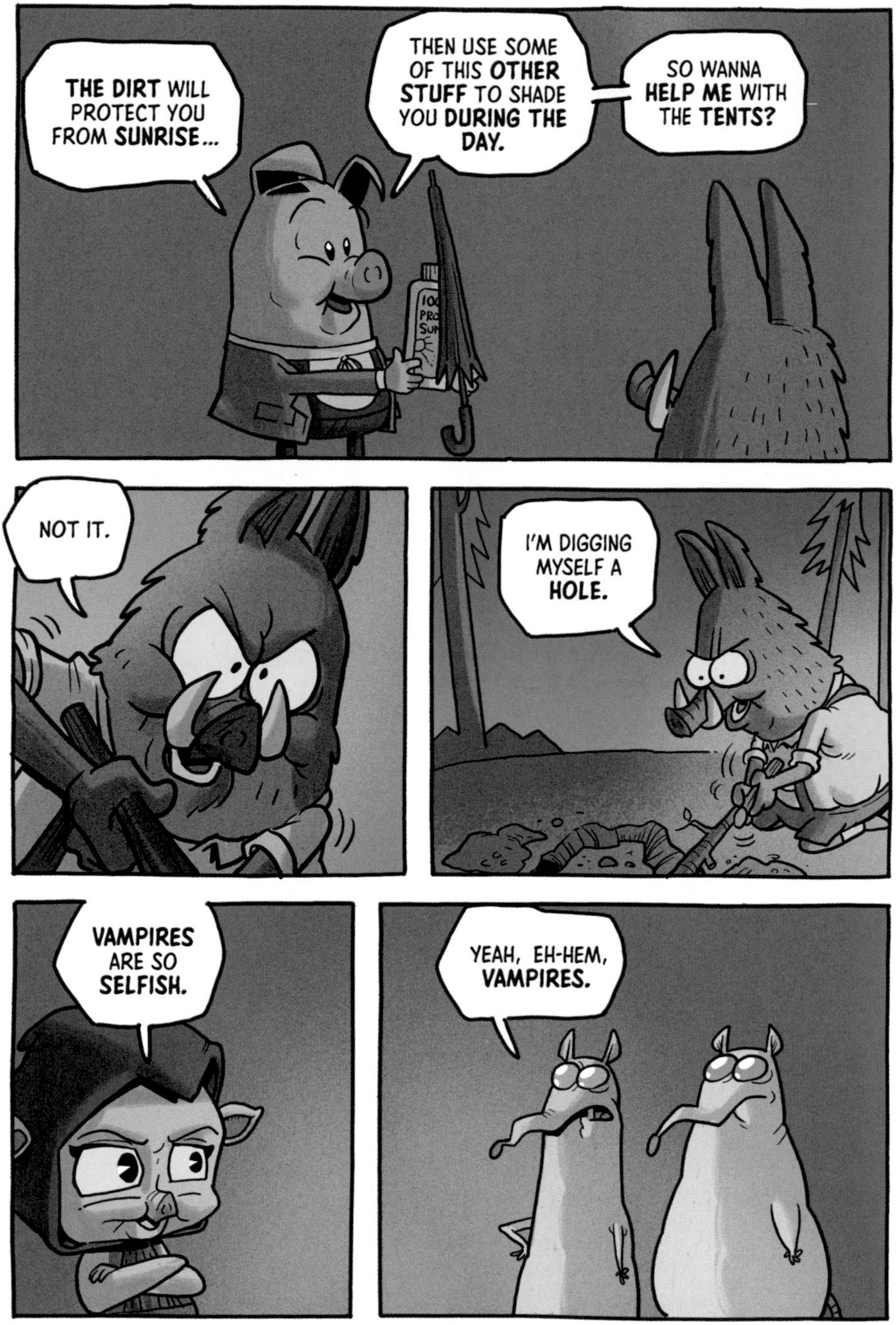
THE DIRT WILL PROTECT YOU FROM SUNRISE...
THEN USE SOME OF THIS OTHER STUFF TO SHADE YOU DURING THE DAY.
SO WANNA HELP ME WITH THE TENTS?
100 PRO SUN
NOT IT.
I'M DIGGING MYSELF A HOLE.
VAMPIRES ARE SO SELFISH.
YEAH, EH-HEM, VAMPIRES.

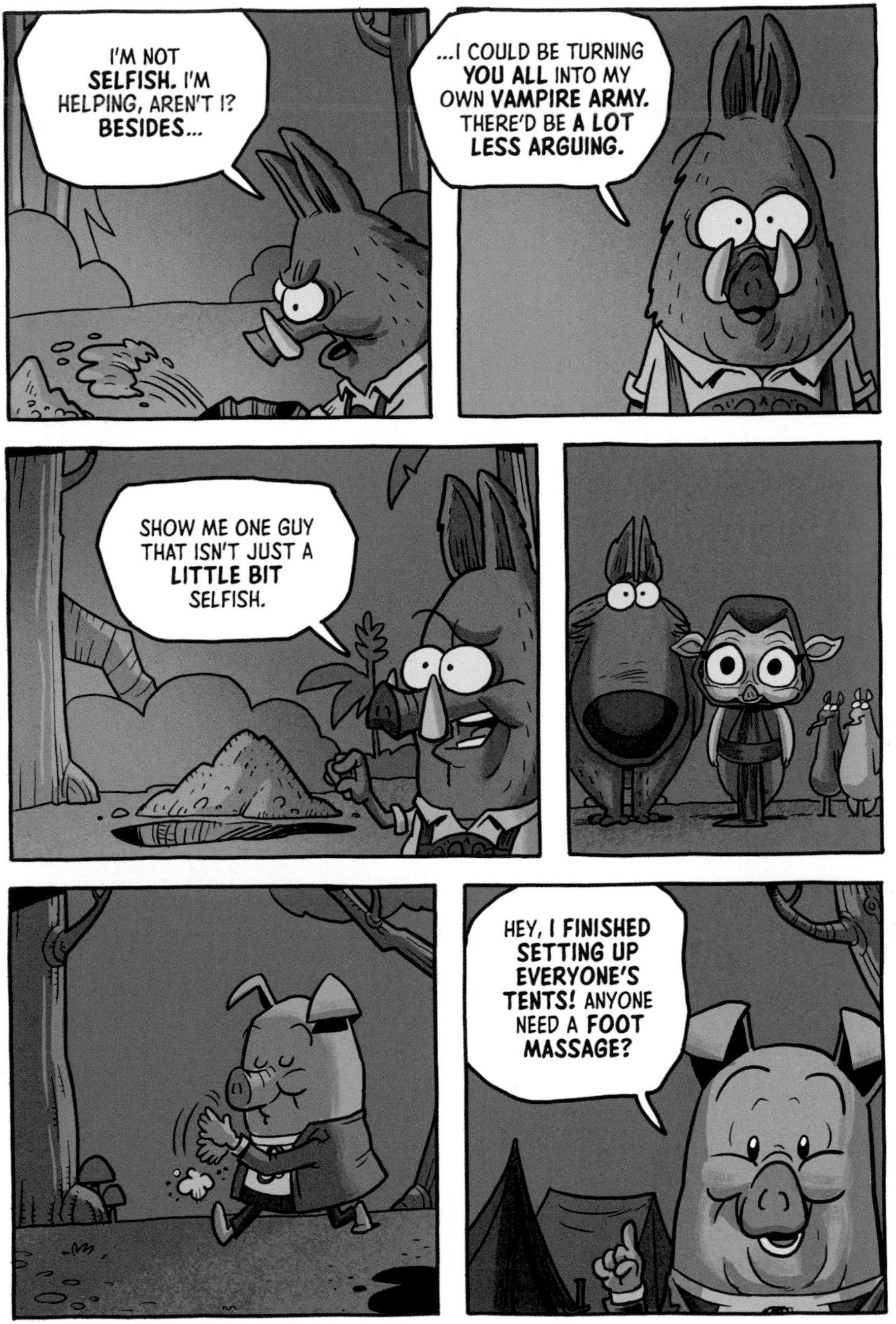
I'M NOT SELFISH. I'M HELPING, AREN'T I? BESIDES...
...I COULD BE TURNING YOU ALL INTO MY OWN VAMPIRE ARMY. THERE'D BE A LOT LESS ARGUING.
SHOW ME ONE GUY THAT ISN'T JUST A LITTLE BIT SELFISH.
HEY, I FINISHED SETTING UP EVERYONE'S TENTS! ANYONE NEED A FOOT MASSAGE?

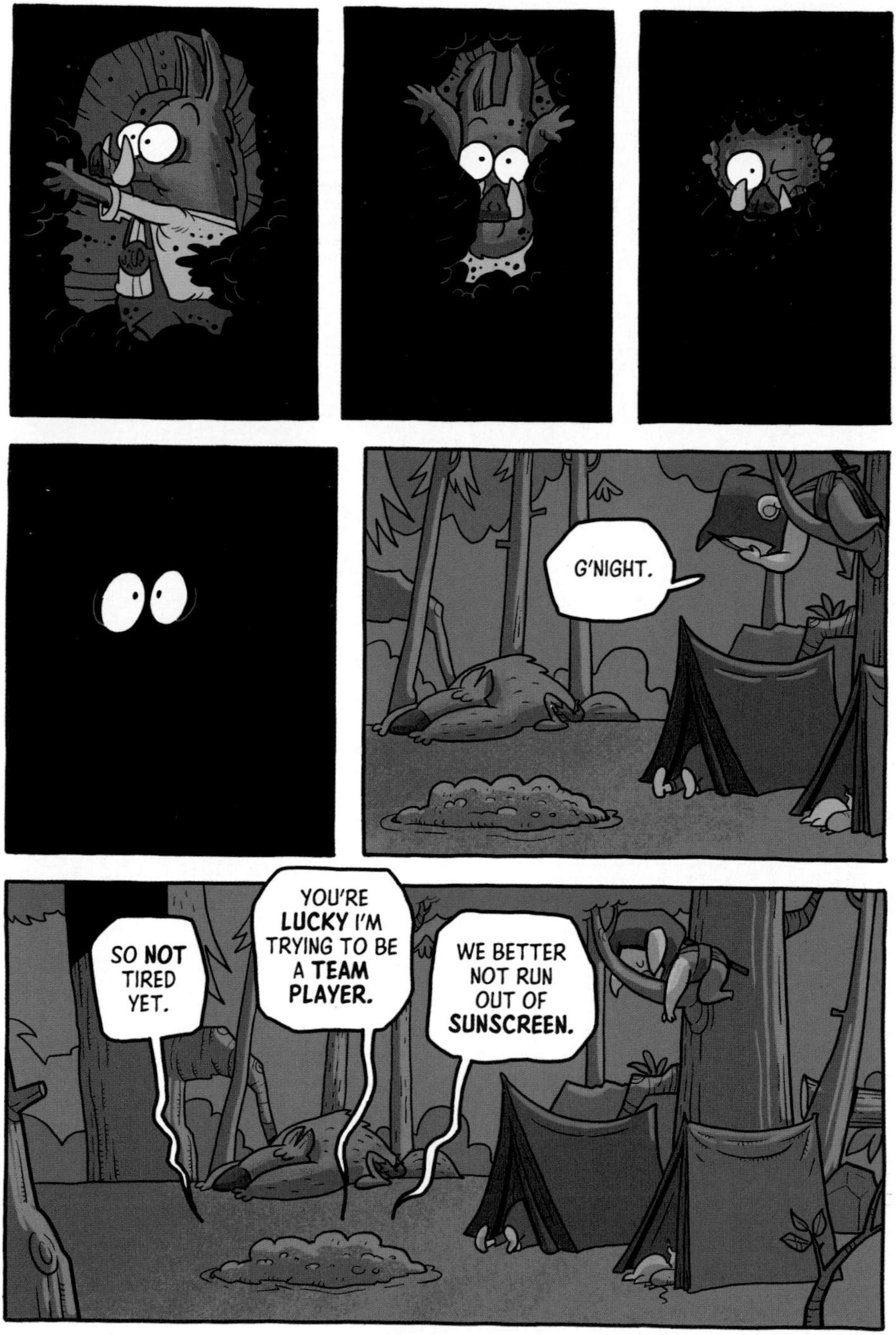
G'NIGHT.
SO NOT TIRED YET.
YOU'RE LUCKY I'M TRYING TO BE A TEAM PLAYER.
WE BETTER NOT RUN OUT OF SUNSCREEN.

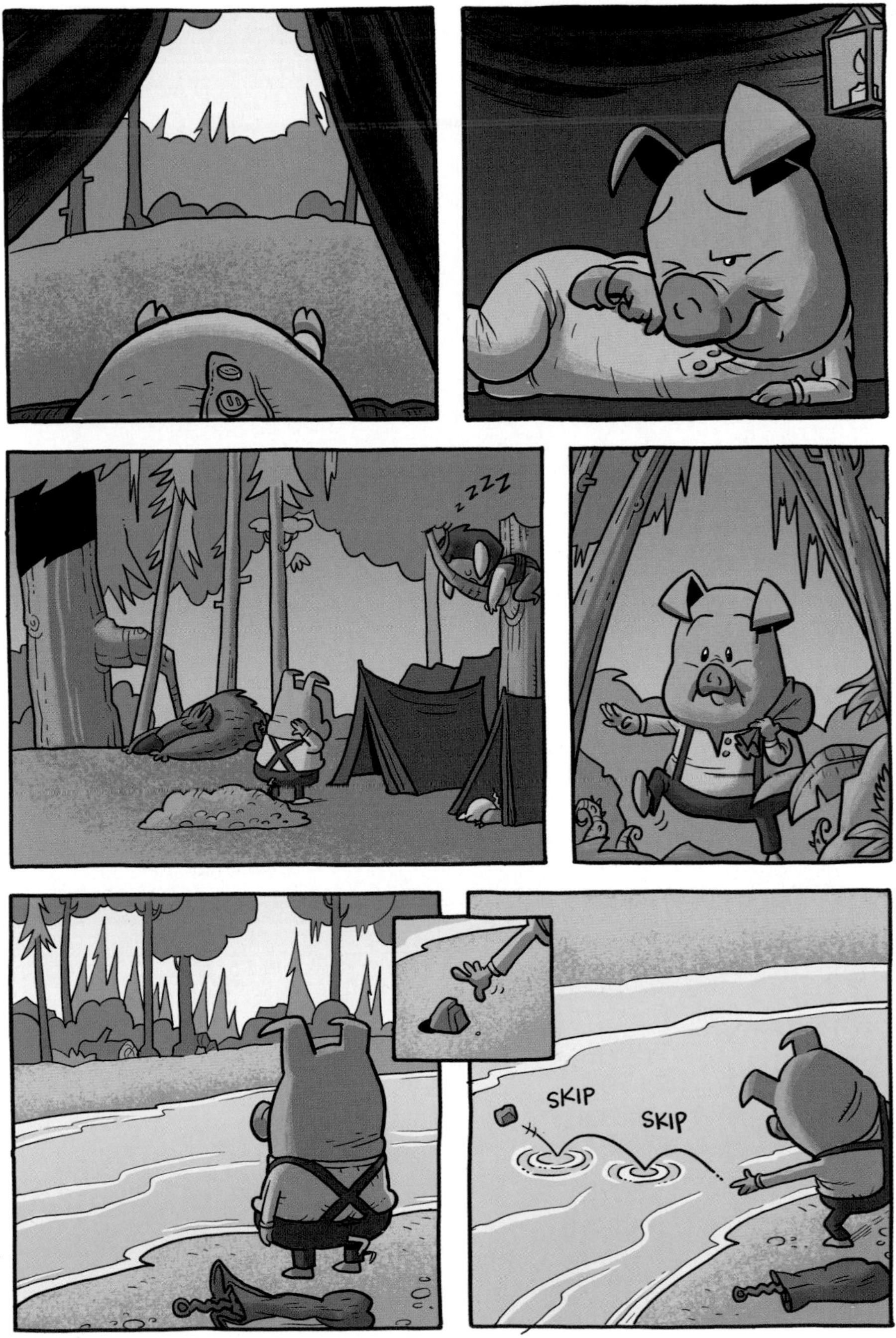
ZZZZ
SKIP
SKIP

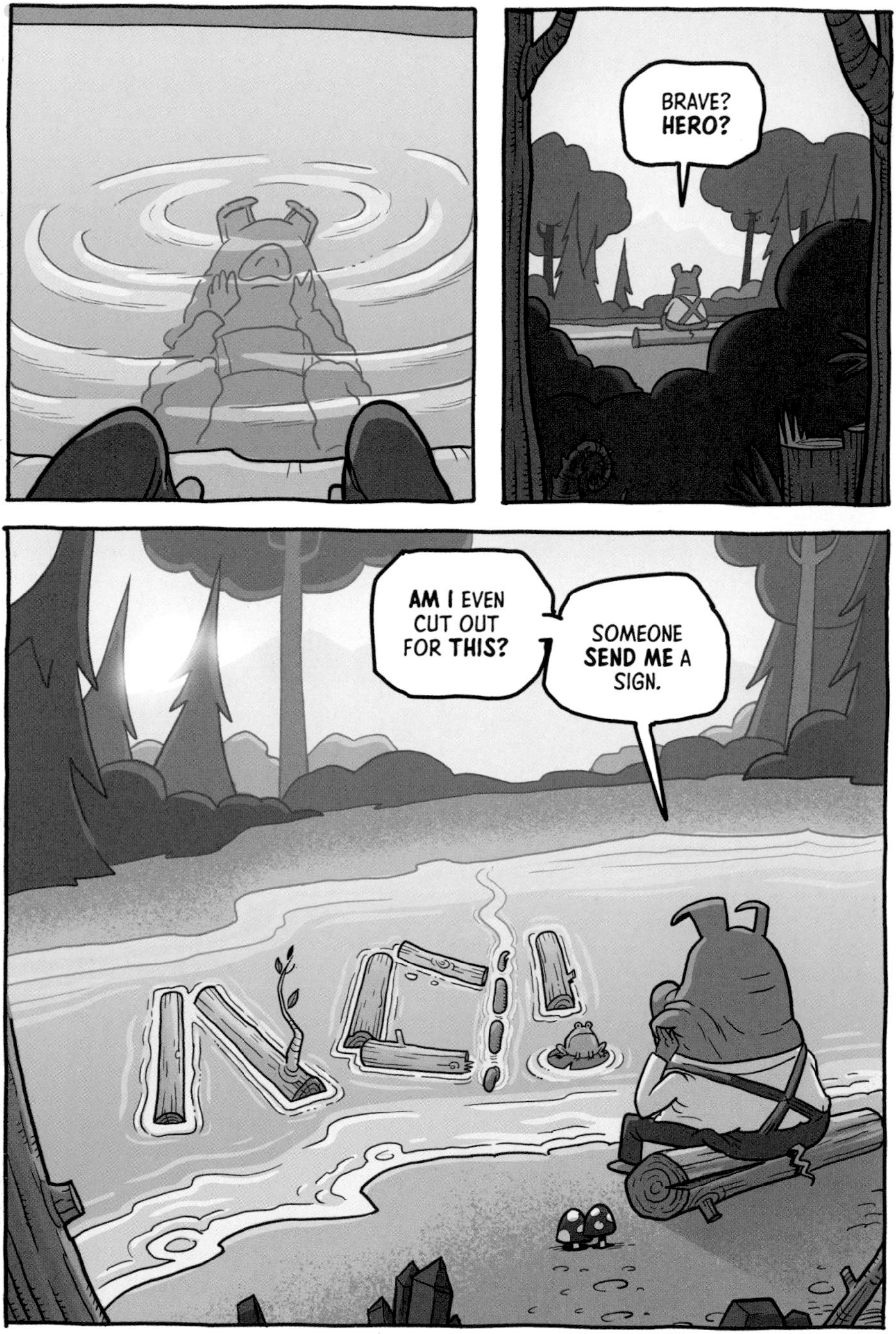
BRAVE? HERO?
AM I EVEN CUT OUT FOR THIS?
SOMEONE SEND ME A SIGN.
NO!

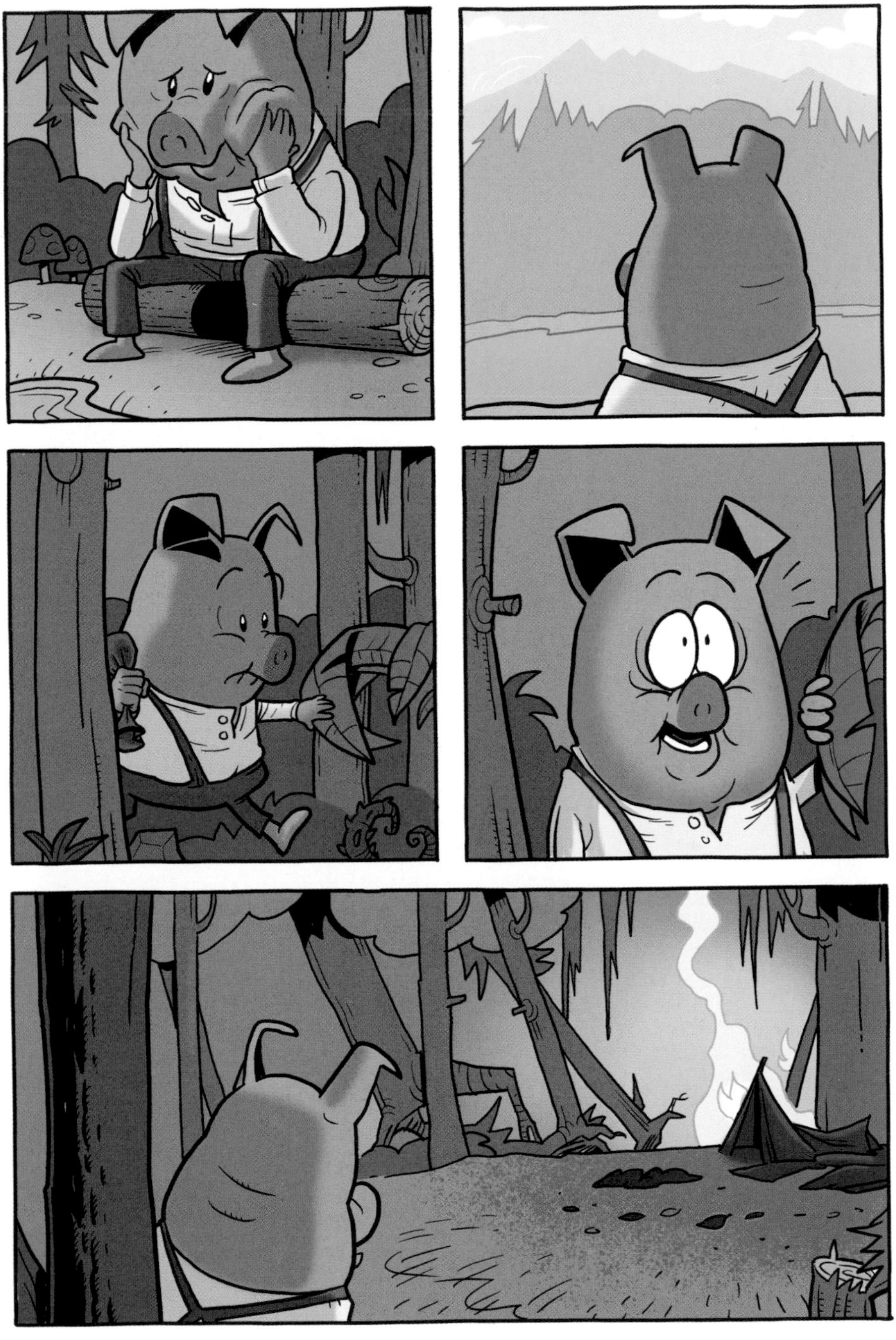

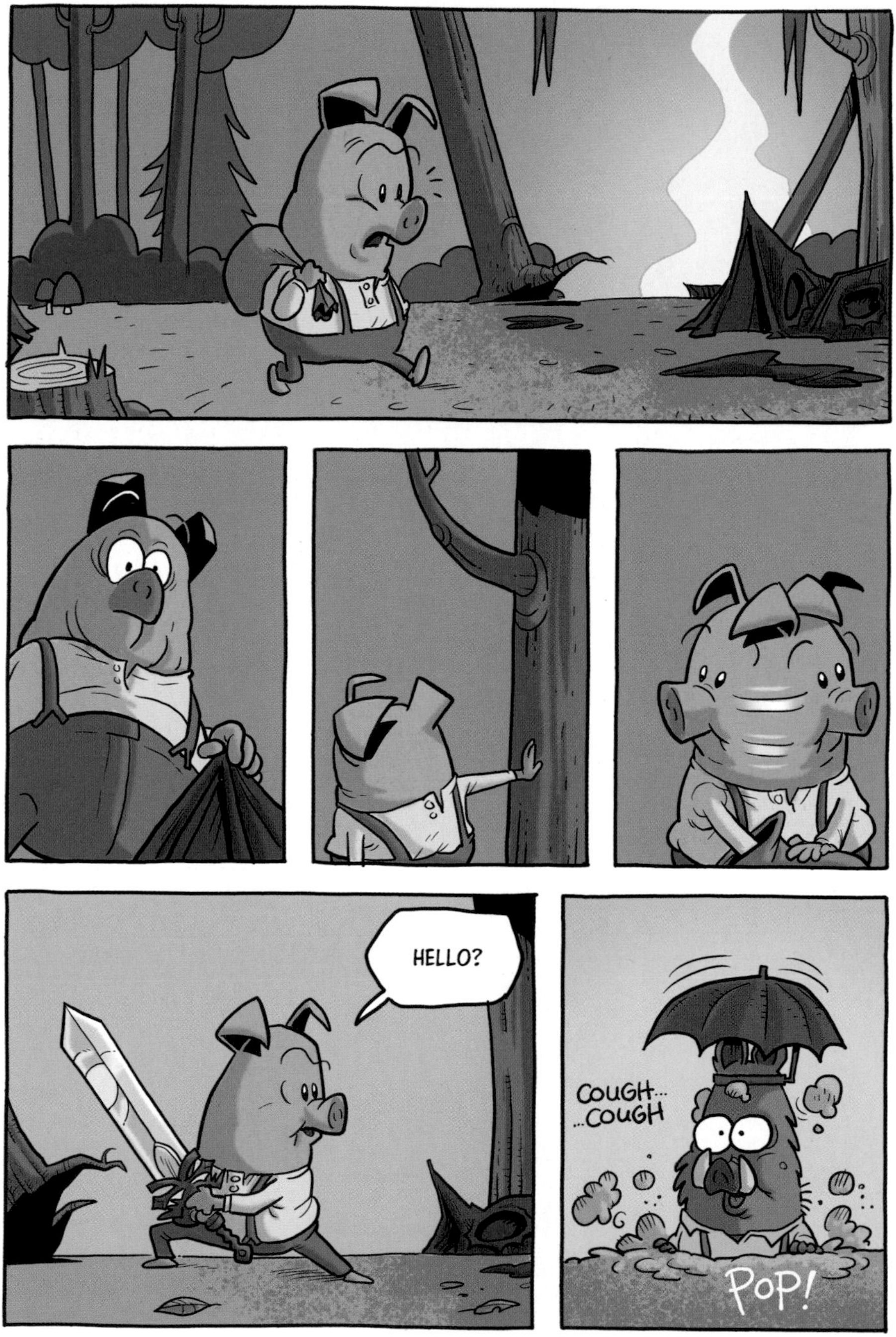
HELLO?
COUGH...
...COUGH
POP!

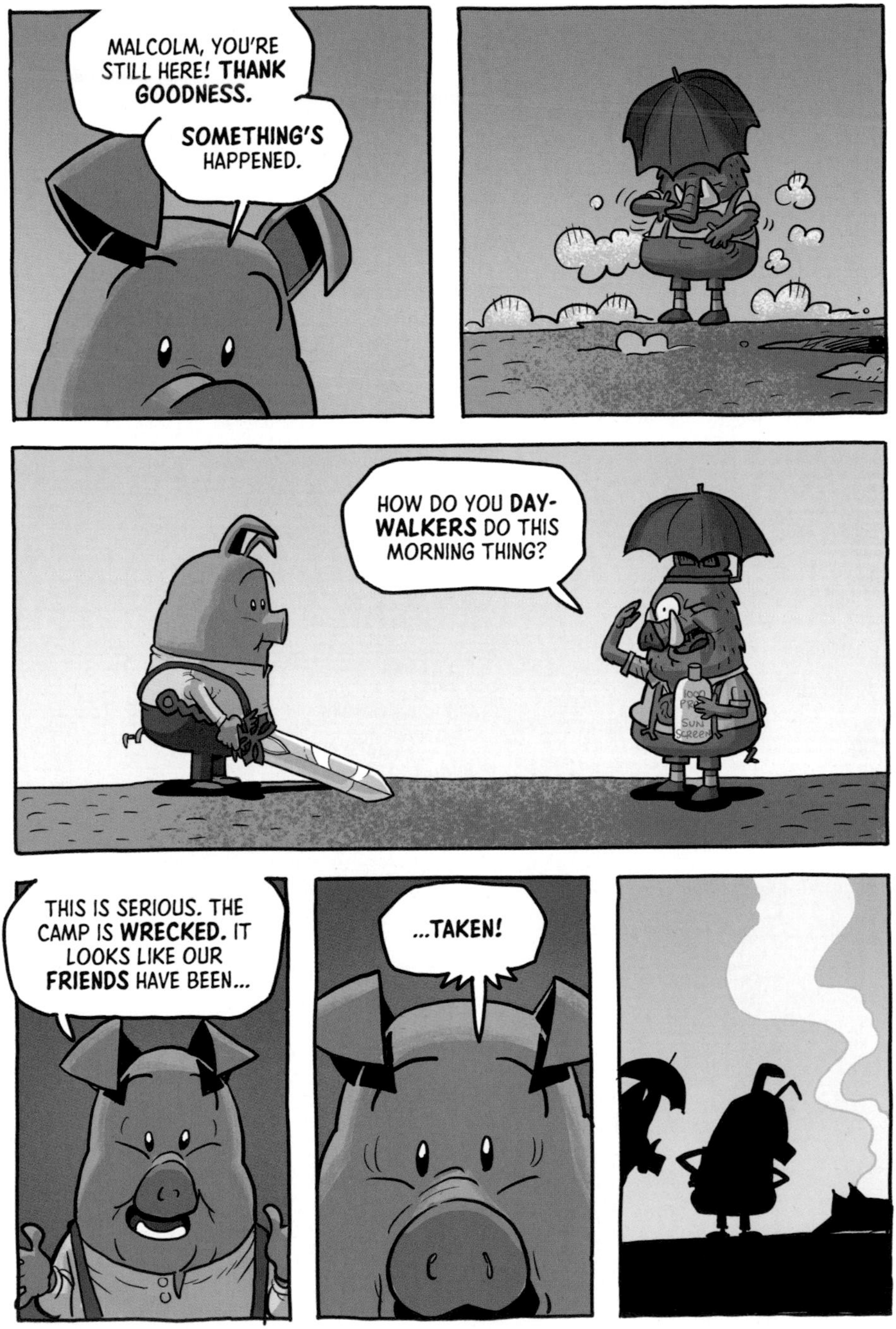
MALCOLM, YOU'RE STILL HERE! **THANK GOODNESS.**
SOMETHING'S HAPPENED.
HOW DO YOU **DAY-WALKERS** DO THIS MORNING THING?
1000 PF SUN SCREEN
THIS IS SERIOUS. THE CAMP IS **WRECKED.** IT LOOKS LIKE OUR **FRIENDS** HAVE BEEN...
...TAKEN!

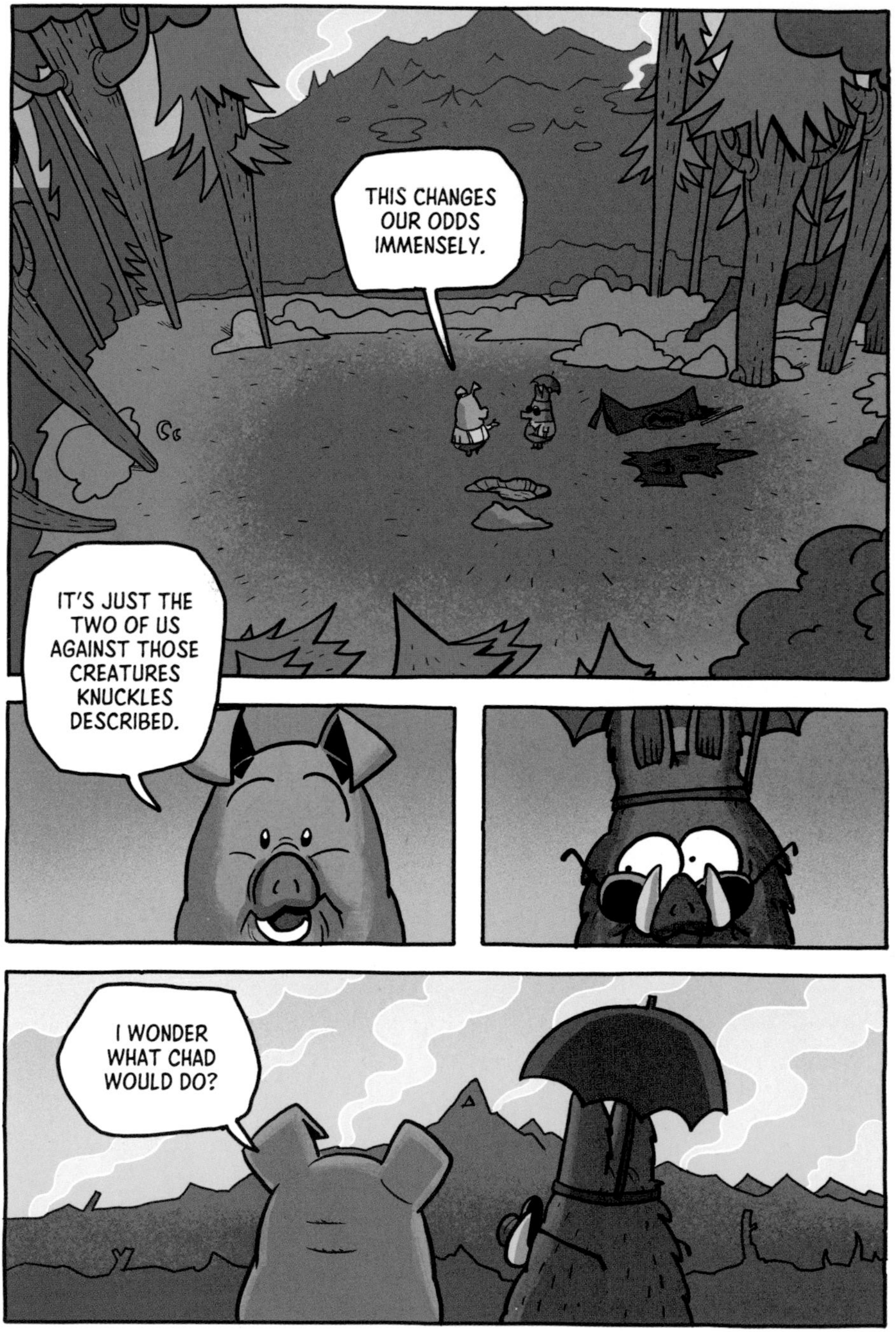
THIS CHANGES OUR ODDS IMMENSELY.
IT'S JUST THE TWO OF US AGAINST THOSE CREATURES KNUCKLES DESCRIBED.
I WONDER WHAT CHAD WOULD DO?

CHAPTER TEN

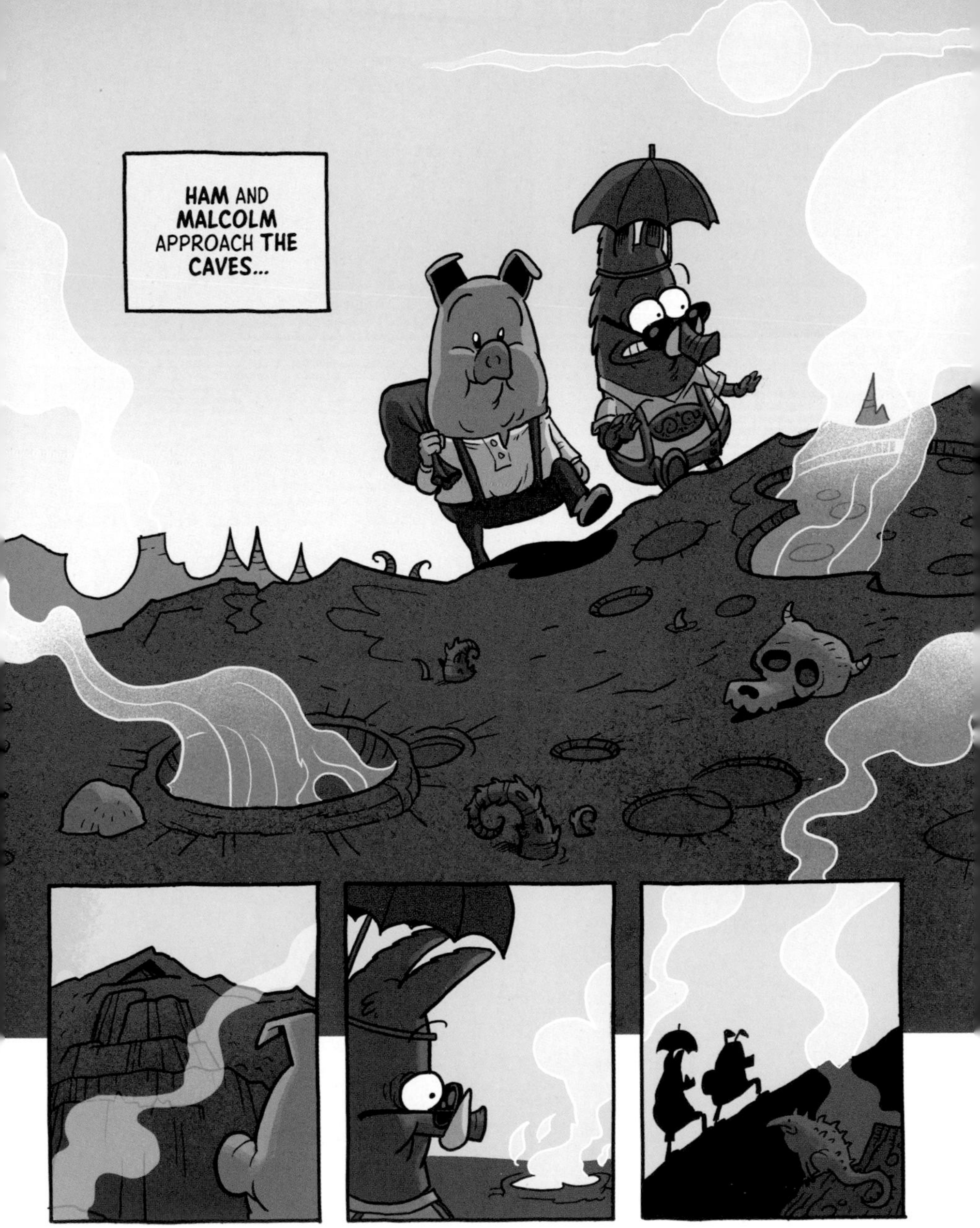
HAM AND MALCOLM APPROACH THE CAVES...

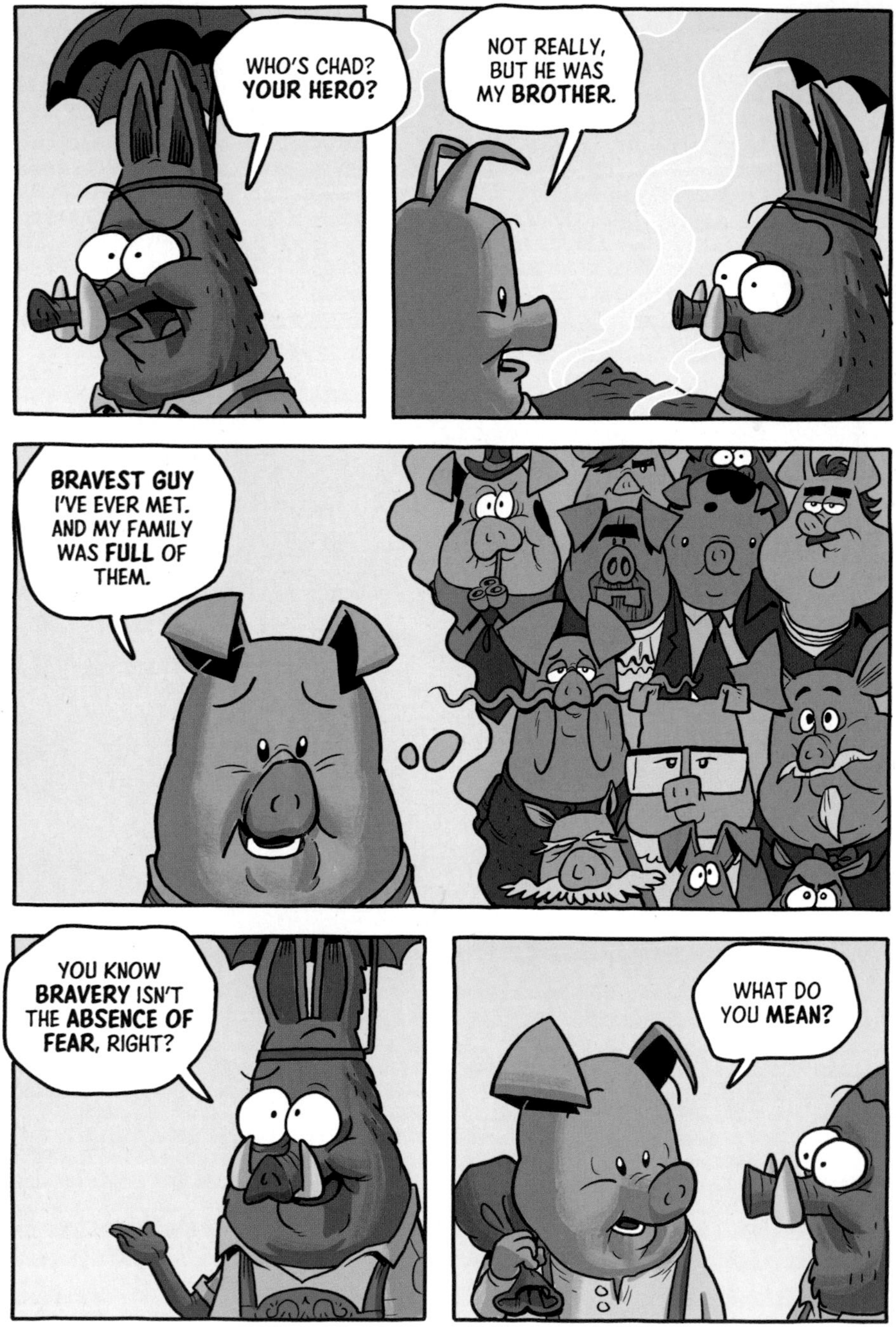
WHO'S CHAD? YOUR HERO?
NOT REALLY, BUT HE WAS MY BROTHER.
BRAVEST GUY I'VE EVER MET. AND MY FAMILY WAS FULL OF THEM.
YOU KNOW BRAVERY ISN'T THE ABSENCE OF FEAR, RIGHT?
WHAT DO YOU MEAN?

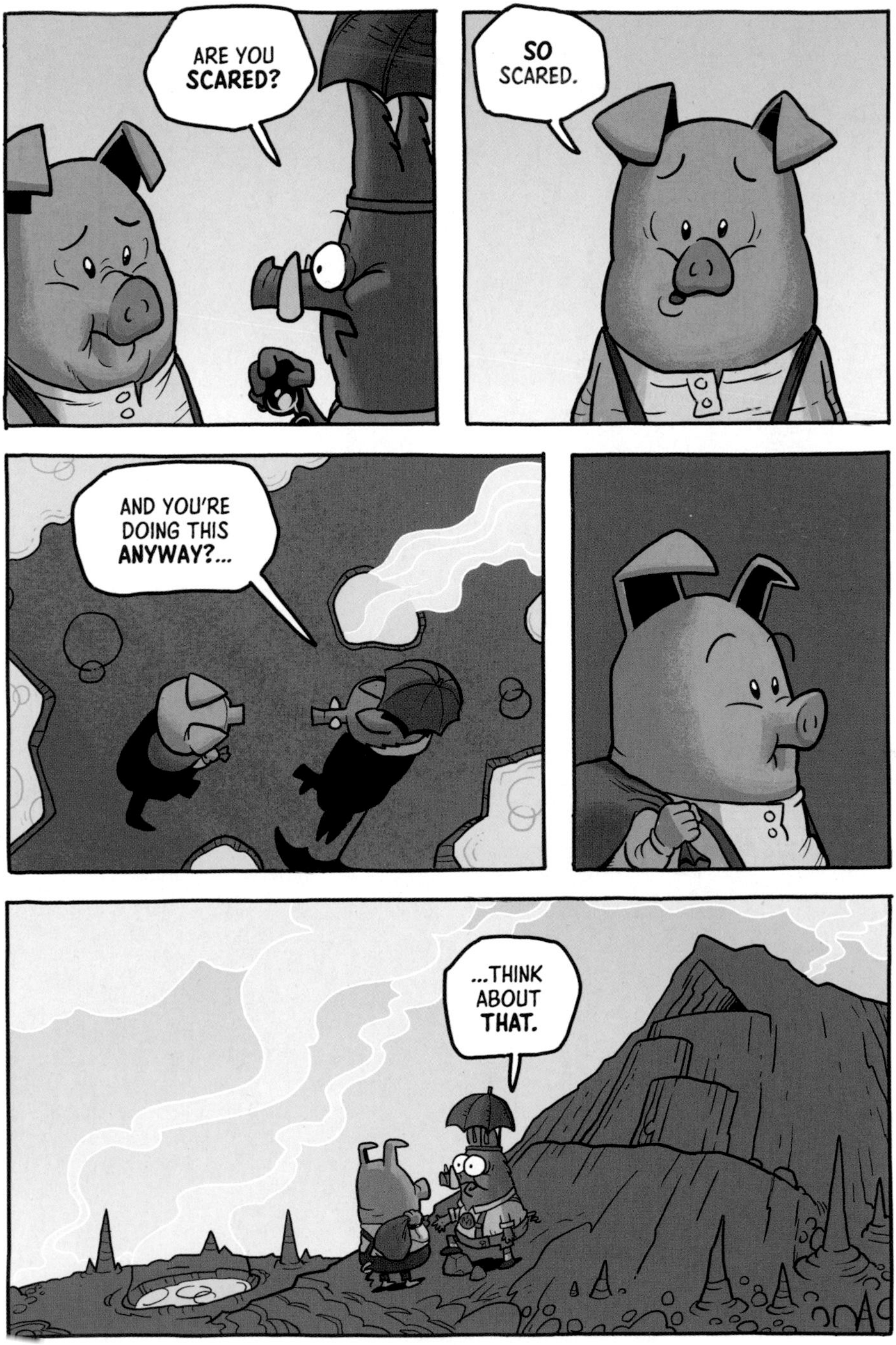
ARE YOU SCARED?
SO SCARED.
AND YOU'RE DOING THIS ANYWAY?...
...THINK ABOUT THAT.

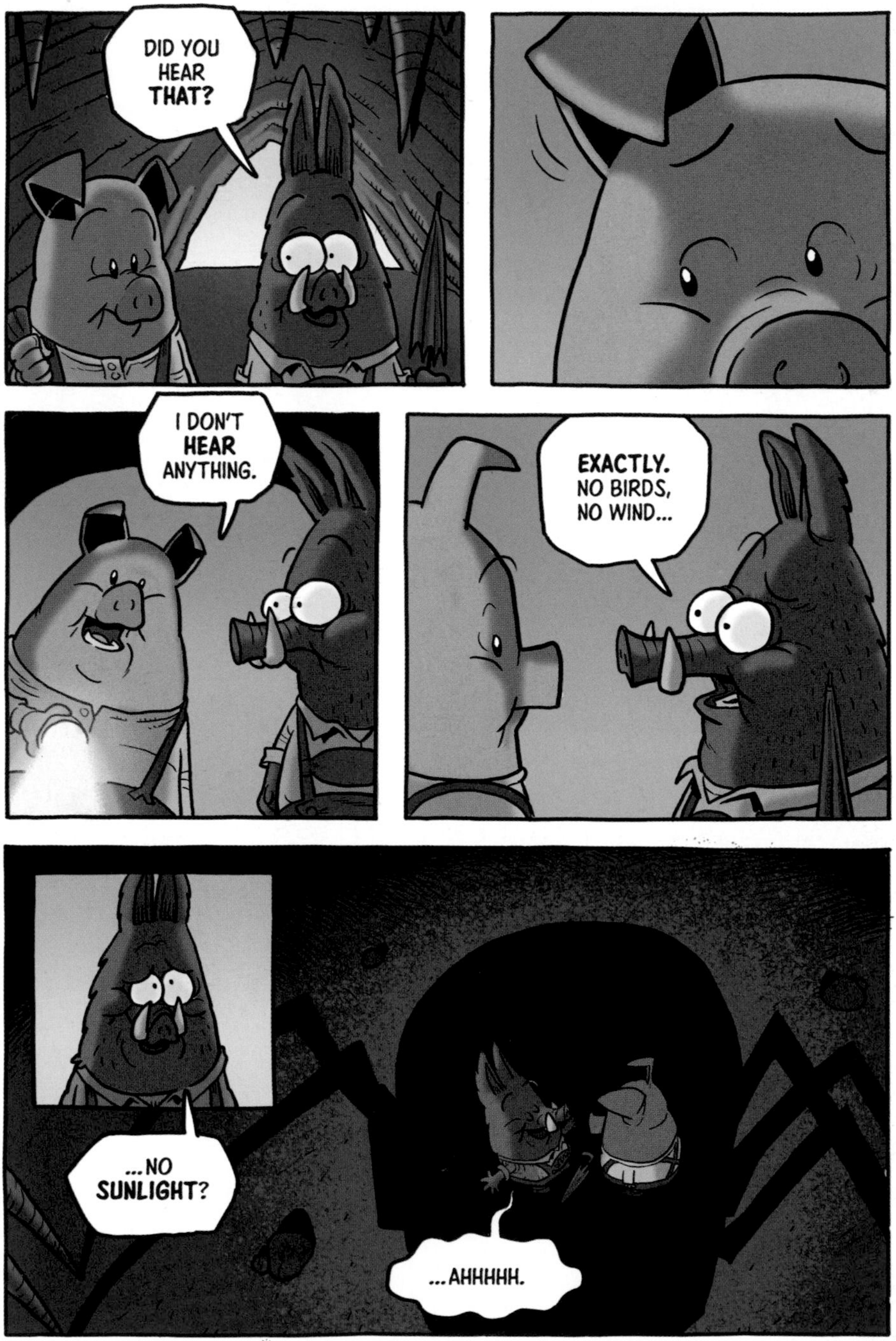
DID YOU HEAR THAT?
I DON'T HEAR ANYTHING.
EXACTLY. NO BIRDS, NO WIND...
...NO SUNLIGHT?
...AHHHHH.

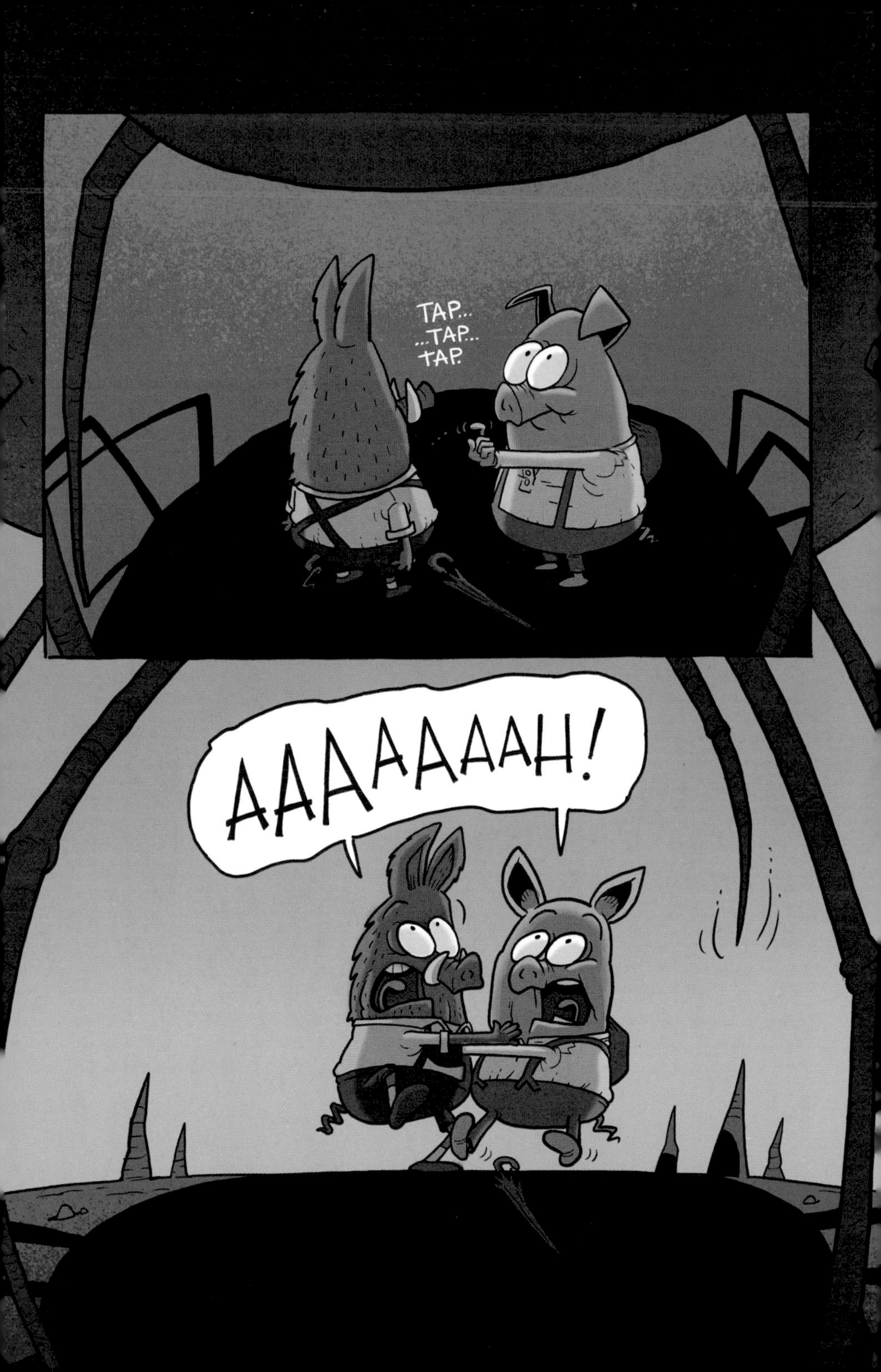
TAP...
...TAP...
TAP.
AAAAAAAH!

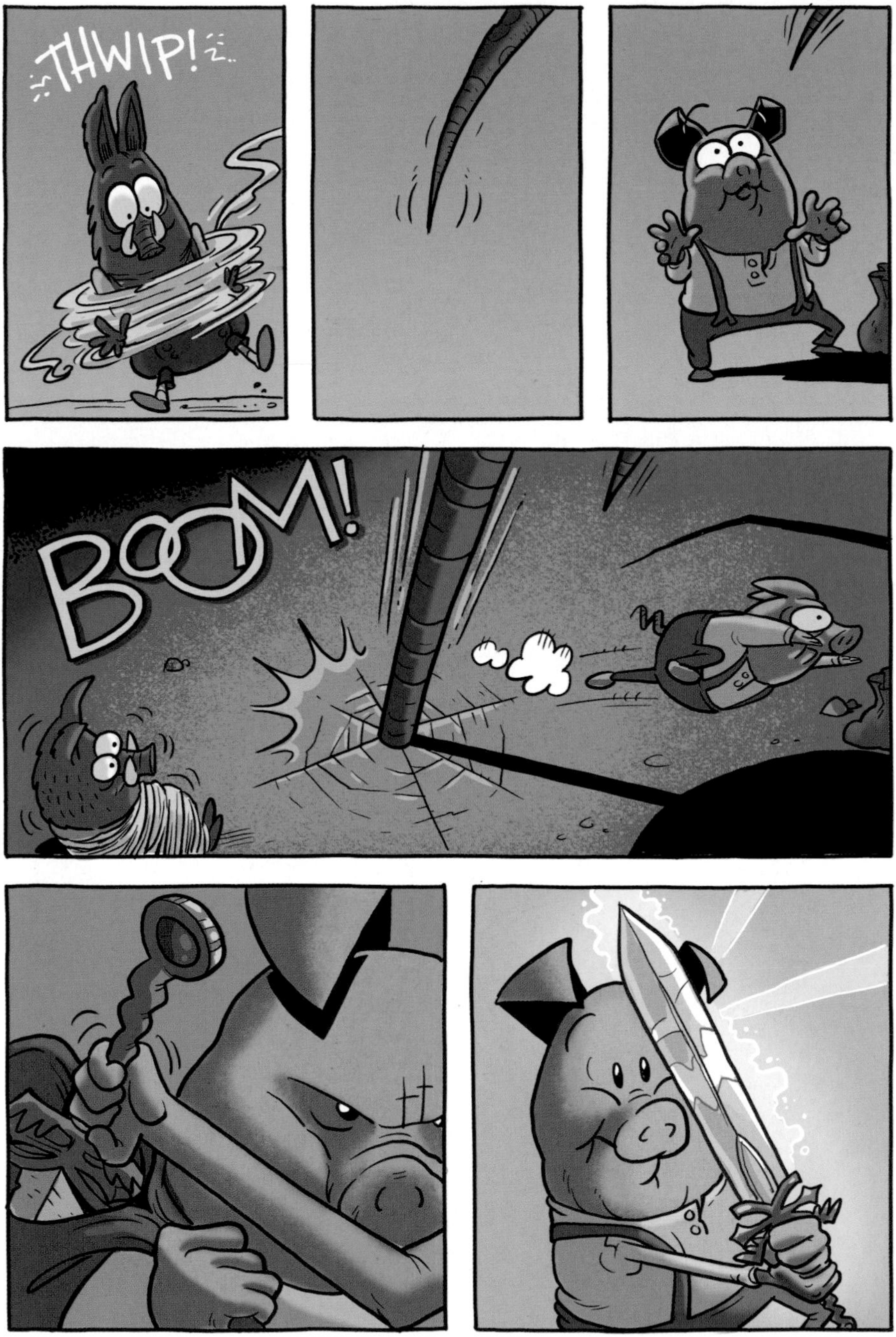
THWIP!
BOOM!

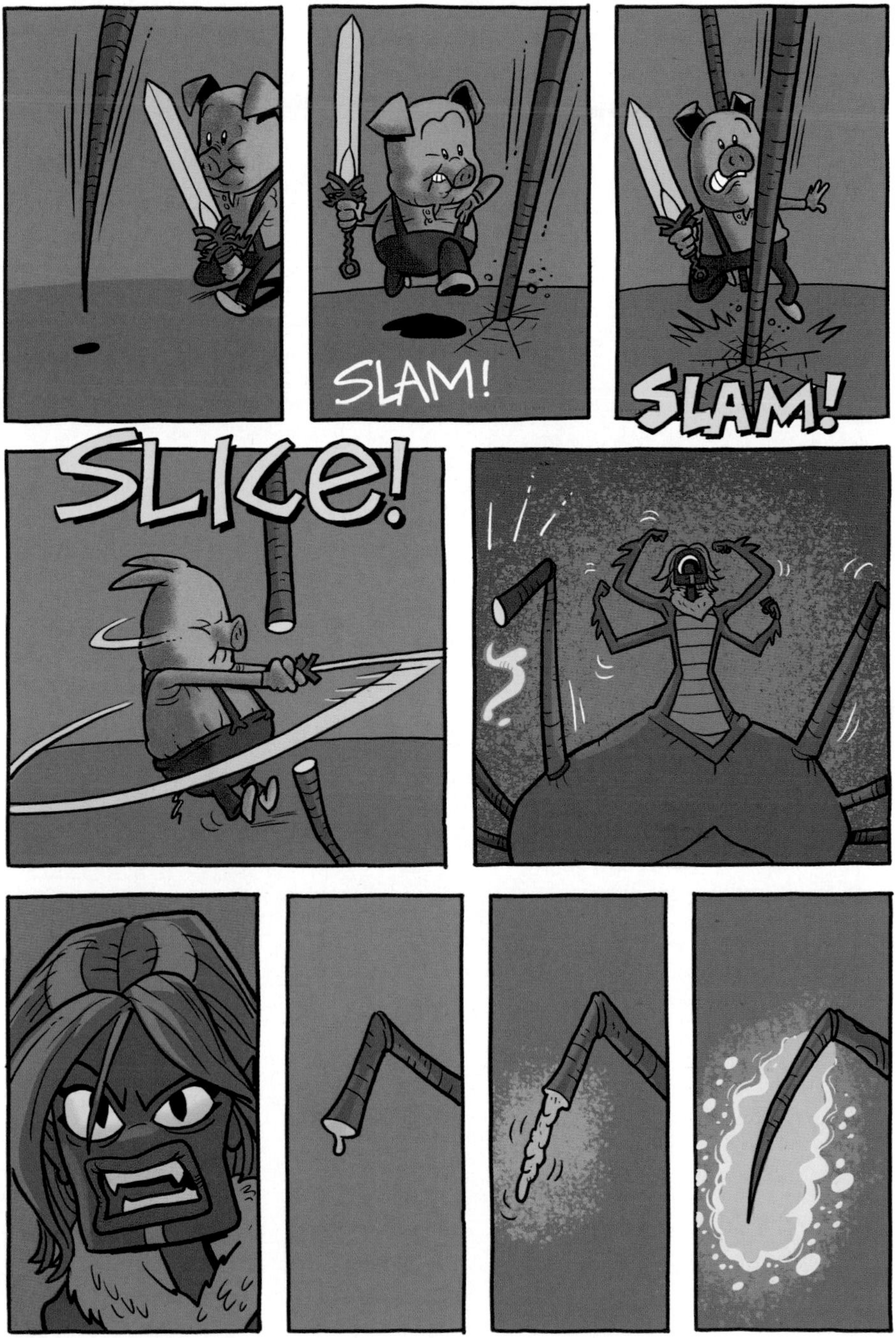
SLAM!
SLAM!
SLICE!
?

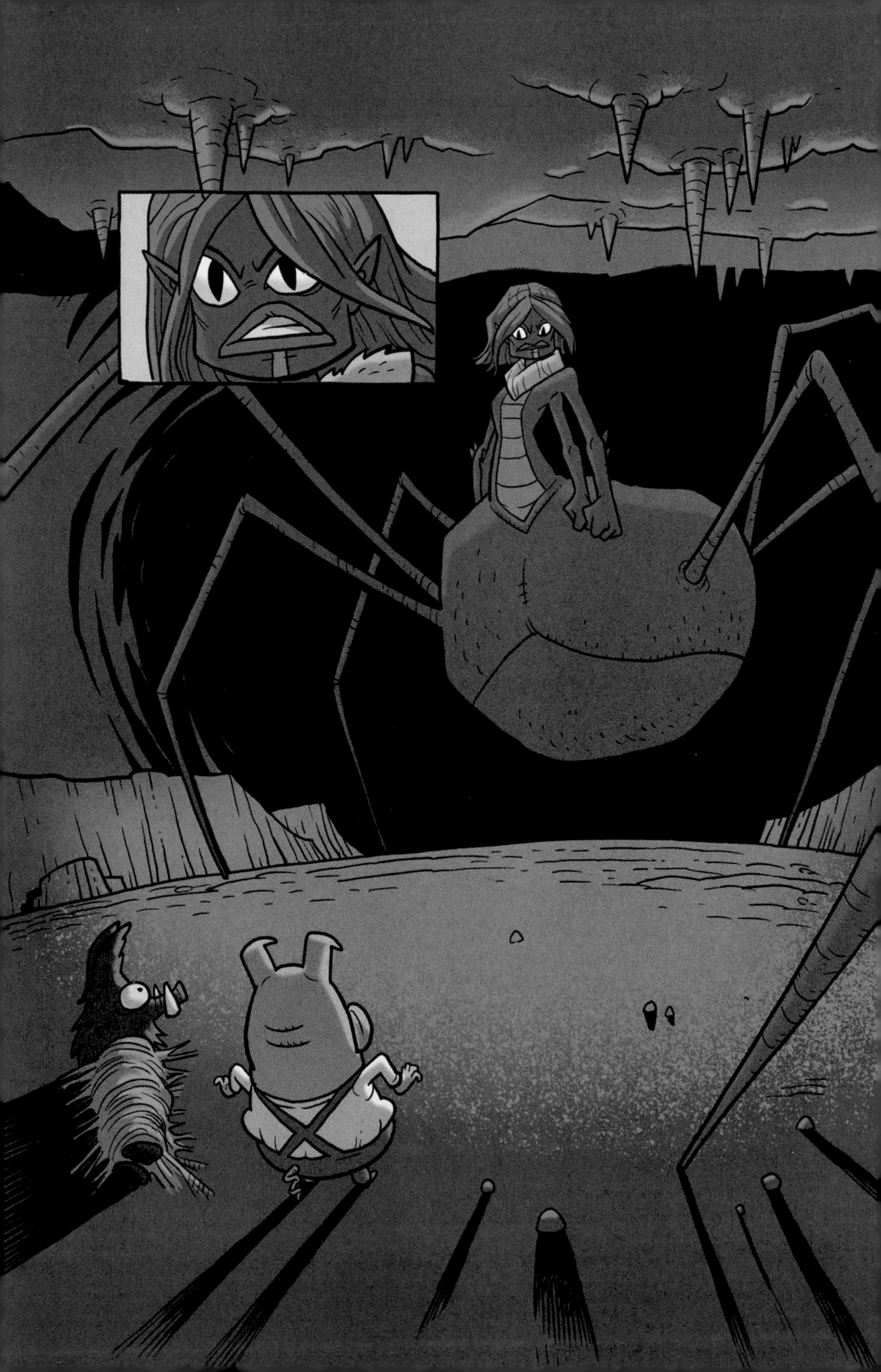

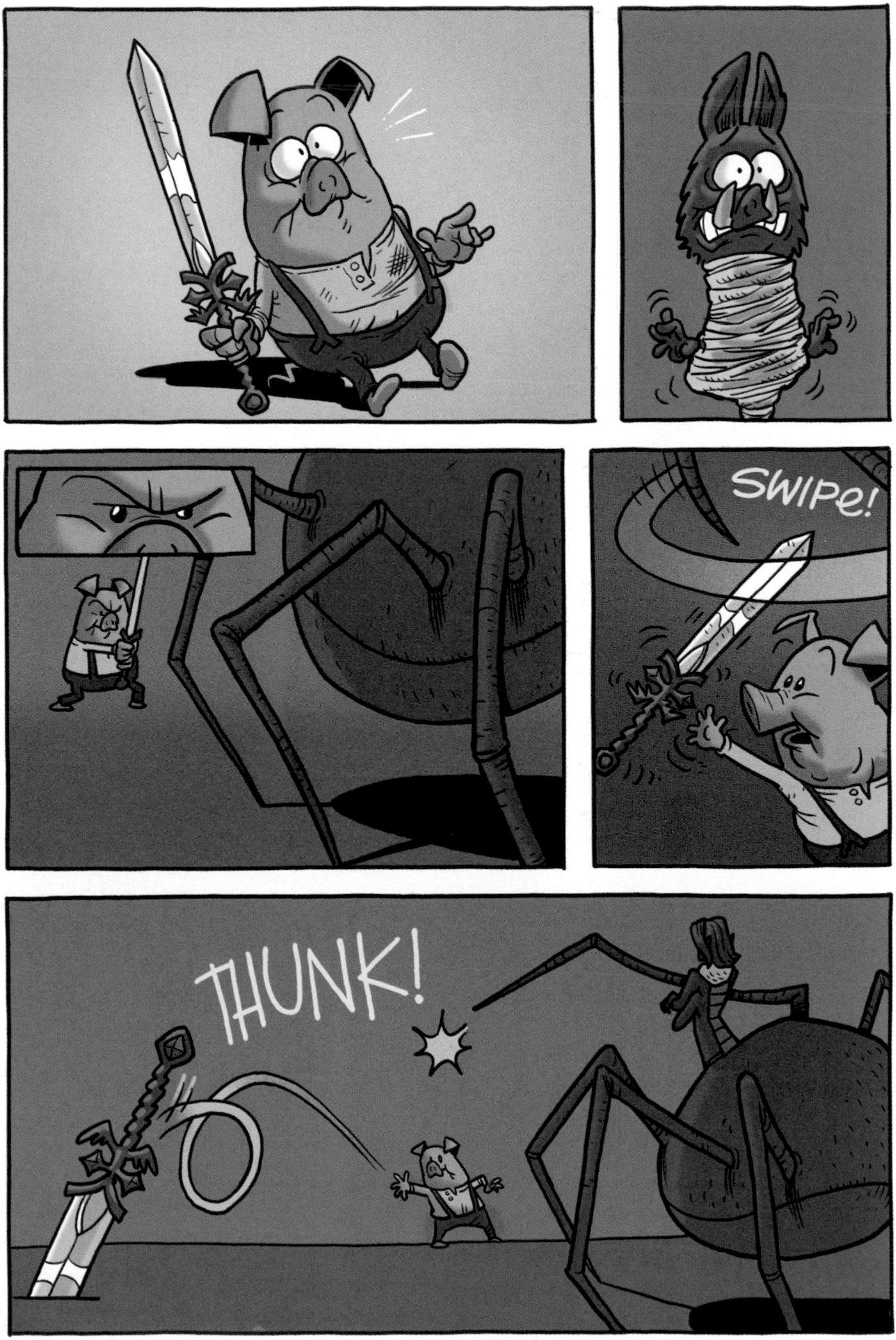
SWIPE!
THUNK!

SKITTER...
SKITTER...
...SKITTER

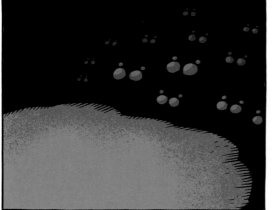

SKITTER...
SKITTER...

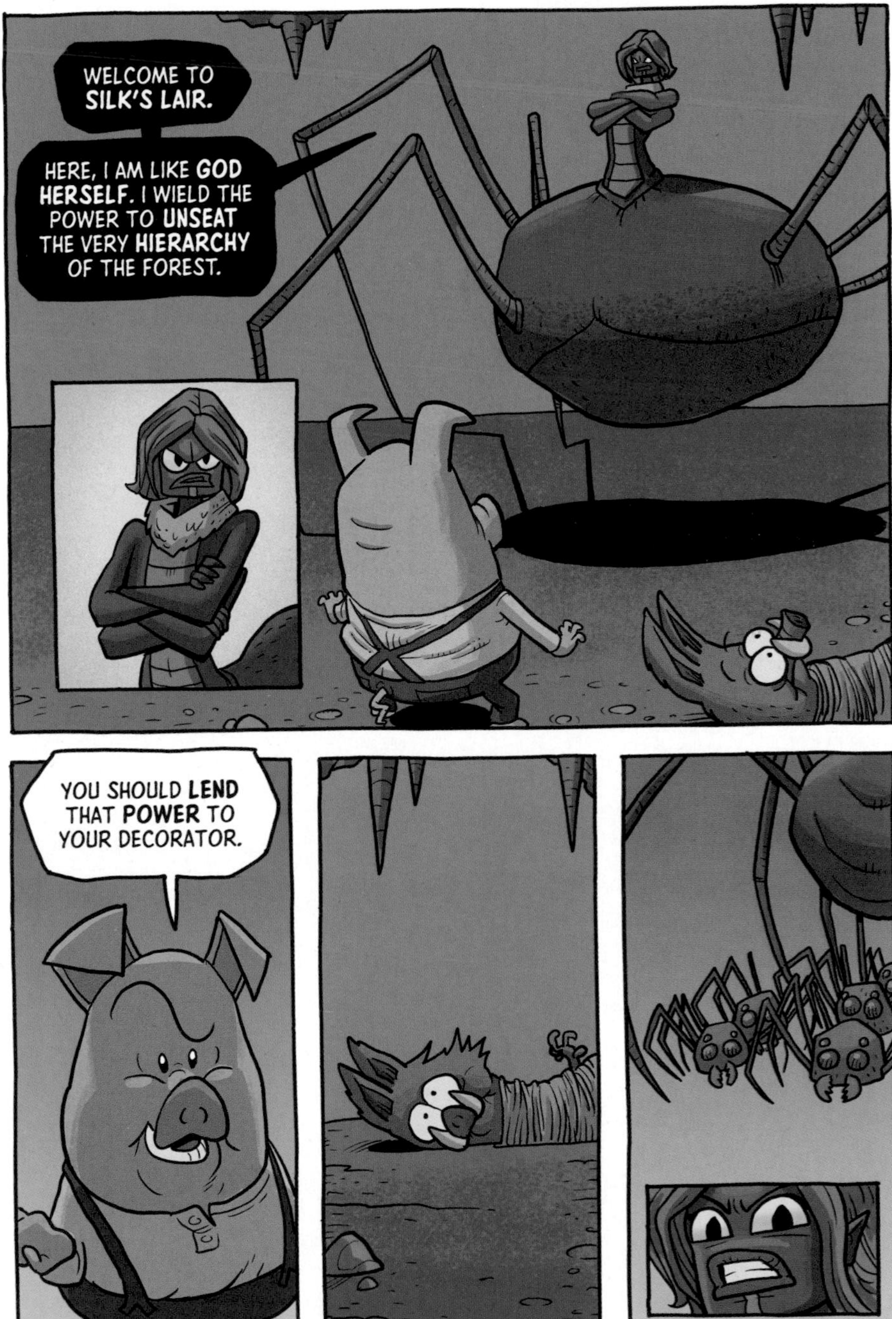
WELCOME TO SILK'S LAIR.
HERE, I AM LIKE GOD HERSELF. I WIELD THE POWER TO UNSEAT THE VERY HIERARCHY OF THE FOREST.
YOU SHOULD LEND THAT POWER TO YOUR DECORATOR.

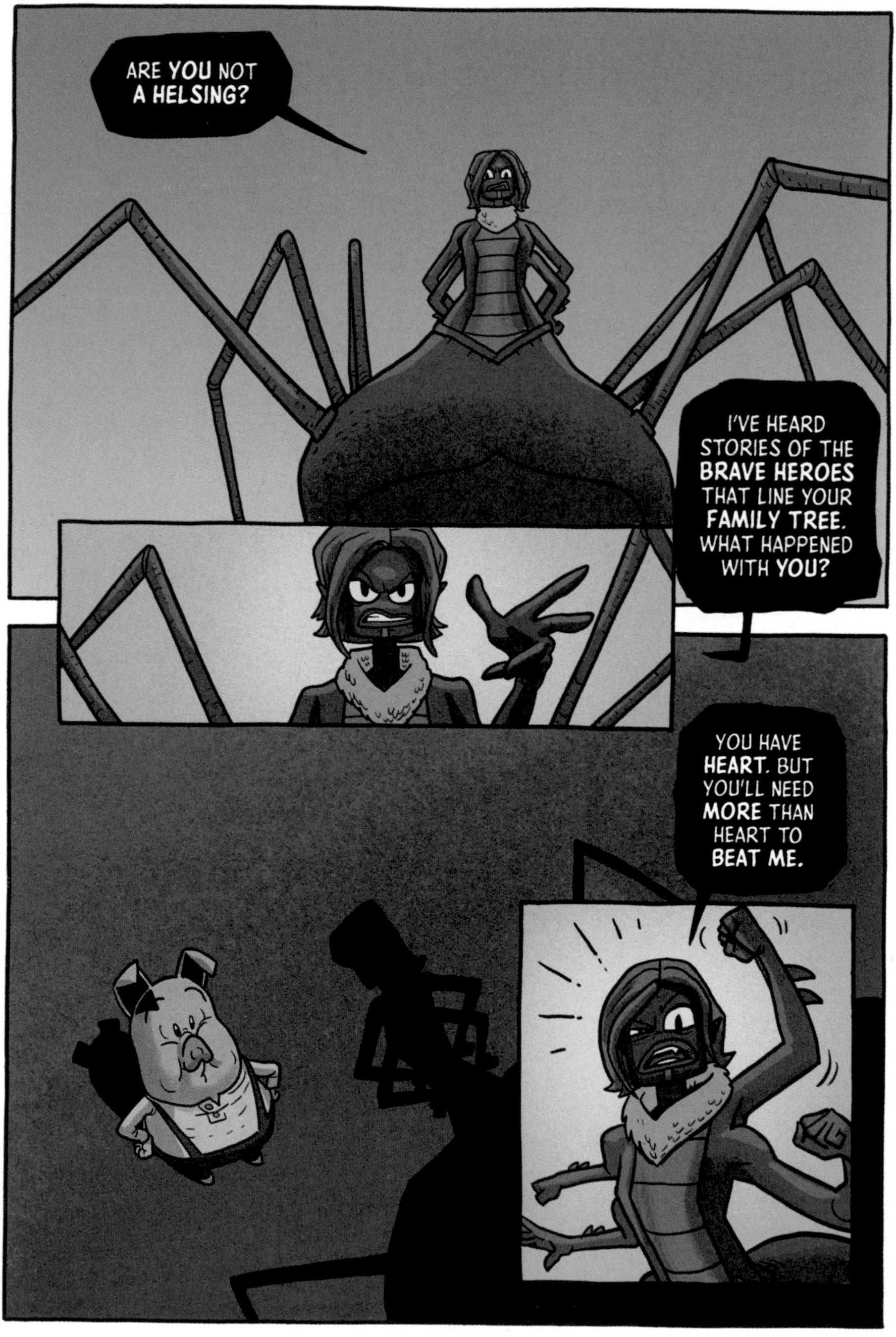
ARE YOU NOT A HELSING?
I'VE HEARD STORIES OF THE BRAVE HEROES THAT LINE YOUR FAMILY TREE. WHAT HAPPENED WITH YOU?
YOU HAVE HEART. BUT YOU'LL NEED MORE THAN HEART TO BEAT ME.

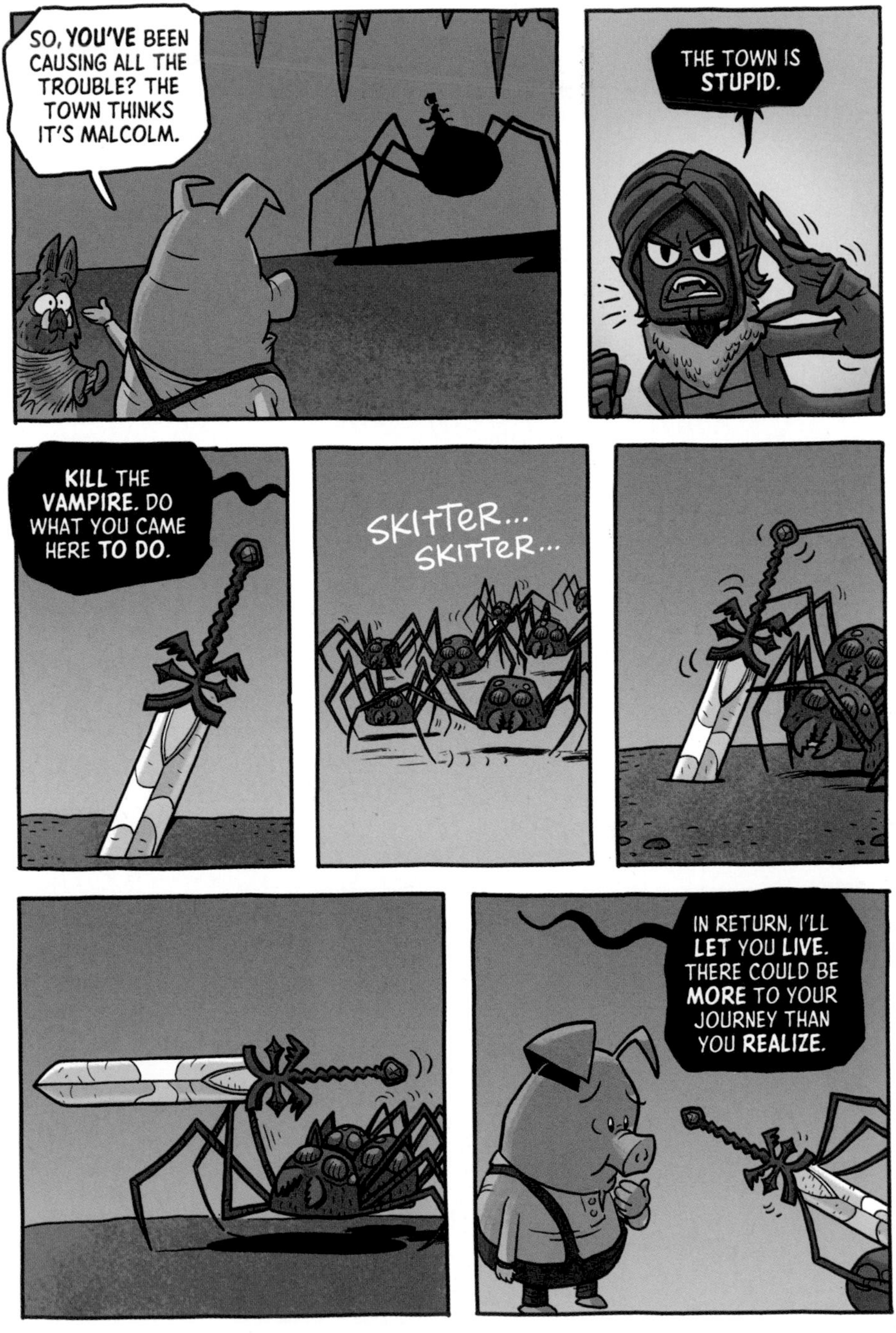
SO, YOU'VE BEEN CAUSING ALL THE TROUBLE? THE TOWN THINKS IT'S MALCOLM.
THE TOWN IS STUPID.
KILL THE VAMPIRE. DO WHAT YOU CAME HERE TO DO.
SKITTER... SKITTER...
IN RETURN, I'LL LET YOU LIVE. THERE COULD BE MORE TO YOUR JOURNEY THAN YOU REALIZE.

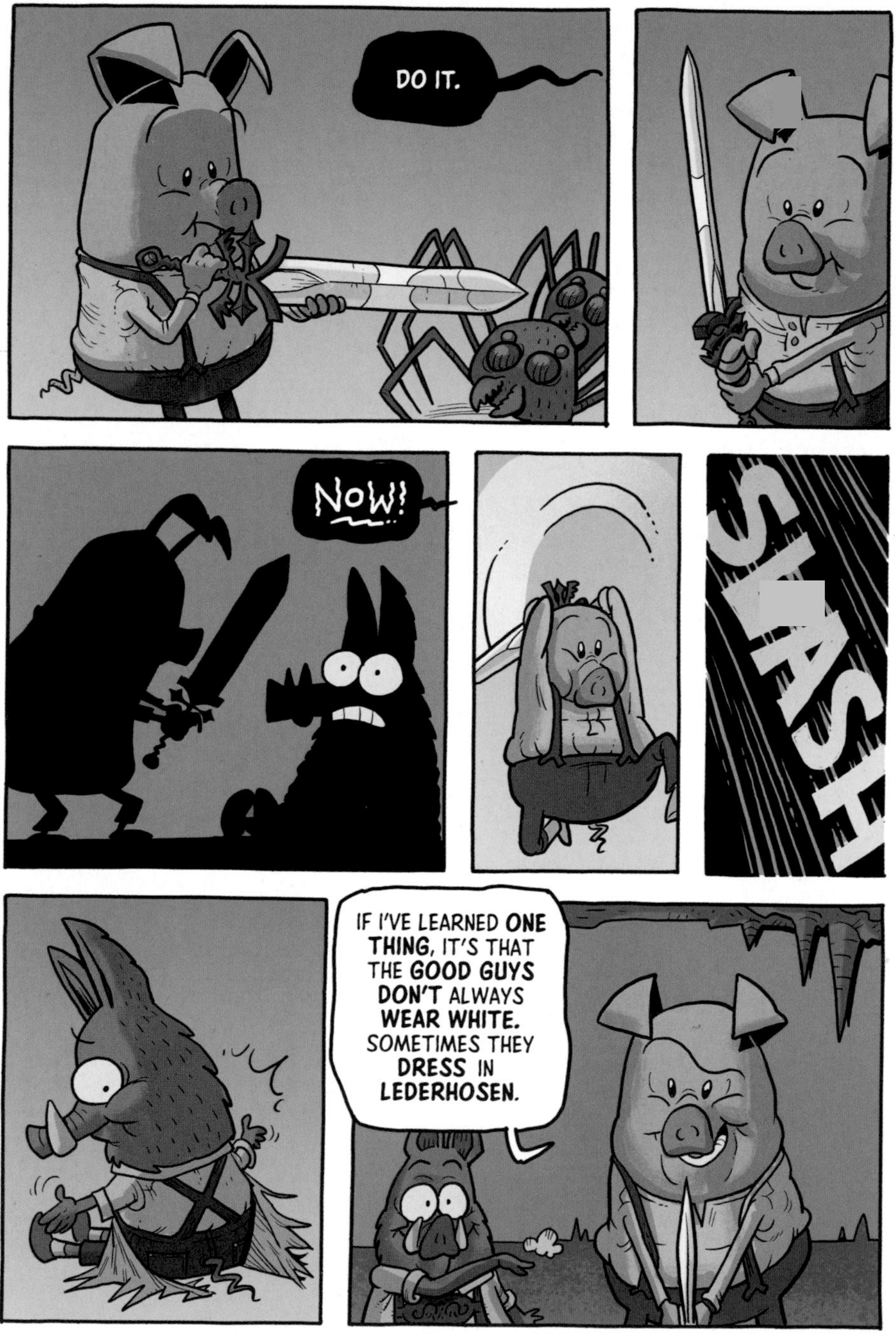
DO IT.
NOW!
SLASH
IF I'VE LEARNED ONE THING, IT'S THAT THE GOOD GUYS DON'T ALWAYS WEAR WHITE. SOMETIMES THEY DRESS IN LEDERHOSEN.

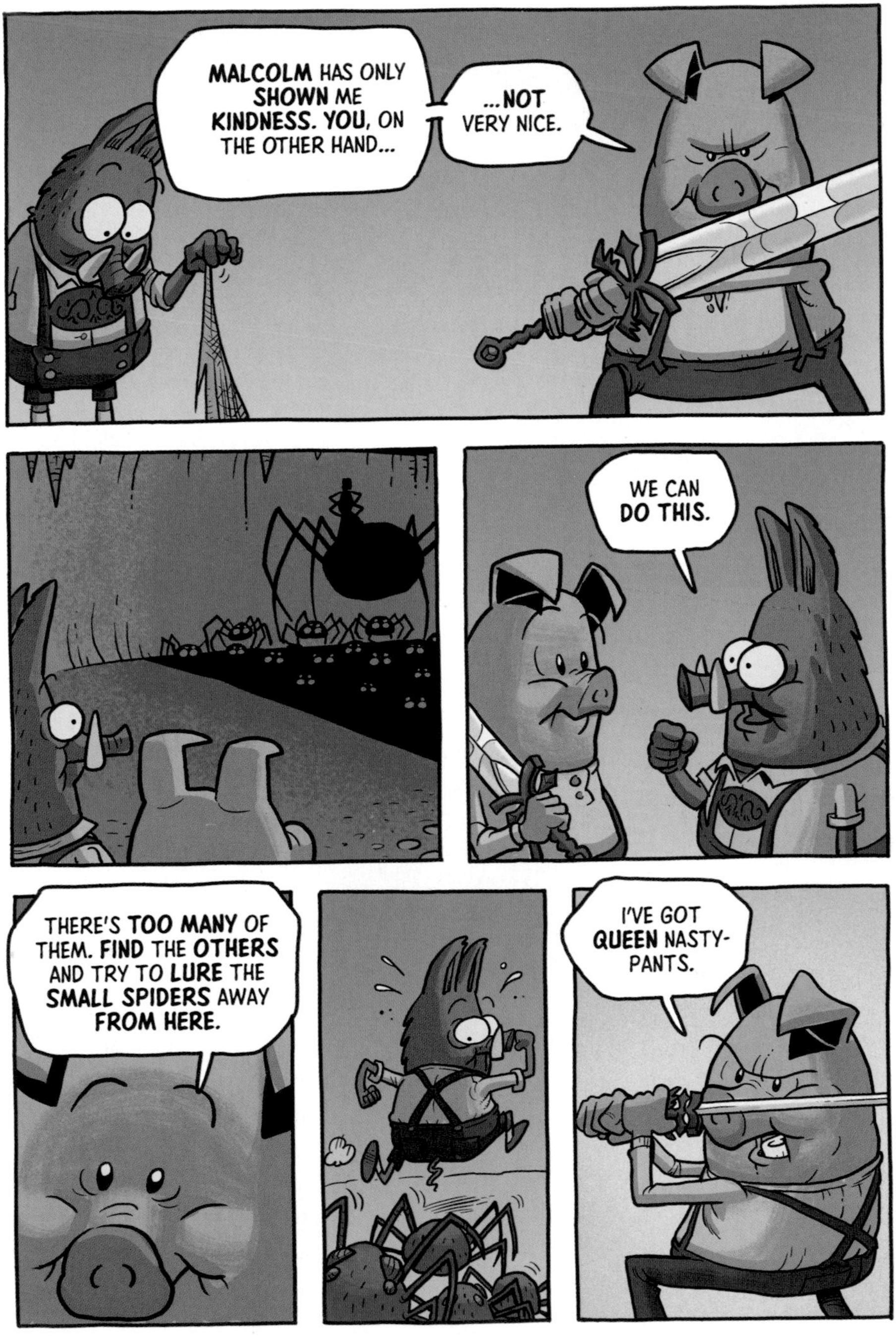
MALCOLM HAS ONLY SHOWN ME KINDNESS. YOU, ON THE OTHER HAND...
...NOT VERY NICE.
WE CAN DO THIS.
THERE'S TOO MANY OF THEM. FIND THE OTHERS AND TRY TO LURE THE SMALL SPIDERS AWAY FROM HERE.
I'VE GOT QUEEN NASTY-PANTS.

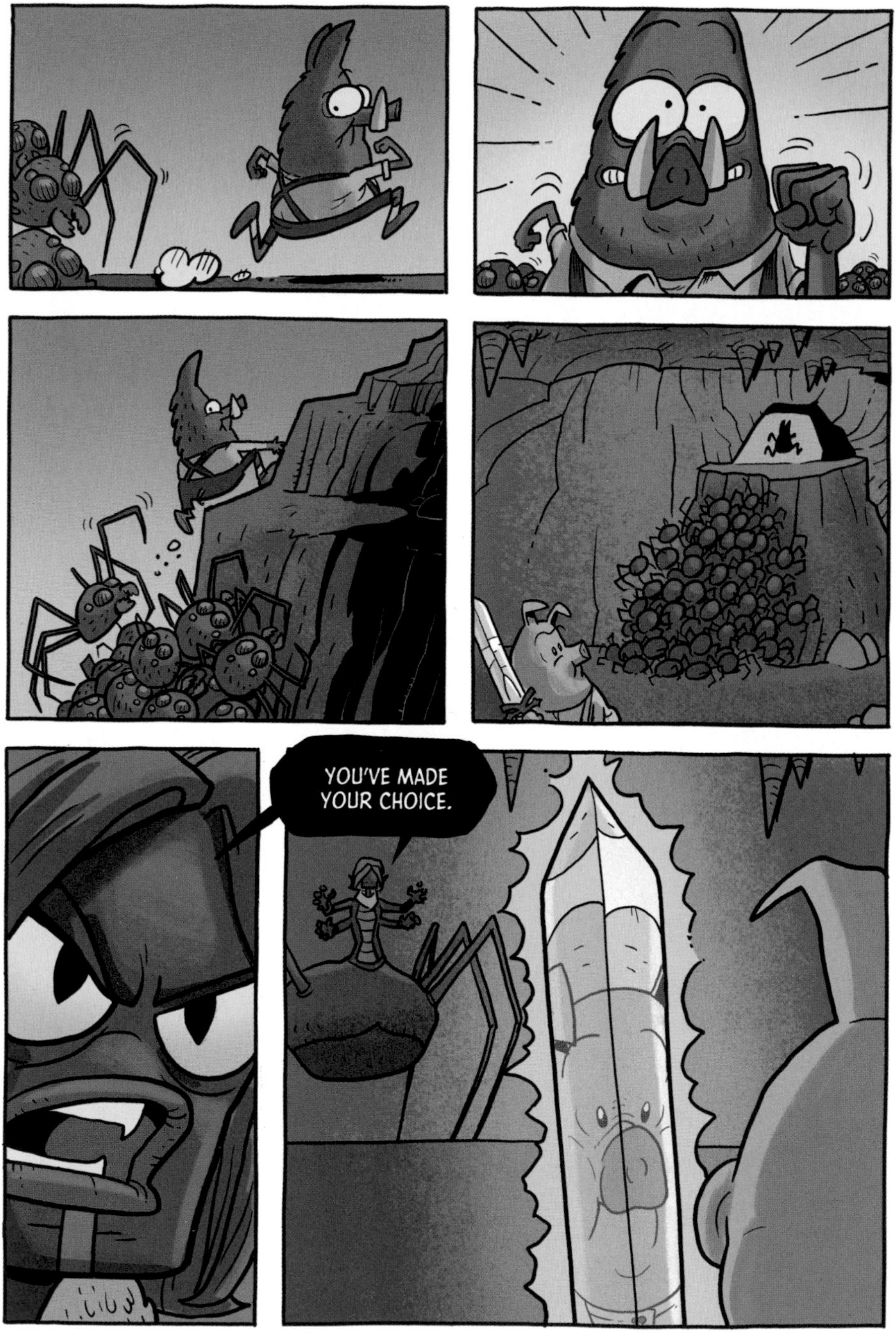
YOU'VE MADE YOUR CHOICE.

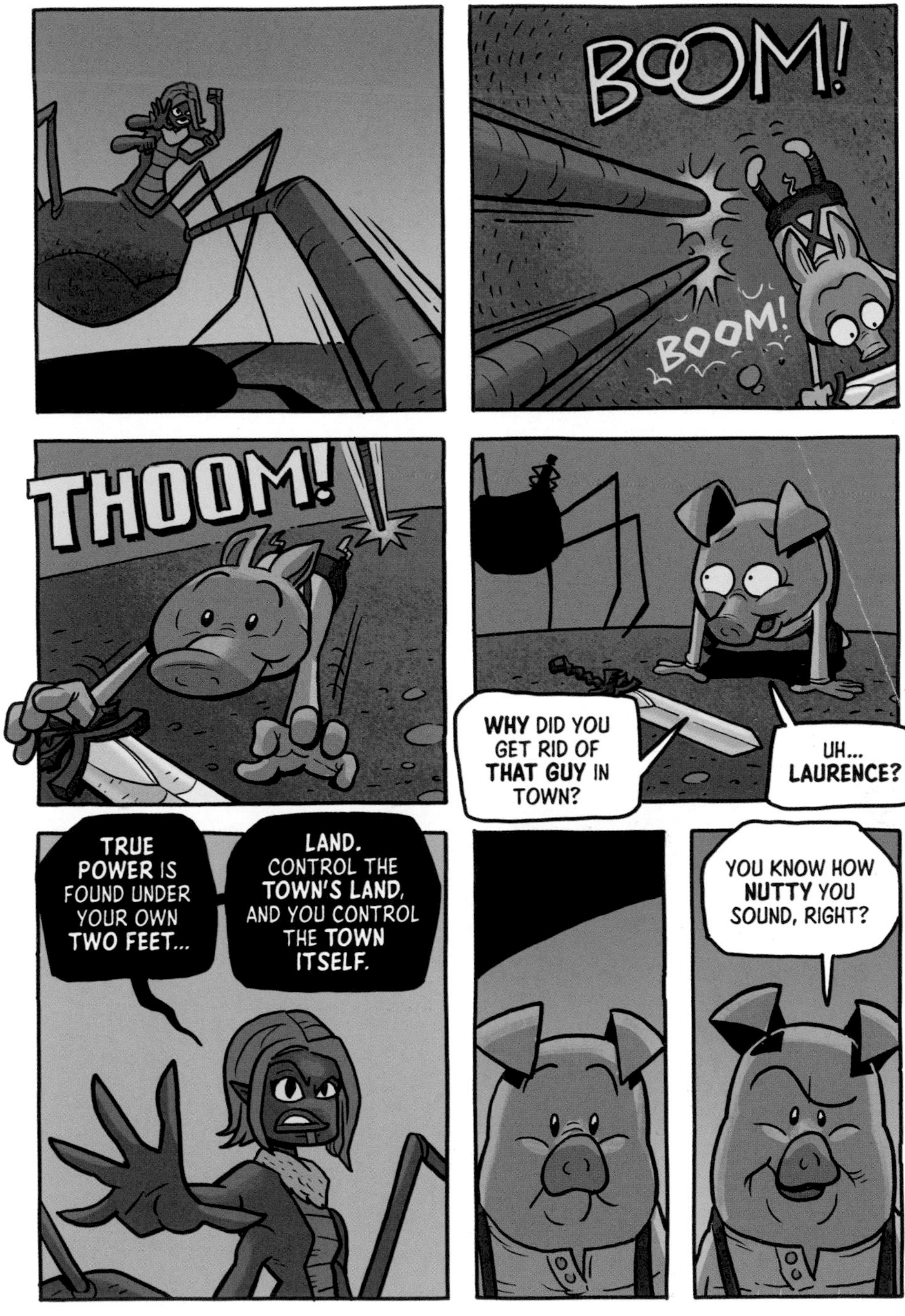
BOOM!
BOOM!
THOOM!
WHY DID YOU GET RID OF THAT GUY IN TOWN?
UH... LAURENCE?
TRUE POWER IS FOUND UNDER YOUR OWN TWO FEET...
LAND. CONTROL THE TOWN'S LAND, AND YOU CONTROL THE TOWN ITSELF.
YOU KNOW HOW NUTTY YOU SOUND, RIGHT?

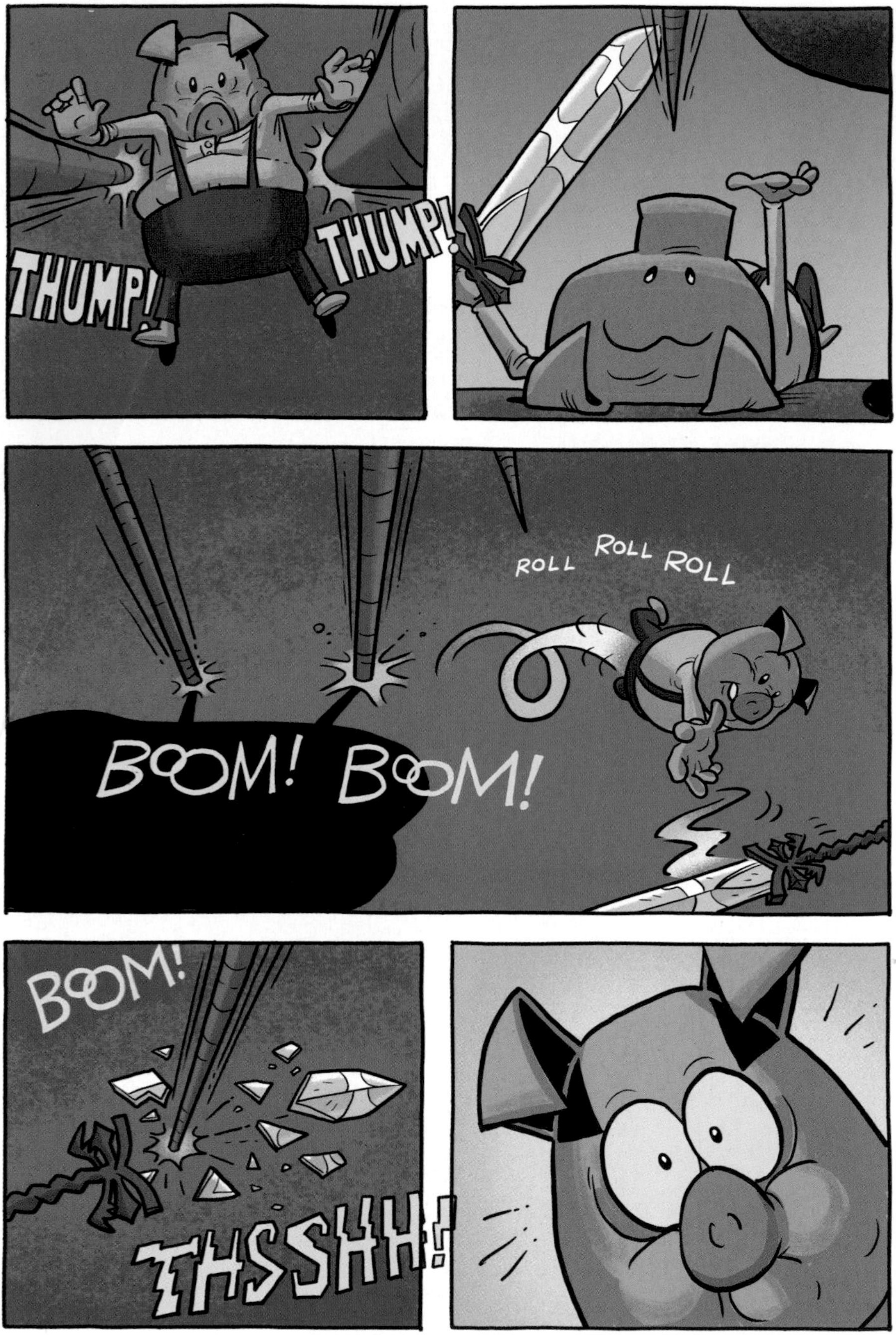
THUMP!
THUMP!
ROLL
ROLL ROLL
BOOM! BOOM!
BOOM!
THSSHH!

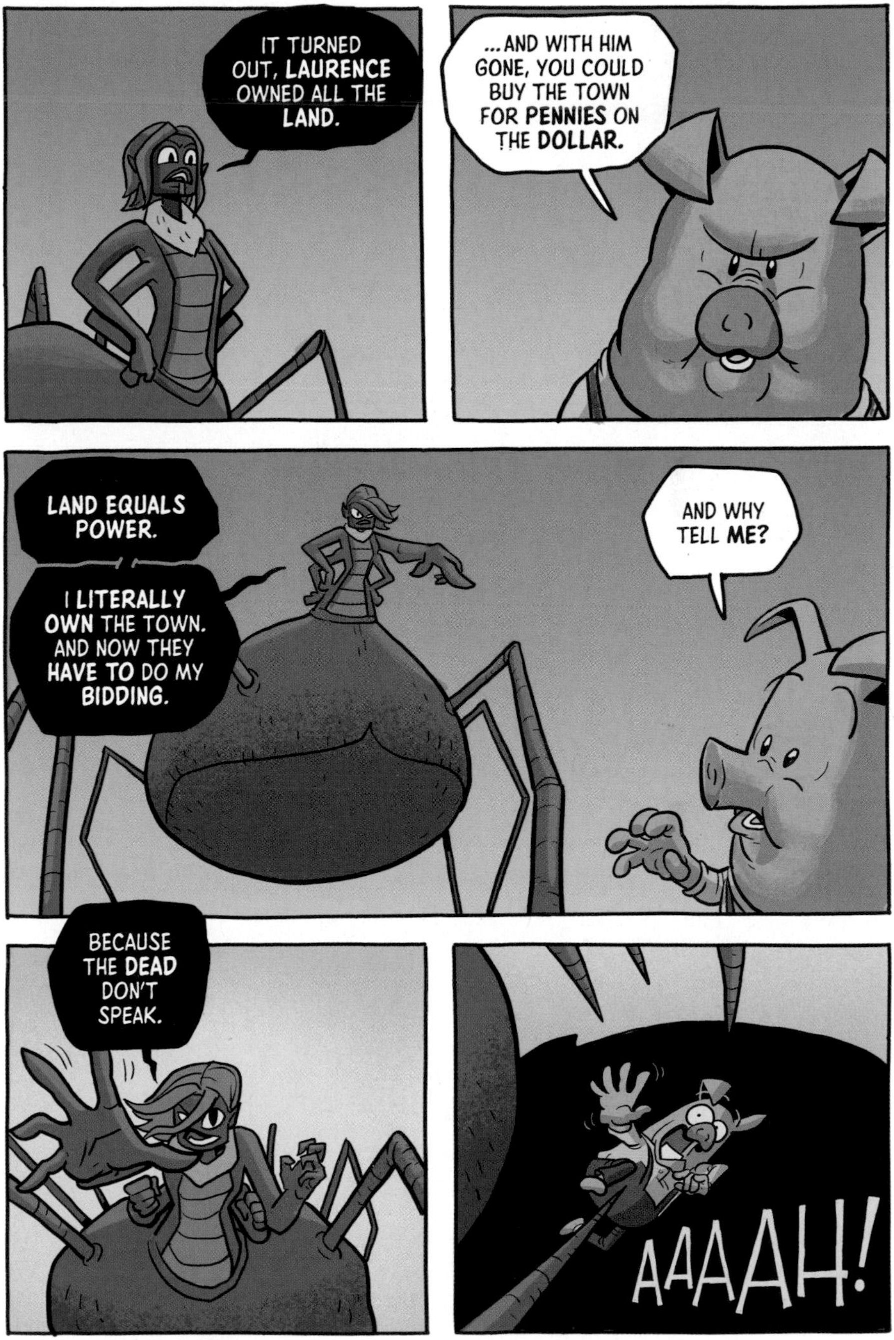
IT TURNED OUT, LAURENCE OWNED ALL THE LAND.
...AND WITH HIM GONE, YOU COULD BUY THE TOWN FOR PENNIES ON THE DOLLAR.
LAND EQUALS POWER.
I LITERALLY OWN THE TOWN. AND NOW THEY HAVE TO DO MY BIDDING.
AND WHY TELL ME?
BECAUSE THE DEAD DON'T SPEAK.
AAAAH!

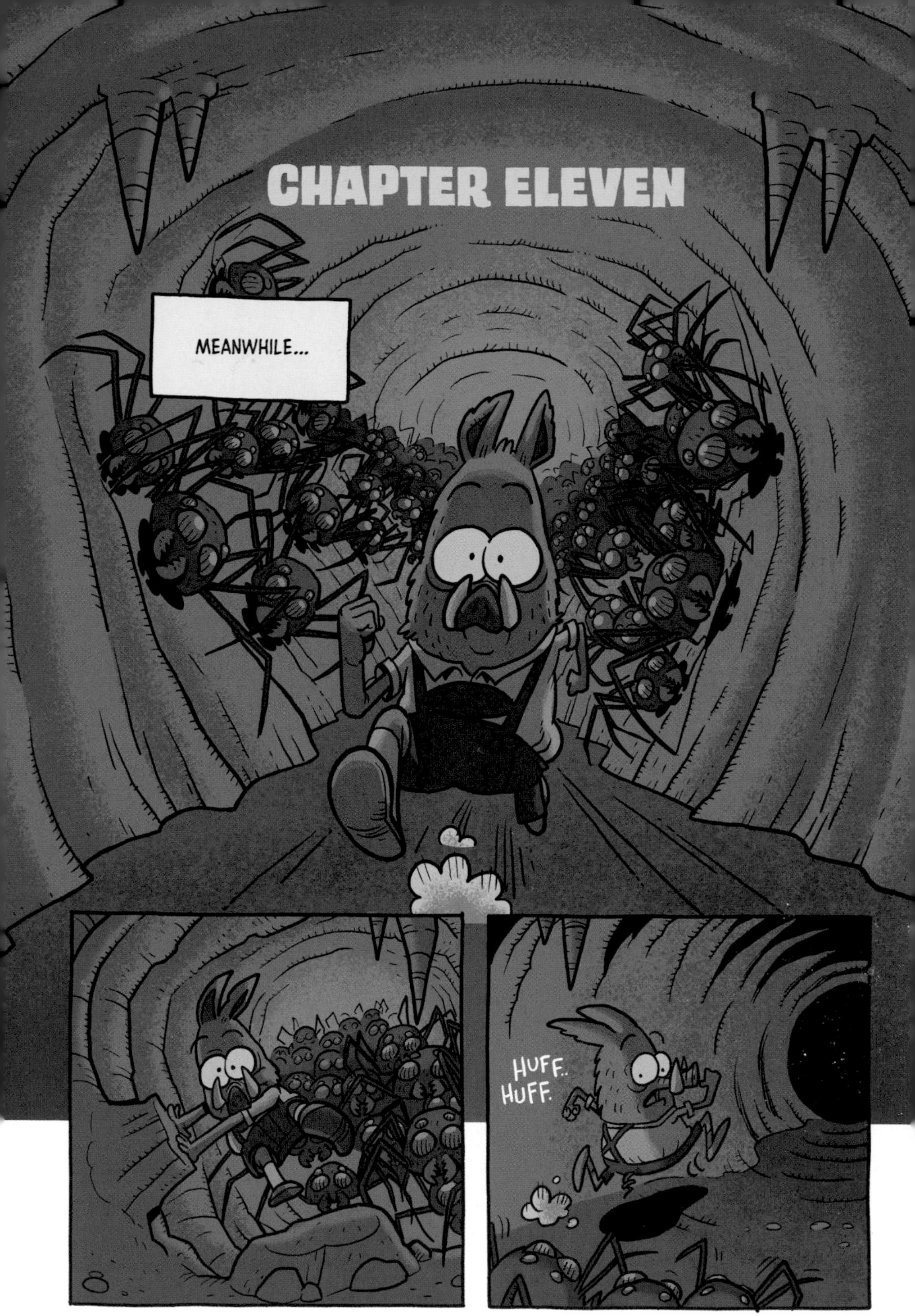
CHAPTER ELEVEN
MEANWHILE...
HUFF..
HUFF.

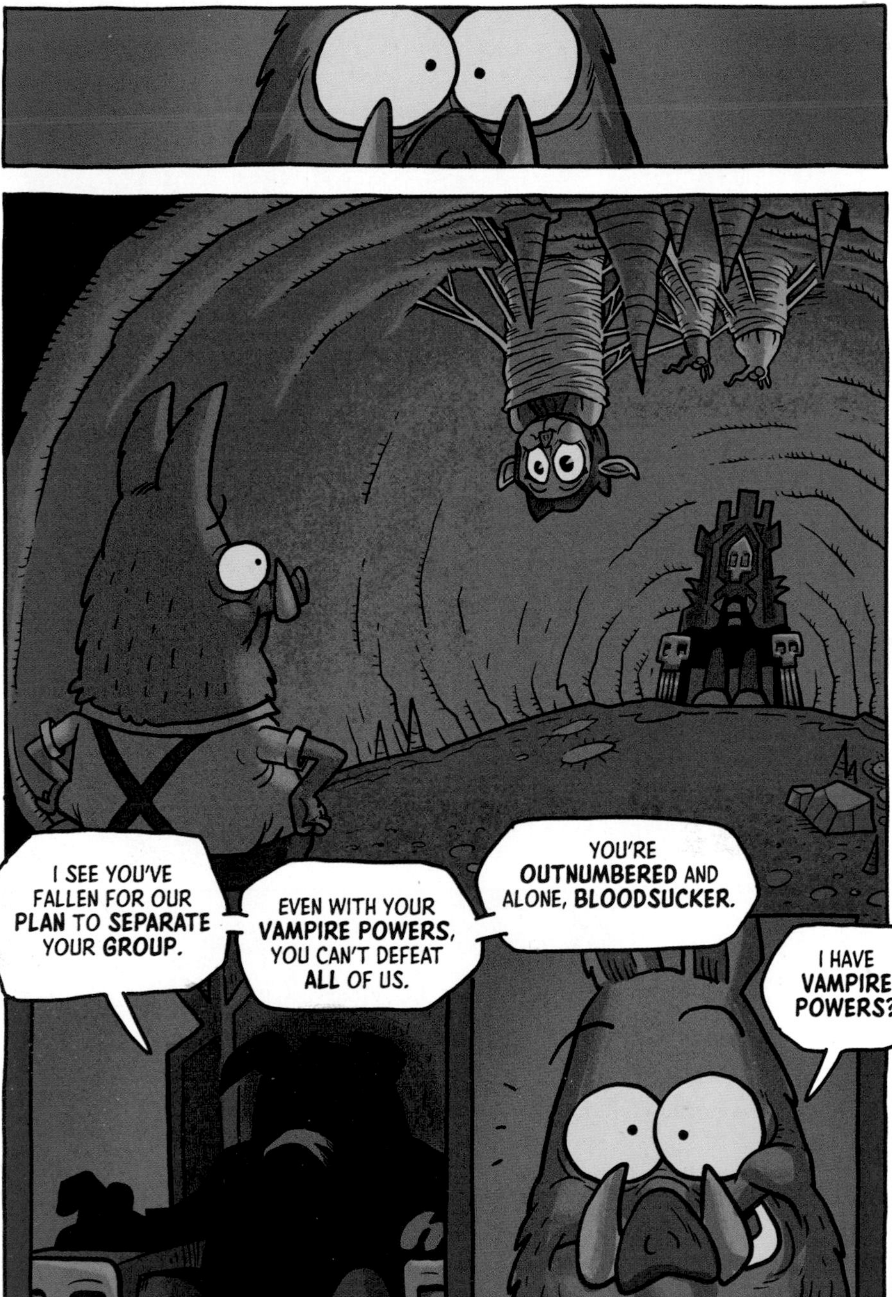
I SEE YOU'VE FALLEN FOR OUR PLAN TO SEPARATE YOUR GROUP.
EVEN WITH YOUR VAMPIRE POWERS, YOU CAN'T DEFEAT ALL OF US.
YOU'RE OUTNUMBERED AND ALONE, BLOODSUCKER.
I HAVE VAMPIRE POWERS?

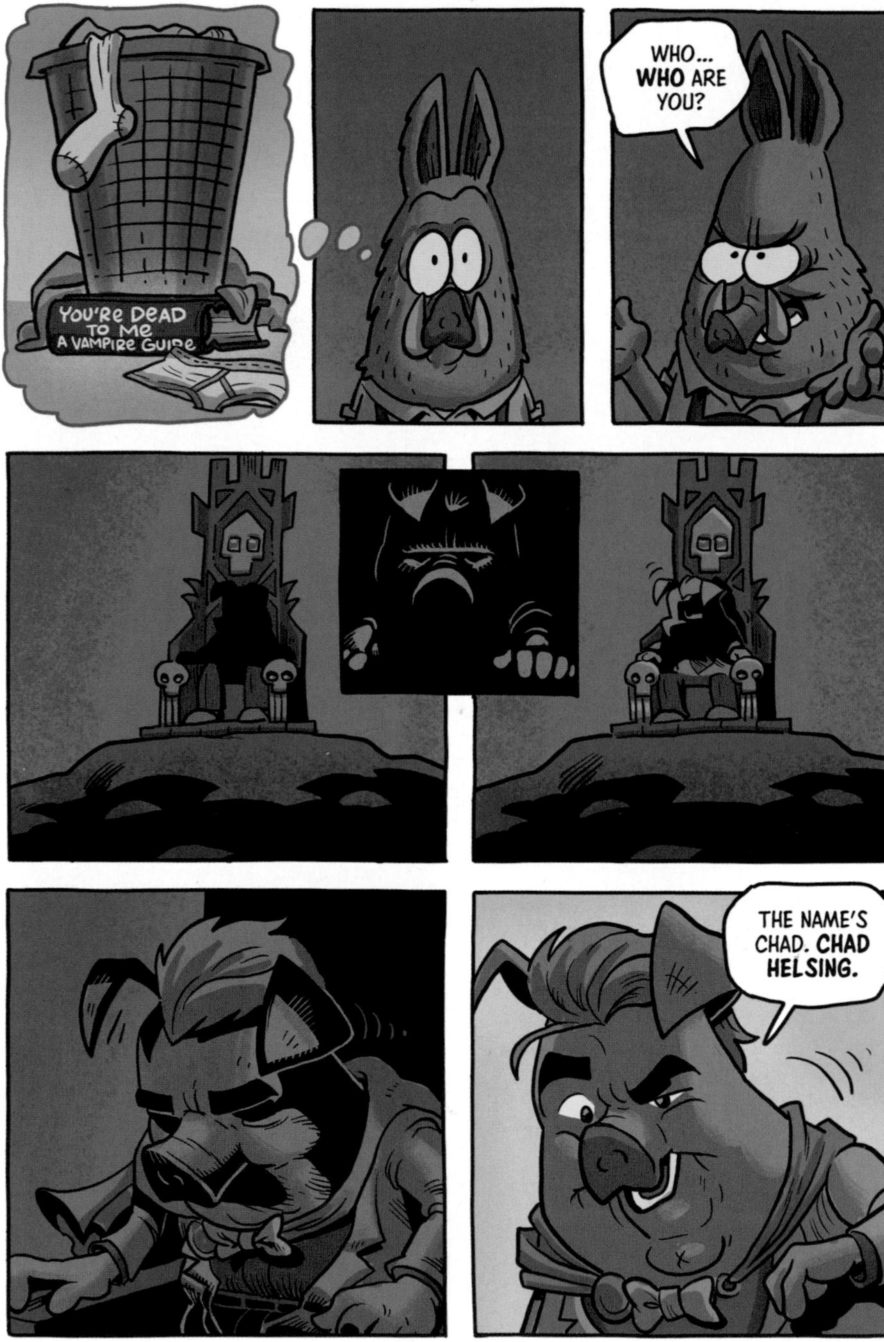
YOU'RE DEAD TO ME A VAMPIRE GUIDE
WHO... WHO ARE YOU?
THE NAME'S CHAD. CHAD HELSING.

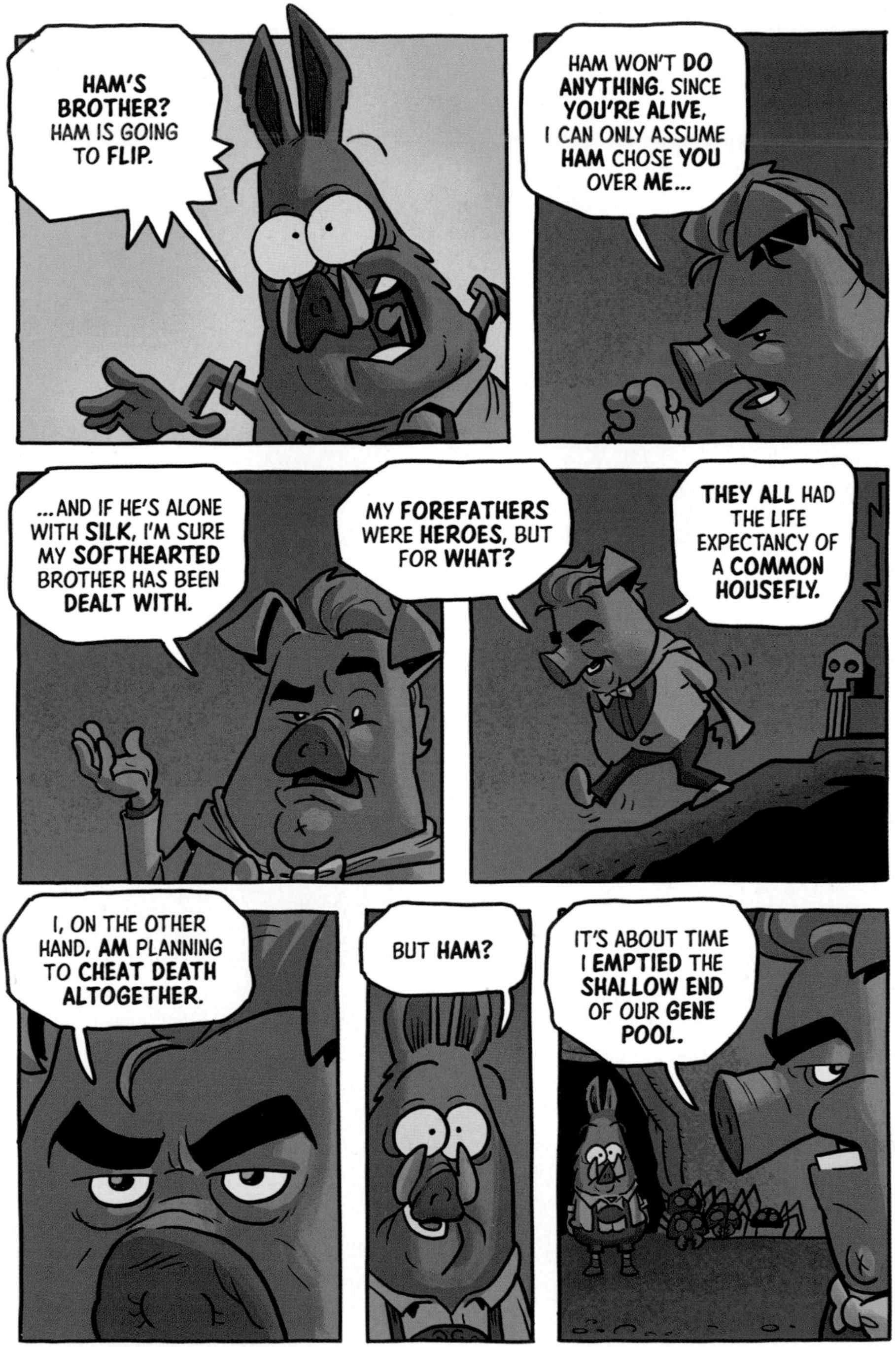
HAM'S BROTHER? HAM IS GOING TO FLIP.
HAM WON'T DO ANYTHING. SINCE YOU'RE ALIVE, I CAN ONLY ASSUME HAM CHOSE YOU OVER ME...
...AND IF HE'S ALONE WITH SILK, I'M SURE MY SOFTHEARTED BROTHER HAS BEEN DEALT WITH.
MY FOREFATHERS WERE HEROES, BUT FOR WHAT?
THEY ALL HAD THE LIFE EXPECTANCY OF A COMMON HOUSEFLY.
I, ON THE OTHER HAND, AM PLANNING TO CHEAT DEATH ALTOGETHER.
BUT HAM?
IT'S ABOUT TIME I EMPTIED THE SHALLOW END OF OUR GENE POOL.

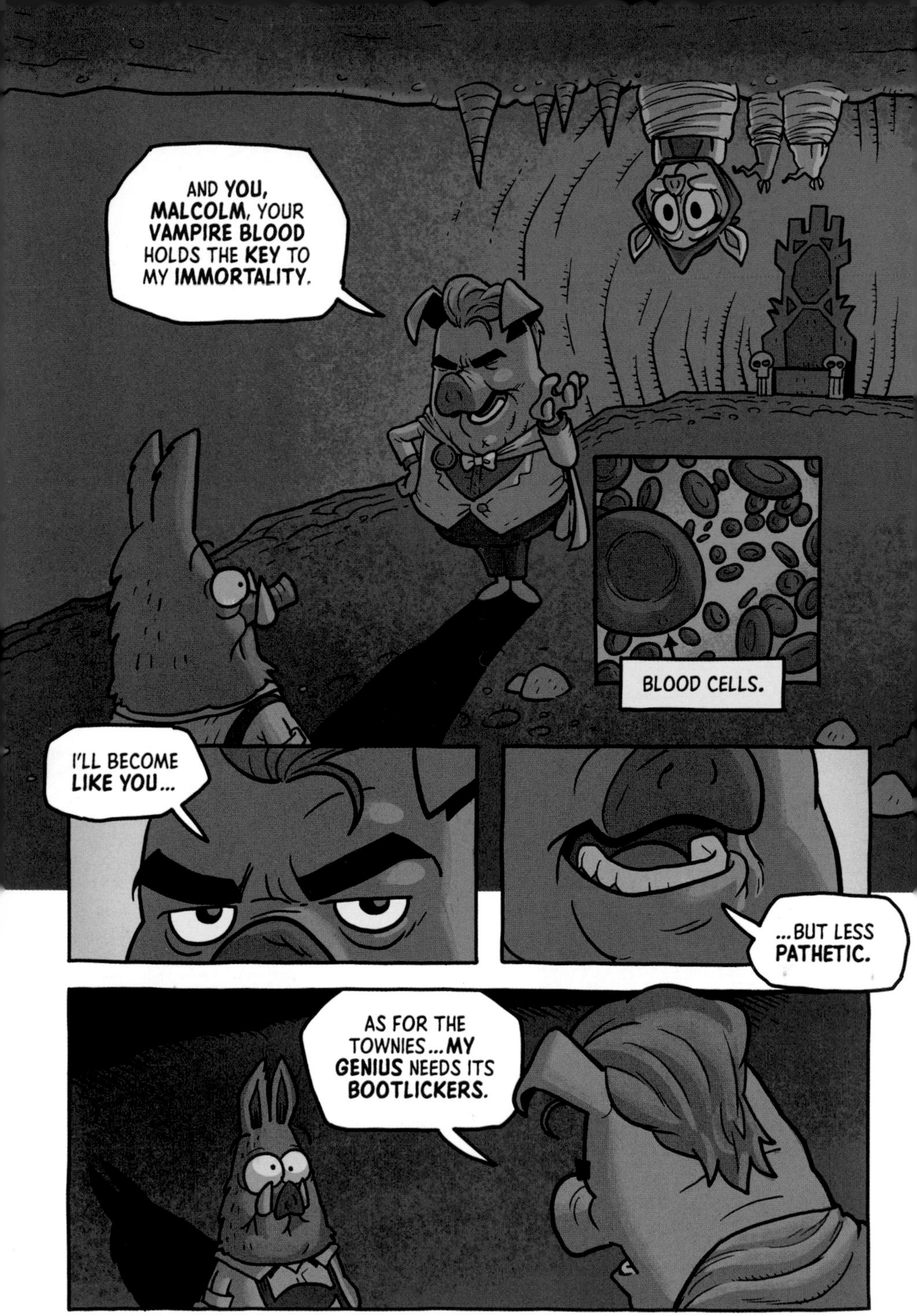
AND YOU, MALCOLM, YOUR VAMPIRE BLOOD HOLDS THE KEY TO MY IMMORTALITY.
BLOOD CELLS.
I'LL BECOME LIKE YOU...
...BUT LESS PATHETIC.
AS FOR THE TOWNIES...MY GENIUS NEEDS ITS BOOTLICKERS.

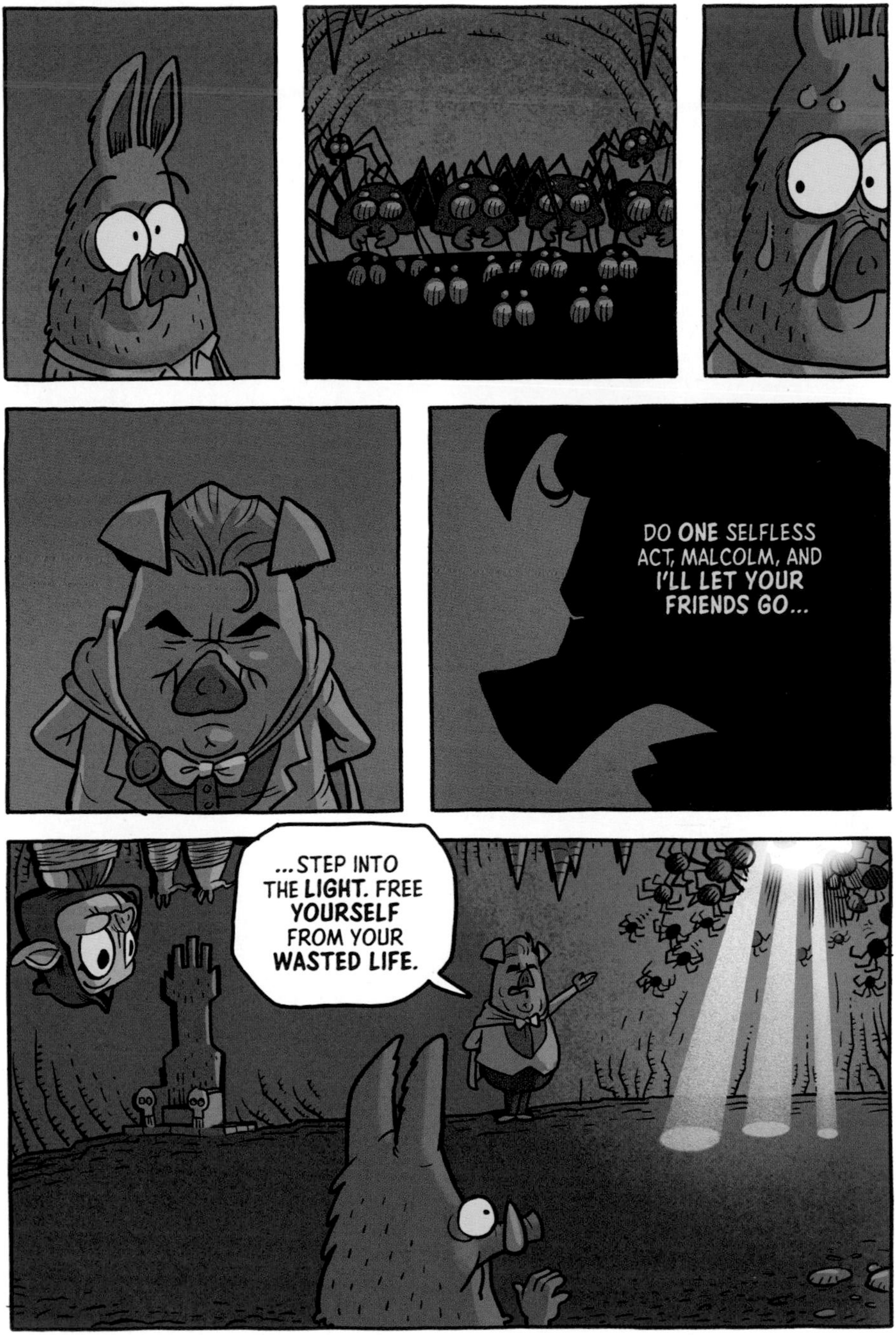
DO ONE SELFLESS ACT, MALCOLM, AND I'LL LET YOUR FRIENDS GO...
...STEP INTO THE LIGHT. FREE YOURSELF FROM YOUR WASTED LIFE.

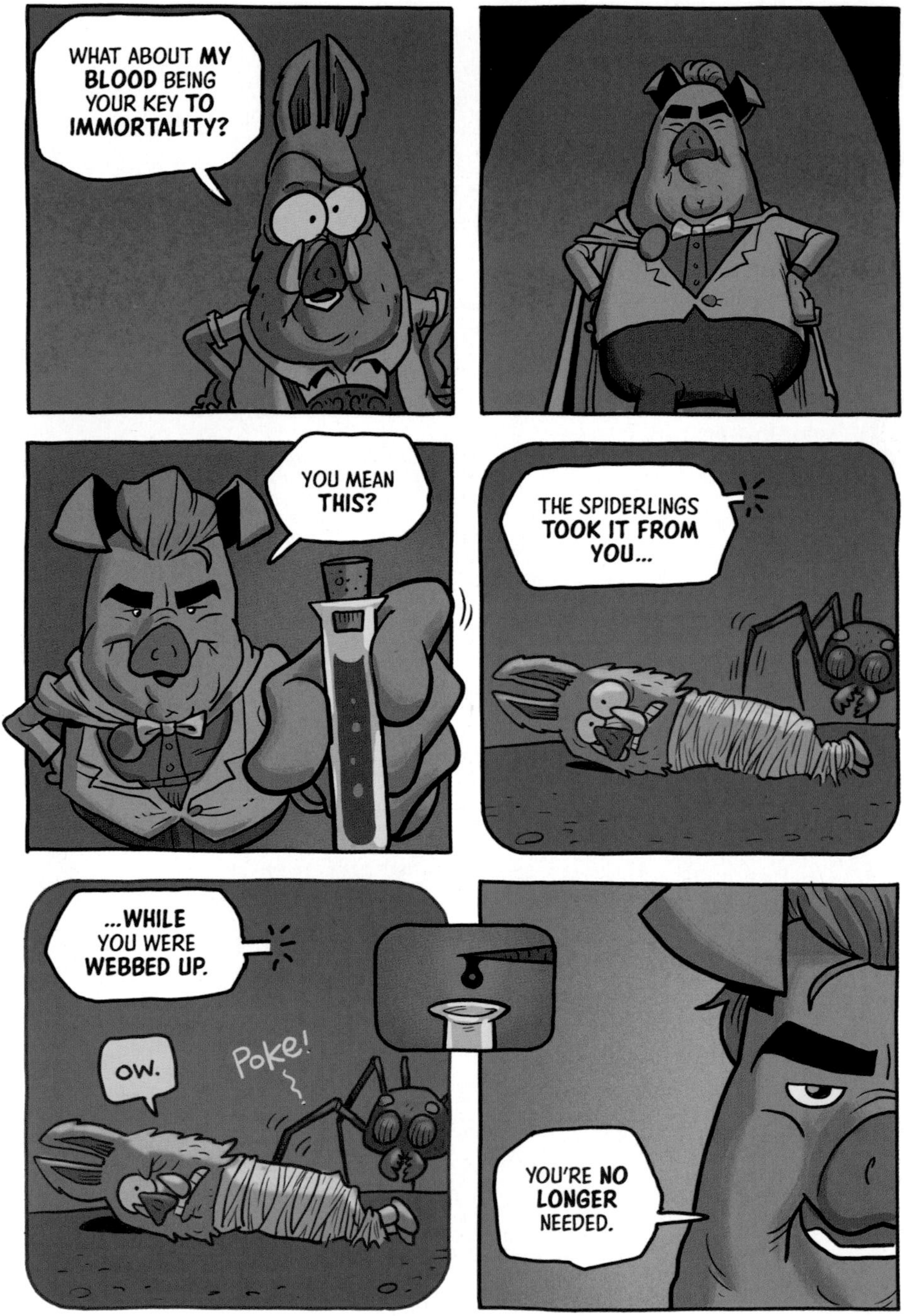
WHAT ABOUT MY BLOOD BEING YOUR KEY TO IMMORTALITY?
YOU MEAN THIS?
THE SPIDERLINGS TOOK IT FROM YOU...
...WHILE YOU WERE WEBBED UP.
OW.
Poke!
YOU'RE NO LONGER NEEDED.

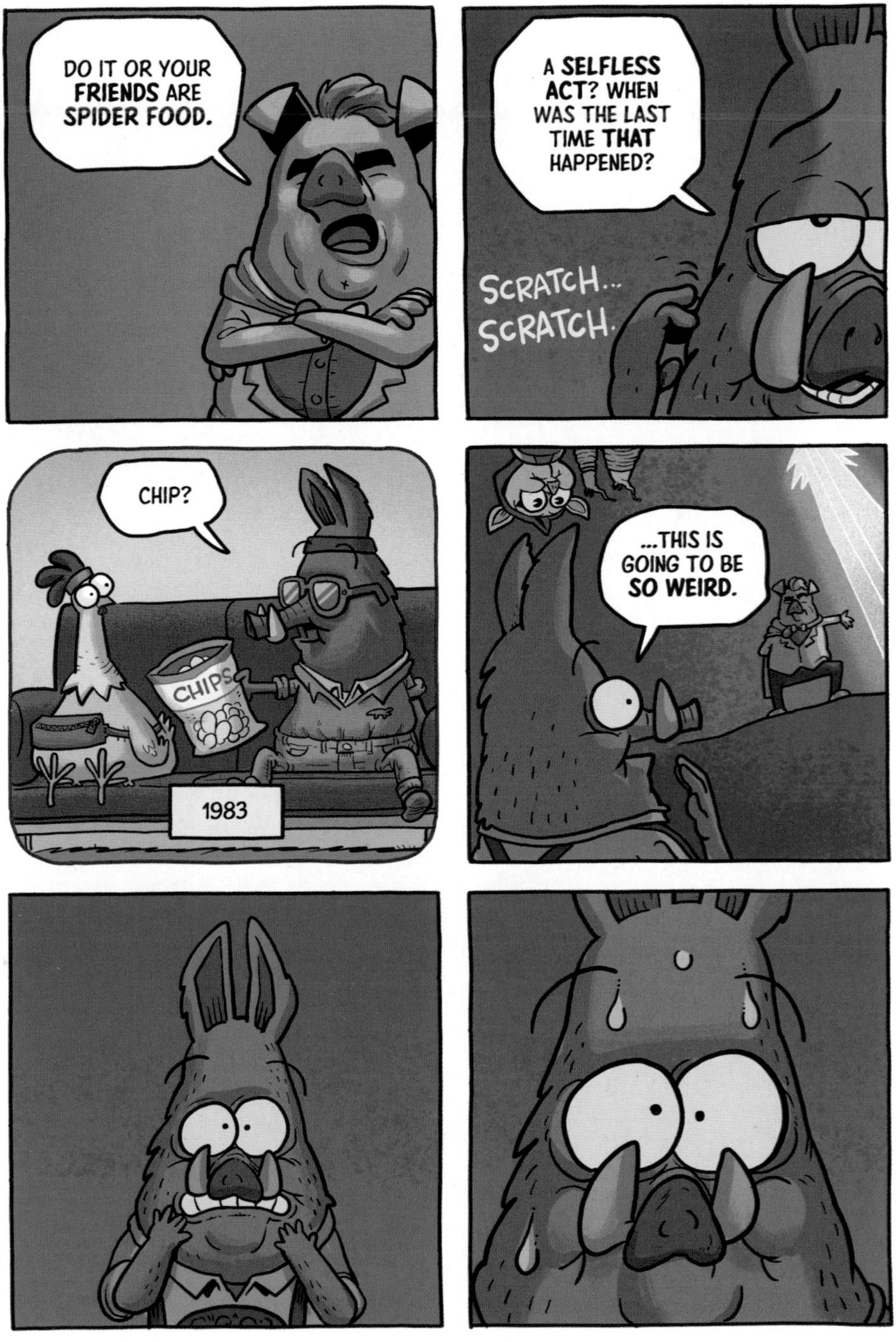
DO IT OR YOUR FRIENDS ARE SPIDER FOOD.
A SELFLESS ACT? WHEN WAS THE LAST TIME THAT HAPPENED?
SCRATCH... SCRATCH.
CHIP?
CHIPS
1983
...THIS IS GOING TO BE SO WEIRD.

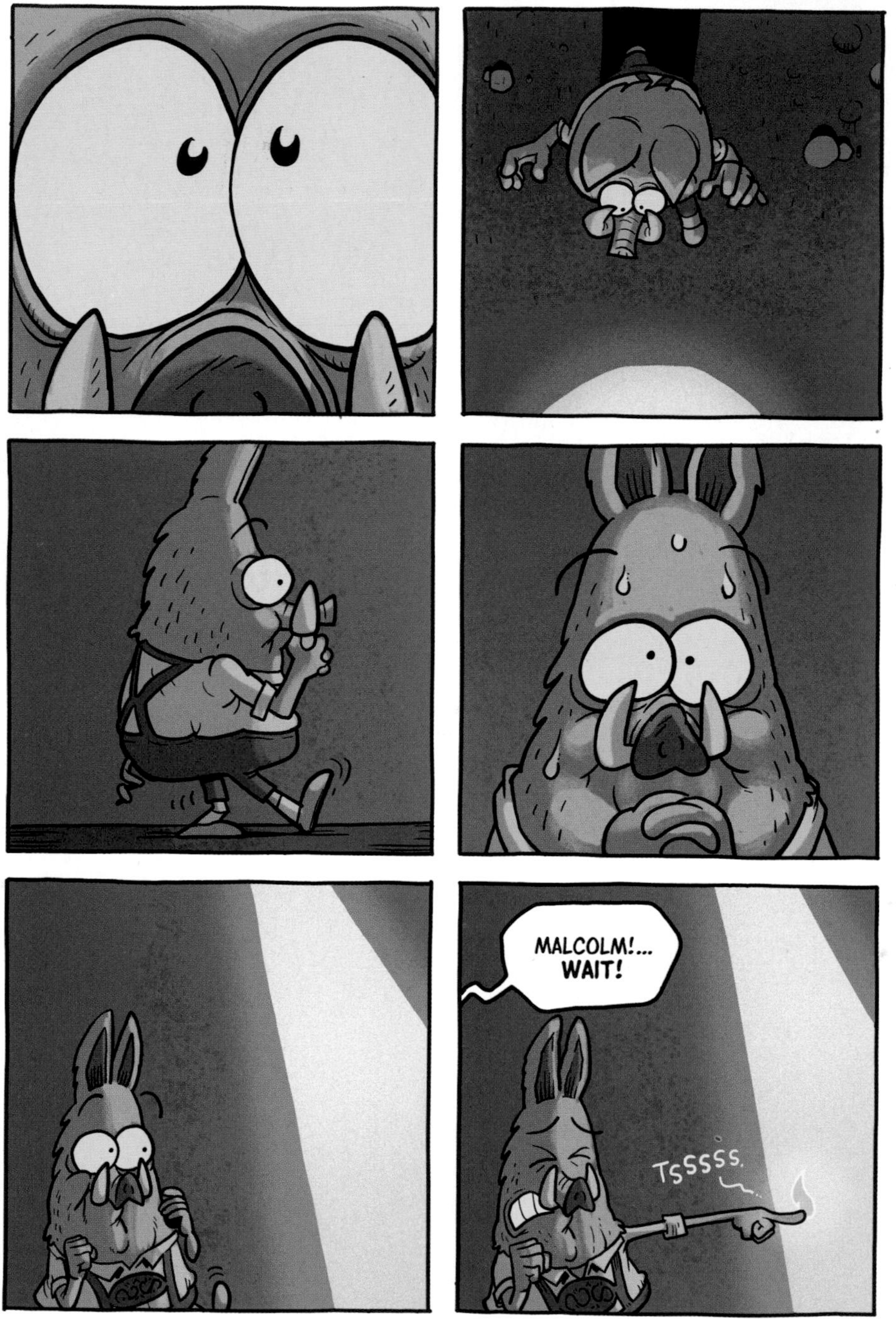
MALCOLM!...
WAIT!
TSSSSS.

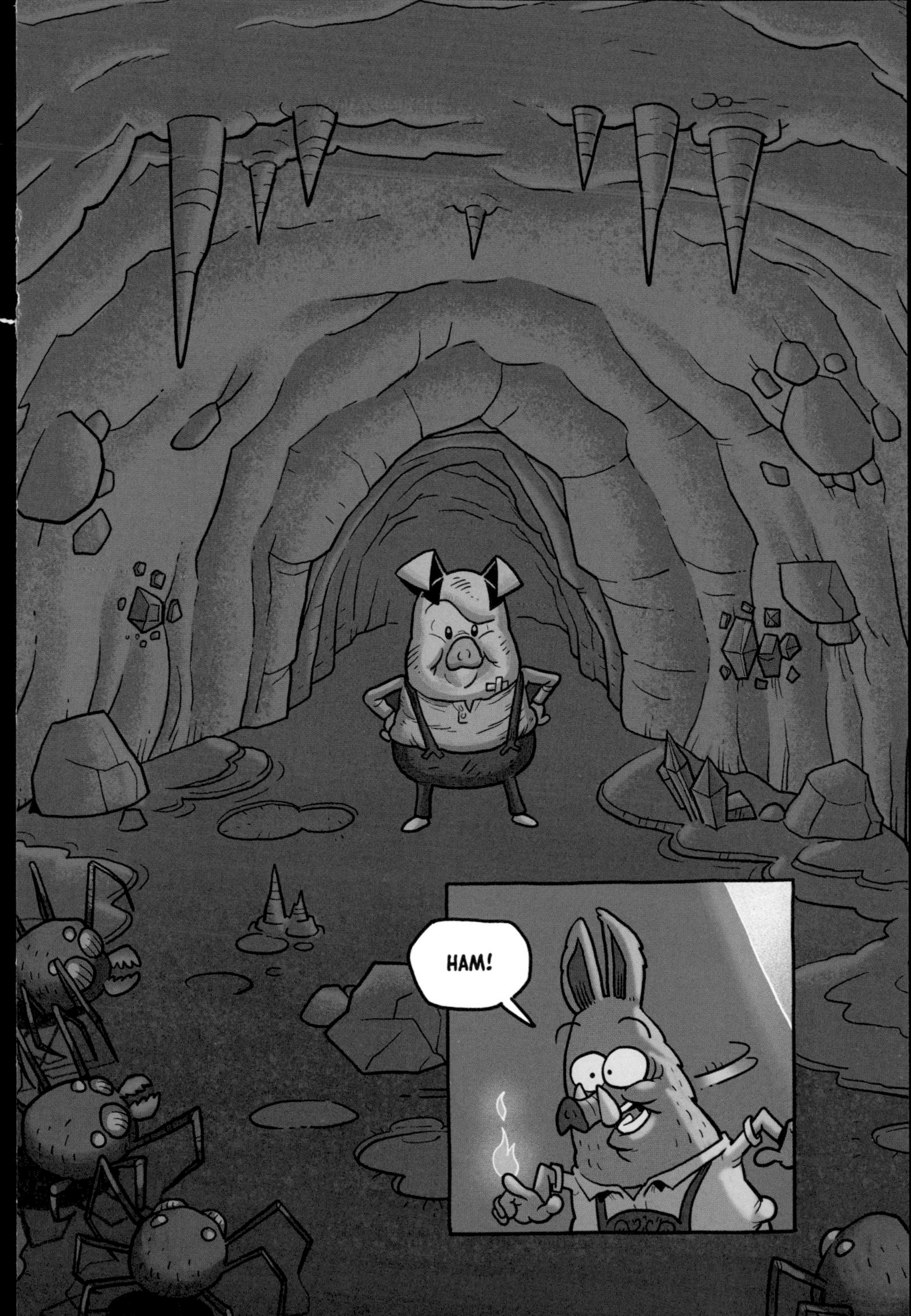
HAM!

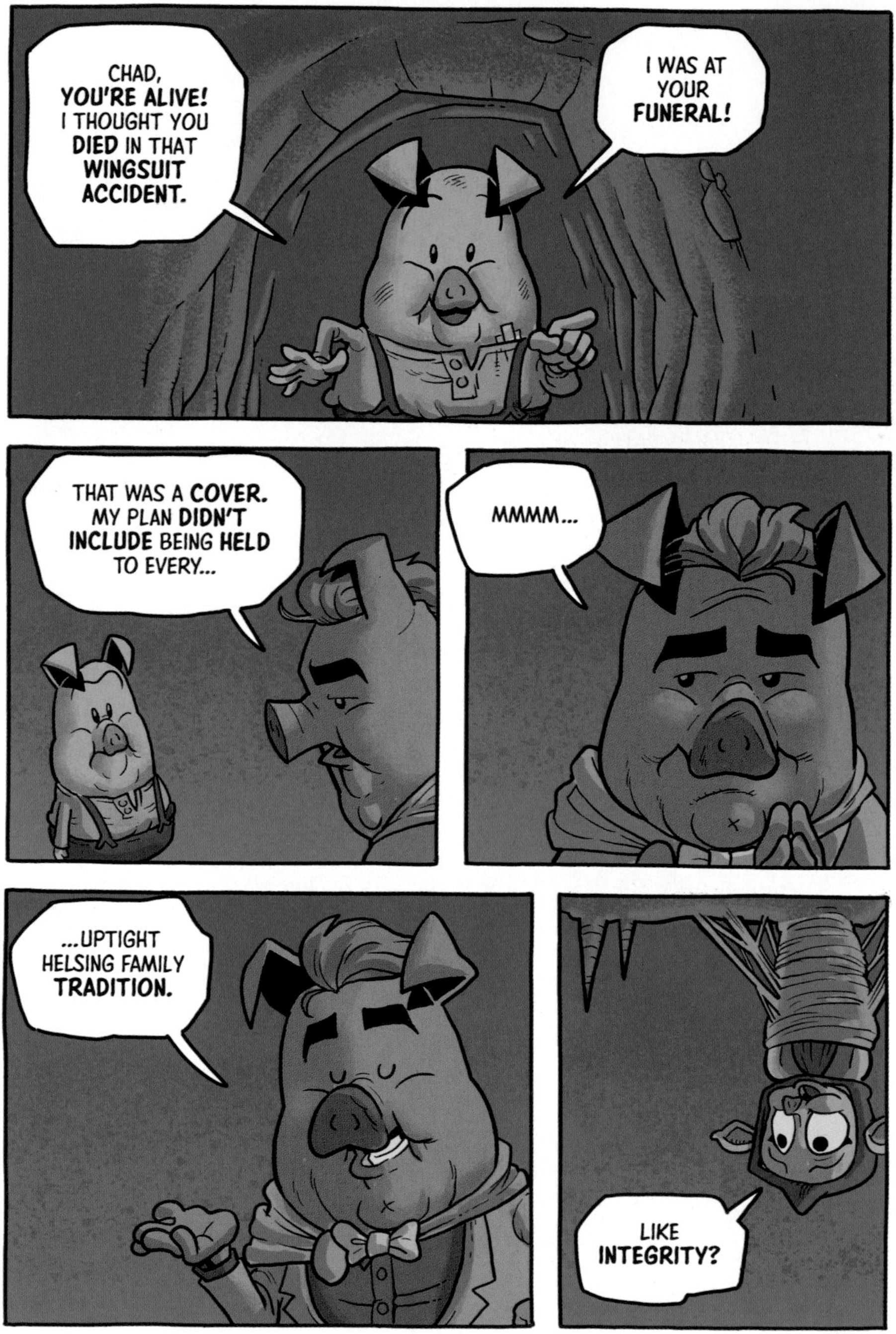
CHAD, **YOU'RE ALIVE!** I THOUGHT YOU **DIED** IN THAT **WINGSUIT ACCIDENT.**
I WAS AT YOUR **FUNERAL!**
THAT WAS A **COVER.** MY PLAN **DIDN'T INCLUDE** BEING **HELD** TO EVERY...
MMMM...
...UPTIGHT HELSING FAMILY **TRADITION.**
LIKE **INTEGRITY?**

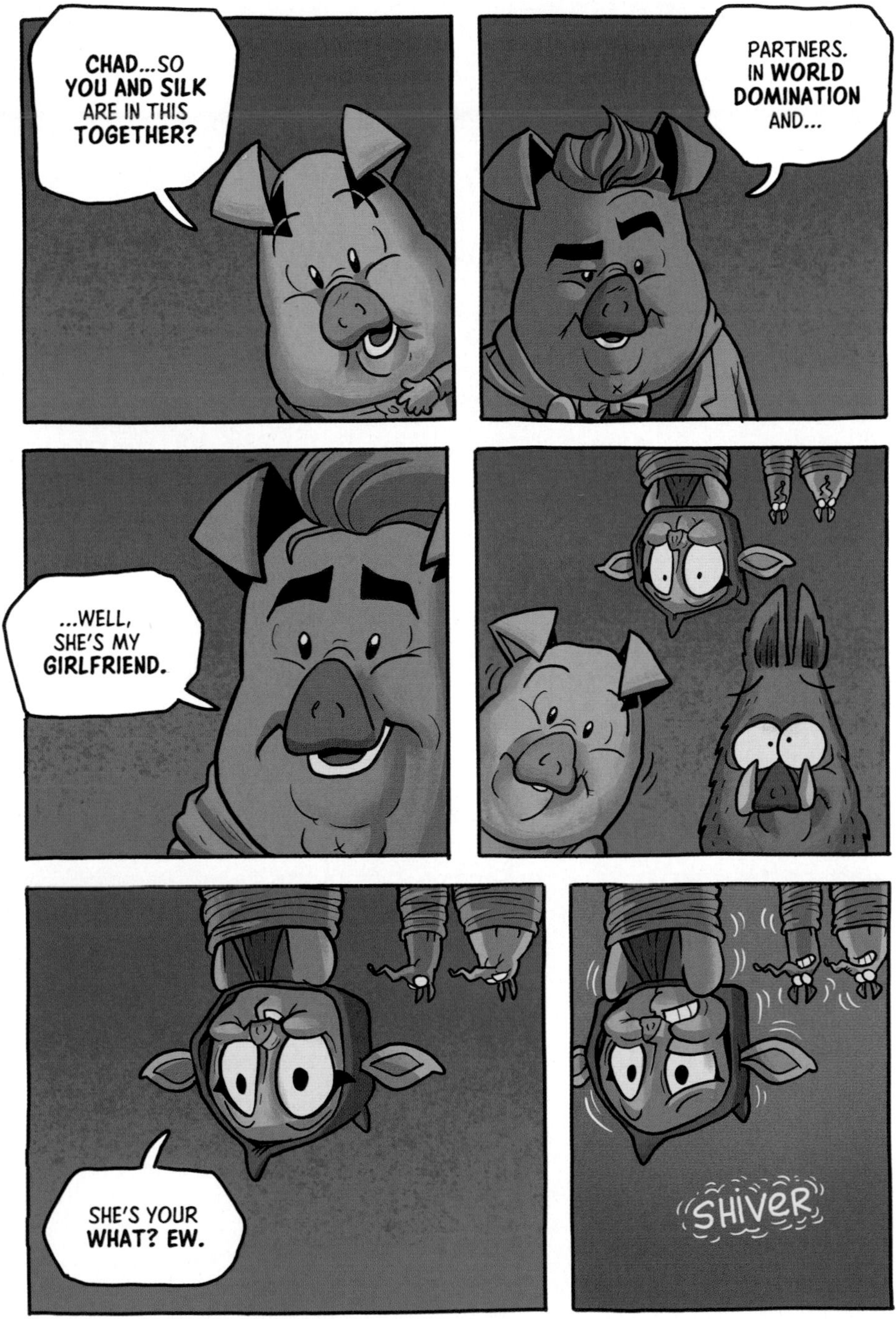

CHAD...SO YOU AND SILK ARE IN THIS TOGETHER?
PARTNERS. IN WORLD DOMINATION AND...
...WELL, SHE'S MY GIRLFRIEND.
SHE'S YOUR WHAT? EW.
SHIVER

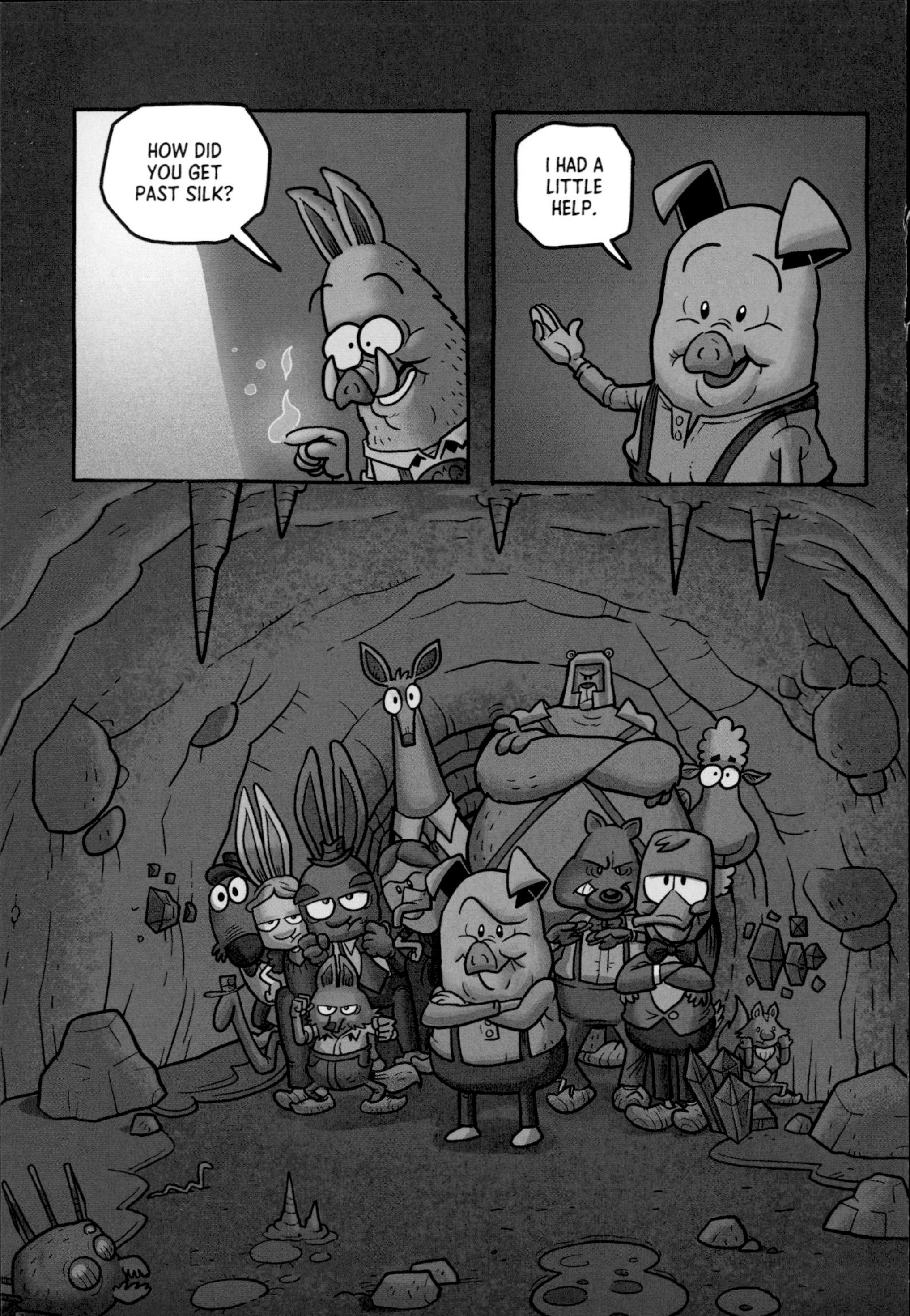
HOW DID YOU GET PAST SILK?
I HAD A LITTLE HELP.

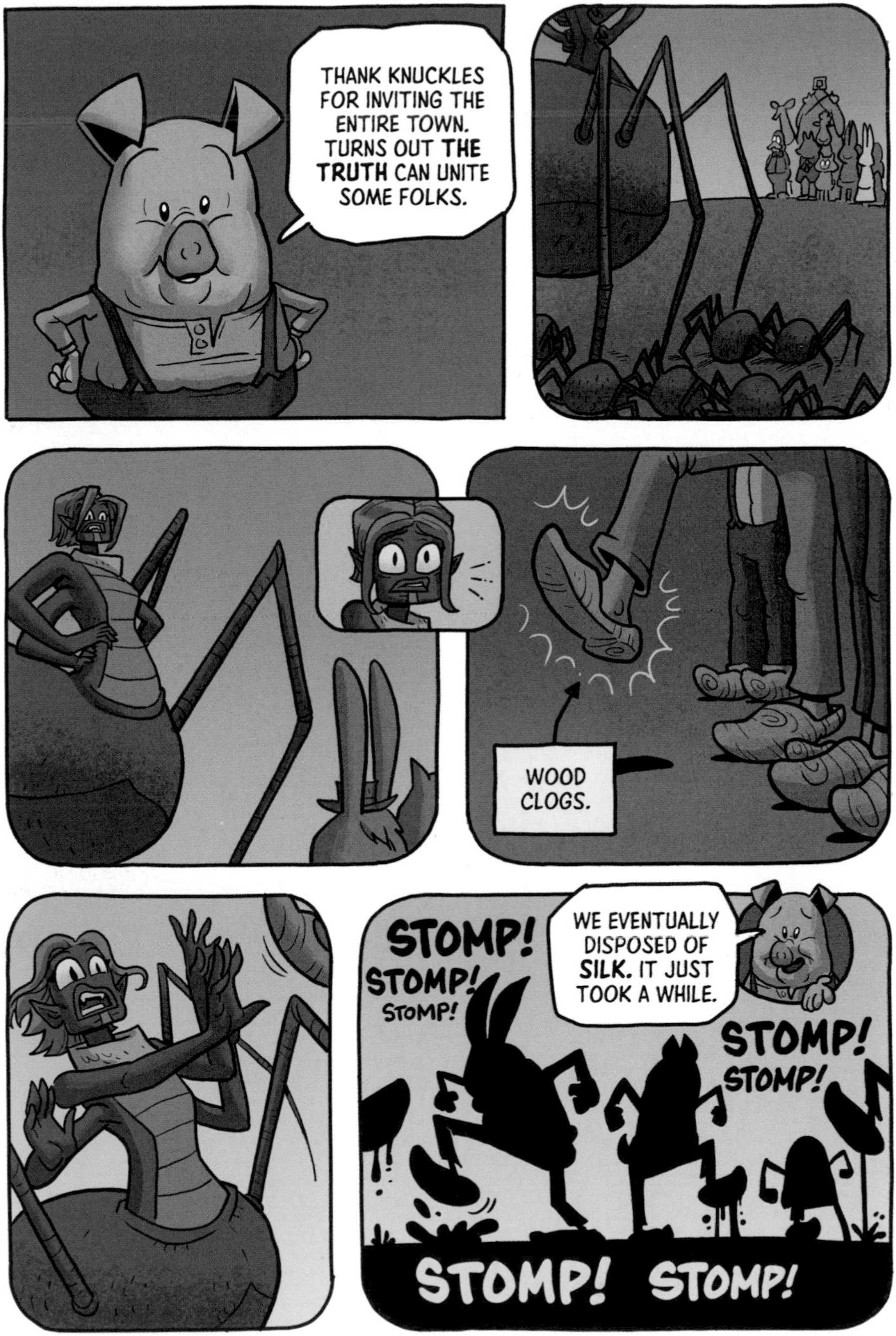
THANK KNUCKLES FOR INVITING THE ENTIRE TOWN. TURNS OUT **THE TRUTH** CAN UNITE SOME FOLKS.
WOOD CLOGS.
STOMP!
STOMP!
STOMP!
WE EVENTUALLY DISPOSED OF **SILK.** IT JUST TOOK A WHILE.
STOMP!
STOMP!
STOMP! STOMP!

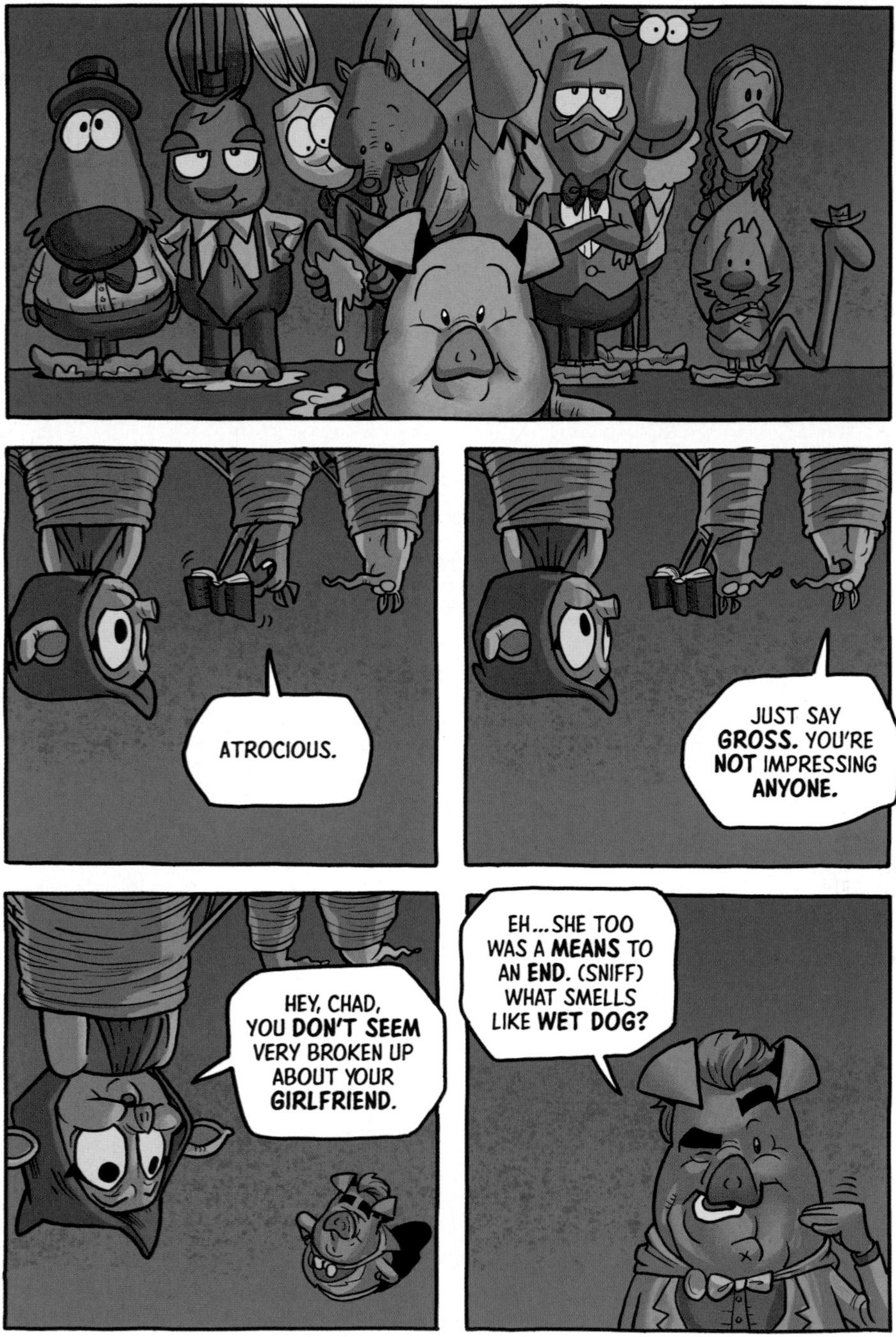

ATROCIOUS.
JUST SAY GROSS. YOU'RE NOT IMPRESSING ANYONE.
HEY, CHAD, YOU DON'T SEEM VERY BROKEN UP ABOUT YOUR GIRLFRIEND.
EH...SHE TOO WAS A MEANS TO AN END. (SNIFF) WHAT SMELLS LIKE WET DOG?

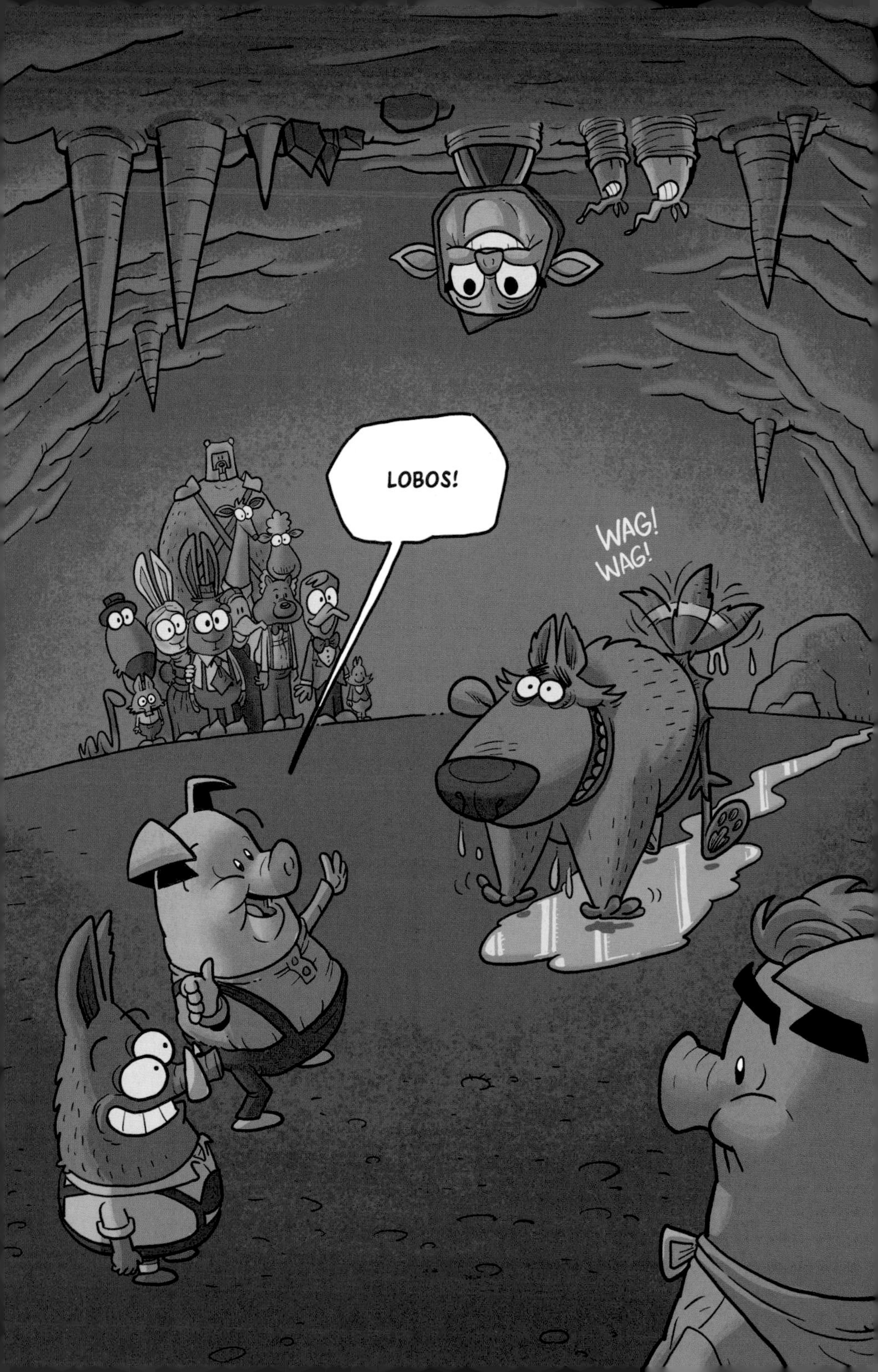
LOBOS!
WAG! WAG!

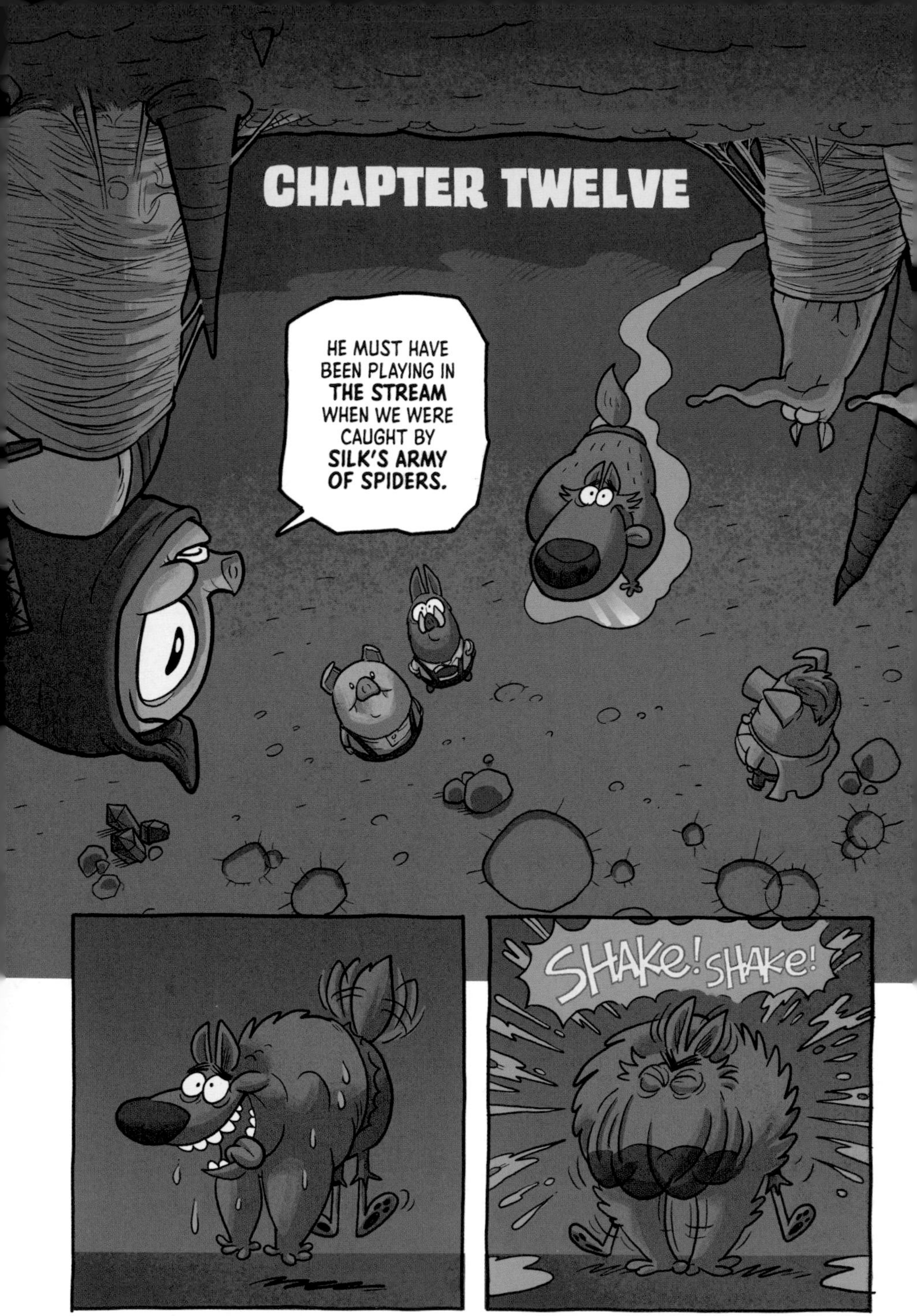
CHAPTER TWELVE
HE MUST HAVE BEEN PLAYING IN THE STREAM WHEN WE WERE CAUGHT BY SILK'S ARMY OF SPIDERS.
SHAKE! SHAKE!

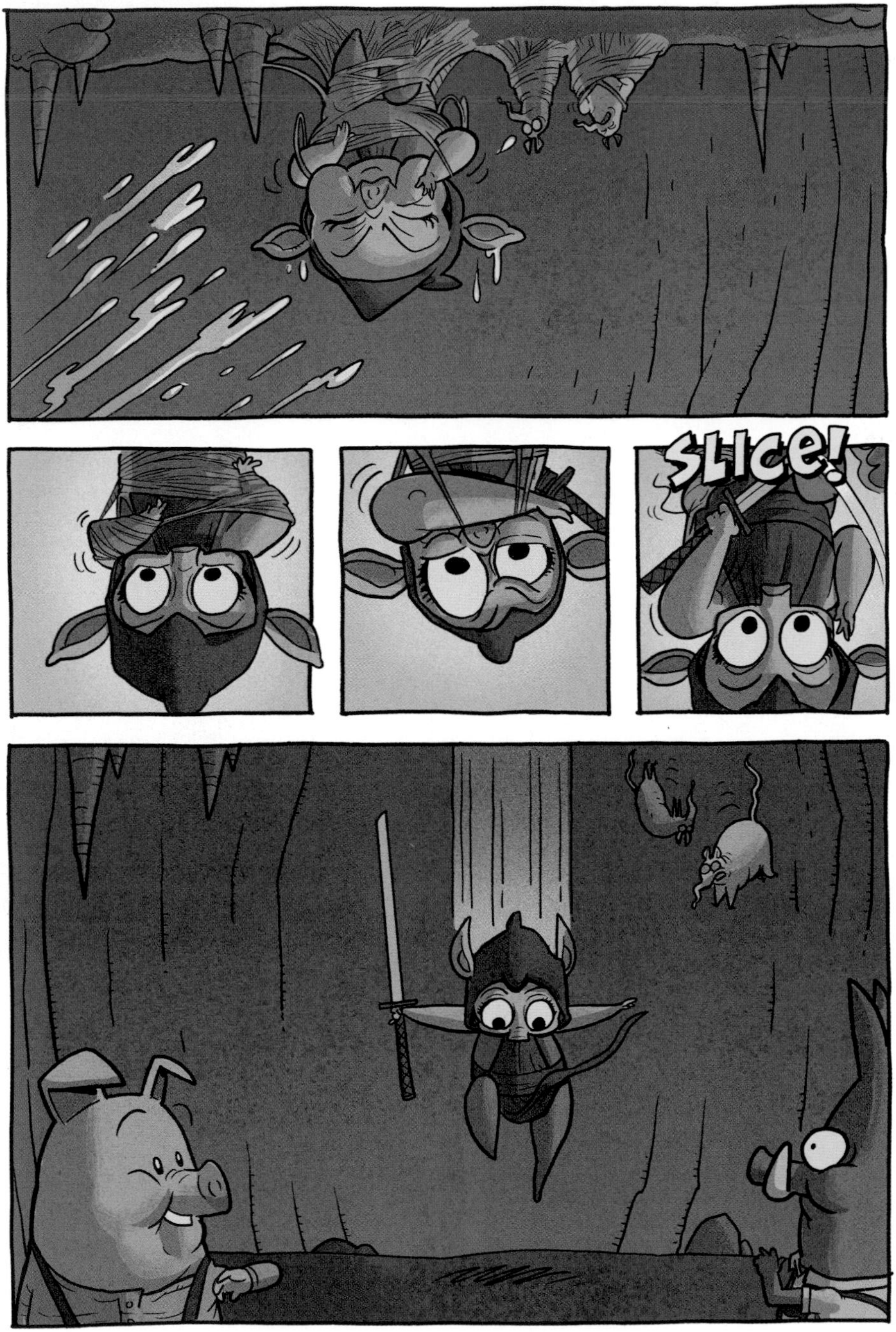
SLICE!

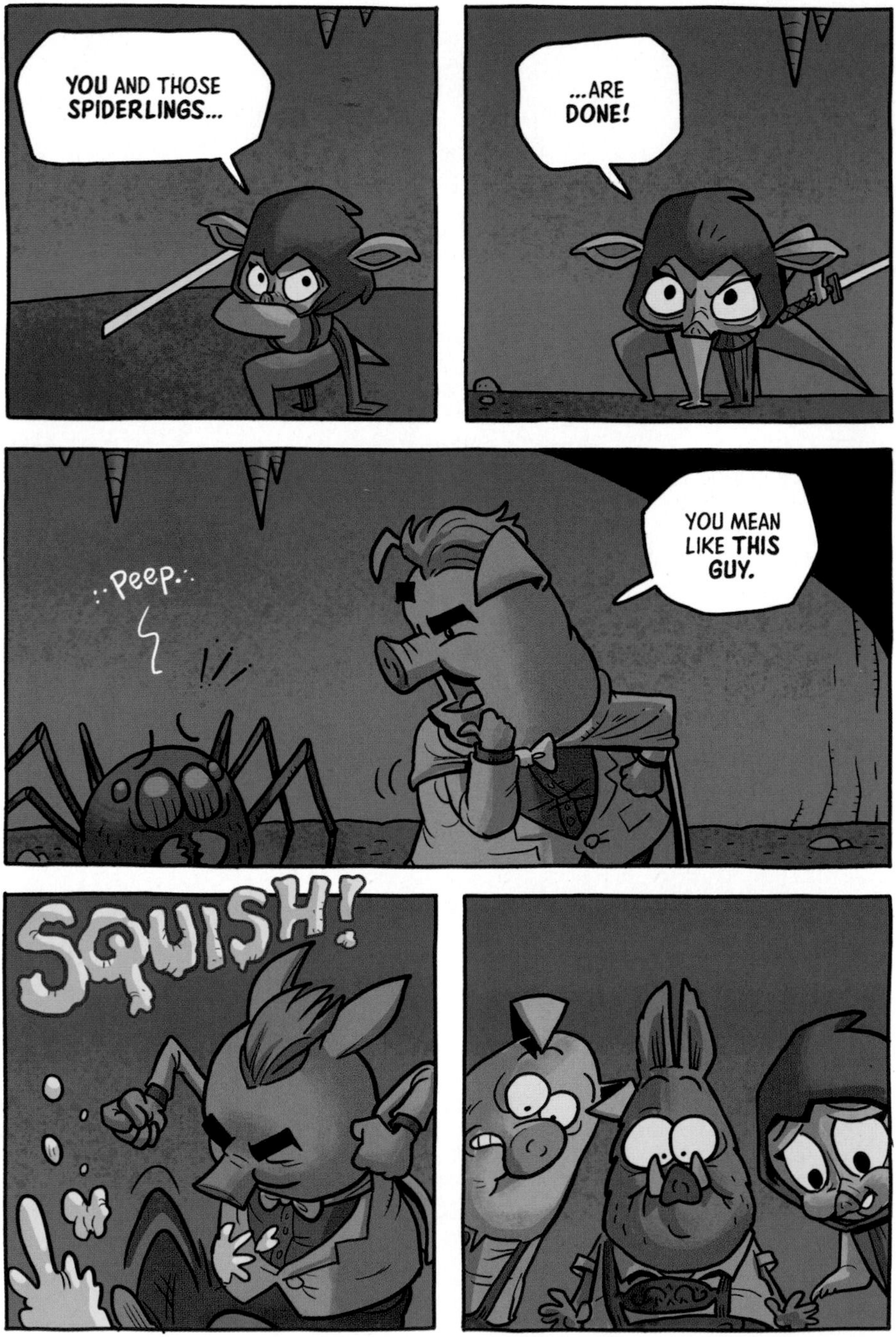
YOU AND THOSE SPIDERLINGS...
...ARE DONE!
Peep.
YOU MEAN LIKE THIS GUY.
SQUISH!

SILK AND HER LITTLE MINIONS WERE USEFUL.
TO A POINT.
USEFUL...
...BUT EXPENDABLE.
AW.
BROTHER OR NOT, YOU HAVE TO ANSWER FOR WHAT YOU'VE DONE.

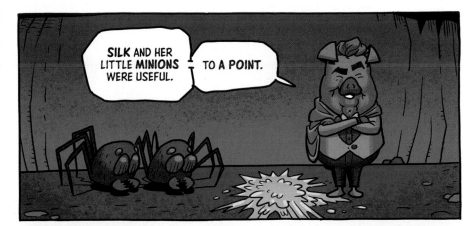

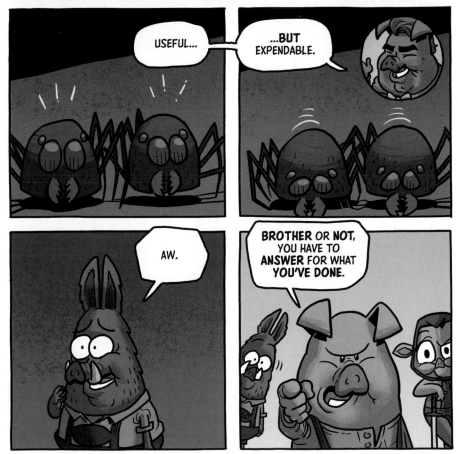

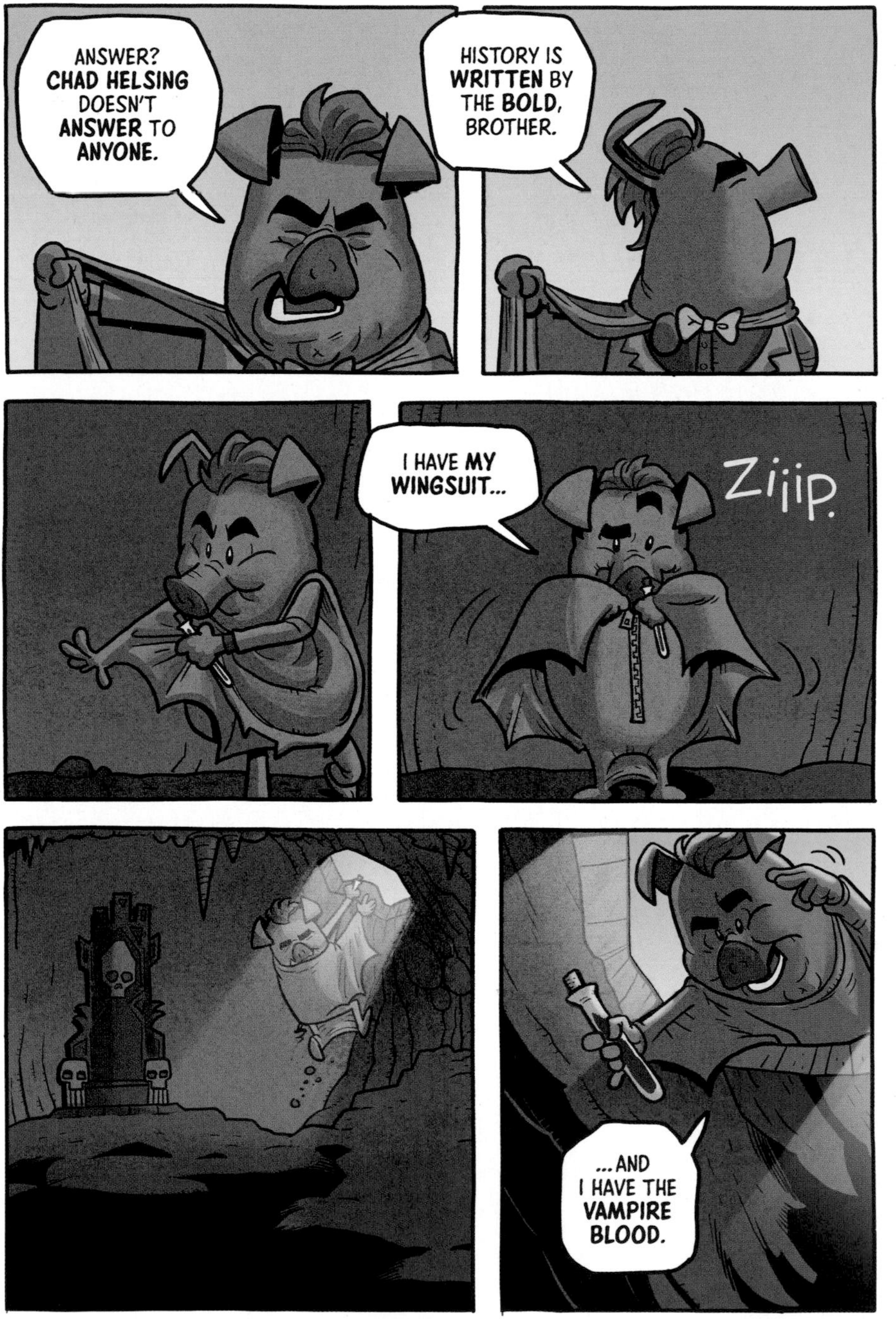
ANSWER? CHAD HELSING DOESN'T ANSWER TO ANYONE.
HISTORY IS WRITTEN BY THE BOLD, BROTHER.
I HAVE MY WINGSUIT...
Ziiip.
...AND I HAVE THE VAMPIRE BLOOD.

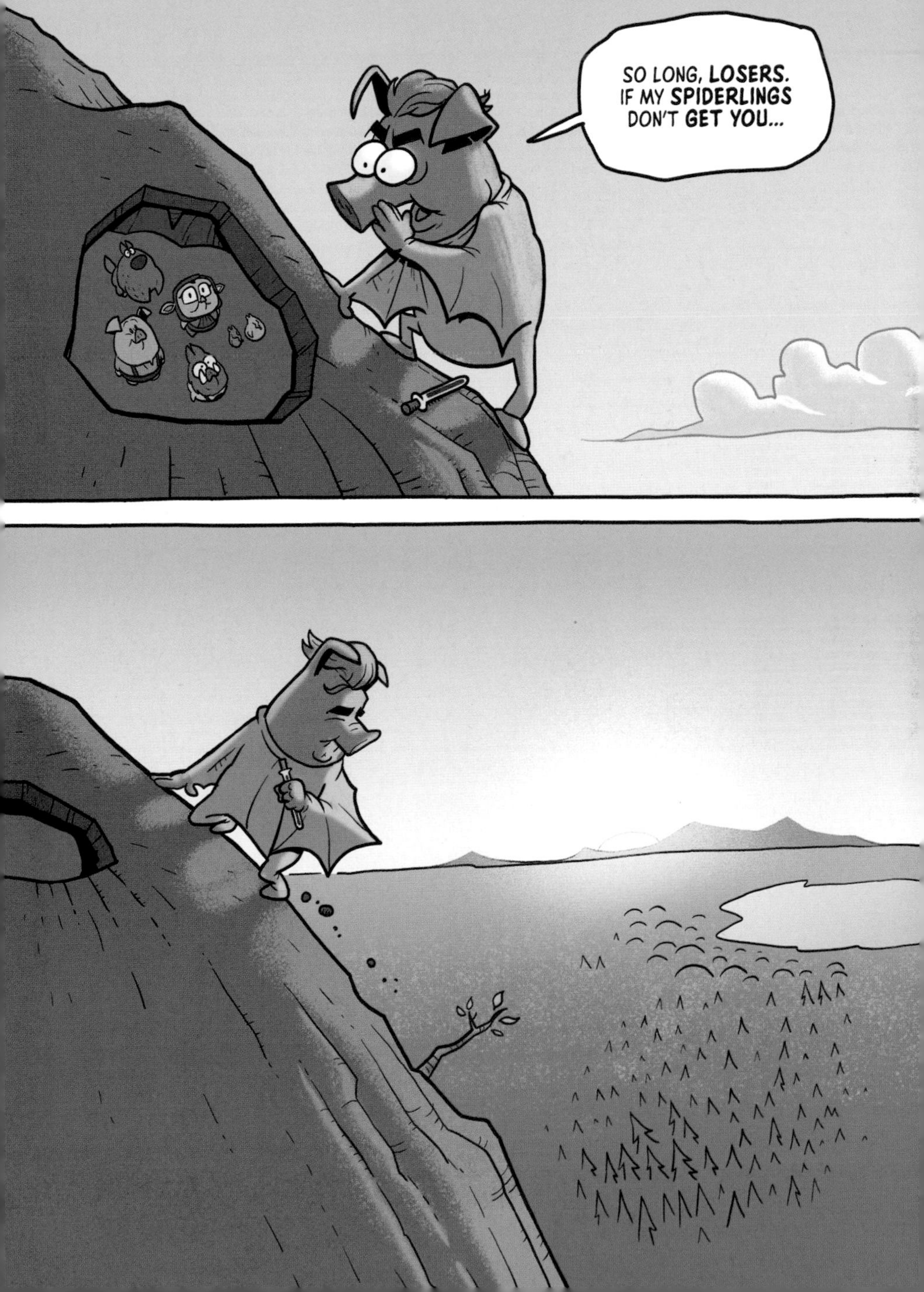
SO LONG, LOSERS. IF MY SPIDERLINGS DON'T GET YOU...

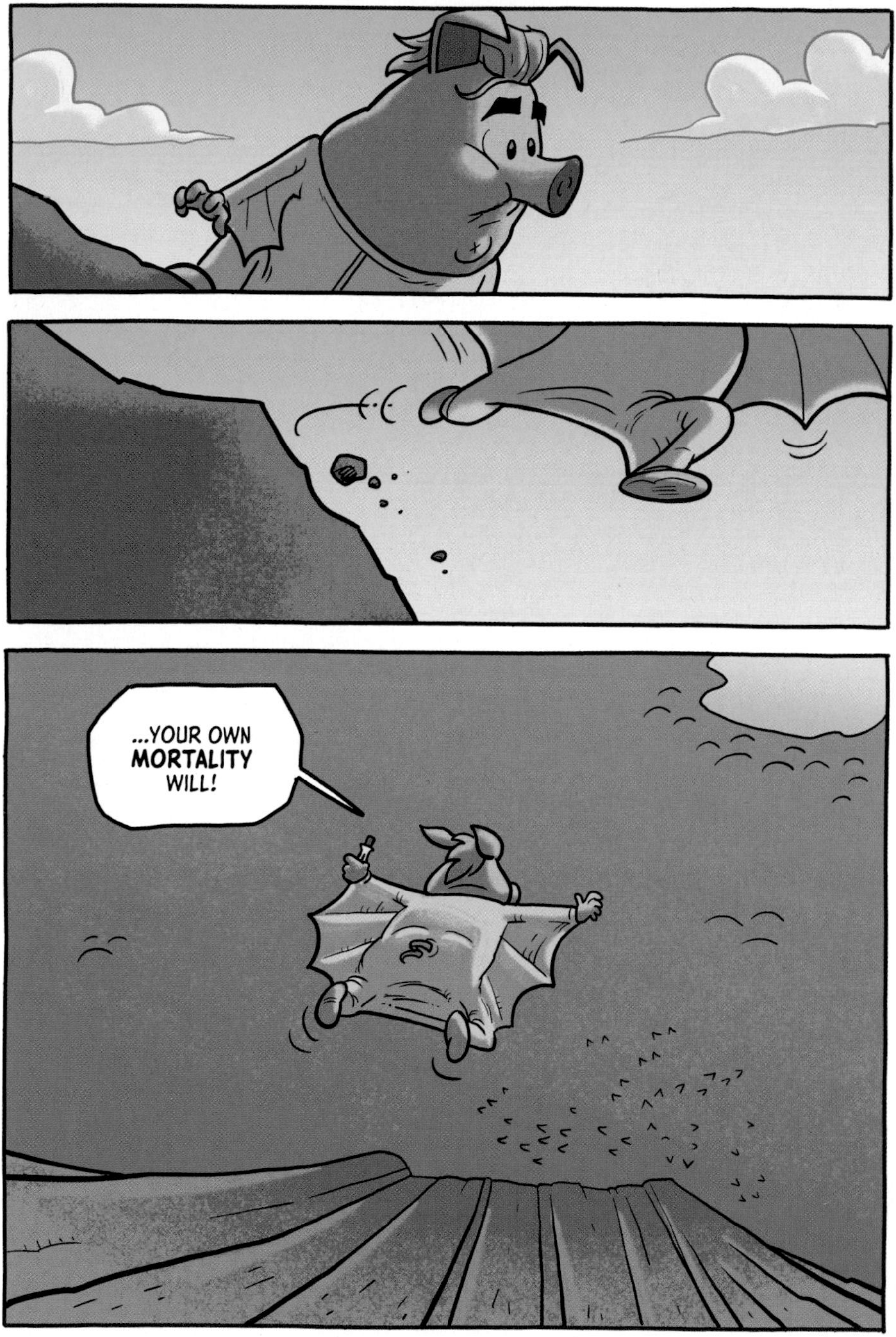
...YOUR OWN MORTALITY WILL!

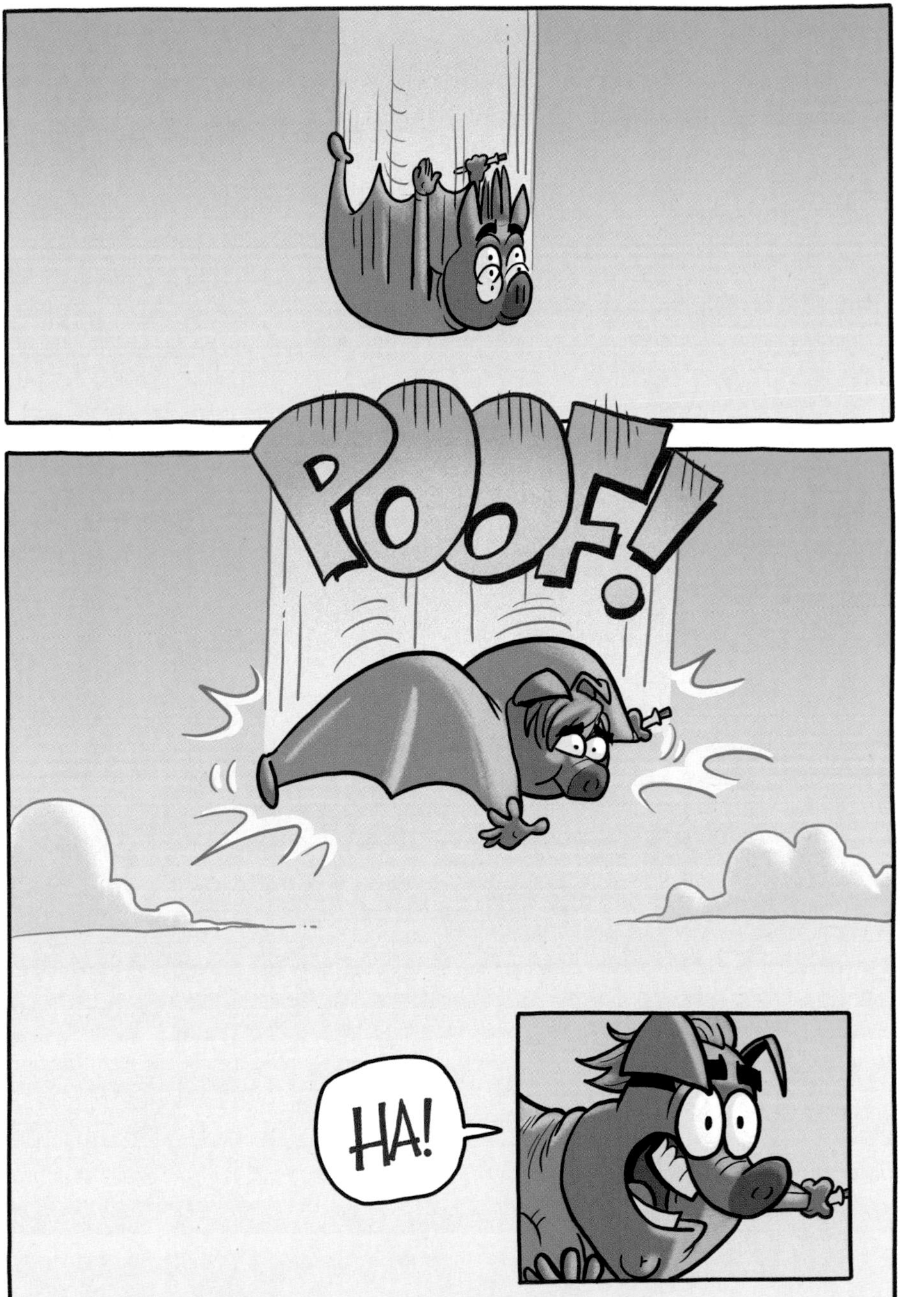
POOF!
HA!

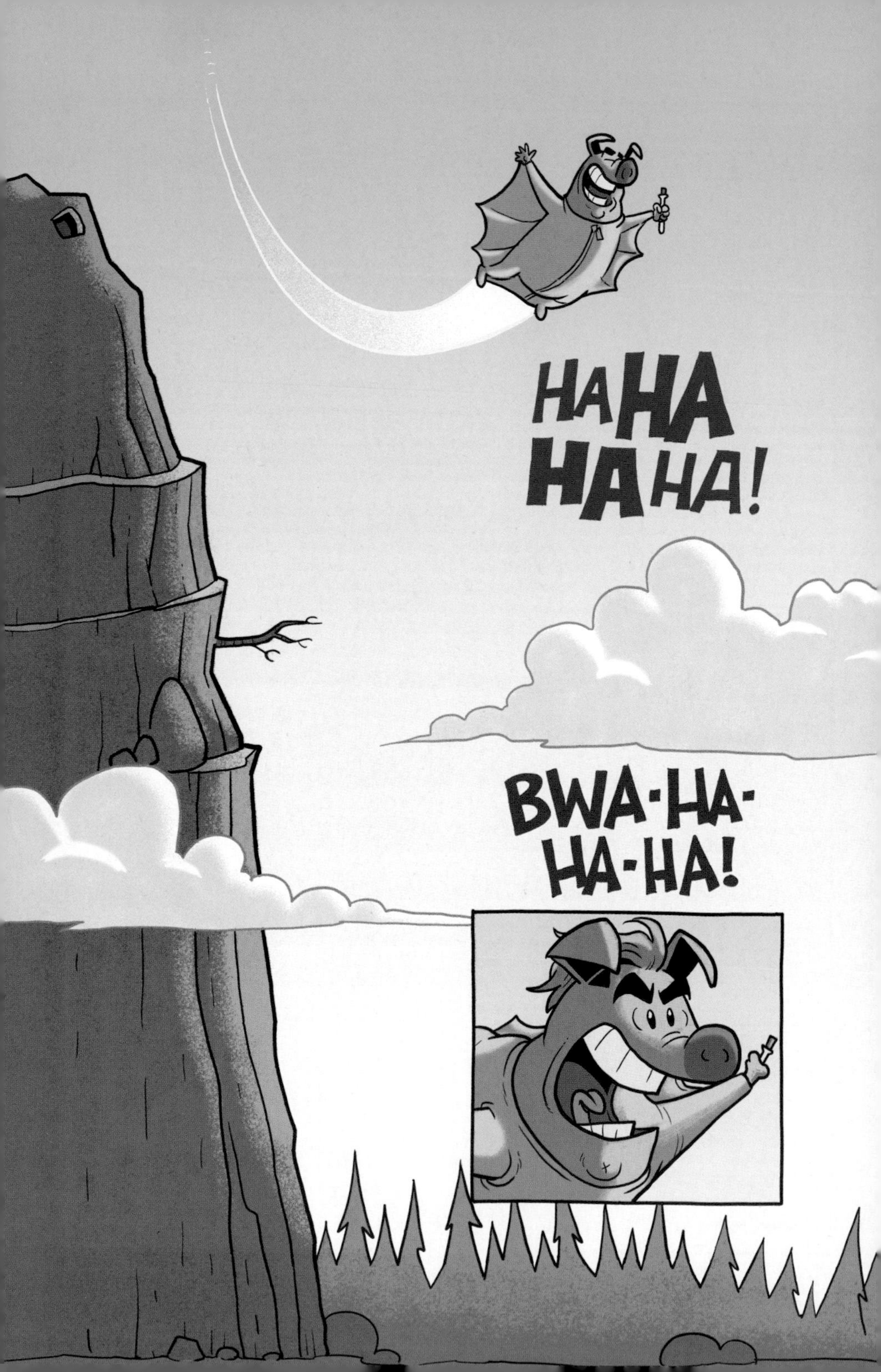
HAHA
HAHA!
BWA-HA-
HA-HA!

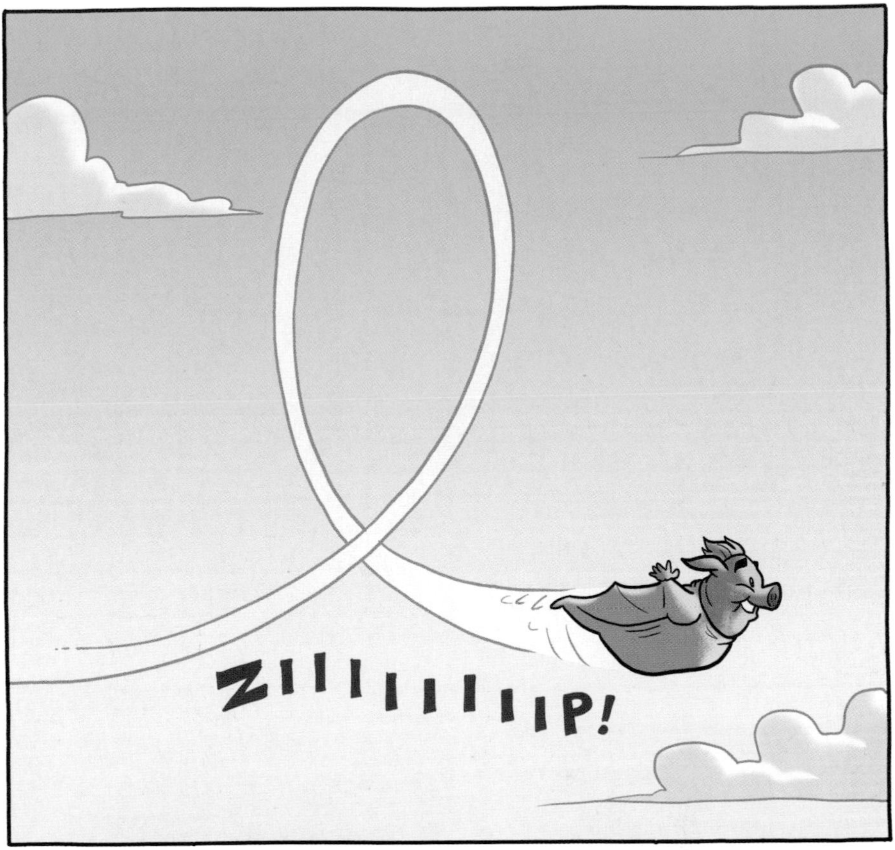
ZIIIIIIIIIP!

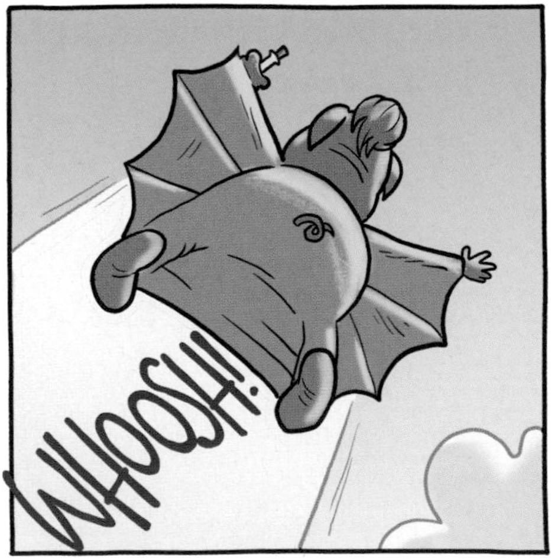
WHOOSH!

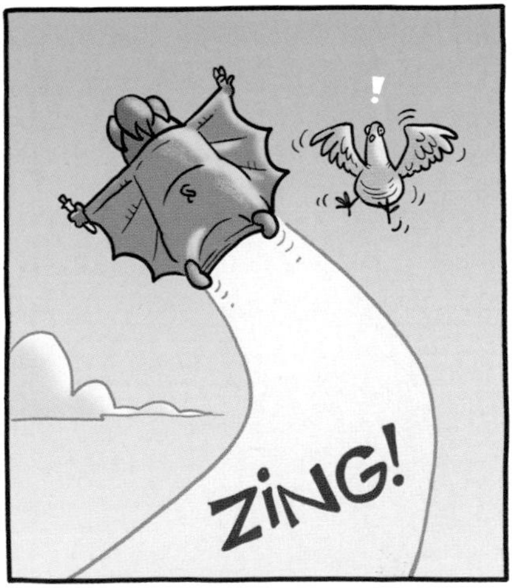
!
ZING!

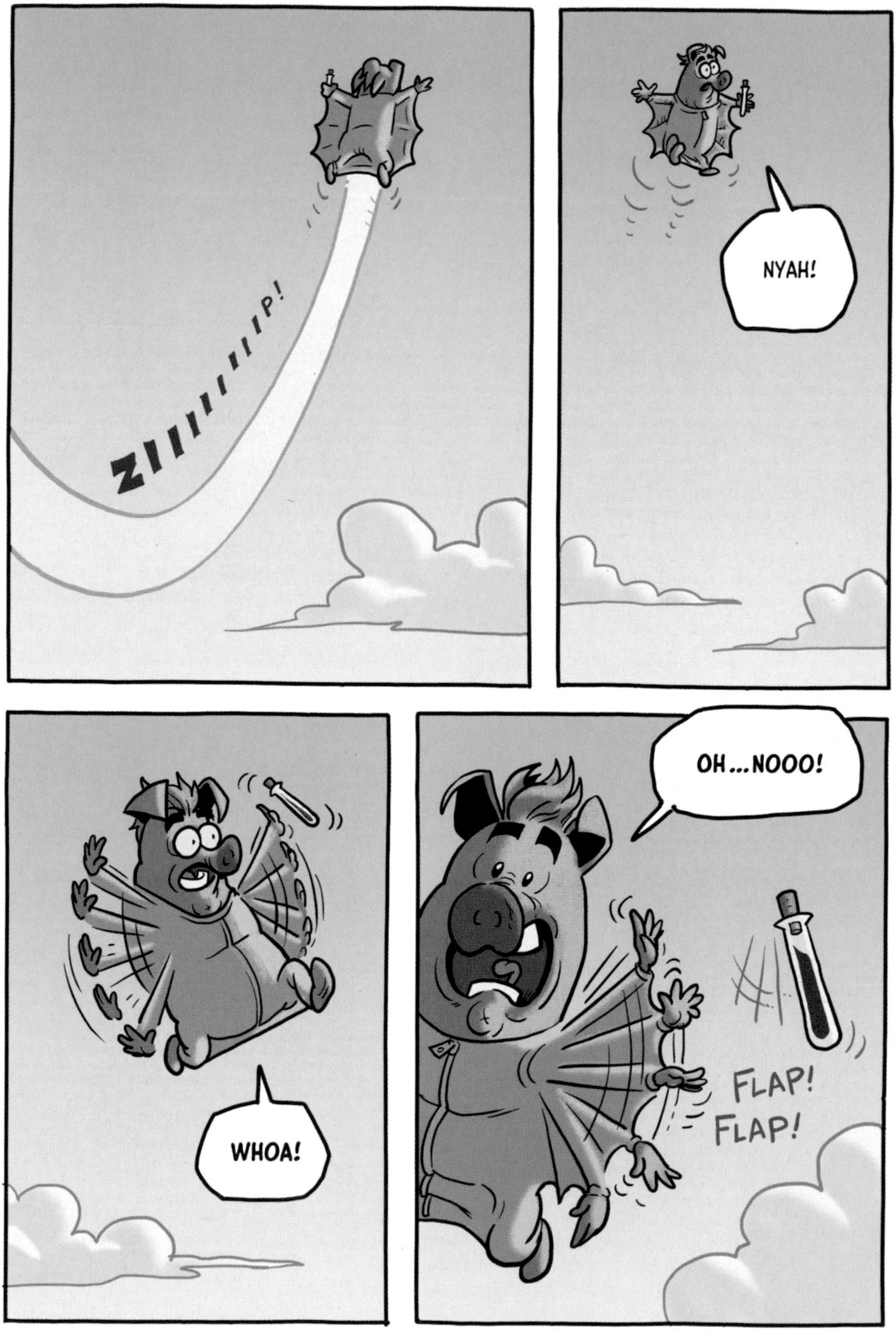
ZIIIIIIIIP!
NYAH!
WHOA!
OH...NOOO!
FLAP!
FLAP!

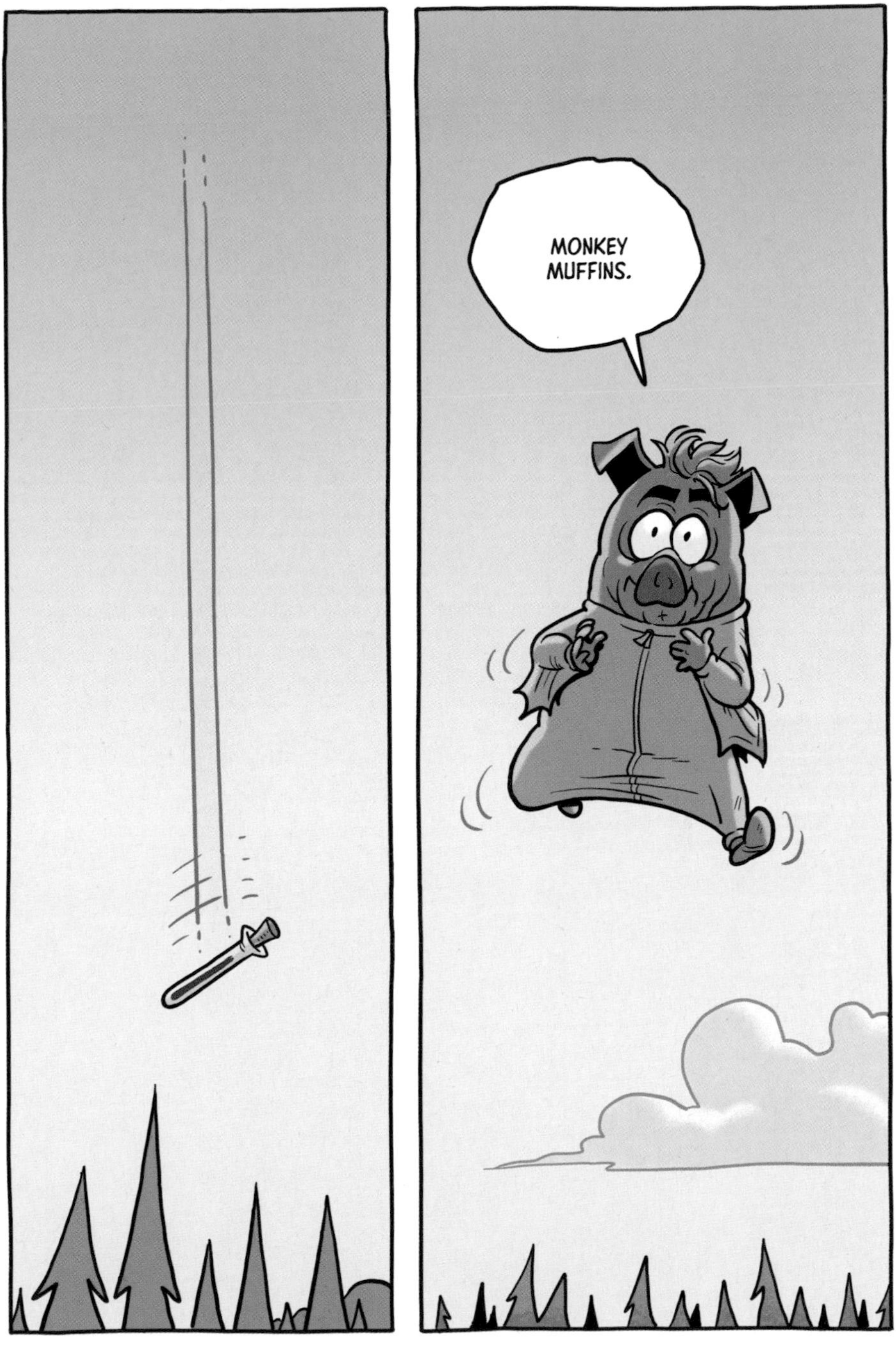
MONKEY
MUFFINS.

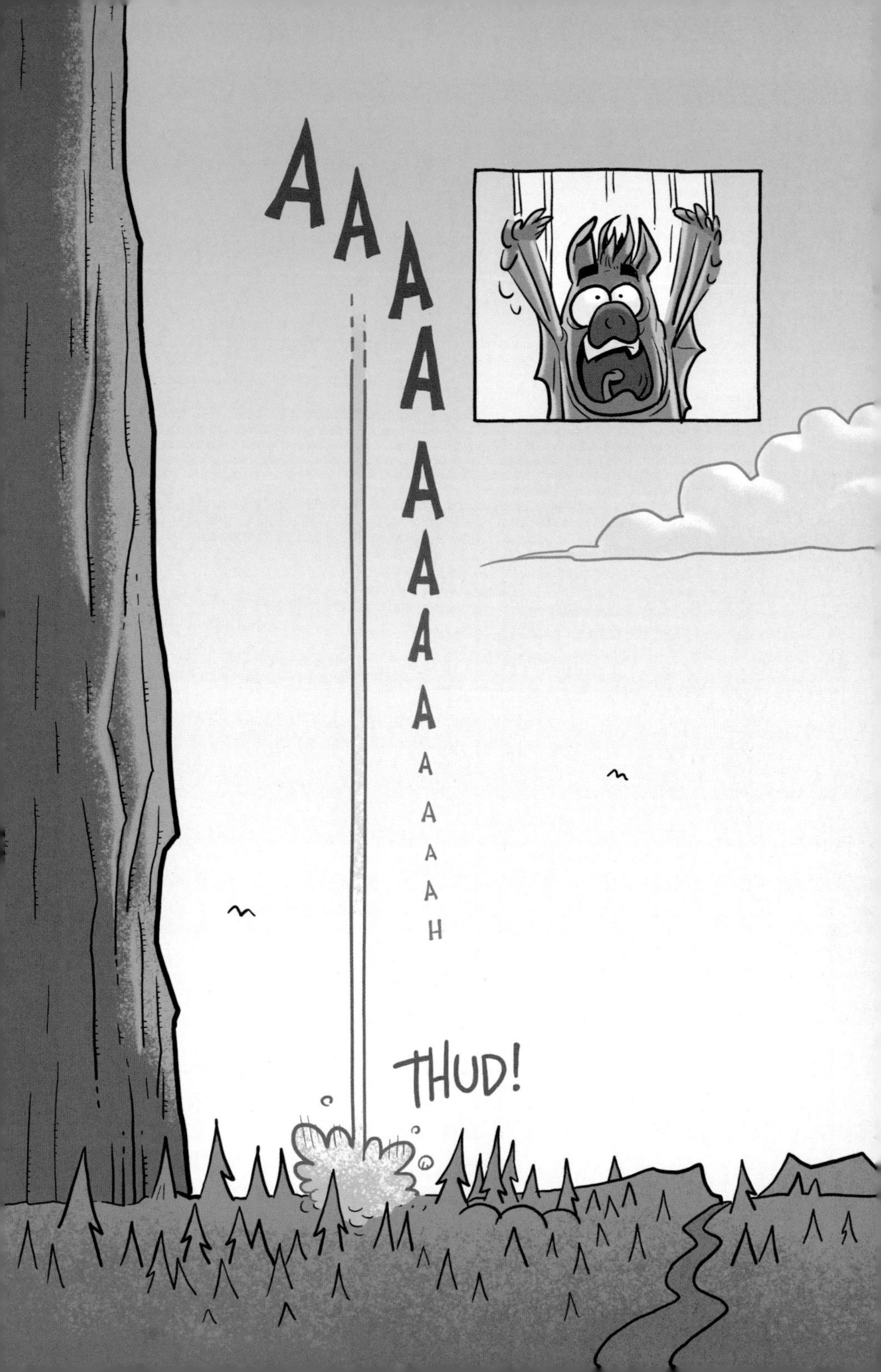
AAAAAAAAAAAAAH
THUD!

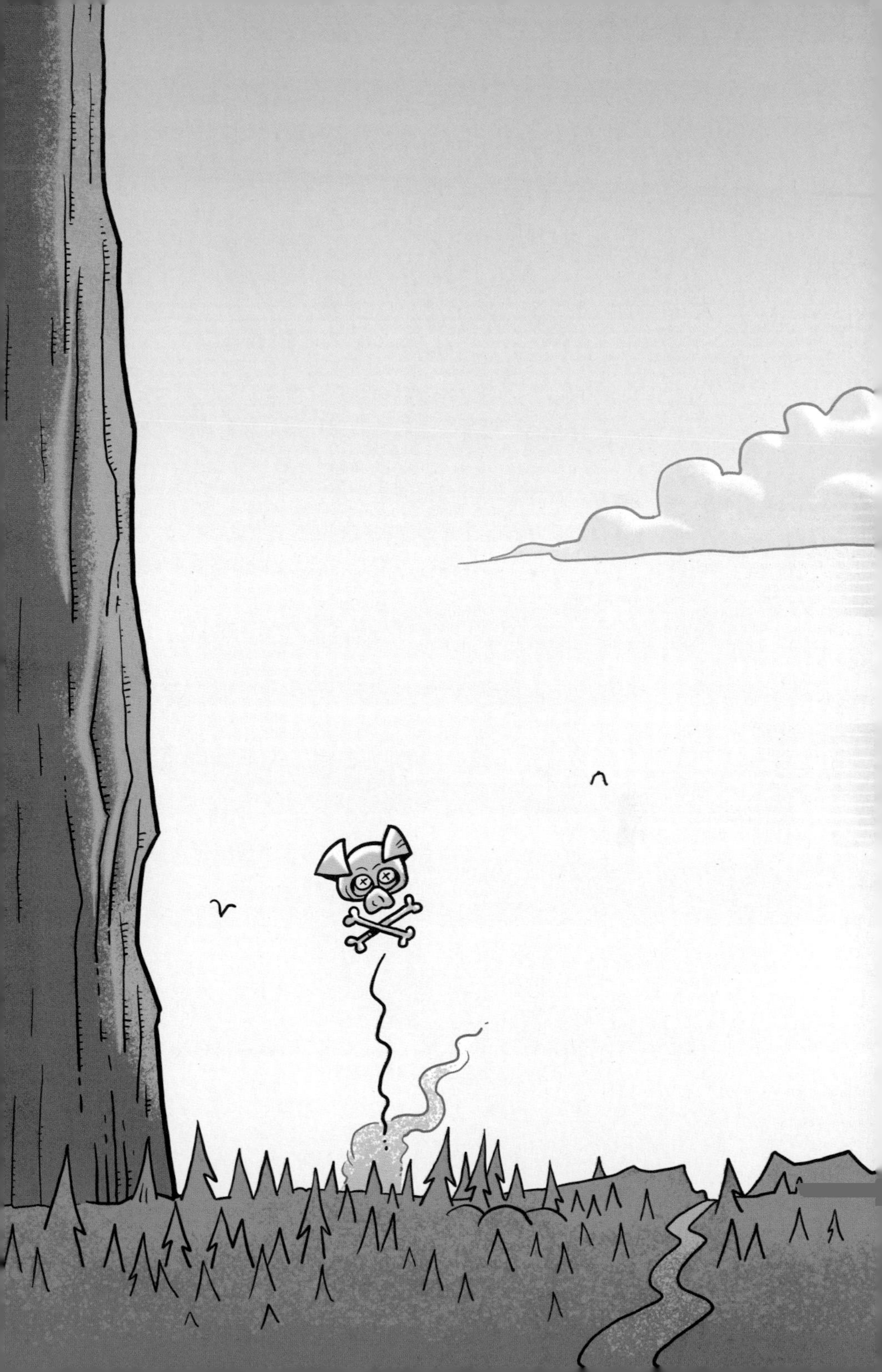

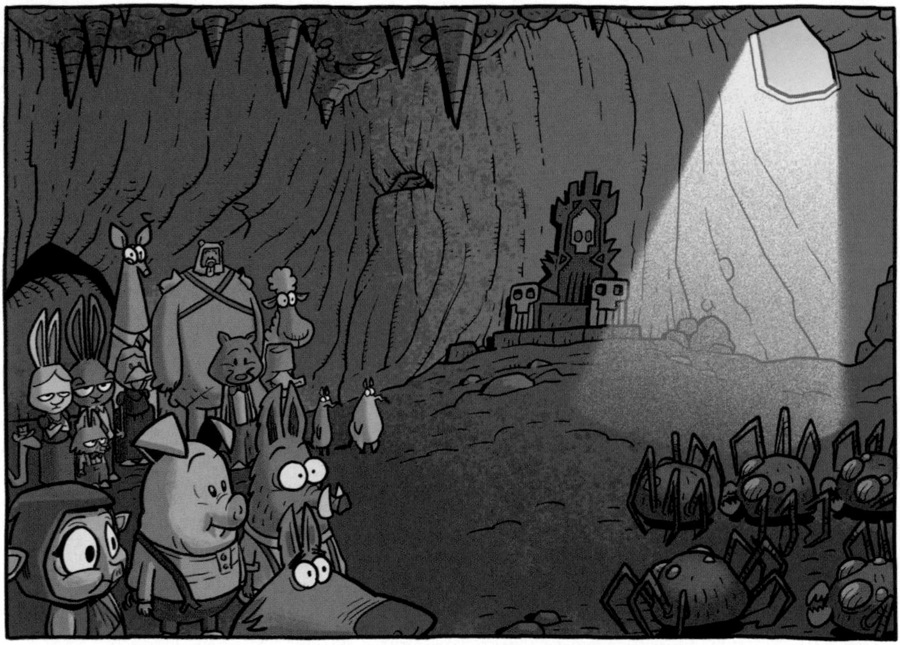

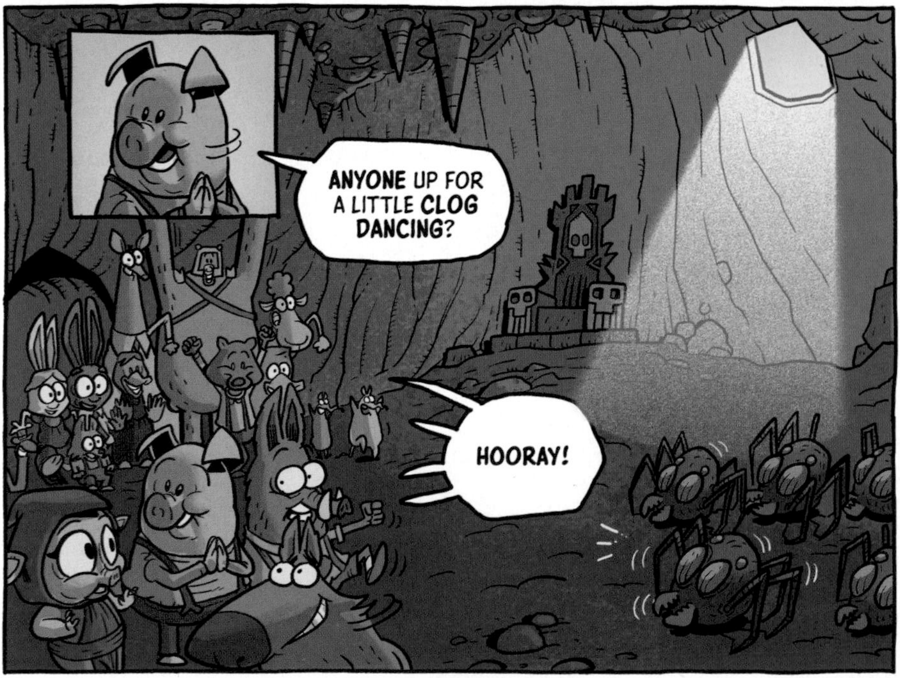
ANYONE UP FOR A LITTLE CLOG DANCING?
HOORAY!

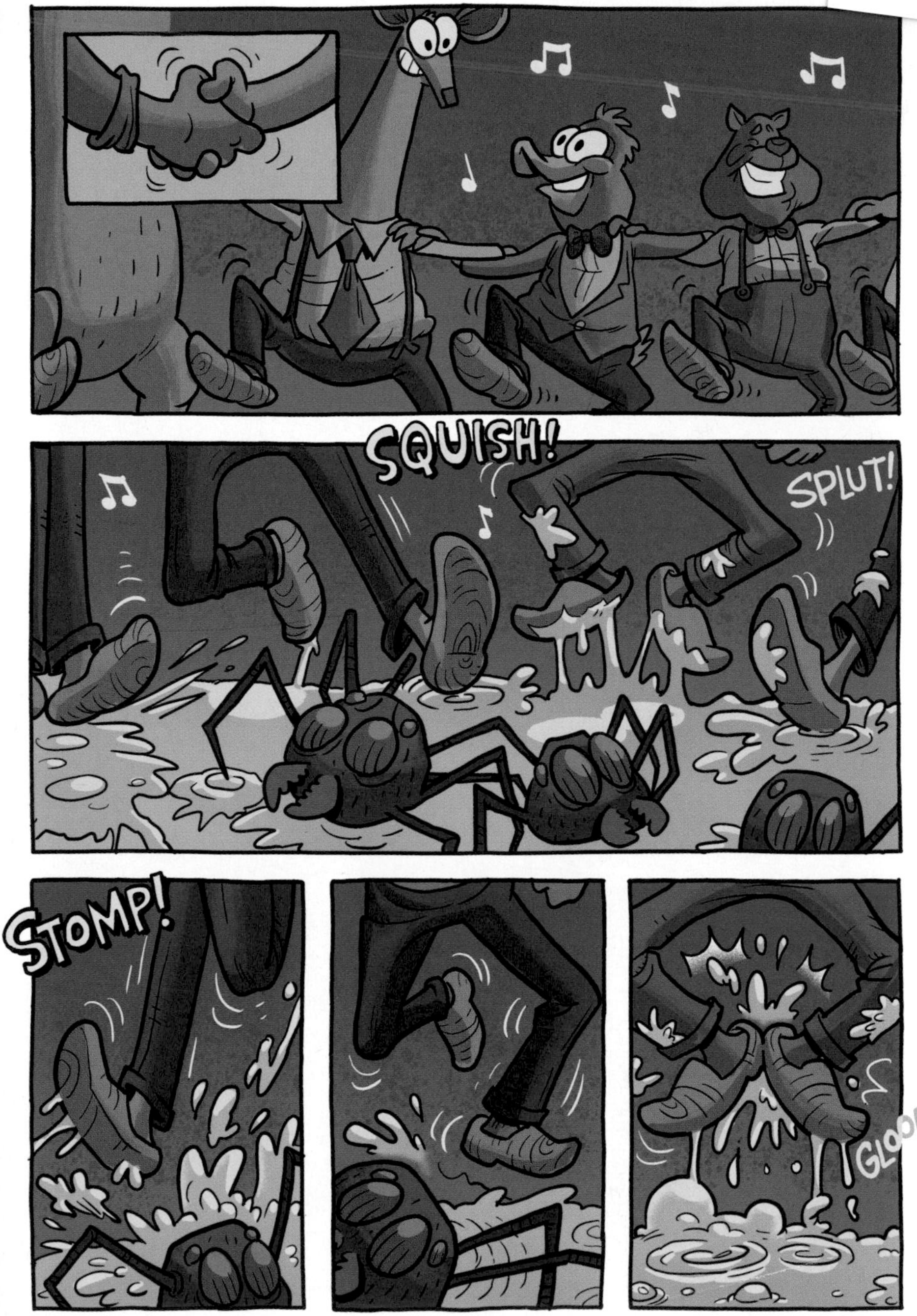
SQUISH!
SPLUT!
STOMP!
GLOOP!

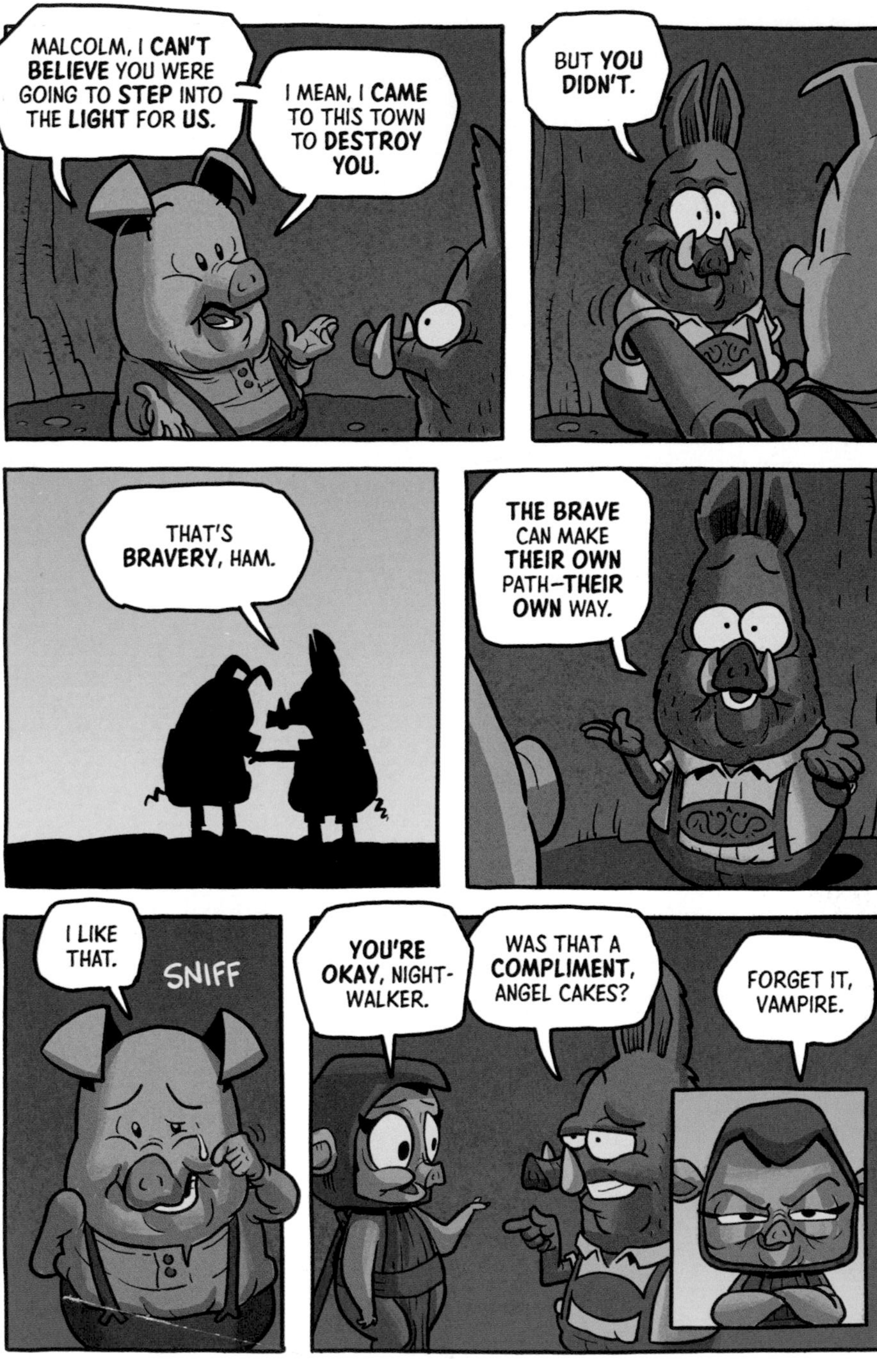
MALCOLM, I CAN'T BELIEVE YOU WERE GOING TO STEP INTO THE LIGHT FOR US.
I MEAN, I CAME TO THIS TOWN TO DESTROY YOU.
BUT YOU DIDN'T.
THAT'S BRAVERY, HAM.
THE BRAVE CAN MAKE THEIR OWN PATH—THEIR OWN WAY.
I LIKE THAT.
SNIFF
YOU'RE OKAY, NIGHT-WALKER.
WAS THAT A COMPLIMENT, ANGEL CAKES?
FORGET IT, VAMPIRE.

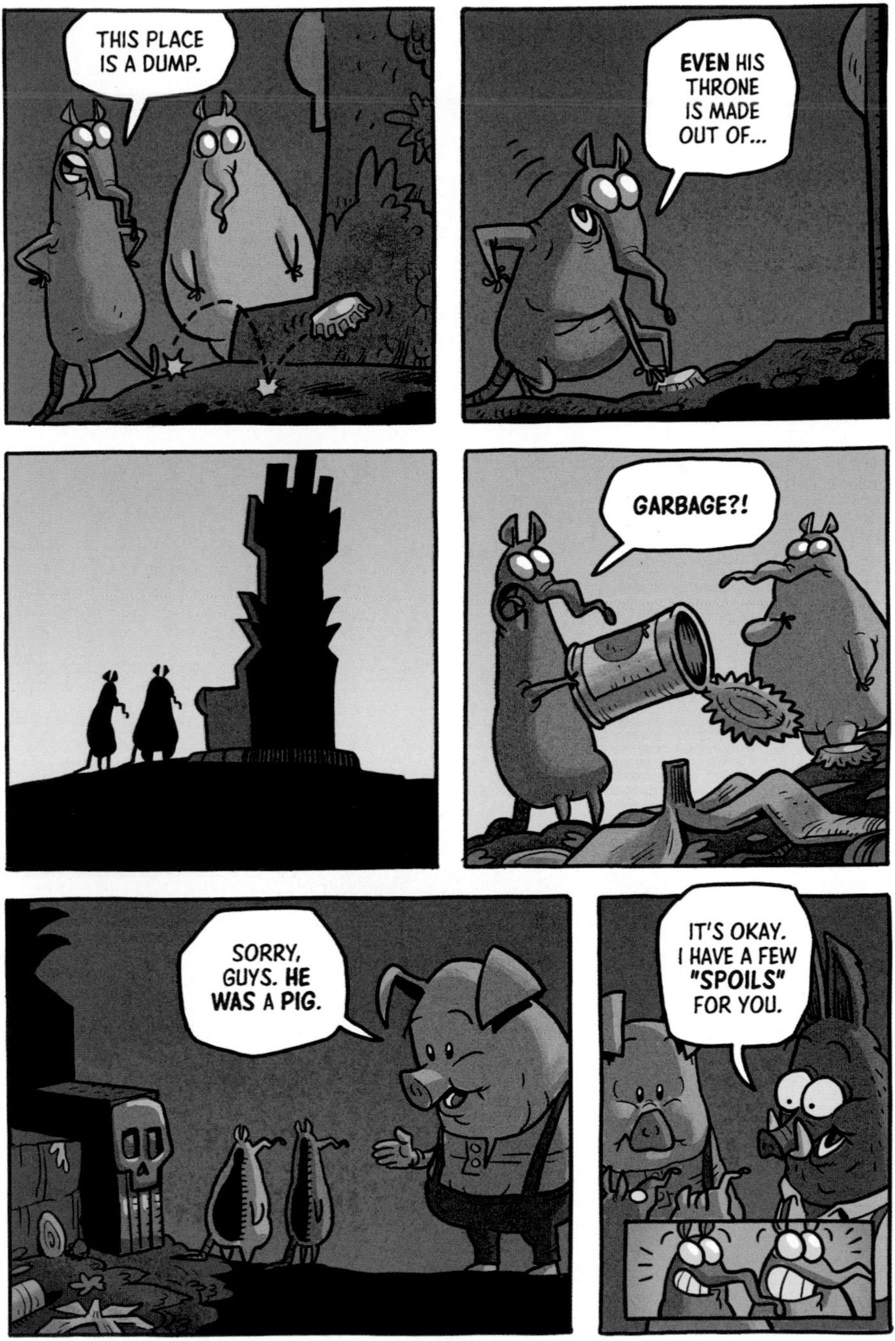
THIS PLACE IS A DUMP.
EVEN HIS THRONE IS MADE OUT OF...
GARBAGE?!
SORRY, GUYS. HE WAS A PIG.
IT'S OKAY. I HAVE A FEW "SPOILS" FOR YOU.

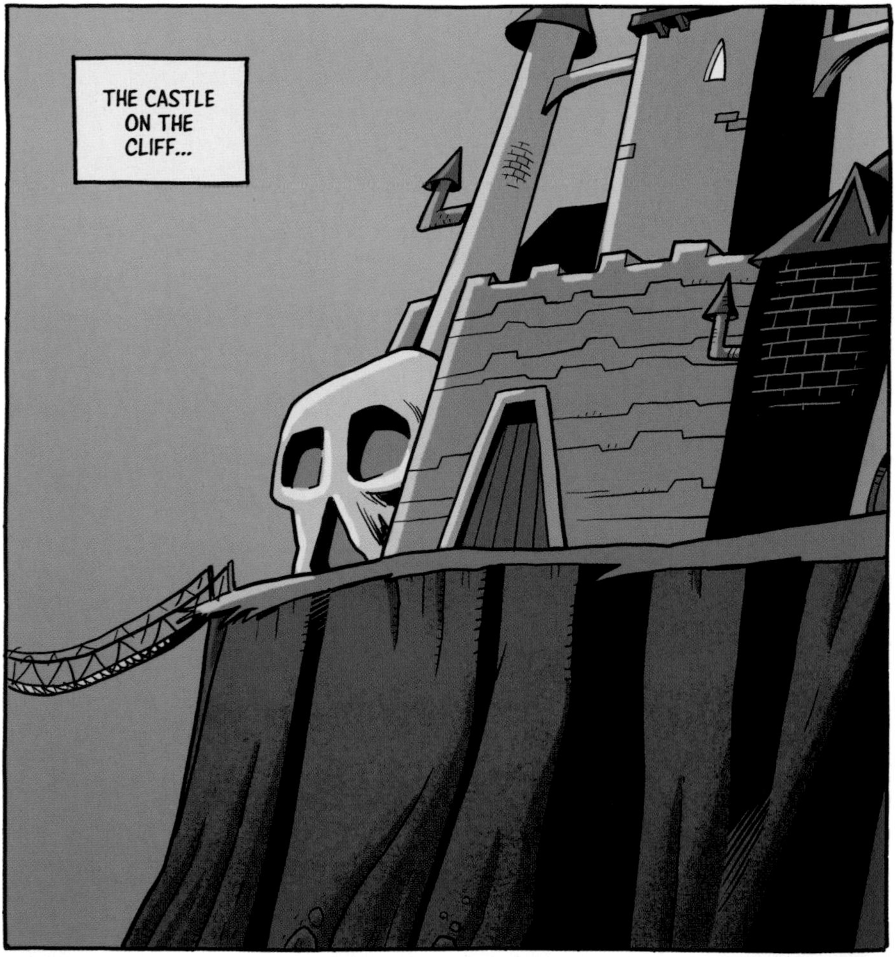
THE CASTLE ON THE CLIFF...

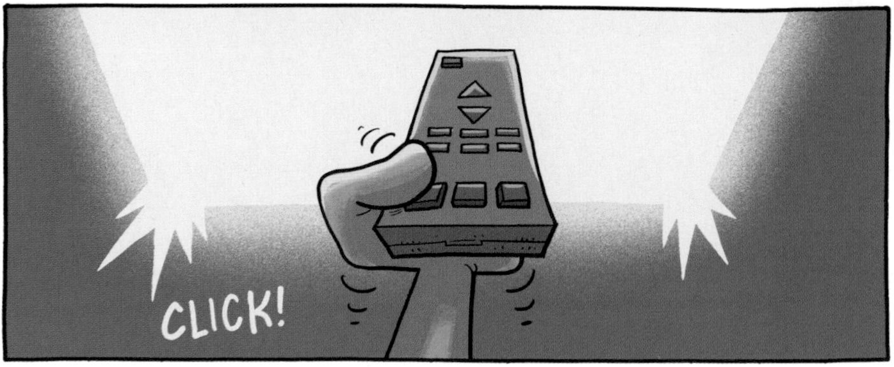
CLICK!

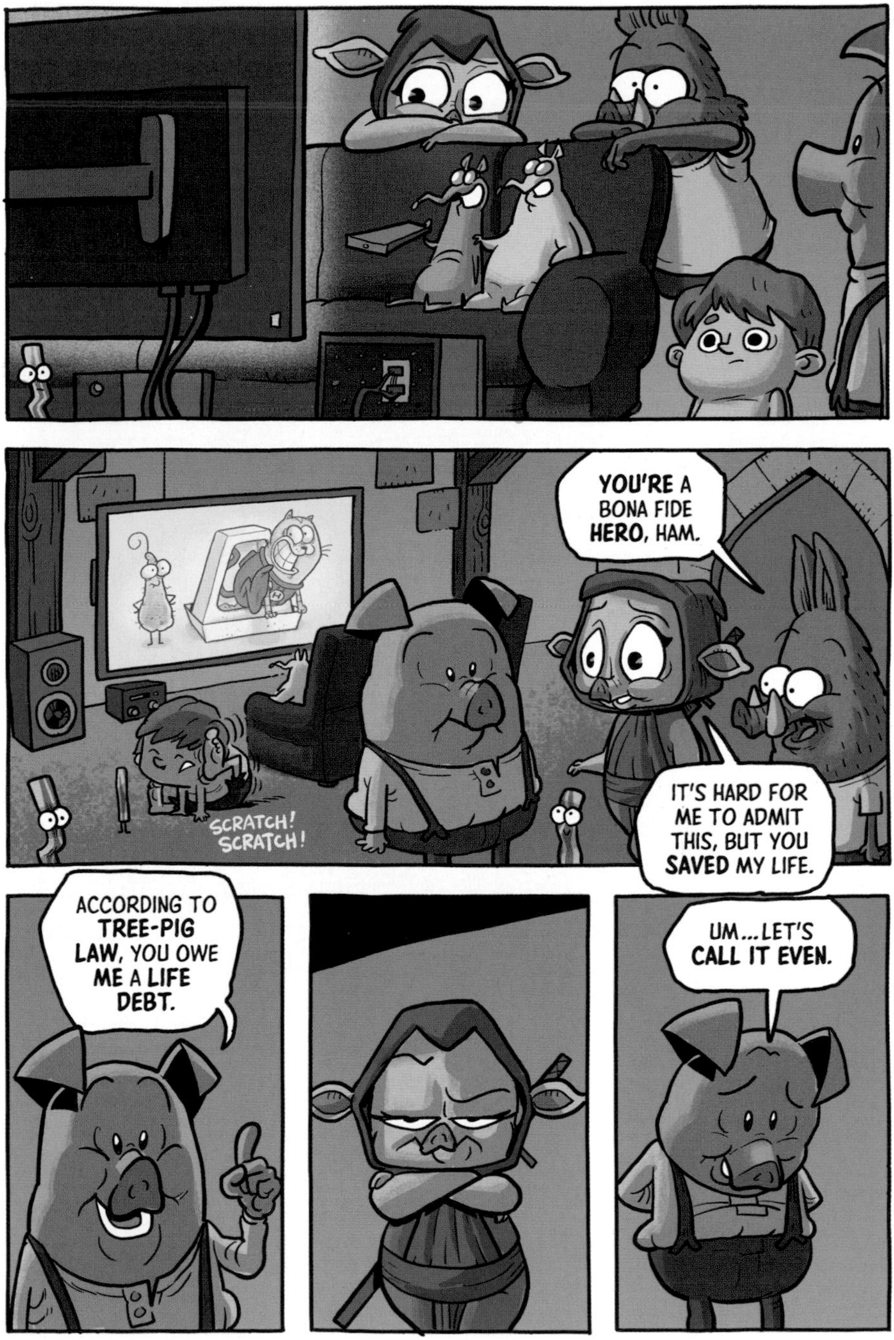

YOU'RE A BONA FIDE HERO, HAM.
SCRATCH! SCRATCH!
IT'S HARD FOR ME TO ADMIT THIS, BUT YOU SAVED MY LIFE.
ACCORDING TO TREE-PIG LAW, YOU OWE ME A LIFE DEBT.
UM...LET'S CALL IT EVEN.

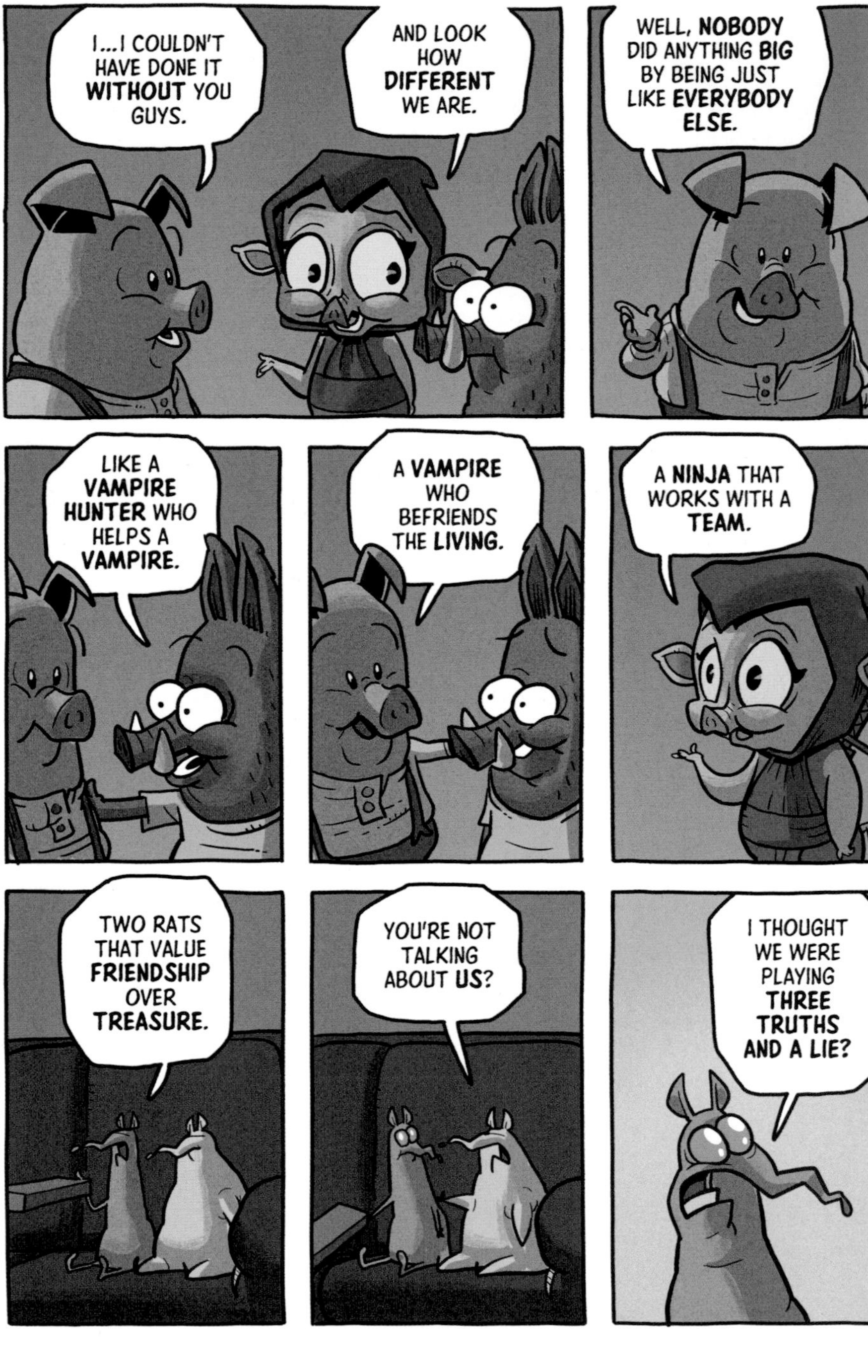
I...I COULDN'T HAVE DONE IT **WITHOUT** YOU GUYS.
AND LOOK HOW **DIFFERENT** WE ARE.
WELL, **NOBODY** DID ANYTHING **BIG** BY BEING JUST LIKE **EVERYBODY ELSE**.
LIKE A **VAMPIRE HUNTER** WHO HELPS A **VAMPIRE**.
A **VAMPIRE** WHO BEFRIENDS THE **LIVING**.
A **NINJA** THAT WORKS WITH A **TEAM**.
TWO RATS THAT VALUE **FRIENDSHIP** OVER **TREASURE**.
YOU'RE NOT TALKING ABOUT **US**?
I THOUGHT WE WERE PLAYING **THREE TRUTHS AND A LIE**?

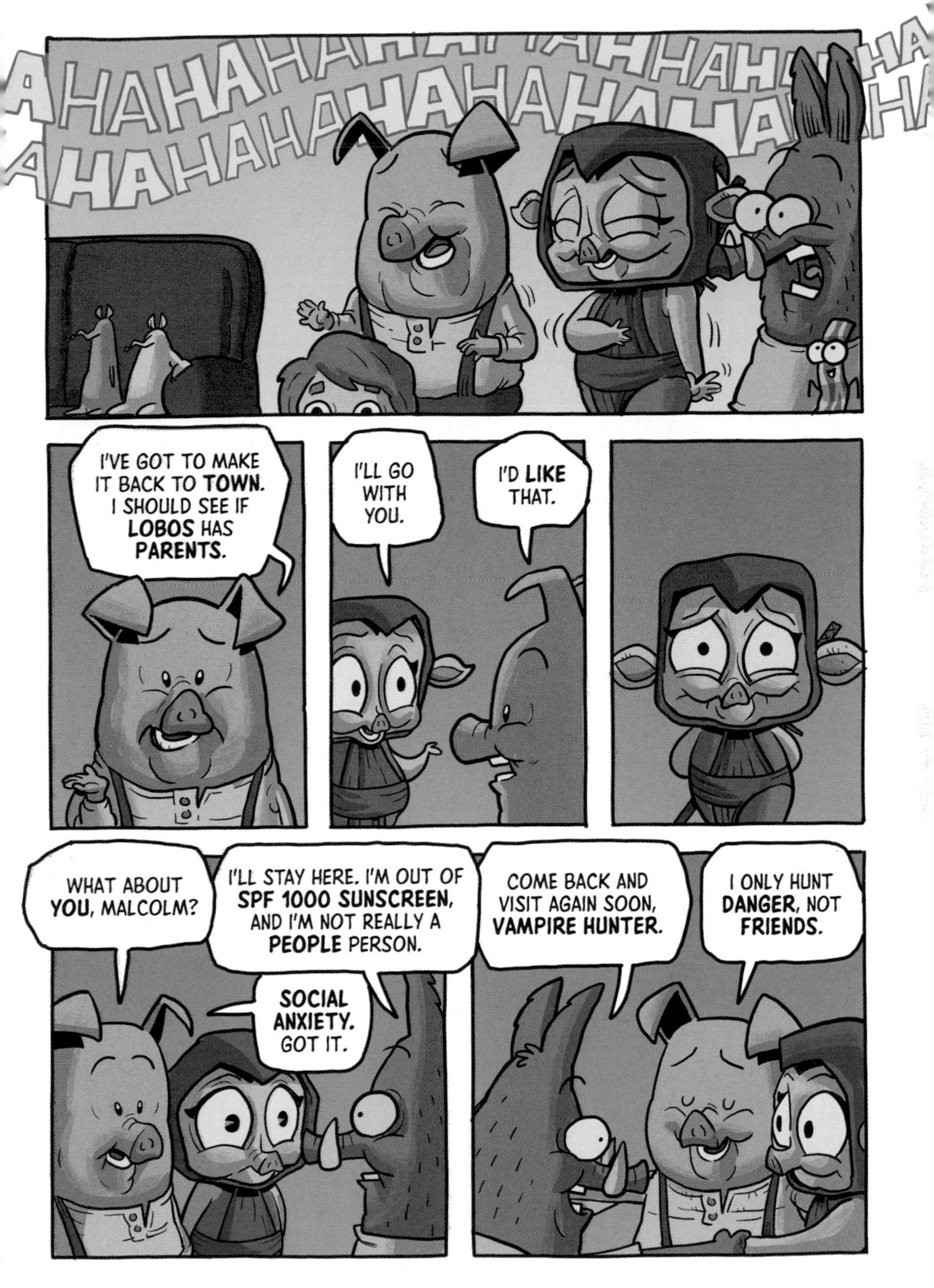
AHAHAHAHAHAHAHAHAHAHA
AHAHAHAHAHAHAHAHAHAHA
I'VE GOT TO MAKE IT BACK TO TOWN. I SHOULD SEE IF LOBOS HAS PARENTS.
I'LL GO WITH YOU.
I'D LIKE THAT.
WHAT ABOUT YOU, MALCOLM?
I'LL STAY HERE. I'M OUT OF SPF 1000 SUNSCREEN, AND I'M NOT REALLY A PEOPLE PERSON.
SOCIAL ANXIETY. GOT IT.
COME BACK AND VISIT AGAIN SOON, VAMPIRE HUNTER.
I ONLY HUNT DANGER, NOT FRIENDS.

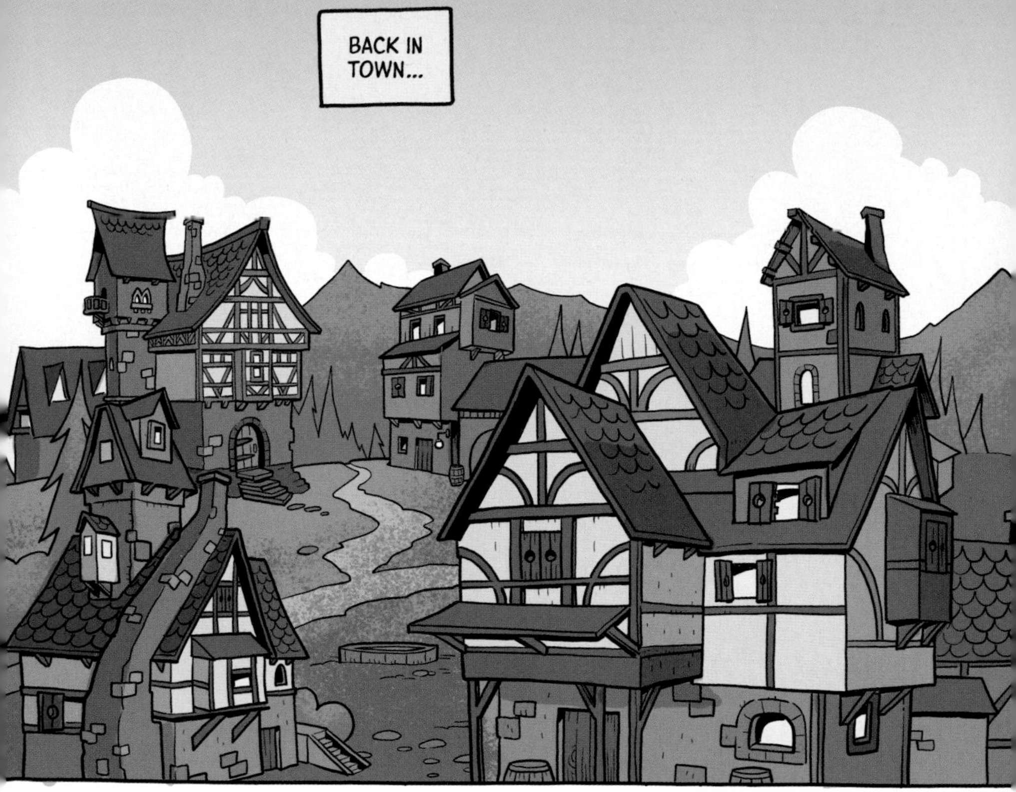
BACK IN TOWN...

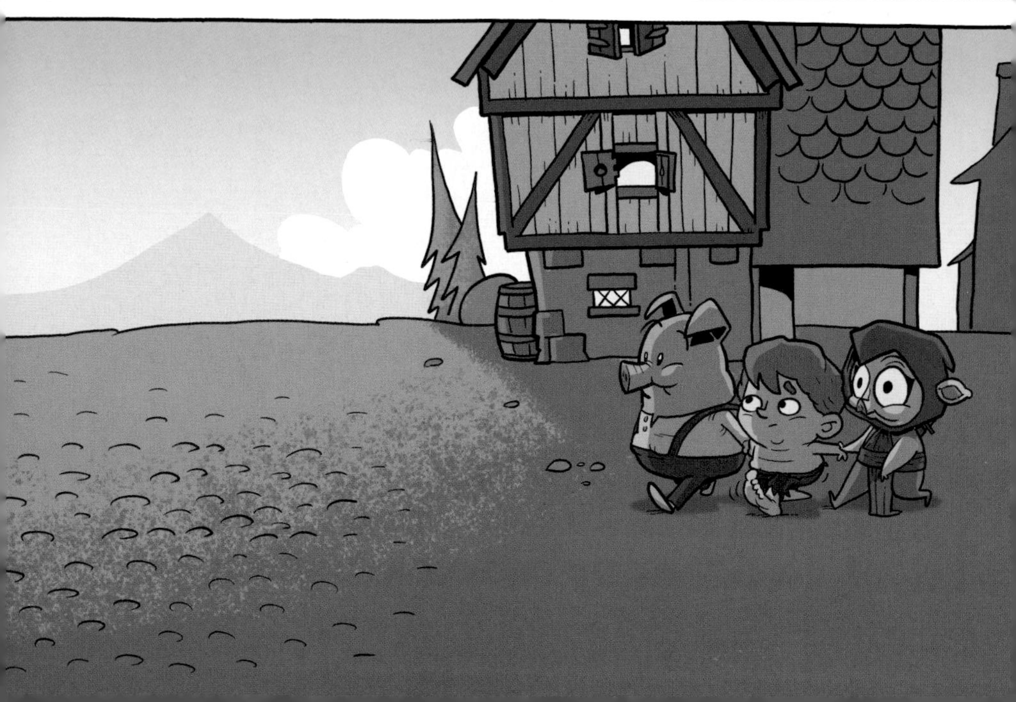

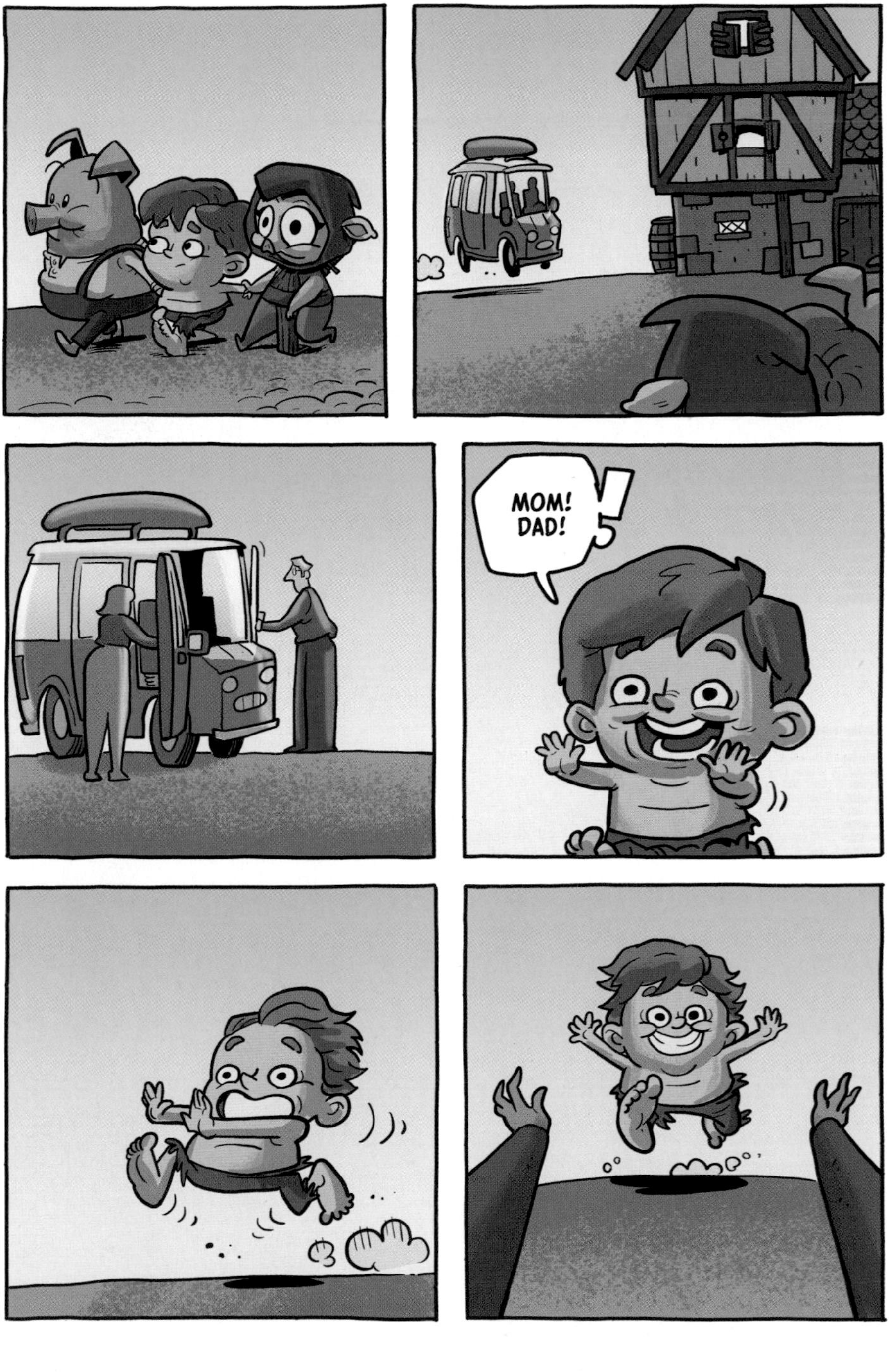
MOM!
DAD!

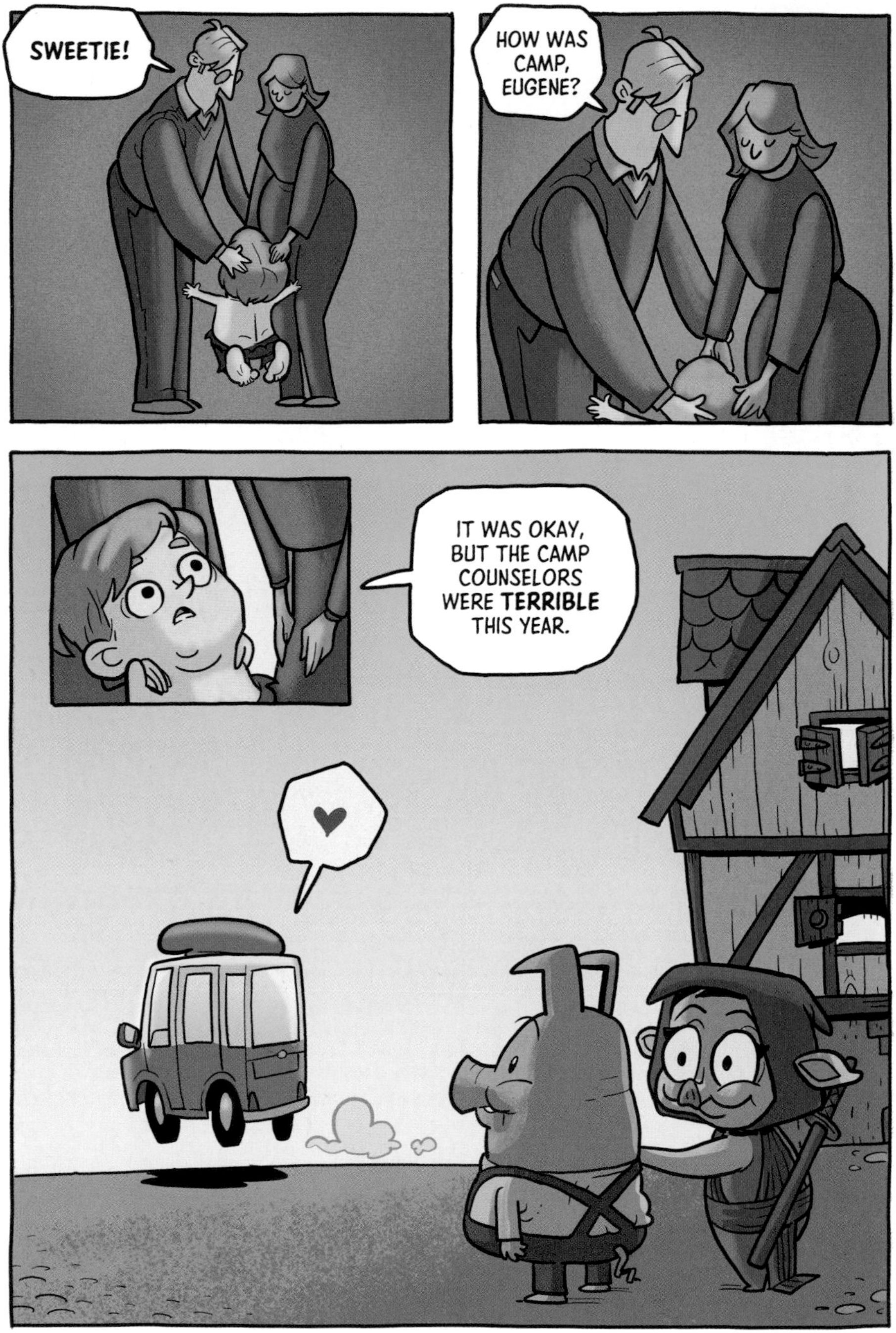
SWEETIE!
HOW WAS CAMP, EUGENE?
IT WAS OKAY, BUT THE CAMP COUNSELORS WERE **TERRIBLE** THIS YEAR.
♥

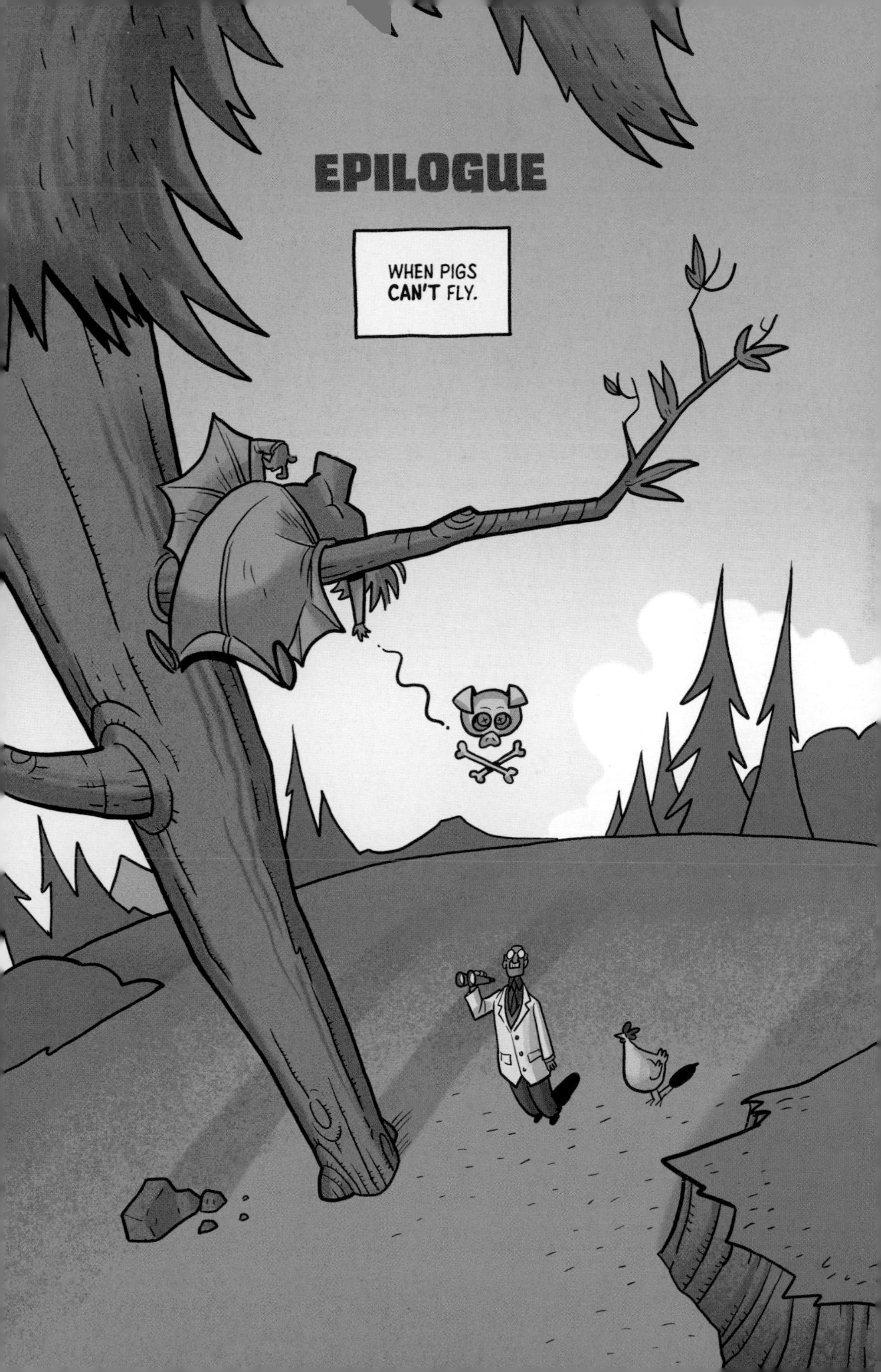
EPILOGUE
WHEN PIGS CAN'T FLY.

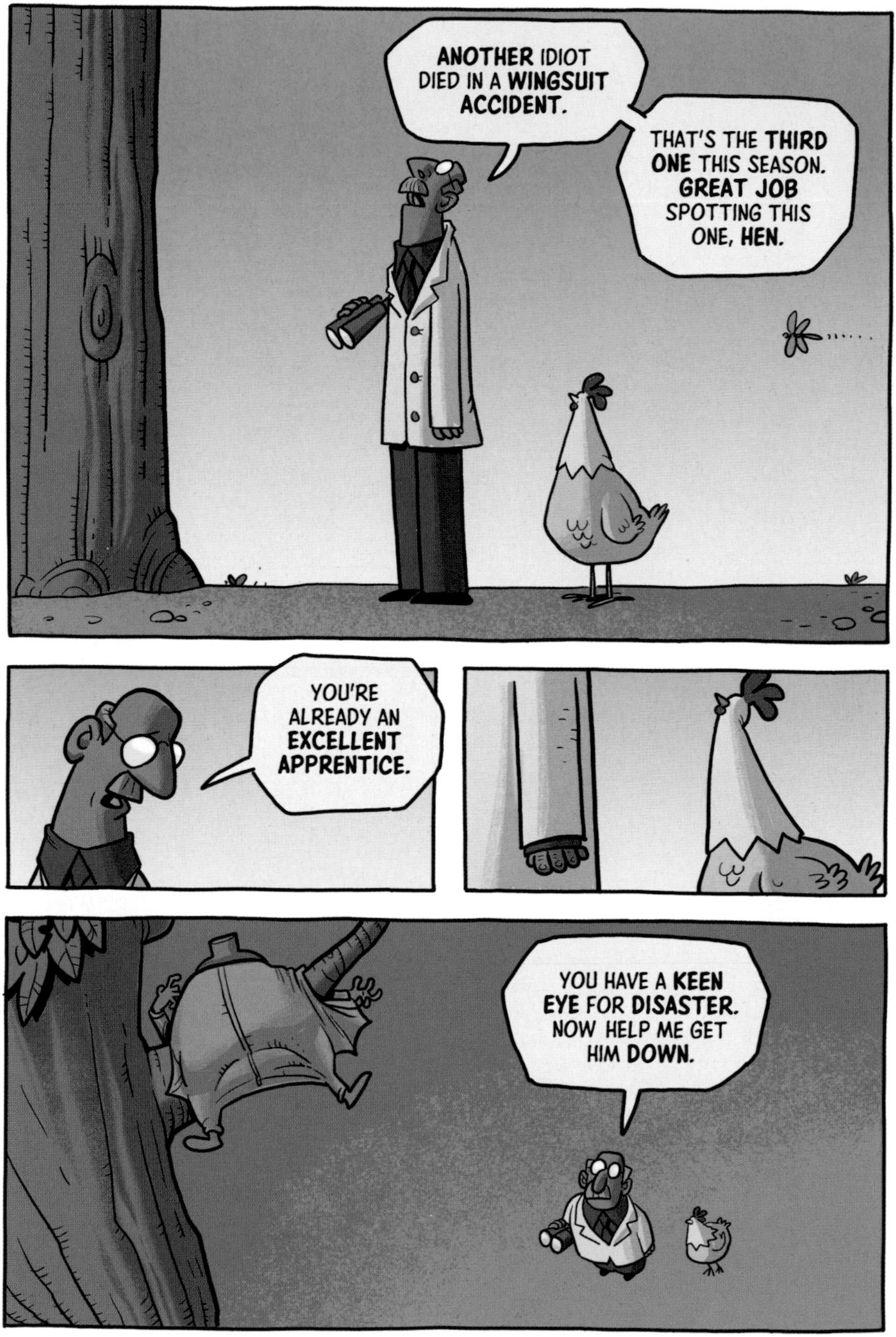
ANOTHER IDIOT DIED IN A WINGSUIT ACCIDENT.
THAT'S THE THIRD ONE THIS SEASON. GREAT JOB SPOTTING THIS ONE, HEN.
YOU'RE ALREADY AN EXCELLENT APPRENTICE.
YOU HAVE A KEEN EYE FOR DISASTER. NOW HELP ME GET HIM DOWN.

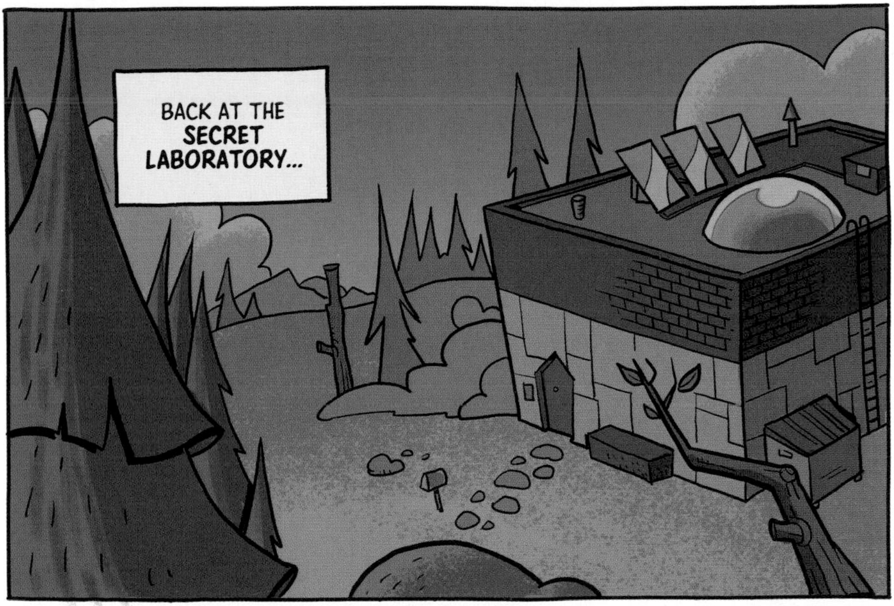
BACK AT THE SECRET LABORATORY...

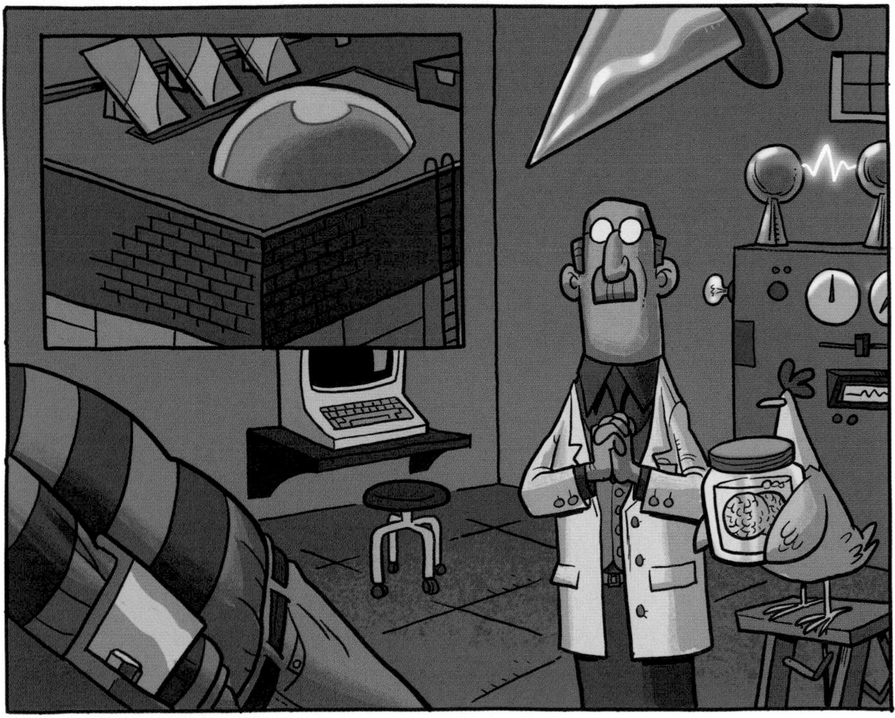

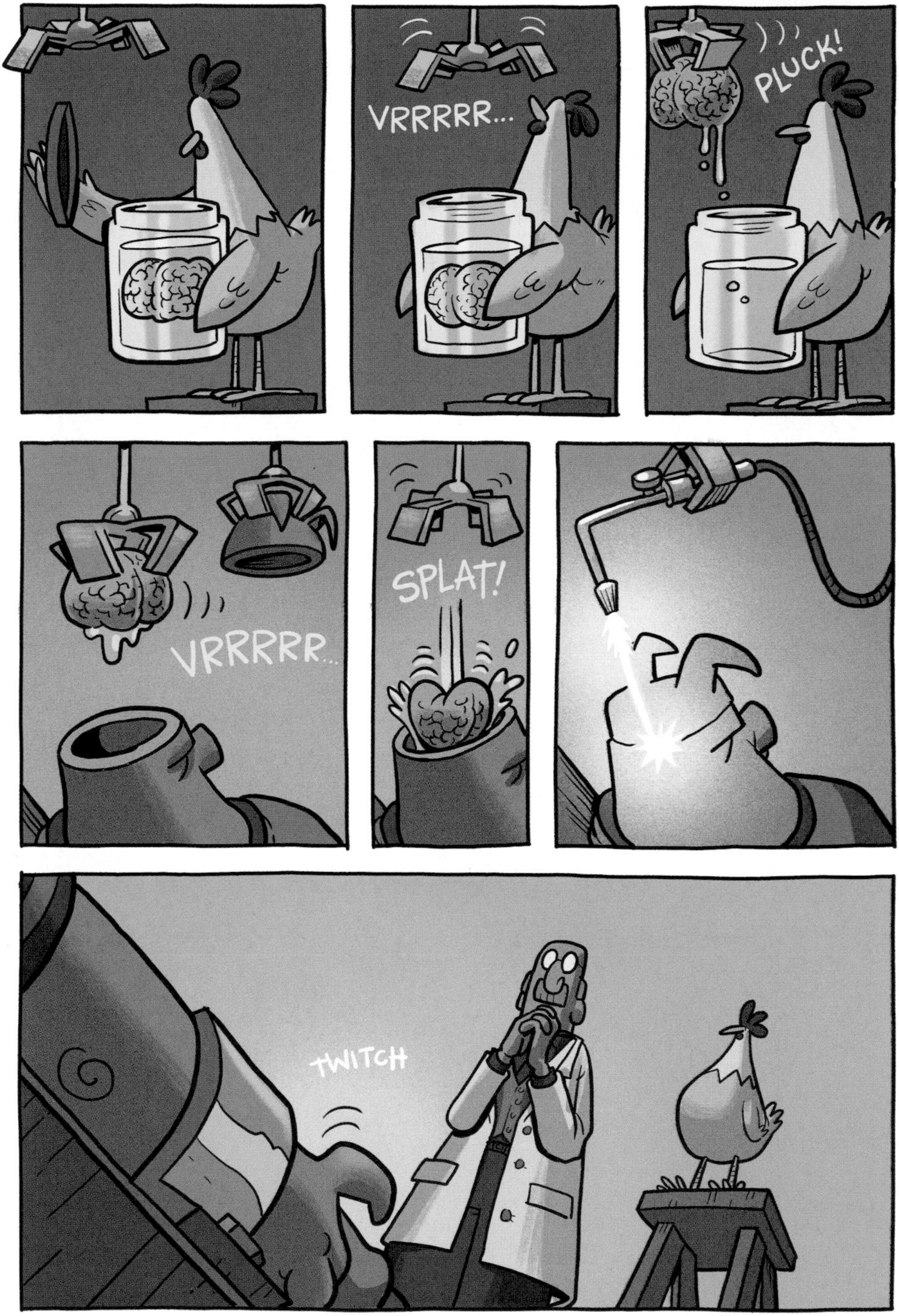
VRRRRR...
PLUCK!
VRRRRR...
SPLAT!
TWITCH

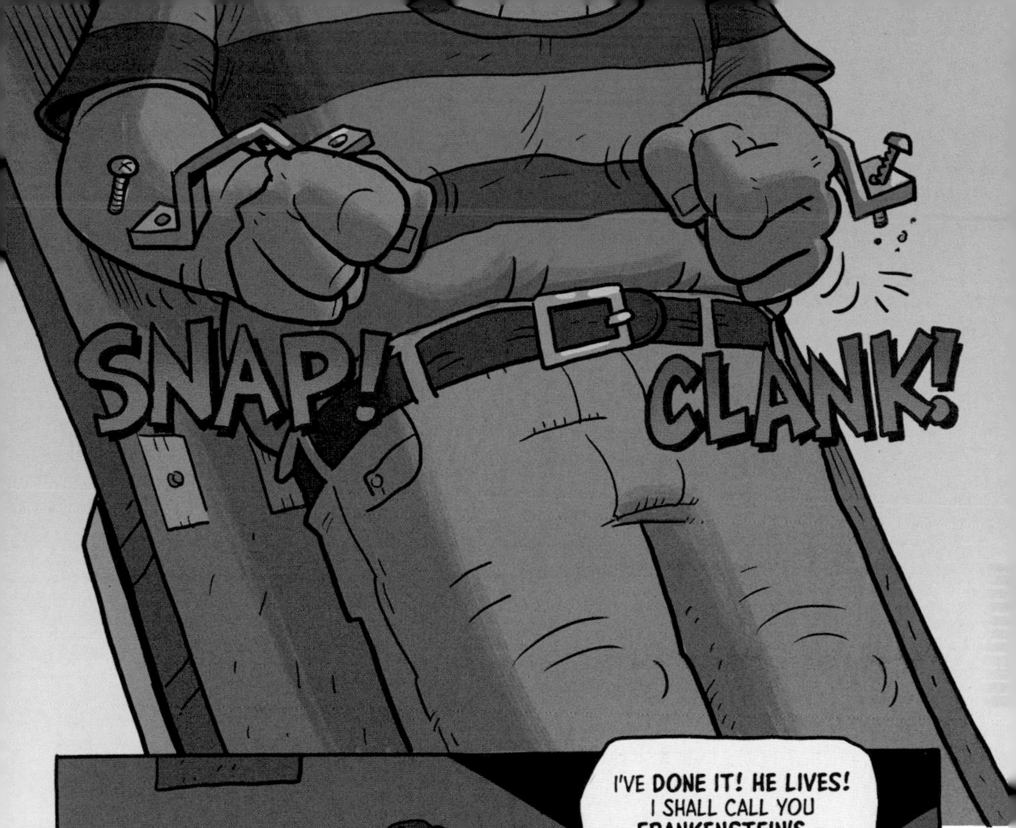
SNAP!
CLANK!

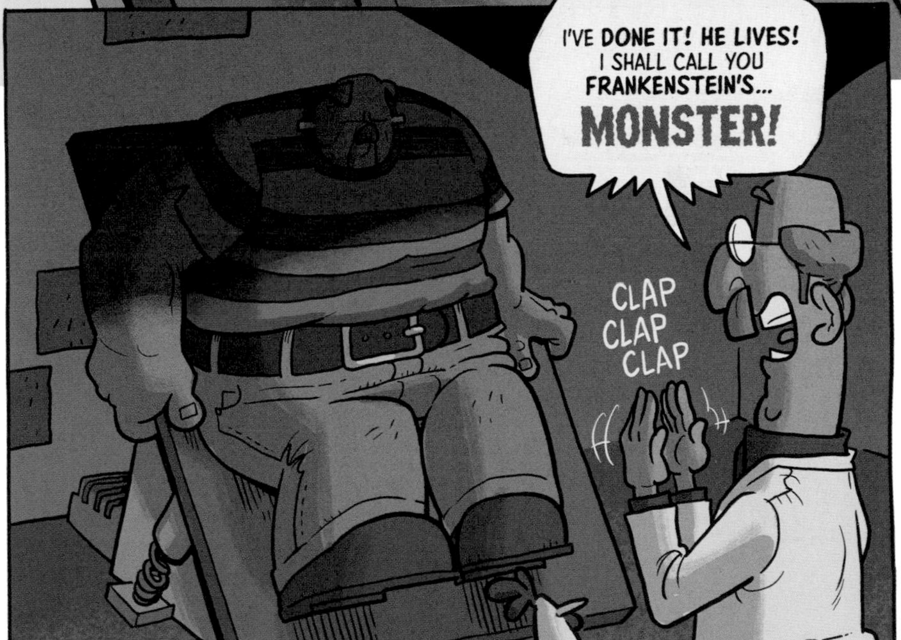
I'VE DONE IT! HE LIVES! I SHALL CALL YOU FRANKENSTEIN'S... MONSTER!
CLAP CLAP CLAP

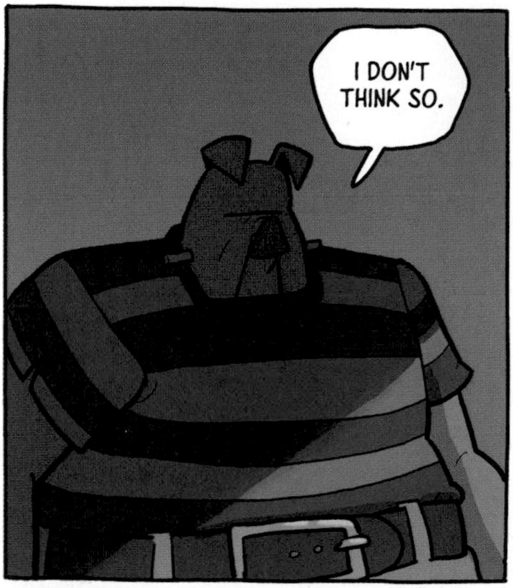
I DON'T THINK SO.
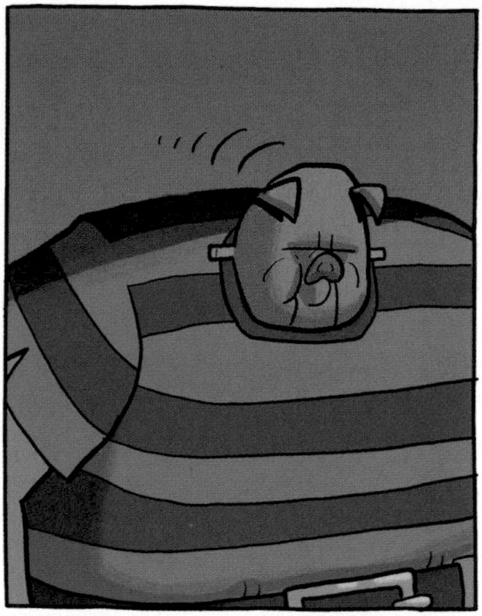
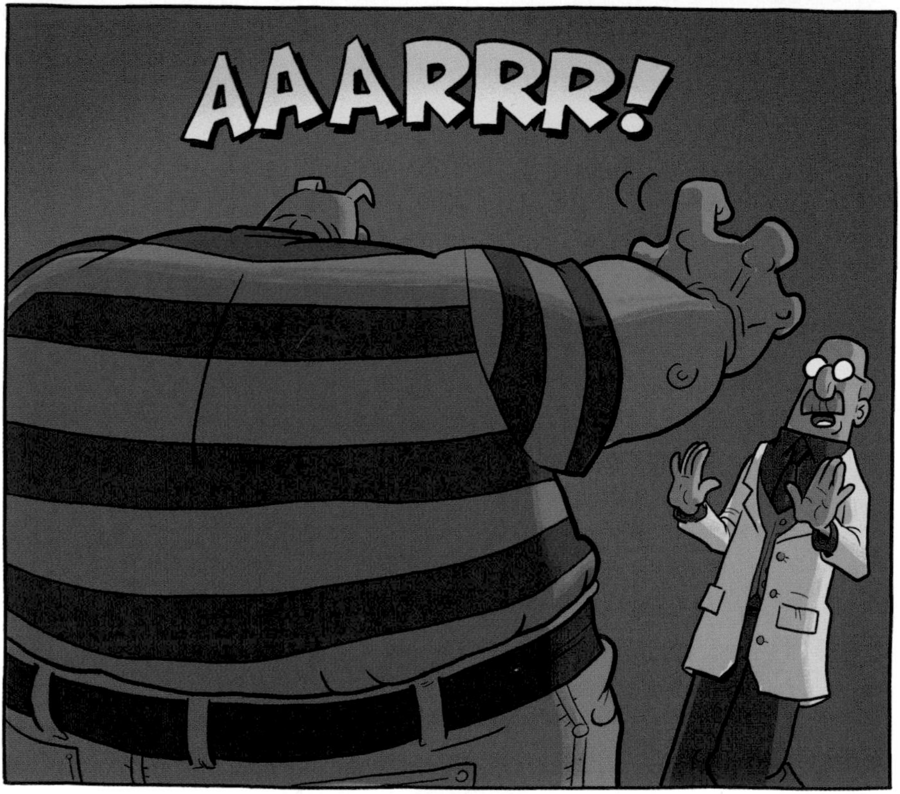
AAARRR!

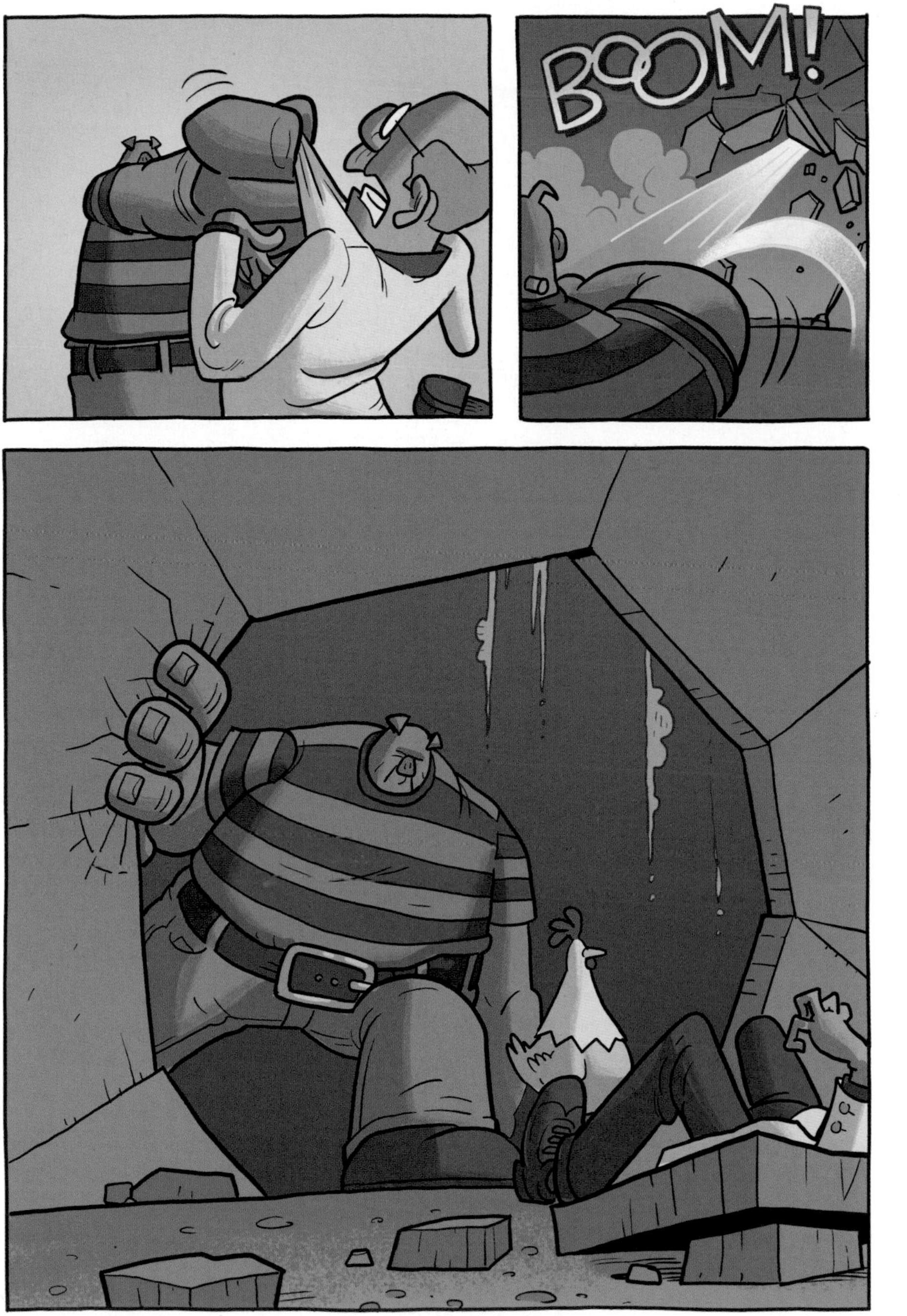
BOOM!

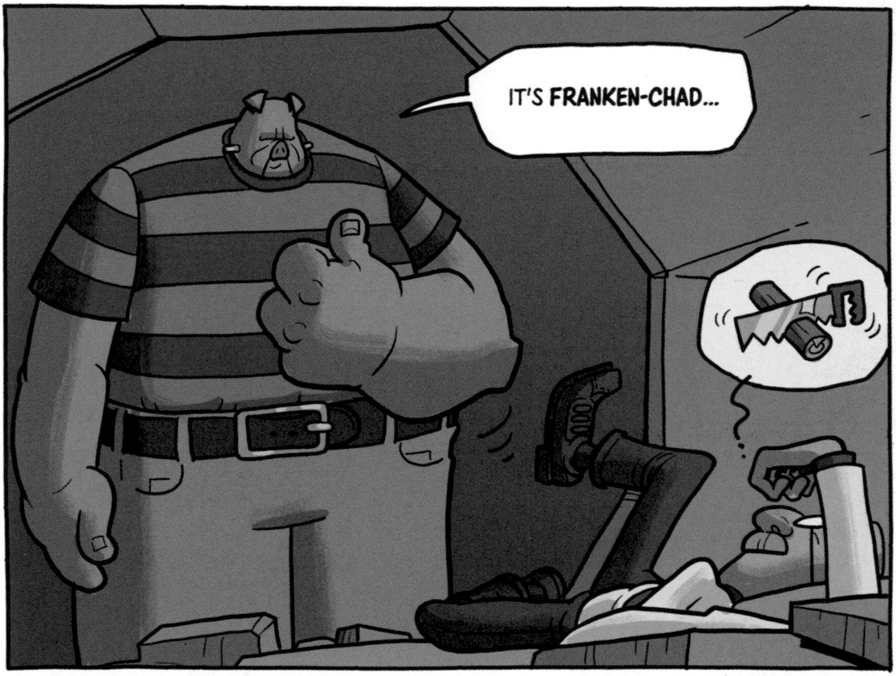
IT'S FRANKEN-CHAD...

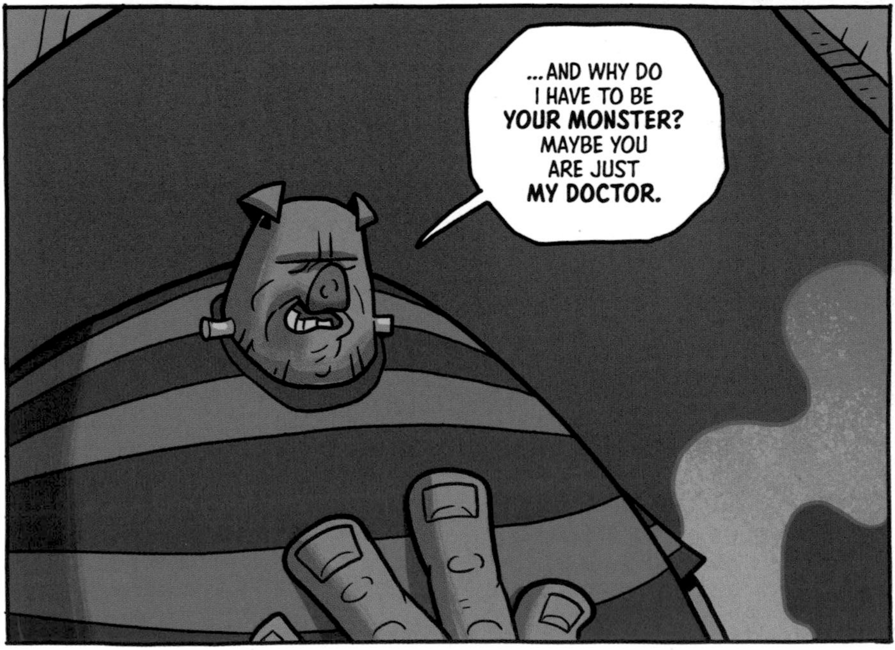
...AND WHY DO I HAVE TO BE YOUR MONSTER? MAYBE YOU ARE JUST MY DOCTOR.

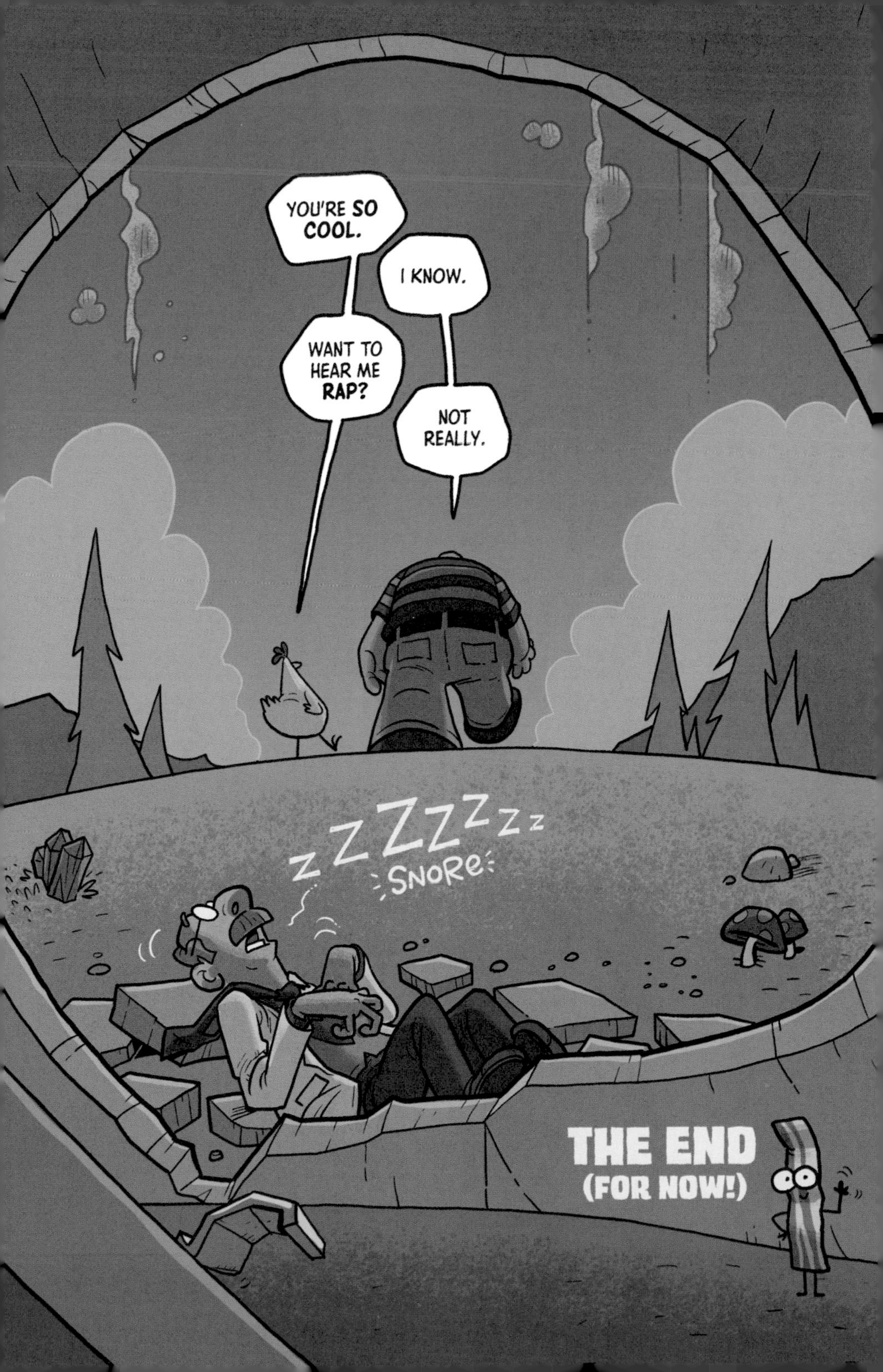
YOU'RE SO COOL.
I KNOW.
WANT TO HEAR ME RAP?
NOT REALLY.
zZZZZzz
SNORE
THE END
(FOR NOW!)

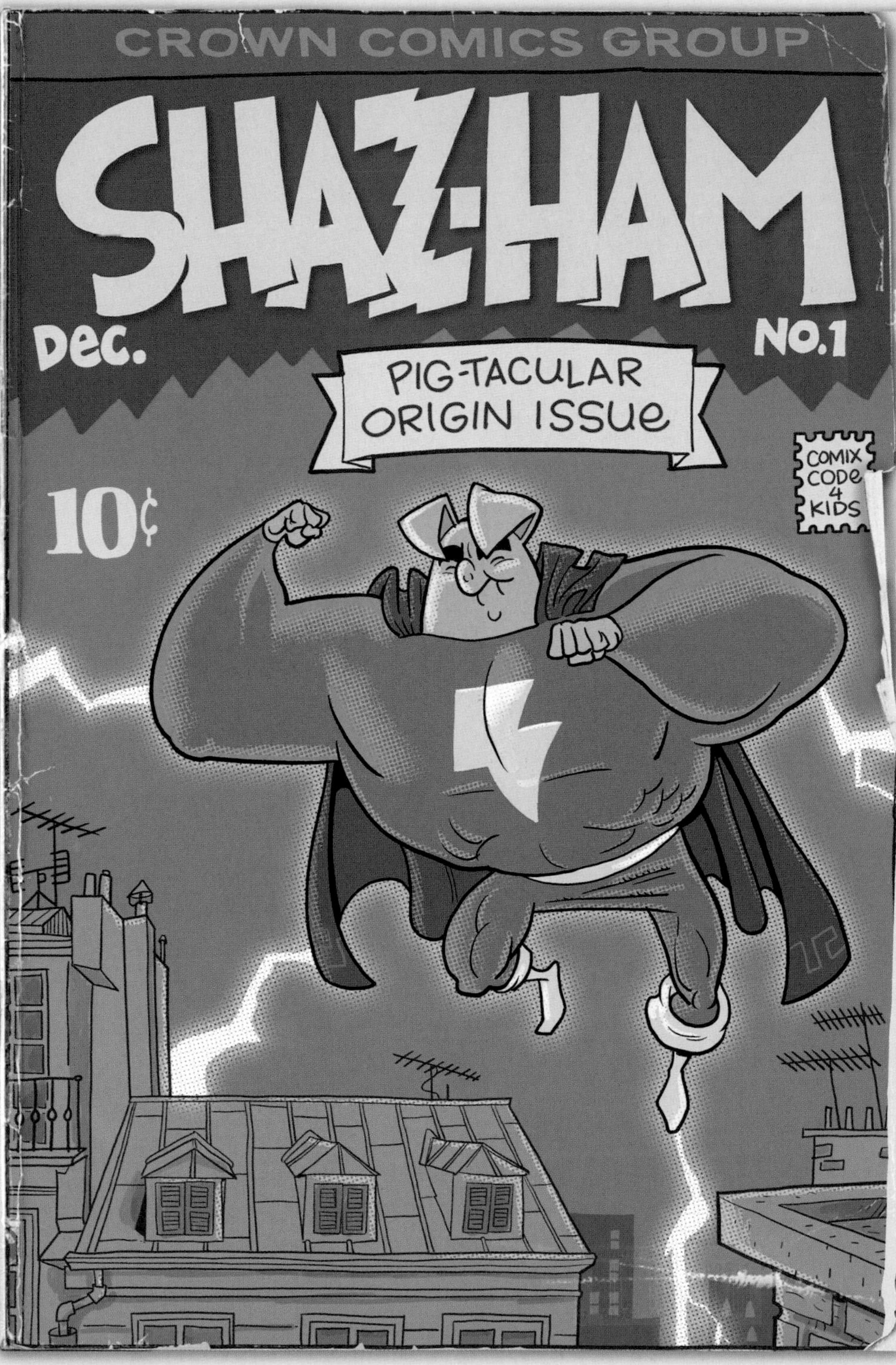
CROWN COMICS GROUP
SHAZ-HAM
DEC.
NO.1
PIG-TACULAR
ORIGIN ISSUE
COMIX CODE 4 KIDS
10¢

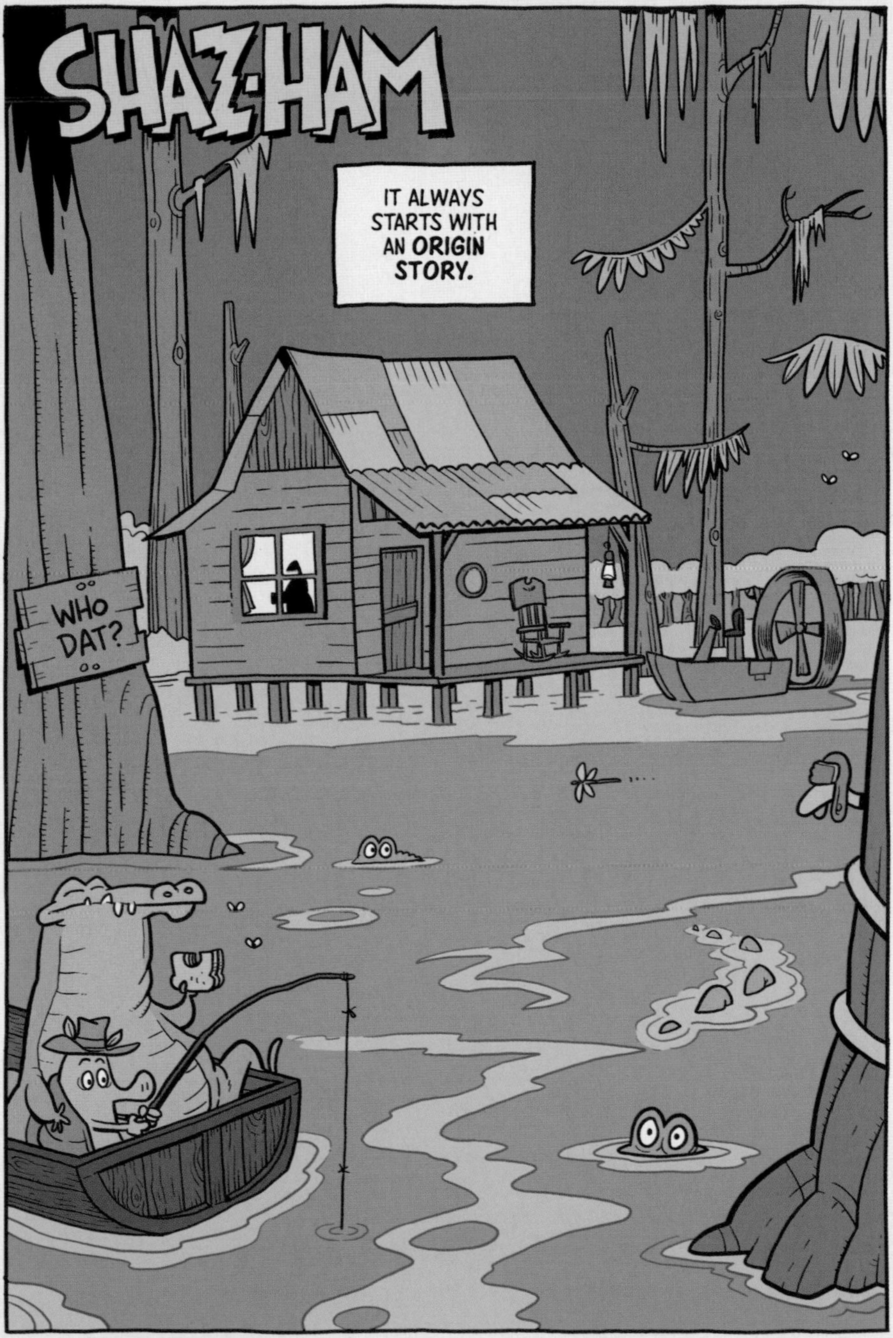
SHAZ-HAM
IT ALWAYS STARTS WITH AN ORIGIN STORY.
WHO DAT?

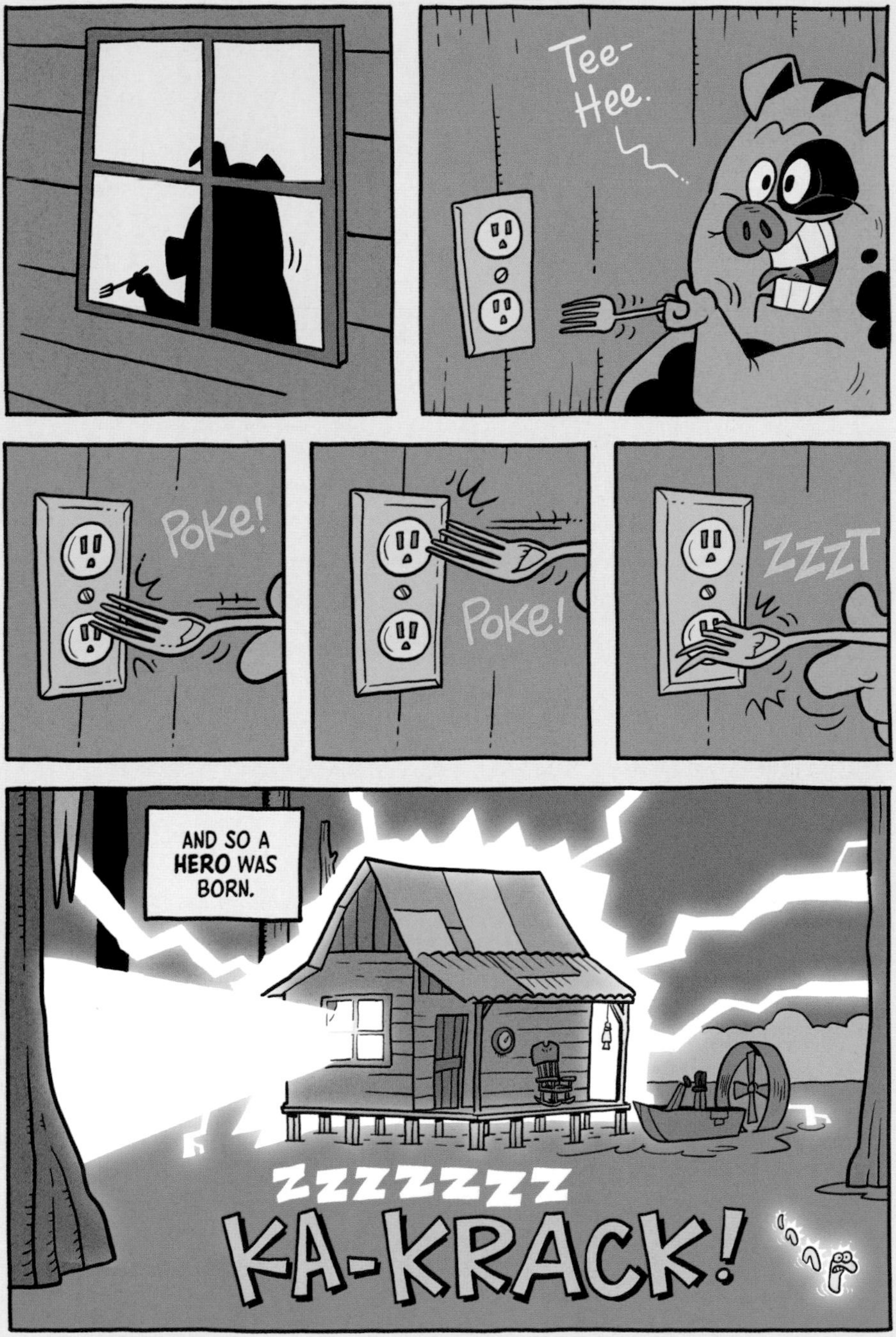

Tee-Hee.
Poke!
Poke!
ZZZT
AND SO A HERO WAS BORN.
ZZZZZZZ
KA-KRACK!

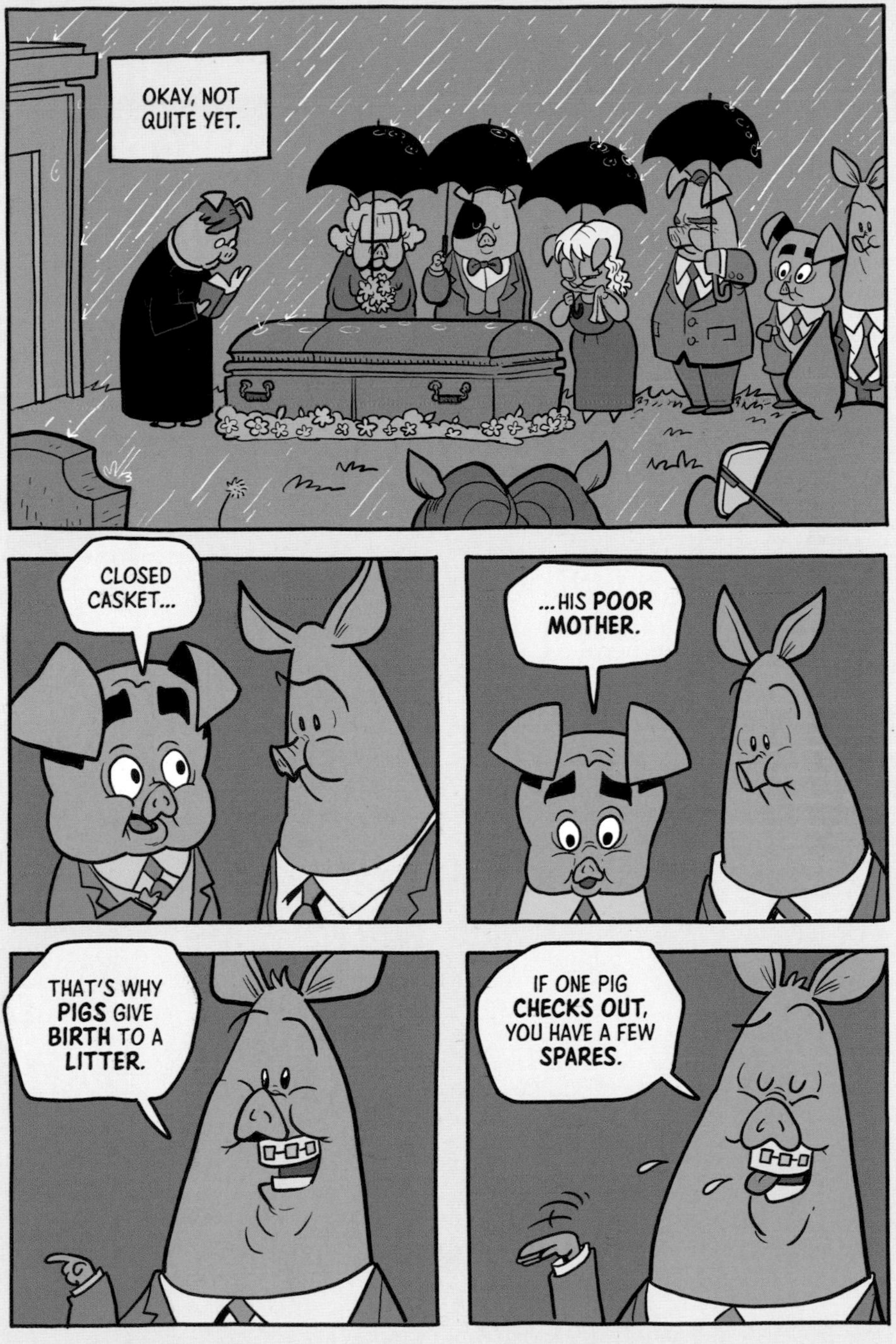
OKAY, NOT QUITE YET.
CLOSED CASKET...
...HIS POOR MOTHER.
THAT'S WHY PIGS GIVE BIRTH TO A LITTER.
IF ONE PIG CHECKS OUT, YOU HAVE A FEW SPARES.

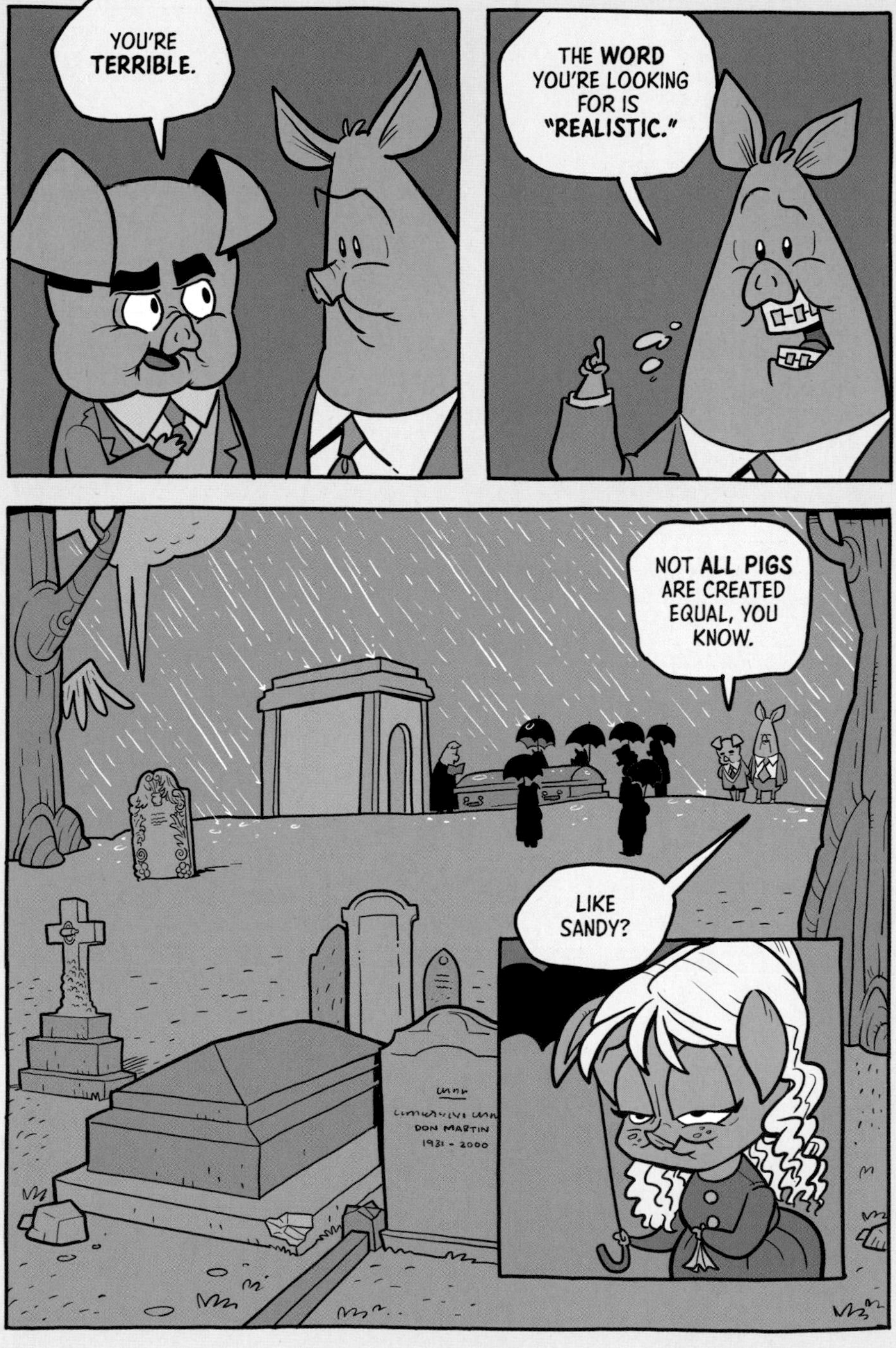
YOU'RE TERRIBLE.
THE WORD YOU'RE LOOKING FOR IS "REALISTIC."
NOT ALL PIGS ARE CREATED EQUAL, YOU KNOW.
LIKE SANDY?
DON MARTIN
1931 - 2000

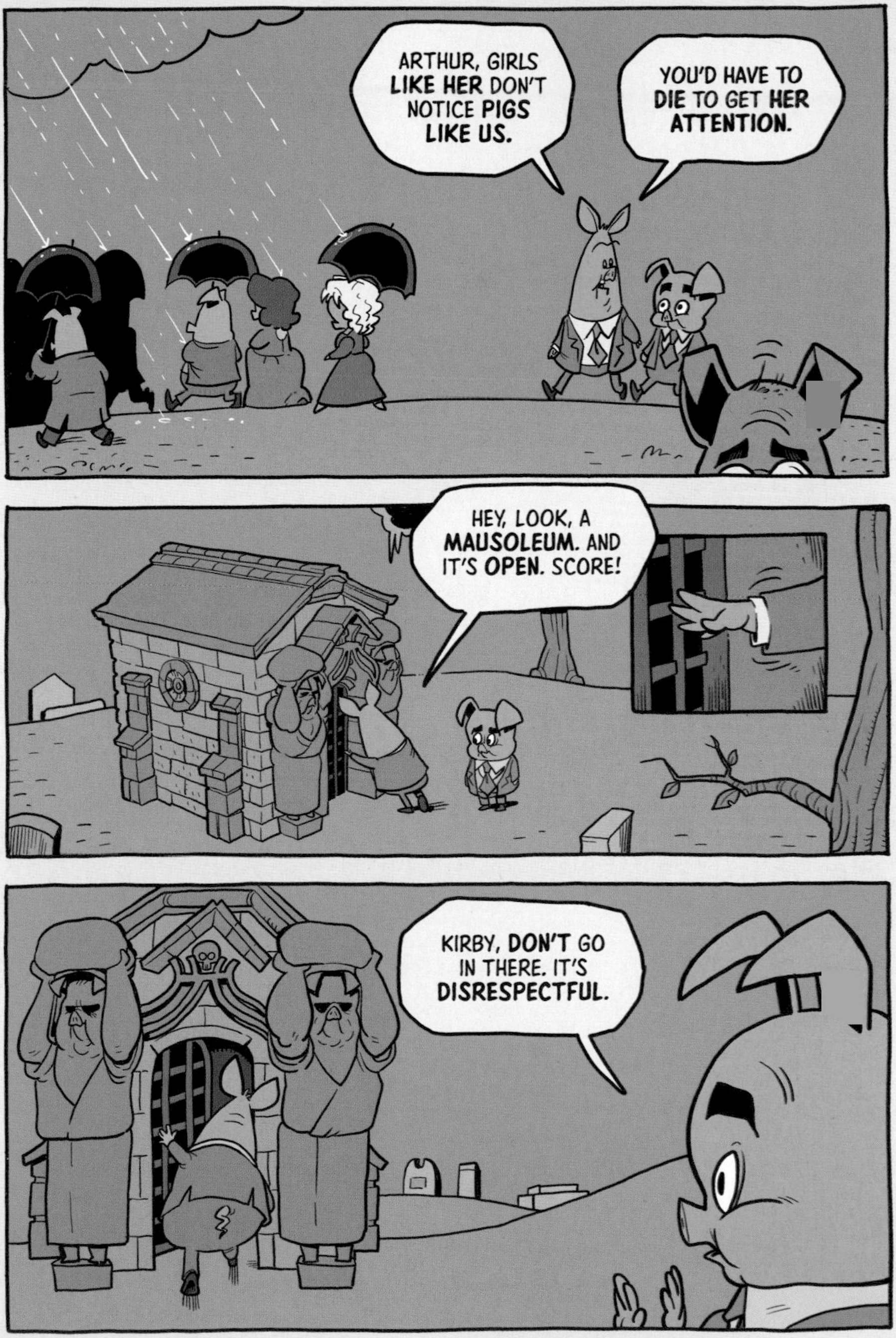
ARTHUR, GIRLS LIKE HER DON'T NOTICE PIGS LIKE US.
YOU'D HAVE TO DIE TO GET HER ATTENTION.
HEY, LOOK, A MAUSOLEUM. AND IT'S OPEN. SCORE!
KIRBY, DON'T GO IN THERE. IT'S DISRESPECTFUL.

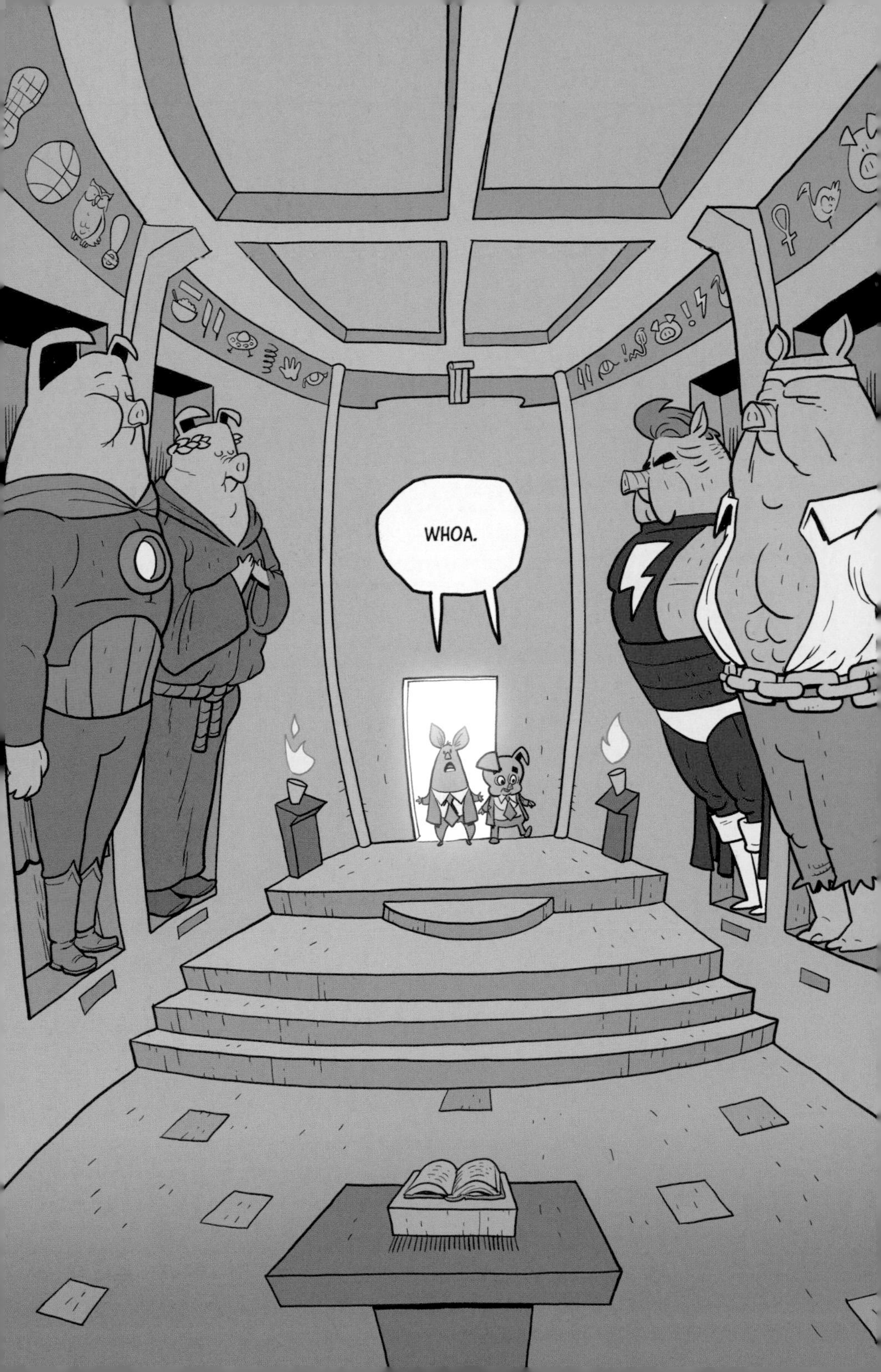
WHOA.

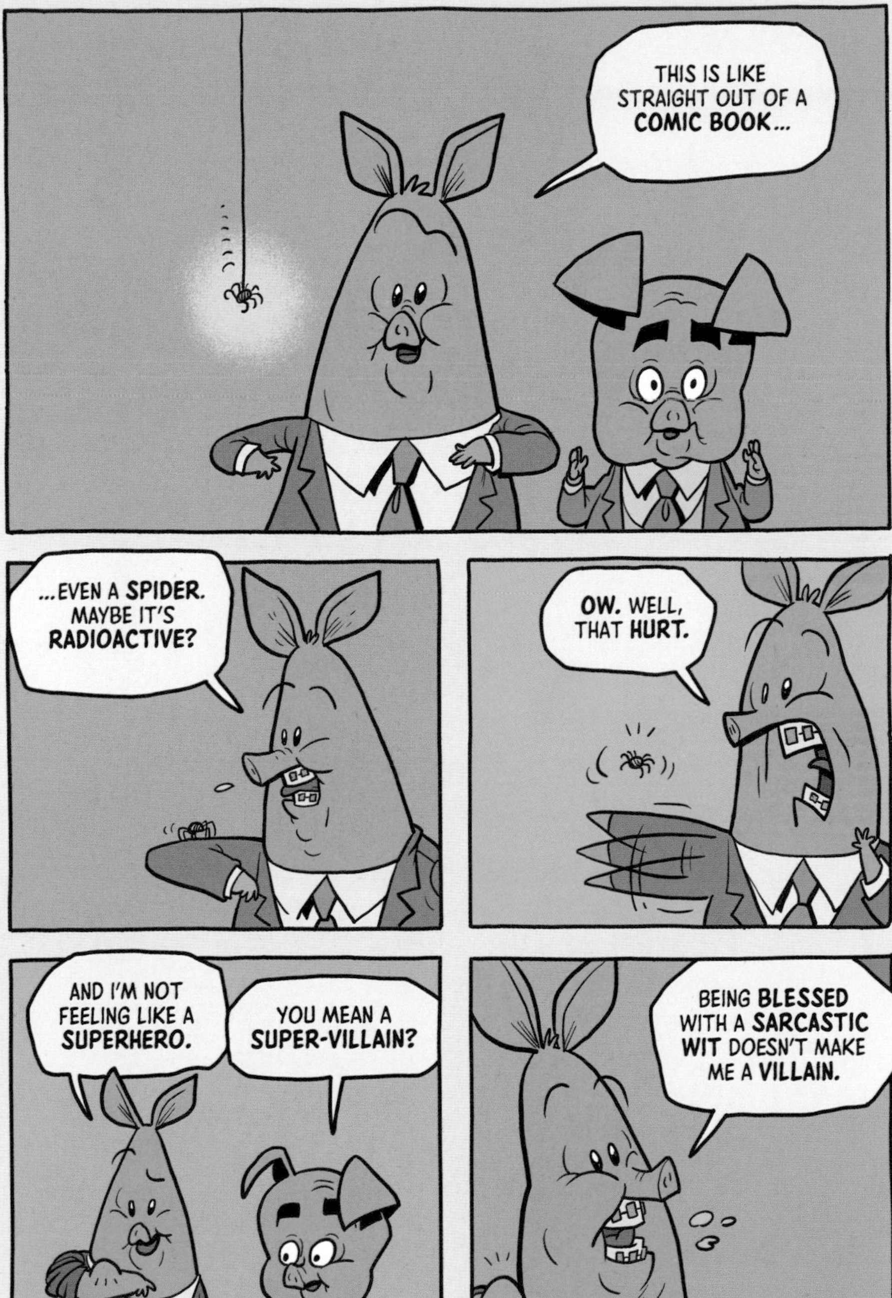
THIS IS LIKE STRAIGHT OUT OF A **COMIC BOOK...**
...EVEN A **SPIDER.** MAYBE IT'S **RADIOACTIVE?**
OW. WELL, THAT **HURT.**
AND I'M NOT FEELING LIKE A **SUPERHERO.**
YOU MEAN A **SUPER-VILLAIN?**
BEING **BLESSED** WITH A **SARCASTIC WIT** DOESN'T MAKE ME A **VILLAIN.**

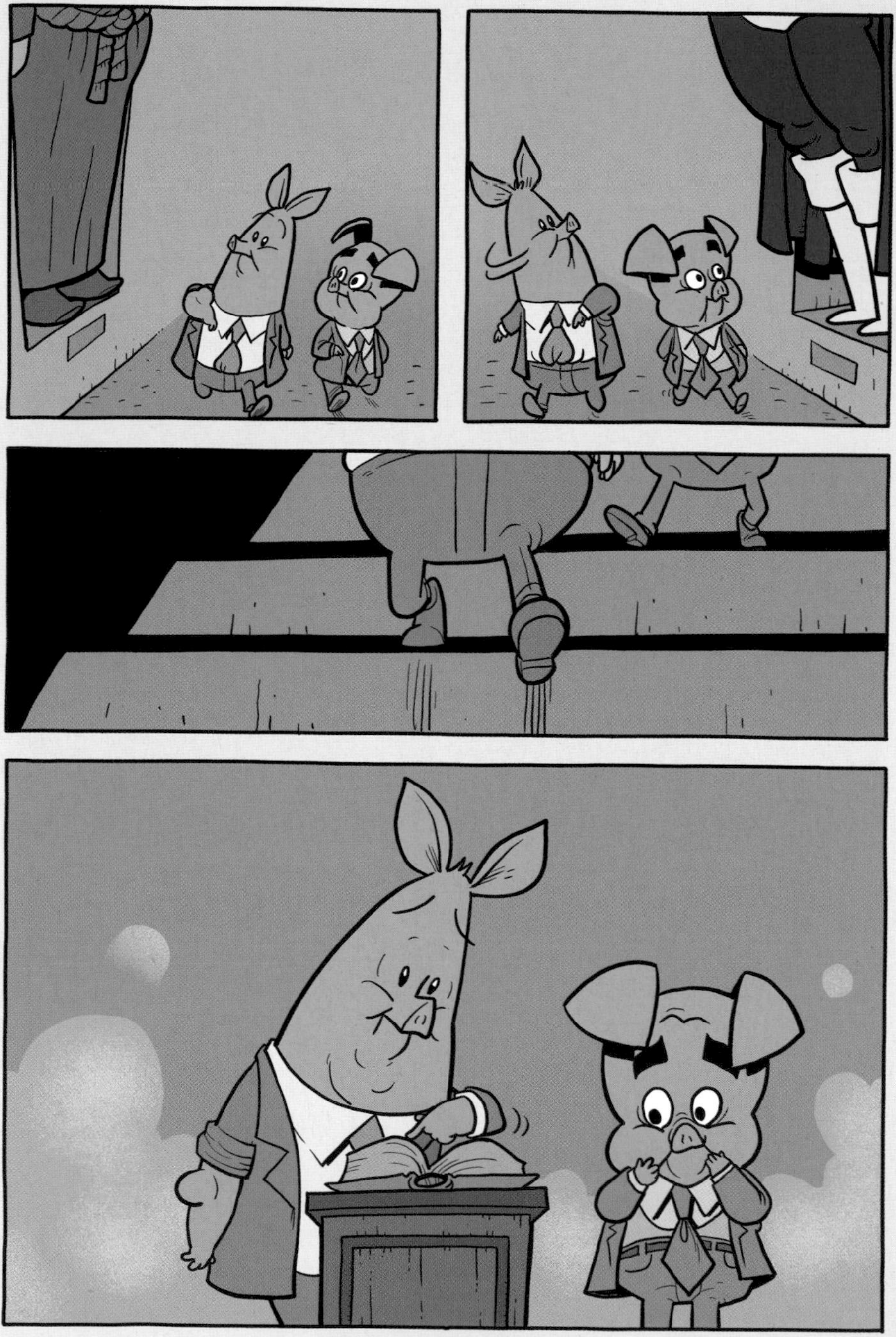

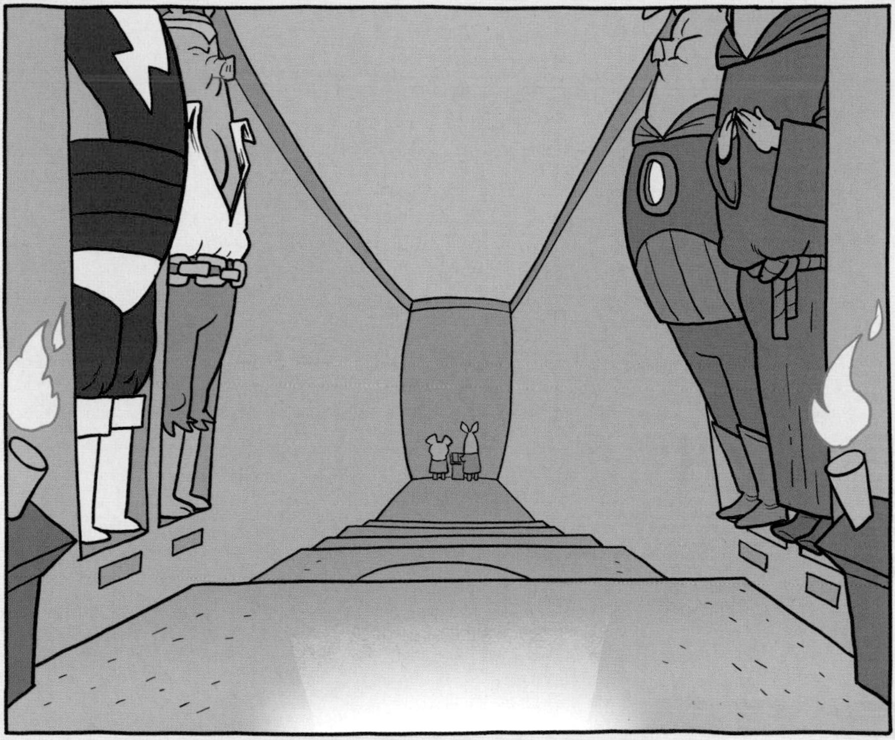

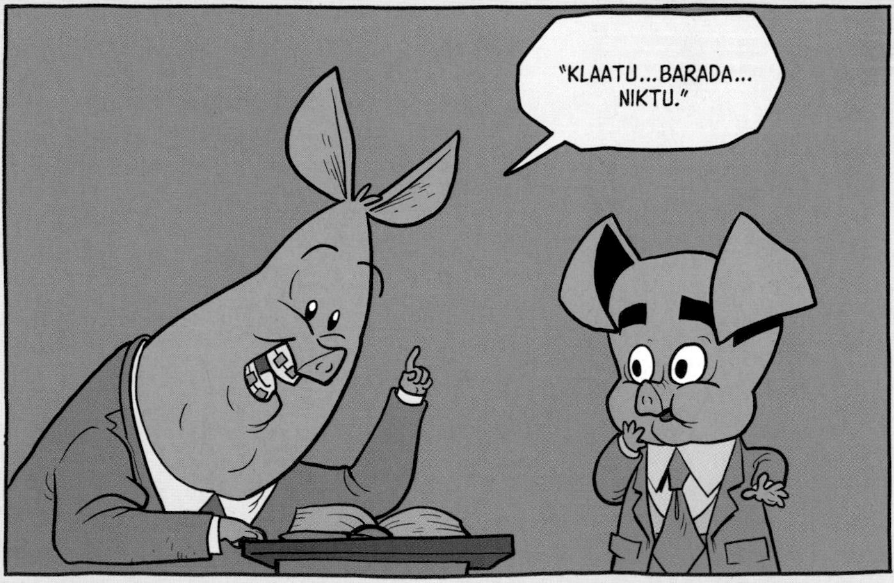
"KLAATU...BARADA... NIKTU."

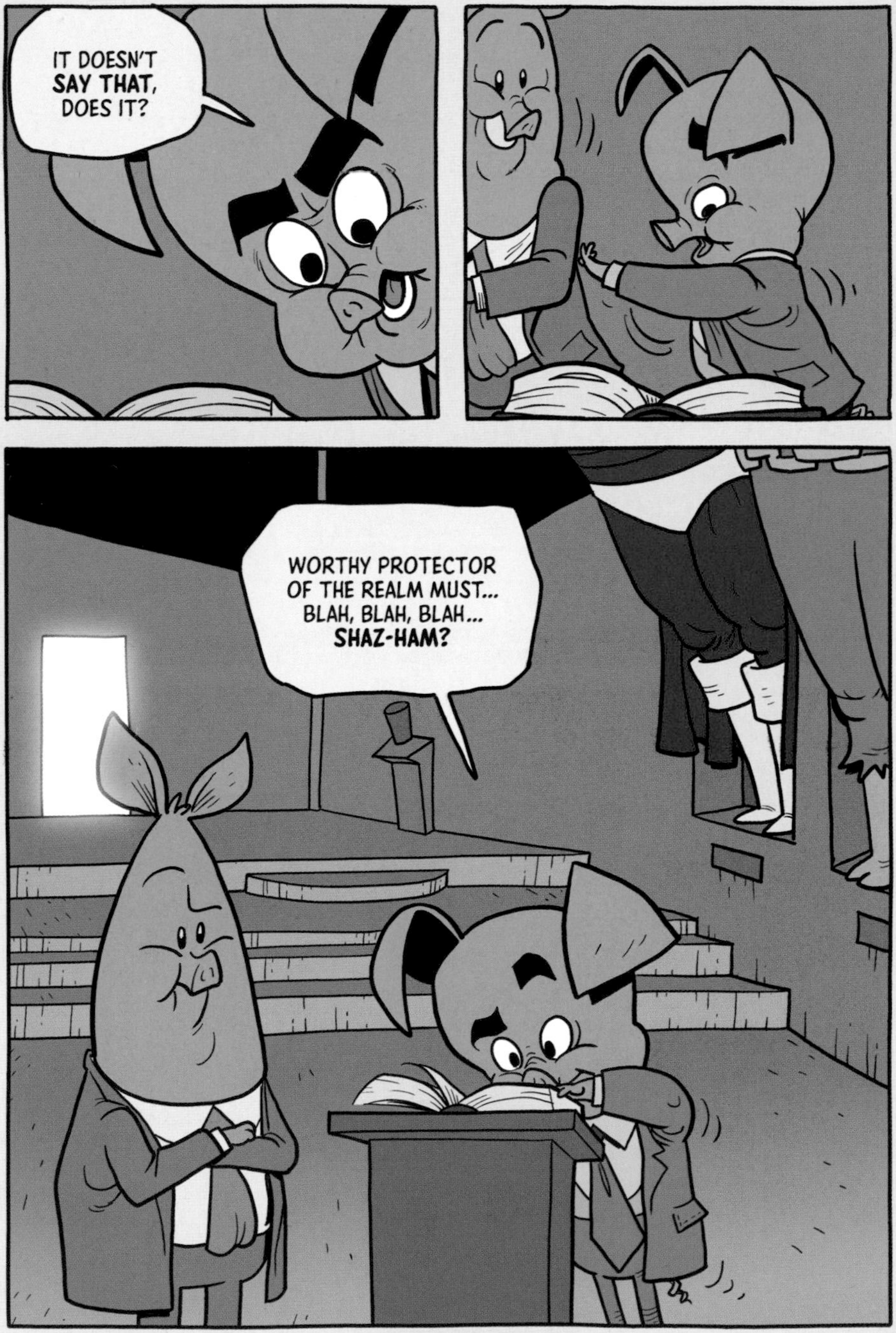
IT DOESN'T SAY THAT, DOES IT?
WORTHY PROTECTOR OF THE REALM MUST... BLAH, BLAH, BLAH... SHAZ-HAM?

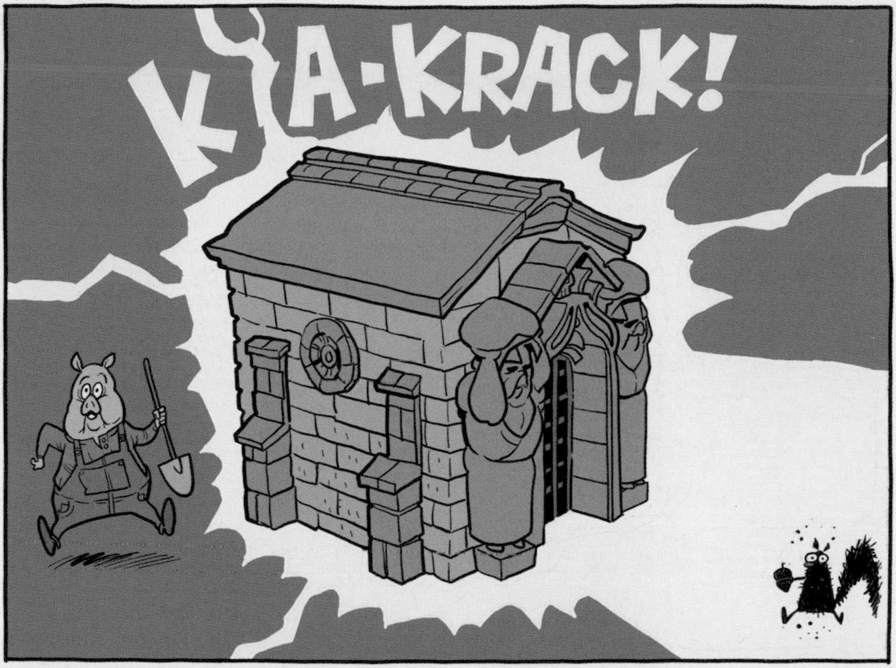
KA-KRACK!

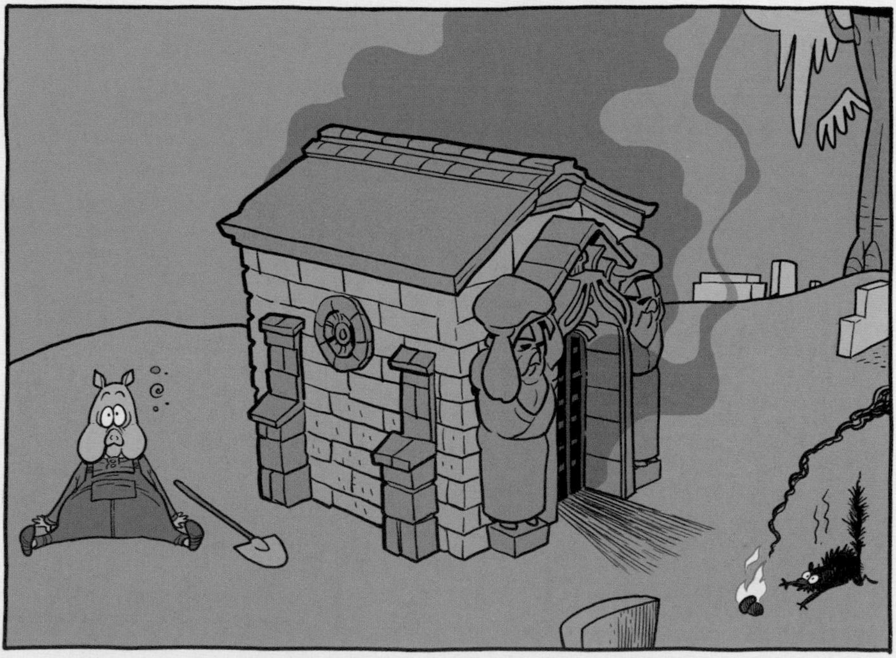

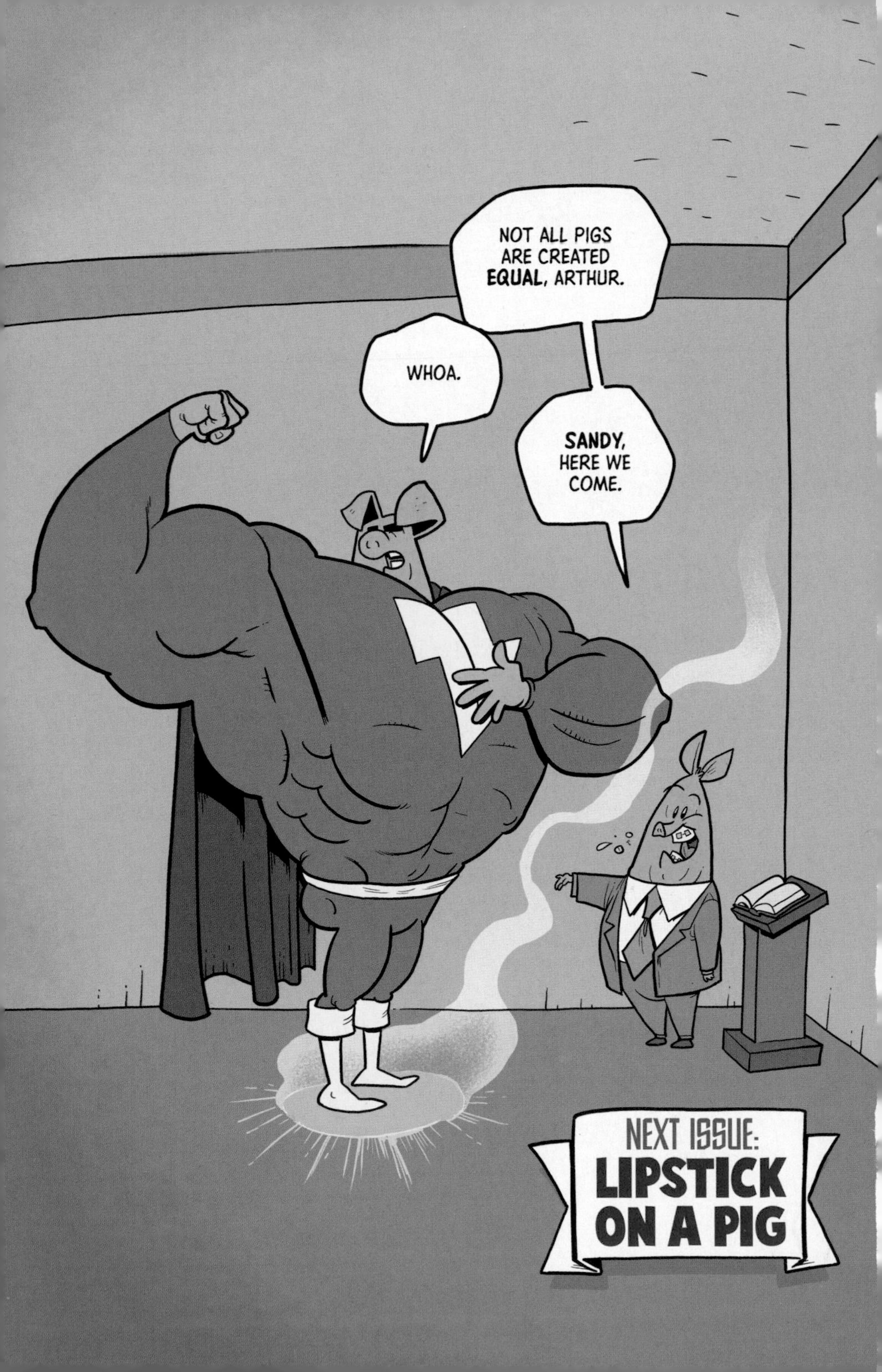
WHOA.
NOT ALL PIGS ARE CREATED **EQUAL**, ARTHUR.
SANDY, HERE WE COME.
NEXT ISSUE:
LIPSTICK ON A PIG